A Longman Cultural Edition

Mary Wollstonecraft Shelley's

FRANKENSTEIN;

or,

The Modern Prometheus

Second Edition

Edited by

Susan J. Wolfson

PEARSON
Longman

New York   Boston   San Francisco
London   Toronto   Sydney   Tokyo   Singapore   Madrid
Mexico City   Munich   Paris   Cape Town   Hong Kong   Montreal

Editor-in-Chief: Joseph P. Terry
Development Editor: Christine Halsey
Executive Marketing Manager: Ann Stypuloski
Production Coordinator: Virginia Riker
Project Coordination, Text Design, and Electronic Page Makeup: Dianne Hall
Cover Designer/Manager: John Callahan
Manufacturing Buyer: Lucy Hebard
Printer and Binder: R R Donnelley and Sons Company / Harrisonburg
Cover Printer: Coral Graphics Services, Inc.

Cover Illustration/Photo: Henry Fuseli, *The Nightmare*, 1781, Founders Society. Purchased with funds from Mr. and Mrs. Bert L. Smokler and Mr. and Mrs. Lawrence A. Fleischman. Photograph 1997 The Detroit Institute of Arts.

For permission to use copyrighted material, grateful acknowledgment is made to the copyright holders on p. ix, which is hereby made part of this copyright page.

Library of Congress Cataloging-in-Publication Data

Shelley, Mary Wollstonecraft, 1797–1851.
   [Frankenstein]
   Mary Wollstonecraft Shelley's Frankenstein, or, The modern Prometheus.—2nd
ed. / edited by Susan J. Wolfson.
       p. cm. — (A Longman cultural edition)
   ISBN 0-321-39953-6 (alk. paper)
     1. Frankenstein (Fictitious character)—Fiction. 2. Geneva (Switzerland)—Fiction.
3. Scientists—Fiction. 4. Monsters—Fiction. I. Wolfson, Susan J., 1948– II. Title.
III. Title: Mary Wollstonecraft Shelley's Frankenstein. IV. Title: Modern Prometheus.
V. Series.

PR5397.F7 2007
823'.7—dc22

                                                                        2006007928

Please visit our Web site at www.ablongman.com

ISBN 0-321-39953-6

18—DOH—15

To the Onlie Begetter of
Frankenstein
and all the progeny,
Mary Wollstonecraft Shelley

Contents

     Victor's childhood and the adoption of Elizabeth—Victor's
     enchantment with occult science and his encounter with
     modern science—Victor's departure for University of
     Ingolstadt—Clerval's straits—Victor meets Professors
     Krempe and Waldman—Victor's health suffers—Elizabeth's
     report on Ernest Frankenstein—Clerval's lament for
     William—Victor's anguish over Justine and William—

List of Illustrations

The Cover:
Henry Fuseli, *The Nightmare* (The Detroit Institute of Arts)

The Nightmare (1782) is the most famous painting of Henry Fuseli, a sardonic and erotically frank artist and scholar whom Shelley's parents knew quite well. Her mother, Mary Wollstonecraft, met Fuseli in 1788 and developed such a passionate attachment to his company and correspondence that in 1792 she proposed to his wife that she join their household (Madame Fuseli threw her out).

Erotic energy flashes in the painting, which puns the "nightmare" doubly: as the "mare" (a female goblin that sits on the chest of the dreamer, with a suffocating weight); and as the eyeless head of the female horse (mare) that peers blindly, or with supernatural vision, on the spectacle of suffocation. The seeming suffocation is more than a bit ambiguous: the dreamer looks like she might be in the throes of erotic ravishment, as normally repressed desires find a demonic outlet.

The painting's imagery figures in at least two key moments in *Frankenstein*. In Volume I, Chapter IV, Victor recounts awaking from a horrible dream on the night he animated his Creature (a dream in which he kisses his beloved Elizabeth only to see her change into the corpse of his mother) to behold "the miserable monster whom I had created" parting the bed curtains and fixing his eyes upon him. In Volume III, Chapter VI, Victor beholds this same "monster" seeming to grin and jeer as he points to the corpse of Elizabeth: "She was there, lifeless and inanimate, thrown across the bed, her head hanging down . . . her bloodless arms and relaxed form flung by the murderer on its bridal bier."

In 1799, *The Nightmare* was parodied in *The Anti-Jacobin Review* (vol. 3, pp. 88–89) in the form of a political cartoon titled "The Nightmare" with the sleeper as the opposition (Whig) leader in parliament, Charles James Fox, vexed by three goblins wearing the caps of the French Jacobins (the radical faction of the Revolution that sponsored the Reign of Terror). One of them rides the horse of death (from the Apocalypse) across his body, spearing his chest with a flag emblazoned "VIVE LA LIBERTÉ" (Let Liberty Live). At the foot of the bed, popping out of the sleeper's jacket pocket, is the anarchist treatise, *Political Justice*, by Shelley's father, William Godwin.

About Longman Cultural Editions

Reading always seems to vibrate with the transformation of the day—now, yesterday, and centuries ago, when the presses first put printed language into wide circulation. Correspondingly, literary culture has always been a matter of change: of new practices confronting established traditions; of texts transforming under the pressure of new techniques of reading and new perspectives of understanding; of canons shifting and expanding; of informing traditions getting reviewed and renewed, recast and reformed by emerging cultural interests and concerns; of culture, too, as a variable "text"—a reading. Inspired by the innovative *Longman Anthology of British Literature,* Longman Cultural Editions respond creatively to the changes, past and recent, by presenting key texts in contexts that illuminate the lively intersections of literature, tradition, and culture. A principal work is made more interesting by materials that place it in relation to its past, present, and future, enabling us to see how it may be reworking traditional debates and practices, how it appears amid the conversations and controversies of its own historical moment, how it gains new significances in subsequent eras of reading and reaction. Readers new to the work will discover attractive paths for exploration, while those more experienced will encounter fresh perspectives and provocative juxtapositions.

Longman Cultural Editions serve not only several kinds of readers but also (appropriately) their several contexts, from various courses of study to independent adventure. Handsomely produced and affordably priced, our volumes offer appealing companions to *The Longman Anthology of British Literature,* in some cases enriching and expanding units originally developed for the *Anthology*, and in other cases presenting this wealth for the first time. The logic and composition of the contexts vary across the series. The constants are the complete text of an important literary work, reliably edited, headed by an inviting introduction, and supplemented by helpful annotation; a table of dates to track its composition, publication, and public reception in relation to biographical, cultural, and historical events; and a guide for further inquiry and study. With these common measures and uncommon assets, Longman Cultural Editions encourage your literary pleasures with resources for lively reflection and adventurous inquiry.

SUSAN J. WOLFSON
General Editor
Professor of English
Princeton University

About This Edition

This edition of *Frankenstein; or, The Modern Prometheus* presents Mary Shelley's remarkable novel in several provocative and illuminating contexts. *Frankenstein* was published in two related but different versions. Mary Godwin began her novel in a story-writing compact at Lord Byron's villa, during the stormy Alpine summer of 1816. Her companions included not only Byron, a sensationally popular poet and subject of scandal, but also her lover and husband-to-be, Percy Shelley. When she and Percy Shelley returned to England at the end of the summer, she continued to work on the novel, which was published in 1818. After Percy Shelley's sudden death in 1822, Mary Shelley began to revise parts of the novel, and a new version appeared in 1831, prefaced by a retrospective "Introduction" on the novel's genesis in 1816. Until the 1970s or so, the 1831 version was the only one available. The text presented here is the Romantic-era publication of 1818, with some half-dozen obvious printer's errors silently corrected (with reference to the text of 1831). The 1831 novel is just as interesting, and from it we supply the Introduction, and a selection of other noteworthy revisions and reconceptions. My own introduction is complemented by a chronology coordinating Shelley's life with key historical events, and a speculative calendar of the novel's events in the late eighteenth century.

From its title page on, *Frankenstein* involves a network of significant allusions, chiefly to John Milton's *Paradise Lost* and Samuel Taylor Coleridge's *The Rime of the Ancyent Marinere* (so it was titled in the first version of 1798). *Frankenstein* also converses with other contemporary texts, by Mary Shelley's parents, husband, and friends. "Monsters, Visionaries, and Mary Shelley," the first contextual section, provides some of these intertextual links as well as illumination from Shelley's own writing, in her journal, her travelogue, and letters to friends. The section closes with an excerpt of the work from which critic Ellen Moers drew the epigraph for her groundbreaking essay on "Female Gothic": Dr. Benjamin Spock's *Baby and Child Care*.

Both the Preface of 1818 and the Introduction of 1831 refer to the story-telling compact that was conceived at Lord Byron's villa, in the Swiss alps, in the summer of 1816. *Frankenstein* was the most famous progeny of this project, but Lord Byron and his physician, John William Polidori, also got involved, and we include their efforts. At the other end of the century, Bram Stoker read Polidori's vampiretale, and wrote *Dracula*.

Shelley's title-page epigraph from *Paradise Lost* signals the vital involvement of Milton's epic in her conception. As a convenience for reference, this contextual section assembles the passages that figure into and sometimes are directly quoted in *Frankenstein*, along with the text which is Milton's reference, the book of Genesis, chapters 2 and 3. Milton's Adam, Eve, and God shape the characters of *Frankenstein*, but the figure that most powerfully possesses its linked creator (Frankenstein) and his Creature is the great antihero, the boldly transgressive, eternally suffering Satan. Shelley, like many in her day, read Satan less as a moral antagonist, the architect of evil, than as a sublime psychological study, a prototype of modern alienation. The unit on "God, Adam, and Satan" presents some other representations in this key by Shelley's contemporaries. One genre of response was popular stage versions of the novel's basic story, ranging from melodramas to pastiches of comedy and catastrophe. Richard Brinsley Peake's *Frankenstein, A Romantic Drama* was a hit in London in the summer of 1823, and remained a favorite well into midcentury.

Contemporary reviewers did not suspect that so heterodox a novel could have a female author; even granting a male author (surmising Percy Shelley), they were shocked, troubled, and impressed. The section "Reviews and Reactions" assembles their comments, as well as Percy Shelley's "ghost" review, written in 1817–18 but not printed until 1832, well after his death, in the wake of the novel's successful republication in 1831. "Frankenstein" continues to figure in our language today, as we describe new developments in science, technology, art, government, fashion, and food. "Frankentalk" offers a sample of this monstrously large universe. "Further Reading and Viewing" provides information about biography, editions, critical studies, films, and Web sites.

For counsel, advice, encouragement, and support in preparing this edition, developed from a popular unit in *The Romantics and Their Contemporaries* (vol. 2a of *The Longman Anthology of British Literature*), I thank my colleagues at Longman: Joe Terry, David Damrosch, Mark Getlein, Peter Manning; for inspiration and illumination, my graduate seminars at Princeton, spring 1997 (especially Jessica Richard, Chris Rovee, Andrew Krull, and Denise Gigante) and spring 2002 (Jack Cragwall, Roger Schwartz, and John Bugg); for intrepid research assistance, Andrew Krull; for advice on polar exploration, Jessica Richard; for advice on Dr. Spock, Deborah Nord; for material services, Firestone Library and the Department of English at Princeton University. And for everything, and everything more, Ronald Levao.

Susan J. Wolfson
Princeton University

Introduction

Mary Wollstonecraft Shelley, 1797–1851

"My husband was, from the first, very anxious that I should prove myself worthy of my parentage, and enrol myself on the page of fame. He was for ever inciting me to obtain literary reputation." Though less anxious for this consequence than he, Mary Shelley succeeded with a vengeance in *Frankenstein,* a sensational novel that has been in print ever since its publication in 1818, as well as the subject of numerous films, take-offs, and parodies. Her parentage was no small burden. It was not just that they were two leading intellectuals of the 1790s, William Godwin and Mary Wollstonecraft, whose social and political writing made them both famous and infamous. It was also that her mother died soon after giving birth to her, a tragedy that made her a monster in her father's eyes, and which she later evoked in the story of the creature whom Victor Frankenstein can regard only as a monster. Mary Godwin never felt loved by her father, though she was passionately attached to him. When she was fourteen, he sent her to live with the family of an admirer in Scotland, feeling that he could not support her along with his family by his second wife, Mary Jane Clairmont (who also wanted to distance Mary from her father). On a six-month visit to the Godwin home in 1812–13, she met an ardent disciple of his, Percy Shelley, and resumed the acquaintance when she returned in spring 1814. She was sixteen; he was twenty-one and unhappily married. They fell in love, courted secretly, and Mary was soon pregnant. At the end of July, they eloped to France, taking along Mary's stepsister, Claire Clairmont. Godwin was furious, and scarcely warmer when they returned a few months later and married at the end of 1816, even as he continued to pester Percy for loans. The journey across the natural beauties and war-ravaged landscapes of Europe was recorded in Mary's first book, *History of a Six Weeks' Tour*, published anonymously in 1817.

Mary's life with Percy was exciting, tempestuous, and fraught with pain. Their first child, born prematurely, died within weeks; Mary had a dream of bringing her back to life. Claire got involved with Lord Byron, became pregnant, and bore a daughter; a year and a half later, she sent this daughter to live with Byron, who after a few months placed her in a convent, where she died of typhoid fever a few years later, an event that horrified Mary and Percy. Meanwhile Percy had lost custody of his two children by his first wife, and from 1814 to 1822, Mary was almost continuously pregnant or nursing. Their second child, William, born in 1816, died in 1819; her third child, born in 1817, died even sooner, in 1818. She suffered a nearly fatal miscarriage in 1822, and a few weeks later Percy, who had been increasingly distant from her, drowned in a storm at sea.

Devastated, impoverished, and with one surviving child (Percy Florence) to support, Shelley returned to London at age twenty-four, longing for anonymity and propriety. She had admired her mother's writings, but she felt the stigma of her notoriety and radical political opinions. Godwin, declined from his celebrity in the 1790s, was regarded as an eccentric thinker wedded to radical ideas. The scandals of Percy's life and opinions and her unconventional life with him were acute social embarrassments—even as she devoted herself to rehabilitating his reputation with editions of his writings that downplayed his politics and idealized (and idolized) his character. Though never matching the success of *Frankenstein*, Shelley developed a capable career as a writer, supplementing the small annuity (£100) from her father-in-law that was contingent on her agreeing not to publish a biography of her husband. (When Percy's eldest son, by Harriet, died in 1826, Percy Florence became the Shelley heir, and the annuity slowly increased.)

Mary Shelley published poems, a mythological drama, some two dozen short tales, many of which she placed in handsomely paying gift-book annuals, as well as encyclopedia articles, essays, reviews, travel books, and several novels. The most famous of her later novels is *The Last Man* (1826), a fable about the sole survivor of a plague-ravaged human race that reflected her own acute sense of isolation. "Shelley died and I was alone," she wrote in her journal;

"My total friendlessness . . . has sunk me in a state of loneliness no other human being ever before, I believe endured—except Robinson Crusoe." Her most sustained labors were her editions of her husband's works, beginning in 1824 with *Posthumous Poems,* a publication immediately suppressed by his father. With his approval, *Poetical Works,* embellished with notes (lightly biographical, anecdotal, and explanatory), appeared in 1839, followed in 1840 by a volume of prose, including essays (the first publication of *A Defence of Poetry*), letters, translations, and fragments. Working on these editions gave Shelley a sense of atonement for her deep feeling of inadequacy to her husband's needs, as well as a sense of continuing relationship with him. As she hoped, her editions were instrumental in recasting the dangerous radical and atheist into a misunderstood idealist and inspired author of beautiful verse. Although these editions were superseded within a few decades by more scholarly ones, her notes were often reprinted, and *Frankenstein* always so—a fate she may have intuited from the "prodigious success" of a London stage version she saw in 1823: "lo & behold!" she exclaimed to a friend, "I found myself famous."

Frankenstein; or, The Modern Prometheus

It is no exaggeration to say that *Frankenstein* is the most famous work of imagination from the Romantic era. It is also a vibrant intersection of interlocking cultural concerns: the claims of humanity against scientific exploration; the relationship between "monsters" and their creators; the questionable judgments by which physical difference is termed monstrous; the responsibility of society for the violent behavior of those to whom it refuses care, compassion, even basic decency; the relationships between men and women, and parents and children (and the symbolic version in care-givers and care-receivers); and the psychological dynamics of repression, doubling, and alter egos. Shelley shaped these issues from her wide reading in modern literature and philosophy, as well as ancient myths, particularly the two indicated on her title page: the biblical story of the creation of life and the Fall from Paradise on which Milton based *Paradise Lost,* and the old myth of Prometheus, who created man out of clay, then when the king of the gods, Jupiter, mistreated man, stole fire from heaven and gave it to man, instructing him in the knowledge and arts that enabled his civilization. Jupiter punished Prometheus by condemning him to perpetual torment on a mountaintop and afflicting mankind with Pandora's box of evils.

Shelley's subtitle, "The Modern Prometheus," folds in several meanings. Boldly experimental investigators of the times, such as Benjamin Franklin, who attempted to tap electrical energy from lightning, earned the title of "Modern Prometheus." The ancient Greek god Prometheus was the first to bring fire from heaven, but his story is a complex reference. The god's actions prefigure those not only of Milton's Satan (like him, punished for disobeying divine law), but also of Christ, especially in the political perspective of Shelley's age: the benefactor of humanity martyred for his compassion. But if in his role of would-be benefactor, Prometheus patterns both the scientist Victor Frankenstein and his Creature, one of the surprises of the novel to those reading it for the first time is that "Frankenstein" is the name of the scientist only and not his creature, who never has a name; when Shelley saw him listed in the dramatis personae of a play-version of her novel as "———," she approved of "this nameless mode of naming the un[n]ameable." Another surprise is the Creature himself, who is not initially a depraved monster at all, but a poignantly abandoned infant with only the most benevolent of impulses, horribly abused by everyone for no reason other than his unusual physical appearance.

In describing this alienation, Shelley provokes attention to the differences that were fracturing modern society—the view of political radicals as monsters; the class differences that made the poor seem monstrous, particularly when they agitated for better treatment; the racial differences that made African slaves seem subhuman to those profiting from the slave trade. Shelley also depicts the deep psychic monstrosities in Victor himself—haunted by unresolved grief over his mother's death, virtually turned monstrous during his scientific studies and, in his own progressive isolation from humanity, becoming more and more like his creature. Moreover, unlike almost every cinematic representation, Shelley makes the Creature educated and articulate: he learns to read and gets a basic course in "Western Civ" from a satchel of books he finds in the forest, among them *Paradise Lost*. From this education, he develops a liberal critique of social corruptions and injustices, as well as a rhetorical power that renowned parliamentarian Edmund Burke might have envied.

Shelley conceived *Frankenstein* in the summer of 1816, in Switzerland, as part of a ghost-story writing compact between herself, Claire, her husband, Byron, and Byron's doctor, John Polidori. As the others went to work, she wrestled with "mortifying" paralysis. Then her imagination came to life with a nightmare of "a pale student of unhallowed arts" who has created life from death and is "horror-stricken" at his "odious handiwork." In 1831 she would call the novel itself "her hideous progeny." Percy saw the potential of this progeny right away, encouraged its development, edited the text (whether he improved it is debatable), and took it to London to seek a publisher. When the novel appeared anonymously in 1818, it created a sensation. Some were fascinated and others appalled by its transgressive horror. Reviewers, including Sir Walter Scott, assumed that its author could only be male, many guessing Percy. In 1823, still in deep mourning over Percy's sudden death the year before, Shelley began to revise her novel, many of her changes creating a more idealistic and idealized, less morally culpable Victor Frankenstein (in whose visionary enthusiasms many saw the image of Percy). Other changes elaborate her concern with social benevolence to the poor, the outcast, the helpless. The revised version, to which she signed her name, was published in 1831, with an Introduction about "the origin of the story," both the circumstances of its inspiration and the materials that influenced its composition.

Shelley wrote her fable partly in the popular genre of the "gothic novel." She was drawn to this mode not only for its association with mystery, sensational events, and the supernatural, but also because it tapped the painful horrors of her own life—all its losses and failed creations, from her accidental responsibility for her mother's death in 1797, to the deaths, abandonments, and suicides that she and her family suffered in her adult life. More public contexts also shape the novel. It opens in 1798, as Victor is rescued from near death by an explorer on a voyage to the North Pole; this is the year that Napoleon, at war with England and already the conqueror of Italy, was dramatically expanding his campaign into Switzerland. Victor's story starts with his birth in the 1770s in the Swiss city of Geneva, the home of Jean-Jacques Rousseau, whose political writings had enormous influence on the French Republican politics. Victor's scientific studies begin in 1789, the year the storming of the Bastille prison inaugurated the French Revolution, and the centennial of England's

Glorious Revolution. This context is nowhere mentioned in the novel, but Shelley's readers, with less than twenty years' distance, would have grasped the significance of making the 1790s the decade for a sequence of catastrophic actions descending from an idealistic project gone awry. *Edinburgh Magazine* saw this significance immediately, discerning a Godwinian "model" for the novel and reading the story of Napoleon's egotism in Victor's career, which ends in isolation on an islandlike iceberg, then icebound boat.

Frankenstein combines myth with personal, literary, and social history to produce an enigmatic, multi-layered fable. Its chronological story terminates at Robert Walton's ship in the Arctic, while its narrative structure uses that terminus as a frame for the interplay of alter egos and mutually reflecting episodes: outcasts and wanderers; scenes of care-giving and nurture, of the dead and the near dead brought back to life; trials and other scenes of judgment; tales told to elicit sympathy, not always with success. Walton, the explorer whose letters open the novel and whose journal entries close it, is an embryonic Frankenstein, for example, eager to explore the unknown, regardless of danger. When he asks the sister to whom he writes his letters to marvel at his encounter with Frankenstein, and when Frankenstein then asks him to "listen to my tale" and learn from his errors, Shelley inaugurates a chain of tale-telling and listening that climaxes in the Creature's demand that Frankenstein listen to his tale—a narration that radically complicates our sense of who is the monster and who is the victim.

Table of Dates

Mary Shelley, The Age, and Events in Frankenstein

{Frankenstein chronology builds on Anne K. Mellor, Mary Shelley, 237n22; the quotations of poetry in the novel are anachronistic.}

MG/MS: Mary Godwin/Mary Shelley
PBS: Percy Bysshe Shelley
{VF: Victor Frankenstein   C: Creature   RW: Robert Walton}

1765	Horace Walpole, *The Castle of Otranto* (the first "gothic" novel) published.
1769	Robert Walton born.
1772	{Victor Frankenstein born.}
1777	{Elizabeth Lavenza joins the Frankenstein family.}
1778	{Ernest Frankenstein born.}
1781	Jean-Jacques Rousseau, *Confessions*. Henri Fuseli's painting, *The Nightmare*. American Revolution ends with the British surrender at Yorktown.
1785	{VF reading occult science: Cornelius Agrippa, Albertus Magnus, Paracelsus.}
1786	William Beckford's gothic novel, *Vathek*.
1787	{VF sees lightning destroy an oak tree and becomes interested in electricity.}
1788	{? William Frankenstein born.}
1789	The storming of the Bastille, 14 July, launches the French Revolution. Mutiny on the HMS *Bounty*. Luigi Galvani's experiments on electrically induced muscular contractions.
	{Summer–autumn after his mother's death from scarlet fever, VF, age 17, resumes his plans to attend university at Ingolstadt.}
1790	Radical Jacobins ascend to power in France; capture of the royal family as they attempt to flee. Published: Edmund Burke,

Reflections on the Revolution in France; Mary Wollstonecraft, *A Vindication of the Rights of Men.*

{January: VF begins his studies at the University; late 1790: RW resolves to undertake a polar voyage, and trains by accompanying whalers on North Sea expeditions.}

1791   Mary Wollstonecraft meets William Godwin. Published: Comte de Volney, *The Ruins of Empires.*

{February: VF's science project; he discovers the secret of life.}

1792   September Massacres of suspected Royalists in France; arrest of the royal family; abolition of the monarchy. P. B. Shelley born. Published: Wollstonecraft, *Vindication of the Rights of Woman.* Wollstonecraft infatuated with Swiss painter Henri Fuseli.

{November: VF animates then abandons Creature; Clerval arrives in Ingolstadt and VF has breakdown; C lives in the woods; De Laceys exiled from Paris.}

1793   Executions of Louis XVI (January) and Marie Antoinette (October); Marat murdered; Reign of Terror begins. France declares war on Britain. In Paris Wollstonecraft begins an affair with American adventurer Gilbert Imlay. Published: Godwin, *Political Justice.*

{Winter: C discovers the De Laceys, is their secret cohabitant; spring: VF recovers from physical collapse; late fall/early winter: C is rejected by the De Laceys.}

1794   Danton and Robespierre executed; the Terror ends. Wollstonecraft's daughter, Fanny Imlay, born. Published: Wollstonecraft, *Historical and Moral View of the French Revolution;* Godwin, *Caleb Williams;* Erasmus Darwin, *Zoonomia; or, The Laws of Organic Life* (–96); Ann Radcliffe, *The Mysteries of Udolpho.*

{May: C kills little William Frankenstein; the middle of August: C encounters VF in the Alps; VF, postponing his marriage to Elizabeth, departs for England at the end of the summer, journeying down the Rhine, and arriving in London in October, where he spends the winter.}

1795   Wollstonecraft returns to London and, in despair over Imlay's new lover, attempts suicide in May; travels to Scandinavia, and attempts suicide in October, when she discovers Imlay with yet another lover. Napoleon invades Italy.

{Spring: VF travels north, stopping at Windsor and Oxford; July–November: VF, in the remote Orkney Islands, constructs a female creature, then destroys it; C kills Henry Clerval.}

1796   Wollstonecraft publishes her Scandinavian travelogue, *Letters*, meets Godwin again; they become lovers by the summer; she becomes pregnant (with Mary Godwin) early in December. Published: Matthew Lewis's gothic novel, *The Monk*.

{11 December: RW in St. Petersburg, preparing for polar voyage; January–March: VF arrested for the murder of Clerval, in prison in Ireland; June: VF marries Elizabeth, whom C kills on their wedding night; July: VF begins his pursuit of C, north along the Rhine, eventually into Russia.}

1797   Wollstonecraft and Godwin marry, 29 March; 30 August: MG born; 10 September: Wollstonecraft dies from septic poisoning incurred during childbirth. May: Napoleon proclaims the end of the Venetian Republic. Published: Radcliffe, *The Italian*.

{28 March: RW in Archangel; 7 July: voyaging North; 31 July: from their nearly icebound ship, the crew sees C on the far ice, driving a dogsled; 1 August: VF appears shipside, nearly frozen to death, is taken on board; 5 August: VF begins to recover; 13–26 August: VF tells his story; 2–5 September: VF urges RW's crew northward; 7 September: RW, at the insistence of his crew, abandons his polar quest and consents to return; 9 September: the ice begins to move; 11 September: passage to the south opens, VF dies; 12 September: C appears and then leaves on an ice raft, supposedly to kill himself.}

1798   Irish Rebellion; Napoleon invades Rome, then Switzerland, a Republic *{home of the Frankenstein family}*. Published: *Lyrical Ballads*, including Samuel Taylor Coleridge's *The Rime of the Ancyent Marinere* and William Wordsworth's *Tintern Abbey*; Joanna Baillie, *Plays on the Passions*; Godwin, *Memoir of Wollstonecraft*; Wollstonecraft, *Maria; or, the Wrongs of Woman*. Scathing attacks on Wollstonecraft in the reactionary press.

1799   Napoleon returns to France and in a coup becomes first consul. Godwin, *St. Leon* (in which the hero discovers both how to transmute base metals into gold, and the elixir of life, granting immortality). Cuvier begins study of comparative anatomy. Rosetta Stone found in Egypt.

1800   Published: Second edition of *Lyrical Ballads* (with Preface). Napoleon crosses the Alps with 4,000 men to attack Austria.

woke one morning to find myself famous"); Baillie, vol. 3 of *Plays;* Grimm's *Fairy Tales;* Davy, *Elements of Chemical Philosophy.* Turner's painting, *Hannibal Crossing the Alps.* Napoleon's Grand Army invades Russia in June and retreats from Moscow in December, with catastrophic losses (500,000 of 600,000 troops).

1813   MG back in Scotland with the Baxters for 10 months. Leigh Hunt imprisoned until 1815 for libeling the Prince Regent. Massive Luddite trial in York, with many sentenced to death or transportation. Byron in the whirl of London society; publishes two sensational "Eastern Tales," *The Giaour* in June and *The Bride of Abydos* in December. Southey publishes *Life of Nelson* and becomes Poet Laureate; PBS's daughter Ianthe born. Published: PBS, *Queen Mab;* Austen, *Pride and Prejudice* (anon.); Mme de Staël, *De l'Allemagne* (suppressed by Napoleon in 1810). Austria joins the Alliance against France; Napoleon defeated at Leipzig, retreats from Spain, Holland, Italy, and Switzerland. Wars of liberation throughout Europe.

1814   Harriet Shelley becomes pregnant by PBS in February. MG returns from Scotland 30 March; PBS courts her with a copy of *Queen Mab;* MG becomes pregnant in May, elopes with PBS and her stepsister Claire in July; they travel in Europe until the end of the summer, and return to an enraged Godwin. Charles born to Harriet in November. Byron sees record-breaking sales of *The Corsair* in February, publishes *Lara* in August, becomes engaged to wealthy heiress Annabella Milbanke in September. PBS, *A Refutation of Deism.* Allies invade France; Napoleon abdicates and is exiled to Elba; Bourbons restored. Published: Wordsworth, *The Excursion;* Austen, *Mansfield Park* (anon.); Scott, *Waverley* (anon.); Cary, translation of *The Divine Comedy.*

1815   22 February: premature birth of MG's and PBS's daughter, who dies 6 March. MG and PBS move to Bishop's Gate, Windsor, in August. January: Byron marries; daughter Ada born in December. Published: Wordsworth, collected *Poems;* Austen, *Emma* (anon.). Napoleon escapes Elba, enters France, is defeated at Waterloo and exiled to St. Helena; restoration of European monarchies.

1816   24 January: William born to MG and PBS; they travel to Continental Europe in the summer, make Byron's acquaintance in Geneva, and spend a great deal of time with him at Villa Diodati, on Lake Geneva, the site of a ghost-story compact (16 June) during which MG begins *Frankenstein.* July: Claire, MG, PBS take a week-long excursion to Chamounix (Mont Blanc and Mer de Glace). September: They return to England. MG works on

Frankenstein throughout the fall; 9 October: MG's half-sister Fanny Imlay commits suicide; MG reading sea-voyaging literature, perhaps drafting the Walton frame for *Frankenstein*, reading Davy on chemistry. November: PBS's wife, Harriet, pregnant by someone else and still wearing PBS's wedding ring, commits suicide (her body is discovered 10 December); 30 December: MG and PBS marry, Mary is already pregnant again.

January: Lady Byron leaves Byron, taking their daughter; April: with a decree of separation, Byron leaves England forever; begins an affair with Claire Clairmont, who becomes pregnant; *Childe Harold's Pilgrimage III* published in December; Byron works on *Manfred* and *Prometheus*. Published: PBS, *Alastor* (February); Leigh Hunt, *The Story of Rimini*; Caroline Lamb, *Glenarvon* (with a Satanic/Byronic hero); Coleridge, *Christabel* and *Kubla Khan*. June: Byron recites some of *Christabel*, and PBS reacts in terror.

Elgin Marbles displayed; prosecution of William Hone (tried in 1817); Spa Field Riots (December).

1817   January: Claire gives birth to a daughter, Alba Allegra. March: PBS and MS move to Marlow, with Claire and Allegra; PBS denied custody of his children by Harriet; MS completes *Frankenstein* (May); Byron's publisher John Murray, though he likes it, declines to publish it; it is accepted by a lesser firm in August. Shelleys' friendship with Leigh Hunt flourishes; daughter Clara born (2 September); a few weeks later MS gives PBS "carte blanche" to correct the proofs for *Frankenstein* and make whatever "alterations you please." November: *History of a Six Weeks' Tour* published (with PBS's *Mont Blanc* and MS's descriptive letters); December: *Frankenstein* advertised in the London papers (*Observer, Times*). Published: Byron, *Manfred* (June); PBS, *Laon and Cythna* (December), then withdrawn; Coleridge, *Biographia Literaria* and *Sibylline Leaves* (including *The Rime of the Ancient Mariner* with the satiric marginal gloss); Hazlitt, *Characters of Shakespear's Plays*.

Blackwood's Edinburgh Magazine founded. Habeas corpus suspended in England (March). Death of Princess Charlotte, the Prince Regent's only legitimate issue, from complications in the delivery of a stillborn child.

1818   Lackington & c., a publisher known for ghost stories and occult material, issues *Frankenstein*, unsigned, in 3 vols., priced at 16 shillings, 6 pence, in a print run of 500. PBS and MS send a copy to Scott, who reviews it favorably in *Blackwood's* (March), assuming PBS the author; other reviews in *Edinburgh Magazine* and *Quarterly Review.* March: MS, PBS, Claire, and children leave for Italy, moving from Milan to Pisa to Livorno, settling in Bagni (Baths) di Lucca in June; travel to Este; PBS brings Claire and Allegra to Venice to meet Byron; MS and children follow in August; baby Clara dies 24 September; move to Este (PBS begins *Prometheus Unbound*), Rome in November, Naples in December. Financially distressed, Godwin hounds the Shelleys for money.

Published: PBS, *The Revolt of Islam* (recast *Laon and Cythna*); Byron, *Childe Harold IV*; Austen, *Northanger Abbey* (posthumous); Peacock, *Nightmare Abbey.* Z's articles on the "Cockney School" in *Blackwood's*, attacking Leigh Hunt, Keats, and eventually Shelley.

European Alliance; habeas corpus restored in England.

1819   March: the Shelleys go to Rome; June: son William dies, move to Livorno (Leghorn), then Montenero; PBS writes his play about incest-rape and murder, *The Cenci.* MS writes her novel *Mathilda.* August: PBS, *Prometheus Unbound* published. October: Move to Florence; November: Percy Florence born, the only of their four children to survive into adulthood.

Byron's "Fragment" published, a piece from that ghost-story compact. He tells Murray that MS, not PBS (as most reviews assumed), is the author of *Frankenstein.* April: John William Polidori's *The Vampyre: A Tale by Lord Byron*, another issue of the compact, appears in *New Monthly Magazine.* Scathing review of PBS's *The Revolt of Islam* in the *Quarterly*, with a vicious attack on his character.

August: "Peterloo Massacre" (a militia charge at a peaceful workers' demonstration near Manchester), and Shelley responds with *The Mask of Anarchy* (not published until 1832); December: Six Acts (repressive measures) passed; birth of Queen Victoria. William Parry's Arctic expedition.

1820   The Shelleys move to Pisa (January), Livorno (June–August), Bagni di San Giuliano (August–October) and back to Pisa; MS writes poetic dramas, *Proserpine* and *Midas.* Byron sends Allegra to live in the country, separating her from her mother. Published: PBS's *Prometheus Unbound and Other Poems,* and *The Cenci;* Keats's last lifetime volume (including *Lamia*).

Death of George III; Regent becomes George IV. Dissolution of Parliament, Cato Street conspiracy in England. Queen Caroline tried for adultery. Royalist reactions throughout Europe; revolution in Spain and Portugal.

1821 PBS enamored of Teresa (Emilia) Viviani, writes *Epipsychidion* (published anon. in May), a visionary romance of union with her, with harsh lines about MS's coldness. Shelleys meet Edward and Jane Williams; PBS enraptured with Jane. Move to Bagni di San Giuliano (April); PBS visits Byron at Ravenna (August), and the Shelleys and the Williamses move to Pisa (October) to be near Byron. Byron publishes *Cain* in December and sends Allegra to a convent.

   Deaths of Napoleon and Keats; Shelley's elegy for Keats, *Adonais,* hooted at in *Blackwood's.*

   Greek War of Liberation (from the Ottoman Empire) begins. Polidori commits suicide.

1822 PBS writes amorous lyrics to Jane. Allegra dies of typhus in April; Shelleys move to Casa Magni, with the Williamses, on the Bay of Lerici (May); MS suffers a nearly fatal miscarriage (16 June); Leigh Hunt and his large family arrive in Pisa in July, to join Byron and Shelley in publishing *The Liberal.* PBS and Edward Williams sail to Pisa to greet them, and drown in a storm at sea on the return to Lerici (8 July). MS moves, with Byron and the Hunts, to Genoa (September). Byron works on his drama, *The Deformed Transformed.*

   Published: PBS, *Hellas* (February); Thomas De Quincey, *Confessions of an English Opium-Eater.*

1823 February: MS publishes her second novel, *Valperga.* MS quarrels with Byron and returns to London in the summer, where a redaction of *Frankenstein* is staged at the Royal Opera House and attended by MS. Another redaction, *The Demon of Switzerland,* is staged at the Royal Coburg. August: Second, two-vol. edition of *Frankenstein,* managed by Godwin and now with MS's name on the title page, is published, with some revisions by him, most later accepted by MS. Other stagings ensue: *Humgumption; or, Dr. Frankenstein and the Hobgoblin* at the New Surrey, and *Presumption and the Blue Demon* at Davis's Royal Amphitheatre. MS receives a £100 annuity from PBS's father. Byron becomes involved in the War for Greek Independence.

1824 16 March: Foreign Secretary George Canning invokes *Frankenstein* in Parliament, to warn of the dangers of liberating West Indian plantation slaves. Byron dies in Greece in April; his body is taken to England, where he is buried in July, with his ancestors near Newstead Abbey, having been refused interment at Westminster Abbey. MS publishes PBS's *Posthumous Poems,* which his father immediately suppresses, forbidding her to write anything about PBS as a condition of the annuity. The Hunts publish Byron's *The Deformed Transformed*. *Frank-in-Steam; or The Modern Promise to Pay* (a burlesque) is staged.

1825   Godwin declares bankruptcy. The gift-book annual craze begins with *Forget-Me-Not*.

1826   Published: MS's novel, *The Last Man*. When PBS's eldest son (by Harriet) dies, Percy Florence becomes heir. June: *Le Monstre et le Magicien* opens in Paris for 94 performances. July, in London: Milner's *The Man and the Monster* staged at the Royal Coburg, and *The Monster and the Magician* opens at the Royal West.

1827   MS helps Thomas Moore with his *Life of Byron* (published 1830). Edward Parry gets closer to the North Pole than any attempt in the previous 50 years.

1828   Published: Leigh Hunt, *Lord Byron and Some of His Contemporaries* (with a chapter on PBS). MS contracts smallpox, begins to publish in the annuals, with a tale in *The Keepsake*. Over the next ten years, MS will publish previously unknown poems and essays by PBS, as well as her own poetry and tales in these volumes.

1830   Published: MS, *Perkin Warbeck*.

1831   31 October (Halloween), second edition of *Frankenstein* published (much revised, with Introduction), bound with Frederick Schiller's *The Ghost-Seer*, in Bentley and Coburn's Standard Novels Series, in a run of 4,000 copies; also published in Edinburgh and Dublin. First Reform Bill, which would have given the vote to some of the unpropertied working class, defeated—amidst often-violent debates.

1832   Second Reform Bill is passed, increasing the representation in Parliament and expanding the vote to middle-class property-holders. William Godwin Jr. dies in the cholera epidemic (1831–33). Percy Florence at Harrow. Death of Scott. PBS's review of *Frankenstein* (1817–18) appears in *The Athenæum* as part of his posthumous papers.

1833   Emancipation of slaves in the British colonies.

1835   MS's *Lodore* published. MS writes biographies for *Lardner's Cabinet Encyclopedia*.

1836   Death of William Godwin, age 80. MS back in London.

1837   MS's last novel, *Falkner*, published; Percy Florence at Trinity College, Cambridge. Coronation of Queen Victoria.

1838   William Hazlitt Jr. asks to publish *Frankenstein* in his series, *The Best Works of the Best Authors*.

1839–40   MS's editions of PBS's *Poetical Works* and *Essays and Letters* appear, including material not previously published.

1840   MS travels to Continental Europe with Percy Florence and his friends.

1842–43   Another trip to Continental Europe.

1844   PBS's father dies, and Percy Florence succeeds to the estate. Published: MS, *Rambles in Germany and Italy.*

1848   Percy Florence marries.

1849   MS moves to Field Place (the Shelley family home) with Percy Florence and his wife. *Frankenstein; or, the Model Man* opens at Adelphi Theatre. Herman Melville reads *Frankenstein.*

1851   1 February: Death of MS in London, from a brain tumor. She is buried next to her parents, whose graves were relocated to St. Peters churchyard in Bournemouth. Melville publishes *Moby Dick.*

1887   *Frankenstein; or The Vampire's Victim* is staged.

1910   Valentine's day: Thomas Edison's *Frankenstein.*

1931   James Whale's *Frankenstein.*

1935   James Whale's *The Bride of Frankenstein*, with Elsa Lanchester playing both Mary Shelley and the bride.

FRANKENSTEIN;

OR,

THE MODERN PROMETHEUS.

———◆———

IN THREE VOLUMES.

———◆———

> Did I request thee, Maker, from my clay
> To mould me man ? Did I solicit thee
> From darkness to promote me ?——
> PARADISE LOST.

———

VOL. I.

═══════

London :

PRINTED FOR

LACKINGTON, HUGHES, HARDING, MAVOR, & JONES,
FINSBURY SQUARE.

———

1818.

The verse is *Paradise Lost* 10.743–45: Adam, in soliloquy, expostulating with an absent God after the Fall. Like many novels of the day, *Frankenstein* was published in three volumes, to facilitate reading by more than one person at a time. Volume 1 of *Frankenstein* had 181 pages plus 12 front-matter pages, Volume 2 had 156 pages, and Volume 3 had 192 pages, for a total of about 530. These pages were printed in the highly economical form of duodecimo ("12mo"): 12 pages on each side of a sheet of paper, front and back, to yield a 24-page bundle that was then stitched together with other such bundles before binding. The pages were not crowded: each held about 100 words to the page, only 5 to 8 words per line, to enable easy reading. *Frankenstein* was priced at 16 shillings, 6 pence, and the Shelleys realized a profit of £41/13/10. Jane Austen's *Emma*, published by John Murray in 1815, also three-volume duodecimo, was priced at £1/1 (or 21 shillings); by this time, Austen was a known success.

TO

WILLIAM GODWIN,

AUTHOR OF POLITICAL JUSTICE, CALEB WILLIAMS, &c.

THESE VOLUMES

Are respectfully inscribed

BY

THE AUTHOR.

Godwin is Shelley's father. *Enquiry Concerning Political Justice*, an intellectually if not politically influential work, was published in 1793 in the wake of the execution of Louis XVI of France, during the Terror that followed the Revolution. It was an emphatic English statement of "anarchist" political philosophy: a disdain of government and institutions as the source of corruption and manifold evils, and an argument for government by rational deliberation of free individuals. *The Adventures of Caleb Williams*, a novel published in 1794, deploys Godwin's political themes into an adventure/detective fiction involving haunted psychologies, crime, and punishment.

Frankenstein;
or,
The Modern Prometheus

～⌇～

by Mary Wollstonecraft Shelley

Preface[1]

The event on which this fiction is founded has been supposed, by Dr Darwin, and some of the physiological writers of Germany, as not of impossible occurrence.[2] I shall not be supposed as according the remotest degree of serious faith to such an imagination; yet, in assuming it as the basis of a work of fancy, I have not considered myself as merely weaving a series of supernatural terrors. The event on which the interest of the story depends is exempt from the disadvantages of

---

[1]In her 1831 Introduction, Shelley says this Preface was "entirely written by" Percy.

[2]Erasmus Darwin (1731–1802), poet, physician, botanist, and grandfather of Charles Darwin, was the most popular scientific writer of Shelley's age. He was a friend of Godwin, and Shelley may have known him in her girlhood. His encyclopedic *Zoonomia* (1794–96) proposed the genetic transmission of environmentally induced diseases and adaptations, including the influence on an embryo of a father's psychology and imagination at conception. In *The Temple of Nature* (1803), Darwin speculated further about "spontaneous vital production" (contradicting Creationism), and asexual male reproduction: "In these lone births no tender mothers blend / Their genial powers to nourish or defend. . . . Birth after birth the line unchanging runs, / And fathers live transmitted in their sons" (2.103–8).

a mere tale of spectres or enchantment. It was recommended by the novelty of the situations which it developes; and, however impossible as a physical fact, affords a point of view to the imagination for the delineating of human passions more comprehensive and commanding than any which the ordinary relations of existing events can yield.

I have thus endeavoured to preserve the truth of the elementary principles of human nature, while I have not scrupled to innovate upon their combinations. The *Iliad*, the tragic poetry of Greece,—Shakespeare, in the *Tempest* and *Midsummer Night's Dream*,—and most especially Milton, in *Paradise Lost*, conform to this rule; and the most humble novelist, who seeks to confer or receive amusement from his labours, may, without presumption, apply to prose fiction a licence, or rather a rule, from the adoption of which so many exquisite combinations of human feeling have resulted in the highest specimens of poetry.

The circumstance on which my story rests was suggested in casual conversation. It was commenced, partly as a source of amusement, and partly as an expedient for exercising any untried resources of mind. Other motives were mingled with these, as the work proceeded. I am by no means indifferent to the manner in which whatever moral tendencies exist in the sentiments or characters it contains shall affect the reader; yet my chief concern in this respect has been limited to the avoiding the enervating effects of the novels of the present day, and to the exhibition of the amiableness of domestic affection, and the excellence of universal virtue. The opinions which naturally spring from the character and situation of the hero are by no means to be conceived as existing always in my own conviction; nor is any inference justly to be drawn from the following pages as prejudicing any philosophical doctrine of whatever kind.

It is a subject also of additional interest to the author, that this story was begun in the majestic region where the scene is principally laid, and in society which cannot cease to be regretted. I passed the summer of 1816 in the environs of Geneva. The season was cold and rainy, and in the evenings we crowded around a blazing wood fire, and occasionally amused ourselves with some German stories of ghosts, which happened to fall into our hands.[3] These tales excited in us a playful desire of imitation. Two other friends[4] (a tale from the

---

[3]The stories were a French translation of *Fantasmagoriana; or Collected Stories of Apparitions of Specters, Ghosts, Phantoms, etc.* (1812).

[4]Percy Shelley and Lord Byron. See "The Story-Telling Compact," p. 273.

pen of one of whom would be far more acceptable to the public than any thing I can ever hope to produce) and myself agreed to write each a story, founded on some supernatural occurrence.

The weather, however, suddenly became serene; and my two friends left me on a journey among the Alps, and lost, in the magnificent scenes which they present, all memory of their ghostly visions. The following tale is the only one which has been completed.

Frankenstein;
or,
The Modern Prometheus

Volume I

Letter I

To Mrs SAVILLE, England.   St. Petersburgh,[1] Dec. 11th, 17—.

You will rejoice to hear that no disaster has accompanied the commencement of an enterprise which you have regarded with such evil forebodings. I arrived here yesterday; and my first task is to assure my dear sister of my welfare, and increasing confidence in the success of my undertaking.

I am already far north of London; and as I walk in the streets of Petersburgh, I feel a cold northern breeze play upon my cheeks, which braces my nerves, and fills me with delight. Do you understand this feeling? This breeze, which has travelled from the regions towards which I am advancing, gives me a foretaste of those icy climes. Inspirited by this wind of promise, my day dreams become more fervent and vivid. I try in vain to be persuaded that the pole is the seat of frost and desolation; it ever presents itself to my imagination as the region of beauty and delight. There, Margaret, the sun is for ever visible; its broad disk just skirting the horizon, and diffusing a perpetual splendour.[2] There—for with your leave, my sister, I will

---

[1] The capital of Russia, and major seaport, at the top of the gulf of Finland. For a speculative calendar, coordinating the careers of Robert Walton, Victor Frankenstein, and the Creature across the 1790s, see the Table of Dates. Godwin and Wollstonecraft conceived their daughter Mary in December 1796.

[2] A popular belief.

put some trust in preceding navigators—there snow and frost are banished; and, sailing over a calm sea, we may be wafted to a land surpassing in wonders and in beauty every region hitherto discovered on the habitable globe. Its productions and features may be without example, as the phaenomena of the heavenly bodies undoubtedly are in those undiscovered solitudes. What may not be expected in a country of eternal light? I may there discover the wondrous power which attracts the needle;[3] and may regulate a thousand celestial observations, that require only this voyage to render their seeming eccentricities consistent for ever. I shall satiate my ardent curiosity with the sight of a part of the world never before visited, and may tread a land never before imprinted by the foot of man. These are my enticements, and they are sufficient to conquer all fear of danger or death, and to induce me to commence this laborious voyage with the joy a child feels when he embarks in a little boat, with his holiday mates, on an expedition of discovery up his native river. But, supposing all these conjectures to be false, you cannot contest the inestimable benefit which I shall confer on all mankind to the last generation, by discovering a passage near the pole to those countries, to reach which at present so many months are requisite; or by ascertaining the secret of the magnet, which, if at all possible, can only be effected by an undertaking such as mine.

These reflections have dispelled the agitation with which I began my letter, and I feel my heart glow with an enthusiasm which elevates me to heaven; for nothing contributes so much to tranquillize the mind as a steady purpose,—a point on which the soul may fix its intellectual eye. This expedition has been the favourite dream of my early years. I have read with ardour the accounts of the various voyages which have been made in the prospect of arriving at the North Pacific Ocean through the seas which surround the pole. You may remember, that a history of all the voyages made for purposes of discovery composed the whole of our good uncle Thomas's library. My education was neglected, yet I was passionately fond of reading. These volumes were my study day and night, and my familiarity with them increased that regret which I had felt, as a child, on learning that my father's dying injunction had forbidden my uncle to allow me to embark in a sea-faring life.

These visions faded when I perused, for the first time, those poets whose effusions entranced my soul, and lifted it to heaven. I also

[3]Compass needle; electromagnetism was among Darwin's interests.

became a poet, and for one year lived in a Paradise of my own creation; I imagined that I also might obtain a niche in the temple where the names of Homer and Shakespeare are consecrated. You are well acquainted with my failure, and how heavily I bore the disappointment. But just at that time I inherited the fortune of my cousin, and my thoughts were turned into the channel of their earlier bent.

Six years have passed since I resolved on my present undertaking. I can, even now, remember the hour from which I dedicated myself to this great enterprise. I commenced by inuring my body to hardship. I accompanied the whale-fishers on several expeditions to the North Sea; I voluntarily endured cold, famine, thirst, and want of sleep; I often worked harder than the common sailors during the day, and devoted my nights to the study of mathematics, the theory of medicine, and those branches of physical science from which a naval adventurer might derive the greatest practical advantage. Twice I actually hired myself as an under-mate in a Greenland whaler, and acquitted myself to admiration. I must own I felt a little proud, when my captain offered me the second dignity in the vessel, and entreated me to remain with the greatest earnestness; so valuable did he consider my services.

And now, dear Margaret, do I not deserve to accomplish some great purpose. My life might have been passed in ease and luxury; but I preferred glory to every enticement that wealth placed in my path. Oh, that some encouraging voice would answer in the affirmative! My courage and my resolution is firm; but my hopes fluctuate, and my spirits are often depressed. I am about to proceed on a long and difficult voyage; the emergencies of which will demand all my fortitude: I am required not only to raise the spirits of others, but sometimes to sustain my own, when their's are failing.

This is the most favourable period for travelling in Russia. They fly quickly over the snow in their sledges; the motion is pleasant, and, in my opinion, far more agreeable than that of an English stage-coach. The cold is not excessive, if you are wrapt in furs, a dress which I have already adopted; for there is a great difference between walking the deck and remaining seated motionless for hours, when no exercise prevents the blood from actually freezing in your veins. I have no ambition to lose my life on the post-road between St. Petersburgh and Archangel.[4]

[4]Archangel, a major port on the White Sea (an inlet of the Arctic Ocean), was so named in 1613 for the monastery of Archangel Michael.

I shall depart for the latter town in a fortnight or three weeks; and my intention is to hire a ship there, which can easily be done by paying the insurance for the owner, and to engage as many sailors as I think necessary among those who are accustomed to the whale-fishing. I do not intend to sail until the month of June: and when shall I return? Ah, dear sister, how can I answer this question? If I succeed, many, many months, perhaps years, will pass before you and I may meet. If I fail, you will see me again soon, or never.

Farewell, my dear, excellent, Margaret. Heaven shower down blessings on you, and save me, that I may again and again testify my gratitude for all your love and kindness.

Your affectionate brother,
R. WALTON.

Letter II

To Mrs SAVILLE, England.   Archangel, 28th March, 17—.[5]

How slowly the time passes here, encompassed as I am by frost and snow; yet a second step is taken towards my enterprise. I have hired a vessel, and am occupied in collecting my sailors; those whom I have already engaged appear to be men on whom I can depend, and are certainly possessed of dauntless courage.

But I have one want which I have never yet been able to satisfy; and the absence of the object of which I now feel as a most severe evil. I have no friend, Margaret: when I am glowing with the enthusiasm of success, there will be none to participate my joy; if I am assailed by disappointment, no one will endeavour to sustain me in dejection. I shall commit my thoughts to paper, it is true; but that is a poor medium for the communication of feeling. I desire the company of a man who could sympathize with me; whose eyes would reply to mine. You may deem me romantic, my dear sister, but I bitterly feel the want of a friend. I have no one near me, gentle yet courageous, possessed of a cultivated as well as of a capacious mind, whose tastes are like my own, to approve or amend my plans. How would such a friend repair the faults of your poor brother! I am too ardent in execution, and too impatient of difficulties. But it is a still greater

[5]Shelley's parents were married 29 March 1797 (the year indicated by 17—).

evil to me that I am self-educated: for the first fourteen years of my life I ran wild on a common, and read nothing but our uncle Thomas's books of voyages. At that age I became acquainted with the celebrated poets of our own country; but it was only when it had ceased to be in my power to derive its most important benefits from such a conviction, that I perceived the necessity of becoming acquainted with more languages than that of my native country. Now I am twenty-eight, and am in reality more illiterate than many schoolboys of fifteen. It is true that I have thought more, and that my day dreams are more extended and magnificent; but they want (as the painters call it) *keeping*;[6] and I greatly need a friend who would have sense enough not to despise me as romantic, and affection enough for me to endeavour to regulate my mind.

Well, these are useless complaints; I shall certainly find no friend on the wide ocean, nor even here in Archangel, among merchants and seamen. Yet some feelings, unallied to the dross of human nature, beat even in these rugged bosoms. My lieutenant, for instance, is a man of wonderful courage and enterprise; he is madly desirous of glory. He is an Englishman, and in the midst of national and professional prejudices, unsoftened by cultivation, retains some of the noblest endowments of humanity. I first became acquainted with him on board a whale vessel: finding that he was unemployed in this city, I easily engaged him to assist in my enterprise.

The master is a person of an excellent disposition, and is remarkable in the ship for his gentleness, and the mildness of his discipline. He is, indeed, of so amiable a nature, that he will not hunt (a favourite, and almost the only amusement here), because he cannot endure to spill blood. He is, moreover, heroically generous. Some years ago he loved a young Russian lady, of moderate fortune; and having amassed a considerable sum in prize-money,[7] the father of the girl consented to the match. He saw his mistress once before the destined ceremony; but she was bathed in tears, and, throwing herself at his feet, entreated him to spare her, confessing at the same time that she loved another, but that he was poor, and that her father would never consent to the union. My generous friend reassured the suppliant, and on being informed of the name of her lover instantly abandoned his pursuit. He had already bought a farm with his money, on which he had designed to pass the

---

[6]Perspective; harmony of composition.

[7]The bounty (plunder) from a captured enemy ship.

remainder of his life; but he bestowed the whole on his rival, together with the remains of his prize-money to purchase stock, and then himself solicited the young woman's father to consent to her marriage with her lover. But the old man decidedly refused, thinking himself bound in honour to my friend; who, when he found the father inexorable, quitted his country, nor returned until he heard that his former mistress was married according to her inclinations. "What a noble fellow!" you will exclaim. He is so; but then he has passed all his life on board a vessel, and has scarcely an idea beyond the rope and the shroud.[8]

But do not suppose that, because I complain a little, or because I can conceive a consolation for my toils which I may never know, that I am wavering in my resolutions. Those are as fixed as fate; and my voyage is only now delayed until the weather shall permit my embarkation. The winter has been dreadfully severe; but the spring promises well, and it is considered as a remarkably early season; so that, perhaps, I may sail sooner than I expected. I shall do nothing rashly; you know me sufficiently to confide in my prudence and considerateness whenever the safety of others is committed to my care.

I cannot describe to you my sensations on the near prospect of my undertaking. It is impossible to communicate to you a conception of the trembling sensation, half pleasurable and half fearful, with which I am preparing to depart. I am going to unexplored regions, to "the land of mist and snow;" but I shall kill no albatross,[9] therefore do not be alarmed for my safety.[10]

Shall I meet you again, after having traversed immense seas, and returned by the most southern cape of Africa or America? I dare not expect such success, yet I cannot bear to look on the reverse of the picture. Continue to write to me by every opportunity: I may receive your letters (though the chance is very doubtful) on some occasions when I need them most to support my spirits. I love you very tenderly. Remember me with affection, should you never hear from me again.

Your affectionate brother,
ROBERT WALTON.

[8]1831 text] he is silent as a Turk; and a kind of ignorant carelessness attends him, which, while it renders his conduct the more astonishing, detracts from the interest and sympathy which otherwise he would command.

[9]"Coleridge's Ancient Mariner" [Shelley's note, 1823]. She heard Coleridge recite *The Rime* when he visited her father in 1806. After the Mariner kills an albatross, all, save him, die.

[10]For another 1831 addition, an elaborated self-heroizing, see p. 191.

Letter III

To Mrs SAVILLE, England.   July 7th, 17—.

My Dear Sister,

I write a few lines in haste, to say that I am safe, and well advanced on my voyage. This letter will reach England by a merchant-man now on its homeward voyage from Archangel; more fortunate than I, who may not see my native land, perhaps, for many years. I am, however, in good spirits: my men are bold, and apparently firm of purpose; nor do the floating sheets of ice that continually pass us, indicating the dangers of the region towards which we are advancing, appear to dismay them. We have already reached a very high latitude; but it is the height of summer, and although not so warm as in England, the southern gales, which blow us speedily towards those shores which I so ardently desire to attain, breathe a degree of renovating warmth which I had not expected.

No incidents have hitherto befallen us, that would make a figure in a letter. One or two stiff gales, and the breaking of a mast, are accidents which experienced navigators scarcely remember to record; and I shall be well content, if nothing worse happen to us during our voyage.

Adieu, my dear Margaret. Be assured, that for my own sake, as well as your's, I will not rashly encounter danger. I will be cool, persevering, and prudent.[11]

Remember me to all my English friends.

Most affectionately yours,
R.W.

Letter IV

To Mrs SAVILLE, England.   August 5th, 17—.

So strange an accident has happened to us, that I cannot forbear recording it, although it is very probable that you will see me before these papers can come into your possession.

Last Monday (July 31st), we were nearly surrounded by ice, which closed in the ship on all sides, scarcely leaving her the sea room in which she floated. Our situation was somewhat dangerous, especially as we

[11]See the text added in 1831, again, an expansion of self-heroizing, p. 192.

were compassed round by a very thick fog. We accordingly lay to, hoping that some change would take place in the atmosphere and weather.

About two o'clock the mist cleared away, and we beheld, stretched out in every direction, vast and irregular plains of ice, which seemed to have no end. Some of my comrades groaned, and my own mind began to grow watchful with anxious thoughts, when a strange sight suddenly attracted our attention, and diverted our solicitude from our own situation. We perceived a low carriage, fixed on a sledge and drawn by dogs, pass on towards the north, at the distance of half a mile: a being which had the shape of a man, but apparently of gigantic stature, sat in the sledge, and guided the dogs. We watched the rapid progress of the traveller with our telescopes, until he was lost among the distant inequalities of the ice.

This appearance excited our unqualified wonder. We were, as we believed, many hundred miles from any land; but this apparition seemed to denote that it was not, in reality, so distant as we had supposed. Shut in, however, by ice, it was impossible to follow his track, which we had observed with the greatest attention.

About two hours after this occurrence, we heard the ground sea;[12] and before night the ice broke, and freed our ship. We, however, lay to until the morning, fearing to encounter in the dark those large loose masses which float about after the breaking up of the ice. I profited of this time to rest for a few hours.

In the morning, however, as soon as it was light, I went upon deck, and found all the sailors busy on one side of the vessel, apparently talking to some one in the sea. It was, in fact, a sledge, like that we had seen before, which had drifted towards us in the night, on a large fragment of ice. Only one dog remained alive; but there was a human being within it, whom the sailors were persuading to enter the vessel. He was not, as the other traveller seemed to be, a savage inhabitant of some undiscovered island, but an European. When I appeared on deck, the master said, "Here is our captain, and he will not allow you to perish on the open sea."

On perceiving me, the stranger addressed me in English, although with a foreign accent. "Before I come on board your vessel," said he, "will you have the kindness to inform me whither you are bound?"

You may conceive my astonishment on hearing such a question addressed to me from a man on the brink of destruction, and to

[12]A stormy sea with heavy waves.

whom I should have supposed that my vessel would have been a re-source which he would not have exchanged for the most precious wealth the earth can afford. I replied, however, that we were on a voyage of discovery towards the northern pole.

Upon hearing this he appeared satisfied, and consented to come on board. Good God! Margaret, if you had seen the man who thus capitulated for his safety, your surprise would have been boundless. His limbs were nearly frozen, and his body dreadfully emaciated by fatigue and suffering. I never saw a man in so wretched a condition. We attempted to carry him into the cabin; but as soon as he had quit-ted the fresh air, he fainted. We accordingly brought him back to the deck, and restored him to animation by rubbing him with brandy, and forcing him to swallow a small quantity. As soon as he shewed signs of life, we wrapped him up in blankets, and placed him near the chimney of the kitchen-stove.[13] By slow degrees he recovered, and ate a little soup, which restored him wonderfully.

Two days passed in this manner before he was able to speak; and I often feared that his sufferings had deprived him of understanding. When he had in some measure recovered, I removed him to my own cabin, and attended on him as much as my duty would permit. I never saw a more interesting creature: his eyes have generally an ex-pression of wildness, and even madness; but there are moments when, if any one performs an act of kindness towards him, or does him any the most trifling service, his whole countenance is lighted up, as it were, with a beam of benevolence and sweetness that I never saw equalled. But he is generally melancholy and despairing; and sometimes he gnashes his teeth, as if impatient of the weight of woes that oppresses him.

When my guest was a little recovered, I had great trouble to keep off the men, who wished to ask him a thousand questions; but I would not allow him to be tormented by their idle curiosity, in a state of body and mind whose restoration evidently depended upon entire repose. Once, however, the lieutenant asked, Why he had come so far upon the ice in so strange a vehicle?

His countenance instantly assumed an aspect of the deepest gloom; and he replied, "To seek one who fled from me."

"And did the man whom you pursued travel in the same fashion?"

[13]See Shelley's journal, 19 March 1815, on her dream of restoring her dead baby to life (p. 246).

"Yes."

"Then I fancy we have seen him; for, the day before we picked you up, we saw some dogs drawing a sledge, with a man in it, across the ice."

This aroused the stranger's attention; and he asked a multitude of questions concerning the route which the daemon,[14] as he called him, had pursued. Soon after, when he was alone with me, he said, "I have, doubtless, excited your curiosity, as well as that of these good people; but you are too considerate to make inquiries."

"Certainly; it would indeed be very impertinent and inhuman in me to trouble you with any inquisitiveness of mine."

"And yet you rescued me from a strange and perilous situation; you have benevolently restored me to life."

Soon after this he inquired, if I thought that the breaking up of the ice had destroyed the other sledge? I replied, that I could not answer with any degree of certainty; for the ice had not broken until near midnight, and the traveller might have arrived at a place of safety before that time; but of this I could not judge.

From this time the stranger seemed very eager to be upon deck, to watch for the sledge which had before appeared; but I have persuaded him to remain in the cabin, for he is far too weak to sustain the rawness of the atmosphere. But I have promised that some one should watch for him, and give him instant notice if any new object should appear in sight.

Such is my journal of what relates to this strange occurrence up to the present day. The stranger has gradually improved in health, but is very silent, and appears uneasy when any one except myself enters his cabin. Yet his manners are so conciliating and gentle, that the sailors are all interested in him, although they have had very little communication with him. For my own part, I begin to love him as a brother; and his constant and deep grief fills me with sympathy and compassion. He must have been a noble creature in his better days, being even now in wreck so attractive and amiable.

I said in one of my letters, my dear Margaret, that I should find no friend on the wide ocean; yet I have found a man who, before his spirit had been broken by misery, I should have been happy to have possessed as the brother of my heart.

[14]In Greek mythology, daemons are supernatural, halfway between men and gods; the term also evokes "demon."

I shall continue my journal concerning the stranger at intervals, should I have any fresh incidents to record.

August 13th, 17—.

My affection for my guest increases every day. He excites at once my admiration and my pity to an astonishing degree. How can I see so noble a creature destroyed by misery without feeling the most poignant grief? He is so gentle, yet so wise; his mind is so cultivated; and when he speaks, although his words are culled with the choicest art, yet they flow with rapidity and unparalleled eloquence.

He is now much recovered from his illness, and is continually on the deck, apparently watching for the sledge that preceded his own. Yet, although unhappy, he is not so utterly occupied by his own misery, but that he interests himself deeply in the employments of others. He has asked me many questions concerning my design;[15] and I have related my little history frankly to him. He appeared pleased with the confidence, and suggested several alterations in my plan, which I shall find exceedingly useful. There is no pedantry in his manner; but all he does appears to spring solely from the interest he instinctively takes in the welfare of those who surround him. He is often overcome by gloom, and then he sits by himself, and tries to overcome all that is sullen or unsocial in his humour. These paroxysms pass from him like a cloud from before the sun, though his dejection never leaves him. I have endeavoured to win his confidence; and I trust that I have succeeded. One day I mentioned to him the desire I had always felt of finding a friend who might sympathize with me, and direct me by his counsel. I said, I did not belong to that class of men who are offended by advice. "I am self-educated, and perhaps I hardly rely sufficiently upon my own powers. I wish therefore that my companion should be wiser and more experienced than myself, to confirm and support me; nor have I believed it impossible to find a true friend."

"I agree with you," replied the stranger, "in believing that friendship is not only a desirable, but a possible acquisition. I once had a friend, the most noble of human creatures, and am entitled, therefore, to judge respecting friendship. You have hope, and the world

---

[15]For Shelley's rewriting of the rest of this paragraph in 1831, elaborating the alter-ego sympathy, see p. 192.

before you,[16] and have no cause for despair. But I—I have lost every thing, and cannot begin life anew."

As he said this, his countenance became expressive of a calm settled grief, that touched me to the heart. But he was silent, and presently retired to his cabin.

Even broken in spirit as he is, no one can feel more deeply than he does the beauties of nature. The starry sky, the sea, and every sight afforded by these wonderful regions, seems still to have the power of elevating his soul from earth. Such a man has a double existence: he may suffer misery, and be overwhelmed by disappointments; yet when he has retired into himself, he will be like a celestial spirit, that has a halo around him, within whose circle no grief or folly ventures.

Will you laugh at the enthusiasm I express concerning this divine wanderer?[17] If you do, you must have certainly lost that simplicity which was once your characteristic charm. Yet, if you will, smile at the warmth of my expressions, while I find every day new causes for repeating them.

August 19th, 17—.

Yesterday the stranger said to me, "You may easily perceive, Captain Walton, that I have suffered great and unparalleled misfortunes. I had determined, once, that the memory of these evils should die with me; but you have won me to alter my determination. You seek for knowledge and wisdom, as I once did; and I ardently hope that the gratification of your wishes may not be a serpent to sting you, as mine has been.[18] I do not know that the relation of my misfortunes will be useful to you, yet, if you are inclined, listen to my tale.[19] I believe that the strange incidents connected with it will afford a view of nature, which may enlarge your faculties and understanding. You will hear of powers and occurrences, such as you have been accustomed to believe impossible: but I do not doubt that my tale conveys in its series internal evidence of the truth of the events of which it is composed."

[16]An echo of the last lines of *Paradise Lost* (12.646).

[17]By cross-lingual pun (the Latin verb "wander" is *errare*), Shelley evokes the errant and erring Satan.

[18]In *Paradise Lost* 9, Eve's desire for the knowledge and wisdom invested in Adam makes her vulnerable to Satan's seduction in the guise of a rationally talking snake.

[19]For the 1831 elaboration, see p. 193.

You may easily conceive that I was much gratified by the offered communication; yet I could not endure that he should renew his grief by a recital of his misfortunes. I felt the greatest eagerness to hear the promised narrative, partly from curiosity, and partly from a strong desire to ameliorate his fate, if it were in my power. I expressed these feelings in my answer.

"I thank you," he replied, "for your sympathy, but it is useless; my fate is nearly fulfilled. I wait but for one event, and then I shall repose in peace. I understand your feeling," continued he, perceiving that I wished to interrupt him; "but you are mistaken, my friend, if thus you will allow me to name you; nothing can alter my destiny: listen to my history, and you will perceive how irrevocably it is determined."

He then told me, that he would commence his narrative the next day when I should be at leisure. This promise drew from me the warmest thanks. I have resolved every night, when I am not engaged, to record, as nearly as possible in his own words, what he has related during the day. If I should be engaged, I will at least make notes. This manuscript will doubtless afford you the greatest pleasure: but to me, who know him, and who hear it from his own lips, with what interest and sympathy shall I read it in some future day![20]

Frankenstein;
or,
The Modern Prometheus

Chapter I

I am by birth a Genevese;[1] and my family is one of the most distinguished of that republic. My ancestors had been for many years counsellors and syndics;[2] and my father had filled several public situations with honour and reputation. He was respected by all who

[20]For additions in 1831, elaborating Victor's appearance and affect, see p. 193.

[1]From Geneva; Switzerland was a rare republic in a continent of monarchies, and home of Rousseau, the philosophical father of the French Revolution, who referred to himself as "Citizen of Geneva."
[2]Ruling elite.

knew him for his integrity and indefatigable attention to public business. He passed his younger days perpetually occupied by the affairs
of his country; and it was not until the decline of life that he thought
of marrying, and bestowing on the state sons who might carry his
virtues and his name down to posterity.

As the circumstances of his marriage illustrate his character, I cannot
refrain from relating them. One of his most intimate friends was a merchant, who, from a flourishing state, fell, through numerous mischances,
into poverty. This man, whose name was Beaufort, was of a proud and
unbending disposition, and could not bear to live in poverty and oblivion in the same country where he had formerly been distinguished for
his rank and magnificence. Having paid his debts, therefore, in the most
honourable manner, he retreated with his daughter to the town of
Lucerne, where he lived unknown and in wretchedness. My father loved
Beaufort with the truest friendship, and was deeply grieved by his retreat
in these unfortunate circumstances. He grieved also for the loss of his society, and resolved to seek him out and endeavour to persuade him to
begin the world again through his credit and assistance.

Beaufort had taken effectual measures to conceal himself; and it
was ten months before my father discovered his abode. Overjoyed at
this discovery, he hastened to the house, which was situated in a
mean street, near the Reuss. But when he entered, misery and despair
alone welcomed him. Beaufort had saved but a very small sum of
money from the wreck of his fortunes; but it was sufficient to provide
him with sustenance for some months, and in the mean time he
hoped to procure some respectable employment in a merchant's
house. The interval was consequently spent in inaction; his grief only
became more deep and rankling, when he had leisure for reflection;
and at length it took so fast hold of his mind, that at the end of three
months he lay on a bed of sickness, incapable of any exertion.

His daughter attended him with the greatest tenderness; but she
saw with despair that their little fund was rapidly decreasing, and
that there was no other prospect of support. But Caroline Beaufort
possessed a mind of an uncommon mould; and her courage rose to
support her in her adversity. She procured plain work;[3] she plaited
straw; and by various means contrived to earn a pittance scarcely
sufficient to support life.

[3] Basic sewing.

Several months passed in this manner. Her father grew worse; her time was more entirely occupied in attending him; her means of subsistence decreased; and in the tenth month her father died in her arms, leaving her an orphan and a beggar. This last blow overcame her; and she knelt by Beaufort's coffin, weeping bitterly, when my father entered the chamber. He came like a protecting spirit to the poor girl, who committed herself to his care, and after the interment of his friend he conducted her to Geneva, and placed her under the protection of a relation. Two years after this event Caroline became his wife.

When my father became a husband and a parent, he found his time so occupied by the duties of his new situation, that he relinquished many of his public employments, and devoted himself to the education of his children. Of these I was the eldest, and the destined successor to all his labours and utility. No creature could have more tender parents than mine. My improvement and health were their constant care, especially as I remained for several years their only child. But before I continue my narrative, I must record an incident which took place when I was four years of age.[4]

My father had a sister, whom he tenderly loved, and who had married early in life an Italian gentleman. Soon after her marriage, she had accompanied her husband into his native country, and for some years my father had very little communication with her. About the time I mentioned she died; and a few months afterwards he received a letter from her husband, acquainting him with his intention of marrying an Italian lady, and requesting my father to take charge of the infant Elizabeth, the only child of his deceased sister. "It is my wish," he said, "that you should consider her as your own daughter, and educate her thus. Her mother's fortune is secured to her, the documents of which I will commit to your keeping. Reflect upon this proposition; and decide whether you would prefer educating your niece yourself to her being brought up by a stepmother."

My father did not hesitate, and immediately went to Italy, that he might accompany the little Elizabeth to her future home. I have often heard my mother say, that she was at that time the most beautiful child she had ever seen, and shewed signs even then of a gentle and affectionate disposition. These indications, and a desire to bind as closely as possible the ties of domestic love, determined my mother to

---

[4]For the 1831 revision of this episode, and of Victor's boyhood, see pp. 194–99.

consider Elizabeth as my future wife; a design which she never found reason to repent.[5]

From this time Elizabeth Lavenza became my playfellow, and, as we grew older, my friend. She was docile and good tempered, yet gay and playful as a summer insect. Although she was lively and animated, her feelings were strong and deep, and her disposition uncommonly affectionate. No one could better enjoy liberty, yet no one could submit with more grace than she did to constraint and caprice. Her imagination was luxuriant, yet her capability of application was great. Her person was the image of her mind; her hazel eyes, although as lively as a bird's, possessed an attractive softness. Her figure was light and airy; and, though capable of enduring great fatigue, she appeared the most fragile creature in the world. While I admired her understanding and fancy, I loved to tend on her, as I should on a favourite animal; and I never saw so much grace both of person and mind united to so little pretension.

Every one adored Elizabeth. If the servants had any request to make, it was always through her intercession. We were strangers to any species of disunion and dispute; for although there was a great dissimilitude in our characters, there was an harmony in that very dissimilitude. I was more calm and philosophical than my companion; yet my temper was not so yielding. My application was of longer endurance; but it was not so severe whilst it endured. I delighted in investigating the facts relative to the actual world; she busied herself in following the aërial creations of the poets. The world was to me a secret, which I desired to discover; to her it was a vacancy, which she sought to people with imaginations of her own.[6]

My brothers were considerably younger than myself; but I had a friend in one of my schoolfellows, who compensated for this deficiency. Henry Clerval was the son of a merchant of Geneva, an intimate friend of my father. He was a boy of singular talent and fancy. I remember, when he was nine years old, he wrote a fairy tale, which was the delight and amazement of all his companions. His favourite study consisted in books of chivalry and romance; and when very young, I can remember, that we used to act plays composed by him out of these favourite books, the principal characters of which were Orlando, Robin Hood, Amadis, and St. George.

[5]First-cousin marriages were not unusual during this time.
[6]Percy Shelley wrote the last two sentences of this paragraph.

No youth could have passed more happily than mine. My parents were indulgent, and my companions amiable. Our studies were never forced; and by some means we always had an end placed in view, which excited us to ardour in the prosecution of them. It was by this method, and not by emulation, that we were urged to application. Elizabeth was not incited to apply herself to drawing, that her companions might not outstrip her; but through the desire of pleasing her aunt, by the representation of some favourite scene done by her own hand. We learned Latin and English, that we might read the writings in those languages; and so far from study being made odious to us through punishment, we loved application, and our amusements would have been the labours of other children. Perhaps we did not read so many books, or learn languages so quickly, as those who are disciplined according to the ordinary methods; but what we learned was impressed the more deeply on our memories.

In this description of our domestic circle I include Henry Clerval; for he was constantly with us. He went to school with me, and generally passed the afternoon at our house; for being an only child, and destitute of companions at home, his father was well pleased that he should find associates at our house; and we were never completely happy when Clerval was absent.

I feel pleasure in dwelling on the recollections of childhood, before misfortune had tainted my mind, and changed its bright visions of extensive usefulness into gloomy and narrow reflections upon self. But, in drawing the picture of my early days, I must not omit to record those events which led, by insensible steps to my after tale of misery: for when I would account to myself for the birth of that passion, which afterwards ruled my destiny, I find it arise, like a mountain river, from ignoble and almost forgotten sources; but, swelling as it proceeded, it became the torrent which, in its course, has swept away all my hopes and joys.

Natural philosophy is the genius[7] that has regulated my fate; I desire therefore, in this narration, to state those facts which led to my predilection for that science. When I was thirteen years of age, we all went on a party of pleasure to the baths near Thonon: the inclemency of the weather obliged us to remain a day confined to the inn. In this house I chanced to find a volume of the works of

[7]Natural philosophy is science (the study of nature); genius: divine spirit, but also with the modern sense of intellectual power.

Cornelius Agrippa.[8] I opened it with apathy; the theory which he attempts to demonstrate, and the wonderful facts which he relates, soon changed this feeling into enthusiasm. A new light seemed to dawn upon my mind; and, bounding with joy, I communicated my discovery to my father. I cannot help remarking here the many opportunities instructors possess of directing the attention of their pupils to useful knowledge, which they utterly neglect. My father looked carelessly at the title-page of my book, and said, "Ah! Cornelius Agrippa! My dear Victor, do not waste your time upon this; it is sad trash."

If, instead of this remark, my father had taken the pains to explain to me, that the principles of Agrippa had been entirely exploded, and that a modern system of science had been introduced, which possessed much greater powers than the ancient, because the powers of the latter where chimerical, while those of the former were real and practical; under such circumstances, I should certainly have thrown Agrippa aside, and, with my imagination warmed as it was, should probably have applied myself to the more rational theory of chemistry which has resulted from modern discoveries. It is even possible, that the train of my ideas would never have received the fatal impulse that led to my ruin. But the cursory glance my father had taken of my volume by no means assured me that he was acquainted with its contents; and I continued to read with the greatest avidity.

When I returned home, my first care was to procure the whole works of this author, and afterwards of Paracelsus and Albertus Magnus.[9] I read and studied the wild fancies of these writers with delight; they appeared to me treasures known to few beside myself;[10] and although I often wished to communicate these secret stores of knowledge to my father, yet his indefinite censure of my favourite Agrippa always withheld me. I disclosed my discoveries to Elizabeth,

[8]Controversial, persecuted German occultist and skeptic (1486–1535), author of *De Occulta Philosophia* (of Occult Science), 1513.

[9]Paracelsus (?1493–1541), Swiss mystic and physician, whose interests ranged from magic and alchemy to modern medicine and chemistry, believed that it was possible to create human life by scientific process. Albertus Magnus (c. 1193–1280), German monk, theologian, and scholastic philosopher. P. Shelley told Godwin of his boyhood rapture with "the reveries of Albertus Magnus & Paracelsus" (letter; 3 June 1812). Books were very expensive. It is remarkable for a young teenager to have this purchasing power.

[10]For the 1831 version of the rest of this paragraph, and the next four, see pp. 199–200. Shelley expands Victor's secret romance with occult science.

therefore, under a promise of strict secrecy; but she did not interest herself in the subject, and I was left by her to pursue my studies alone.

It may appear very strange, that a disciple of Albertus Magnus should arise in the eighteenth century; but our family was not scientifical, and I had not attended any of the lectures given at the schools of Geneva. My dreams were therefore undisturbed by reality; and I entered with the greatest diligence into the search of the philosopher's stone and the elixir of life.[11] But the latter obtained my most undivided attention: wealth was an inferior object; but what glory would attend the discovery, if I could banish disease from the human frame, and render man invulnerable to any but a violent death!

Nor were these my only visions. The raising of ghosts or devils was a promise liberally accorded by my favourite authors,[12] the fulfilment of which I most eagerly sought; and if my incantations were always unsuccessful, I attributed the failure rather to my own inexperience and mistake, than to a want of skill or fidelity in my instructors.

The natural phaenomena that take place every day before our eyes did not escape my examinations. Distillation, and the wonderful effects of steam, processes of which my favourite authors were utterly ignorant, excited my astonishment; but my utmost wonder was engaged by some experiments on an air-pump, which I saw employed by a gentleman whom we were in the habit of visiting.[13]

The ignorance of the early philosophers on these and several other points served to decrease their credit with me: but I could not entirely throw them aside, before some other system should occupy their place in my mind.

When I was about fifteen years old, we had retired to our house near Belrive,[14] when we witnessed a most violent and terrible thunder-storm. It advanced from behind the mountains of Jura; and the thunder burst at once with frightful loudness from various quarters of the heavens.[15] I remained, while the storm lasted, watching its progress with curiosity and delight. As I stood at the door, on a sudden

[11]Medieval alchemists sought the elixir of life, to restore youth; the philosopher's stone would change base metals to gold. The hero of Godwin's novel *St. Leon* (1799) uncovers both secrets.

[12]Percy Shelley conducted such experiments.

[13]Erasmus Darwin speculated about steam-power.

[14]"Beautiful shore" (French), about 4 miles from Geneva.

[15]For Byron's famous rendering of such events, see pp. 267–69.

I beheld a stream of fire issue from an old and beautiful oak, which stood about twenty yards from our house; and so soon as the dazzling light vanished, the oak had disappeared, and nothing remained but a blasted stump.[16] When we visited it the next morning, we found the tree shattered in a singular manner. It was not splintered by the shock, but entirely reduced to thin ribbands of wood. I never beheld any thing so utterly destroyed.

The catastrophe of this tree excited my extreme astonishment;[17] and I eagerly inquired of my father the nature and origin of thunder and lightning. He replied, "Electricity," describing at the same time the various effects of that power. He constructed a small electrical machine, and exhibited a few experiments; he made also a kite, with a wire and string, which drew down that fluid from the clouds.[18]

This last stroke completed the overthrow of Cornelius Agrippa, Albertus Magnus, and Paracelsus, who had so long reigned the lords of my imagination. But by some fatality I did not feel inclined to commence the study of any modern system; and this disinclination was influenced by the following circumstance.

My father expressed a wish that I should attend a course of lectures upon natural philosophy,[19] to which I cheerfully consented. Some accident prevented my attending these lectures until the course was nearly finished. The lecture, being therefore one of the last, was entirely incomprehensible to me. The professor discoursed with the greatest fluency of potassium and boron, of sulphates and oxyds, terms to which I could affix no idea; and I became disgusted with the science of natural philosophy, although I still read Pliny and Buffon with delight, authors, in my estimation, of nearly equal interest and utility.[20]

My occupations at this age were principally the mathematics, and most of the branches of study appertaining to that science. I was busily employed in learning languages; Latin was already familiar to

[16]An omen of Victor's fate after his experiment with electricity. See pp. 65, 125, 149, 174.

[17]For the 1831 revision of this passage, elaborating Victor's fatal rapture with modern science, see p. 200.

[18]An allusion to the famous experiments that earned Benjamin Franklin the nickname "The Modern Prometheus"; Erasmus Darwin was also interested in electricity, a new science that excited many, including Alessandro Volta, who experimented with electric currents in 1800, and Humphry Davy, who was working on electroplating in 1807.

[19]The 18th-c. term for natural sciences.

[20]Pliny (1st c.) and Comte de Buffon (18th c.) were naturalists and rationalists who influenced Percy; Mary read both in 1817.

me, and I began to read some of the easiest Greek authors without the help of a lexicon. I also perfectly understood English and German. This is the list of my accomplishments at the age of seventeen; and you may conceive that my hours were fully employed in acquiring and maintaining a knowledge of this various literature.

Another task also devolved upon me, when I became the instructor of my brothers. Ernest was six years younger than myself, and was my principal pupil. He had been afflicted with ill health from his infancy, through which Elizabeth and I had been his constant nurses: his disposition was gentle, but he was incapable of any severe application. William, the youngest of our family, was yet an infant, and the most beautiful little fellow in the world;[21] his lively blue eyes, dimpled cheeks, and endearing manners, inspired the tenderest affection.

Such was our domestic circle, from which care and pain seemed for ever banished. My father directed our studies, and my mother partook of our enjoyments. Neither of us possessed the slightest preeminence over the other; the voice of command was never heard amongst us; but mutual affection engaged us all to comply with and obey the slightest desire of each other.

Chapter II

When I had attained the age of seventeen, my parents resolved that I should become a student at the university of Ingolstadt.[1] I had hitherto attended the schools of Geneva; but my father thought it necessary, for the completion of my education, that I should be made acquainted with other customs than those of my native country. My departure was therefore fixed at an early date; but, before the day resolved upon could arrive, the first misfortune of my life occurred—an omen, as it were, of my future misery.

Elizabeth had caught the scarlet fever; but her illness was not severe, and she quickly recovered. During her confinement, many arguments had been urged to persuade my mother to refrain from attending upon

[21]The Shelleys' son William, named for William Godwin, was born January 1816; his mother conceived *Frankenstein* in June.

[1]The University of Ingolstadt, in Bavaria, Germany, housed a medical school, and was a well-known center of progressive learning. One of its professors founded a secret society there, the Order of the Illuminati. Its advocacy of free-thinking and radical politics got it outlawed in 1785.

her. She had, at first, yielded to our entreaties; but when she heard that her favourite was recovering, she could no longer debar herself from her society, and entered her chamber long before the danger of infection was past. The consequences of this imprudence were fatal. On the third day my mother sickened; her fever was very malignant, and the looks of her attendants prognosticated the worst event. On her death-bed the fortitude and benignity of this admirable woman did not desert her. She joined the hands of Elizabeth and myself: "My children," she said, "my firmest hopes of future happiness were placed on the prospect of your union. This expectation will now be the consolation of your father. Elizabeth, my love, you must supply my place to your younger cousins. Alas! I regret that I am taken from you; and, happy and beloved as I have been, is it not hard to quit you all? But these are not thoughts befitting me; I will endeavour to resign myself cheerfully to death, and will indulge a hope of meeting you in another world."

She died calmly; and her countenance expressed affection even in death. I need not describe the feelings of those whose dearest ties are rent by that most irreparable evil, the void that presents itself to the soul, and the despair that is exhibited on the countenance. It is so long before the mind can persuade itself that she, whom we saw every day, and whose very existence appeared a part of our own, can have departed for ever—that the brightness of a beloved eye can have been extinguished, and the sound of a voice so familiar, and dear to the ear, can be hushed, never more to be heard. These are the reflections of the first days; but when the lapse of time proves the reality of the evil, then the actual bitterness of grief commences. Yet from whom has not that rude hand rent away some dear connexion; and why should I describe a sorrow which all have felt, and must feel? The time at length arrives, when grief is rather an indulgence than a necessity; and the smile that plays upon the lips, although it may be deemed a sacrilege, is not banished. My mother was dead, but we had still duties which we ought to perform; we must continue our course with the rest, and learn to think ourselves fortunate, whilst one remains whom the spoiler[2] has not seized.

My journey to Ingolstadt, which had been deferred by these events, was now again determined upon. I obtained from my father a respite of some weeks. This period was spent sadly; my mother's death, and my speedy departure, depressed our spirits; but Elizabeth

[2]An old allegorical term for death.

endeavoured to renew the spirit of cheerfulness in our little society. Since the death of her aunt, her mind had acquired new firmness and vigour. She determined to fulfil her duties with the greatest exactness; and she felt that that most imperious duty, of rendering her uncle and cousins happy, had devolved upon her. She consoled me, amused her uncle, instructed my brothers; and I never beheld her so enchanting as at this time, when she was continually endeavouring to contribute to the happiness of others, entirely forgetful of herself.

The day of my departure at length arrived. I had taken leave of all my friends, excepting Clerval, who spent the last evening with us.[3] He bitterly lamented that he was unable to accompany me; but his father could not be persuaded to part with him, intending that he should become a partner with him in business, in compliance with his favourite theory, that learning was superfluous in the commerce of ordinary life. Henry had a refined mind; he had no desire to be idle, and was well pleased to become his father's partner, but he believed that a man might be a very good trader, and yet possess a cultivated understanding.

We sat late, listening to his complaints, and making many little arrangements for the future. The next morning early I departed. Tears gushed from the eyes of Elizabeth; they proceeded partly from sorrow at my departure, and partly because she reflected that the same journey was to have taken place three months before, when a mother's blessing would have accompanied me.

I threw myself into the chaise that was to convey me away, and indulged in the most melancholy reflections. I, who had ever been surrounded by amiable companions, continually engaged in endeavouring to bestow mutual pleasure, I was now alone. In the university, whither I was going, I must form my own friends, and be my own protector. My life had hitherto been remarkably secluded and domestic; and this had given me invincible repugnance to new countenances. I loved my brothers, Elizabeth, and Clerval; these were "old familiar faces";[4] but I believed myself totally unfitted for the company of strangers. Such were my reflections as I commenced my journey; but as I proceeded, my spirits and hopes rose. I ardently desired the acquisition of knowledge. I had often, when at home, thought it hard to remain during my

[3]For the 1831 version of the rest of this paragraph, and the next, see p. 201. Shelley elaborates the friends' painful departure and different prospects.

[4]A reference to a poem (1798) of the same title by Charles Lamb: "For some they have died, and some they have left me, / And some are taken from me; all are departed; / All, all are gone, the old familiar faces."

youth cooped up in one place, and had longed to enter the world, and take my station among other human beings. Now my desires were complied with, and it would, indeed, have been folly to repent.

I had sufficient leisure for these and many other reflections during my journey to Ingolstadt, which was long and fatiguing. At length the high white steeple of the town met my eyes. I alighted, and was conducted to my solitary apartment, to spend the evening as I pleased.

The next morning I delivered my letters of introduction, and paid a visit to some of the principal professors,[5] and among others to M. Krempe, professor of natural philosophy. He received me with politeness, and asked me several questions concerning my progress in the different branches of science appertaining to natural philosophy. I mentioned, it is true, with fear and trembling, the only authors I had ever read upon those subjects. The professor stared: "Have you," he said, "really spent your time in studying such nonsense?"

I replied in the affirmative. "Every minute," continued M. Krempe with warmth, "every instant that you have wasted on those books is utterly and entirely lost. You have burdened your memory with exploded systems, and useless names. Good God! in what desert land have you lived, where no one was kind enough to inform you that these fancies, which you have so greedily imbibed, are a thousand years old, and as musty as they are ancient? I little expected in this enlightened and scientific age to find a disciple of Albertus Magnus and Paracelsus. My dear Sir, you must begin your studies entirely anew."

So saying, he stept aside, and wrote down a list of several books treating of natural philosophy, which he desired me to procure, and dismissed me, after mentioning that in the beginning of the following week he intended to commence a course of lectures upon natural philosophy in its general relations, and that M. Waldman, a fellow-professor, would lecture upon chemistry the alternate days that he missed.

I returned home, not disappointed, for I had long considered those authors useless whom the professor had so strongly reprobated; but I did not feel much inclined to study the books which I procured at his recommendation. M. Krempe was a little squat man, with a gruff voice and repulsive countenance; the teacher, therefore, did not prepossess me in favour of his doctrine. Besides, I had a contempt for the

---

[5]For the 1831 version, see p. 202. Shelley gives Victor a self-exculpating rhetoric of destiny.

uses of modern natural philosophy. It was very different, when the masters of the science sought immortality and power; such views, although futile, were grand: but now the scene was changed. The ambition of the inquirer seemed to limit itself to the annihilation of those visions on which my interest in science was chiefly founded. I was required to exchange chimeras of boundless grandeur for realities of little worth.

Such were my reflections during the first two or three days spent almost in solitude. But as the ensuing week commenced, I thought of the information which M. Krempe had given me concerning the lectures. And although I could not consent to go and hear that little conceited fellow deliver sentences out of a pulpit, I recollected what he had said of M. Waldman, whom I had never seen, as he had hitherto been out of town.

Partly from curiosity, and partly from idleness, I went into the lecturing room, which M. Waldman entered shortly after. This professor was very unlike his colleague. He appeared about fifty years of age, but with an aspect expressive of the greatest benevolence; a few gray hairs covered his temples, but those at the back of his head were nearly black. His person was short, but remarkably erect; and his voice the sweetest I had ever heard. He began his lecture by a recapitulation of the history of chemistry and the various improvements made by different men of learning, pronouncing with fervour the names of the most distinguished discoverers. He then took a cursory view of the present state of the science, and explained many of its elementary terms. After having made a few preparatory experiments, he concluded with a panegyric upon modern chemistry, the terms of which I shall never forget:—

"The ancient teachers of this science," said he, "promised impossibilities, and performed nothing. The modern masters promise very little; they know that metals cannot be transmuted, and that the elixir of life is a chimera. But these philosophers, whose hands seem only made to dabble in dirt, and their eyes to pour over the microscope or crucible, have indeed performed miracles. They penetrate into the recesses of nature, and shew how she works in her hiding places. They ascend into the heavens; they have discovered how the blood circulates, and the nature of the air we breathe. They have acquired new and almost unlimited powers; they can command the thunders of heaven, mimic the earthquake, and even mock the invisible world with its own shadows."

I departed highly pleased with the professor and his lecture,[6] and paid him a visit the same evening. His manners in private were even more mild and attractive than in public; for there was a certain dignity in his mien during his lecture, which in his own house was replaced by the greatest affability and kindness. He heard with attention my little narration concerning my studies, and smiled at the names of Cornelius Agrippa, and Paracelsus, but without the contempt that M. Krempe had exhibited. He said, that "these were men to whose indefatigable zeal modern philosophers were indebted for most of the foundations of their knowledge. They had left to us, as an easier task, to give new names, and arrange in connected classifications, the facts which they in a great degree had been the instruments of bringing to light. The labours of men of genius, however erroneously directed, scarcely ever fail in ultimately turning to the solid advantage of mankind." I listened to his statement, which was delivered without any presumption or affection; and then added, that his lecture had removed my prejudices against modern chemists; and I, at the same time, requested his advice concerning the books I ought to procure.

"I am happy," said M. Waldman, "to have gained a disciple; and if your application equals your ability, I have no doubt of your success. Chemistry is that branch of natural philosophy in which the greatest improvements have been and may be made; it is on that account that I have made it my peculiar study; but at the same time I have not neglected the other branches of science. A man would make but a very sorry chemist, if he attended to that department of human knowledge alone. If your wish is to become really a man of science, and not merely a petty experimentalist, I should advise you to apply to every branch of natural philosophy, including mathematics."

He then took me into his laboratory, and explained to me the uses of his various machines; instructing me as to what I ought to procure, and promising me the use of his own, when I should have advanced far enough in the science not to derange their mechanism. He also gave me the list of books which I had requested; and I took my leave.

Thus ended a day memorable to me; it decided my future destiny.

[6]For new text in 1831, see p. 202. Again, Shelley gives Victor a fuller view of himself as a victim of fate. This is also, in 1831, the first time the name "Frankenstein" appears in the text proper.

Chapter III

From this day natural philosophy, and particularly chemistry, in the most comprehensive sense of the term, became nearly my sole occupation. I read with ardour those works, so full of genius and discrimination, which modern inquirers have written on these subjects. I attended the lectures, and cultivated the acquaintance, of the men of science of the university; and I found even in M. Krempe a great deal of sound sense and real information, combined, it is true, with a repulsive physiognomy and manners, but not on that account the less valuable. In M. Waldman I found a true friend. His gentleness was never tinged by dogmatism; and his instructions were given with an air of frankness and good nature, that banished every idea of pedantry. It was, perhaps, the amiable character of this man that inclined me more to that branch of natural philosophy which he professed, than an intrinsic love for the science itself. But this state of mind had place only in the first steps towards knowledge: the more fully I entered into the science, the more exclusively I pursued it for its own sake. That application, which at first had been a matter of duty and resolution, now became so ardent and eager, that the stars often disappeared in the light of morning whilst I was yet engaged in my laboratory.

As I applied so closely, it may be easily conceived that I improved rapidly. My ardour was indeed the astonishment of the students; and my proficiency, that of the masters. Professor Krempe often asked me, with a sly smile, how Cornelius Agrippa went on? whilst M. Waldman expressed the most heartfelt exultation in my progress. Two years passed in this manner, during which I paid no visit to Geneva, but was engaged, heart and soul, in the pursuit of some discoveries, which I hoped to make. None but those who have experienced them can conceive of the enticements of science. In other studies you go as far as others have gone before you, and there is nothing more to know; but in a scientific pursuit there is continual food for discovery and wonder. A mind of moderate capacity, which closely pursues one study, must infallibly arrive at great proficiency in that study; and I, who continually sought the attainment of one object of pursuit, and was solely wrapt up in this, improved so rapidly, that, at the end of two years, I made some discoveries in the improvement of some chemical instruments, which procured me great esteem and admiration at the university. When I had arrived at this point, and had become as well acquainted with the theory and practice of natural philosophy as depended on the lessons of any of the professors at Ingolstadt, my residence there being no longer conducive to my improvements, I thought of returning to my friends and my native town, when an incident happened that protracted my stay.

One of the phaenomena which had peculiarly attracted my attention was the structure of the human frame, and, indeed, any animal endued with life. Whence, I often asked myself, did the principle of life proceed? It was a bold question, and one which has ever been considered as a mystery; yet with how many things are we upon the brink of becoming acquainted, if cowardice or carelessness did not restrain our inquiries. I revolved these circumstances in my mind, and determined thenceforth to apply myself more particularly to those branches of natural philosophy which relate to physiology. Unless I had been animated by an almost supernatural enthusiasm, my application to this study would have been irksome, and almost intolerable. To examine the causes of life, we must first have recourse to death. I became acquainted with the science of anatomy: but this was not sufficient; I must also observe the natural decay and corruption of the human body. In my education my father had taken the greatest precautions that my mind should be impressed with no supernatural horrors. I do not ever remember to have trembled at a tale of superstition, or to have feared the apparition of a spirit. Darkness had no effect upon my fancy; and a church-yard was to me merely the receptacle of bodies deprived of life, which, from being the seat of beauty and strength, had become food for the worm. Now I was led to examine the cause and progress of this decay, and forced to spend days and nights in vaults and charnel houses.[1] My attention was fixed upon every object the most insupportable to the delicacy of the human feelings. I saw how the fine form of man was degraded and wasted; I beheld the corruption of death succeed to the blooming cheek of life; I saw how the worm inherited the wonders of the eye and brain. I paused, examining and analysing all the minutiae of causation, as exemplified in the change from life to death, and death to life, until from the midst of this darkness a sudden light broke in upon me—a light so brilliant and wondrous, yet so simple, that while

[1]As does the frame-poet of Percy Shelley's *Alastor* (23–29); see p. 249.

I became dizzy with the immensity of the prospect which it illustrated, I was surprised that among so many men of genius, who had directed their inquiries towards the same science, that I alone should be reserved to discover so astonishing a secret.

Remember, I am not recording the vision of a madman. The sun does not more certainly shine in the heavens, than that which I now affirm is true. Some miracle might have produced it, yet the stages of the discovery were distinct and probable. After days and nights of incredible labour and fatigue, I succeeded in discovering the cause of generation and life; nay, more, I became myself capable of bestowing animation upon lifeless matter.

The astonishment which I had at first experienced on this discovery soon gave place to delight and rapture. After so much time spent in painful labour, to arrive at once at the summit of my desires, was the most gratifying consummation of my toils. But this discovery was so great and overwhelming, that all the steps by which I had been progressively led to it were obliterated, and I beheld only the result. What had been the study and desire of the wisest men since the creation of the world, was now within my grasp. Not that, like a magic scene, it all opened upon me at once: the information I had obtained was of a nature rather to direct my endeavours so soon as I should point them towards the object of my search, than to exhibit that object already accomplished. I was like the Arabian who had been buried with the dead, and found a passage to life aided only by one glimmering, and seemingly ineffectual, light.[2]

I see by your eagerness, and the wonder and hope which your eyes express, my friend, that you expect to be informed of the secret with which I am acquainted; that cannot be: listen patiently until the end of my story, and you will easily perceive why I am reserved upon that subject. I will not lead you on, unguarded and ardent as I then was, to your destruction and infallible misery. Learn from me, if not by my precepts, at least by my example, how dangerous is the acquirement of knowledge, and how much happier that man is who believes his native town to be the world, than he who aspires to become greater than his nature will allow.

When I found so astonishing a power placed within my hands, I hesitated a long time concerning the manner in which I should employ

---

[2]A tale told in "The Fourth Voyage of Sindbad," in *A Thousand and One Nights*.

it. Although I possessed the capacity of bestowing animation, yet to prepare a frame for the reception of it, with all its intricacies of fibres, muscles, and veins, still remained a work of inconceivable difficulty and labour. I doubted at first whether I should attempt the creation of a being like myself or one of simpler organization; but my imagination was too much exalted by my first success to permit me to doubt of my ability to give life to an animal as complex and wonderful as man. The materials at present within my command hardly appeared adequate to so arduous an undertaking; but I doubted not that I should ultimately succeed. I prepared myself for a multitude of reverses; my operations might be incessantly baffled, and at last my work be imperfect: yet, when I considered the improvement which every day takes place in science and mechanics, I was encouraged to hope my present attempts would at least lay the foundations of future success. Nor could I consider the magnitude and complexity of my plan as any argument of its impracticability. It was with these feelings that I began the creation of a human being. As the minuteness of the parts formed a great hindrance to my speed, I resolved, contrary to my first intention, to make the being of a gigantic stature; that is to say, about eight feet in height, and proportionably large. After having formed this determination, and having spent some months in successfully collecting and arranging my materials, I began.

No one can conceive the variety of feelings which bore me onwards, like a hurricane, in the first enthusiasm of success. Life and death appeared to me ideal bounds, which I should first break through, and pour a torrent of light into our dark world. A new species would bless me as its creator and source; many happy and excellent natures would owe their being to me. No father could claim the gratitude of his child so completely as I should deserve their's. Pursuing these reflections, I thought, that if I could bestow animation upon lifeless matter, I might in process of time (although I now found it impossible) renew life where death had apparently devoted the body to corruption.

These thoughts supported my spirits, while I pursued my undertaking with unremitting ardour. My cheek had grown pale with study, and my person had become emaciated with confinement. Sometimes, on the very brink of certainty, I failed; yet still I clung to the hope which the next day or the next hour might realize. One secret which I alone possessed was the hope to which I had dedicated myself; and the moon gazed on my midnight labours, while, with unrelaxed and breathless eagerness, I pursued nature to her hiding places. Who shall conceive the horrors of my secret toil, as I dabbled among the unhallowed damps of the grave, or tortured the living animal to animate the lifeless clay?[3] My limbs now tremble, and my eyes swim with the remembrance; but then a resistless, and almost frantic impulse, urged me forward; I seemed to have lost all soul or sensation but for this one pursuit. It was indeed but a passing trance, that only made me feel with renewed acuteness so soon as, the unnatural stimulus ceasing to operate, I had returned to my old habits. I collected bones from charnel houses; and disturbed, with profane fingers, the tremendous secrets of the human frame. In a solitary chamber, or rather cell, at the top of the house, and separated from all the other apartments by a gallery and staircase, I kept my workshop of filthy creation; my eyeballs were starting from their sockets in attending to the details of my employment. The dissecting room and the slaughter-house furnished many of my materials; and often did my human nature turn with loathing from my occupation, whilst, still urged on by an eagerness which perpetually increased, I brought my work near to a conclusion.

The summer months passed while I was thus engaged, heart and soul, in one pursuit. It was a most beautiful season; never did the fields bestow a more plentiful harvest, or the vines yield a more luxuriant vintage: but my eyes were insensible to the charms of nature. And the same feelings which made me neglect the scenes around me caused me also to forget those friends who were so many miles absent, and whom I had not seen for so long a time. I knew my silence disquieted them; and I well remembered the words of my father: "I know that while you are pleased with yourself, you will think of us with affection, and we shall hear regularly from you. You must pardon me, if I regard any interruption in your correspondence as a proof that your other duties are equally neglected."

I knew well therefore what would be my father's feelings; but I could not tear my thoughts from my employment, loathsome in itself, but which had taken an irresistible hold of my imagination. I wished, as it were, to procrastinate all that related to my feelings of affection until the great object, which swallowed up every habit of my nature, should be completed.

---

[3]The animation of clay refers to the myths of Prometheus's creation of man, and of God's creation of Adam in Genesis (2.7). Percy Shelley strongly opposed vivisection.

I then thought that my father would be unjust if he ascribed my neglect to vice, or faultiness on my part; but I am now convinced that he was justified in conceiving that I should not be altogether free from blame. A human being in perfection ought always to preserve a calm and peaceful mind, and never to allow passion or a transitory desire to disturb his tranquillity. I do not think that the pursuit of knowledge is an exception to this rule. If the study to which you apply yourself has a tendency to weaken your affections, and to destroy your taste for those simple pleasures in which no alloy can possibly mix, then that study is certainly unlawful, that is to say, not befitting the human mind. If this rule were always observed; if no man allowed any pursuit whatsoever to interfere with the tranquillity of his domestic affections, Greece had not been enslaved; Caesar would have spared his country; America would have been discovered more gradually; and the empires of Mexico and Peru had not been destroyed.[4]

But I forget that I am moralizing in the most interesting part of my tale; and your looks remind me to proceed.

My father made no reproach in his letters; and only took notice of my silence by inquiring into my occupations more particularly than before. Winter, spring, and summer, passed away during my labours; but I did not watch the blossom or the expanding leaves—sights which before always yielded me supreme delight, so deeply was I engrossed in my occupation. The leaves of that year had withered before my work drew near to a close; and now every day shewed me more plainly how well I had succeeded. But my enthusiasm was checked by my anxiety, and I appeared rather like one doomed by slavery to toil in the mines, or any other unwholesome trade, than an artist occupied by his favourite employment. Every night I was oppressed by a slow fever, and I became nervous to a most painful degree; a disease that I regretted the more because I had hitherto enjoyed most excellent health, and had always boasted of the firmness of my nerves.[5] But I believed that exercise and amusement would soon drive away such symptoms; and I promised myself both of these, when my creation should be complete.

[4]Referring to the domination of Greece by the Ottoman empire; the civil war that followed the republicans' assassination of Julius Caesar in 44 B.C.E.; the treatment of native Americans by European settlers; the violent subjugations of Mexico and Peru by Spanish conquistadors. This argument was advanced in *The Ruins . . . of Empires* (1791), a critique of imperialism by Comte de Volney that was a major influence on Percy Shelley.

[5]For new text in 1831, augmenting these effects, see p. 202.

Chapter IV

It was on a dreary night of November, that I beheld the accomplishment of my toils. With an anxiety that almost amounted to agony, I collected the instruments of life around me, that I might infuse a spark of being into the lifeless thing that lay at my feet. It was already one in the morning; the rain pattered dismally against the panes, and my candle was nearly burnt out, when, by the glimmer of the half-extinguished light, I saw the dull yellow eye of the creature open; it breathed hard, and a convulsive motion agitated its limbs.[1]

How can I describe my emotions at this catastrophe, or how delineate the wretch whom with such infinite pains and care I had endeavoured to form? His limbs were in proportion, and I had selected his features as beautiful. Beautiful!—Great God! His yellow skin scarcely covered the work of muscles and arteries beneath; his hair was of a lustrous black, and flowing; his teeth of a pearly whiteness; but these luxuriances only formed a more horrid contrast with his watery eyes, that seemed almost of the same colour as the dun white sockets in which they were set, his shrivelled complexion, and straight black lips.

The different accidents of life are not so changeable as the feelings of human nature. I had worked hard for nearly two years, for the sole purpose of infusing life into an inanimate body. For this I had deprived myself of rest and health. I had desired it with an ardour that far exceeded moderation; but now that I had finished, the beauty of the dream vanished, and breathless horror and disgust filled my heart. Unable to endure the aspect of the being I had created, I rushed out of the room, and continued a long time traversing my bedchamber, unable to compose my mind to sleep. At length lassitude succeeded to the tumult I had before endured; and I threw myself on the bed in my clothes, endeavouring to seek a few moments of forgetfulness. But it was in vain: I slept indeed, but I was disturbed by the wildest dreams. I thought I saw Elizabeth, in the bloom of health, walking in the streets of Ingolstadt. Delighted and surprised, I embraced her; but as I imprinted the first kiss on her lips, they became livid with the hue of death; her features appeared to change, and I thought that I held the corpse of my dead mother in my arms; a shroud enveloped her form, and I saw the graveworms crawling in the folds of the flannel. I

---

[1] In the 1831 "Introduction" Shelley says that this image, appearing to her in a dream, was the inspiration for the novel.

started from my sleep with horror; a cold dew covered my forehead, my teeth chattered, and every limb became convulsed; when, by the dim and yellow light of the moon, as it forced its way through the window-shutters, I beheld the wretch—the miserable monster whom I had created. He held up the curtain of the bed; and his eyes, if eyes they may be called, were fixed on me. His jaws opened, and he muttered some inarticulate sounds, while a grin wrinkled his cheeks. He might have spoken, but I did not hear; one hand was stretched out, seemingly to detain me, but I escaped, and rushed down stairs. I took refuge in the court-yard belonging to the house which I inhabited; where I remained during the rest of the night, walking up and down in the greatest agitation, listening attentively, catching and fearing each sound as if it were to announce the approach of the demoniacal corpse to which I had so miserably given life.

Oh! no mortal could support the horror of that countenance. A mummy again endued with animation could not be so hideous as that wretch. I had gazed on him while unfinished; he was ugly then; but when those muscles and joints were rendered capable of motion, it became a thing such as even Dante could not have conceived.

I passed the night wretchedly. Sometimes my pulse beat so quickly and hardly, that I felt the palpitation of every artery; at others, I nearly sank to the ground through languor and extreme weakness. Mingled with this horror, I felt the bitterness of disappointment: dreams that had been my food and pleasant rest for so long a space, were now become a hell to me; and the change was so rapid, the overthrow so complete!

Morning, dismal and wet, at length dawned, and discovered to my sleepless and aching eyes the church of Ingolstadt, its white steeple and clock, which indicated the sixth hour. The porter opened the gates of the court, which had that night been my asylum, and I issued into the streets, pacing them with quick steps, as if I sought to avoid the wretch whom I feared every turning of the street would present to my view. I did not dare return to the apartment which I inhabited, but felt impelled to hurry on, although wetted by the rain, which poured from a black and comfortless sky.

I continued walking in this manner for some time, endeavouring, by bodily exercise, to ease the load that weighed upon my mind. I traversed the streets, without any clear conception of where I was, or what I was doing. My heart palpitated in the sickness of fear; and I hurried on with irregular steps, not daring to look about me:

> Like one who, on a lonely road,
>   Doth walk in fear and dread,
> And, having once turn'd round, walks on,
>   And turns no more his head;
> Because he knows a frightful fiend
>   Doth close behind him tread.[2]

Continuing thus, I came at length opposite to the inn at which the various diligences[3] and carriages usually stopped. Here I paused, I knew not why; but I remained some minutes with my eyes fixed on a coach that was coming towards me from the other end of the street. As it drew nearer, I observed that it was the Swiss diligence: it stopped just where I was standing; and, on the door being opened, I perceived Henry Clerval, who, on seeing me, instantly sprung out. "My dear Frankenstein,"[4] exclaimed he, "how glad I am to see you! how fortunate that you should be here at the very moment of my alighting!"

Nothing could equal my delight on seeing Clerval; his presence brought back to my thoughts my father, Elizabeth, and all those scenes of home so dear to my recollection. I grasped his hand, and in a moment forgot my horror and misfortune; I felt suddenly, and for the first time during many months, calm and serene joy. I welcomed my friend, therefore, in the most cordial manner, and we walked towards my college. Clerval continued talking for some time about our mutual friends, and his own good fortune in being permitted to come to Ingolstadt. "You may easily believe," said he, "how great was the difficulty to persuade my father that it was not absolutely necessary for a merchant not to understand any thing except book-keeping; and, indeed, I believe I left him incredulous to the last, for his constant answer to my unwearied entreaties was the same as that of the Dutch schoolmaster in the Vicar of Wakefield: 'I have ten thousand florins a year without Greek, I eat heartily without Greek.'[5] But his affection for me at length overcame his dislike of learning, and he has permitted me to undertake a voyage of discovery to the land of knowledge."

"It gives me the greatest delight to see you; but tell me how you left my father, brothers, and Elizabeth."

---

[2] "Coleridge's 'Ancient Mariner' " [M. Shelley's note]; lines 451–56 (see p. 222).
[3] Stagecoaches.
[4] This is the first naming of Frankenstein in the body of the novel.
[5] Oliver Goldsmith, *The Vicar of Wakefield* (1766), ch. 20.

"Very well, and very happy, only a little uneasy that they hear from you so seldom. By the bye, I mean to lecture you a little upon their account myself.—But, my dear Frankenstein," continued he, stopping short, and gazing full in my face, "I did not before remark how very ill you appear; so thin and pale; you look as if you had been watching for several nights."

"You have guessed right; I have lately been so deeply engaged in one occupation, that I have not allowed myself sufficient rest, as you see: but I hope, I sincerely hope, that all these employments are now at an end, and that I am at length free."

I trembled excessively; I could not endure to think of, and far less to allude to the occurrences of the preceding night. I walked with a quick pace, and we soon arrived at my college. I then reflected, and the thought made me shiver, that the creature whom I had left in my apartment might still be there, alive, and walking about. I dreaded to behold this monster; but I feared still more that Henry should see him. Entreating him therefore to remain a few minutes at the bottom of the stairs, I darted up towards my own room. My hand was already on the lock of the door before I recollected myself. I then paused; and a cold shivering came over me. I threw the door forcibly open, as children are accustomed to do when they expect a spectre to stand in waiting for them on the other side; but nothing appeared. I stepped fearfully in: the apartment was empty; and my bedroom was also freed from its hideous guest. I could hardly believe that so great a good-fortune could have befallen me; but when I became assured that my enemy had indeed fled, I clapped my hands for joy, and ran down to Clerval.

We ascended into my room, and the servant presently brought breakfast; but I was unable to contain myself. It was not joy only that possessed me; I felt my flesh tingle with excess of sensitiveness, and my pulse beat rapidly. I was unable to remain for a single instant in the same place; I jumped over the chairs, clapped my hands, and laughed aloud. Clerval at first attributed my unusual spirits to joy on his arrival; but when he observed me more attentively, he saw a wildness in my eyes for which he could not account; and my loud, unrestrained, heartless laughter, frightened and astonished him.

"My dear Victor," cried he, "what, for God's sake, is the matter? Do not laugh in that manner. How ill you are! What is the cause of all this?"

"Do not ask me," cried I, putting my hands before my eyes, for I thought I saw the dreaded spectre glide into the room; "*he* can tell.— Oh, save me! save me!" I imagined that the monster seized me; I struggled furiously, and fell down in a fit.

Poor Clerval! what must have been his feelings? A meeting, which he anticipated with such joy, so strangely turned to bitterness. But I was not the witness of his grief; for I was lifeless, and did not recover my senses for a long, long time.

This was the commencement of a nervous fever, which confined me for several months. During all that time Henry was my only nurse. I afterwards learned that, knowing my father's advanced age, and unfitness for so long a journey, and how wretched my sickness would make Elizabeth, he spared them this grief by concealing the extent of my disorder. He knew that I could not have a more kind and attentive nurse than himself; and, firm in the hope he felt of my recovery, he did not doubt that, instead of doing harm, he performed the kindest action that he could towards them.

But I was in reality very ill; and surely nothing but the unbounded and unremitting attentions of my friend could have restored me to life. The form of the monster on whom I had bestowed existence was for ever before my eyes, and I raved incessantly concerning him. Doubtless my words surprised Henry: he at first believed them to be the wanderings of my disturbed imagination; but the pertinacity with which I continually recurred to the same subject persuaded him that my disorder indeed owed its origin to some uncommon and terrible event.

By very slow degrees, and with frequent relapses, that alarmed and grieved my friend, I recovered. I remember the first time I became capable of observing outward objects with any kind of pleasure, I perceived that the fallen leaves had disappeared, and that the young buds were shooting forth from the trees that shaded my window. It was a divine spring; and the season contributed greatly to my convalescence. I felt also sentiments of joy and affection revive in my bosom; my gloom disappeared, and in a short time I became as cheerful as before I was attacked by the fatal passion.

"Dearest Clerval," exclaimed I, "how kind, how very good you are to me. This whole winter, instead of being spent in study, as you promised yourself, has been consumed in my sick room. How shall I ever repay you? I feel the greatest remorse for the disappointment of which I have been the occasion; but you will forgive me."

"You will repay me entirely, if you do not discompose yourself, but get well as fast as you can; and since you appear in such good spirits, I may speak to you on one subject, may I not?"

I trembled. One subject! what could it be? Could he allude to an object on whom I dared not even think?

"Compose yourself," said Clerval, who observed my change of colour, "I will not mention it, if it agitates you; but your father and cousin would be very happy if they received a letter from you in your own hand-writing. They hardly know how ill you have been, and are uneasy at your long silence."

"Is that all? my dear Henry. How could you suppose that my first thought would not fly towards those dear, dear friends whom I love, and who are so deserving of my love."

"If this is your present temper, my friend, you will perhaps be glad to see a letter that has been lying here some days for you: it is from your cousin, I believe."

Chapter V

CLERVAL then put the following letter into my hands.

To V. FRANKENSTEIN.

"MY DEAR COUSIN,

"I cannot describe to you the uneasiness we have all felt concerning your health. We cannot help imagining that your friend Clerval conceals the extent of your disorder: for it is now several months since we have seen your hand-writing; and all this time you have been obliged to dictate your letters to Henry. Surely, Victor, you must have been exceedingly ill; and this makes us all very wretched, as much so nearly as after the death of your dear mother. My uncle was almost persuaded that you were indeed dangerously ill, and could hardly be restrained from undertaking a journey to Ingolstadt. Clerval always writes that you are getting better; I eagerly hope that you will confirm this intelligence soon in your own hand-writing; for indeed, indeed, Victor, we are all very miserable on this account. Relieve us from this fear, and we shall be the happiest creatures in the world. Your father's health is now so vigorous, that he appears ten years younger since last winter. Ernest also is so much improved, that you would hardly know him: he is now nearly sixteen, and has lost that sickly appearance which he had some years ago; he is grown quite robust and active.

My uncle and I conversed a long time last night about what profession Ernest should follow.[1] His constant illness when young has deprived him of the habits of application; and now that he enjoys good health, he is continually in the open air, climbing the hills, or rowing on the lake. I therefore proposed that he should be a farmer; which you know, Cousin, is a favourite scheme of mine. A farmer's is a very healthy happy life; and the least hurtful, or rather the most beneficial profession of any. My uncle had an idea of his being educated as an advocate, that through his interest he might become a judge. But, besides that he is not at all fitted for such an occupation, it is certainly more creditable to cultivate the earth for the sustenance of man, than to be the confidant, and sometimes the accomplice, of his vices; which is the profession of a lawyer. I said, that the employments of a prosperous farmer, if they were not a more honourable, they were at least a happier species of occupation than that of a judge, whose misfortune it was always to meddle with the dark side of human nature. My uncle smiled, and said, that I ought to be an advocate myself, which put an end to the conversation on that subject.

And now I must tell you a little story that will please, and perhaps amuse you. Do you not remember Justine Moritz? Probably you do not; I will relate her history, therefore, in a few words. Madame Moritz, her mother, was a widow with four children, of whom Justine was the third. This girl had always been the favourite of her father; but, through a strange perversity, her mother could not endure her, and, after the death of M. Moritz, treated her very ill. My aunt observed this; and, when Justine was twelve years of age, prevailed on her mother to allow her to live at her house. The republican institutions of our country have produced simpler and happier manners than those which prevail in the great monarchies that surround it.[2] Hence there is less distinction between the several classes of its inhabitants; and the lower orders being neither so poor nor so despised, their manners are more refined and moral. A servant in Geneva does not mean the same thing as a servant in France and England. Justine,

[1]For the 1831 report on Ernest, see p. 203.

[2]The paragraph from this sentence to the end was written by Percy Shelley. These are views expressed in Volney's *Ruins of Empires;* see n. 4 on p. 36.

thus received in our family, learned the duties of a servant; a condition which, in our fortunate country, does not include the idea of ignorance, and a sacrifice of the dignity of a human being.

After what I have said, I dare say you well remember the heroine of my little tale: for Justine was a great favourite of your's; and I recollect you once remarked, that if you were in an ill humour, one glance from Justine could dissipate it, for the same reason that Ariosto gives concerning the beauty of Angelica[3]—she looked so frank-hearted[4] and happy. My aunt conceived a great attachment for her, by which she was induced to give her an education superior to that which she had at first intended. This benefit was fully repaid; Justine was the most grateful little creature in the world: I do not mean that she made any professions, I never heard one pass her lips; but you could see by her eyes that she almost adored her protectress. Although her disposition was gay, and in many respects inconsiderate, yet she paid the greatest attention to every gesture of my aunt. She thought her the model of all excellence, and endeavoured to imitate her phraseology and manners, so that even now she often reminds me of her.

When my dearest aunt died, every one was too much occupied in their own grief to notice poor Justine, who had attended her during her illness with the most anxious affection. Poor Justine was very ill; but other trials were reserved for her.

One by one, her brothers and sister died; and her mother, with the exception of her neglected daughter, was left childless. The conscience of the woman was troubled; she began to think that the deaths of her favourites was a judgment from heaven to chastise her partiality. She was a Roman Catholic; and I believe her confessor confirmed the idea which she had conceived.[5] Accordingly, a few months after your departure for Ingolstadt, Justine was called home by her repentant mother. Poor girl! she wept when she quitted our house: she was much altered since the death of my aunt; grief had given softness and a winning mildness to her manners, which had before been remarkable for vivacity. Nor was her residence at her

[3]The heroine of Ariosto's *Orlando Furioso* (1532); Orlando's fury-unto-madness is provoked by Angelica's marriage to another.

[4]Open-hearted; Shelley may have meant to pun on Justine's innate affinity for the Frankenstein family. Compare Elizabeth herself, pp. 56–57.

[5]The Shelleys, like many theological liberals, regarded Roman Catholicism as a religion of "superstition."

mother's house of a nature to restore her gaiety. The poor woman was very vacillating in her repentance. She sometimes begged Justine to forgive her unkindness, but much oftener accused her of having caused the deaths of her brothers and sister. Perpetual fretting at length threw Madame Moritz into a decline, which at first increased her irritability, but she is now at peace for ever. She died on the first approach of cold weather, at the beginning of this last winter. Justine has returned to us; and I assure you I love her tenderly. She is very clever and gentle, and extremely pretty; as I mentioned before, her mien and her expressions continually remind me of my dear aunt.

I must say also a few words to you, my dear cousin, of little darling William. I wish you could see him; he is very tall of his age, with sweet laughing blue eyes, dark eye-lashes, and curling hair. When he smiles, two little dimples appear on each cheek, which are rosy with health. He has already had one or two little *wives*, but Louisa Biron is his favourite, a pretty little girl of five years of age.

Now, dear Victor, I dare say you wish to be indulged in a little gossip concerning the good people of Geneva. The pretty Miss Mansfield has already received the congratulatory visits on her approaching marriage with a young Englishman, John Melbourne, Esq. Her ugly sister, Manon, married M. Duvillard, the rich banker, last autumn. Your favourite schoolfellow, Louis Manoir, has suffered several misfortunes since the departure of Clerval from Geneva. But he has already recovered his spirits, and is reported to be on the point of marrying a very lively pretty Frenchwoman, Madame Tavernier. She is a widow, and much older than Manoir; but she is very much admired, and a favourite with every body.

I have written myself into good spirits, dear cousin; yet I cannot conclude without again anxiously inquiring concerning your health. Dear Victor, if you are not very ill, write yourself, and make your father and all of us happy; or—I cannot bear to think of the other side of the question; my tears already flow. Adieu, my dearest cousin.

Geneva, March 18th, 17—.   ELIZABETH LAVENZA."

"Dear, dear Elizabeth!" I exclaimed when I had read her letter, "I will write instantly, and relieve them from the anxiety they must feel." I wrote, and this exertion greatly fatigued me; but my convalescence had commenced, and proceeded regularly. In another fortnight I was able to leave my chamber.

One of my first duties on my recovery was to introduce Clerval to the several professors of the university. In doing this, I underwent a kind of rough usage, ill befitting the wounds that my mind had sustained. Ever since the fatal night, the end of my labours, and the beginning of my misfortunes, I had conceived a violent antipathy even to the name of natural philosophy. When I was otherwise quite restored to health, the sight of a chemical instrument would renew all the agony of my nervous symptoms. Henry saw this, and had removed all my apparatus from my view. He had also changed my apartment; for he perceived that I had acquired a dislike for the room which had previously been my laboratory. But these cares of Clerval were made of no avail when I visited the professors. M. Waldman inflicted torture when he praised, with kindness and warmth, the astonishing progress I had made in the sciences. He soon perceived that I disliked the subject; but, not guessing the real cause, he attributed my feelings to modesty, and changed the subject from my improvement to the science itself, with a desire, as I evidently saw, of drawing me out. What could I do? He meant to please, and he tormented me. I felt as if he had placed carefully, one by one, in my view those instruments which were to be afterwards used in putting me to a slow and cruel death. I writhed under his words, yet dared not exhibit the pain I felt. Clerval, whose eyes and feelings were always quick in discerning the sensations of others, declined the subject, alleging, in excuse, his total ignorance; and the conversation took a more general turn. I thanked my friend from my heart, but I did not speak. I saw plainly that he was surprised, but he never attempted to draw my secret from me; and although I loved him with a mixture of affection and reverence that knew no bounds, yet I could never persuade myself to confide to him that event which was so often present to my recollection, but which I feared the detail to another would only impress more deeply.

M. Krempe was not equally docile; and in my condition at that time, of almost insupportable sensitiveness, his harsh blunt encomiums gave me even more pain than the benevolent approbation of M. Waldman. "D—n the fellow!" cried he; "why, M. Clerval, I assure you he has outstript us all. Aye, stare if you please; but it is nevertheless true. A youngster who, but a few years ago, believed Cornelius Agrippa as firmly as the gospel, has now set himself at the head of the university; and if he is not soon pulled down, we shall all be out of countenance.— Aye, aye," continued he, observing my face expressive of suffering,

"M. Frankenstein is modest; an excellent quality in a young man. Young men should be diffident of themselves, you know, M. Clerval; I was myself when young: but that wears out in a very short time."

M. Krempe had now commenced an eulogy on himself, which happily turned the conversation from a subject that was so annoying to me.

Clerval was no natural philosopher. His imagination was too vivid for the minutiae of science. Languages were his principal study; and he sought, by acquiring their elements, to open a field for self-instruction on his return to Geneva. Persian, Arabic, and Hebrew, gained his attention, after he had made himself perfectly master of Greek and Latin. For my own part, idleness had ever been irksome to me; and now that I wished to fly from reflection, and hated my former studies, I felt great relief in being the fellow-pupil with my friend, and found not only instruction but consolation in the works of the orientalists. Their melancholy is soothing, and their joy elevating to a degree I never experienced in studying the authors of any other country. When you read their writings, life appears to consist in a warm sun and garden of roses,—in the smiles and frowns of a fair enemy, and the fire that consumes your own heart. How different from the manly and heroical poetry of Greece and Rome.

Summer passed away in these occupations, and my return to Geneva was fixed for the latter end of autumn; but being delayed by several accidents, winter and snow arrived, the roads were deemed impassable, and my journey was retarded until the ensuing spring. I felt this delay very bitterly; for I longed to see my native town, and my beloved friends. My return had only been delayed so long from an unwillingness to leave Clerval in a strange place, before he had become acquainted with any of its inhabitants. The winter, however, was spent cheerfully; and although the spring was uncommonly late, when it came, its beauty compensated for its dilatoriness.

The month of May had already commenced, and I expected the letter daily which was to fix the date of my departure, when Henry proposed a pedestrian tour in the environs of Ingolstadt that I might bid a personal farewell to the country I had so long inhabited. I acceded with pleasure to this proposition: I was fond of exercise, and Clerval had always been my favourite companion in the rambles of this nature that I had taken among the scenes of my native country.

We passed a fortnight in these perambulations: my health and spirits had long been restored, and they gained additional strength from the salubrious air I breathed, the natural incidents of our progress, and the conversation of my friend. Study had before secluded me from the intercourse of my fellow-creatures, and rendered me unsocial; but Clerval called forth the better feelings of my heart; he again taught me to love the aspect of nature, and the cheerful faces of children. Excellent friend! how sincerely did you love me, and endeavour to elevate my mind, until it was on a level with your own. A selfish pursuit had cramped and narrowed me, until your gentleness and affection warmed and opened my senses; I became the same happy creature who, a few years ago, loving and beloved by all, had no sorrow or care. When happy, inanimate nature had the power of bestowing on me the most delightful sensations. A serene sky and verdant fields filled me with ecstasy. The present season was indeed divine; the flowers of spring bloomed in the hedges, while those of summer were already in bud: I was undisturbed by thoughts which during the preceding year had pressed upon me, notwithstanding my endeavours to throw them off, with an invincible burden.

Henry rejoiced in my gaiety, and sincerely sympathized in my feelings: he exerted himself to amuse me, while he expressed the sensations that filled his soul. The resources of his mind on this occasion were truly astonishing: his conversation was full of imagination; and very often, in imitation of the Persian and Arabic writers, he invented tales of wonderful fancy and passion. At other times he repeated my favourite poems, or drew me out into arguments, which he supported with great ingenuity.

We returned to our college on a Sunday afternoon: the peasants were dancing, and every one we met appeared gay and happy. My own spirits were high, and I bounded along with feelings of unbridled joy and hilarity.

Chapter VI

On my return, I found the following letter from my father:—

To V. FRANKENSTEIN.

"MY DEAR VICTOR,

"You have probably waited impatiently for a letter to fix the date of your return to us; and I was at first tempted to write only a few lines, merely mentioning the day on which I should expect you. But that would be a cruel kindness, and I dare not do it. What would be your surprise, my son, when you expected a happy and gay welcome, to behold, on the contrary, tears and wretchedness? And how, Victor, can I relate our misfortune? Absence cannot have rendered you callous to our joys and griefs; and how shall I inflict pain on an absent child? I wish to prepare you for the woeful news, but I know it is impossible; even now your eye skims over the page, to seek the words which are to convey to you the horrible tidings.

William is dead!—that sweet child, whose smiles delighted and warmed my heart, who was so gentle, yet so gay! Victor, he is murdered!

I will not attempt to console you; but will simply relate the circumstances of the transaction.

Last Thursday (May 7th) I, my niece, and your two brothers, went to walk in Plainpalais.[1] The evening was warm and serene, and we prolonged our walk farther than usual. It was already dusk before we thought of returning; and then we discovered that William and Ernest, who had gone on before, were not to be found. We accordingly rested on a seat until they should return. Presently Ernest came, and inquired if we had seen his brother: he said, that they had been playing together, that William had run away to hide himself, and that he vainly sought for him, and afterwards waited for him a long time, but that he did not return.

This account rather alarmed us, and we continued to search for him until night fell, when Elizabeth conjectured that he might have returned to the house. He was not there. We returned again, with torches; for I could not rest, when I thought that my sweet boy had lost himself, and was exposed to all the damps and dews of night: Elizabeth also suffered extreme anguish. About five in the morning I discovered my lovely boy, whom the night before I had seen blooming and active in health, stretched on the grass livid and motionless: the print of the murderer's finger was on his neck.

He was conveyed home, and the anguish that was visible in my countenance betrayed the secret to Elizabeth. She was very earnest to see the corpse. At first I attempted to prevent her; but she persisted, and entering the room where it lay, hastily examined the neck of the victim, and clasping her hands exclaimed, 'O God! I have murdered my darling infant!'

[1] A grassy plain south of Geneva.

She fainted, and was restored with extreme difficulty. When she again lived, it was only to weep and sigh. She told me, that that same evening William had teazed her to let him wear a very valuable miniature that she possessed of your mother. This picture is gone, and was doubtless the temptation which urged the murderer to the deed. We have no trace of him at present, although our exertions to discover him are unremitted; but they will not restore my beloved William.

Come, dearest Victor; you alone can console Elizabeth. She weeps continually, and accuses herself unjustly as the cause of his death; her words pierce my heart. We are all unhappy; but will not that be an additional motive for you, my son, to return and be our comforter? Your dear mother! Alas, Victor! I now say, Thank God she did not live to witness the cruel, miserable death of her youngest darling!

Come, Victor; not brooding thoughts of vengeance against the assassin, but with feelings of peace and gentleness, that will heal, instead of festering the wounds of our minds. Enter the house of mourning, my friend, but with kindness and affection for those who love you, and not with hatred for your enemies.

> Your affectionate and afflicted father,
Geneva, May 12th, 17—. ALPHONSE FRANKENSTEIN."

Clerval, who had watched my countenance as I read this letter, was surprised to observe the despair that succeeded to the joy I at first expressed on receiving news from my friends. I threw the letter on the table, and covered my face with my hands.

"My dear Frankenstein," exclaimed Henry, when he perceived me weep with bitterness, "are you always to be unhappy? My dear friend, what has happened?"

I motioned to him to take up the letter, while I walked up and down the room in the extremest agitation. Tears also gushed from the eyes of Clerval, as he read the account of my misfortune.

"I can offer you no consolation, my friend," said he; "your disaster is irreparable. What do you intend to do?"

"To go instantly to Geneva: come with me, Henry, to order the horses."

During our walk, Clerval endeavoured to raise my spirits. He did not do this by common topics of consolation, but by exhibiting the truest sympathy. "Poor William!" said he, "that dear child; he now sleeps with his angel mother. His friends mourn and weep, but he is at rest: he does not now feel the murderer's grasp; a sod covers his gentle form, and he knows no pain. He can no longer be a fit subject for pity; the survivors are the greatest sufferers, and for them time is the only consolation. Those maxims of the Stoics, that death was no evil, and that the mind of man ought to be superior to despair on the eternal absence of a beloved object, ought not to be urged. Even Cato wept over the dead body of his brother."[2]

Clerval spoke thus as we hurried through the streets; the words impressed themselves on my mind, and I remembered them afterwards in solitude. But now, as soon as the horses arrived, I hurried into a cabriole,[3] and bade farewell to my friend.

My journey was very melancholy. At first I wished to hurry on, for I longed to console and sympathize with my loved and sorrowing friends; but when I drew near my native town, I slackened my progress. I could hardly sustain the multitude of feelings that crowded into my mind. I passed through scenes familiar to my youth, but which I had not seen for nearly six years. How altered every thing might be during that time? One sudden and desolating change had taken place; but a thousand little circumstances might have by degrees worked other alterations, which, although they were done more tranquilly, might not be the less decisive. Fear overcame me; I dared not advance, dreading a thousand nameless evils that made me tremble, although I was unable to define them.

I remained two days at Lausanne, in this painful state of mind. I contemplated the lake: the waters were placid; all around was calm, and the snowy mountains, "the palaces of nature,"[4] were not changed. By degrees the calm and heavenly scene restored me, and I continued my journey towards Geneva.

[2]The grief of Roman statesman Cato the Younger (1st c. B.C.E.) for his beloved brother is recounted in *Plutarch's Lives* (which the Creature reads; see II.VII). Although Cato professed Stoicism (moderation of temper and restraint of passion), Plutarch reports that he "showed himself more a fond brother than a philosopher, not only in the excess of his grief, bewailing, and embracing the dead body, but also in the extravagant expenses of the funeral. . . . there were some who took upon them to cavil at all this, as not consistent with his usual calmness and moderation, not discerning that though he were steadfast, firm, and inflexible to pleasure, fear or foolish entreaties, yet he was full of natural tenderness and brotherly affection." In the 1831 text, Shelley dropped this allusion and wrote new text; see p. 203.

[3]Small, two-wheel, one-horse carriage.

[4]Byron, *Childe Harold's Pilgrimage III* (1816): "the Alps, / The palaces of Nature" (lxii).

The road ran by the side of the lake, which became narrower as I approached my native town. I discovered more distinctly the black sides of Jura, and the bright summit of Mont Blanc;[5] I wept like a child: "Dear mountains! my own beautiful lake! how do you welcome your wanderer? Your summits are clear; the sky and lake are blue and placid. Is this to prognosticate peace, or to mock at my unhappiness?"

I fear, my friend, that I shall render myself tedious by dwelling on these preliminary circumstances; but they were days of comparative happiness, and I think of them with pleasure. My country, my beloved country! who but a native can tell the delight I took in again beholding thy streams, thy mountains, and, more than all, thy lovely lake.

Yet, as I drew nearer home, grief and fear again overcame me. Night also closed around; and when I could hardly see the dark mountains, I felt still more gloomily. The picture appeared a vast and dim scene of evil, and I foresaw obscurely that I was destined to become the most wretched of human beings. Alas! I prophesied truly, and failed only in one single circumstance, that in all the misery I imagined and dreaded, I did not conceive the hundredth part of the anguish I was destined to endure.

It was completely dark when I arrived in the environs of Geneva; the gates of the town were already shut; and I was obliged to pass the night at Secheron, a village half a league to the east of the city.[6] The sky was serene; and, as I was unable to rest, I resolved to visit the spot where my poor William had been murdered. As I could not pass through the town, I was obliged to cross the lake in a boat to arrive at Plainpalais. During this short voyage I saw the lightnings playing on the summit of Mont Blanc in the most beautiful figures. The storm appeared to approach rapidly; and, on landing, I ascended a low hill, that I might observe its progress. It advanced; the heavens were clouded, and I soon felt the rain coming slowly in large drops, but its violence quickly increased.

I quitted my seat, and walked on, although the darkness and storm increased every minute, and the thunder burst with a terrific crash over my head. It was echoed from Salêve, the Juras, and the Alps of Savoy; vivid flashes of lightning dazzled my eyes, illuminating

[5]Mont Blanc, the highest peak in the Alps and the subject of a poem by Percy Shelley. See p. 258.

[6]Victor is confused; it's actually to the north. A league is a variable measure, 2.5 to 4.5 miles.

the lake, making it appear like a vast sheet of fire;[7] then for an instant every thing seemed of a pitchy darkness, until the eye recovered itself from the preceding flash. The storm, as is often the case in Switzerland, appeared at once in various parts of the heavens. The most violent storm hung exactly north of the town, over that part of the lake which lies between the promontory of Belrive and the village of Copêt. Another storm enlighted Jura with faint flashes; and another darkened and sometimes disclosed the Môle, a peaked mountain to the east of the lake.

While I watched the storm, so beautiful yet terrific, I wandered on with a hasty step. This noble war in the sky elevated my spirits; I clasped my hands, and exclaimed aloud, "William, dear angel! this is thy funeral, this thy dirge!" As I said these words, I perceived in the gloom a figure which stole from behind a clump of trees near me; I stood fixed, gazing intently: I could not be mistaken. A flash of lightning illuminated the object, and discovered its shape plainly to me; its gigantic stature, and the deformity of its aspect, more hideous than belongs to humanity, instantly informed me that it was the wretch, the filthy daemon to whom I had given life. What did he there? Could he be (I shuddered at the conception) the murderer of my brother? No sooner did that idea cross my imagination, than I became convinced of its truth; my teeth chattered, and I was forced to lean against a tree for support. The figure passed me quickly, and I lost it in the gloom. Nothing in human shape could have destroyed that fair child. *He* was the murderer! I could not doubt it. The mere presence of the idea was an irresistible proof of the fact. I thought of pursuing the devil; but it would have been in vain, for another flash discovered him to me hanging among the rocks of the nearly perpendicular ascent of Mont Salêve, a hill that bounds Plainpalais on the south. He soon reached the summit, and disappeared.

I remained motionless. The thunder ceased; but the rain still continued, and the scene was enveloped in an impenetrable darkness. I revolved in my mind the events which I had until now sought to forget: the whole train of my progress towards the creation; the appearance of the work of my own hands alive at my bed side; its departure. Two years had now nearly elapsed since the night on which he

[7]A lake of fire is one of the features of Hell in *Paradise Lost* (1.52, 210). See also Byron's famous stanzas on the Alpine thunderstorm in *Childe Harold III*, pp. 267–69, and Mary Shelley's description in *Six Weeks' Tour*, pp. 257–58.

first received life; and was this his first crime? Alas! I had turned loose into the world a depraved wretch, whose delight was in carnage and misery; had he not murdered my brother?

No one can conceive the anguish I suffered during the remainder of the night, which I spent, cold and wet, in the open air. But I did not feel the inconvenience of the weather; my imagination was busy in scenes of evil and despair. I considered the being whom I had cast among mankind, and endowed with the will and power to effect purposes of horror, such as the deed which he had now done, nearly in the light of my own vampire,[8] my own spirit let loose from the grave, and forced to destroy all that was dear to me.

Day dawned; and I directed my steps towards the town. The gates were open; and I hastened to my father's house. My first thought was to discover what I knew of the murderer, and cause instant pursuit to be made. But I paused when I reflected on the story that I had to tell. A being whom I myself had formed, and endued with life, had met me at midnight among the precipices of an inaccessible mountain. I remembered also the nervous fever with which I had been seized just at the time that I dated my creation, and which would give an air of delirium to a tale otherwise so utterly improbable. I well knew that if any other had communicated such a relation to me, I should have looked upon it as the ravings of insanity. Besides, the strange nature of the animal would elude all pursuit, even if I were so far credited as to persuade my relatives to commence it. Besides, of what use would be pursuit? Who could arrest a creature capable of scaling the overhanging sides of Mont Salêve? These reflections determined me, and I resolved to remain silent.

It was about five in the morning when I entered my father's house. I told the servants not to disturb the family, and went into the library to attend their usual hour of rising.

Six years had elapsed, passed as a dream but for one indelible trace, and I stood in the same place where I had last embraced my father before my departure for Ingolstadt. Beloved and respectable parent! He still remained to me. I gazed on the picture of my mother,

---

[8]Byron recounts this legendary specter in his popular poem *The Giaour* (1813); the hero is cursed with a dire fate: "on earth as vampire sent, / Thy corse shall from its tomb be rent: / Then ghastly haunt thy native place, / And suck the blood of all thy race; / . . . / Yet loathe the banquet which perforce / Must feed thy living livid corse: / Thy victims ere they yet expire / Shall know the demon for their sire" (755–64).

which stood over the mantle-piece. It was an historical subject, painted at my father's desire, and represented Caroline Beaufort in an agony of despair, kneeling by the coffin of her dead father. Her garb was rustic, and her cheek pale; but there was an air of dignity and beauty, that hardly permitted the sentiment of pity. Below this picture was a miniature of William; and my tears flowed when I looked upon it. While I was thus engaged, Ernest entered: he had heard me arrive, and hastened to welcome me. He expressed a sorrowful delight to see me: "Welcome, my dearest Victor," said he. "Ah! I wish you had come three months ago, and then you would have found us all joyous and delighted. But we are now unhappy; and, I am afraid, tears instead of smiles will be your welcome. Our father looks so sorrowful: this dreadful event seems to have revived in his mind his grief on the death of Mamma. Poor Elizabeth also is quite inconsolable." Ernest began to weep as he said these words.

"Do not," said I, "welcome me thus; try to be more calm, that I may not be absolutely miserable the moment I enter my father's house after so long an absence. But, tell me, how does my father support his misfortunes? and how is my poor Elizabeth?"

"She indeed requires consolation; she accused herself of having caused the death of my brother, and that made her very wretched. But since the murderer has been discovered."

"The murderer discovered! Good God! how can that be? who could attempt to pursue him? It is impossible; one might as well try to overtake the winds, or confine a mountain-stream with a straw."

"I do not know what you mean; but we were all very unhappy when she was discovered. No one would believe it at first; and even now Elizabeth will not be convinced, notwithstanding all the evidence. Indeed, who would credit that Justine Moritz, who was so amiable, and fond of all the family, could all at once become so extremely wicked?"

"Justine Moritz! Poor, poor girl, is she the accused? But it is wrongfully; every one knows that; no one believes it, surely, Ernest?"

"No one did at first; but several circumstances came out, that have almost forced conviction upon us: and her own behaviour has been so confused, as to add to the evidence of facts a weight that, I fear, leaves no hope for doubt. But she will be tried to-day, and you will then hear all."

He related that, the morning on which the murder of poor William had been discovered, Justine had been taken ill, and confined to her bed; and, after several days, one of the servants, happening to examine the apparel she had worn on the night of the murder, had discovered in her pocket the picture of my mother, which had been judged to be the temptation of the murderer. The servant instantly shewed it to one of the others, who, without saying a word to any of the family, went to a magistrate; and, upon their deposition, Justine was apprehended. On being charged with the fact, the poor girl confirmed the suspicion in a great measure by her extreme confusion of manner.

This was a strange tale, but it did not shake my faith; and I replied earnestly, "You are all mistaken; I know the murderer. Justine, poor, good Justine, is innocent."

At that instant my father entered. I saw unhappiness deeply impressed on his countenance, but he endeavoured to welcome me cheerfully; and, after we had exchanged our mournful greeting, would have introduced some other topic than that of our disaster, had not Ernest exclaimed, "Good God, Papa! Victor says that he knows who was the murderer of poor William."

"We do also, unfortunately," replied my father; "for indeed I had rather have been for ever ignorant than have discovered so much depravity and ingratitude in one I valued so highly."

"My dear father, you are mistaken; Justine is innocent."

"If she is, God forbid that she should suffer as guilty. She is to be tried to-day, and I hope, I sincerely hope, that she will be acquitted."

This speech calmed me. I was firmly convinced in my own mind that Justine, and indeed every human being, was guiltless of this murder. I had no fear, therefore, that any circumstantial evidence could be brought forward strong enough to convict her;[9] and, in this assurance, I calmed myself, expecting the trial with eagerness, but without prognosticating an evil result.

We were soon joined by Elizabeth. Time had made great alterations in her form since I had last beheld her. Six years before she had been a pretty, good-humoured girl, whom every one loved and caressed. She was now a woman in stature and expression of countenance, which was uncommonly lovely. An open and capacious forehead gave indications of a good understanding, joined to great frankness of disposition. Her eyes were hazel, and expressive of mildness, now through recent

[9]For the 1831 text for the rest of this paragraph, see p. 203. In 1831, Victor is far more self-incriminating.

affliction allied to sadness. Her hair was of a rich dark auburn, her complexion fair, and her figure slight and graceful. She welcomed me with the greatest affection. "Your arrival, my dear cousin," said she, "fills me with hope. You perhaps will find some means to justify my poor guiltless Justine. Alas! who is safe, if she be convicted of crime? I rely on her innocence as certainly as I do upon my own. Our misfortune is doubly hard to us; we have not only lost that lovely darling boy, but this poor girl, whom I sincerely love, is to be torn away by even a worse fate. If she is condemned, I never shall know joy more. But she will not, I am sure she will not; and then I shall be happy again, even after the sad death of my little William."

"She is innocent, my Elizabeth," said I, "and that shall be proved; fear nothing, but let your spirits be cheered by the assurance of her acquittal."

"How kind you are! every one else believes in her guilt, and that made me wretched; for I knew that it was impossible: and to see every one else prejudiced in so deadly a manner, rendered me hopeless and despairing." She wept.

"Sweet niece," said my father, "dry your tears. If she is, as you believe, innocent, rely on the justice of our judges, and the activity with which I shall prevent the slightest shadow of partiality."

Chapter VII

We passed a few sad hours, until eleven o'clock, when the trial was to commence. My father and the rest of the family being obliged to attend as witnesses, I accompanied them to the court. During the whole of this wretched mockery of justice, I suffered living torture. It was to be decided, whether the result of my curiosity and lawless devices would cause the death of two of my fellow-beings: one a smiling babe, full of innocence and joy; the other far more dreadfully murdered, with every aggravation of infamy that could make the murder memorable in horror. Justine also was a girl of merit, and possessed qualities which promised to render her life happy: now all was to be obliterated in an ignominious grave; and I the cause! A thousand times rather would I have confessed myself guilty of the crime ascribed to Justine; but I was absent when it was committed, and such a declaration would have been considered as the ravings of a madman, and would not have exculpated her who suffered through me.

The appearance of Justine was calm. She was dressed in mourning; and her countenance, always engaging, was rendered, by the solemnity of her feelings, exquisitely beautiful. Yet she appeared confident in innocence, and did not tremble, although gazed on and execrated by thousands; for all the kindness which her beauty might otherwise have excited, was obliterated in the minds of the spectators by the imagination of the enormity she was supposed to have committed. She was tranquil, yet her tranquility was evidently constrained; and as her confusion had before been adduced as a proof of her guilt, she worked up her mind to an appearance of courage. When she entered the court, she threw her eyes round it, and quickly discovered where we were seated. A tear seemed to dim her eye when she saw us; but she quickly recovered herself, and a look of sorrowful affection seemed to attest her utter guiltlessness.

The trial began; and after the advocate against her had stated the charge, several witnesses were called. Several strange facts combined against her, which might have staggered any one who had not such proof of her innocence as I had. She had been out the whole of the night on which the murder had been committed, and towards morning had been perceived by a market-woman not far from the spot where the body of the murdered child had been afterwards found. The woman asked her what she did there; but she looked very strangely, and only returned a confused and unintelligible answer. She returned to the house about eight o'clock; and when one inquired where she had passed the night, she replied, that she had been looking for the child, and demanded earnestly, if any thing had been heard concerning him. When shewn the body, she fell into violent hysterics, and kept her bed for several days. The picture was then produced, which the servant had found in her pocket; and when Elizabeth, in a faltering voice, proved that it was the same which, an hour before the child had been missed, she had placed round his neck, a murmur of horror and indignation filled the court.

Justine was called on for her defence. As the trial had proceeded, her countenance had altered. Surprise, horror, and misery, were strongly expressed. Sometimes she struggled with her tears; but when she was desired to plead, she collected her powers, and spoke in an audible although variable voice:—

"God knows," she said, "how entirely I am innocent. But I do not pretend that my protestations should acquit me: I rest my innocence on a plain and simple explanation of the facts which have been adduced against me; and I hope the character I have always borne will incline my judges to a favorable interpretation, where any circumstance appears doubtful or suspicious."

She then related that, by the permission of Elizabeth, she had passed the evening of the night on which the murder had been committed, at the house of an aunt at Chêne, a village situated at about a league from Geneva. On her return, at about nine o'clock, she met a man, who asked her if she had seen any thing of the child who was lost. She was alarmed by this account, and passed several hours in looking for him, when the gates of Geneva were shut, and she was forced to remain several hours of the night in a barn belonging to a cottage, being unwilling to call up the inhabitants, to whom she was well known. Unable to rest or sleep, she quitted her asylum early, that she might again endeavour to find my brother. If she had gone near the spot where his body lay, it was without her knowledge. That she had been bewildered when questioned by the market-woman, was not surprising, since she had passed a sleepless night, and the fate of poor William was yet uncertain. Concerning the picture she could give no account.

"I know," continued the unhappy victim, "how heavily and fatally this one circumstance weighs against me, but I have no power of explaining it; and when I have expressed my utter ignorance, I am only left to conjecture concerning the probabilities by which it might have been placed in my pocket. But here also I am checked. I believe that I have no enemy on earth, and none surely would have been so wicked as to destroy me wantonly. Did the murderer place it there? I know of no opportunity afforded him for so doing; or if I had, why should he have stolen the jewel, to part with it again so soon?

"I commit my cause to the justice of my judges, yet I see no room for hope. I beg permission to have a few witnesses examined concerning my character; and if their testimony shall not overweigh my supposed guilt, I must be condemned, although I would pledge my salvation on my innocence."

Several witnesses were called, who had known her for many years, and they spoke well of her; but fear, and hatred of the crime of which they supposed her guilty, rendered them timorous, and unwilling to come forward. Elizabeth saw even this last resource, her excellent dispositions and irreproachable conduct, about to fail the accused, when, although violently agitated, she desired permission to address the court.

"I am," said she, "the cousin of the unhappy child who was murdered, or rather his sister, for I was educated by and have lived with his parents ever since and even long before his birth. It may therefore be judged indecent in me to come forward on this occasion; but when I see a fellow-creature about to perish through the cowardice of her pretended friends, I wish to be allowed to speak, that I may say what I know of her character. I am well acquainted with the accused. I have lived in the same house with her, at one time for five, and at another for nearly two years. During all that period she appeared to me the most amiable and benevolent of human creatures. She nursed Madame Frankenstein, my aunt, in her last illness with the greatest affection and care; and afterwards attended her own mother during a tedious illness, in a manner that excited the admiration of all who knew her. After which she again lived in my uncle's house, where she was beloved by all the family. She was warmly attached to the child who is now dead, and acted towards him like a most affectionate mother. For my own part, I do not hesitate to say, that, notwithstanding all the evidence produced against her, I believe and rely on her perfect innocence. She had no temptation for such an action: as to the bauble on which the chief proof rests, if she had earnestly desired it, I should have willingly given it to her; so much do I esteem and value her."

Excellent Elizabeth! A murmur of approbation was heard; but it was excited by her generous interference, and not in favour of poor Justine, on whom the public indignation was turned with renewed violence, charging her with the blackest ingratitude. She herself wept as Elizabeth spoke, but she did not answer. My own agitation and anguish was extreme during the whole trial. I believed in her innocence; I knew it. Could the daemon, who had (I did not for a minute doubt) murdered my brother, also in his hellish sport have betrayed the innocent to death and ignominy. I could not sustain the horror of my situation; and when I perceived that the popular voice, and the countenances of the judges, had already condemned my unhappy victim, I rushed out of the court in agony. The tortures of the accused did not equal mine; she was sustained by innocence, but the fangs of remorse tore my bosom, and would not forego their hold.

I passed a night of unmingled wretchedness. In the morning I went to the court; my lips and throat were parched. I dared not ask the fatal question; but I was known, and the officer guessed the cause of my visit. The ballots had been thrown; they were all black, and Justine was condemned.

I cannot pretend to describe what I then felt. I had before experienced sensations of horror; and I have endeavoured to bestow upon them adequate expressions, but words cannot convey an idea of the heart-sickening despair that I then endured. The person to whom I addressed myself added, that Justine had already confessed her guilt. "That evidence," he observed, "was hardly required in so glaring a case, but I am glad of it; and, indeed, none of our judges like to condemn a criminal upon circumstantial evidence, be it ever so decisive."

When I returned home, Elizabeth eagerly demanded the result.

"My cousin," replied I, "it is decided as you may have expected; all judges had rather that ten innocent should suffer, than that one guilty should escape. But she has confessed."

This was a dire blow to poor Elizabeth, who had relied with firmness upon Justine's innocence. "Alas!" said she, "how shall I ever again believe in human benevolence? Justine, whom I loved and esteemed as my sister, how could she put on those smiles of innocence only to betray; her mild eyes seemed incapable of any severity or ill-humour, and yet she has committed a murder."

Soon after we heard that the poor victim had expressed a wish to see my cousin. My father wished her not to go; but said, that he left it to her own judgment and feelings to decide. "Yes," said Elizabeth, "I will go, although she is guilty; and you, Victor, shall accompany me: I cannot go alone." The idea of this visit was torture to me, yet I could not refuse.

We entered the gloomy prison-chamber, and beheld Justine sitting on some straw at the further end; her hands were manacled, and her head rested on her knees. She rose on seeing us enter; and when we were left alone with her, she threw herself at the feet of Elizabeth, weeping bitterly. My cousin wept also.

"Oh, Justine!" said she, "why did you rob me of my last consolation. I relied on your innocence; and although I was then very wretched, I was not so miserable as I am now."

"And do you also believe that I am so very, very wicked? Do you also join with my enemies to crush me?" Her voice was suffocated with sobs.

"Rise, my poor girl," said Elizabeth, "why do you kneel, if you are innocent? I am not one of your enemies; I believed you guiltless, notwithstanding every evidence, until I heard that you had yourself declared your guilt. That report, you say, is false; and be assured, dear Justine, that nothing can shake my confidence in you for a moment, but your own confession."

"I did confess; but I confessed a lie. I confessed, that I might obtain absolution; but now that falsehood lies heavier at my heart than all my other sins. The God of heaven forgive me! Ever since I was condemned, my confessor has besieged me; he threatened and menaced, until I almost began to think that I was the monster that he said I was. He threatened excommunication and hell fire in my last moments, if I continued obdurate. Dear lady, I had none to support me; all looked on me as a wretch doomed to ignominy and perdition. What could I do? In an evil hour[1] I subscribed to a lie; and now only am I truly miserable."

She paused, weeping, and then continued—"I thought with horror, my sweet lady, that you should believe your Justine, whom your blessed aunt had so highly honoured, and whom you loved, was a creature capable of a crime which none but the devil himself could have perpetrated. Dear William! dearest blessed child! I soon shall see you again in heaven, where we shall all be happy; and that consoles me, going as I am to suffer ignominy and death."

"Oh, Justine! forgive me for having for one moment distrusted you. Why did you confess? But do not mourn, my dear girl; I will every where proclaim your innocence, and force belief. Yet you must die; you, my playfellow, my companion, my more than sister. I never can survive so horrible a misfortune."

"Dear, sweet Elizabeth, do not weep. You ought to raise me with thoughts of a better life, and elevate me from the petty cares of this world of injustice and strife. Do not you, excellent friend, drive me to despair."

"I will try to comfort you; but this, I fear, is an evil too deep and poignant to admit of consolation, for there is no hope. Yet heaven bless thee, my dearest Justine, with resignation, and a confidence elevated beyond this world. Oh! how I hate its shews and mockeries! when one creature is murdered, another is immediately deprived of life in a slow torturing manner; then the executioners, their hands yet reeking with the blood of innocence, believe that they have done a

---

[1]Milton's punning description for the fall of Eve, *Paradise Lost* 9.780.

great deed. They call this *retribution*. Hateful name! When that word is pronounced, I know greater and more horrid punishments are going to be inflicted than the gloomiest tyrant has ever invented to satiate his utmost revenge. Yet this is not consolation for you, my Justine, unless indeed that you may glory in escaping from so miserable a den. Alas! I would I were in peace with my aunt and my lovely William, escaped from a world which is hateful to me, and the visages of men which I abhor."

Justine smiled languidly. "This, dear lady, is despair, and not resignation. I must not learn the lesson that you would teach me. Talk of something else, something that will bring peace, and not increase of misery."

During this conversation I had retired to a corner of the prison-room, where I could conceal the horrid anguish that possessed me. Despair! Who dared talk of that? The poor victim, who on the morrow was to pass the dreary boundary between life and death, felt not as I did, such deep and bitter agony. I gnashed my teeth, and ground them together, uttering a groan that came from my inmost soul. Justine started. When she saw who it was, she approached me, and said, "Dear Sir, you are very kind to visit me; you, I hope, do not believe that I am guilty."

I could not answer. "No, Justine," said Elizabeth; "he is more convinced of your innocence than I was; for even when he heard that you had confessed, he did not credit it."

"I truly thank him. In these last moments I feel the sincerest gratitude towards those who think of me with kindness. How sweet is the affection of others to such a wretch as I am! It removes more than half my misfortune; and I feel as if I could die in peace, now that my innocence is acknowledged by you, dear lady, and your cousin."

Thus the poor sufferer tried to comfort others and herself. She indeed gained the resignation she desired. But I, the true murderer, felt the never-dying worm alive in my bosom, which allowed of no hope or consolation.[2] Elizabeth also wept, and was unhappy; but her's also was the misery of innocence, which, like a cloud that passes over

[2]Jesus refers to Hell as a place "where their worm dieth not, and the fire is not quenched" (Mark 9.44), echoed in *Paradise Lost* 6.739 in the Son's reference to Satan's eternal torment as "th'undying Worm"; in *The Bride of Abydos* (1813), Byron describes remorse as "the worm that will not sleep—and never dies . . . That winds around and tears the quivering heart!" (2.644–49).

the fair moon, for a while hides, but cannot tarnish its brightness. Anguish and despair had penetrated into the core of my heart; I bore a hell within me, which nothing could extinguish.[3] We staid several hours with Justine; and it was with great difficulty that Elizabeth could tear herself away. "I wish," cried she, "that I were to die with you; I cannot live in this world of misery."

Justine assumed an air of cheerfulness, while she with difficulty repressed her bitter tears. She embraced Elizabeth, and said, in a voice of half-suppressed emotion, "Farewell, sweet lady, dearest Elizabeth, my beloved and only friend; may heaven in its bounty bless and preserve you; may this be the last misfortune that you will ever suffer. Live, and be happy, and make others so."

As we returned, Elizabeth said, "You know not, my dear Victor, how much I am relieved, now that I trust in the innocence of this unfortunate girl. I never could again have known peace, if I had been deceived in my reliance on her. For the moment that I did believe her guilty, I felt an anguish that I could not have long sustained. Now my heart is lightened. The innocent suffers; but she whom I thought amiable and good has not betrayed the trust I reposed in her, and I am consoled."

Amiable cousin! such were your thoughts, mild and gentle as your own dear eyes and voice. But I—I was a wretch, and none ever conceived of the misery that I then endured.[4]

Frankenstein;
or,
The Modern Prometheus
Volume II
Chapter I

Nothing is more painful to the human mind, than, after the feelings have been worked up by a quick succession of events, the dead calmness of inaction and certainty which follows, and deprives the soul both of hope and fear. Justine died; she rested; and I was alive. The

---

[3]Echoing Satan: see *Paradise Lost* 4.75 and 9.467.
[4]For the 1831 volume-closer, elaborating Victor's torments, see p. 203.

blood flowed freely in my veins, but a weight of despair and remorse pressed on my heart, which nothing could remove. Sleep fled from my eyes; I wandered like an evil spirit, for I had committed deeds of mischief beyond description horrible, and more, much more, (I persuaded myself) was yet behind.[1] Yet my heart overflowed with kindness, and the love of virtue. I had begun life with benevolent intentions, and thirsted for the moment when I should put them in practice, and make myself useful to my fellow-beings. Now all was blasted: instead of that serenity of conscience, which allowed me to look back upon the past with self-satisfaction, and from thence to gather promise of new hopes, I was seized by remorse and the sense of guilt, which hurried me away to a hell of intense tortures, such as no language can describe.

This state of mind preyed upon my health, which had entirely recovered from the first shock it had sustained. I shunned the face of man; all sound of joy or complacency was torture to me; solitude was my only consolation—deep, dark, death-like solitude.

My father observed with pain the alteration perceptible in my disposition and habits, and endeavoured to reason with me on the folly of giving way to immoderate grief. "Do you think, Victor," said he, "that I do not suffer also? No one could love a child more than I loved your brother" (tears came into his eyes as he spoke); "but is it not a duty to the survivors, that we should refrain from augmenting their unhappiness by an appearance of immoderate grief? It is also a duty owed to yourself; for excessive sorrow prevents improvement or enjoyment, or even the discharge of daily usefulness, without which no man is fit for society."

This advice, although good, was totally inapplicable to my case; I should have been the first to hide my grief, and console my friends, if remorse had not mingled its bitterness with my other sensations. Now I could only answer my father with a look of despair, and endeavour to hide myself from his view.

About this time we retired to our house at Belrive. This change was particularly agreeable to me. The shutting of the gates regularly at ten o'clock, and the impossibility of remaining on the lake after that hour, had rendered our residence within the walls of Geneva very irksome to me. I was now free. Often, after the rest of the family

[1]An allegorical conception of time from the classical era: the future occurs as "Time" moves forward, from behind.

had retired for the night, I took the boat, and passed many hours upon the water. Sometimes, with my sails set, I was carried by the wind; and sometimes, after rowing into the middle of the lake, I left the boat to pursue its own course, and gave way to my own miserable reflections. I was often tempted, when all was at peace around me, and I the only unquiet thing that wandered restless in a scene so beautiful and heavenly, if I except some bat, or the frogs, whose harsh and interrupted croaking was heard only when I approached the shore—often, I say, I was tempted to plunge into the silent lake, that the waters might close over me and my calamities for ever. But I was restrained, when I thought of the heroic and suffering Elizabeth, whom I tenderly loved, and whose existence was bound up in mine. I thought also of my father, and surviving brother: should I by my base desertion leave them exposed and unprotected to the malice of the fiend whom I had let loose among them?

At these moments I wept bitterly, and wished that peace would revisit my mind only that I might afford them consolation and happiness. But that could not be. Remorse extinguished every hope. I had been the author of unalterable evils; and I lived in daily fear, lest the monster whom I had created should perpetrate some new wickedness. I had an obscure feeling that all was not over, and that he would still commit some signal crime, which by its enormity should almost efface the recollection of the past. There was always scope for fear, so long as any thing I loved remained behind. My abhorrence of this fiend cannot be conceived. When I thought of him, I gnashed my teeth, my eyes became inflamed, and I ardently wished to extinguish that life which I had so thoughtlessly bestowed. When I reflected on his crimes and malice, my hatred and revenge burst all bounds of moderation. I would have made a pilgrimage to the highest peak of the Andes, could I, when there, have precipitated him to their base. I wished to see him again, that I might wreak the utmost extent of anger on his head, and avenge the deaths of William and Justine.

Our house was the house of mourning. My father's health was deeply shaken by the horror of the recent events. Elizabeth was sad and desponding; she no longer took delight in her ordinary occupations; all pleasure seemed to her sacrilege toward the dead; eternal woe and tears she then thought was the just tribute she should pay to innocence so blasted and destroyed. She was no longer that happy creature, who in earlier youth wandered with me on the banks of the lake, and talked with ecstacy of our future prospects. She had become grave, and often conversed of the inconstancy of fortune, and the instability of human life.

"When I reflect, my dear cousin," said she, "on the miserable death of Justine Moritz, I no longer see the world and its works as they before appeared to me. Before, I looked upon the accounts of vice and injustice, that I read in books or heard from others, as tales of ancient days, or imaginary evils; at least they were remote, and more familiar to reason than to the imagination; but now misery has come home, and men appear to me as monsters thirsting for each other's blood. Yet I am certainly unjust. Every body believed that poor girl to be guilty; and if she could have committed the crime for which she suffered, assuredly she would have been the most depraved of human creatures. For the sake of a few jewels, to have murdered the son of her benefactor and friend, a child whom she had nursed from its birth, and appeared to love as if it had been her own! I could not consent to the death of any human being; but certainly I should have thought such a creature unfit to remain in the society of men. Yet she was innocent. I know, I feel she was innocent; you are of the same opinion, and that confirms me. Alas! Victor, when falsehood can look so like the truth, who can assure themselves of certain happiness? I feel as if I were walking on the edge of a precipice, towards which thousands are crowding, and endeavouring to plunge me into the abyss. William and Justine were assassinated, and the murderer escapes; he walks about the world free, and perhaps respected. But even if I were condemned to suffer on the scaffold for the same crimes, I would not change places with such a wretch."

I listened to this discourse with the extremest agony. I, not in deed, but in effect, was the true murderer. Elizabeth read my anguish in my countenance, and kindly taking my hand said, "My dearest cousin, you must calm yourself. These events have affected me, God knows how deeply; but I am not so wretched as you are. There is an expression of despair, and sometimes of revenge, in your countenance, that makes me tremble. Be calm, my dear Victor; I would sacrifice my life to your peace. We surely shall be happy: quiet in our native country, and not mingling in the world, what can disturb our tranquillity?"[2]

---

[2]In 1831 Shelley elaborates Victor's alternation between anguish and self-forgetfulness; see p. 204.

She shed tears as she said this, distrusting the very solace that she gave; but at the same time she smiled, that she might chase away the fiend that lurked in my heart. My father, who saw in the unhappiness that was painted in my face only an exaggeration of that sorrow which I might naturally feel, thought that an amusement suited to my taste would be the best means of restoring to me my wonted serenity. It was from this cause that he had removed to the country; and, induced by the same motive, he now proposed that we should all make an excursion to the valley of Chamounix.[3] I had been there before, but Elizabeth and Ernest never had; and both had often expressed an earnest desire to see the scenery of this place, which had been described to them as so wonderful and sublime. Accordingly we departed from Geneva on this tour about the middle of the month of August, nearly two months after the death of Justine.

The weather was uncommonly fine; and if mine had been a sorrow to be chased away by any fleeting circumstance, this excursion would certainly have had the effect intended by my father. As it was, I was somewhat interested in the scene; it sometimes lulled, although it could not extinguish my grief. During the first day we travelled in a carriage. In the morning we had seen the mountains at a distance, towards which we gradually advanced. We perceived that the valley through which we wound, and which was formed by the river Arve, whose course we followed, closed in upon us by degrees; and when the sun had set, we beheld immense mountains and precipices overhanging us on every side, and heard the sound of the river raging among rocks, and the dashing of waterfalls around.[4]

The next day we pursued our journey upon mules; and as we ascended still higher, the valley assumed a more magnificent and astonishing character. Ruined castles hanging on the precipices of piny mountains; the impetuous Arve, and cottages every here and there peeping forth from among the trees, formed a scene of singular beauty. But it was augmented and rendered sublime by the mighty Alps, whose white and shining pyramids and domes towered above all, as belonging to another earth, the habitations of another race of beings.

We passed the bridge of Pelissier, where the ravine, which the river forms, opened before us, and we began to ascend the mountain

---

[3]Whence rises the sublime Mont Blanc.

[4]The Shelleys toured this region in 1814; see Percy's response in *Mont Blanc*. For Victor's worship of "a power mighty as Omnipotence," see the 1831 revision, p. 205.

that overhangs it. Soon after we entered the valley of Chamounix. This valley is more wonderful and sublime, but not so beautiful and picturesque as that of Servox, through which we had just passed. The high and snowy mountains were its immediate boundaries; but we saw no more ruined castles and fertile fields. Immense glaciers approached the road; we heard the rumbling thunder of the falling avelânche, and marked the smoke of its passage. Mont Blanc, the supreme and magnificent Mont Blanc, raised itself from the surrounding *aiguilles*,[5] and its tremendous *dome* overlooked the valley.

During this journey, I sometimes joined Elizabeth, and exerted myself to point out to her the various beauties of the scene. I often suffered my mule to lag behind, and indulged in the misery of reflection. At other times I spurred on the animal before my companions, that I might forget them, the world, and, more than all, myself. When at a distance, I alighted, and threw myself on the grass, weighted down by horror and despair. At eight in the evening I arrived at Chamounix. My father and Elizabeth were very much fatigued; Ernest, who accompanied us, was delighted, and in high spirits: the only circumstance that detracted from his pleasure was the south wind, and the rain it seemed to promise for the next day.

We retired early to our apartments, but not to sleep; at least I did not. I remained many hours at the window, watching the pallid lightning that played above Mont Blanc, and listening to the rushing of the Arve, which ran below my window.

Chapter II

The next day, contrary to the prognostications of our guides, was fine, although clouded. We visited the source of the Arveiron,[1] and rode about the valley until evening. These sublime and magnificent scenes afforded me the greatest consolation that I was capable of receiving. They elevated me from all littleness of feeling; and although they did not remove my grief, they subdued and tranquillized it. In some degree, also they diverted my mind from the thoughts over which it had brooded for the last month. I returned in the evening, fatigued, but less unhappy, and conversed with my family with more cheerfulness

[5]Peaks.

[1]The various branches from the Arve river.

than had been my custom for some time. My father was pleased, and Elizabeth overjoyed. "My dear cousin," said she, "you see what happiness you diffuse when you are happy; do not relapse again!"[2]

The following morning the rain poured down in torrents, and thick mists hid the summits of the mountains. I rose early, but felt unusually melancholy. The rain depressed me; my old feelings recurred, and I was miserable. I knew how disappointed my father would be at this sudden change, and I wished to avoid him until I had recovered myself so far as to be enabled to conceal those feelings that overpowered me. I knew that they would remain that day at the inn; and as I had ever inured myself to rain, moisture, and cold, I resolved to go alone to the summit of Montanvert. I remembered the effect that the view of the tremendous and ever-moving glacier had produced upon my mind when I first saw it. It had then filled me with a sublime ecstacy that gave wings to the soul, and allowed it to soar from the obscure world to light and joy. The sight of the awful and majestic in nature had indeed always the effect of solemnizing my mind, and causing me to forget the passing cares of life. I determined to go alone, for I was well acquainted with the path, and the presence of another would destroy the solitary grandeur of the scene.

The ascent is precipitous, but the path is cut into continual and short windings, which enable you to surmount the perpendicularity of the mountain. It is a scene terrifically desolate. In a thousand spots the traces of the winter avelânche may be perceived, where trees lie broken and strewed on the ground; some entirely destroyed, others bent, leaning upon the jutting rocks of the mountain, or transversely upon other trees. The path, as you ascend higher, is intersected by ravines of snow, down which stones continually roll from above; one of them is particularly dangerous, as the slightest sound, such as even speaking in a loud voice, produces a concussion of air sufficient to draw destruction upon the head of the speaker. The pines are not tall or luxuriant, but they are sombre, and add an air of severity to the scene. I looked on the valley beneath; vast mists were rising from the rivers which ran through it, and curling in thick wreaths around the opposite mountains, whose summits were hid in the uniform clouds, while rain poured from the dark sky, and added to the melancholy impression I received from the objects around me. Alas! why does man boast of sensibilities superior to those apparent in the brute; it

[2]For the 1831 elaboration of Victor's mood-swings, see p. 205.

only renders them more necessary beings. If our impulses were confined to hunger, thirst, and desire, we might be nearly free; but now we are moved by every wind that blows, and a chance word or scene that that word may convey to us.

> We rest; a dream has power to poison sleep.
> We rise; one wand'ring thought pollutes the day.
> We feel, conceive, or reason; laugh, or weep,
>> Embrace fond woe, or cast our cares away;
>
>> It is the same: for, be it joy or sorrow,
>> The path of its departure still is free.
> Man's yesterday may ne'er be like his morrow;
> Nought may endure but mutability![3]

It was nearly noon when I arrived at the top of the ascent. For some time I sat upon the rock that overlooks the sea of ice.[4] A mist covered both that and the surrounding mountains. Presently a breeze dissipated the cloud, and I descended upon the glacier. The surface is very uneven, rising like the waves of a troubled sea, descending low, and interspersed by rifts that sink deep. The field of ice is almost a league in width, but I spent nearly two hours in crossing it. The opposite mountain is a bare perpendicular rock. From the side where I now stood Montanvert was exactly opposite, at the distance of a league; and above it rose Mont Blanc, in awful majesty. I remained in a recess of the rock, gazing on this wonderful and stupendous scene. The sea, or rather the vast river of ice, wound among its dependent mountains, whose aërial summits hung over its recesses. Their icy and glittering peaks shone in the sunlight over the clouds. My heart, which was before sorrowful, now swelled with something like joy; I exclaimed—"Wandering spirits, if indeed ye wander, and do not rest in your narrow beds, allow me this faint happiness, or take me, as your companion, away from the joys of life."

---

[3] "Shelley's Poems."—'On Mutability.'" [M. Shelley's note, 1831]. Victor quotes the last half of a 16-line poem, *Mutability* (actually written two decades after the time of the story and first published in P. B. Shelley's *Alastor* volume, Feb. 1816). Mary Shelley's inclusion of this verse is partly an advertisement for Percy Shelley's volume, which was not selling well, and partly a play to the coterie who would recognize the verse.

[4] Mer de Glace (Sea of Ice) is the glacier descending from Mont Blanc. "This is the most desolate place in the world—iced mountains surround it—no sign of vegetation," Shelley wrote of her visit (journal, 25 July 1816). See *Mont Blanc* for another description.

As I said this, I suddenly beheld the figure of a man, at some distance, advancing towards me with superhuman speed. He bounded over the crevices in the ice, among which I had walked with caution; his stature also, as he approached, seemed to exceed that of man. I was troubled: a mist came over my eyes, and I felt a faintness seize me; but I was quickly restored by the cold gale of the mountains. I perceived, as the shape came nearer, (sight tremendous and abhorred!) that it was the wretch whom I had created. I trembled with rage and horror, resolving to wait his approach, and then close with him in mortal combat. He approached; his countenance bespoke bitter anguish, combined with disdain and malignity, while its unearthly ugliness rendered it almost too horrible for human eyes. But I scarcely observed this; anger and hatred had at first deprived me of utterance, and I recovered only to overwhelm him with words expressive of furious detestation and contempt.

"Devil!" I exclaimed, "do you dare approach me? and do not you fear the fierce vengeance of my arm wreaked on your miserable head? Begone, vile insect! or rather stay, that I may trample you to dust! and, oh, that I could, with the extinction of your miserable existence, restore those victims whom you have so diabolically murdered!"

"I expected this reception," said the daemon. "All men hate the wretched; how then must I be hated, who am miserable beyond all living things! Yet you, my creator, detest and spurn me, thy creature, to whom thou art bound by ties only dissoluble by the annihilation of one of us. You purpose to kill me. How dare you sport thus with life? Do your duty towards me, and I will do mine towards you and the rest of mankind. If you will comply with my conditions, I will leave them and you at peace; but if you refuse, I will glut the maw of death, until it be satiated with the blood of your remaining friends."

"Abhorred monster! fiend that thou art! the tortures of hell are too mild a vengeance for thy crimes. Wretched devil! you reproach me with your creation; come on then, that I may extinguish the spark which I so negligently bestowed."

My rage was without bounds; I sprang on him, impelled by all the feelings which can arm one being against the existence of another.

He easily eluded me, and said,

"Be calm! I entreat you to hear me, before you give vent to your hatred on my devoted head. Have I not suffered enough, that you seek to increase my misery? Life, although it may only be an accumulation of anguish, is dear to me, and I will defend it. Remember, thou hast made me more powerful than thyself; my height is superior to thine; my joints more supple. But I will not be tempted to set myself in opposition to thee. I am thy creature, and I will be even mild and docile to my natural lord and king, if thou wilt also perform thy part, the which thou owest me. Oh, Frankenstein, be not equitable to every other, and trample upon me alone, to whom thy justice, and even thy clemency and affection, is most due. Remember, that I am thy creature: I ought to be thy Adam; but I am rather the fallen angel, whom thou drivest from joy for no misdeed. Every where I see bliss, from which I alone am irrevocably excluded.[5] I was benevolent and good; misery made me a fiend. Make me happy, and I shall again be virtuous."

"Begone! I will not hear you. There can be no community between you and me; we are enemies. Begone, or let us try our strength in a fight, in which one must fall."

"How can I move thee? Will no entreaties cause thee to turn a favourable eye upon thy creature, who implores thy goodness and compassion. Believe me, Frankenstein: I was benevolent; my soul glowed with love and humanity: but am I not alone, miserably alone? You, my creator, abhor me; what hope can I gather from your fellow-creatures, who owe me nothing? they spurn and hate me. The desert mountains and dreary glaciers are my refuge. I have wandered here many days; the caves of ice, which I only do not fear, are a dwelling to me, and the only one which man does not grudge. These bleak skies I hail, for they are kinder to me than your fellow-beings. If the multitude of mankind knew of my existence, they would do as you do, and arm themselves for my destruction. Shall I not then hate them who abhor me? I will keep no terms with my enemies. I am miserable, and they shall share my wretchedness. Yet it is in your power to recompense me, and deliver them from an evil which it only remains for you to make so great, that not only you and your family, but thousands of others, shall be swallowed up in the whirlwinds of its rage. Let your compassion be moved, and do not disdain me. Listen to my tale: when you have heard that, abandon or commiserate me, as you shall judge that I deserve. But hear me. The guilty are allowed, by human laws, bloody as they may be, to speak in their own defence before they are condemned. Listen to me, Frankenstein. You accuse me of murder; and yet you would, with a

[5]See Satan in *Paradise Lost* (which the Creature has read) 9.468–70.

satisfied conscience, destroy your own creature. Oh, praise the eternal justice of man! Yet I ask you not to spare me: listen to me; and then, if you can, and if you will, destroy the work of your hands."

"Why do you call to my remembrance circumstances of which I shudder to reflect, that I have been the miserable origin and author? Cursed be the day, abhorred devil, in which you first saw light! Cursed (although I curse myself) be the hands that formed you! You have made me wretched beyond expression. You have left me no power to consider whether I am just to you, or not. Begone! Relieve me from the sight of your detested form."

"Thus I relieve thee, my creator," he said, and placed his hated hands before my eyes, which I flung from me with violence; "thus I take from thee a sight which you abhor. Still thou canst listen to me, and grant me thy compassion. By the virtues that I once possessed, I demand this from you. Hear my tale; it is long and strange, and the temperature of this place is not fitting to your fine sensations; come to the hut upon the mountain. The sun is yet high in the heavens; before it descends to hide itself behind yon snowy precipices, and illuminate another world, you will have heard my story, and can decide. On you it rests, whether I quit for ever the neighbourhood of man, and lead a harmless life, or become the scourge of your fellow-creatures, and the author of your own speedy ruin."

As he said this, he led the way across the ice: I followed. My heart was full, and I did not answer him; but, as I proceeded, I weighed the various arguments that he had used, and determined at least to listen to his tale. I was partly urged by curiosity, and compassion confirmed my resolution. I had hitherto supposed him to be the murderer of my brother, and I eagerly sought a confirmation or denial of this opinion. For the first time, also, I felt what the duties of a creator towards his creature were, and that I ought to render him happy before I complained of his wickedness.[6] These motives urged me to comply with his demand. We crossed the ice, therefore, and ascended the opposite rock. The air was cold, and the rain again began to descend: we entered the hut, the fiend with an air of exultation, I with a heavy heart, and depressed spirits. But I consented to listen;

[6]An ethic that Wollstonecraft (Shelley's mother) advocated. See Jemima's story from *The Wrongs of Woman* (p. 229) and *A Vindication of the Rights of Woman* (1792): "A great proportion of the misery that wanders, in hideous forms, around the world, is allowed to arise from the negligence of parents" (Ch. 11).

and, seating myself by the fire which my odious companion had lighted, he thus began his tale.

Chapter III

"It is with considerable difficulty that I remember the original aera of my being: all the events of that period appear confused and indistinct.[1] A strange multiplicity of sensations seized me, and I saw, felt, heard, and smelt, at the same time; and it was, indeed, a long time before I learned to distinguish between the operations of my various senses. By degrees, I remember, a stronger light pressed upon my nerves, so that I was obliged to shut my eyes. Darkness then came over me, and troubled me; but hardly had I felt this, when, by opening my eyes, as I now suppose, the light poured in upon me again. I walked, and, I believe, descended; but I presently found a great alteration in my sensations. Before, dark and opaque bodies had surrounded me, impervious to my touch or sight; but I now found that I could wander on at liberty, with no obstacles which I could not either surmount or avoid. The light became more and more oppressive to me; and, the heat wearying me as I walked, I sought a place where I could receive shade. This was the forest near Ingolstadt; and here I lay by the side of a brook resting from my fatigue, until I felt tormented by hunger and thirst. This roused me from my nearly dormant state, and I ate some berries which I found hanging on the trees, or lying on the ground. I slaked my thirst at the brook; and then lying down, was overcome by sleep.

"It was dark when I awoke; I felt cold also, and half-frightened as it were instinctively, finding myself so desolate. Before I had quitted your apartment, on a sensation of cold, I had covered myself with some clothes; but these were insufficient to secure me from the dews of night. I was a poor, helpless, miserable wretch; I knew, and could distinguish, nothing; but, feeling pain invade me on all sides, I sat down and wept.

"Soon a gentle light stole over the heavens, and gave me a sensation of pleasure. I started up, and beheld a radiant form[2] rise from among

---

[1]Shelley evokes the contrast of Adam's account of his awakening and earliest memories in Paradise (see *Paradise Lost* 8.250–300) and also echoes Volney's description of primitive humanity in *Ruins of Empires* (1792), the book from which the Creature learns to read (see II.V).

[2]Shelley's footnote in 1831] The moon.

the trees. I gazed with a kind of wonder. It moved slowly, but it enlightened my path; and I again went out in search of berries. I was still cold, when under one of the trees I found a huge cloak, with which I covered myself, and sat down upon the ground. No distinct ideas occupied my mind; all was confused. I felt light, and hunger, and thirst, and darkness; innumerable sounds rung in my ears, and on all sides various scents saluted me: the only object that I could distinguish was the bright moon, and I fixed my eyes on that with pleasure.

"Several changes of day and night passed, and the orb of night had greatly lessened when I began to distinguish my sensations from each other. I gradually saw plainly the clear stream that supplied me with drink, and the trees that shaded me with their foliage. I was delighted when I first discovered that a pleasant sound, which often saluted my ears, proceeded from the throats of the little winged animals who had often intercepted the light from my eyes. I began also to observe, with greater accuracy, the forms that surrounded me, and to perceive the boundaries of the radiant roof of light which canopied me. Sometimes I tried to imitate the pleasant songs of the birds, but was unable. Sometimes I wished to express my sensations in my own mode, but the uncouth and inarticulate sounds which broke from me frightened me into silence again.[3]

"The moon had disappeared from the night, and again, with a lessened form, shewed itself, while I still remained in the forest. My sensations had, by this time, become distinct, and my mind received every day additional ideas. My eyes became accustomed to the light, and to perceive objects in their right forms; I distinguished the insect from the herb, and, by degrees, one herb from another. I found that the sparrow uttered none but harsh notes, whilst those of the blackbird and thrush were sweet and enticing.

"One day, when I was oppressed by cold, I found a fire which had been left by some wandering beggars, and was overcome with delight at the warmth I experienced from it. In my joy I thrust my hand into the live embers, but quickly drew it out again with a cry of pain. How strange, I thought, that the same cause should produce such opposite effects! I examined the materials of the fire, and to my joy found it to be composed of wood. I quickly collected some branches;

[3]Shelley may be glancing at the contrasting case of Wordsworth's "Boy of Winander" (*Lyrical Ballads*, 1800), whose "responsive" calling back and forth to birds and whose communion with nature even in silence convey spiritual intimacy.

but they were wet, and would not burn. I was pained at this, and sat still watching the operation of the fire. The wet wood which I had placed near the heat dried, and itself became inflamed. I reflected on this; and, by touching the various branches, I discovered the cause, and busied myself in collecting a great quantity of wood, that I might dry it, and have a plentiful supply of fire. When night came on, and brought sleep with it, I was in the greatest fear lest my fire should be extinguished. I covered it carefully with dry wood and leaves, and placed wet branches upon it; and then, spreading my cloak, I lay on the ground, and sunk into sleep.

"It was morning when I awoke, and my first care was to visit the fire. I uncovered it, and a gentle breeze quickly fanned it into a flame. I observed this also, and contrived a fan of branches, which roused the embers when they were nearly extinguished. When night came again, I found, with pleasure, that the fire gave light as well as heat; and that the discovery of this element was useful to me in my food; for I found some of the offals that the travellers had left had been roasted, and tasted much more savoury than the berries I gathered from the trees. I tried, therefore, to dress my food in the same manner, placing it on the live embers. I found that the berries were spoiled by this operation, and the nuts and roots much improved.

"Food, however, became scarce; and I often spent the whole day searching in vain for a few acorns to assuage the pangs of hunger. When I found this, I resolved to quit the place that I had hitherto inhabited, to seek for one where the few wants I experienced would be more easily satisfied. In this emigration, I exceedingly lamented the loss of the fire which I had obtained through accident, and knew not how to re-produce it. I gave several hours to the serious consideration of this difficulty; but I was obliged to relinquish all attempt to supply it; and, wrapping myself up in my cloak, I struck across the wood towards the setting sun. I passed three days in these rambles, and at length discovered the open country. A great fall of snow had taken place the night before, and the fields were of one uniform white; the appearance was disconsolate, and I found my feet chilled by the cold damp substance that covered the ground.

"It was about seven in the morning, and I longed to obtain food and shelter; at length I perceived a small hut, on a rising ground, which had doubtless been built for the convenience of some shepherd. This was a new sight to me; and I examined the structure with great curiosity. Finding the door open, I entered. An old man sat in it, near a fire, over which he was preparing his breakfast. He turned on hearing a noise; and, perceiving me, shrieked loudly, and, quitting the hut, ran across the fields with a speed of which his debilitated form hardly appeared capable. His appearance, different from any I had ever before seen, and his flight, somewhat surprised me. But I was enchanted by the appearance of the hut: here the snow and rain could not penetrate; the ground was dry; and it presented to me then as exquisite and divine a retreat as Pandaemonium[4] appeared to the daemons of hell after their sufferings in the lake of fire. I greedily devoured the remnants of the shepherd's breakfast, which consisted of bread, cheese, milk, and wine; the latter, however, I did not like. Then overcome by fatigue, I lay down among some straw, and fell asleep.

"It was noon when I awoke; and, allured by the warmth of the sun, which shone brightly on the white ground, I determined to recommence my travels; and, depositing the remains of the peasant's breakfast in a wallet[5] I found, I proceeded across the fields for several hours, until at sunset I arrived at a village. How miraculous did this appear! the huts, the neater cottages, and stately houses, engaged my admiration by turns. The vegetables in the gardens, the milk and cheese that I saw placed at the windows of some of the cottages, allured my appetite. One of the best of these I entered; but I had hardly placed my foot within the door, before the children shrieked, and one of the women fainted. The whole village was roused; some fled, some attacked me, until, grievously bruised by stones and many other kinds of missile weapons, I escaped to the open country, and fearfully took refuge in a low hovel, quite bare, and making a wretched appearance after the palaces I had beheld in the village. This hovel, however, joined a cottage of a neat and pleasant appearance; but, after my late dearly-bought experience, I dared not enter it. My place of refuge was constructed of wood, but so low, that I could with difficulty sit upright in it. No wood, however, was placed on the earth, which formed the floor, but it was dry; and although the wind entered it by innumerable chinks, I found it an agreeable asylum from the snow and rain.

---

[4]Milton's coinage: "city of all the demons"; Milton depicts Hell as a stormy lake of fire in *Paradise Lost* Book I, which ends with the building of "Pandemonium, / The high Capitol of Satan and his Peers," a city whose pomp is a parody of Heaven.
[5]Satchel.

"Here then I retreated, and lay down, happy to have found a shelter, however miserable, from the inclemency of the season, and still more from the barbarity of man.

"As soon as morning dawned, I crept from my kennel, that I might view the adjacent cottage, and discover if I could remain in the habitation I had found. It was situated against the back of the cottage, and surrounded on the sides which were exposed by a pig-stye and a clear pool of water. One part was open, and by that I had crept in; but now I covered every crevice by which I might be perceived with stones and wood, yet in such a manner that I might move them on occasion to pass out: all the light I enjoyed came through the stye, and that was sufficient for me.

"Having thus arranged my dwelling, and carpeted it with clean straw, I retired; for I saw the figure of a man at a distance, and I remembered too well my treatment the night before, to trust myself in his power. I had first, however, provided for my sustenance for that day, by a loaf of coarse bread, which I purloined, and a cup with which I could drink, more conveniently than from my hand, of the pure water which flowed by my retreat. The floor was a little raised, so that it was kept perfectly dry, and by its vicinity to the chimney of the cottage it was tolerably warm.

"Being thus provided, I resolved to reside in this hovel, until something should occur which might alter my determination. It was indeed a paradise, compared to the bleak forest, my former residence, the rain-dropping branches, and dank earth. I ate my breakfast with pleasure, and was about to remove a plank to procure myself a little water, when I heard a step, and, looking through a small chink, I beheld a young creature, with a pail on her head, passing before my hovel. The girl was young and of gentle demeanour, unlike what I have since found cottagers and farm-house servants to be. Yet she was meanly[6] dressed, a coarse blue petticoat and a linen jacket being her only garb; her fair hair was plaited, but not adorned; she looked patient, yet sad. I lost sight of her; and in about a quarter of an hour she returned, bearing the pail, which was now partly filled with milk. As she walked along, seemingly incommoded by the burden, a young man met her, whose countenance expressed a deeper despondence. Uttering a few sounds with an air of melancholy, he took the pail from her head, and bore it to the cottage himself. She followed, and

[6]Plainly.

they disappeared. Presently I saw the young man again, with some tools in his hand, cross the field behind the cottage; and the girl was also busied, sometimes in the house, and sometimes in the yard.

"On examining my dwelling, I found that one of the windows of the cottage had formerly occupied a part of it, but the panes had been filled up with wood. In one of these was a small and almost imperceptible chink, through which the eye could just penetrate. Through this crevice, a small room was visible, white-washed and clean, but very bare of furniture. In one corner, near a small fire, sat an old man, leaning his head on his hands in a disconsolate attitude. The young girl was occupied in arranging the cottage; but presently she took something out of a drawer, which employed her hands, and she sat down beside the old man, who, taking up an instrument, began to play, and to produce sounds, sweeter than the voice of the thrush or the nightingale. It was a lovely sight, even to me, poor wretch! who had never beheld aught beautiful before. The silver hair and benevolent countenance of the aged cottager, won my reverence; while the gentle manners of the girl enticed my love. He played a sweet mournful air, which I perceived drew tears from the eyes of his amiable companion, of which the old man took no notice, until she sobbed audibly; he then pronounced a few sounds, and the fair creature, leaving her work, knelt at his feet. He raised her, and smiled with such kindness and affection, that I felt sensations of a peculiar and overpowering nature: they were a mixture of pain and pleasure, such as I had never before experienced, either from hunger or cold, warmth or food; and I withdrew from the window, unable to bear these emotions.

"Soon after this the young man returned, bearing on his shoulders a load of wood. The girl met him at the door, helped to relieve him of his burden, and, taking some of the fuel into the cottage, placed it on the fire; then she and the youth went apart into a nook of the cottage, and he shewed her a large loaf and a piece of cheese. She seemed pleased; and went into the garden for some roots and plants, which she placed in water, and then upon the fire. She afterwards continued her work, whilst the young man went into the garden, and appeared busily employed in digging and pulling up roots. After he had been employed thus about an hour, the young woman joined him, and they entered the cottage together.

"The old man had, in the mean time, been pensive; but, on the appearance of his companions, he assumed a more cheerful air, and they sat down to eat. The meal was quickly dispatched. The young woman was again occupied in arranging the cottage; the old man walked before the cottage in the sun for a few minutes, leaning on the arm of the youth. Nothing could exceed in beauty the contrast between these two excellent creatures. One was old, with silver hairs and a countenance beaming with benevolence and love: the younger was slight and graceful in his figure, and his features were moulded with the finest symmetry; yet his eyes and attitude expressed the utmost sadness and despondency. The old man returned to the cottage; and the youth, with tools different from those he had used in the morning, directed his steps across the fields.

"Night quickly shut in; but, to my extreme wonder, I found that the cottagers had a means of prolonging light, by the use of tapers, and was delighted to find, that the setting of the sun did not put an end to the pleasure I experienced in watching my human neighbours. In the evening, the young girl and her companion were employed in various occupations which I did not understand; and the old man again took up the instrument, which produced the divine sounds that had enchanted me in the morning. So soon as he had finished, the youth began, not to play, but to utter sounds that were monotonous, and neither resembling the harmony of the old man's instrument or the songs of the birds; I since found that he read aloud, but at that time I knew nothing of the science of words or letters.

"The family, after having been thus occupied for a short time, extinguished their lights, and retired, as I conjectured, to rest.

Chapter IV

"I lay on my straw, but I could not sleep. I thought of the occurrence of the day. What chiefly struck me was the gentle manners of these people; and I longed to join them, but dared not. I remembered too well the treatment I had suffered the night before from the barbarous villagers, and resolved, whatever course of conduct I might hereafter think it right to pursue, that for the present I would remain quietly in my hovel, watching, and endeavouring to discover the motives which influenced their actions.

"The cottagers arose the next morning before the sun. The young woman arranged the cottage, and prepared the food; and the youth departed after the first meal.

"This day was passed in the same routine as that which preceded it. The young man was constantly employed out of doors, and the girl in various laborious occupations within. The old man, whom I soon perceived to be blind, employed his leisure hours on his instrument, or in contemplation. Nothing could exceed the love and respect which the younger cottagers exhibited towards their venerable companion. They performed towards him every little office of affection and duty with gentleness; and he rewarded them by his benevolent smiles.

"They were not entirely happy. The young man and his companion often went apart, and appeared to weep. I saw no cause for their unhappiness; but I was deeply affected by it. If such lovely creatures were miserable, it was less strange that I, an imperfect and solitary being, should be wretched. Yet why were these gentle beings unhappy? They possessed a delightful house (for such it was in my eyes), and every luxury; they had a fire to warm them when chill, and delicious viands when hungry; they were dressed in excellent clothes; and, still more, they enjoyed one another's company and speech, interchanging each day looks of affection and kindness. What did their tears imply? Did they really express pain? I was at first unable to solve these questions; but perpetual attention, and time, explained to me many appearances which were at first enigmatic.

"A considerable period elapsed before I discovered one of the causes of the uneasiness of this amiable family; it was poverty: and they suffered that evil in a very distressing degree. Their nourishment consisted entirely of the vegetables of their garden, and the milk of one cow, who gave very little during the winter, when its masters could scarcely procure food to support it. They often, I believe, suffered the pangs of hunger very poignantly, especially the two younger cottagers; for several times they placed food before the old man, when they reserved none for themselves.

"This trait of kindness moved me sensibly. I had been accustomed, during the night, to steal a part of their store for my own consumption; but when I found that in doing this I inflicted pain on the cottagers, I abstained, and satisfied myself with berries, nuts, and roots, which I gathered from a neighbouring wood.

"I discovered also another means through which I was enabled to assist their labours. I found that the youth spent a great part of each day in collecting wood for the family fire; and, during the night, I often took his tools, the use of which I quickly discovered, and brought home firing sufficient for the consumption of several days.

"I remember, the first time that I did this, the young woman, when she opened the door in the morning, appeared greatly astonished on seeing a great pile of wood on the outside. She uttered some words in a loud voice, and the youth joined her, who also expressed surprise. I observed, with pleasure, that he did not go to the forest that day, but spent it in repairing the cottage, and cultivating the garden.

"By degrees I made a discovery of still greater moment. I found that these people possessed a method of communicating their experience and feelings to one another by articulate sounds. I perceived that the words they spoke sometimes produced pleasure or pain, smiles or sadness, in the minds and countenances of the hearers. This was indeed a godlike science, and I ardently desired to become acquainted with it. But I was baffled in every attempt I made for this purpose. Their pronunciation was quick; and the words they uttered, not having any apparent connexion with visible objects, I was unable to discover any clue by which I could unravel the mystery of their reference. By great application, however, and after having remained during the space of several revolutions of the moon in my hovel, I discovered the names that were given to some of the most familiar objects of discourse: I learned and applied the words *fire, milk, bread,* and *wood.* I learned also the names of the cottagers themselves. The youth and his companion had each of them several names, but the old man had only one, which was *father.* The girl was called *sister,* or *Agatha;* and the youth *Felix, brother,* or *son.*[1] I cannot describe the delight I felt when I learned the ideas appropriated to each of these sounds, and was able to pronounce them. I distinguished several other words, without being able as yet to understand or apply them; such as *good, dearest, unhappy.*

"I spent the winter in this manner. The gentle manners and beauty of the cottagers greatly endeared them to me: when they were unhappy, I felt depressed; when they rejoiced, I sympathized in their joys. I saw few human beings beside them; and if any other happened to enter the cottage, their harsh manners and rude gait only enhanced to me the superior accomplishments of my friends. The old man, I could perceive, often endeavoured to encourage his children, as sometimes I found that he called them, to cast off their melancholy. He would talk in a cheerful accent, with an expression of goodness

---

[1] *Felix* means "fortunate"; *Agatha* means "beautiful." U. C. Knoepflmacher marks the asymmetry of *daughter* not being among Agatha's names, an absence that reflects Mary Shelley's feeling of rejection by her father.

that bestowed pleasure even upon me. Agatha listened with respect, her eyes sometimes filled with tears, which she endeavoured to wipe away unperceived; but I generally found that her countenance and tone were more cheerful after having listened to the exhortations of her father. It was not thus with Felix. He was always the saddest of the groupe; and, even to my unpractised senses, he appeared to have suffered more deeply than his friends. But if his countenance was more sorrowful, his voice was more cheerful than that of his sister, especially when he addressed the old man.

"I could mention innumerable instances, which, although slight, marked the dispositions of these amiable cottagers. In the midst of poverty and want, Felix carried with pleasure to his sister the first little white flower that peeped out from beneath the snowy ground. Early in the morning before she had risen, he cleared away the snow that obstructed her path to the milk-house, drew water from the well, and brought the wood from the out-house,[2] where, to his perpetual astonishment, he found his store always replenished by an invisible hand. In the day, I believe, he worked sometimes for a neighbouring farmer, because he often went forth, and did not return until dinner, yet brought no wood with him. At other times he worked in the garden; but, as there was little to do in the frosty season, he read to the old man and Agatha.

"This reading had puzzled me extremely at first; but, by degrees, I discovered that he uttered many of the same sounds when he read as when he talked. I conjectured, therefore, that he found on the paper signs for speech which he understood, and I ardently longed to comprehend these also; but how was that possible, when I did not even understand the sounds for which they stood as signs? I improved, however, sensibly in this science, but not sufficiently to follow up any kind of conversation, although I applied my whole mind to the endeavour: for I easily perceived that, although I eagerly longed to discover myself to the cottagers, I ought not to make the attempt until I had first become master of their language; which knowledge might enable me to make them overlook the deformity of my figure; for with this also the contrast perpetually presented to my eyes had made me acquainted.

"I had admired the perfect forms of my cottagers—their grace, beauty, and delicate complexions: but how was I terrified, when I

[2]Shed.

viewed myself in a transparent pool![3] At first I started back, unable to believe that it was indeed I who was reflected in the mirror; and when I became fully convinced that I was in reality the monster that I am, I was filled with the bitterest sensations of despondence and mortification. Alas! I did not yet entirely know the fatal effects of this miserable deformity.

"As the sun became warmer, and the light of day longer, the snow vanished, and I beheld the bare trees and the black earth. From this time Felix was more employed; and the heart-moving indications of impending famine disappeared. Their food, as I afterwards found, was coarse, but it was wholesome; and they procured a sufficiency of it. Several new kinds of plants sprung up in the garden, which they dressed; and these signs of comfort increased daily as the season advanced.

"The old man, leaning on his son, walked each day at noon, when it did not rain, as I found it was called when the heavens poured forth its waters. This frequently took place; but a high wind quickly dried the earth, and the season became far more pleasant than it had been.

"My mode of life in my hovel was uniform. During the morning I attended the motions of the cottagers; and when they were dispersed in various occupations, I slept: the remainder of the day was spent in observing my friends. When they had retired to rest, if there was any moon, or the night was star-light, I went into the woods, and collected my own food and fuel for the cottage. When I returned, as often as it was necessary, I cleared their path from the snow, and performed those offices that I had seen done by Felix. I afterwards found that these labours, performed by an invisible hand, greatly astonished them; and once or twice I heard them, on these occasions, utter the words *good spirit, wonderful;* but I did not then understand the signification of these terms.

"My thoughts now became more active, and I longed to discover the motives and feelings of these lovely creatures; I was inquisitive to know why Felix appeared so miserable, and Agatha so sad. I thought (foolish wretch!) that it might be in my power to restore happiness to these deserving people. When I slept, or was absent, the forms of the venerable blind father, the gentle Agatha, and the excellent Felix, flitted before me. I looked upon them as superior beings, who would be

[3]Alluding, by contrast, to Narcissus and to Eve's infatuation with her reflection; see *Paradise Lost* 4.449–80.

the arbiters of my future destiny. I formed in my imagination a thousand pictures of presenting myself to them, and their reception of me. I imagined that they would be disgusted, until, by my gentle demeanour and conciliating words, I should first win their favour, and afterwards their love.

"These thoughts exhilarated me, and led me to apply with fresh ardour to the acquiring the art of language. My organs were indeed harsh, but supple; and although my voice was very unlike the soft music of their tones, yet I pronounced such words as I understood with tolerable ease. It was as the ass and the lap-dog; yet surely the gentle ass, whose intentions were affectionate, although his manners were rude, deserved better treatment than blows and execration.[4]

"The pleasant showers and genial warmth of spring greatly altered the aspect of the earth. Men, who before this change seemed to have been hid in caves, dispersed themselves, and were employed in various arts of cultivation. The birds sang in more cheerful notes, and the leaves began to bud forth on the trees. Happy, happy earth! fit habitation for gods,[5] which, so short a time before, was bleak, damp, and unwholesome. My spirits were elevated by the enchanting appearance of nature; the past was blotted from my memory, the present was tranquil, and the future gilded by bright rays of hope, and anticipations of joy.

Chapter V

"I now hasten to the more moving part of my story. I shall relate events that impressed me with feelings which, from what I was, have made me what I am.

"Spring advanced rapidly; the weather became fine, and the skies cloudless. It surprised me, that what before was desert and gloomy should now bloom with the most beautiful flowers and verdure. My senses were gratified and refreshed by a thousand scents of delight, and a thousand sights of beauty.

"It was on one of these days, when my cottagers periodically rested from labour—the old man played on his guitar, and the children lis-

[4]A reference to one of La Fontaine's immensely popular *Fables* (1668–94) (Book IV.5). As in Aesop's, animal fables satirize contemporary mores.

[5]Rewriting *Paradise Lost*: "Hell this fit habitation fraught with fire / Unquenchable, the house of woe and pain" (6.876–77).

tened to him—I observed that the countenance of Felix was melancholy beyond expression: he sighed frequently; and once his father paused in his music, and I conjectured by his manner that he inquired the cause of his son's sorrow. Felix replied in a cheerful accent, and the old man was recommencing his music, when some one tapped at the door.

"It was a lady on horseback, accompanied by a countryman as a guide. The lady was dressed in a dark suit, and covered with a thick black veil. Agatha asked a question; to which the stranger only replied by pronouncing, in a sweet accent, the name of Felix. Her voice was musical, but unlike that of either of my friends. On hearing this word, Felix came up hastily to the lady; who, when she saw him, threw up her veil, and I beheld a countenance of angelic beauty and expression. Her hair of a shining raven black, and curiously braided; her eyes were dark, but gentle, although animated; her features of a regular proportion, and her complexion wondrously fair, each cheek tinged with a lovely pink.

"Felix seemed ravished with delight when he saw her, every trait of sorrow vanished from his face, and it instantly expressed a degree of ecstatic joy, of which I could hardly have believed it capable; his eyes sparkled, as his cheek flushed with pleasure; and at that moment I thought him as beautiful as the stranger. She appeared affected by different feelings; wiping a few tears from her lovely eyes, she held out her hand to Felix, who kissed it rapturously, and called her, as well as I could distinguish, his sweet Arabian. She did not appear to understand him, but smiled. He assisted her to dismount, and, dismissing her guide, conducted her into the cottage. Some conversation took place between him and his father; and the young stranger knelt at the old man's feet, and would have kissed his hand, but he raised her, and embraced her affectionately.

"I soon perceived, that although the stranger uttered articulate sounds, and appeared to have a language of her own, she was neither understood by, or herself understood, the cottagers. They made many signs which I did not comprehend; but I saw that her presence diffused gladness through the cottage, dispelling their sorrow as the sun dissipates the morning mists. Felix seemed peculiarly happy, and with smiles of delight welcomed his Arabian. Agatha, the ever-gentle Agatha, kissed the hands of the lovely stranger; and, pointing to her brother, made signs which appeared to me to mean that he had been sorrowful until she came. Some hours passed thus, while they, by their countenances, expressed joy, the cause of which I did not comprehend. Presently I found, by the frequent recurrence of one sound which the stranger repeated after them, that she was endeavouring to learn their language; and the idea instantly occurred to me, that I should make use of the same instructions to the same end. The stranger learned about twenty words at the first lesson, most of them indeed were those which I had before understood, but I profited by the others.

"As night came on, Agatha and the Arabian retired early. When they separated, Felix kissed the hand of the stranger, and said, 'Good night, sweet Safie.'[1] He sat up much longer, conversing with his father; and, by the frequent repetition of her name, I conjectured that their lovely guest was the subject of their conversation. I ardently desired to understand them, and bent every faculty towards that purpose, but found it utterly impossible.

"The next morning Felix went out to his work; and, after the usual occupations of Agatha were finished, the Arabian sat at the feet of the old man, and, taking his guitar, played some airs so entrancingly beautiful, that they at once drew tears of sorrow and delight from my eyes. She sang, and her voice flowed in a rich cadence, swelling or dying away, like a nightingale of the woods.

"When she had finished, she gave the guitar to Agatha, who at first declined it. She played a simple air, and her voice accompanied it in sweet accents, but unlike the wondrous strain of the stranger. The old man appeared enraptured, and said some words, which Agatha endeavoured to explain to Safie, and by which he appeared to wish to express that she bestowed on him the greatest delight by her music.

"The days now passed as peaceably as before, with the sole alteration, that joy had taken place of sadness in the countenances of my friends. Safie was always gay and happy; she and I improved rapidly in the knowledge of language, so that in two months I began to comprehend most of the words uttered by my protectors.

"In the meanwhile also the black ground was covered with herbage, and the green banks interspersed with innumerable flowers, sweet to the scent and the eyes, stars of pale radiance among the moonlight woods; the sun became warmer, the nights clear and

---

[1]"Safie" derives from the Greek word for "learning" and plays against "Sophie," the simple, obedient wife idealized in Rousseau's *Émile*, a character acidly critiqued by Wollstonecraft in *Rights of Woman*.

balmy; and my nocturnal rambles were an extreme pleasure to me, although they were considerably shortened by the late setting and early rising of the sun; for I never ventured abroad during daylight, fearful of meeting with the same treatment as I had formerly endured in the first village which I entered.

"My days were spent in close attention, that I might more speedily master the language; and I may boast that I improved more rapidly than the Arabian, who understood very little, and conversed in broken accents, whilst I comprehended and could imitate almost every word that was spoken.

"While I improved in speech, I also learned the science of letters, as it was taught to the stranger; and this opened before me a wide field for wonder and delight.

"The book from which Felix instructed Safie was Volney's *Ruins of Empires.* I should not have understood the purport of this book, had not Felix, in reading it, given very minute explanations. He had chosen this work, he said, because the declamatory style was framed in imitation of the eastern authors. Through this work I obtained a cursory knowledge of history, and a view of the several empires at present existing in the world; it gave me an insight into the manners, governments, and religions of the different nations of the earth. I heard of the slothful Asiatics; of the stupendous genius and mental activity of the Grecians; of the wars and wonderful virtue of the early Romans—of their subsequent degeneration—of the decline of that mighty empire; of chivalry, christianity, and kings. I heard of the discovery of the American hemisphere, and wept with Safie over the hapless fate of its original inhabitants.[2]

"These wonderful narrations inspired me with strange feelings. Was man, indeed, at once so powerful, so virtuous, and magnificent, yet so vicious and base? He appeared at one time a mere scion of the evil principle, and at another as all that can be conceived of noble and godlike. To be a great and virtuous man appeared the highest honour that can befall a sensitive being; to be base and vicious, as many on record have been, appeared the lowest degradation, a condition more abject than that of the blind mole or harmless worm. For a long

---

[2]*Les Ruines; ou Méditations sur les révolutions des empires* was published in 1791, in the wake of the French Revolution (Volney was part of the Revolutionary government); the English translation *Ruins, or Meditations on the Revolutions of Empires* appeared a year later. In this influential work, Volney surveys world history up to the Revolution and, in the vein of principled atheism, gives a contemptuous comparison of the world's religions. The views reported in this paragraph are voiced by a Muslim in Book 2.

time I could not conceive how one man could go forth to murder his fellow, or even why there were laws and governments; but when I heard details of vice and bloodshed, my wonder ceased, and I turned away with disgust and loathing.

"Every conversation of the cottagers now opened new wonders to me. While I listened to the instructions which Felix bestowed upon the Arabian, the strange system of human society was explained to me. I heard of the division of property, of immense wealth and squalid poverty; of rank, descent, and noble blood.

"The words induced me to turn towards myself. I learned that the possessions most esteemed by your fellow-creatures were, high and un-sullied descent united with riches. A man might be respected with only one of these acquisitions; but without either he was considered, except in very rare instances, as a vagabond and a slave, doomed to waste his powers for the profit of the chosen few. And what was I? Of my creation and creator I was absolutely ignorant; but I knew that I possessed no money, no friends, no kind of property.[3] I was, besides, endowed with a figure hideously deformed and loathsome; I was not even of the same nature as man. I was more agile than they, and could subsist upon coarser diet; I bore the extremes of heat and cold with less injury to my frame; my stature far exceeded their's. When I looked around, I saw and heard of none like me. Was I then a monster, a blot upon the earth, from which all men fled, and whom all men disowned?

"I cannot describe to you the agony that these reflections inflicted upon me; I tried to dispel them, but sorrow only increased with knowledge.[4] Oh, that I had for ever remained in my native wood, nor known or felt beyond the sensations of hunger, thirst, and heat!

"Of what a strange nature is knowledge! It clings to the mind, when it has once seized on it, like a lichen on the rock. I wished some-times to shake off all thought and feeling; but I learned that there was but one means to overcome the sensation of pain, and that was death—a state which I feared yet did not understand. I admired virtue and good feelings, and loved the gentle manners and amiable qualities of my cottagers; but I was shut out from intercourse[5] with them, except

[3]A social critique voiced by Wollstonecraft in her two *Vindications* and Godwin in *Political Justice*.

[4]Alluding to Adam and Eve's gain of knowledge, including knowledge of their mortal-ity, and echoing the laments of Byron's Manfred (1.1.10); see p. 264.

[5]Social interaction.

through means which I obtained by stealth, when I was unseen and unknown, and which rather increased than satisfied the desire I had of becoming one among my fellows. The gentle words of Agatha, and the animated smiles of the charming Arabian, were not for me. The mild exhortations of the old man, and the lively conversation of the loved Felix, were not for me. Miserable, unhappy wretch!

"Other lessons were impressed upon me even more deeply. I heard of the difference of sexes; of the birth and growth of children; how the father doated on the smiles of the infant, and the lively sallies of the older child; how all the life and cares of the mother were wrapt up in the precious charge; how the mind of youth expanded and gained knowledge; of brother, sister, and all the various relationships which bind one human being to another in mutual bonds.[6]

"But where were my friends and relations? No father had watched my infant days, no mother had blessed me with smiles and caresses; or if they had, all my past life was now a blot, a blind vacancy in which I distinguished nothing.[7] From my earliest remembrance I had been as I then was in height and proportion. I had never yet seen a being resembling me, or who claimed any intercourse with me. What was I? The question again recurred, to be answered only with groans.

"I will soon explain to what these feelings tended; but allow me now to return to the cottagers, whose story excited in me such various feelings of indignation, delight, and wonder, but which all terminated in additional love and reverence for my protectors (for so I loved, in an innocent, half painful self-deceit, to call them).

Chapter VI

"Some time elapsed before I learned the history of my friends. It was one which could not fail to impress itself deeply on my mind, unfolding as it did a number of circumstances each interesting and wonderful to one so utterly inexperienced as I was.

"The name of the old man was De Lacey. He was descended from a good family in France, where he had lived for many years in affluence, respected by his superiors, and beloved by his equals. His son was

[6]Themes in Wollstonecraft's *Rights of Woman* and Jemima's narrative in *The Wrongs of Woman*.
[7]Echoing Wordsworth's "Intimations" Ode (1815), stanzas 5–9; the Creature gives a dark version of the Wordsworthian myth of a childhood fostered by "Nature."

bred in the service of his country; and Agatha had ranked with ladies of the highest distinction. A few months before my arrival, they had lived in a large and luxurious city, called Paris, surrounded by friends, and possessed of every enjoyment which virtue, refinement of intellect, or taste, accompanied by a moderate fortune, could afford.

"The father of Safie had been the cause of their ruin. He was a Turkish merchant, and had inhabited Paris for many years, when, for some reason which I could not learn, he became obnoxious to the government. He was seized and cast into prison the very day that Safie arrived from Constantinople[1] to join him. He was tried, and condemned to death. The injustice of his sentence was very flagrant; all Paris was indignant; and it was judged that his religion and wealth, rather than the crime alleged against him, had been the cause of his condemnation.

"Felix had been present at the trial; his horror and indignation were uncontrollable, when he heard the decision of the court. He made, at that moment, a solemn vow to deliver him, and then looked around for the means. After many fruitless attempts to gain admittance to the prison, he found a strongly grated window in an unguarded part of the building, which lighted the dungeon of the unfortunate Mahometan; who, loaded with chains, waited in despair the execution of the barbarous sentence. Felix visited the grate at night, and made known to the prisoner his intentions in his favour. The Turk,[2] amazed and delighted, endeavoured to kindle the zeal of his deliverer by promises of reward and wealth. Felix rejected his offers with contempt; yet when he saw the lovely Safie, who was allowed to visit her father, and who, by her gestures, expressed her lively gratitude, the youth could not help owning to his own mind, that the captive possessed a treasure which would fully reward his toil and hazard.

"The Turk quickly perceived the impression that his daughter had made on the heart of Felix, and endeavoured to secure him more entirely in his interests by the promise of her hand in marriage, so soon as he should be conveyed to a place of safety. Felix was too delicate to

[1]In the 18th c., the capital of the Ottoman Empire; formerly called "Byzantium," it is now known as "Istanbul."

[2]In shifting the ethnic term from exotic "Arabian," Shelley draws on "Turk" as a byword for a cruel, ruthless barbarian. The government that persecutes him is the new French Republic during the Reign of Terror. A Mahometan is a follower of the prophet Muhammad; a Muslim.

accept this offer; yet he looked forward to the probability of that event as to the consummation of his happiness.

"During the ensuing days, while the preparations were going forward for the escape of the merchant, the zeal of Felix was warmed by several letters that he received from this lovely girl, who found means to express her thoughts in the language of her lover by the aid of an old man, a servant of her father's, who understood French. She thanked him in the most ardent terms for his intended services towards her father; and at the same time she gently deplored her own fate.

"I have copies of these letters; for I found means, during my residence in the hovel, to procure the implements of writing; and the letters were often in the hands of Felix or Agatha. Before I depart, I will give them to you, they will prove the truth of my tale; but at present, as the sun is already far declined, I shall only have time to repeat the substance of them to you.

"Safie related, that her mother was a Christian Arab, seized and made a slave by the Turks; recommended by her beauty, she had won the heart of the father of Safie, who married her. The young girl spoke in high and enthusiastic terms of her mother, who, born in freedom spurned the bondage to which she was now reduced. She instructed her daughter in the tenets of her religion, and taught her to aspire to higher powers of intellect, and an independence of spirit, forbidden to the female followers of Mahomet.[3] This lady died; but her lessons were indelibly impressed on the mind of Safie, who sickened at the prospect of again returning to Asia, and the being immured within the walls of a harem, allowed only to occupy herself with puerile amusements, ill suited to the temper of her soul, now accustomed to grand ideas and a noble emulation for virtue. The prospect of marrying a Christian, and remaining in a country where women were allowed to take a rank in society, was enchanting to her.

"The day for the execution of the Turk was fixed; but, on the night previous to it, he had quitted prison, and before morning was distant many leagues from Paris. Felix had procured passports in the name of his father, sister, and himself. He had previously communicated his plan to the former, who aided the deceit by quitting his house, under the pretence of a journey, and concealed himself, with his daughter, in an obscure part of Paris.

[3]A view of Islam stated in Wollstonecraft's *Rights of Woman*.

"Felix conducted the fugitives through France to Lyons, and across Mont Cenis to Leghorn,[4] where the merchant had decided to wait a favourable opportunity of passing into some part of the Turkish dominions.

"Safie resolved to remain with her father until the moment of his departure, before which time the Turk renewed his promise that she should be united to his deliverer; and Felix remained with them in expectation of that event; and in the mean time he enjoyed the society of the Arabian, who exhibited towards him the simplest and tenderest affection. They conversed with one another through the means of an interpreter, and sometimes with the interpretation of looks; and Safie sang to him the divine airs of her native country.

"The Turk allowed this intimacy to take place, and encouraged the hopes of the youthful lovers, while in his heart he had formed far other plans. He loathed the idea that his daughter should be united to a Christian; but he feared the resentment of Felix if he should appear lukewarm; for he knew that he was still in the power of his deliverer, if he should choose to betray him to the Italian state which they inhabited. He revolved a thousand plans by which he should be enabled to prolong the deceit until it might be no longer necessary, and secretly to take his daughter with him when he departed. His plans were greatly facilitated by the news which arrived from Paris.

"The government of France were greatly enraged at the escape of their victim, and spared no pains to detect and punish his deliverer. The plot of Felix was quickly discovered, and De Lacey and Agatha were thrown into prison. The news reached Felix, and roused him from his dream of pleasure. His blind and aged father, and his gentle sister, lay in a noisome dungeon, while he enjoyed the free air, and the society of her whom he loved. This idea was torture to him. He quickly arranged with the Turk, that if the latter should find a favourable opportunity for escape before Felix could return to Italy, Safie should remain as a boarder at a convent at Leghorn; and then, quitting the lovely Arabian, he hastened to Paris, and delivered himself up to the vengeance of the law, hoping to free De Lacey and Agatha by this proceeding.

"He did not succeed. They remained confined for five months before the trial took place; the result of which deprived them of their fortune, and condemned them to a perpetual exile from their native country.

[4]Mount Cenis is in southern France. Leghorn is a major port in the Tuscan region of Italy.

"They found a miserable asylum in the cottage in Germany, where I discovered them. Felix soon learned that the treacherous Turk, for whom he and his family endured such unheard-of oppression, on discovering that his deliverer was thus reduced to poverty and impotence, became a traitor to good feeling and honour, and had quitted Italy with his daughter, insultingly sending Felix a pittance of money to aid him, as he said, in some plan of future maintenance.

"Such were the events that preyed on the heart of Felix, and rendered him, when I first saw him, the most miserable of his family. He could have endured poverty, and when this distress had been the meed of his virtue, he would have gloried in it: but the ingratitude of the Turk, and the loss of his beloved Safie, were misfortunes more bitter and irreparable. The arrival of the Arabian now infused new life into his soul.

"When the news reached Leghorn, that Felix was deprived of his wealth and rank, the merchant commanded his daughter to think no more of her lover, but to prepare to return with him to her native country. The generous nature of Safie was outraged by this command; she attempted to expostulate with her father, but he left her angrily, reiterating his tyrannical mandate.

"A few days after, the Turk entered his daughter's apartment, and told her hastily, that he had reason to believe that his residence at Leghorn had been divulged, and that he should speedily be delivered up to the French government; he had, consequently, hired a vessel to convey him to Constantinople, for which city he should sail in a few hours. He intended to leave his daughter under the care of a confidential servant, to follow at her leisure with the greater part of his property, which had not yet arrived at Leghorn.

"When alone, Safie resolved in her own mind the plan of conduct that it would become her to pursue in this emergency. A residence in Turkey was abhorrent to her; her religion and feelings were alike adverse to it. By some papers of her father's, which fell into her hands, she heard of the exile of her lover, and learnt the name of the spot where he then resided. She hesitated some time, but at length she formed her determination. Taking with her some jewels that belonged to her, and a small sum of money, she quitted Italy, with an attendant, a native of Leghorn, but who understood the common language of Turkey, and departed for Germany.

"She arrived in safety at a town about twenty leagues from the cottage of De Lacey, when her attendant fell dangerously ill. Safie nursed her with the most devoted affection; but the poor girl died, and the Arabian was left alone, unacquainted with the language of the country, and utterly ignorant of the customs of the world. She fell, however, into good hands. The Italian had mentioned the name of the spot for which they were bound; and, after her death, the woman of the house in which they had lived took care that Safie should arrive in safety at the cottage of her lover.

Chapter VII

"Such was the history of my beloved cottagers. It impressed me deeply. I learned, from the views of social life which it developed, to admire their virtues, and to deprecate the vices of mankind.

"As yet I looked upon crime as a distant evil; benevolence and generosity were ever present before me, inciting within me a desire to become an actor in the busy scene where so many admirable qualities were called forth and displayed. But, in giving an account of the progress of my intellect, I must not omit a circumstance which occurred in the beginning of the month of August of the same year.

"One night, during my accustomed visit to the neighbouring wood, where I collected my own food, and brought home firing for my protectors, I found on the ground a leathern portmanteau, containing several articles of dress and some books. I eagerly seized the prize, and returned with it to my hovel. Fortunately the books were written in the language the elements of which I had acquired at the cottage;[1] they consisted of *Paradise Lost,* a volume of *Plutarch's Lives,* and the *Sorrows of Werter.* The possession of these treasures gave me extreme delight; I now continually studied and exercised my mind upon these histories, whilst my friends were employed in their ordinary occupations.

"I can hardly describe to you the effect of these books. They produced in me an infinity of new images and feelings, that sometimes raised me to ecstasy, but more frequently sunk me into the lowest dejection. In the *Sorrows of Werter,* besides the interest of its simple and affecting story, so many opinions are canvassed, and so many

[1]French. In *Lives,* Greek biographer Plutarch (c. 46–120) analyzed notable Greeks and Romans in terms of character strengths and weaknesses. One of the most sensationally popular novels of Shelley's day was Goethe's *The Sorrows of Werter* (1774; rev. 1787), a semi-autobiographical account of the hero's passion for Charlotte, betrothed to another. In despair, Werter blows his brains out, a suicide reputed to have sparked a vogue among the romantically alienated youth of Europe; Shelley described her mother as "a female Werter," referring to her suicidal despair over her jilting by her lover, Gilbert Imlay.

lights thrown upon what had hitherto been to me obscure subjects, that I found in it a never-ending source of speculation and astonishment. The gentle and domestic manners it described, combined with lofty sentiments and feelings, which had for their object something out of self, accorded well with my experience among my protectors, and with the wants which were for ever alive in my own bosom. But I thought Werter himself a more divine being than I had ever beheld or imagined; his character contained no pretension, but it sunk deep. The disquisitions upon death and suicide were calculated to fill me with wonder. I did not pretend to enter into the merits of the case, yet I inclined towards the opinions of the hero, whose extinction I wept, without precisely understanding it.

"As I read, however, I applied much personally to my own feelings and condition. I found myself similar, yet at the same time strangely unlike the beings concerning whom I read, and to whose conversation I was a listener. I sympathized with, and partly understood them, but I was unformed in mind; I was dependent on none, and related to none. 'The path of my departure was free';[2] and there was none to lament my annihilation. My person was hideous, and my stature gigantic: what did this mean? Who was I? What was I? Whence did I come? What was my destination? These questions continually recurred, but I was unable to solve them.

"The volume of *Plutarch's Lives* which I possessed, contained the histories of the first founders of the ancient republics. This book had a far different effect upon me from the *Sorrows of Werter*. I learned from Werter's imaginations despondency and gloom: but Plutarch taught me high thoughts; he elevated me above the wretched sphere of my own reflections, to admire and love the heroes of past ages. Many things I read surpassed my understanding and experience. I had a very confused knowledge of kingdoms, wide extents of country, mighty rivers, and boundless seas. But I was perfectly unacquainted with towns, and large assemblages of men. The cottage of my protectors had been the only school in which I had studied human nature; but this book developed new and mightier scenes of action. I read of men concerned in public affairs governing or massacring their species. I felt the greatest ardour for virtue rise within me, and abhorrence for vice, as far as I understood the signification of those terms, relative as they

[2]Like Victor, the Creature apparently has had prophetic access to P. Shelley's "Mutability," slightly misquoting line 14 (see II.II, p. 71).

were, as I applied them, to pleasure and pain alone. Induced by these feelings, I was of course led to admire peaceable law-givers, Numa, Solon, and Lycurgus, in preference to Romulus and Theseus.[3] The patriarchal lives[4] of my protectors caused these impressions to take a firm hold on my mind; perhaps, if my first introduction to humanity had been made by a young soldier, burning for glory and slaughter, I should have been imbued with different sensations.

"But *Paradise Lost* excited different and far deeper emotions. I read it, as I had read the other volumes which had fallen into my hands, as a true history. It moved every feeling of wonder and awe, that the picture of an omnipotent God warring with his creatures was capable of exciting. I often referred the several situations, as their similarity struck me, to my own. Like Adam, I was created apparently[5] united by no link to any other being in existence; but his state was far different from mine in every other respect. He had come forth from the hands of God a perfect creature, happy and prosperous, guarded by the especial care of his Creator; he was allowed to converse with, and acquire knowledge from beings of a superior nature:[6] but I was wretched, helpless, and alone. Many times I considered Satan as the fitter emblem of my condition; for often, like him, when I viewed the bliss of my protectors, the bitter gall of envy rose within me.[7]

"Another circumstance strengthened and confirmed these feelings. Soon after my arrival in the hovel, I discovered some papers in the pocket of the dress[8] which I had taken from your laboratory. At first I

[3]Theseus was a semidivine legendary king of Athens, famous for slaying the Minotaur. Romulus was the semidivine cofounder of Rome, succeeded by Numa Pompilius, legendary king famed for wisdom, piety, and a long, peaceful reign. Lycurgus (c. 7th c. B.C.E.) is the famed law-giver of Sparta, who brought peace to the Greek city-state. Another Lycurgus is the 4th-c. B.C.E. Athenian orator, statesman, and prosecutor of official corruption. Athenian statesman and poet Solon (c. 639–559 B.C.E.) was famed for reforms ending serfdom and introducing more humane civil law. Romulus and Theseus were infamously violent, and cruel to women: Romulus murdered his twin brother Remus and led the mass rape of the Sabine women; Theseus was a serial rapist, and faithless spouse of Ariadne, whom he abandoned. For a long time, neither ruler, moreover, was certain of his paternity.

[4]Literally, governed by fathers, and as a conventional ideal, government by a wise, venerable, benign man.

[5]The 1831 text deletes "created apparently."

[6]In Book 8 (250–559), Adam recounts several conversations with his Creator, and he is tutored in Eden by the "affable" Archangel Raphael.

[7]See *Paradise Lost* 4.358–69.

[8]Lab coat.

had neglected them; but now that I was able to decypher the characters in which they were written, I began to study them with diligence. It was your journal of the four months that preceded my creation. You minutely described in these papers every step you took in the progress of your work; this history was mingled with accounts of domestic occurrences. You, doubtless, recollect these papers. Here they are. Every thing is related in them which bears reference to my accursed origin; the whole detail of that series of disgusting circumstances which produced it is set in view; the minutest description of my odious and loathsome person is given, in language which painted your own horrors, and rendered mine ineffaceable. I sickened as I read. 'Hateful day when I received life!' I exclaimed in agony. 'Cursed creator! Why did you form a monster so hideous that even you turned from me in disgust? God in pity made man beautiful and alluring, after his own image;[9] but my form is a filthy type of your's, more horrid from its very resemblance. Satan had his companions, fellow-devils, to admire and encourage him; but I am solitary and detested.'

"These were the reflections of my hours of despondency and solitude; but when I contemplated the virtues of the cottagers, their amiable and benevolent dispositions, I persuaded myself that when they should become acquainted with my admiration of their virtues, they would compassionate me, and overlook my personal deformity. Could they turn from their door one, however monstrous, who solicited their compassion and friendship? I resolved, at least, not to despair, but in every way to fit myself for an interview with them which would decide my fate. I postponed this attempt for some months longer; for the importance attached to its success inspired me with a dread lest I should fail. Besides, I found that my understanding improved so much with every day's experience, that I was unwilling to commence this undertaking until a few more months should have added to my wisdom.

"Several changes, in the mean time, took place in the cottage. The presence of Safie diffused happiness among its inhabitants; and I also found that a greater degree of plenty reigned there. Felix and Agatha spent more time in amusement and conversation, and were assisted in their labours by servants. They did not appear rich, but they were contented and happy; their feelings were serene and peaceful, while mine became every day more tumultuous. Increase of knowledge only discovered to me more clearly what a wretched outcast I was.

[9]Referring to Genesis, "God created man in his own image" (1.27).

I cherished hope, it is true; but it vanished, when I beheld my person reflected in water, or my shadow in the moon-shine, even as that frail image and that inconstant shade.

"I endeavoured to crush these fears, and to fortify myself for the trial which in a few months I resolved to undergo; and sometimes I allowed my thoughts, unchecked by reason, to ramble in the fields of Paradise, and dared to fancy amiable and lovely creatures sympathizing with my feelings and cheering my gloom; their angelic countenances breathed smiles of consolation. But it was all a dream: no Eve soothed my sorrows, or shared my thoughts; I was alone. I remembered Adam's supplication to his Creator; but where was mine? he had abandoned me, and, in the bitterness of my heart, I cursed him.[10]

"Autumn passed thus. I saw, with surprise and grief, the leaves decay and fall, and nature again assume the barren and bleak appearance it had worn when I first beheld the woods and the lovely moon. Yet I did not heed the bleakness of the weather; I was better fitted by my conformation for the endurance of cold than heat. But my chief delights were the sight of the flowers, the birds, and all the gay apparel of summer; when those deserted me, I turned with more attention towards the cottagers. Their happiness was not decreased by the absence of summer. They loved, and sympathized with one another; and their joys, depending on each other, were not interrupted by the casualties that took place around them. The more I saw of them, the greater became my desire to claim their protection and kindness; my heart yearned to be known and loved by these amiable creatures: to see their sweet looks turned towards me with affection, was the utmost limit of my ambition. I dared not think that they would turn them from me with disdain and horror. The poor that stopped at their door were never driven away. I asked, it is true, for greater treasures than a little food or rest; I required kindness and sympathy; but I did not believe myself utterly unworthy of it.

"The winter advanced, and an entire revolution of the seasons had taken place since I awoke into life. My attention, at this time, was solely directed towards my plan of introducing myself into the

---

[10]The Creature refers to Adam's dream of the creation of Eve and his joyous awakening (*Paradise Lost* 8.470–99), as well as to his prior expostulation with God about his desire for a companion (8.379–451, part of which Wollstonecraft quotes in *Rights of Woman*), an argument that wins God's sympathy. The closing phrases allude to Satan's boast to God that he can get faithful Job "to curse thee to thy face" (1.9), and to Job's wife urging him, in the wake of his first afflictions, to "curse God, and die" (2.11), an exhortation that Job refuses even though he rues the day he was born.

cottage of my protectors. I revolved many projects; but that on which I finally fixed was, to enter the dwelling when the blind old man should be alone. I had sagacity enough to discover, that the unnatural hideousness of my person was the chief object of horror with those who had formerly beheld me. My voice, although harsh, had nothing terrible in it; I thought, therefore, that if, in the absence of his children, I could gain the good-will and mediation of the old De Lacey, I might, by his means, be tolerated by my younger protectors.

"One day, when the sun shone on the red leaves that strewed the ground, and diffused cheerfulness, although it denied warmth, Safie, Agatha, and Felix, departed on a long country walk, and the old man, at his own desire, was left alone in the cottage. When his children had departed, he took up his guitar, and played several mournful, but sweet airs, more sweet and mournful than I had ever heard him play before. At first his countenance was illuminated with pleasure, but, as he continued, thoughtfulness and sadness succeeded; at length, laying aside the instrument, he sat absorbed in reflection.

"My heart beat quick; this was the hour and moment of trial, which would decide my hopes, or realize my fears. The servants were gone to a neighbouring fair. All was silent in and around the cottage: it was an excellent opportunity; yet, when I proceeded to execute my plan, my limbs failed me, and I sunk to the ground. Again I rose; and, exerting all the firmness of which I was master, removed the planks which I had placed before my hovel to conceal my retreat. The fresh air revived me, and, with renewed determination, I approached the door of their cottage.

"I knocked. 'Who is there?' said the old man—'Come in.'

"I entered; 'Pardon this intrusion,' said I, 'I am a traveller in want of a little rest; you would greatly oblige me, if you would allow me to remain a few minutes before the fire.'

"'Enter,' said De Lacey; 'and I will try in what manner I can relieve your wants; but, unfortunately, my children are from home, and, as I am blind, I am afraid I shall find it difficult to procure food for you.'

"'Do not trouble yourself, my kind host, I have food; it is warmth and rest only that I need.'

"I sat down, and a silence ensued. I knew that every minute was precious to me, yet I remained irresolute in what manner to commence the interview; when the old man addressed me—

"'By your language, stranger, I suppose you are my countryman;— are you French?'

"'No; but I was educated by a French family, and understand that language only. I am now going to claim the protection of some friends, whom I sincerely love, and of whose favour I have some hopes.'

"'Are these Germans?'

"'No, they are French. But let us change the subject. I am an unfortunate and deserted creature; I look around, and I have no relation or friend upon earth. These amiable people to whom I go have never seen me, and know little of me. I am full of fears; for if I fail there, I am an outcast in the world for ever.'

"'Do not despair. To be friendless is indeed to be unfortunate; but the hearts of men, when unprejudiced by any obvious self-interest, are full of brotherly love and charity. Rely, therefore, on your hopes; and if these friends are good and amiable, do not despair.'

"'They are kind—they are the most excellent creatures in the world; but, unfortunately, they are prejudiced against me. I have good dispositions; my life has been hitherto harmless, and, in some degree, beneficial; but a fatal prejudice clouds their eyes, and where they ought to see a feeling and kind friend, they behold only a detestable monster.'

"'That is indeed unfortunate; but if you are really blameless, cannot you undeceive them?'

"'I am about to undertake that task; and it is on that account that I feel so many overwhelming terrors. I tenderly love these friends; I have, unknown to them, been for many months in the habits of daily kindness towards them; but they believe that I wish to injure them, and it is that prejudice which I wish to overcome.'

"'Where do these friends reside?'

"'Near this spot.'

"The old man paused, and then continued, 'If you will unreservedly confide to me the particulars of your tale, I perhaps may be of use in undeceiving them. I am blind, and cannot judge of your countenance, but there is something in your words which persuades me that you are sincere. I am poor, and an exile; but it will afford me true pleasure to be in any way serviceable to a human creature.'

"'Excellent man! I thank you, and accept your generous offer. You raise me from the dust by this kindness; and I trust that, by your aid, I shall not be driven from the society and sympathy of your fellow-creatures.'

"'Heaven forbid! even if you were really criminal; for that can only drive you to desperation, and not instigate you to virtue. I also am unfortunate; I and my family have been condemned, although innocent: judge, therefore, if I do not feel for your misfortunes.'

"'How can I thank you, my best and only benefactor? from your lips first have I heard the voice of kindness directed towards me; I shall be for ever grateful; and your present humanity assures me of success with those friends whom I am on the point of meeting.'

"'May I know the names and residence of those friends?'

"I paused. This, I thought, was the moment of decision, which was to rob me of, or bestow happiness on me for ever. I struggled vainly for firmness sufficient to answer him, but the effort destroyed all my remaining strength; I sank on the chair, and sobbed aloud. At that moment I heard the steps of my younger protectors. I had not a moment to lose; but, seizing the hand of the old man, I cried, 'Now is the time!—save and protect me! You and your family are the friends whom I seek. Do not you desert me in the hour of trial!'

"'Great God!' exclaimed the old man, 'who are you?'

"At that instant the cottage door was opened, and Felix, Safie, and Agatha entered. Who can describe their horror and consternation on beholding me? Agatha fainted; and Safie, unable to attend to her friend, rushed out of the cottage. Felix darted forward, and with supernatural force tore me from his father, to whose knees I clung: in a transport of fury, he dashed me to the ground, and struck me violently with a stick. I could have torn him limb from limb, as the lion rends the antelope. But my heart sunk within me as with bitter sickness, and I refrained. I saw him on the point of repeating his blow, when, overcome by pain and anguish, I quitted the cottage, and in the general tumult escaped unperceived to my hovel.

Chapter VIII

"Cursed, cursed creator! Why did I live?[1] Why, in that instant, did I not extinguish the spark of existence which you had so wantonly bestowed? I know not; despair had not yet taken possession of me; my feelings were those of rage and revenge. I could with pleasure have destroyed the cottage and its inhabitants, and have glutted myself with their shrieks and misery.

[1]"Let the day perish I was born" (Job 3.3).

"When night came, I quitted my retreat, and wandered in the wood; and now, no longer restrained by the fear of discovery, I gave vent to my anguish in fearful howlings. I was like a wild beast that had broken the toils; destroying the objects that obstructed me, and ranging through the wood with a stag-like swiftness. Oh! what a miserable night I passed! the cold stars shone in mockery, and the bare trees waved their branches above me: now and then the sweet voice of a bird burst forth amidst the universal stillness. All, save I, were at rest or in enjoyment: I, like the arch fiend, bore a hell within me;[2] and, finding myself unsympathized with, wished to tear up the trees, spread havoc and destruction around me, and then to have sat down and enjoyed the ruin.

"But this was a luxury of sensation that could not endure; I became fatigued with excess of bodily exertion, and sank on the damp grass in the sick impotence of despair. There was none among the myriads of men that existed who would pity or assist me; and should I feel kindness towards my enemies? No: from that moment I declared everlasting war against the species,[3] and, more than all, against him who had formed me, and sent me forth to this insupportable misery.

"The sun rose; I heard the voices of men, and knew that it was impossible to return to my retreat during that day. Accordingly I hid myself in some thick underwood, determining to devote the ensuing hours to reflection on my situation.

"The pleasant sunshine, and the pure air of day, restored me to some degree of tranquillity; and when I considered what had passed at the cottage, I could not help believing that I had been too hasty in my conclusions. I had certainly acted imprudently. It was apparent that my conversation had interested the father in my behalf, and I was a fool in having exposed my person to the horror of his children. I ought to have familiarized the old De Lacey to me, and by degrees have discovered myself to the rest of his family, when they should have been prepared for my approach. But I did not believe my errors to be irretrievable; and, after much consideration, I resolved to return to the cottage, seek the old man, and by my representations win him to my party.

[2]Satan's fate in *Paradise Lost* (4.20).

[3]Echoing Satan's enmity to man as well as his despair: "Nor hope to be myself less miserable / By what I seek, but others to make such / As I . . . For only in destroying I find ease / To my relentless thoughts" (*Paradise Lost* 9.126–30).

"These thoughts calmed me, and in the afternoon I sank into a profound sleep; but the fever of my blood did not allow me to be visited by peaceful dreams. The horrible scene of the preceding day was for ever acting before my eyes; the females were flying, and the enraged Felix tearing me from his father's feet. I awoke exhausted; and, finding that it was already night, I crept forth from my hiding-place, and went in search of food.

"When my hunger was appeased, I directed my steps towards the well-known path that conducted to the cottage. All there was at peace. I crept into my hovel, and remained in silent expectation of the accustomed hour when the family arose. That hour past, the sun mounted high in the heavens, but the cottagers did not appear. I trembled violently, apprehending some dreadful misfortune. The inside of the cottage was dark, and I heard no motion; I cannot describe the agony of this suspence.

"Presently two countrymen passed by; but, pausing near the cottage, they entered into conversation, using violent gesticulations; but I did not understand what they said, as they spoke the language of the country, which differed from that of my protectors. Soon after, however, Felix approached with another man: I was surprised, as I knew that he had not quitted the cottage that morning, and waited anxiously to discover, from his discourse, the meaning of these unusual appearances.

"'Do you consider,' said his companion to him, 'that you will be obliged to pay three months' rent, and to lose the produce of your garden? I do not wish to take any unfair advantage, and I beg therefore that you will take some days to consider of your determination.'

"'It is utterly useless,' replied Felix, 'we can never again inhabit your cottage. The life of my father is in the greatest danger, owing to the dreadful circumstance that I have related. My wife and my sister will never recover their horror. I entreat you not to reason with me any more. Take possession of your tenement, and let me fly from this place.'

"Felix trembled violently as he said this. He and his companion entered the cottage, in which they remained for a few minutes, and then departed. I never saw any of the family of De Lacey more.

"I continued for the remainder of the day in my hovel in a state of utter and stupid despair. My protectors had departed, and had broken the only link that held me to the world. For the first time the feelings of revenge and hatred filled my bosom, and I did not strive to controul them; but, allowing myself to be borne away by the stream,

I bent my mind towards injury and death. When I thought of my friends, of the mild voice of De Lacey, the gentle eyes of Agatha, and the exquisite beauty of the Arabian, these thoughts vanished, and a gush of tears somewhat soothed me. But again, when I reflected that they had spurned and deserted me, anger returned, a rage of anger; and, unable to injure any thing human, I turned my fury towards inanimate objects. As night advanced, I placed a variety of combustibles around the cottage; and, after having destroyed every vestige of cultivation in the garden, I waited with forced impatience until the moon had sunk to commence my operations.

"As the night advanced, a fierce wind arose from the woods, and quickly dispersed the clouds that had loitered in the heavens: the blast tore along like a mighty avelanche, and produced a kind of insanity in my spirits, that burst all bounds of reason and reflection. I lighted the dry branch of a tree, and danced with fury around the devoted cottage, my eyes still fixed on the western horizon, the edge of which the moon nearly touched. A part of its orb was at length hid, and I waved my brand; it sunk, and, with a loud scream, I fired the straw, and heath, and bushes, which I had collected. The wind fanned the fire, and the cottage was quickly enveloped by the flames, which clung to it, and licked it with their forked and destroying tongues.[4]

"As soon as I was convinced that no assistance could save any part of the habitation, I quitted the scene, and sought for refuge in the woods.

"And now, with the world before me, whither should I bend my steps?[5] I resolved to fly far from the scene of my misfortunes; but to me, hated and despised, every country must be equally horrible. At length the thought of you crossed my mind. I learned from your papers that you were my father, my creator; and to whom could I apply with more fitness than to him who had given me life? Among the lessons that Felix had bestowed upon Safie geography had not been omitted: I had learned from these the relative situations of the different countries of the earth. You had mentioned Geneva as the name of your native town; and towards this place I resolved to proceed.

"But how was I to direct myself? I knew that I must travel in a south-westerly direction to reach my destination; but the sun was my

[4]Evoking the destruction of Eden at the end of *Paradise Lost* (12.632–44), its virtual transformation into hellfire.

[5]An allusion to the end of *Paradise Lost* (12.646–49); cf. Victor's allusion to the same line in Walton's Letter IV, 13 August (p. 16).

only guide. I did not know the names of the towns that I was to pass through, nor could I ask information from a single human being; but I did not despair. From you only could I hope for succour, although towards you I felt no sentiment but that of hatred. Unfeeling, heartless creator! you had endowed me with perceptions and passions, and then cast me abroad an object for the scorn and horror of mankind. But on you only had I any claim for pity and redress, and from you I determined to seek that justice which I vainly attempted to gain from any other being that wore the human form.

"My travels were long, and the sufferings I endured intense. It was late in autumn when I quitted the district where I had so long resided. I travelled only at night, fearful of encountering the visage of a human being. Nature decayed around me, and the sun became heatless; rain and snow poured around me; mighty rivers were frozen; the surface of the earth was hard, and chill, and bare, and I found no shelter. Oh, earth! how often did I imprecate curses on the cause of my being! The mildness of my nature had fled, and all within me was turned to gall and bitterness. The nearer I approached to your habitation, the more deeply did I feel the spirit of revenge enkindled in my heart. Snow fell, and the waters were hardened, but I rested not. A few incidents now and then directed me, and I possessed a map of the country; but I often wandered wide from my path. The agony of my feelings allowed me no respite: no incident occurred from which my rage and misery could not extract its food; but a circumstance that happened when I arrived on the confines of Switzerland, when the sun had recovered its warmth, and the earth again began to look green, confirmed in an especial manner the bitterness and horror of my feelings.

"I generally rested during the day, and travelled only when I was secured by night from the view of man. One morning, however, finding that my path lay through a deep wood, I ventured to continue my journey after the sun had risen; the day, which was one of the first of spring, cheered even me by the loveliness of its sunshine and the balminess of the air. I felt emotions of gentleness and pleasure, that had long appeared dead, revive within me. Half surprised by the novelty of these sensations, I allowed myself to be borne away by them; and, forgetting my solitude and deformity, dared to be happy. Soft tears again bedewed my cheeks, and I even raised my humid eyes with thankfulness towards the blessed sun which bestowed such joy upon me.

"I continued to wind among the paths of the wood, until I came to its boundary, which was skirted by a deep and rapid river, into which many of the trees bent their branches, now budding with the fresh spring. Here I paused, not exactly knowing what path to pursue, when I heard the sound of voices, that induced me to conceal myself under the shade of a cypress. I was scarcely hid, when a young girl came running towards the spot where I was concealed, laughing as if she ran from some one in sport. She continued her course along the precipitous sides of the river, when suddenly her foot slipt, and she fell into the rapid stream. I rushed from my hiding place, and with extreme labour from the force of the current, saved her, and dragged her to shore. She was senseless; and I endeavoured, by every means in my power, to restore animation, when I was suddenly interrupted by the approach of a rustic, who was probably the person from whom she had playfully fled. On seeing me, he darted towards me, and, tearing the girl from my arms, hastened towards the deeper parts of the wood. I followed speedily, I hardly knew why; but when the man saw me draw near, he aimed a gun, which he carried, at my body, and fired. I sunk to the ground, and my injurer, with increased swiftness, escaped into the wood.

"This was then the reward of my benevolence! I had saved a human being from destruction, and, as a recompence, I now writhed under the miserable pain of a wound, which shattered the flesh and bone. The feelings of kindness and gentleness, which I had entertained but a few moments before, gave place to hellish rage and gnashing of teeth. Inflamed by pain, I vowed eternal hatred and vengeance to all mankind. But the agony of my wound overcame me; my pulses paused, and I fainted.

"For some weeks I led a miserable life in the woods, endeavouring to cure the wound which I had received. The ball had entered my shoulder, and I knew not whether it had remained there or passed through; at any rate I had no means of extracting it. My sufferings were augmented also by the oppressive sense of the injustice and ingratitude of their infliction. My daily vows rose for revenge—a deep and deadly revenge, such as would alone compensate for the outrages and anguish I had endured.

"After some weeks my wound healed, and I continued my journey. The labours I endured were no longer to be alleviated by the bright sun or gentle breezes of spring; all joy was but a mockery, which insulted my desolate state, and made me feel more painfully that I was not made for the enjoyment of pleasure.

"But my toils now drew near a close; and, two months from this time, I reached the environs of Geneva.

"It was evening when I arrived, and I retired to a hiding-place among the fields that surround it, to meditate in what manner I should apply to you. I was oppressed by fatigue and hunger, and far too unhappy to enjoy the gentle breezes of evening, or the prospect of the sun setting behind the stupendous mountains of Jura.

"At this time a slight sleep relieved me from the pain of reflection, which was disturbed by the approach of a beautiful child, who came running into the recess I had chosen with all the sportiveness of infancy. Suddenly, as I gazed on him, an idea seized me, that this little creature was unprejudiced, and had lived too short a time to have imbibed a horror of deformity. If, therefore, I could seize him, and educate him as my companion and friend, I should not be so desolate in this peopled earth.

"Urged by this impulse, I seized on the boy as he passed, and drew him towards me. As soon as he beheld my form, he placed his hands before his eyes, and uttered a shrill scream: I drew his hand forcibly from his face, and said, 'Child, what is the meaning of this? I do not intend to hurt you; listen to me.'

"He struggled violently; 'Let me go,' he cried; 'monster! ugly wretch! you wish to eat me, and tear me to pieces—You are an ogre—Let me go, or I will tell my papa.'

"'Boy, you will never see your father again; you must come with me.'

"'Hideous monster! let me go; My papa is a Syndic—he is M. Frankenstein—he would punish you. You dare not keep me.'

"'Frankenstein! you belong then to my enemy—to him towards whom I have sworn eternal revenge; you shall be my first victim.'

"The child still struggled, and loaded me with epithets which carried despair to my heart: I grasped his throat to silence him, and in a moment he lay dead at my feet.

"I gazed on my victim, and my heart swelled with exultation and hellish triumph: clapping my hands, I exclaimed, 'I, too, can create desolation; my enemy is not impregnable; this death will carry despair to him, and a thousand other miseries shall torment and destroy him.'

"As I fixed my eyes on the child, I saw something glittering on his breast. I took it; it was a portrait of a most lovely woman. In spite of my malignity, it softened and attracted me. For a few moments I gazed with delight on her dark eyes, fringed by deep lashes, and her lovely lips; but presently my rage returned: I remembered that I was for ever deprived of the delights that such beautiful creatures could bestow; and that she whose resemblance I contemplated would, in regarding me, have changed that air of divine benignity to one expressive of disgust and affright.

"Can you wonder that such thoughts transported me with rage? I only wonder that at that moment, instead of venting my sensations in exclamations and agony, I did not rush among mankind, and perish in the attempt to destroy them.

"While I was overcome by these feelings, I left the spot where I had committed the murder, and was seeking a more secluded hiding-place, when I perceived a woman passing near me. She was young, not indeed so beautiful as her whose portrait I held, but of an agreeable aspect, and blooming in the loveliness of youth and health. Here, I thought, is one of those whose smiles are bestowed on all but me; she shall not escape:[6] thanks to the lessons of Felix, and the sanguinary laws of man, I have learned how to work mischief. I approached her unperceived, and placed the portrait securely in one of the folds of her dress.

"For some days I haunted the spot where these scenes had taken place; sometimes wishing to see you, sometimes resolved to quit the world and its miseries for ever. At length I wandered towards these mountains, and have ranged through their immense recesses, consumed by a burning passion which you alone can gratify. We may not part until you have promised to comply with my requisition. I am alone, and miserable; man will not associate with me; but one as deformed and horrible as myself would not deny herself to me. My companion must be of the same species, and have the same defects. This being you must create."

Chapter IX

The being finished speaking, and fixed his looks upon me in expectation of a reply. But I was bewildered, perplexed, and unable to arrange my ideas sufficiently to understand the full extent of his proposition. He continued—

[6]For the more erotic revision of 1831, see p. 205.

"You must create a female for me, with whom I can live in the interchange of those sympathies necessary for my being. This you alone can do; and I demand it of you as a right which you must not refuse."[1]

The latter part of his tale had kindled anew in me the anger that had died away while he narrated his peaceful life among the cottagers, and, as he said this, I could no longer suppress the rage that burned within me.

"I do refuse it," I replied; "and no torture shall ever extort a consent from me. You may render me the most miserable of men, but you shall never make me base in my own eyes. Shall I create another like yourself, whose joint wickedness might desolate the world. Begone! I have answered you; you may torture me, but I will never consent."

"You are in the wrong," replied the fiend; "and, instead of threatening, I am content to reason with you. I am malicious because I am miserable; am I not shunned and hated by all mankind? You, my creator, would tear me to pieces, and triumph; remember that, and tell me why I should pity man more than he pities me? You would not call it murder, if you could precipitate me into one of those ice-rifts, and destroy my frame, the work of your own hands. Shall I respect man, when he contemns me? Let him live with me in the interchange of kindness, and, instead of injury, I would bestow every benefit upon him with tears of gratitude at his acceptance. But that cannot be; the human senses are insurmountable barriers to our union. Yet mine shall not be the submission of abject slavery. I will revenge my injuries: if I cannot inspire love, I will cause fear; and chiefly towards you my arch-enemy, because my creator, do I swear inextinguishable hatred. Have a care: I will work at your destruction, nor finish until I desolate your heart, so that you curse the hour of your birth."[2]

A fiendish rage animated him as he said this; his face was wrinkled into contortions too horrible for human eyes to behold; but presently he calmed himself, and proceeded—

"I intended to reason. This passion is detrimental to me; for you do not reflect that you are the cause of its excess. If any being felt

---

[1]Again referring to Adam's plea to his Creator for a mate, Shelley also echoes her father's famous argument in *Political Justice* (7.6) that "man is a social animal," whose "soul yearns, with inexpressible longings, for the society of its like. . . . Who can tell the sufferings of him who is condemned to uninterrupted solitude? Who can tell that this is not, to the majority of mankind, the bitterest torment that human ingenuity can inflict?"

[2]Another reference to Job.

emotions of benevolence towards me, I should return them an hundred and an hundred fold; for that one creature's sake, I would make peace with the whole kind! But I now indulge in dreams of bliss that cannot be realized. What I ask of you is reasonable and moderate; I demand a creature of another sex, but as hideous as myself: the gratification is small, but it is all that I can receive, and it shall content me. It is true, we shall be monsters, cut off from all the world; but on that account we shall be more attached to one another. Our lives will not be happy, but they will be harmless, and free from the misery I now feel. Oh! my creator, make me happy; let me feel gratitude towards you for one benefit! Let me see that I excite the sympathy of some existing thing; do not deny me my request!"

I was moved. I shuddered when I thought of the possible consequences of my consent; but I felt that there was some justice in his argument. His tale, and the feelings he now expressed, proved him to be a creature of fine sensations; and did I not, as his maker, owe him all the portion of happiness that it was in my power to bestow? He saw my change of feeling, and continued—

"If you consent, neither you nor any other human being shall ever see us again: I will go to the vast wilds of South America. My food is not that of man; I do not destroy the lamb and the kid, to glut my appetite; acorns and berries afford me sufficient nourishment. My companion will be of the same nature as myself, and will be content with the same fare.[3] We shall make our bed of dried leaves; the sun will shine on us as on man, and will ripen our food. The picture I present to you is peaceful and human, and you must feel that you could deny it only in the wantonness of power and cruelty. Pitiless as you have been towards me, I now see compassion in your eyes; let me seize the favourable moment, and persuade you to promise what I so ardently desire."

"You propose," replied I, "to fly from the habitations of man, to dwell in those wilds where the beasts of the field will be your only companions. How can you, who long for the love and sympathy of man, persevere in this exile? You will return, and again seek their kindness, and you will meet with their detestation; your evil passions will be renewed, and you will then have a companion to aid you in the task of destruction. This may not be; cease to argue the point, for I cannot consent."

---

[3]Percy Shelley was a vegetarian.

"How inconstant are your feelings! but a moment ago you were moved by my representations, and why do you again harden yourself to my complaints? I swear to you, by the earth which I inhabit, and by you that made me, that, with the companion you bestow, I will quit the neighbourhood of man, and dwell, as it may chance, in the most savage of places. My evil passions will have fled, for I shall meet with sympathy; my life will flow quietly away, and, in my dying moments, I shall not curse my maker."

His words had a strange effect upon me. I compassionated him, and sometimes felt a wish to console him; but when I looked upon him, when I saw the filthy mass that moved and talked, my heart sickened, and my feelings were altered to those of horror and hatred. I tried to stifle these sensations; I thought, that as I could not sympathize with him, I had no right to withhold from him the small portion of happiness which was yet in my power to bestow.

"You swear," I said, "to be harmless; but have you not already shewn a degree of malice that should reasonably make me distrust you? May not even this be a feint that will increase your triumph by affording a wider scope for your revenge?"

"How is this? I thought I had moved your compassion, and yet you still refuse to bestow on me the only benefit that can soften my heart, and render me harmless. If I have no ties and no affections, hatred and vice must be my portion;[4] the love of another will destroy the cause of my crimes, and I shall become a thing, of whose existence every one will be ignorant. My vices are the children of a forced solitude that I abhor; and my virtues will necessarily arise when I live in communion with an equal. I shall feel the affections of a sensitive being, and become linked to the chain of existence and events, from which I am now excluded."

I paused some time to reflect on all he had related, and the various arguments which he had employed. I thought of the promise of virtues which he had displayed on the opening of his existence, and the subsequent blight of all kindly feeling by the loathing and scorn which his protectors had manifested towards him. His power and threats were not omitted in my calculations: a creature who could exist in the ice caves of the glaciers, and hide himself from pursuit among the ridges of inaccessible precipices, was a being possessing

---

[4]Bestowal.

faculties it would be vain to cope with. After a long pause of reflection, I concluded, that the justice due both to him and my fellow-creatures demanded of me that I should comply with his request. Turning to him, therefore, I said—

"I consent to your demand, on your solemn oath to quit Europe for ever, and every other place in the neighbourhood of man, as soon as I shall deliver into your hands a female who will accompany you in your exile."

"I swear," he cried, "by the sun, and by the blue sky of heaven,[5] that if you grant my prayer, while they exist you shall never behold me again. Depart to your home, and commence your labours: I shall watch their progress with unutterable anxiety; and fear not but that when you are ready I shall appear."

Saying this, he suddenly quitted me, fearful, perhaps, of any change in my sentiments. I saw him descend the mountain with greater speed than the flight of an eagle, and quickly lost him among the undulations of the sea of ice.

His tale had occupied the whole day; and the sun was upon the verge of the horizon when he departed. I knew that I ought to hasten my descent towards the valley, as I should soon be encompassed in darkness; but my heart was heavy, and my steps slow. The labour of winding among the little paths of the mountains, and fixing my feet firmly as I advanced, perplexed me, occupied as I was by the emotions which the occurrences of the day had produced. Night was far advanced, when I came to the half-way resting-place, and seated myself beside the fountain. The stars shone at intervals, as the clouds passed from over them; the dark pines rose before me, and every here and there a broken tree lay on the ground: it was a scene of wonderful solemnity, and stirred strange thoughts within me. I wept bitterly; and, clasping my hands in agony, I exclaimed, "Oh! stars, and clouds, and winds, ye are all about to mock me: if ye really pity me, crush sensation and memory; let me become as nought; but if not, depart, depart and leave me in darkness."

These were wild and miserable thoughts; but I cannot describe to you how the eternal twinkling of the stars weighed upon me, and how I listened to every blast of wind, as if it were a dull ugly siroc[6] on its way to consume me.

[5]1831 addition] and by the fire of love that burns in my heart,

[6]A scorching wind blowing from North African deserts across the Mediterranean into southern Europe.

Morning dawned before I arrived at the village of Chamounix; but my presence, so haggard and strange, hardly calmed the fears of my family, who had waited the whole night in anxious expectation of my return.[7]

The following day we returned to Geneva. The intention of my father in coming had been to divert my mind, and to restore me to my lost tranquillity; but the medicine had been fatal. And, unable to account for the excess of misery I appeared to suffer, he hastened to return home, hoping the quiet and monotony of a domestic life would by degrees alleviate my sufferings from whatsoever cause they might spring.

For myself, I was passive in all their arrangements; and the gentle affection of my beloved Elizabeth was inadequate to draw me from the depth of my despair. The promise I had made to the daemon weighed upon my mind, like Dante's iron cowl on the heads of the hellish hypocrites.[8] All pleasures of earth and sky passed before me like a dream, and that thought only had to me the reality of life. Can you wonder, that sometimes a kind of insanity possessed me, or that I saw continually about me a multitude of filthy animals inflicting on me incessant torture, that often extorted screams and bitter groans?

By degrees, however, these feelings became calmed. I entered again into the every-day scene of life, if not with interest, at least with some degree of tranquillity.

Frankenstein;
or,
The Modern Prometheus

Volume III

Chapter I

Day after day, week after week, passed away on my return to Geneva; and I could not collect the courage to recommence my work. I feared the vengeance of the disappointed fiend, yet I was unable to overcome my repugnance to the task which was enjoined me. I found

[7]new text, 1831] but I answered no question, scarcely did I speak . . .

[8]Victor likens himself to those exhausted by the laborious toil and crushing burden of maintaining an outward gilded appearance (*Inferno* 25.58–67).

that I could not compose a female without again devoting several months to profound study and laborious disquisition. I had heard of some discoveries having been made by an English philosopher, the knowledge of which was material to my success, and I sometimes thought of obtaining my father's consent to visit England for this purpose; but I clung to every pretence of delay, and could not resolve to interrupt my returning tranquillity. My health, which had hitherto declined, was now much restored; and my spirits, when unchecked by the memory of my unhappy promise, rose proportionably. My father saw this change with pleasure, and he turned his thoughts towards the best method of eradicating the remains of my melancholy, which every now and then would return by fits, and with a devouring blackness overcast the approaching sunshine. At these moments I took refuge in the most perfect solitude. I passed whole days on the lake alone in a little boat, watching the clouds, and listening to the rippling of the waves, silent and listless. But the fresh air and bright sun seldom failed to restore me to some degree of composure; and, on my return, I met the salutations of my friends with a readier smile and a more cheerful heart.

It was after my return from one of these rambles that my father, calling me aside, thus addressed me:—

"I am happy to remark, my dear son, that you have resumed your former pleasures, and seem to be returning to yourself. And yet you are still unhappy, and still avoid our society. For some time I was lost in conjecture as to the cause of this; but yesterday an idea struck me, and if it is well founded, I conjure you to avow it. Reserve on such a point would be not only useless, but draw down treble misery on us all."

I trembled violently at this exordium,[1] and my father continued—

"I confess, my son, that I have always looked forward to your marriage with your cousin as the tie of our domestic comfort, and the stay of my declining years. You were attached to each other from your earliest infancy; you studied together, and appeared, in dispositions and tastes, entirely suited to one another. But so blind is the experience of man, that what I conceived to be the best assistants to my plan may have entirely destroyed it. You, perhaps, regard her as your sister, without any wish that she might become your wife. Nay, you

---

[1]Formal introduction to a treatise.

may have met with another whom you may love; and, considering yourself as bound in honour to your cousin, this struggle may occasion the poignant misery which you appear to feel."

"My dear father, re-assure yourself. I love my cousin tenderly and sincerely. I never saw any woman who excited, as Elizabeth does, my warmest admiration and affection. My future hopes and prospects are entirely bound up in the expectation of our union."

"The expression of your sentiments on this subject, my dear Victor, gives me more pleasure than I have for some time experienced. If you feel thus, we shall assuredly be happy, however present events may cast a gloom over us. But it is this gloom, which appears to have taken so strong a hold of your mind, that I wish to dissipate. Tell me, therefore, whether you object to an immediate solemnization of the marriage. We have been unfortunate, and recent events have drawn us from that every-day tranquillity befitting my years and infirmities. You are younger; yet I do not suppose, possessed as you are of a competent fortune, that an early marriage would at all interfere with any future plans of honour and utility that you may have formed. Do not suppose, however, that I wish to dictate happiness to you, or that a delay on your part would cause me any serious uneasiness. Interpret my words with candour, and answer me, I conjure you, with confidence and sincerity."

I listened to my father in silence, and remained for some time incapable of offering any reply. I revolved rapidly in my mind a multitude of thoughts, and endeavoured to arrive at some conclusion. Alas! to me the idea of an immediate union with my cousin was one of horror and dismay. I was bound by a solemn promise, which I had not yet fulfilled, and dared not break; or, if I did, what manifold miseries might not impend over me and my devoted[2] family! Could I enter into a festival with this deadly weight yet hanging round my neck,[3] and bowing me to the ground. I must perform my engagement, and let the monster depart with his mate, before I allowed myself to enjoy the delight of an union from which I expected peace.

I remembered also the necessity imposed upon me of either journeying to England, or entering into a long correspondence with those philosophers of that country, whose knowledge and discoveries were

---

[2]Affectionately linked; doomed.

[3]See *The Rime of the Ancyent Marinere* (1798): "Instead of the Cross the Albatross / About my neck was hung" (137–38).

of indispensable use to me in my present undertaking. The latter method of obtaining the desired intelligence was dilatory and unsatisfactory: besides, any variation was agreeable to me, and I was delighted with the idea of spending a year or two in change of scene and variety of occupation, in absence from my family; during which period some event might happen which would restore me to them in peace and happiness: my promise might be fulfilled, and the monster have departed; or some accident might occur to destroy him, and put an end to my slavery for ever.[4]

These feelings dictated my answer to my father. I expressed a wish to visit England; but, concealing the true reasons of this request, I clothed my desires under the guise of wishing to travel and see the world before I sat down for life within the walls of my native town.

I urged my entreaty with earnestness, and my father was easily induced to comply; for a more indulgent and less dictatorial parent did not exist upon earth. Our plan was soon arranged. I should travel to Strasburgh, where Clerval would join me. Some short time would be spent in the towns of Holland, and our principal stay would be in England. We should return by France; and it was agreed that the tour should occupy the space of two years.

My father pleased himself with the reflection, that my union with Elizabeth should take place immediately on my return to Geneva. "These two years," said he, "will pass swiftly, and it will be the last delay that will oppose itself to your happiness. And, indeed, I earnestly desire that period to arrive, when we shall all be united, and neither hopes or fears arise to disturb our domestic calm."

"I am content," I replied, "with your arrangement. By that time we shall both have become wiser, and I hope happier, than we at present are." I sighed; but my father kindly forbore to question me further concerning the cause of my dejection. He hoped that new scenes, and the amusement of travelling, would restore my tranquillity.

I now made arrangements for my journey; but one feeling haunted me, which filled me with fear and agitation. During my absence I should leave my friends unconscious of the existence of their enemy, and unprotected from his attacks, exasperated as he might be by my departure. But he had promised to follow me wherever I might go; and would he not accompany me to England? This imagination was dreadful in itself, but soothing, inasmuch as it supposed

[4]Shelley increases Victor's agitation in the 1831 version; see p. 206.

the safety of my friends. I was agonized with the idea of the possibility that the reverse of this might happen. But through the whole period during which I was the slave of my creature, I allowed myself to be governed by the impulses of the moment; and my present sensations strongly intimated that the fiend would follow me, and exempt my family from the danger of his machinations.

It was in the latter end of August that I departed, to pass two years of exile. Elizabeth approved of the reasons of my departure, and only regretted that she had not the same opportunities of enlarging her experience, and cultivating her understanding. She wept, however, as she bade me farewell, and entreated me to return happy and tranquil. "We all," said she, "depend upon you; and if you are miserable, what must be our feelings?"

I threw myself into the carriage that was to convey me away, hardly knowing whither I was going, and careless of what was passing around. I remembered only, and it was with a bitter anguish that I reflected on it, to order that my chemical instruments should be packed to go with me: for I resolved to fulfil my promise while abroad, and return, if possible, a free man. Filled with dreary imaginations, I passed through many beautiful and majestic scenes; but my eyes were fixed and unobserving. I could only think of the bourne of my travels, and the work which was to occupy me whilst they endured.

After some days spent in listless indolence, during which I traversed many leagues, I arrived at Strasburgh,[5] where I waited two days for Clerval. He came. Alas, how great was the contrast between us! He was alive to every new scene; joyful when he saw the beauties of the setting sun, and more happy when he beheld it rise, and recommence a new day. He pointed out to me the shifting colours of the landscape, and the appearances of the sky. "This is what it is to live," he cried; "now I enjoy existence! But you, my dear Frankenstein, wherefore are you desponding and sorrowful?" In truth, I was occupied by gloomy thoughts, and neither saw the descent of the evening star, nor the golden sun-rise reflected in the Rhine.—And you, my friend, would be far more amused with the journal of Clerval, who observed the scenery with an eye of feeling and delight, than to listen to my reflections. I, a miserable wretch, haunted by a curse that shut up every avenue to enjoyment.

[5]A major riverport; their course will follow Mary and Percy's trip down the Rhine in 1814.

We had agreed to descend the Rhine in a boat from Strasburgh to Rotterdam, whence we might take shipping for London. During this voyage, we passed by many willowy islands, and saw several beautiful towns. We staid a day at Manheim, and, on the fifth from our departure from Strasburgh, arrived at Mayence.[6] The course of the Rhine below Mayence becomes much more picturesque. The river descends rapidly, and winds between hills, not high, but steep, and of beautiful forms. We saw many ruined castles standing on the edges of precipices, surrounded by black woods, high and inaccessible. This part of the Rhine, indeed, presents a singularly variegated landscape. In one spot you view rugged hills, ruined castles overlooking tremendous precipices, with the dark Rhine rushing beneath; and, on the sudden turn of a promontory, flourishing vineyards, with green sloping banks, and a meandering river, and populous towns, occupy the scene.

We travelled at the time of the vintage, and heard the song of the labourers, as we glided down the stream. Even I, depressed in mind, and my spirits continually agitated by gloomy feelings, even I was pleased. I lay at the bottom of the boat, and, as I gazed on the cloudless blue sky, I seemed to drink in a tranquillity to which I had long been a stranger. And if these were my sensations, who can describe those of Henry? He felt as if he had been transported to Fairyland, and enjoyed a happiness seldom tasted by man. "I have seen," he said, "the most beautiful scenes of my own country; I have visited the lakes of Lucerne and Uri, where the snowy mountains descend almost perpendicularly to the water, casting black and impenetrable shades, which would cause a gloomy and mournful appearance, were it not for the most verdant islands that relieve the eye by their gay appearance; I have seen this lake agitated by a tempest, when the wind tore up whirlwinds of water, and gave you an idea of what the water-spout must be on the great ocean, and the waves dash with fury the base of the mountain, where the priest and his mistress were overwhelmed by an avalanche, and where their dying voices are still said to be heard amid the pauses of the nightly wind;[7] I have seen

[6]East of the Rhine, between Mannheim and Mainz (Mayence), is Castle Frankenstein.
[7]In *History of a Six Weeks' Tour* (1817), an account of her first trip to Europe with Percy, Mary records a local "story of a priest and his mistress, who, flying from persecution, inhabited a cottage at the foot of the snows. One winter night an avalanche overwhelmed them, but their plaintive voices are still heard in stormy nights, calling for succour from the peasants."

the mountains of La Valais, and the Pays de Vaud: but this country, Victor, pleases me more than all those wonders. The mountains of Switzerland are more majestic and strange; but there is a charm in the banks of this divine river, that I never before saw equalled. Look at that castle which overhangs yon precipice; and that also on the island, almost concealed amongst the foliage of those lovely trees; and now that group of labourers coming from among their vines; and that village half-hid in the recess of the mountain. Oh, surely, the spirit that inhabits and guards this place has a soul more in harmony with man, than those who pile the glacier, or retire to the inaccessible peaks of the mountains of our own country."

Clerval! beloved friend! even now it delights me to record your words, and to dwell on the praise of which you are so eminently deserving. He was a being formed in the "very poetry of nature."[8] His wild and enthusiastic imagination was chastened by the sensibility of his heart. His soul overflowed with ardent affections, and his friendship was of that devoted and wondrous nature that the worldly-minded teach us to look for only in the imagination. But even human sympathies were not sufficient to satisfy his eager mind. The scenery of external nature, which others regard only with admiration, he loved with ardour:

> ———The sounding cataract
> Haunted *him* like a passion: the tall rock,
> The mountain, and the deep and gloomy wood,
> Their colours and their forms, were then to him
> An appetite; a feeling, and a love,
> That had no need of a remoter charm,
> By thought supplied, or any interest
> Unborrowed from the eye.[9]

And where does he now exist? Is this gentle and lovely being lost for ever? Has this mind so replete with ideas, imaginations fanciful

[8]"Leigh Hunt's 'Rimini.'" [Shelley's note]; *The Story of Rimini* (1816), a controversial poem drawn from Dante's story in *Inferno* of the adulterous lovers, Paolo and Francesca. Paolo, "a creature / Formed in the very poetry of nature" (2.46–47), is sent to court Francesca in the place of Prince Giovanni, his more sullen, aloof elder brother. Francesca is forced to marry Giovanni, who kills both her and Paolo when he discovers their adultery.

[9]"Wordsworth's 'Tintern Abbey'" [Shelley's note]; see lines 77–84; Clerval is substituted for Wordsworth—by 1816, the famous "Poet of Nature" (so Percy Shelley addresses him in his sonnet "To Wordsworth").

and magnificent, which formed a world, whose existence depended on the life of its creator; has this mind perished? Does it now only exist in my memory? No, it is not thus; your form so divinely wrought, and beaming with beauty, has decayed, but your spirit still visits and consoles your unhappy friend.

Pardon this gush of sorrow; these ineffectual words are but a slight tribute to the unexampled worth of Henry,[10] but they soothe my heart, overflowing with the anguish which his remembrance creates. I will proceed with my tale.

Beyond Cologne we descended to the plains of Holland; and we resolved to post[11] the remainder of our way; for the wind was contrary, and the stream of the river was too gentle to aid us.

Our journey here lost the interest arising from beautiful scenery; but we arrived in a few days at Rotterdam, whence we proceeded by sea to England. It was on a clear morning, in the latter days of December, that I first saw the white cliffs of Britain.[12] The banks of the Thames presented a new scene; they were flat, but fertile, and almost every town was marked by the remembrance of some story. We saw Tilbury Fort, and remembered the Spanish armada; Gravesend, Woolwich, and Greenwich, places which I had heard of even in my country.

At length we saw the numerous steeples of London, St. Paul's towering above all, and the Tower famed in English history.

Chapter II

London was our present point of rest; we determined to remain several months in this wonderful and celebrated city. Clerval desired the intercourse of the men of genius and talent who flourished at this time;[1] but this was with me a secondary object; I was principally occupied with the means of obtaining the information necessary for the completion of my promise, and quickly availed myself of the letters of introduction that I had brought with me, addressed to the most distinguished natural philosophers.

[10]An intimate reference to the friend usually called "Clerval."
[11]Travel by relays of horses.
[12]At Dover.

[1]Shelley's compliment to her father Godwin and his contemporaries: her mother, Blake, Paine, Darwin, and others.

If this journey had taken place during my days of study and happiness, it would have afforded me inexpressible pleasure. But a blight had come over my existence, and I only visited these people for the sake of the information they might give me on the subject in which my interest was so terribly profound. Company was irksome to me; when alone, I could fill my mind with the sights of heaven and earth; the voice of Henry soothed me, and I could thus cheat myself into a transitory peace. But busy uninteresting joyous faces brought back despair to my heart. I saw an insurmountable barrier placed between me and my fellow-men; this barrier was sealed with the blood of William and Justine; and to reflect on the events connected with those names filled my soul with anguish.

But in Clerval I saw the image of my former self;[2] he was inquisitive, and anxious to gain experience and instruction. The difference of manners which he observed was to him an inexhaustible source of instruction and amusement. He was for ever busy; and the only check to his enjoyments was my sorrowful and dejected mien. I tried to conceal this as much as possible, that I might not debar him from the pleasures natural to one who was entering on a new scene of life, undisturbed by any care or bitter recollection. I often refused to accompany him, alleging another engagement, that I might remain alone. I now also began to collect the materials necessary for my new creation, and this was to me like the torture of single drops of water continually falling on the head. Every thought that was devoted to it was an extreme anguish, and every word that I spoke in allusion to it caused my lips to quiver, and my heart to palpitate.

After passing some months in London, we received a letter from a person in Scotland, who had formerly been our visitor at Geneva. He mentioned the beauties of his native country, and asked us if those were not sufficient allurements to induce us to prolong our journey as far north as Perth, where he resided. Clerval eagerly desired to accept this invitation; and I, although I abhorred society, wished to view again mountains and streams, and all the wondrous works with which Nature adorns her chosen dwelling-places.

[2]An oblique echo of *Tintern Abbey* 117–21: "My dear, dear Friend, . . . in thy voice I catch / The language of my former heart, and read / My former pleasures . . . what I was once." Wordsworth is addressing his younger sister. In 1831, Shelley elaborates the value of this trip abroad to Clerval's imperial ambitions. See p. 206.

We had arrived in England at the beginning of October,[3] and it was now February. We accordingly determined to commence our journey towards the north at the expiration of another month. In this expedition we did not intend to follow the great road to Edinburgh, but to visit Windsor, Oxford, Matlock, and the Cumberland lakes, resolving to arrive at the completion of this tour about the end of July. I packed my chemical instruments, and the materials I had collected, resolving to finish my labours in some obscure nook in the northern Highlands of Scotland.

We quitted London on the 27th of March, and remained a few days at Windsor, rambling in its beautiful forest. This was a new scene to us mountaineers; the majestic oaks, the quantity of game, and the herds of stately deer, were all novelties to us.

From thence we proceeded to Oxford. As we entered this city, our minds were filled with the remembrance of the events that had been transacted there more than a century and a half before. It was here that Charles I. had collected his forces. This city had remained faithful to him, after the whole nation had forsaken his cause to join the standard of parliament and liberty. The memory of that unfortunate king, and his companions, the amiable Falkland, the insolent Goring, his queen, and son, gave a peculiar interest to every part of the city, which they might be supposed to have inhabited.[4] The spirit of elder days found a dwelling here, and we delighted to trace its footsteps. If these feelings had not found an imaginary gratification, the appearance of the city had yet in itself sufficient beauty to obtain our admiration. The colleges are ancient and picturesque; the streets are almost magnificent; and the lovely Isis,[5] which flows beside it

---

[3]Victor's chronology is getting confused. He has just given their arrival as late December (p. 122), a discrepancy Shelley lets stand in the 1831 text. The imagination of a longer delay in commencing the second creature suggests Victor's anxiety, even in retrospect.

[4]Oxford, seat of Oxford University, was Charles I's base during the Civil Wars of the 1640s against Cromwell's Parliamentary faction; Charles was defeated and brought to London, where he was beheaded in 1649. Falkland, one of his chief advisors, was said to have let himself, in despair over the Civil Wars, be slain in battle in 1643; Godwin modeled a character on him in his political novel *Caleb Williams* (see Shelley's dedication). Goring, one of Charles I's generals, was notoriously ambitious and self-serving; before the war, irritated that he had been given a secondary role in Charles's plot against Parliament, he betrayed the plot to the rebels. In a novel set in the revolutionary 1790s, Victor's sympathies for the doomed champions of the Royal Cause seem a form of unrecognized self-pity.

[5]The name of the Thames in Oxford.

through meadows of exquisite verdure, is spread forth into a placid expanse of waters, which reflects its majestic assemblage of towers, and spires, and domes, embosomed among aged trees.

I enjoyed this scene; and yet my enjoyment was embittered both by the memory of the past, and the anticipation of the future. I was formed for peaceful happiness. During my youthful days discontent never visited my mind; and if I was ever overcome by *ennui*,[6] the sight of what is beautiful in nature, or the study of what is excellent and sublime in the productions of man, could always interest my heart, and communicate elasticity to my spirits. But I am a blasted tree; the bolt has entered my soul; and I felt then that I should survive to exhibit, what I shall soon cease to be—a miserable spectacle of wrecked humanity, pitiable to others, and abhorrent to myself.

We passed a considerable period at Oxford, rambling among its environs, and endeavouring to identify every spot which might relate to the most animating epoch of English history. Our little voyages of discovery were often prolonged by the successive objects that presented themselves. We visited the tomb of the illustrious Hampden, and the field on which that patriot fell.[7] For a moment my soul was elevated from its debasing and miserable fears to contemplate the divine ideas of liberty and self-sacrifice, of which these sights were the monuments and the remembrancers. For an instant I dared to shake off my chains, and look around me with a free and lofty spirit; but the iron had eaten into my flesh, and I sank again, trembling and hopeless, into my miserable self.

We left Oxford with regret, and proceeded to Matlock, which was our next place of rest. The country in the neighbourhood of this village resembled, to a greater degree, the scenery of Switzerland; but every thing is on a lower scale; and the green hills want the crown of distant white Alps, which always attend on the piny mountains of my native country. We visited the wondrous cave, and the little cabinets of natural history, where the curiosities are disposed in the same manner as in the collections at Servox and Chamounix. The latter name made me tremble, when pronounced by Henry; and I hastened to quit Matlock, with which that terrible scene was thus associated.

[6]French: boredom, world-weariness.

[7]Hampden (1594–1643), a cousin and supporter of Cromwell, and a popular hero of the Parliamentary cause, was killed in a skirmish near Oxford. Victor appears to have sympathies for idealistic, self-sacrificing revolutionaries, too.

From Derby still journeying northward, we passed two months in Cumberland and Westmoreland. I could now almost fancy myself among the Swiss mountains. The little patches of snow which yet lingered on the northern sides of the mountains, the lakes, and the dashing of the rocky streams, were all familiar and dear sights to me. Here also we made some acquaintances, who almost contrived to cheat me into happiness. The delight of Clerval was proportionably greater than mine; his mind expanded in the company of men of talent,[8] and he found in his own nature greater capacities and resources than he could have imagined himself to have possessed while he associated with his inferiors. "I could pass my life here," said he to me; "and among these mountains I should scarcely regret Switzerland and the Rhine."

But he found that a traveller's life is one that includes much pain amidst its enjoyments. His feelings are for ever on the stretch; and when he begins to sink into repose, he finds himself obliged to quit that on which he rests in pleasure for something new, which again engages his attention, and which also he forsakes for other novelties.

We had scarcely visited the various lakes of Cumberland and Westmoreland, and conceived an affection for some of the inhabitants, when the period of our appointment with our Scotch friend approached, and we left them to travel on. For my own part I was not sorry. I had now neglected my promise for some time, and I feared the effects of the daemon's disappointment. He might remain in Switzerland, and wreak his vengeance on my relatives. This idea pursued me, and tormented me at every moment from which I might otherwise have snatched repose and peace. I waited for my letters with feverish impatience: if they were delayed, I was miserable, and overcome by a thousand fears; and when they arrived, and I saw the superscription of Elizabeth or my father, I hardly dared to read and ascertain my fate. Sometimes I thought that the fiend followed me, and might expedite my remissness by murdering my companion. When these thoughts possessed me, I would not quit Henry for a moment, but followed him as his shadow, to protect him from the fancied rage of his destroyer. I felt as if I had committed some great crime, the consciousness of which haunted me. I was guiltless, but I had indeed drawn down a horrible curse upon my head, as mortal as that of crime.

[8] A compliment to the writers associated with Lake District (Westmoreland and Cumberland) in the 1790s: Wordsworth and Coleridge; Southey in his radical youth; and abolitionist Clarkson.

I visited Edinburgh with languid eyes and mind; and yet that city might have interested the most unfortunate being. Clerval did not like it so well as Oxford; for the antiquity of the latter city was more pleasing to him. But the beauty and regularity of the new town of Edinburgh, its romantic castle, and its environs, the most delightful in the world, Arthur's Seat, St. Bernard's Well, and the Pentland Hills, compensated him for the change, and filled him with cheerfulness and admiration. But I was impatient to arrive at the termination of my journey.

We left Edinburgh in a week, passing through Coupar, St. Andrews, and along the banks of the Tay, to Perth, where our friend expected us. But I was in no mood to laugh and talk with strangers, or enter into their feelings or plans with the good humour expected from a guest; and accordingly I told Clerval that I wished to make the tour of Scotland alone. "Do you," said I, "enjoy yourself, and let this be our rendezvous. I may be absent a month or two; but do not interfere with my motions, I entreat you: leave me to peace and solitude for a short time; and when I return, I hope it will be with a lighter heart, more congenial to your own temper."

Henry wished to dissuade me; but, seeing me bent on this plan, ceased to remonstrate. He entreated me to write often. "I had rather be with you," he said, "in your solitary rambles, than with these Scotch people, whom I do not know: hasten then, my dear friend, to return, that I may again feel myself somewhat at home, which I cannot do in your absence."

Having parted from my friend, I determined to visit some remote spot of Scotland, and finish my work in solitude. I did not doubt but that the monster followed me, and would discover himself to me when I should have finished, that he might receive his companion.

With this resolution I traversed the northern highlands, and fixed on one of the remotest of the Orkneys[9] as the scene of my labours. It was a place fitted for such a work, being hardly more than a rock, whose high sides were continually beaten upon by the waves. The soil was barren, scarcely affording pasture for a few miserable cows, and oatmeal for its inhabitants, which consisted of five persons, whose gaunt and scraggy limbs gave tokens of their miserable fare. Vegetables and bread, when they indulged in such luxuries, and even fresh water, was to be procured from the main land, which was about five miles distant.

[9]Islands off the north coast of Scotland.

On the whole island there were but three miserable huts, and one of these was vacant when I arrived. This I hired. It contained but two rooms, and these exhibited all the squalidness of the most miserable penury. The thatch had fallen in, the walls were unplastered, and the door was off its hinges. I ordered it to be repaired, bought some furniture, and took possession; an incident which would, doubtless, have occasioned some surprise, had not all the senses of the cottagers been benumbed by want and squalid poverty. As it was, I lived ungazed at and unmolested, hardly thanked for the pittance of food and clothes which I gave; so much does suffering blunt even the coarsest sensations of men.

In this retreat I devoted the morning to labour; but in the evening, when the weather permitted, I walked on the stony beach of the sea, to listen to the waves as they roared, and dashed at my feet. It was a monotonous, yet ever-changing scene. I thought of Switzerland; it was far different from this desolate and appalling landscape. Its hills are covered with vines, and its cottages are scattered thickly in the plains. Its fair lakes reflect a blue and gentle sky; and, when troubled by the winds, their tumult is but as the play of a lively infant, when compared to the roarings of the giant ocean.

In this manner I distributed my occupations when I first arrived; but, as I proceeded in my labour, it became every day more horrible and irksome to me. Sometimes I could not prevail on myself to enter my laboratory for several days; and at other times I toiled day and night in order to complete my work. It was indeed a filthy process in which I was engaged. During my first experiment, a kind of enthusiastic frenzy had blinded me to the horror of my employment; my mind was intently fixed on the sequel of[10] my labour, and my eyes were shut to the horror of my proceedings. But now I went to it in cold blood, and my heart often sickened at the work of my hands.

Thus situated, employed in the most detestable occupation, immersed in a solitude where nothing could for an instant call my attention from the actual scene in which I was engaged, my spirits became unequal; I grew restless and nervous. Every moment I feared to meet my persecutor. Sometimes I sat with my eyes fixed on the ground, fearing to raise them lest they should encounter the object which I so much dreaded to behold. I feared to wander from the sight of my fellow-creatures, lest when alone he should come to claim his companion.

[10]1831] consummation of

In the mean time I worked on, and my labour was already considerably advanced. I looked towards its completion with a tremulous and eager hope, which I dared not trust myself to question, but which was intermixed with obscure forebodings of evil, that made my heart sicken in my bosom.

Chapter III

I sat one evening in my laboratory; the sun had set, and the moon was just rising from the sea; I had not sufficient light for my employment, and I remained idle, in a pause of consideration of whether I should leave my labour for the night, or hasten its conclusion by an unremitting attention to it. As I sat, a train of reflection occurred to me, which led me to consider the effects of what I was now doing. Three years before I was engaged in the same manner, and had created a fiend whose unparalleled barbarity had desolated my heart, and filled it for ever with the bitterest remorse. I was now about to form another being, of whose dispositions I was alike ignorant; she might become ten thousand times more malignant than her mate, and delight, for its own sake, in murder and wretchedness. He had sworn to quit the neighbourhood of man, and hide himself in deserts; but she had not; and she, who in all probability was to become a thinking and reasoning animal, might refuse to comply with a compact made before her creation. They might even hate each other; the creature who already lived loathed his own deformity, and might he not conceive a greater abhorence for it when it came before his eyes in the female form? She also might turn with disgust from him to the superior beauty of man; she might quit him, and he be again alone, exasperated by the fresh provocation of being deserted by one of his own species.

Even if they were to leave Europe, and inhabit the deserts of the new world, yet one of the first results of those sympathies for which the daemon thirsted would be children, and a race of devils would be propagated upon the earth, who might make the very existence of the species of man a condition precarious and full of terror. Had I a right, for my own benefit, to inflict this curse upon everlasting generations? I had before been moved by the sophisms of the being I had created; I had been struck senseless by his fiendish threats: but now, for the first time, the wickedness of my promise burst upon me; I shuddered to think that future ages might curse me as their pest, whose selfishness had not hesitated to buy its own peace at the price perhaps of the existence of the whole human race.

I trembled, and my heart failed within me; when, on looking up, I saw, by the light of the moon, the daemon at the casement. A ghastly grin wrinkled his lips as he gazed on me, where I sat fulfilling the task which he had allotted to me. Yes, he had followed me in my travels; he had loitered in forests, hid himself in caves, or taken refuge in wide and desert heaths; and he now came to mark my progress, and claim the fulfilment of my promise.

As I looked on him, his countenance expressed the utmost extent of malice and treachery. I thought with a sensation of madness on my promise of creating another like to him, and, trembling with passion, tore to pieces the thing on which I was engaged. The wretch saw me destroy the creature on whose future existence he depended for happiness, and, with a howl of devilish despair and revenge, withdrew.

I left the room, and, locking the door, made a solemn vow in my own heart never to resume my labours; and then, with trembling steps, I sought my own apartment. I was alone; none were near me to dissipate the gloom, and relieve me from the sickening oppression of the most terrible reveries.

Several hours past, and I remained near my window gazing on the sea; it was almost motionless, for the winds were hushed, and all nature reposed under the eye of the quiet moon. A few fishing vessels alone specked the water, and now and then the gentle breeze wafted the sound of voices, as the fisherman called to one another. I felt the silence, although I was hardly conscious of its extreme profundity, until my ear was suddenly arrested by the paddling of oars near the shore, and a person landed close to my house.

In a few minutes after, I heard the creaking of my door, as if some one endeavoured to open it softly. I trembled from head to foot; I felt a presentiment of who it was, and wished to rouse one of the peasants who dwelt in a cottage not far from mine; but I was overcome by the sensation of helplessness, so often felt in frightful dreams, when you in vain endeavour to fly from an impending danger, and was rooted to the spot.

Presently I heard the sound of footsteps along the passage; the door opened, and the wretch whom I dreaded appeared. Shutting the door, he approached me, and said, in a smothered voice—

"You have destroyed the work which you began; what is it that you intend? Do you dare to break your promise? I have endured toil and misery: I left Switzerland with you; I crept along the shores of the Rhine, among its willow islands, and over the summits of its hills. I have dwelt many months in the heaths of England, and among the deserts of Scotland. I have endured incalculable fatigue, and cold, and hunger; do you dare destroy my hopes?"

"Begone! I do break my promise; never will I create another like yourself, equal in deformity and wickedness."

"Slave, I before reasoned with you, but you have proved yourself unworthy of my condescension. Remember that I have power; you believe yourself miserable, but I can make you so wretched that the light of day will be hateful to you. You are my creator, but I am your master;—obey!"

"The hour of my weakness is past, and the period of your power is arrived. Your threats cannot move me to do an act of wickedness; but they confirm me in a resolution of not creating you a companion in vice. Shall I, in cool blood, set loose upon the earth a daemon, whose delight is in death and wretchedness. Begone! I am firm, and your words will only exasperate my rage."

The monster saw my determination in my face, and gnashed his teeth in the impotence of anger. "Shall each man," cried he, "find a wife for his bosom, and each beast have his mate, and I be alone? I had feelings of affection, and they were requited by detestation and scorn. Man, you may hate; but beware! Your hours will pass in dread and misery, and soon the bolt will fall which must ravish from you your happiness for ever. Are you to be happy, while I grovel in the intensity of my wretchedness? You can blast my other passions; but revenge remains—revenge, henceforth dearer than light or food! I may die; but first you, my tyrant and tormentor, shall curse the sun that gazes on your misery. Beware; for I am fearless, and therefore powerful. I will watch with the wiliness of a snake, that I may sting with its venom. Man, you shall repent of the injuries you inflict."

"Devil, cease; and do not poison the air with these sounds of malice. I have declared my resolution to you, and I am no coward to bend beneath words. Leave me; I am inexorable."

"It is well. I go; but remember, I shall be with you on your wedding-night."

I started forward, and exclaimed, "Villain! before you sign my death-warrant, be sure that you are yourself safe."

I would have seized him; but he eluded me, and quitted the house with precipitation: in a few moments I saw him in his boat, which shot across the waters with an arrowy swiftness, and was soon lost amidst the waves.

All was again silent; but his words rung in my ears. I burned with rage to pursue the murderer of my peace, and precipitate him into the ocean. I walked up and down my room hastily and perturbed, while my imagination conjured up a thousand images to torment and sting me. Why had I not followed him, and closed with him in mortal strife? But I had suffered him to depart, and he had directed his course towards the main land. I shuddered to think who might be the next victim sacrificed to his insatiate revenge. And then I thought again of his words—*"I will be with you on your wedding-night."* That then was the period fixed for the fulfilment of my destiny. In that hour I should die, and at once satisfy and extinguish his malice. The prospect did not move me to fear; yet when I thought of my beloved Elizabeth,—of her tears and endless sorrow, when she should find her lover so barbarously snatched from her,—tears, the first I had shed for many months, streamed from my eyes, and I resolved not to fall before my enemy without a bitter struggle.

The night passed away, and the sun rose from the ocean; my feelings became calmer, if it may be called calmness, when the violence of rage sinks into the depths of despair. I left the house, the horrid scene of the last night's contention, and walked on the beach of the sea, which I almost regarded as an insuperable barrier between me and my fellow-creatures; nay, a wish that such should prove the fact stole across me. I desired that I might pass my life on that barren rock, wearily it is true, but uninterrupted by any sudden shock of misery. If I returned, it was to be sacrificed, or to see those whom I most loved die under the grasp of a daemon whom I had myself created.

I walked about the isle like a restless spectre, separated from all it loved, and miserable in the separation. When it became noon, and the sun rose higher, I lay down on the grass, and was overpowered by a deep sleep. I had been awake the whole of the preceding night, my nerves were agitated, and my eyes inflamed by watching and misery. The sleep into which I now sunk refreshed me; and when I woke, I again felt as if I belonged to a race of human beings like myself, and I began to reflect upon what had passed with greater composure; yet still the words of the fiend rung in my ears like a death-knell, they appeared like a dream, yet distinct and oppressive as a reality.

The sun had far descended, and I still sat on the shore, satisfying my appetite, which had become ravenous, with an oaten cake, when I saw a fishing-boat land close to me, and one of the men brought me a packet; it contained letters from Geneva, and one from Clerval, entreating me to join him. He said that nearly a year had elapsed since we had quitted Switzerland, and France was yet unvisited. He entreated me, therefore, to leave my solitary isle, and meet him at Perth, in a week from that time, when we might arrange the plan of our future proceedings. This letter in a degree recalled me to life, and I determined to quit my island at the expiration of two days.

Yet, before I departed, there was a task to perform, on which I shuddered to reflect: I must pack my chemical instruments; and for that purpose I must enter the room which had been the scene of my odious work, and I must handle those utensils, the sight of which was sickening to me. The next morning, at day-break, I summoned sufficient courage, and unlocked the door of my laboratory. The remains of the half-finished creature, whom I had destroyed, lay scattered on the floor, and I almost felt as if I had mangled the living flesh of a human being. I paused to collect myself, and then entered the chamber. With trembling hand I conveyed the instruments out of the room; but I reflected that I ought not to leave the relics of my work to excite the horror and suspicion of the peasants, and I accordingly put them into a basket, with a great quantity of stones, and laying them up, determined to throw them into the sea that very night; and in the mean time I sat upon the beach, employed in cleaning and arranging my chemical apparatus.

Nothing could be more complete than the alteration that had taken place in my feelings since the night of the appearance of the daemon. I had before regarded my promise with a gloomy despair, as a thing that, with whatever consequences, must be fulfilled; but I now felt as if a film had been taken from before my eyes, and that I, for the first time, saw clearly. The idea of renewing my labours did not for one instant occur to me; the threat I had heard weighed on my thoughts, but I did not reflect that a voluntary act of mine could avert it. I had resolved in my own mind, that to create another like the fiend I had first made would be an act of the basest and most atrocious selfishness; and I banished from my mind every thought that could lead to a different conclusion.

Between two and three in the morning the moon rose; and I then, putting my basket aboard a little skiff, sailed out about four miles from the shore. The scene was perfectly solitary: a few boats were returning towards land, but I sailed away from them. I felt as if I was about the commission of a dreadful crime, and avoided with shuddering anxiety any encounter with my fellow-creatures. At one time the moon, which had before been clear, was suddenly overspread by a thick cloud, and I took advantage of the moment of darkness, and cast my basket into the sea; I listened to the gurgling sound as it sunk, and then sailed away from the spot. The sky became clouded; but the air was pure, although chilled by the north-east breeze that was then rising. But it refreshed me, and filled me with such agreeable sensations, that I resolved to prolong my stay on the water, and fixing the rudder in a direct position, stretched myself at the bottom of the boat. Clouds hid the moon, every thing was obscure, and I heard only the sound of the boat, as its keel cut through the waves; the murmur lulled me, and in a short time I slept soundly.

I do not know how long I remained in this situation, but when I awoke I found that the sun had already mounted considerably. The wind was high, and the waves continually threatened the safety of my little skiff. I found that the wind was north-east, and must have driven me far from the coast from which I had embarked. I endeavoured to change my course, but quickly found that if I again made the attempt the boat would be instantly filled with water. Thus situated, my only resource was to drive before the wind. I confess that I felt a few sensations of terror. I had no compass with me, and was so little acquainted with the geography of this part of the world that the sun was of little benefit to me. I might be driven into the wide Atlantic, and feel all the tortures of starvation, or be swallowed up in the immeasurable waters that roared and buffeted around me. I had already been out many hours, and felt the torment of a burning thirst, a prelude to my other sufferings. I looked on the heavens, which were covered by clouds that flew before the wind only to be replaced by others: I looked upon the sea, it was to be my grave. "Fiend," I exclaimed, "your task is already fulfilled!" I thought of Elizabeth, of my father, and of Clerval; and sunk into[1] a reverie, so despairing and frightful, that even now, when the scene is on the point of closing before me for ever, I shudder to reflect on it.

---

[1]1831 after "Clerval"] all left behind, on whom the monster might satisfy his sanguinary and merciless passions. The idea plunged me into . . .

Some hours passed thus; but by degrees, as the sun declined towards the horizon, the wind died away into a gentle breeze, and the sea became free from breakers. But these gave place to a heavy swell; I felt sick, and hardly able to hold the rudder, when suddenly I saw a line of high land towards the south.

Almost spent, as I was, by fatigue, and the dreadful suspense I endured for several hours, this sudden certainty of life rushed like a flood of warm joy to my heart, and tears gushed from my eyes.

How mutable are our feelings, and how strange is that clinging love we have of life even in the excess of misery! I constructed another sail with a part of my dress, and eagerly steered my course towards the land. It had a wild and rocky appearance; but as I approached nearer, I easily perceived the traces of cultivation. I saw vessels near the shore, and found myself suddenly transported back to the neighbourhood of civilized man. I eagerly traced the windings of the land, and hailed a steeple which I at length saw issuing from behind a small promontory. As I was in a state of extreme debility, I resolved to sail directly towards the town as a place where I could most easily procure nourishment. Fortunately I had money with me. As I turned the promontory, I perceived a small neat town and a good harbour, which I entered, my heart bounding with joy at my unexpected escape.

As I was occupied in fixing the boat and arranging the sails, several people crowded towards the spot. They seemed very much surprised at my appearance; but, instead of offering me any assistance, whispered together with gestures that at any other time might have produced in me a slight sensation of alarm. As it was, I merely remarked that they spoke English; and I therefore addressed them in that language: "My good friends," said I, "will you be so kind as to tell me the name of this town, and inform me where I am?"

"You will know that soon enough," replied a man with a gruff voice. "May be you are come to a place that will not prove much to your taste; but you will not be consulted as to your quarters, I promise you."

I was exceedingly surprised on receiving so rude an answer from a stranger; and I was also disconcerted on perceiving the frowning and angry countenances of his companions. "Why do you answer me so roughly?" I replied: "surely it is not the custom of Englishmen to receive strangers so inhospitably."

"I do not know," said the man, "what the custom of the English may be; but it is the custom of the Irish to hate villains."

While this strange dialogue continued, I perceived the crowd rapidly increase. Their faces expressed a mixture of curiosity and anger, which annoyed, and in some degree alarmed me. I inquired the way to the inn; but no one replied. I then moved forward, and a murmuring sound arose from the crowd as they followed and surrounded me; when an ill-looking man approaching, tapped me on the shoulder, and said, "Come, Sir, you must follow me to Mr Kirwin's, to give an account of yourself."

"Who is Mr Kirwin? Why am I to give an account of myself? Is not this a free country?"

"Aye, Sir, free enough for honest folks. Mr Kirwin is a magistrate; and you are to give an account of the death of a gentleman who was found murdered here last night."

This answer startled me; but I presently recovered myself. I was innocent; that could easily be proved: accordingly I followed my conductor in silence, and was led to one of the best houses in the town. I was ready to sink from fatigue and hunger; but, being surrounded by a crowd, I thought it politic to rouse all my strength, that no physical debility might be construed into apprehension or conscious guilt. Little did I then expect the calamity that was in a few moments to overwhelm me, and extinguish in horror and despair all fear of ignominy or death.

I must pause here; for it requires all my fortitude to recall the memory of the frightful events which I am about to relate, in proper detail, to my recollection.

Chapter IV

I was soon introduced into the presence of the magistrate, an old benevolent man, with calm and mild manners. He looked upon me, however, with some degree of severity; and then, turning towards my conductors, he asked who appeared as witnesses on this occasion.

About half a dozen men came forward; and one being selected by the magistrate, he deposed, that he had been out fishing the night before with his son and brother-in-law, Daniel Nugent, when, about ten o'clock, they observed a strong northerly blast rising, and they accordingly put in for port. It was a very dark night, as the moon had not yet risen; they did not land at the harbour, but, as they had been accustomed, at a creek about two miles below. He walked on first, carrying a part of the fishing tackle, and his companions followed him at some distance. As he was proceeding along the sands, he struck his foot against something, and fell all his length on the ground. His companions came to assist him; and, by the light of their lantern, they found that he had fallen on the body of a man, who was to all appearance dead. Their first supposition was, that it was the corpse of some person who had been drowned, and was thrown on shore by the waves; but, upon examination, they found that the clothes were not wet, and even that the body was not then cold. They instantly carried it to the cottage of an old woman near the spot, and endeavoured, but in vain, to restore it to life. He appeared to be a handsome young man, about five and twenty years of age. He had apparently been strangled; for there was no sign of any violence, except the black mark of fingers on his neck.

The first part of this deposition did not in the least interest me; but when the mark of the fingers was mentioned, I remembered the murder of my brother, and felt myself extremely agitated; my limbs trembled, and a mist came over my eyes, which obliged me to lean on a chair for support. The magistrate observed me with a keen eye, and of course drew an unfavourable augury from my manner.

The son confirmed his father's account: but when Daniel Nugent was called, he swore positively that, just before the fall of his companion, he saw a boat, with a single man in it, at a short distance from the shore; and, as far as he could judge by the light of a few stars, it was the same boat in which I had just landed.

A woman deposed, that she lived near the beach, and was standing at the door of her cottage, waiting for the return of the fishermen, about an hour before she heard of the discovery of the body, when she saw a boat, with only one man in it, push off from that part of the shore where the corpse was afterwards found.

Another woman confirmed the account of the fisherman having brought the body into her house; it was not cold. They put it into a bed, and rubbed it; and Daniel went to the town for an apothecary, but life was quite gone.

Several other men were examined concerning my landing; and they agreed, that, with the strong north wind that had arisen during the night, it was very probable that I had beaten about for many hours, and had been obliged to return nearly to the same spot from which I had departed. Besides, they observed that it appeared that I had brought the body from another place, and it was likely, that as I did not appear to know the shore, I might have put into the harbour ignorant of the distance of the town of ———— from the place where I had deposited the corpse.

Mr Kirwin, on hearing this evidence, desired that I should be taken into the room where the body lay for interment, that it might be observed what effect the sight of it would produce upon me. This idea was probably suggested by the extreme agitation I had exhibited when the mode of the murder had been described. I was accordingly conducted, by the magistrate and several other persons, to the inn. I could not help being struck by the strange coincidences that had taken place during this eventful night; but, knowing that I had been conversing with several persons in the island I had inhabited about the time that the body had been found, I was perfectly tranquil as to the consequences of the affair.

I entered the room where the corpse lay, and was led up to the coffin. How can I describe my sensations on beholding it? I feel yet parched with horror, nor can I reflect on that terrible moment without shuddering and agony, that faintly reminds me of the anguish of the recognition. The trial, the presence of the magistrate and witnesses, passed like a dream from my memory, when I saw the lifeless form of Henry Clerval stretched before me. I gasped for breath; and, throwing myself on the body, I exclaimed, "Have my murderous machinations deprived you also, my dearest Henry, of life? Two I have already destroyed; other victims await their destiny: but you, Clerval, my friend, my benefactor"—

The human frame could no longer support the agonizing suffering that I endured, and I was carried out of the room in strong convulsions.

A fever succeeded to this. I lay for two months on the point of death: my ravings, as I afterwards heard, were frightful; I called myself the murderer of William, of Justine, and of Clerval. Sometimes I entreated my attendants to assist me in the destruction of the fiend by whom I was tormented; and, at others, I felt the fingers of the monster already grasping my neck, and screamed aloud with agony and terror. Fortunately, as I spoke my native language, Mr Kirwin alone understood me; but my gestures and bitter cries were sufficient to affright the other witnesses.

Why did I not die? More miserable than man ever was before, why did I not sink into forgetfulness and rest? Death snatches away many blooming children, the only hopes of their doating parents: how many brides and youthful lovers have been one day in the bloom of health and hope, and the next a prey for worms and the decay of the tomb! Of what materials was I made, that I could thus resist so many shocks, which, like the turning of the wheel, continually renewed the torture.

But I was doomed to live; and, in two months, found myself as awaking from a dream, in a prison, stretched on a wretched bed, surrounded by gaolers, turnkeys, bolts, and all the miserable apparatus of a dungeon. It was morning, I remember, when I thus awoke to understanding: I had forgotten the particulars of what had happened, and only felt as if some great misfortune had suddenly overwhelmed me; but when I looked around, and saw the barred windows, and the squalidness of the room in which I was, all flashed across my memory, and I groaned bitterly.

This sound disturbed an old woman who was sleeping in a chair beside me. She was a hired nurse, the wife of one of the turnkeys, and her countenance expressed all those bad qualities which often characterize that class. The lines of her face were hard and rude, like that of persons accustomed to see without sympathizing in sights of misery. Her tone expressed her entire indifference; she addressed me in English, and the voice struck me as one that I had heard during my sufferings:

"Are you better now, Sir?" said she.

I replied in the same language, with a feeble voice, "I believe I am; but if it be all true, if indeed I did not dream, I am sorry that I am still alive to feel this misery and horror."

"For that matter," replied the old woman, "if you mean about the gentleman you murdered, I believe that it were better for you if you were dead, for I fancy it will go hard with you; but you will be hung when the next sessions come on. However, that's none of my business, I am sent to nurse you, and get you well; I do my duty with a safe conscience, it were well if every body did the same."

I turned with loathing from the woman who could utter so unfeeling a speech to a person just saved, on the very edge of death; but I felt languid, and unable to reflect on all that had passed. The whole series of my life appeared to me as a dream; I sometimes doubted if indeed it were all true, for it never presented itself to my mind with the force of reality.

As the images that floated before me became more distinct, I grew feverish; a darkness pressed around me; no one was near me who soothed me with the gentle voice of love; no dear hand supported me. The physician came and prescribed medicines, and the old woman prepared them for me; but utter carelessness was visible in the first, and the expression of brutality was strongly marked in the visage of the second. Who could be interested in the fate of a murderer, but the hangman who would gain his fee?

These were my first reflections; but I soon learned that Mr Kirwin had shewn me extreme kindness. He had caused the best room in the prison to be prepared for me (wretched indeed was the best); and it was he who had provided a physician and a nurse. It is true, he seldom came to see me; for, although he ardently desired to relieve the sufferings of every human creature, he did not wish to be present at the agonies and miserable ravings of a murderer. He came, therefore, sometimes to see that I was not neglected; but his visits were short, and at long intervals.

One day, when I was gradually recovering, I was seated in a chair, my eyes half open, and my cheeks livid like those in death, I was overcome by gloom and misery, and often reflected I had better seek death than remain miserably pent up only to be let loose in a world replete with wretchedness. At one time I considered whether I should not declare myself guilty, and suffer the penalty of the law, less innocent than poor Justine had been. Such were my thoughts, when the door of my apartment was opened, and Mr Kirwin entered. His countenance expressed sympathy and compassion; he drew a chair close to mine, and addressed me in French—

"I fear that this place is very shocking to you; can I do any thing to make you more comfortable?"

"I thank you; but all that you mention is nothing to me: on the whole earth there is no comfort which I am capable of receiving."

"I know that the sympathy of a stranger can be but of little relief to one borne down as you are by so strange a misfortune. But you will, I hope, soon quit this melancholy abode; for, doubtless, evidence can easily be brought to free you from the criminal charge."

"That is my least concern: I am, by a course of strange events, become the most miserable of mortals. Persecuted and tortured as I am and have been, can death be any evil to me?"

"Nothing indeed could be more unfortunate and agonizing than the strange chances that have lately occurred. You were thrown, by some surprising accident, on this shore, renowned for its hospitality; seized immediately, and charged with murder. The first sight that was presented to your eyes was the body of your friend, murdered in so unaccountable a manner, and placed, as it were, by some fiend across your path."

As Mr Kirwin said this, notwithstanding the agitation I endured on this retrospect of my sufferings, I also felt considerable surprise at the knowledge he seemed to possess concerning me. I suppose some astonishment was exhibited in my countenance; for Mr Kirwin hastened to say—

"It was not until a day or two after your illness that I thought of examining your dress, that I might discover some trace by which I could send to your relations an account of your misfortune and illness. I found several letters, and, among others, one which I discovered from its commencement to be from your father. I instantly wrote to Geneva: nearly two months have elapsed since the departure of my letter.—But you are ill; even now you tremble: you are unfit for agitation of any kind."

"This suspense is a thousand times worse than the most horrible event: tell me what new scene of death has been acted, and whose murder I am now to lament."

"Your family is perfectly well," said Mr Kirwin, with gentleness; "and some one, a friend, is come to visit you."

I know not by what chain of thought the idea presented itself, but it instantly darted into my mind that the murderer had come to mock at my misery, and taunt me with the death of Clerval, as a new incitement for me to comply with his hellish desires. I put my hand before my eyes, and cried out in agony—

"Oh! take him away! I cannot see him; for God's sake, do not let him enter!"

Mr Kirwin regarded me with a troubled countenance. He could not help regarding my exclamation as a presumption of my guilt, and said, in rather a severe tone—

"I should have thought, young man, that the presence of your father would have been welcome, instead of inspiring such violent repugnance."

"My father!" cried I, while every feature and every muscle was relaxed from anguish to pleasure. "Is my father, indeed, come? How kind, how very kind. But where is he, why does he not hasten to me?"

My change of manner surprised and pleased the magistrate; perhaps he thought that my former exclamation was a momentary return of delirium, and now he instantly resumed his former benevolence. He rose, and quitted the room with my nurse, and in a moment my father entered it.

Nothing, at this moment, could have given me greater pleasure than the arrival of my father. I stretched out my hand to him, and cried—

"Are you then safe—and Elizabeth—and Ernest?"

My father calmed me with assurances of their welfare, and endeavoured, by dwelling on these subjects so interesting to my heart, to raise my desponding spirits; but he soon felt that a prison cannot be the abode of cheerfulness. "What a place is this that you inhabit, my son!" said he, looking mournfully at the barred windows, and wretched appearance of the room. "You travelled to seek happiness, but a fatality seems to pursue you. And poor Clerval—"

The name of my unfortunate and murdered friend was an agitation too great to be endured in my weak state; I shed tears.

"Alas! yes, my father," replied I; "some destiny of the most horrible kind hangs over me, and I must live to fulfil it, or surely I should have died on the coffin of Henry."

We were not allowed to converse for any length of time, for the precarious state of my health rendered every precaution necessary that could insure tranquillity. Mr Kirwin came in, and insisted that my strength should not be exhausted by too much exertion. But the appearance of my father was to me like that of my good angel, and I gradually recovered my health.

As my sickness quitted me, I was absorbed by a gloomy and black melancholy, that nothing could dissipate. The image of Clerval was for ever before me, ghastly and murdered. More than once the agitation into which these reflections threw me made my friends dread a dangerous relapse. Alas! why did they preserve so miserable and detested a life? It was surely that I might fulfil my destiny, which is now drawing to a close. Soon, oh, very soon, will death extinguish these throbbings, and relieve me from the mighty weight of anguish that bears me to the dust; and, in executing the award of justice, I shall also sink to rest. Then the appearance of death was distant, although the wish was ever present to my thoughts; and I often sat for hours motionless and speechless, wishing for some mighty revolution that might bury me and my destroyer in its ruins.

The season of the assizes[1] approached. I had already been three months in prison; and although I was still weak, and in continual danger of a relapse, I was obliged to travel nearly a hundred miles to the county-town, where the court was held. Mr Kirwin charged himself with every care of collecting witnesses, and arranging my defence. I was spared the disgrace of appearing publicly as a criminal, as the case was not brought before the court that decides on life and death. The grand jury rejected the bill, on its being proved that I was on the Orkney Islands at the hour the body of my friend was found, and a fortnight after my removal I was liberated from prison.

My father was enraptured on finding me freed from the vexations of a criminal charge, that I was again allowed to breathe the fresh atmosphere, and allowed to return to my native country. I did not participate in these feelings; for to me the walls of a dungeon or a palace were alike hateful. The cup of life was poisoned for ever; and although the sun shone upon me, as upon the happy and gay of heart, I saw around me nothing but a dense and frightful darkness, penetrated by no light but the glimmer of two eyes that glared upon me. Sometimes they were the expressive eyes of Henry, languishing in death, the dark orbs nearly covered by the lids, and the long black lashes that fringed them; sometimes it was the watery clouded eyes of the monster, as I first saw them in my chamber at Ingolstadt.

My father tried to awaken in me the feelings of affection. He talked of Geneva, which I should soon visit—of Elizabeth, and Ernest; but these words only drew deep groans from me. Sometimes, indeed, I felt a wish for happiness; and thought, with melancholy delight, of my beloved cousin; or longed, with a devouring *maladie du pays*,[2] to see once more the blue lake and rapid Rhone, that had been so dear to me in early childhood: but my general state of feeling was a torpor, in which a prison was as welcome a residence as the divinest scene in nature; and these fits were seldom interrupted, but by paroxysms of anguish and despair. At these moments I often endeavoured to put an end to the existence I loathed; and it required unceasing attendance and vigilance to restrain me from committing some dreadful act of violence.

[1] County-court sessions.
[2] French: homesickness.

I remember, as I quitted the prison, I heard one of the men say, "He may be innocent of the murder, but he has certainly a bad conscience." These words struck me. A bad conscience! yes, surely I had one. William, Justine, and Clerval, had died through my infernal machinations; "And whose death," cried I, "is to finish the tragedy? Ah! my father, do not remain in this wretched country; take me where I may forget myself, my existence, and all the world."

My father easily acceded to my desire; and, after having taken leave of Mr Kirwin, we hastened to Dublin. I felt as if I was relieved from a heavy weight, when the packet sailed with a fair wind from Ireland, and I had quitted for ever the country which had been to me the scene of so much misery.[3]

It was midnight. My father slept in the cabin; and I lay on the deck, looking at the stars, and listening to the dashing of the waves. I hailed the darkness that shut Ireland from my sight, and my pulse beat with a feverish joy, when I reflected that I should soon see Geneva. The past appeared to me in the light of a frightful dream; yet the vessel in which I was, the wind that blew me from the detested shore of Ireland, and the sea which surrounded me, told me too forcibly that I was deceived by no vision, and that Clerval, my friend and dearest companion, had fallen a victim to me and the monster of my creation. I repassed, in my memory, my whole life; my quiet happiness while residing with my family in Geneva, the death of my mother, and my departure for Ingolstadt. I remembered shuddering at the mad enthusiasm that hurried me on to the creation of my hideous enemy, and I called to mind the night during which he first lived. I was unable to pursue the train of thought; a thousand feelings pressed upon me, and I wept bitterly.

Ever since my recovery from the fever I had been in the custom of taking every night a small quantity of laudanum;[4] for it was by means of this drug only that I was enabled to gain the rest necessary for the preservation of life. Oppressed by the recollection of my various misfortunes, I now took a double dose, and soon slept profoundly. But sleep did not afford me respite from thought and misery; my dreams presented a thousand objects that scared me.

[3]For the 1831 revision, giving much more emphasis to Victor's desire to return home to protect his family, see p. 206.

[4]First used by Paracelsus, this is opium dissolved in alcohol, a powerful painkiller, sedative, and psychadelic agent.

Towards morning I was possessed by a kind of nightmare;[5] I felt the fiend's grasp in my neck, and could not free myself from it; groans and cries rung in my ears. My father, who was watching over me, perceiving my restlessness, awoke me, and pointed to the port of Holyhead, which we were now entering.[6]

Chapter V

We had resolved not to go to London, but to cross the country to Portsmouth, and thence to embark for Havre. I preferred this plan principally because I dreaded to see again those places in which I had enjoyed a few moments of tranquillity with my beloved Clerval. I thought with horror of seeing again those persons whom we had been accustomed to visit together, and who might make inquiries concerning an event, the very remembrance of which made me again feel the pang I endured when I gazed on his lifeless form in the inn at ——————.

As for my father, his desires and exertions were bounded to the again[1] seeing me restored to health and peace of mind. His tenderness and attentions were unremitting; my grief and gloom was obstinate, but he would not despair. Sometimes he thought that I felt deeply the degradation of being obliged to answer a charge of murder, and he endeavoured to prove to me the futility of pride.[2]

"Alas! my father," said I, "how little do you know me. Human beings, their feelings and passions, would indeed be degraded, if such a wretch as I felt pride. Justine, poor unhappy Justine, was as innocent as I, and she suffered the same charge; she died for it; and I am the cause of this—I murdered her. William, Justine, and Henry—they all died by my hands."

My father had often, during my imprisonment, heard me make the same assertion; when I thus accused myself, he sometimes seemed to desire an explanation, and at others he appeared to consider it as caused by delirium, and that, during my illness, some idea of this kind had presented itself to my imagination, the remembrance of which I preserved

---

[5]In its original meaning, an evil spirit that attacked during sleep.

[6]For the 1831 additions to this paragraph, on Victor's renewed longing for forgetfulness, see p. 207.

---

[1]"again" is an adjective.

[2]For the expansion of Victor's anguish in 1831, see p. 207.

in my convalescence. I avoided explanation, and maintained a continual silence concerning the wretch I had created. I had a feeling that I should be supposed mad, and this for ever chained my tongue,[3] when I would have given the whole world to have confided the fatal secret.

Upon this occasion my father said, with an expression of unbounded wonder, "What do you mean, Victor? are you mad? My dear son, I entreat you never to make such an assertion again."

"I am not mad," I cried energetically; "the sun and the heavens, who have viewed my operations, can bear witness of my truth. I am the assassin of those most innocent victims; they died by my machinations. A thousand times would I have shed my own blood, drop by drop, to have saved their lives; but I could not, my father, indeed I could not sacrifice the whole human race."

The conclusion of this speech convinced my father that my ideas were deranged, and he instantly changed the subject of our conversation, and endeavoured to alter the course of my thoughts. He wished as much as possible to obliterate the memory of the scenes that had taken place in Ireland, and never alluded to them, or suffered me to speak of my misfortunes.

As time passed away I became more calm: misery had her dwelling in my heart, but I no longer talked in the same incoherent manner of my own crimes; sufficient for me was the consciousness of them. By the utmost self-violence, I curbed the imperious voice of wretchedness, which sometimes desired to declare itself to the whole world; and my manners were calmer and more composed than they had ever been since my journey to the sea of ice.[4]

We arrived at Havre on the 8th of May, and instantly proceeded to Paris, where my father had some business which detained us a few weeks. In this city, I received the following letter from Elizabeth:—

To VICTOR FRANKENSTEIN.

My Dearest Friend,

It gave me the greatest pleasure to receive a letter from my uncle dated at Paris; you are no longer at a formidable distance, and I may hope to see you in less than a fortnight. My poor cousin, how much

---

[3]For new sentences in 1831 on Victor's secret anguish, see p. 207.

[4]*Mer de glace*: the glacier descending from Mont Blanc, where Victor reencountered his Creature.

you must have suffered! I expect to see you looking even more ill than when you quitted Geneva. This winter has been passed most miserably, tortured as I have been by anxious suspense; yet I hope to see peace in your countenance, and to find that your heart is not totally devoid of comfort and tranquillity.

Yet I fear that the same feelings now exist that made you so miserable a year ago, even perhaps augmented by time. I would not disturb you at this period, when so many misfortunes weigh upon you; but a conversation that I had with my uncle previous to his departure renders some explanation necessary before we meet.

Explanation! you may possibly say; what can Elizabeth have to explain? If you really say this, my questions are answered, and I have no more to do than to sign myself your affectionate cousin. But you are distant from me, and it is possible that you may dread, and yet be pleased with this explanation; and, in a probability of this being the case, I dare not any longer postpone writing what, during your absence, I have often wished to express to you, but have never had the courage to begin.

You well know, Victor, that our union had been the favourite plan of your parents even since our infancy. We were told this when young, and taught to look forward to it as an event that would certainly take place. We were affectionate playfellows during childhood, and, I believe, dear and valued friends to one another as we grew older. But as brother and sister often entertain a lively affection towards each other, without desiring a more intimate union, may not such also be our case? Tell me, dearest Victor. Answer me, I conjure you, by our mutual happiness, with simple truth—do you not love another?

You have travelled; you have spent several years of your life at Ingolstadt; and I confess to you, my friend, that when I saw you last autumn so unhappy, flying to solitude, from the society of every creature, I could not help supposing that you might regret our connexion, and believe yourself bound in honour to fulfil the wishes of your parents, although they opposed themselves to your inclinations. But this is false reasoning. I confess to you, my cousin, that I love you, and that in my airy dreams of futurity you have been my constant friend and companion. But it is your happiness I desire as well as my own, when I declare to you, that our marriage would render me eternally miserable, unless it were the dictate of your own free choice. Even now I weep to think, that, borne down as you are by the cruelest misfortunes, you may stifle, by the word *honour*, all hope of that love and happiness which would alone restore you to yourself. I, who have so interested an affection for you, may increase your miseries ten-fold, by being an obstacle to your wishes. Ah, Victor, be assured that your cousin and playmate has too sincere a love for you not to be made miserable by this supposition. Be happy, my friend; and if you obey me in this one request, remain satisfied that nothing on earth will have the power to interrupt my tranquillity.

Do not let this letter disturb you; do not answer it to-morrow, or the next day, or even until you come, if it will give you pain. My uncle will send me news of your health; and if I see but one smile on your lips when we meet, occasioned by this or any other exertion of mine, I shall need no other happiness.

ELIZABETH LAVENZA.
Geneva, May 18th, 17—.

This letter revived in my memory what I had before forgotten, the threat of the fiend—"*I will be with you on your wedding-night!*" Such was my sentence, and on that night would the daemon employ every art to destroy me, and tear me from the glimpse of happiness which promised partly to console my sufferings. On that night he had determined to consummate his crimes by my death. Well, be it so; a deadly struggle would then assuredly take place, in which if he was victorious, I should be at peace, and his power over me be at an end. If he were vanquished, I should be a free man. Alas! what freedom? such as the peasant enjoys when his family have been massacred before his eyes, his cottage burnt, his lands laid waste, and he is turned adrift, homeless, pennyless, and alone, but free. Such would be my liberty, except that in my Elizabeth I possessed a treasure; alas! balanced by those horrors of remorse and guilt, which would pursue me until death.

Sweet and beloved Elizabeth! I read and re-read her letter, and some softened feelings stole into my heart, and dared to whisper paradisaical dreams of love and joy; but the apple was already eaten, and the angel's arm bared to drive me from all hope.[5] Yet I would die to make her happy. If the monster executed his threat, death was inevitable; yet, again, I considered whether my marriage

---

[5]An allusion to the expulsion from Eden. See Genesis 3.24 and *Paradise Lost* 12.632–44.

would hasten my fate. My destruction might indeed arrive a few months sooner; but if my torturer should suspect that I postponed it, influenced by his menaces, he would surely find other, and perhaps more dreadful means of revenge. He had vowed *to be with me on my wedding-night,* yet he did not consider that threat as binding him to peace in the mean time; for, as if to shew me that he was not yet satiated with blood, he had murdered Clerval immediately after the enunciation of his threats. I resolved, therefore, that if my immediate union with my cousin would conduce either to her's or my father's happiness, my adversary's designs against my life should not retard it a single hour.

In this state of mind I wrote to Elizabeth. My letter was calm and affectionate. "I fear, my beloved girl," I said, "little happiness remains for us on earth; yet all that I may one day enjoy is concentered in you. Chase away your idle fears; to you alone do I consecrate my life, and my endeavours for contentment. I have one secret, Elizabeth, a dreadful one; when revealed to you, it will chill your frame with horror, and then, far from being surprised at my misery, you will only wonder that I survive what I have endured. I will confide this tale of misery and terror to you the day after our marriage shall take place; for, my sweet cousin, there must be perfect confidence between us. But until then, I conjure you, do not mention or allude to it. This I most earnestly entreat, and I know you will comply."

In about a week after the arrival of Elizabeth's letter, we returned to Geneva. My cousin welcomed me with warm affection; yet tears were in her eyes, as she beheld my emaciated frame and feverish cheeks. I saw a change in her also. She was thinner, and had lost much of that heavenly vivacity that had before charmed me; but her gentleness, and soft looks of compassion, made her a more fit companion for one blasted and miserable as I was.

The tranquillity which I now enjoyed did not endure. Memory brought madness with it; and when I thought on what had passed, a real insanity possessed me; sometimes I was furious, and burnt with rage, sometimes low and despondent. I neither spoke or looked, but sat motionless, bewildered by the multitude of miseries that overcame me.

Elizabeth alone had the power to draw me from these fits; her gentle voice would soothe me when transported by passion, and inspire me with human feelings when sunk in torpor. She wept with me, and for me. When reason returned, she would remonstrate, and endeavour to inspire me with resignation. Ah! it is well for the unfortunate to be resigned, but for the guilty there is no peace. The agonies of remorse poison the luxury there is otherwise sometimes found in indulging the excess of grief.

Soon after my arrival my father spoke of my immediate marriage with my cousin. I remained silent.

"Have you, then, some other attachment?"

"None on earth. I love Elizabeth, and look forward to our union with delight. Let the day therefore be fixed; and on it I will consecrate myself, in life or death, to the happiness of my cousin."

"My dear Victor, do not speak thus. Heavy misfortunes have befallen us; but let us only cling closer to what remains, and transfer our love for those whom we have lost to those who yet live. Our circle will be small, but bound close by the ties of affection and mutual misfortune. And when time shall have softened your despair, new and dear objects of care will be born to replace those of whom we have been so cruelly deprived."

Such were the lessons of my father. But to me the remembrance of the threat returned: nor can you wonder, that, omnipotent as the fiend had yet been in his deeds of blood, I should almost regard him as invincible; and that when he had pronounced the words, "*I shall be with you on your wedding-night,*" I should regard the threatened fate as unavoidable. But death was no evil to me, if the loss of Elizabeth were balanced with it; and I therefore, with a contented and even cheerful countenance, agreed with my father, that if my cousin would consent, the ceremony should take place in ten days, and thus put, as I imagined, the seal to my fate.

Great God! if for one instant I had thought what might be the hellish intention of my fiendish adversary, I would rather have banished myself for ever from my native country, and wandered a friendless outcast over the earth, than have consented to this miserable marriage. But, as if possessed of magic powers, the monster had blinded me to his real intentions; and when I thought that I prepared only my own death, I hastened that of a far dearer victim.

As the period fixed for our marriage drew nearer, whether from cowardice or a prophetic feeling, I felt my heart sink within me. But I concealed my feelings by an appearance of hilarity, that brought smiles and joy to the countenance of my father, but hardly deceived the ever-watchful and nicer eye of Elizabeth. She looked forward to our union with placid contentment, not unmingled with a little fear, which past misfortunes had impressed, that what now appeared certain and tangible happiness, might soon dissipate into an airy dream, and leave no trace but deep and everlasting regret.

Preparations were made for the event; congratulatory visits were received; and all wore a smiling appearance. I shut up, as well as I could, in my own heart the anxiety that preyed there, and entered with seeming earnestness into the plans of my father, although they might only serve as the decorations of my tragedy. A house was purchased for us near Cologny, by which we should enjoy the pleasures of the country, and yet be so near Geneva as to see my father every day; who would still reside within the walls, for the benefit of Ernest, that he might follow his studies at the schools.[6]

In the mean time I took every precaution to defend my person, in case the fiend should openly attack me. I carried pistols and a dagger constantly about me, and was ever on the watch to prevent artifice; and by these means gained a greater degree of tranquillity. Indeed, as the period approached, the threat appeared more as a delusion, not to be regarded as worthy to disturb my peace, while the happiness I hoped for in my marriage wore a greater appearance of certainty, as the day fixed for its solemnization drew nearer, and I heard it continually spoken of as an occurrence which no accident could possibly prevent.

Elizabeth seemed happy; my tranquil demeanour contributed greatly to calm her mind. But on the day that was to fulfil my wishes and my destiny, she was melancholy, and a presentiment of evil pervaded her; and perhaps also she thought of the dreadful secret, which I had promised to reveal to her the following day. My father was in the mean time overjoyed, and, in the bustle of preparation, only observed in the melancholy of his niece the diffidence of a bride.

After the ceremony was performed, a large party assembled at my father's; but it was agreed that Elizabeth and I should pass the afternoon and night at Evian, and return to Cologny the next morning. As the day was fair, and the wind favourable, we resolved to go by water.

Those were the last moments of my life during which I enjoyed the feeling of happiness. We passed rapidly along: the sun was hot,

---

[6]In the 1831 version, Alphonse gets the Austrian government to restore Villa Lavenza, on the shores of Lake Como, to Elizabeth, and the newlyweds agree to honeymoon there.

but we were sheltered from its rays by a kind of canopy, while we enjoyed the beauty of the scene, sometimes on one side of the lake, where we saw Mont Salêve, the pleasant banks of Montalêgre, and at a distance, surmounting all, the beautiful Mont Blânc, and the assemblage of snowy mountains that in vain endeavour to emulate her; sometimes coasting the opposite banks, we saw the mighty Jura opposing its dark side to the ambition that would quit its native country, and an almost insurmountable barrier to the invader who should wish to enslave it.[7]

I took the hand of Elizabeth: "You are sorrowful, my love. Ah! if you knew what I have suffered, and what I may yet endure, you would endeavour to let me taste the quiet, and freedom from despair, that this one day at least permits me to enjoy."

"Be happy, my dear Victor," replied Elizabeth; "there is, I hope, nothing to distress you; and be assured that if a lively joy is not painted in my face, my heart is contented. Something whispers to me not to depend too much on the prospect that is opened before us; but I will not listen to such a sinister voice. Observe how fast we move along, and how the clouds which sometimes obscure, and sometimes rise above the dome of Mont Blânc, render this scene of beauty still more interesting. Look also at the innumerable fish that are swimming in the clear waters, where we can distinguish every pebble that lies at the bottom. What a divine day! how happy and serene all nature appears!"

Thus Elizabeth endeavoured to divert her thoughts and mine from all reflection upon melancholy subjects. But her temper was fluctuating; joy for a few instants shone in her eyes, but it continually gave place to distraction and reverie.

The sun sunk lower in the heavens; we passed the river Drance, and observed its path through the chasms of the higher, and the glens of the lower hills. The Alps here come closer to the lake, and we approached the amphitheatre of mountains which forms its eastern boundary. The spire of Evian shone under the woods that surrounded it, and the range of mountain above mountain by which it was overhung.

The wind, which had hitherto carried us along with amazing rapidity, sunk at sunset to a light breeze; the soft air just ruffled the water, and caused a pleasant motion among the trees as we approached

[7]Napoleon invaded Switzerland in 1798, another shock for sympathizers with the French Revolution.

the shore, from which it wafted the most delightful scent of flowers and hay. The sun sunk beneath the horizon as we landed; and as I touched the shore, I felt those cares and fears revive, which soon were to clasp me, and cling to me for ever.

Chapter VI

It was eight o'clock when we landed; we walked for a short time on the shore, enjoying the transitory light, and then retired to the inn, and contemplated the lovely scene of waters, woods, and mountains, obscured in darkness, yet still displaying their black outlines.

The wind, which had fallen in the south, now rose with great violence in the west. The moon had reached her summit in the heavens, and was beginning to descend; the clouds swept across it swifter than the flight of the vulture, and dimmed her rays, while the lake reflected the scene of the busy heavens, rendered still busier by the restless waves that were beginning to rise. Suddenly a heavy storm of rain descended.

I had been calm during the day; but so soon as night obscured the shapes of objects, a thousand fears arose in my mind. I was anxious and watchful, while my right hand grasped a pistol which was hidden in my bosom; every sound terrified me; but I resolved that I would sell my life dearly, and not relax[1] the impending conflict until my own life, or that of my adversary, were extinguished.

Elizabeth observed my agitation for some time in timid and fearful silence; at length she said, "What is it that agitates you, my dear Victor? What is it you fear?"

"Oh! peace, peace, my love," replied I, "this night, and all will be safe: but this night is dreadful, very dreadful."

I passed an hour in this state of mind, when suddenly I reflected how dreadful the combat which I momentarily expected would be to my wife, and I earnestly entreated her to retire, resolving not to join her until I had obtained some knowledge as to the situation of my enemy.

She left me, and I continued some time walking up and down the passages of the house, and inspecting every corner that might afford a retreat to my adversary. But I discovered no trace of him, and was beginning to conjecture that some fortunate chance had

---

[1] 1831] shrink from

intervened to prevent the execution of his menaces; when suddenly I heard a shrill and dreadful scream. It came from the room into which Elizabeth had retired. As I heard it, the whole truth rushed into my mind, my arms dropped, the motion of every muscle and fibre was suspended; I could feel the blood trickling in my veins, and tingling in the extremities of my limbs. This state lasted but for an instant; the scream was repeated, and I rushed into the room.

Great God! why did I not then expire! Why am I here to relate the destruction of the best hope, and the purest creature of earth. She was there, lifeless and inanimate, thrown across the bed, her head hanging down, and her pale and distorted features half covered by her hair. Every where I turn I see the same figure—her bloodless arms and relaxed form flung by the murderer on its bridal bier.[2] Could I behold this, and live? Alas! life is obstinate, and clings closest where it is most hated. For a moment only did I lose recollection; I fainted.

When I recovered, I found myself surrounded by the people of the inn; their countenances expressed a breathless terror: but the horror of others appeared only as a mockery, a shadow of the feelings that oppressed me. I escaped from them to the room where lay the body of Elizabeth, my love, my wife, so lately living, so dear, so worthy. She had been moved from the posture in which I had first beheld her; and now, as she lay, her head upon her arm, and a handkerchief thrown across her face and neck, I might have supposed her asleep. I rushed towards her, and embraced her with ardour; but the deathly languor and coldness of the limbs told me, that what I now held in my arms had ceased to be the Elizabeth whom I had loved and cherished. The murderous mark of the fiend's grasp was on her neck, and the breath had ceased to issue from her lips.

While I still hung over her in the agony of despair, I happened to look up. The windows of the room had before been darkened; and I felt a kind of panic on seeing the pale yellow light of the moon illuminate the chamber. The shutters had been thrown back; and, with a sensation of horror not to be described, I saw at the open window a figure the most hideous and abhorred. A grin was on the face of the monster; he seemed to jeer, as with his fiendish finger he pointed towards the corpse of my wife. I rushed towards the window, and

---

[2]Shelley describes Elizabeth's corpse in the pose of *The Nightmare*, the famous painting by Henry Fuseli represented on our cover.

drawing a pistol from my bosom, shot; but he eluded me, leaped from his station, and, running with the swiftness of lightning, plunged into the lake.

The report of the pistol brought a crowd into the room. I pointed to the spot where he had disappeared, and we followed the track with boats; nets were cast, but in vain. After passing several hours, we returned hopeless, most of my companions believing it to have been a form conjured by my fancy. After having landed, they proceeded to search the country, parties going in different directions among the woods and vines.

I did not accompany them; I was exhausted: a film covered my eyes, and my skin was parched with the heat of fever. In this state I lay on a bed, hardly conscious of what had happened; my eyes wandered round the room, as if to seek something that I had lost.

At length I remembered that my father would anxiously expect the return of Elizabeth and myself, and that I must return alone. This reflection brought tears into my eyes, and I wept for a long time; but my thoughts rambled to various subjects, reflecting on my misfortunes, and their cause. I was bewildered in a cloud of wonder and horror. The death of William, the execution of Justine, the murder of Clerval, and lastly of my wife; even at that moment I knew not that my only remaining friends were safe from the malignity of the fiend; my father even now might be writhing under his grasp, and Ernest might be dead at his feet. This idea made me shudder, and recalled me to action. I started up, and resolved to return to Geneva with all possible speed.

There were no horses to be procured, and I must return by the lake; but the wind was unfavourable, and the rain fell in torrents. However, it was hardly morning, and I might reasonably hope to arrive by night. I hired men to row, and took an oar myself, for I had always experienced relief from mental torment in bodily exercise. But the overflowing misery I now felt, and the excess of agitation that I endured, rendered me incapable of any exertion. I threw down the oar; and, leaning my head upon my hands, gave way to every gloomy idea that arose. If I looked up, I saw the scenes which were familiar to me in my happier time, and which I had contemplated but the day before in the company of her who was now but a shadow and a recollection. Tears streamed from my eyes. The rain had ceased for a moment, and I saw the fish play in the waters as they had done a few hours before; they had then been observed by Elizabeth. Nothing is so painful to the human mind as a great and sudden change. The sun might shine, or the clouds might lour; but nothing could appear to me as it had done the day before. A fiend had snatched from me every hope of future happiness: no creature had ever been so miserable as I was; so frightful an event is single in the history of man.

But why should I dwell upon the incidents that followed this last overwhelming event. Mine has been a tale of horrors; I have reached their *acme,* and what I must now relate can but be tedious to you. Know that, one by one, my friends were snatched away; I was left desolate. My own strength is exhausted; and I must tell, in a few words, what remains of my hideous narration.

I arrived at Geneva. My father and Ernest yet lived; but the former sunk under the tidings that I bore. I see him now, excellent and venerable old man! his eyes wandered in vacancy, for they had lost their charm and their delight—his niece, his more than daughter, whom he doated on with all that affection which a man feels, who, in the decline of life, having few affections, clings more earnestly to those that remain. Cursed, cursed be the fiend that brought misery on his grey hairs, and doomed him to waste in wretchedness! He could not live under the horrors that were accumulated around him; an apoplectic fit was brought on, and in a few days he died in my arms.

What then became of me? I know not; I lost sensation, and chains and darkness were the only objects that pressed upon me. Sometimes, indeed, I dreamt that I wandered in flowery meadows and pleasant vales with the friends of my youth; but awoke, and found myself in a dungeon. Melancholy followed, but by degrees I gained a clear conception of my miseries and situation, and was then released from my prison. For they had called me mad; and during many months, as I understood, a solitary cell had been my habitation.

But liberty had been a useless gift to me had I not, as I awakened to reason, at the same time awakened to revenge. As the memory of past misfortunes pressed upon me, I began to reflect on their cause— the monster whom I had created, the miserable daemon whom I had sent abroad into the world for my destruction. I was possessed by a maddening rage when I thought of him, and desired and ardently prayed that I might have him within my grasp to wreak a great and signal revenge on his cursed head.

Nor did my hate long confine itself to useless wishes; I began to reflect on the best means of securing him; and for this purpose, about a month after my release, I repaired to a criminal judge in the town, and told him that I had an accusation to make; that I knew the destroyer of my family; and that I required him to exert his whole authority for the apprehension of the murderer.

The magistrate listened to me with attention and kindness: "Be assured, sir," said he, "no pains or exertions on my part shall be spared to discover the villain."

"I thank you," replied I; "listen, therefore, to the deposition that I have to make. It is indeed a tale so strange, that I should fear you would not credit it, were there not something in truth which, however wonderful, forces conviction. The story is too connected to be mistaken for a dream, and I have no motive for falsehood." My manner, as I thus addressed him, was impressive, but calm; I had formed in my own heart a resolution to pursue my destroyer to death; and this purpose quieted my agony, and provisionally reconciled me to life. I now related my history briefly, but with firmness and precision, marking the dates with accuracy, and never deviating into invective or exclamation.

The magistrate appeared at first perfectly incredulous, but as I continued he became more attentive and interested; I saw him sometimes shudder with horror, at others a lively surprise, unmingled with disbelief, was painted on his countenance.

When I had concluded my narration, I said, "This is the being whom I accuse, and for whose detection and punishment I call upon you to exert your whole power. It is your duty as a magistrate, and I believe and hope that your feelings as a man will not revolt from the execution of those functions on this occasion."

This address caused a considerable change in the physiognomy of my auditor. He had heard my story with that half kind of belief that is given to a tale of spirits and supernatural events; but when he was called upon to act officially in consequence, the whole tide of his incredulity returned. He, however, answered mildly, "I would willingly afford you every aid in your pursuit; but the creature of whom you speak appears to have powers which would put all my exertions to defiance. Who can follow an animal which can traverse the sea of ice, and inhabit caves and dens, where no man would venture to intrude? Besides, some months have elapsed since the commission of his crimes, and no one can conjecture to what place he has wandered, or what region he may now inhabit."

"I do not doubt that he hovers near the spot which I inhabit; and if he has indeed taken refuge in the Alps, he may be hunted like the chamois,[3] and destroyed as a beast of prey. But I perceive your thoughts: you do not credit my narrative, and do not intend to pursue my enemy with the punishment which is his desert."

As I spoke, rage sparkled in my eyes; the magistrate was intimidated; "You are mistaken," said he, "I will exert myself; and if it is in my power to seize the monster, be assured that he shall suffer punishment proportionate to his crimes. But I fear, from what you have yourself described to be his properties, that this will prove impracticable, and that, while every proper measure is pursued, you should endeavour to make up your mind to disappointment."

"That cannot be; but all that I can say will be of little avail. My revenge is of no moment to you; yet, while I allow it to be a vice, I confess that it is the devouring and only passion of my soul. My rage is unspeakable, when I reflect that the murderer, whom I have turned loose upon society, still exists. You refuse my just demand: I have but one resource; and I devote myself, either in my life or death, to his destruction."

I trembled with excess of agitation as I said this; there was a phrenzy in my manner, and something, I doubt not, of that haughty fierceness, which the martyrs of old are said to have possessed. But to a Genevan magistrate, whose mind was occupied by far other ideas than those of devotion and heroism, this elevation of mind had much the appearance of madness. He endeavoured to soothe me as a nurse does a child, and reverted to my tale as the effects of delirium.

"Man," I cried, "how ignorant art thou in thy pride of wisdom! Cease; you know not what it is you say."

I broke from the house angry and disturbed, and retired to meditate on some other mode of action.

Chapter VII

My present situation was one in which all voluntary thought was swallowed up and lost. I was hurried away by fury; revenge alone endowed me with strength and composure; it modelled my feelings, and allowed me to be calculating and calm, at periods when otherwise delirium or death would have been my portion.

---

[3]Small mountain antelope.

My first resolution was to quit Geneva for ever; my country, which, when I was happy and beloved, was dear to me, now, in my adversity, became hateful. I provided myself with a sum of money, together with a few jewels which had belonged to my mother, and departed.

And now my wanderings began, which are to cease but with life. I have traversed a vast portion of the earth, and have endured all the hardships which travellers, in deserts and barbarous countries, are wont to meet. How I have lived I hardly know; many times have I stretched my failing limbs upon the sandy plain, and prayed for death. But revenge kept me alive; I dared not die, and leave my adversary in being.

When I quitted Geneva, my first labour was to gain some clue by which I might trace the steps of my fiendish enemy. But my plan was unsettled; and I wandered many hours around the confines of the town, uncertain what path I should pursue. As night approached, I found myself at the entrance of the cemetery where William, Elizabeth, and my father, reposed. I entered it, and approached the tomb which marked their graves. Every thing was silent, except the leaves of the trees, which were gently agitated by the wind; the night was nearly dark; and the scene would have been solemn and affecting even to an uninterested observer. The spirits of the departed seemed to flit around, and to cast a shadow, which was felt but seen not, around the head of the mourner.

The deep grief which this scene had at first excited quickly gave way to rage and despair. They were dead, and I lived; their murderer also lived, and to destroy him I must drag out my weary existence. I knelt on the grass, and kissed the earth, and with quivering lips exclaimed, "By the sacred earth on which I kneel, by the shades that wander near me, by the deep and eternal grief that I feel, I swear; and by thee, O Night, and by the spirits that preside over thee, I swear to pursue the daemon, who caused this misery, until he or I shall perish in mortal conflict. For this purpose I will preserve my life: to execute this dear revenge, will I again behold the sun, and tread the green herbage of earth, which otherwise should vanish from my eyes for ever. And I call on you, spirits of the dead; and on you, wandering ministers of vengeance, to aid and conduct me in my work. Let the cursed and hellish monster drink deep of agony; let him feel the despair that now torments me."

I had begun my adjuration with solemnity, and an awe which almost assured me that the shades of my murdered friends heard and approved my devotion; but the furies possessed me as I concluded, and rage choked my utterance.

I was answered through the stillness of night by a loud and fiendish laugh. It rung on my ears long and heavily; the mountains re-echoed it, and I felt as if all hell surrounded me with mockery and laughter. Surely in that moment I should have been possessed by phrenzy, and have destroyed my miserable existence, but that my vow was heard, and that I was reserved for vengeance. The laughter died away; when a well-known and abhorred voice, apparently close to my ear, addressed me in an audible whisper—"I am satisfied: miserable wretch! you have determined to live, and I am satisfied."

I darted towards the spot from which the sound proceeded; but the devil eluded my grasp. Suddenly the broad disk of the moon arose, and shone full upon his ghastly and distorted shape, as he fled with more than mortal speed.

I pursued him; and for many months this has been my task. Guided by a slight clue, I followed the windings of the Rhone, but vainly. The blue Mediterranean appeared; and, by a strange chance, I saw the fiend enter by night, and hide himself in a vessel bound for the Black Sea. I took my passage in the same ship; but he escaped, I know not how.

Amidst the wilds of Tartary and Russia, although he still evaded me, I have ever followed in his track. Sometimes the peasants, scared by this horrid apparition, informed me of his path; sometimes he himself, who feared that if I lost all trace I should despair and die, often left some mark to guide me. The snows descended on my head, and I saw the print of his huge step on the white plain. To you first entering on life, to whom care is new, and agony unknown, how can you understand what I have felt, and still feel? Cold, want, and fatigue, were the least pains which I was destined to endure; I was cursed by some devil, and carried about with me my eternal hell;[1] yet still a spirit of good followed and directed my steps, and, when I most murmured, would suddenly extricate me from seemingly insurmountable difficulties. Sometimes, when nature, overcome by hunger, sunk under the exhaustion, a repast was prepared for me in the desert, that restored and inspirited me. The fare was indeed coarse, such as the peasants of the country ate; but I may not doubt

---

[1]Echoing Satan, *Paradise Lost* 4.75 and 9.467.

that it was set there by the spirits that I had invoked to aid me. Often, when all was dry, the heavens cloudless, and I was parched by thirst, a slight cloud would bedim the sky, shed the few drops that revived me, and vanish.

I followed, when I could, the courses of the rivers; but the daemon generally avoided these, as it was here that the population of the country chiefly collected. In other places human beings were seldom seen; and I generally subsisted on the wild animals that crossed my path. I had money with me, and gained the friendship of the villagers by distributing it, or bringing with me some food that I had killed, which, after taking a small part, I always presented to those who had provided me with fire and utensils for cooking.

My life, as it passed thus, was indeed hateful to me, and it was during sleep alone that I could taste joy. O blessed sleep! often, when most miserable, I sank to repose, and my dreams lulled me even to rapture. The spirits that guarded me had provided these moments, or rather hours, of happiness, that I might retain strength to fulfil my pilgrimage. Deprived of this respite, I should have sunk under my hardships. During the day I was sustained and inspirited by the hope of night: for in sleep I saw my friends, my wife, and my beloved country; again I saw the benevolent countenance of my father, heard the silver tones of my Elizabeth's voice, and beheld Clerval enjoying health and youth. Often, when wearied by a toilsome march, I persuaded myself that I was dreaming until night should come, and that I should then enjoy reality in the arms of my dearest friends. What agonizing fondness did I feel for them! how did I cling to their dear forms, as sometimes they haunted even my waking hours, and persuade myself that they still lived! At such moments vengeance, that burned within me, died in my heart, and I pursued my path towards the destruction of the daemon, more as a task enjoined by heaven, as the mechanical impulse of some power of which I was unconscious, than as the ardent desire of my soul.

What his feelings were whom I pursued, I cannot know. Sometimes, indeed, he left marks in writing on the barks of the trees, or cut in stone, that guided me, and instigated my fury. "My reign is not yet over," (these words were legible in one of these inscriptions); "you live, and my power is complete. Follow me; I seek the everlasting ices of the north, where you will feel the misery of cold and frost, to which I am impassive. You will find near this place, if you follow not too tardily, a dead hare; eat, and be refreshed. Come on, my enemy; we have yet to wrestle for our lives; but many hard and miserable hours must you endure, until that period shall arrive."

Scoffing devil! Again do I vow vengeance; again do I devote thee, miserable fiend, to torture and death. Never will I omit my search, until he or I perish; and then with what ecstasy shall I join my Elizabeth, and those who even now prepare for me the reward of my tedious toil and horrible pilgrimage.

As I still pursued my journey to the northward, the snows thickened, and the cold increased in a degree almost too severe to support. The peasants were shut up in their hovels, and only a few of the most hardy ventured forth to seize the animals whom starvation had forced from their hiding-places to seek for prey. The rivers were covered with ice, and no fish could be procured; and thus I was cut off from my chief article of maintenance.

The triumph of my enemy increased with the difficulty of my labours. One inscription that he left was in these words: "Prepare! your toils only begin: wrap yourself in furs, and provide food, for we shall soon enter upon a journey where your sufferings will satisfy my everlasting hatred."

My courage and perseverance were invigorated by these scoffing words; I resolved not to fail in my purpose; and, calling on heaven to support me, I continued with unabated fervour to traverse immense deserts, until the ocean appeared at a distance, and formed the utmost boundary of the horizon. Oh! how unlike it was to the blue seas of the south! Covered with ice, it was only to be distinguished from land by its superior wildness and ruggedness. The Greeks wept for joy when they beheld the Mediterranean from the hills of Asia, and hailed with rapture the boundary of their toils.[2] I did not weep; but I knelt down, and, with a full heart, thanked my guiding spirit for conducting me in safety to the place where I hoped, notwithstanding my adversary's gibe, to meet and grapple with him.

Some weeks before this period I had procured a sledge and dogs, and thus traversed the snows with inconceivable speed. I know not whether the fiend possessed the same advantages; but I found that, as before I had daily lost ground in the pursuit, I now gained on him; so

---

[2]A famous incident recorded in Xenophon's *Anabasis*. In 400 B.C.E. Xenophon led his retreating army across the sea and through Armenia.

much so, that when I first saw the ocean, he was but one day's journey in advance, and I hoped to intercept him before he should reach the beach. With new courage, therefore, I pressed on, and in two days arrived at a wretched hamlet on the sea-shore. I inquired of the inhabitants concerning the fiend, and gained accurate information. A gigantic monster, they said, had arrived the night before, armed with a gun and many pistols; putting to flight the inhabitants of a solitary cottage, through fear of his terrific appearance. He had carried off their store of winter food, and, placing it in a sledge, to draw which he had seized on a numerous drove of trained dogs, he had harnessed them, and the same night, to the joy of the horror-struck villagers, had pursued his journey across the sea in a direction that led to no land; and they conjectured that he must speedily be destroyed by the breaking of the ice, or frozen by the eternal frosts.

On hearing this information, I suffered a temporary access of despair. He had escaped me; and I must commence a destructive and almost endless journey across the mountainous ices of the ocean,—amidst cold that few of the inhabitants could long endure, and which I, the native of a genial and sunny climate, could not hope to survive. Yet at the idea that the fiend should live and be triumphant, my rage and vengeance returned, and, like a mighty tide, overwhelmed every other feeling. After a slight repose, during which the spirits of the dead hovered round, and instigated me to toil and revenge, I prepared for my journey.

I exchanged my land sledge for one fashioned for the inequalities of the frozen ocean; and, purchasing a plentiful stock of provisions, I departed from land.

I cannot guess how many days have passed since then; but I have endured misery, which nothing but the eternal sentiment of a just retribution burning within my heart could have enabled me to support. Immense and rugged mountains of ice often barred up my passage, and I often heard the thunder of the ground sea, which threatened my destruction. But again the frost came, and made the paths of the sea secure.

By the quantity of provision which I had consumed I should guess that I had passed three weeks in this journey; and the continual protraction of hope, returning back upon the heart, often wrung bitter drops of despondency and grief from my eyes. Despair had indeed almost secured her prey, and I should soon have sunk beneath this misery; when once, after the poor animals that carried me had with incredible toil gained the summit of a sloping ice mountain, and one sinking under his fatigue died, I viewed the expanse before me with anguish, when suddenly my eye caught a dark speck upon the dusky plain. I strained my sight to discover what it could be, and uttered a wild cry of ecstasy when I distinguished a sledge, and the distorted proportions of a well-known form within. Oh! with what a burning gush did hope revisit my heart! warm tears filled my eyes, which I hastily wiped away, that they might not intercept the view I had of the daemon; but still my sight was dimmed by the burning drops, until, giving way to the emotions that oppressed me, I wept aloud.

But this was not the time for delay; I disencumbered the dogs of their dead companion, gave them a plentiful portion of food; and, after an hour's rest, which was absolutely necessary, and yet which was bitterly irksome to me, I continued my route. The sledge was still visible; nor did I again lose sight of it, except at the moments when for a short time some ice rock concealed it with its intervening crags. I indeed perceptibly gained on it; and when, after nearly two days' journey, I beheld my enemy at no more than a mile distant, my heart bounded within me.

But now, when I appeared almost within grasp of my enemy, my hopes were suddenly extinguished, and I lost all trace of him more utterly than I had ever done before. A ground sea was heard; the thunder of its progress, as the waters rolled and swelled beneath me, became every moment more ominous and terrific. I pressed on, but in vain. The wind arose; the sea roared; and, as with the mighty shock of an earthquake, it split, and cracked with a tremendous and overwhelming sound. The work was soon finished: in a few minutes a tumultuous sea rolled between me and my enemy, and I was left drifting on a scattered piece of ice, that was continually lessening, and thus preparing for me a hideous death.

In this manner many appalling hours passed; several of my dogs died; and I myself was about to sink under the accumulation of distress, when I saw your vessel riding at anchor, and holding forth to me hopes of succour and life. I had no conception that vessels ever came so far north, and was astounded at the sight. I quickly destroyed part of my sledge to construct oars; and by these means was enabled, with infinite fatigue, to move my ice-raft in the direction of your ship. I had determined, if you were going southward, still to trust myself to the mercy of the seas, rather than abandon my purpose. I hoped to induce you to grant me a boat with which I could still pursue my enemy. But your direction was northward. You took me on board when my vigour was exhausted, and I should soon have sunk under my multiplied hardships into a death, which I still dread,—for my task is unfulfilled.

Oh! when will my guiding spirit, in conducting me to the daemon, allow me the rest I so much desire; or must I die, and he yet live? If I do, swear to me, Walton, that he shall not escape; that you will seek him, and satisfy my vengeance in his death. Yet, do I dare ask you to undertake my pilgrimage, to endure the hardships that I have undergone? No; I am not so selfish. Yet, when I am dead, if he should appear; if the ministers of vengeance should conduct him to you, swear that he shall not live—swear that he shall not triumph over my accumulated woes, and live to make another such a wretch as I am. He is eloquent and persuasive; and once his words had even power over my heart: but trust him not. His soul is as hellish as his form, full of treachery and fiend-like malice. Hear him not; call on the manes[3] of William, Justine, Clerval, Elizabeth, my father, and of the wretched Victor, and thrust your sword into his heart. I will hover near, and direct the steel aright.

WALTON, *in continuation.*

August 26th, 17—.

You have read this strange and terrific story, Margaret; and do you not feel your blood congealed with horror, like that which even now curdles mine? Sometimes, seized with sudden agony, he could not continue his tale; at others, his voice broken, yet piercing, uttered with difficulty the words so replete with agony. His fine and lovely eyes were now lighted up with indignation, now subdued to downcast sorrow, and quenched in infinite wretchedness. Sometimes he commanded his countenance and tones, and related the most horrible incidents with a tranquil voice, suppressing every mark of agitation; then, like a volcano bursting forth, his face would suddenly change to an expression of the wildest rage, as he shrieked out imprecations on his persecutor.

[3]In classical mythology, ghosts of dead family members, urging vengeance.

His tale is connected, and told with an appearance of the simplest truth; yet I own to you that the letters of Felix and Safie, which he shewed me, and the apparition of the monster, seen from our ship, brought to me a greater conviction of the truth of his narrative than his asseverations, however earnest and connected. Such a monster has then really existence; I cannot doubt it; yet I am lost in surprise and admiration. Sometimes I endeavoured to gain from Frankenstein the particulars of his creature's formation; but on this point he was impenetrable.

"Are you mad, my friend?" said he, "or whither does your senseless curiosity lead you? Would you also create for yourself and the world a demoniacal enemy? Or to what do your questions tend? Peace, peace! learn my miseries, and do not seek to increase your own."

Frankenstein discovered that I made notes concerning his history: he asked to see them, and then himself corrected and augmented them in many places; but principally in giving the life and spirit to the conversations he held with his enemy. "Since you have preserved my narration," said he, "I would not that a mutilated one should go down to posterity."

Thus has a week passed away, while I have listened to the strangest tale that ever imagination formed. My thoughts, and every feeling of my soul, have been drunk up by the interest for my guest, which this tale, and his own elevated and gentle manners have created. I wish to soothe him; yet can I counsel one so infinitely miserable, so destitute of every hope of consolation, to live? Oh, no! the only joy that he can now know will be when he composes his shattered feelings to peace and death. Yet he enjoys one comfort, the offspring of solitude and delirium: he believes, that, when in dreams he holds converse with his friends, and derives from that communion consolation for his miseries, or excitements to his vengeance, that they are not the creations of his fancy, but the real beings who visit him from the regions of a remote world. This faith gives a solemnity to his reveries that render them to me almost as imposing and interesting as truth.

Our conversations are not always confined to his own history and misfortunes. On every point of general literature he displays unbounded knowledge, and a quick and piercing apprehension. His eloquence is forcible and touching; nor can I hear him, when he relates a pathetic incident, or endeavours to move the passions of pity or love, without tears. What a glorious creature must he have been in the days of his prosperity, when he is thus noble and godlike in ruin.[4] He seems to feel his own worth, and the greatness of his fall.

"When younger," said he, "I felt as if I were destined for some great enterprise. My feelings are profound; but I possessed a coolness of judgment that fitted me for illustrious achievements. This sentiment of the worth of my nature supported me, when others would have been oppressed; for I deemed it criminal to throw away in useless grief those talents that might be useful to my fellow-creatures. When I reflected on the work I had completed, no less a one than the creation of a sensitive and rational animal, I could not rank myself with the herd of common projectors.[5] But this feeling, which supported me in the commencement of my career, now serves only to plunge me lower in the dust. All my speculations and hopes are as nothing; and, like the archangel who aspired to omnipotence, I am chained in an eternal hell.[6] My imagination was vivid, yet my powers of analysis and application were intense; by the union of these qualities I conceived the idea, and executed the creation of a man. Even now I cannot recollect, without passion, my reveries while the work was incomplete. I trod heaven in my thoughts, now exulting in my powers, now burning with the idea of their effects. From my infancy I was imbued with high hopes and a lofty ambition; but how am I sunk! Oh! my friend, if you had known me as I once was, you would not recognize me in this state of degradation. Despondency rarely visited my heart; a high destiny seemed to bear me on, until I fell, never, never again to rise."

Must I then lose this admirable being? I have longed for a friend; I have sought one who would sympathize with and love me. Behold, on these desert seas I have found such a one; but, I fear, I have gained him only to know his value, and lose him. I would reconcile him to life, but he repulses the idea.

"I thank you, Walton," he said, "for your kind intentions towards so miserable a wretch; but when you speak of new ties, and fresh affections, think you that any can replace those who are gone? Can any man be to me as Clerval was; or any woman another Elizabeth? Even where the affections are not strongly moved by any

[4]Echoing Milton's description of Satan in *Paradise Lost* 1.592–94 (see p. 307).

[5]Schemers, experimenters, entrepreneurs.

[6]Satan's torment in Hell; see *Paradise Lost* 1.47–48.

superior excellence, the companions of our childhood always possess
a certain power over our minds, which hardly any later friend can
obtain. They know our infantine dispositions, which, however they
may be afterwards modified, are never eradicated; and they can judge
of our actions with more certain conclusions as to the integrity of our
motives. A sister or a brother can never, unless indeed such symptoms have been shewn early, suspect the other of fraud or false dealing, when another friend, however strongly he may be attached, may,
in spite of himself, be invaded with suspicion. But I enjoyed friends,
dear not only through habit and association, but from their own
merits; and, wherever I am, the soothing voice of my Elizabeth, and
the conversation of Clerval, will be ever whispered in my ear. They
are dead; and but one feeling in such a solitude can persuade me to
preserve my life. If I were engaged in any high undertaking or design,
fraught with extensive utility to my fellow-creatures, then could I live
to fulfil it. But such is not my destiny; I must pursue and destroy the
being to whom I gave existence; then my lot on earth will be fulfilled,
and I may die."

September 2d.[7]

My Beloved Sister,

I write to you, encompassed by peril, and ignorant whether I am ever
doomed to see again dear England, and the dearer friends that inhabit it. I am surrounded by mountains of ice,[8] which admit of no
escape, and threaten every moment to crush my vessel. The brave fellows, whom I have persuaded to be my companions, look towards
me for aid; but I have none to bestow. There is something terribly appalling in our situation, yet my courage and hopes do not desert me.
We may survive; and if we do not, I will repeat the lessons of my
Seneca, and die with a good heart.[9]

Yet what, Margaret, will be the state of your mind? You will not
hear of my destruction, and you will anxiously await my return.
Years will pass, and you will have visitings of despair, and yet be tor-

[7]This is the week that Mary Shelley's mother dies.

[8]The plight of the Ancient Mariner's ship in the Antarctic: "Ice mast-high came floating by" (51).

[9]Seneca, a 1st-c. Roman statesman, tragedian, and Stoic (an advocate of spiritual
peace through even-temperedness), was accused of conspiracy against his former
pupil, Emperor Nero; when Nero ordered him to commit suicide, he slashed his veins
and bled to death.

tured by hope. Oh! my beloved sister, the sickening failings of your heart-felt expectations are, in prospect, more terrible to me than my own death. But you have a husband, and lovely children; you may be happy: heaven bless you, and make you so!

My unfortunate guest regards me with the tenderest compassion. He endeavours to fill me with hope; and talks as if life were a possession which he valued. He reminds me how often the same accidents have happened to other navigators, who have attempted this sea, and, in spite of myself, he fills me with cheerful auguries. Even the sailors feel the power of his eloquence: when he speaks, they no longer despair; he rouses their energies, and, while they hear his voice, they believe these vast mountains of ice are mole-hills, which will vanish before the resolutions of man. These feelings are transitory; each day's expectation delayed fills them with fear, and I almost dread a mutiny caused by this despair.

September 5th.

A scene has just passed of such uncommon interest, that although it is highly probable that these papers may never reach you, yet I cannot forbear recording it.

We are still surrounded by mountains of ice, still in imminent danger of being crushed in their conflict. The cold is excessive, and many of my unfortunate comrades have already found a grave amidst this scene of desolation. Frankenstein has daily declined in health: a feverish fire still glimmers in his eyes;[10] but he is exhausted, and, when suddenly roused to any exertion, he speedily sinks again into apparent lifelessness.

I mentioned in my last letter the fears I entertained of a mutiny. This morning, as I sat watching the wan countenance of my friend— his eyes half closed, and his limbs hanging listlessly,—I was roused by half a dozen of the sailors, who desired admission into the cabin. They entered; and their leader addressed me. He told me that he and his companions had been chosen by the other sailors to come in deputation to me, to make me a demand, which, in justice, I could not refuse. We were immured in ice, and should probably never escape; but they feared that if, as was possible, the ice should dissipate, and a free passage be opened, I should be rash enough to continue my voyage, and lead them into fresh dangers, after they might happily have

---

[10]The symptom of hellish agony in both the Ancient Mariner and Satan.

surmounted this. They desired, therefore, that I should engage with a solemn promise, that if the vessel should be freed, I would instantly direct my course southward.

This speech troubled me. I had not despaired; nor had I yet conceived the idea of returning, if set free. Yet could I, in justice, or even in possibility, refuse this demand? I hesitated before I answered; when Frankenstein, who had at first been silent, and, indeed, appeared hardly to have force enough to attend, now roused himself; his eyes sparkled, and his cheeks flushed with momentary vigour. Turning towards the men, he said—

"What do you mean? What do you demand of your captain? Are you then so easily turned from your design? Did you not call this a glorious expedition? and wherefore was it glorious? Not because the way was smooth and placid as a southern sea, but because it was full of dangers and terror; because, at every new incident, your fortitude was to be called forth, and your courage exhibited; because danger and death surrounded, and these dangers you were to brave and overcome. For this was it a glorious, for this was it an honourable undertaking. You were hereafter to be hailed as the benefactors of your species; your name adored, as belonging to brave men who encountered death for honour and the benefit of mankind. And now, behold, with the first imagination of danger, or, if you will, the first mighty and terrific trial of your courage, you shrink away, and are content to be handed down as men who had not strength enough to endure cold and peril; and so, poor souls, they were chilly, and returned to their warm fire-sides. Why, that requires not this preparation; ye need not have come thus far, and dragged your captain to the shame of a defeat, merely to prove yourselves cowards. Oh! be men, or be more than men. Be steady to your purposes, and firm as a rock. This ice is not made of such stuff as your hearts might be; it is mutable, cannot withstand you, if you say that it shall not. Do not return to your families with the stigma of disgrace marked on your brows.[11] Return as heroes who have fought and conquered, and who know not what it is to turn their backs on the foe."[12]

---

[11] A reference to the mark of Cain, designating him as a social outcast and cautioning that vengeance for his fratricide is God's alone (Genesis 4.15).

[12] Victor echoes the great speech of the Greek hero Ulysses in Dante's *Inferno* (26.112–20), as he recalls his appeal to his comrades to undertake another (ultimately fatal) voyage of adventure; Ulysses is part of the literary lineage of Milton's Satan, especially his grand speeches to his comrades in Hell.

Celebrated French artist Gustave Doré rendered 42 engraved illustrations for Coleridge's poem, *The Rime of the Ancient Mariner* (published in 1875). This one is of the advent of the albatross over the icebound ship.

He spoke this with a voice so modulated to the different feelings expressed in his speech, with an eye so full of lofty design and heroism, that can you wonder that these men were moved. They looked at one another, and were unable to reply. I spoke; I told them to retire, and consider of what had been said: that I would not lead them further north, if they strenuously desired the contrary; but that I hoped that, with reflection, their courage would return.

They retired, and I turned towards my friend; but he was sunk in languor, and almost deprived of life.

How all this will terminate, I know not; but I had rather die, than return shamefully,—my purpose unfulfilled. Yet I fear such will be my fate; the men, unsupported by ideas of glory and honour, can never willingly continue to endure their present hardships.

September 7th.

The die is cast;[13] I have consented to return, if we are not destroyed. Thus are my hopes blasted by cowardice and indecision; I come back ignorant and disappointed. It requires more philosophy than I possess, to bear this injustice with patience.

September 12th.

It is past; I am returning to England. I have lost my hopes of utility and glory;—I have lost my friend. But I will endeavour to detail these bitter circumstances to you, my dear sister; and, while I am wafted towards England, and towards you, I will not despond.

September 9th,[14] the ice began to move, and roarings like thunder were heard at a distance, as the islands split and cracked in every direction. We were in the most imminent peril; but, as we could only remain passive, my chief attention was occupied by my unfortunate guest, whose illness increased in such a degree, that he was entirely confined to his bed. The ice cracked behind us, and was driven with force towards the north; a breeze sprung from the west, and on the 11th the passage towards the south became perfectly free. When the sailors saw this, and that their return to their native country was

---

[13]An allusion to Julius Caesar's famous remark on crossing the Rubicon river to march against his rival Pompey; the phrase "the die is cast" (plural: dice) indicates a momentous, irrevocable, and possibly fatal gamble.

[14]Just days after giving birth to her, Shelley's mother, Mary Wollstonecraft, died on 10 September 1797, from post-partum poisoning.

apparently assured, a shout of tumultuous joy broke from them, loud and long-continued. Frankenstein, who was dozing, awoke, and asked the cause of the tumult. "They shout," I said, "because they will soon return to England."

"Do you then really return?"

"Alas! yes; I cannot withstand their demands. I cannot lead them unwillingly to danger, and I must return."

"Do so, if you will; but I will not. You may give up your purpose; but mine is assigned to me by heaven, and I dare not. I am weak; but surely the spirits who assist my vengeance will endow me with sufficient strength." Saying this, he endeavoured to spring from the bed, but the exertion was too great for him; he fell back, and fainted.

It was long before he was restored; and I often thought that life was entirely extinct. At length he opened his eyes, but he breathed with difficulty, and was unable to speak. The surgeon gave him a composing draught, and ordered us to leave him undisturbed. In the mean time he told me, that my friend had certainly not many hours to live.

His sentence was pronounced; and I could only grieve, and be patient. I sat by his bed watching him; his eyes were closed, and I thought he slept; but presently he called to me in a feeble voice, and, bidding me come near, said—"Alas! the strength I relied on is gone; I feel that I shall soon die, and he, my enemy and persecutor, may still be in being. Think not, Walton, that in the last moments of my existence I feel that burning hatred, and ardent desire of revenge, I once expressed, but I feel myself justified in desiring the death of my adversary. During these last days I have been occupied in examining my past conduct; nor do I find it blameable. In a fit of enthusiastic madness I created a rational creature, and was bound towards him, to assure, as far as was in my power, his happiness and well-being. This was my duty; but there was another still paramount to that. My duties towards my fellow-creatures[15] had greater claims to my attention, because they included a greater proportion of happiness or misery. Urged by this view, I refused, and I did right in refusing, to create a companion for the first creature. He shewed unparalleled malignity and selfishness, in evil: he destroyed my friends; he devoted to destruction beings who possessed exquisite sensations, happiness, and

---

[15]1831] the beings of my own species

wisdom; nor do I know where this thirst for vengeance may end. Miserable himself, that he may render no other wretched, he ought to die. The task of his destruction was mine, but I have failed. When actuated by selfish and vicious motives, I asked you to undertake my unfinished work; and I renew this request now, when I am only induced by reason and virtue.

Yet I cannot ask you to renounce your country and friends, to fulfill this task; and now, that you are returning to England, you will have little chance of meeting with him. But the consideration of these points, and the well-balancing of what you may esteem your duties, I leave to you; my judgment and ideas are already disturbed by the near approach of death. I dare not ask you to do what I think right, for I may still be misled by passion.

That he should live to be an instrument of mischief disturbs me; in other respects this hour, when I momentarily expect my release, is the only happy one which I have enjoyed for several years. The forms of the beloved dead flit before me, and I hasten to their arms. Farewell, Walton! Seek happiness in tranquillity, and avoid ambition, even if it be only the apparently innocent one of distinguishing yourself in science and discoveries. Yet why do I say this? I have myself been blasted in these hopes, yet another may succeed."

His voice became fainter as he spoke; and at length, exhausted by his effort, he sunk into silence. About half an hour afterwards he attempted again to speak, but was unable; he pressed my hand feebly, and his eyes closed for ever, while the irradiation of a gentle smile passed away from his lips.

Margaret, what comment can I make on the untimely extinction of this glorious spirit? What can I say, that will enable you to understand the depth of my sorrow? All that I should express would be inadequate and feeble. My tears flow; my mind is overshadowed by a cloud of disappointment. But I journey towards England, and I may there find consolation.

I am interrupted. What do these sounds portend? It is midnight; the breeze blows fairly, and the watch on deck scarcely stir. Again; there is a sound as of a human voice, but hoarser; it comes from the cabin where the remains of Frankenstein still lie. I must arise, and examine. Good night, my sister.

Great God! what a scene has just taken place! I am yet dizzy with the remembrance of it. I hardly know whether I shall have the power to detail it; yet the tale which I have recorded would be incomplete without this final and wonderful catastrophe.

I entered the cabin, where lay the remains of my ill-fated and admirable friend. Over him hung a form which I cannot find words to describe; gigantic in stature, yet uncouth and distorted in its proportions. As he hung over the coffin, his face was concealed by long locks of ragged hair; but one vast hand was extended, in colour and apparent texture like that of a mummy. When he heard the sound of my approach, he ceased to utter exclamations of grief and horror, and sprung towards the window. Never did I behold a vision so horrible as his face, of such loathsome, yet appalling hideousness. I shut my eyes involuntarily, and endeavoured to recollect what were my duties with regard to this destroyer. I called on him to stay.

He paused, looking on me with wonder; and, again turning towards the lifeless form of his creator, he seemed to forget my presence, and every feature and gesture seemed instigated by the wildest rage of some uncontrollable passion.

"That is also my victim!" he exclaimed; "in his murder my crimes are consummated; the miserable series of my being is wound to its close! Oh, Frankenstein! generous and self-devoted[16] being! what does it avail that I now ask thee to pardon me? I, who irretrievably destroyed thee by destroying all thou lovedst. Alas! he is cold; he may not answer me."

His voice seemed suffocated; and my first impulses, which had suggested to me the duty of obeying the dying request of my friend, in destroying his enemy, were now suspended by a mixture of curiosity and compassion. I approached this tremendous being; I dared not again raise my looks upon his face, there was something so scaring and unearthly in his ugliness. I attempted to speak, but the words died away on my lips. The monster continued to utter wild and incoherent self-reproaches. At length I gathered resolution to address him, in a pause of the tempest of his passion: "Your repentance," I said, "is now superfluous. If you had listened to the voice of conscience, and heeded the stings of remorse, before you had urged your diabolical vengeance to this extremity, Frankenstein would yet have lived."

[16]Both "generous" (devotion of self) and, ironically, "selfish" (devoted to self). Percy Shelley wrote to Leigh Hunt in December 1816 of feeling himself as an "object" whom all "abhor & avoid," except to those very "few" who "believe in self-devotion and generosity because they are themselves generous & self devoted."

"And do you dream?" said the daemon; "do you think that I was then dead to agony and remorse?—He," he continued, pointing to the corpse, "he suffered not more in the consummation of the deed;—oh! not the ten-thousandth portion of the anguish that was mine during the lingering detail of its execution. A frightful selfishness hurried me on, while my heart was poisoned with remorse. Think ye that the groans of Clerval were music to my ears? My heart was fashioned to be susceptible of love and sympathy; and, when wrenched by misery to vice and hatred, it did not endure the violence of the change without torture, such as you cannot even imagine.

"After the murder of Clerval, I returned to Switzerland, heart-broken and overcome. I pitied Frankenstein; my pity amounted to horror: I abhorred myself. But when I discovered that he, the author at once of my existence and of its unspeakable torments, dared to hope for happiness; that while he accumulated wretchedness and despair upon me, he sought his own enjoyment in feelings and passions from the indulgence of which I was for ever barred, then impotent envy and bitter indignation filled me with an insatiable thirst for vengeance. I recollected my threat, and resolved that it should be accomplished. I knew that I was preparing for myself a deadly torture; but I was the slave, not the master of an impulse, which I detested, yet could not disobey. Yet when she died!—nay, then I was not miserable. I had cast off all feeling, subdued all anguish to riot in the excess of my despair. Evil thenceforth became my good.[17] Urged thus far, I had no choice but to adapt my nature to an element which I had willingly chosen. The completion of my demoniacal design became an insatiable passion. And now it is ended; there is my last victim!"

I was at first touched by the expressions of his misery; yet when I called to mind what Frankenstein had said of his powers of eloquence and persuasion, and when I again cast my eyes on the lifeless form of my friend, indignation was re-kindled within me. "Wretch!" I said, "it is well that you come here to whine over the desolation that you have made. You throw a torch into a pile of buildings, and when they are consumed you sit among the ruins, and lament the fall. Hypocritical fiend! if he whom you mourn still lived, still would he be the object, again would he become the prey of your accursed vengeance. It is not pity that you feel; you lament only because the victim of your malignity is withdrawn from your power."

[17]Satan's principle; see *Paradise Lost* 4.110.

"Oh, it is not thus—not thus," interrupted the being; "yet such must be the impression conveyed to you by what appears to be the purport of my actions. Yet I seek not a fellow-feeling in my misery. No sympathy may I ever find. When I first sought it, it was the love of virtue, the feelings of happiness and affection with which my whole being overflowed, that I wished to be participated. But now, that virtue has become to me a shadow, and that happiness and affection are turned into bitter and loathing despair, in what should I seek for sympathy? I am content to suffer alone, while my sufferings shall endure: when I die, I am well satisfied that abhorrence and opprobrium should load my memory. Once my fancy was soothed with dreams of virtue, of fame, and of enjoyment. Once I falsely hoped to meet with beings, who, pardoning my outward form, would love me for the excellent qualities which I was capable of bringing forth. I was nourished with high thoughts of honour and devotion. But now vice has degraded me beneath the meanest animal. No crime, no mischief, no malignity, no misery, can be found comparable to mine. When I call over the frightful catalogue of my deeds, I cannot believe that I am he[18] whose thoughts were once filled with sublime and transcendent visions of the beauty and the majesty of goodness. But it is even so; the fallen angel becomes a malignant devil.[19] Yet even that enemy of God and man had friends and associates in his desolation; I am quite alone.

"You, who call Frankenstein your friend, seem to have a knowledge of my crimes and his misfortunes. But, in the detail which he gave you of them, he could not sum up the hours and months of misery which I endured, wasting in impotent passions. For whilst I destroyed his hopes, I did not satisfy my own desires. They were for ever ardent and craving; still I desired love and fellowship, and I was still spurned. Was there no injustice in this? Am I to be thought the only criminal, when all human kind sinned against me? Why do you not hate Felix, who drove his friend from his door with contumely? Why do you not execrate the rustic who sought to destroy the saviour of his child? Nay, these are virtuous and immaculate beings! I, the miserable and the abandoned, am an abortion, to be spurned at, and

[18]1831] the same creature

[19]Satan had been archangel Lucifer (light-bearer, a version of Prometheus): "*Lucifer* from Heav'n ... Fell with his flaming legions through the Deep" (*Paradise Lost* 7.131–34).

kicked, and trampled on. Even now my blood boils at the recollection of this injustice.

"But it is true that I am a wretch. I have murdered the lovely and the helpless; I have strangled the innocent as they slept, and grasped to death his throat who never injured me or any other living thing. I have devoted my creator, the select specimen of all that is worthy of love and admiration among men, to misery; I have pursued him even to that irremediable ruin. There he lies, white and cold in death. You hate me; but your abhorrence cannot equal that with which I regard myself. I look on the hands which executed the deed; I think on the heart in which the imagination of it was conceived, and long for the moment when they will meet my eyes, when it will haunt my thoughts, no more.

"Fear not that I shall be the instrument of future mischief. My work is nearly complete. Neither your's nor any man's death is needed to consummate the series of my being, and accomplish that which must be done; but it requires my own. Do not think that I shall be slow to perform this sacrifice. I shall quit your vessel on the ice-raft which brought me hither, and shall seek the most northern extremity of the globe; I shall collect my funeral pile, and consume to ashes this miserable frame, that its remains may afford no light to any curious and unhallowed wretch, who would create such another as I have been. I shall die. I shall no longer feel the agonies which now consume me, or be the prey of feelings unsatisfied, yet unquenched. He is dead who called me into being; and when I shall be no more, the very remembrance of us both will speedily vanish. I shall no longer see the sun or stars, or feel the winds play on my cheeks. Light, feeling, and sense, will pass away; and in this condition must I find my happiness. Some years ago, when the images which this world affords first opened upon me, when I felt the cheering warmth of summer, and heard the rustling of the leaves and the chirping of the birds, and these were all to me, I should have wept to die; now it is my only consolation. Polluted by crimes, and torn by the bitterest remorse, where can I find rest but in death?

"Farewell! I leave you, and in you the last of human kind whom these eyes will ever behold. Farewell, Frankenstein! If thou wert yet alive, and yet cherished a desire of revenge against me, it would be better satiated in my life than in my destruction. But it was not so; thou didst seek my extinction, that I might not cause greater wretchedness; and if yet, in some mode unknown to me, thou hast not yet ceased to think and feel, thou desirest not my life for my own misery. Blasted as thou wert, my agony was still superior to thine; for the bitter sting of remorse may not cease to rankle in my wounds until death shall close them for ever.

"But soon," he cried, with sad and solemn enthusiasm, "I shall die, and what I now feel be no longer felt. Soon these burning miseries will be extinct. I shall ascend my funeral pile triumphantly, and exult in the agony of the torturing flames. The light of that conflagration will fade away; my ashes will be swept into the sea by the winds. My spirit will sleep in peace; or if it thinks, it will not surely think thus. Farewell."

He sprung from the cabin-window, as he said this, upon the ice-raft which lay close to the vessel. He was soon borne away by the waves, and lost in darkness and distance.[20]

THE END.

[20]Mary Shelley had first written: ". . . he was carried away by the waves and I soon lost sight of him in the darkness & distance."

from FRANKENSTEIN, BY MARY W. SHELLEY
(London: Colburn and Bentley, 1831)

So reads the first title page of Bentley's Standard Novels, No. IX, two volumes, presenting *Frankenstein* in Vol. 1, bound with the first part of an English translation of Friedrich Schiller's German tale, *The Ghost-Seer*. (Vol. 2 completed *The Ghost-Seer* and offered Charles Brockden Brown's American gothic novel, *Edgar Huntley*.) By 1831, it is clear, Shelley was a "standard," in the company of peers, and *Frankenstein* was pegged as a gothic thriller. Following the title page was this second one, elaborating Shelley's credentials:

FRANKENSTEIN:
OR,
THE MODERN PROMETHEUS.

BY THE AUTHOR OF
THE LAST MAN, PERKIN WARBECK,
&c. &c.

REVISED, CORRECTED,
AND ILLUSTRATED WITH A NEW INTRODUCTION
BY THE AUTHOR.

Although the first reviews of the 1818 novel were controversial and even dismissive, *Frankenstein* was clearly taking the pulse of the times: science vs. society; intellectual adventure vs. moral reflection; domestic affections vs. secret knowledge; tensions of class, culture, gender, even race; a critique of the romantic sublime and a romance with the same; a dark recasting of the Wordsworthian myth of childhood; a skepticism about the Enlightenment ideology of rational education.

July 1821 saw it translated into French as *Frankenstein, ou le Prométhée moderne*. In February 1823 William Godwin was proud to report to his daughter, still in Italy, "Your talents are truly extraordinary. 'Frankenstein' is universally known, and . . . everywhere respected." With his eye ever on the market, a few months later he noted the impending staging of *Frankenstein* at the English Opera House: "I know not whether it will succeed," he murmurs to Shelley, but hastens to add, "If it does, it will be some sort of feather in the cap of the author of the novel, a recommendation in your future negociacions with booksellers." When R. B. Peake's stage version proved a success in the summer of 1823, *Frankenstein*, with a push from Godwin, was quickly republished, the author now identified: "Mary Wollstonecraft Shelley." When the title page of her next novel, *The Last Man* (1826), blazoned "By the Author of Frankenstein," the fame was confirmed. A French Frankenstein was flourishing, too. In 1826, *Le Monstre et le magicien* opened on the Paris stage, followed by another staging in London. And then H. M. Milner's *The Man and the Monster; or, the Fate of Frankenstein* opened at the Royal Coburg.

Across the 1820s "Frankenstein" was proliferating not only on stage and in print but also as a byword for threatening new social developments. Foreign Secretary Canning summoned it in March 1824 to gloss worries about the emancipated male slave (see p. 394). In November 1830 *Fraser's Magazine* wrote the fiction into the body politic, proposing that "a state without religion is like a human body without a soul, or rather like an unnatural body of the species of the Frankenstein monster . . . a horrible and heterogeneous compound, full of corruption, and exciting our disgust" (p. 481).

This public circulation plugs the "Introduction" Shelley constructed for the new version of 1831 into a complex double chronology. Its narrative "account" is of the novel's inception, back in 1816, and even before then, in the nurture of young Mary Godwin's imagination. But its composition is charged by the life and fame of the novel since 1818. While Shelley was somewhat uneasy about the fame of authorship, especially in tandem with the catastrophic loss of Percy Shelley, she enjoyed her accomplishment. Thus she writes in April 1829 to her and Percy's friend E. J. Trelawny (responding to his hope that she would help write a life of the poet):

> There is nothing I shrink from more fearfully than publicity—I have too much of it—& what is worse I am forced by my hard situation to meet it in a thousand ways . . . I am—a silly goose— who far from wishing to stand forward to assert myself in any way, now than I am alone in the world, have but the desire to

wrap night and the obscurity of insignificance around me. This is
weakness—but I cannot help it—to be in print—the subject of
<u>men's</u> observations—of the bitter hard world's commentaries, to
be attacked or defended!—this ill becomes one who knows how
little she possesses worthy to attract attention—and whose chief
merit—if it be one—is a love of that privacy which no woman can
emerge from without regret— . . . I only seek to be forgotten—[1]

By February 1831, however, Shelley was approaching Charles Ollier,
chief literary adviser to the firm of Colburn and Bentley, to test interest in a revised version of *Frankenstein* for its Standard Novels family. When Ollier responded favorably, she exercised no small degree
of authorial self-interest:

If there is another <u>real</u> ~~introd~~ edition of Frankenstein—that is if it
goes to press again—will you remember that I have a short passage to add to the Introduction. Do not fail me with regard to
this—it will be only a few lines—& those not disagreeable to
C.&B.—but the contrary.[2]

Short passage became short story, a prequel-sequel displacing the
Preface of 1818 ghost-written by Percy Shelley (this text now de-
moted to an appendage).

Framed as an autobiographical history, the new Introduction was
also a strategic narrative. Retailing the novel's genesis, Shelley trades on
and promotes its celebrity, answering curiosity about the "Author" of
such a "hideous progeny" (so she is happy to dub *Frankenstein*). Her
recounting of the tale's origins in the summer of 1816 produces a canny
supplement to the novel, echoing in her own authorial inspirations and
excitements Frankenstein's transgressive studies and throes of conception, and casting her appetitive listening to famous poets' conversations
on the pattern of her Creature's secret education in the De Lacey household. The Introduction at once amplifies the original tale and advertises
(as preface and publicity) the 1831 scion.

The publishers ran with the promise. Early in September 1831, a
notice on the front page of the *Morning Chronicle* announced "Mrs.
Shelley's popular Romance, Frankenstein, Revised by the Author, with

[1]*Letters*, ed. Betty T. Bennett. 2: 72.
[2]*Letters* 2: 129.

a New Introduction explanatory of the origin of the Story; and the Castle of Otranto, with a Life of Horace Walpole, written by Sir Walter Scott, will appear in an early volume" of the Standard Novels. It was a great package, and over the next three weeks, Colburn's *Court Journal* replayed the notice. The pairing was then reworked, to partner *Frankenstein* (Scott-graced though *Otranto* was) with Schiller's *Ghost-Seer*.[3] Just as cheerily, the 15 October *Chronicle* advertised the new nuptials: "A more attractive book could hardly be formed than will be produced by a union of two stories, which, as is the case with Frankenstein and The Ghost-Seer, have each had such marked effect on society" (p. 4). Colburn amplified the buzz by pre-publishing Shelley's "new Introduction" the next week in his *Court Journal* (22 October, p. 724), barely after Shelley blotted the copytext.

A front-page advertisement in the *Chronicle* a week later, 29 October, repeated the news of the "new Introduction, explanatory of the origin of the Story, by the Author, and containing original anecdotes of Lord Byron, &c." even as another item in the same issue (on Thomas Moore's recently published *Life of Byron*) fanned the fame with this quotation from Moore: "The most memorable result, indeed of their story-telling compact was Mrs. Shelley's powerful romance of 'Frankenstein'—one of those original conceptions that take hold of the public mind at once, and for ever" (p. 4). *Frankenstein* arrived in bookstores two days later, on Halloween, and within days its publishers coaxed the *Chronicle* to report that "demand" had been "so great as to absorb on the first day the whole supply"—a preface to their assurance to "those who were disappointed in their applications for the volume" that "another impression has been produced, and copies may be had either at the publishers, or at the retail booksellers" (p. 4).

The 1831 novel (now in 24 consecutive chapters) tells the same tale as the 1818, but with many revisions (some already given in our footnotes). Many swaths are so substantial as to amount to a re-conception, a re-production of the original text into a new progeny. This unit presents the most arresting, with the framing italics giving the textual coordinates and page numbers in 1818.

---

[3]The advertising information is drawn from *The Frankenstein Notebooks*, ed. Charles E. Robinson (Part A, ciii–civ). The *Chronicle*'s first announcement, 3 September, was nested in an advertisement for Jane Porter's *The Scottish Chiefs*. *Court Journal* propelled notices across successive weeks: 10 September (p. 632), 17 September (p. 648), 24 September (p. 644), and 8 October (p. 696).

C. Holst, del.   W. Chevalier, sculp.

FRANKENSTEIN.

By the glimmer of the half-extinguished light. I saw the dull, yellow eye of the creature open; it breathed hard, and a convulsive motion agitated its limbs, *** *I rushed out of the room.*"

Page 43.

London, Published by H. Colburn and R. Bentley, 1831.

This doublet of pictures juxtaposes Victor's abandonment of his Creature on the night of creation with Victor's earlier departure from Elizabeth as he goes off to college. The mirroring composition (two arches, two figures) underscores the contrasts (pastoral Elizabeth vs. gothic creature; the sorry departure and the panicked flight).

FRANKENSTEIN,

BY

MARY W. SHELLEY.

"The day of my departure at length arrived." page 41.

LONDON:

COLBURN AND BENTLEY.

CUMMING, DUBLIN; BELL & BRADFUTE, EDINBURGH.
GALIGNANI, PARIS.

1831.

INTRODUCTION

The Publishers of the Standard Novels, in selecting "Frankenstein" for one of their series, expressed a wish that I should furnish them with some account of the origin of the story. I am the more willing to comply, because I shall thus give a general answer to the question, so very frequently asked me—"How I, then a young girl, came to think of, and to dilate upon, so very hideous an idea?" It is true that I am very averse to bringing myself forward in print; but as my account will only appear as an appendage to a former production, and as it will be confined to such topics as have connection with my authorship alone, I can scarcely accuse myself of a personal intrusion.

It is not singular that, as the daughter of two persons of distinguished literary celebrity, I should very early in life have thought of writing. As a child I scribbled; and my favourite pastime, during the hours given me for recreation, was to "write stories." Still I had a dearer pleasure than this, which was the formation of castles in the air—the indulging in waking dreams—the following up trains of thought, which had for their subject the formation of a succession of imaginary incidents. My dreams were at once more fantastic and agreeable than my writings. In the latter I was a close imitator— rather doing as others had done, than putting down the suggestions of my own mind. What I wrote was intended at least for one other eye—my childhood's companion and friend;[1] but my dreams were all my own; I accounted for them to nobody; they were my refuge when annoyed—my dearest pleasure when free.

I lived principally in the country as a girl, and passed a considerable time in Scotland. I made occasional visits to the more picturesque parts; but my habitual residence was on the blank and dreary northern shores of the Tay, near Dundee. Blank and dreary on retrospection I call them; they were not so to me then. They were the eyry[2] of freedom, and the pleasant region where unheeded I could commune with the creatures of my fancy. I wrote then—but in a most commonplace style. It was beneath the trees of the grounds belonging to our house, or on the bleak sides of the woodless

---

[1]Isabel Baxter, daughter of William Baxter, an admirer of her father; Godwin felt he could not support Mary and, worried about tensions between her and his second wife, sent her to live with the Baxters from 1812 to 1814.

[2]Eagle's nest, high up in the cliffs.

mountains near, that my true compositions, the airy flights of my imagination, were born and fostered. I did not make myself the heroine of my tales. Life appeared to me too common-place an affair as regarded myself. I could not figure to myself that romantic woes or wonderful events would ever be my lot; but I was not confined to my own identity, and I could people the hours with creations far more interesting to me at that age, than my own sensations.

After this my life became busier, and reality stood in place of fiction. My husband,[3] however, was, from the first, very anxious that I should prove myself worthy of my parentage, and enrol myself on the page of fame. He was for ever inciting me to obtain literary reputation, which even on my own part I cared for then, though since I have become infinitely indifferent to it. At this time he desired that I should write, not so much with the idea that I could produce any thing worthy of notice, but that he might himself judge how far I possessed the promise of better things hereafter. Still I did nothing. Travelling, and the cares of a family, occupied my time; and study, in the way of reading, or improving my ideas in communication with his far more cultivated mind, was all of literary employment that engaged my attention.

In the summer of 1816, we visited Switzerland, and became the neighbours of Lord Byron. At first we spent our pleasant hours on the lake, or wandering on its shores; and Lord Byron, who was writing the third canto of Childe Harold, was the only one among us who put his thoughts upon paper. These, as he brought them successively to us, clothed in all the light and harmony of poetry, seemed to stamp as divine the glories of heaven and earth, whose influences we partook with him.

But it proved a wet, ungenial summer, and incessant rain often confined us for days to the house. Some volumes of ghost stories, translated from the German into French, fell into our hands.[4] There was the History of the Inconstant Lover, who, when he thought to clasp the bride to whom he had pledged his vows, found himself in the arms of the pale ghost of her whom he had deserted. There was the tale of the sinful founder of his race, whose miserable doom it was to bestow the kiss of death on all the younger sons of his fated house, just when they

[3]Percy Shelley was not actually her "husband" when she wrote the novel in the summer of 1816; they married in December, after his first wife committed suicide.

[4]*Fantasmagoria* (French trans. 1812); see the 1818 Preface; the somewhat misrecalled tales are *La Morte Fiancée* (*The Dead Fiancée*) and *Les Portraits de Famille* (*Family Portraits*).

reached the age of promise. His gigantic, shadowy form, clothed like the ghost in Hamlet, in complete armour, but with the beaver[5] up, was seen at midnight, by the moon's fitful beams, to advance slowly along the gloomy avenue. The shape was lost beneath the shadow of the castle walls; but soon a gate swung back, a step was heard, the door of the chamber opened, and he advanced to the couch of the blooming youths, cradled in healthy sleep. Eternal sorrow sat upon his face as he bent down and kissed the forehead of the boys, who from that hour withered like flowers snapt upon the stalk. I have not seen these stories since then; but their incidents are as fresh in my mind as if I had read them yesterday.

"We will each write a ghost story," said Lord Byron; and his proposition was acceded to. There were four of us. The noble author began a tale, a fragment of which he printed at the end of his poem of Mazeppa. Shelley, more apt to embody ideas and sentiments in the radiance of brilliant imagery, and in the music of the most melodious verse that adorns our language, than to invent the machinery of a story, commenced one founded on the experiences of his early life. Poor Polidori had some terrible idea about a skull-headed lady, who was so punished for peeping through a key-hole—what to see I forget—something very shocking and wrong of course; but when she was reduced to a worse condition than the renowned Tom of Coventry, he did not know what to do with her, and was obliged to despatch her to the tomb of the Capulets, the only place for which she was fitted.[6] The illustrious poets also, annoyed by the platitude of prose, speedily relinquished their uncongenial task.

I busied myself *to think of a story*,—a story to rival those which had excited us to this task. One which would speak to the mysterious fears of our nature, and awaken thrilling horror—one to make the reader dread to look round, to curdle the blood, and quicken the beatings of the heart. If I did not accomplish these things, my ghost story would be unworthy of its name. I thought and pondered—vainly. I felt that blank incapability of invention which is the greatest misery of authorship, when dull Nothing replies to our anxious invocations. *Have you thought of a story?* I was asked each morning, and each morning I was forced to reply with a mortifying negative.

[5]Visor; Shelley alludes to the ghost of Hamlet's (murdered, revenge-seeking) father (*Hamlet* 1.2.226–30).

[6]Tom of Coventry is the legendary "Peeping Tom" of the 13th c. who was struck blind for disobeying an edict not to peek at Lady Godiva as she rode naked through Coventry on a white horse; the Capulets are Juliet's family in *Romeo and Juliet,* in whose tomb the tragedy climaxes with the suicides of the young lovers.

Every thing must have a beginning, to speak in Sanchean phrase;[7] and that beginning must be linked to something that went before. The Hindoos give the world an elephant to support it, but they make the elephant stand upon a tortoise.[8] Invention, it must be humbly admitted, does not consist in creating out of void, but out of chaos; the materials must, in the first place, be afforded: it can give form to dark, shapeless substances, but cannot bring into being the substance itself. In all matters of discovery and invention, even of those that appertain to the imagination, we are continually reminded of the story of Columbus and his egg.[9] Invention consists in the capacity of seizing on the capabilities of a subject, and in the power of moulding and fashioning ideas suggested to it.

Many and long were the conversations between Lord Byron and Shelley, to which I was a devout but nearly silent listener.[10] During one of these, various philosophical doctrines were discussed, and among others the nature of the principle of life, and whether there was any probability of its ever being discovered and communicated. They talked of the experiments of Dr Darwin (I speak not of what the Doctor really did, or said that he did, but, as more to my purpose, of what was then spoken of as having been done by him), who preserved a piece of vermicelli in a glass case, till by some extraordinary means it began to move with voluntary motion. Not thus, after all, would life be given. Perhaps a corpse would be re-animated; galvanism had given token of such things: perhaps the component parts of a creature might be manufactured, brought together, and endued with vital warmth.[11]

[7]Don Quixote's squire, Sancho Panza, is convinced that he can govern his own island, even though he has no experience: "in this matter of government everything depends upon the beginning" (2.33); Shelley was reading *Don Quixote* in 1816.

[8]The ancient Hindu myth is cited by Shaftesbury in *Characteristicks* (2nd ed., 1715) and by Wollstonecraft in *Rights of Woman* (V.iv).

[9]Archangel Raphael gives Adam an account of creation of the world from materials in chaos (*Paradise Lost* Book 7.220–42). In a famous legend, recently told in Washington Irving's *The Life and Voyages of Christopher Columbus* (1828), Book 5, Ch. 8, Columbus was challenged to prove his boast that he could stand an egg on end; he tapped off one end and stood it on that, citing the trick to demonstrate how a seemingly impossible task, such as sailing to the Americas, once demonstrated, was easily repeated.

[10]Like the Creature's situation with the De Lacey family.

[11]Erasmus Darwin refers to this pasta experiment ("vermicelli": "little worms") in *The Temple of Nature, or, The Origin of Society: A Poem* (1803). Galvanism, the inducement of spasms in dead tissue with electric current, was given a sensational, widely reported demonstration when Giovanni Aldini (physiologist Luigi Galvani's nephew) "animated" the corpse of an executed convict, causing it to sit upright.

Night waned upon this talk, and even the witching hour had gone by,[12] before we retired to rest. When I placed my head on my pillow, I did not sleep, nor could I be said to think. My imagination, unbidden, possessed and guided me, gifting the successive images that arose in my mind with a vividness far beyond the usual bounds of reverie. I saw—with shut eyes, but acute mental vision,—I saw the pale student of unhallowed arts kneeling beside the thing he had put together. I saw the hideous phantasm of a man stretched out, and then, on the working of some powerful engine, show signs of life, and stir with an uneasy, half vital motion. Frightful must it be; for supremely frightful would be the effect of any human endeavour to mock the stupendous mechanism of the Creator of the world. His success would terrify the artist; he would rush away from his odious handywork, horror-stricken. He would hope that, left to itself, the slight spark of life which he had communicated would fade; that this thing, which had received such imperfect animation, would subside into dead matter; and he might sleep in the belief that the silence of the grave would quench for ever the transient existence of the hideous corpse which he had looked upon as the cradle of life. He sleeps; but he is awakened; he opens his eyes; behold the horrid thing stands at his bedside, opening his curtains, and looking on him with yellow, watery, but speculative eyes.[13]

I opened mine in terror. The idea so possessed my mind, that a thrill of fear ran through me, and I wished to exchange the ghastly image of my fancy for the realities around. I see them still; the very room, the dark *parquet,* the closed shutters, with the moonlight struggling through, and the sense I had that the glassy lake and white high Alps were beyond. I could not so easily get rid of my hideous phantom; still it haunted me. I must try to think of something else. I recurred to my ghost story,—my tiresome unlucky ghost story! O! if I could only contrive one which would frighten my reader as I myself had been frightened that night!

Swift as light and as cheering was the idea that broke in upon me. "I have found it! What terrified me will terrify others; and I need only describe the spectre which had haunted my midnight pillow." On the morrow I announced that I had *thought of a story.* I began that

[12] " 'Tis now the very witching time of night, / When churchyards yawn, and Hell itself breathes out / Contagion to this world" (*Hamlet* 3.2.396–98).

[13] See I.IV, the first three paragraphs.

day with the words, *It was on a dreary night of November,* making only a transcript of the grim terrors of my waking dream.

At first I thought but of a few pages—of a short tale; but Shelley urged me to develope the idea at greater length. I certainly did not owe the suggestion of one incident, nor scarcely of one train of feeling, to my husband, and yet but for his incitement, it would never have taken the form in which it was presented to the world. From this declaration I must except the preface. As far as I can recollect, it was entirely written by him.

And now, once again, I bid my hideous progeny go forth and prosper. I have an affection for it, for it was the offspring of happy days, when death and grief were but words, which found no true echo in my heart. Its several pages speak of many a walk, many a drive, and many a conversation, when I was not alone; and my companion was one who, in this world, I shall never see more. But this is for myself; my readers have nothing to do with these associations.

I will add but one word as to the alterations I have made. They are principally those of style. I have changed no portion of the story, nor introduced any new ideas or circumstances. I have mended the language where it was so bald as to interfere with the interest of the narrative; and these changes occur almost exclusively in the beginning of the first volume. Throughout they are entirely confined to such parts as are mere adjuncts to the story, leaving the core and substance of it untouched.

M.W.S.

London, October 15, 1831.

Additions to Robert Walton's First Letters

The visionary quester and determined, life-risking adventurer

28th March, 17—

(p. 10) *do not be alarmed for my safety,*] or if I should come back to you as worn and woful as the "Ancient Mariner"? You will smile at my allusion, but I will disclose a secret. I have often attributed my attachment to, my passionate enthusiasm for, the dangerous mysteries of ocean to that production of the most imaginative of

modern poets. There is something at work in my soul which I do
not understand. I am practically industrious—pains-taking; a work-
man to execute with perseverance and labour:—but besides this,
there is a love for the marvellous, a belief in the marvellous, intertwined in all my projects, which hurries me out of the common
pathways of men, even to the wild sea and unvisited regions I am
about to explore.

But to return to dearer considerations. [*Shall I meet you again . . .*

July 7th, 17—

(p. 11) *I will be cool, persevering, and prudent.*] But success *shall*
crown my endeavours. Wherefore not? Thus far I have gone, tracing
a secure way over the pathless seas: the very stars themselves being
witnesses and testimonies of my triumph. Why not still proceed over
the untamed yet obedient element? What can stop the determined
heart and resolved will of man?

My swelling heart involuntarily pours itself out thus. But I must
finish. Heaven bless my beloved sister!

The mutual sympathy of Walton and Frankenstein

August 13th, 17—

(pp. 15–16) *He has asked me many questions concerning my design . . .*] He entered attentively into all my arguments in favour of
my eventual success, and into every minute detail of the measures I
had taken to secure it. I was easily led by the sympathy which he
evinced, to use the language of my heart, to give utterance to the
burning ardour of my soul; and to say, with all the fervour that
warmed me, how gladly I would sacrifice my fortune, my existence,
my every hope, to the furtherance of my enterprise. One man's life
or death were but a small price to pay for the acquirement of the
knowledge which I sought; for the dominion I should acquire and
transmit over the elemental foes of our race. As I spoke, a dark
gloom spread over my listener's countenance. At first I perceived
that he tried to suppress his emotion; he placed his hands before his
eyes; and my voice quivered and failed me, as I beheld tears trickle
fast from between his fingers;—a groan burst from his heaving
breast. I paused; at length he spoke, in broken accents:—"Unhappy

man! Do you share my madness? Have you drank also of the intoxicating draught? Hear me,—let me reveal my tale, and you will dash the cup from your lips!"

Such words, you may imagine, strongly excited my curiosity; but the paroxysm of grief that had seized the stranger overcame his weakened powers, and many hours of repose and tranquil conversation were necessary to restore his composure.

Having conquered the violence of his feelings, he appeared to despise himself for being the slave of passion; and quelling the dark tyranny of despair, he led me again to converse concerning myself personally. He asked me the history of my earlier years. The tale was quickly told: but it awakened various trains of reflection. I spoke of my desire of finding a friend—of my thirst for a more intimate sympathy with a fellow mind than had ever fallen to my lot; and expressed my conviction that a man could boast of little happiness who did not enjoy this blessing.

"I agree with you," replied the stranger; "we are unfashioned creatures, but half made up, if one wiser, better, dearer than ourselves—such a friend ought to be—do not lend his aid to perfectionate our weak and faulty natures." [*I once had a friend, the most noble of human creatures,* ...

August 19th, 17—

(p. 16) *if you are inclined*] when I reflect that you are pursuing the same course, exposing yourself to the same dangers which have rendered me what I am, I imagine that you may deduce an apt moral from my tale; one that may direct you if you succeed in your undertaking and console you in case of failure. Prepare to hear of occurrences which are usually deemed marvellous. . . . [*but I do not doubt that my tale*

(p. 17) added to the end of the letter] Even now, as I commence my task, his full-toned voice swells in my ears; his lustrous eyes dwell on me with all their melancholy sweetness; I see his thin hand raised in animation, while the lineaments of his face are irradiated by the soul within. Strange and harrowing must be his story; frightful the storm which embraced the gallant vessel on its course and wrecked it—thus!

Additions and Revisions
to Victor Frankenstein's Narrative

*Throughout Victor elaborates his plight as "victim of destiny,"
caught up in destructive forces beyond his control*

Victor's childhood and the adoption of Elizabeth

*(Chapters I–II) A fuller account of the domestic harmony of his
childhood, his parents' devotion to family, and the adoption of orphan Elizabeth—not a cousin, as in 1816, but embraced as if she
were, even a sibling. She and Henry Clerval balance Victor's solitary
tendencies, his anti-social metaphysical curiosity and passions.*

I.I (pp. 19–21) *When my father became a husband and a parent . . .*]
There was a considerable difference between the ages of my parents,
but this circumstance seemed to unite them only closer in bonds of devoted affection. There was a sense of justice in my father's upright
mind, which rendered it necessary that he should approve highly to
love strongly. Perhaps during former years he had suffered from the
late-discovered unworthiness of one beloved, and so was disposed to
set a greater value on tried worth. There was a show of gratitude and
worship in his attachment to my mother, differing wholly from the
doating fondness of age, for it was inspired by reverence for her
virtues, and a desire to be the means of, in some degree, recompensing
her for the sorrows she had endured, but which gave inexpressible
grace to his behaviour to her. Every thing was made to yield to her
wishes and her convenience. He strove to shelter her, as a fair exotic is
sheltered by the gardener, from every rougher wind, and to surround
her with all that could tend to excite pleasurable emotion in her soft
and benevolent mind. Her health, and even the tranquillity of her hitherto constant spirit, had been shaken by what she had gone through.
During the two years that had elapsed previous to their marriage my
father had gradually relinquished all his public functions; and immediately after their union they sought the pleasant climate of Italy, and
the change of scene and interest attendant on a tour through that land
of wonders, as a restorative for her weakened frame.

From Italy they visited Germany and France. I, their eldest child,
was born at Naples,[1] and as an infant accompanied them in their rambles. I remained for several years their only child. Much as they were

---

[1]Contradicting Victor's initial boast of being "Genevese" (Swiss) "by birth."

attached to each other, they seemed to draw inexhaustible stores of affection from a very mine of love to bestow them upon me. My mother's tender caresses, and my father's smile of benevolent pleasure while regarding me, are my first recollections. I was their plaything and their idol, and something better—their child, the innocent and helpless creature bestowed on them by Heaven, whom to bring up to good, and whose future lot it was in their hands to direct to happiness or misery, according as they fulfilled their duties towards me. With this deep consciousness of what they owed towards the being to which they had given life, added to the active spirit of tenderness that animated both, it may be imagined that while during every hour of my infant life I received a lesson of patience, of charity, and of self-control, I was so guided by a silken cord that all seemed but one train of enjoyment to me.

For a long time I was their only care. My mother had much desired to have a daughter, but I continued their single offspring. When I was about five years old, while making an excursion beyond the frontiers of Italy, they passed a week on the shores of the Lake of Como. Their benevolent disposition often made them enter the cottages of the poor. This, to my mother, was more than a duty; it was a necessity, a passion,—remembering what she had suffered, and how she had been relieved,—for her to act in her turn the guardian angel to the afflicted. During one of their walks a poor cot in the foldings of a vale attracted their notice, as being singularly disconsolate, while the number of half-clothed children gathered about it, spoke of penury in its worst shape. One day, when my father had gone by himself to Milan, my mother, accompanied by me, visited this abode. She found a peasant and his wife, hard working, bent down by care and labour, distributing a scanty meal to five hungry babes. Among these there was one which attracted my mother far above all the rest.[2] She appeared of a different stock. The four others were dark-eyed, hardy little vagrants; this child was thin, and very fair. Her hair was the brightest living gold, and, despite the poverty of her clothing, seemed to set a crown of distinction on her head. Her brow was clear and ample, her blue eyes cloudless, and her lips and the moulding of her face so expressive of sensibility[3] and sweetness, that none could

[2]Recasting Elizabeth as an adopted orphan rather than a blood-cousin, Shelley at once sharpens the contrasts with the Creature's doomed hopes and elaborates the racialized aesthetic values in the Frankenstein family (and implicitly in European culture).

[3]A term with a wide range of meanings in Shelley's day, here indicating emotional sensitivity and spiritual character.

behold her without looking on her as of a distinct species, a being heaven-sent, and bearing a celestial stamp in all her features.

The peasant woman, perceiving that my mother fixed eyes of wonder and admiration on this lovely girl, eagerly communicated her history. She was not her child, but the daughter of a Milanese nobleman. Her mother was a German, and had died on giving her birth.[4] The infant had been placed with these good people to nurse:[5] they were better off then. They had not been long married, and their eldest child was but just born. The father of their charge was one of those Italians nursed in the memory of the antique glory of Italy,—one among the *schiavi ognor frementi*,[6] who exerted himself to obtain the liberty of his country. He became the victim of its weakness. Whether he had died, or still lingered in the dungeons of Austria, was not known. His property was confiscated; his child became an orphan and a beggar.[7] She continued with her foster parents, and bloomed in their rude abode, fairer than a garden rose among dark-leaved brambles.

When my father returned from Milan, he found playing with me in the hall of our villa, a child fairer than pictured cherub—a creature who seemed to shed radiance from her looks, and whose form and motions were lighter than the chamois[8] of the hills. The apparition was soon explained. With his permission my mother prevailed on her rustic guardians to yield their charge to her. They were fond of the sweet orphan. Her presence had seemed a blessing to them; but it would be unfair to her to keep her in poverty and want when Providence afforded her such powerful protection. They consulted their village priest, and the result was that Elizabeth Lavenza became the inmate[9] of my parents' house—my more than sister—the beautiful and adored companion of all my occupations and my pleasures.

Everyone loved Elizabeth. The passionate and almost reverential attachment with which all regarded her became, while I shared it, my pride and my delight. On the evening previous to her being brought

[4]As Shelley's own mother had.

[5]A "wet-nurse" is hired to suckle a child not her own.

[6]A phrase from a sonnet in *Misogallo* by Italian poet and dramatist Vittorio Alfieri (1749–1803), a champion of Italian independence from Austria: "We are slaves, yes, but *slaves still quivering*" with rage and defiance.

[7]Repeating the plight of Caroline Beaufort after her father's death (see p. 19).

[8]Small mountain antelope.

[9]The modern sense of "prisoner" was just emerging; the primary sense in 1831 was still "inhabitant."

to my home, my mother had said playfully,—"I have a pretty present for my Victor—to-morrow he shall have it." And when, on the morrow, she presented Elizabeth to me as her promised gift, I, with childish seriousness, interpreted her words literally, and looked upon Elizabeth as mine—mine to protect, love, and cherish. All praises bestowed on her I received as made to a possession of my own. We called each other familiarly by the name of cousin. No word, no expression could body forth the kind of relation in which she stood to me—my more than sister, since till death she was to be mine only.

Chapter II

We were brought up together; there was not quite a year difference in our ages. I need not say that we were strangers to any species of disunion or dispute. Harmony was the soul of our companionship, and the diversity and contrast that subsisted in our characters drew us nearer together. Elizabeth was of a calmer and more concentrated disposition; but, with all my ardour, I was capable of a more intense application, and was more deeply smitten with the thirst for knowledge. She busied herself with following the aerial creations of the poets; and in the majestic and wondrous scenes which surrounded our Swiss home—the sublime shapes of the mountains; the changes of the seasons, tempest and calm; the silence of winter, and the life and turbulence of our Alpine summers,—she found ample scope for admiration and delight. While my companion contemplated with a serious and satisfied spirit the magnificent appearances of things, I delighted in investigating their causes. The world was to me a secret which I desired to divine. Curiosity, earnest research to learn the hidden laws of nature, gladness akin to rapture, as they were unfolded to me, are among the earliest sensations I can remember.

On the birth of a second son, my junior by seven years, my parents gave up entirely their wandering life, and fixed themselves in their native country. We possessed a house in Geneva, and a *campagne*[10] on Belrive, the eastern shore of the lake, at the distance of rather more than a league from the city. We resided principally in the latter, and the lives of my parents were passed in considerable seclusion. It was my temper to avoid a crowd and to attach myself fervently to a few. I was

[10]Country-house (in distinction from the town house).

indifferent, therefore, to my schoolfellows in general; but I united myself in the bonds of the closest friendship to one among them. Henry Clerval was the son of a merchant of Geneva. He was a boy of singular talent and fancy. He loved enterprise, hardship, and even danger, for its own sake. He was deeply read in books of chivalry and romance.[11] He composed heroic songs and began to write many a tale of enchantment and knightly adventure. He tried to make us act plays, and to enter into masquerades, in which the characters were drawn from the heroes of Roncesvalles,[12] of the Round Table of King Arthur, and the chivalrous train who shed their blood to redeem the holy sepulchre from the hands of the infidels.[13]

No human being could have passed a happier childhood than myself. My parents were possessed by the very spirit of kindness and indulgence. We felt that they were not the tyrants to rule our lot according to their caprice, but the agents and creators of all the many delights which we enjoyed. When I mingled with other families, I distinctly discerned how peculiarly fortunate my lot was, and gratitude assisted the development of filial love.

My temper was sometimes violent, and my passions vehement; but by some law in my temperature they were turned, not towards childish pursuits, but to an eager desire to learn, and not to learn all things indiscriminately. I confess that neither the structure of languages, nor the code of governments, nor the politics of various states possessed attractions for me. It was the secrets of heaven and earth that I desired to learn; and whether it was the outward substance of things or the inner spirit of nature and the mysterious soul of man that occupied me, still my enquiries were directed to the metaphysical, or, in it highest sense, the physical secrets of the world.

[11]The literary genres of knightly exploits and exotic adventures.

[12]Roncesvalles pass in the Pyrenees was famed in Spain's legendary past and in the recent Napoleonic wars. It was here that Roland, the most renowned of Charlemagne's Christian knights, was killed in 778 by a band of Basque mountaineers in an ambush of his retreating army of 20,000—represented in *Chanson de Roland* (11th c.) as an attack force of 400,000 Muslims (another racial polarization).

[13]King Arthur and his Knights of the Round Table are part of England's legendary Christian past. The Crusades of 1095–1243 were a pan-European war to wrest the "Holy Lands" from the "Infidels" (the Muslim populations of these eastern Mediterranean lands); this brutal genocidal campaign involved any Jewish populations along the way. Though celebrated in early modern Romance, by the end of the 18th c., these wars were beginning to be seen as an appalling exercise of imperialism under the aegis of the cross.

Meanwhile Clerval occupied himself, so to speak, with the moral[14] relations of things. The busy stage of life, the virtues of heroes, and the actions of men, were his theme; and his hope and his dream was to become one among those whose names are recorded in story, as the gallant and adventurous benefactors of our species.[15] The saintly soul of Elizabeth shone like a shrine-dedicated lamp in our peaceful home. Her sympathy was ours; her smile, her soft voice, the sweet glance of her celestial eyes, were ever there to bless and animate us. She was the living spirit of love to soften and attract; I might have become sullen in my study, through the ardour of my nature, but that she was there to subdue me to a semblance of her own gentleness. And Clerval—could aught ill entrench on the noble spirit of Clerval?—yet he might not have been so perfectly humane, so thoughtful in his generosity—so full of kindness and tenderness amidst his passion for adventurous exploit, had she not unfolded to him the real loveliness of beneficence, and made the doing good the end and aim of his soaring ambition.

[*I feel pleasure in dwelling on the recollections of childhood* . . .

Victor's enchantment with occult science and his encounter with modern science (Ch. II)

I.I (pp. 22–23) *I read and studied the wild fancies of these writers with delight; they appeared to me treasures known to few beside myself.*] I have described myself as always having been embued with a fervent longing to penetrate the secrets of nature. In spite of the intense labour and wonderful discoveries of modern philosophers, I always came from my studies discontented and unsatisfied. Sir Isaac Newton is said to have avowed that he felt like a child picking up shells beside the great and unexplored ocean of truth.[1] Those of his successors in each branch of natural philosophy with whom I was acquainted, appeared even to my boy's apprehensions, as tyros engaged in the same pursuit.

The untaught peasant beheld the elements around him and was acquainted with their practical uses. The most learned philosopher

[14]In the 18th-c. sense of "socially ethical."

[15]Compare Robert Walton's self-representation on p. 6.

[1]Sir Isaac Newton (1642–1727), the great mathematician and physicist (natural philosopher).

knew little more. He had partially unveiled the face of Nature, but her immortal lineaments were still a wonder and a mystery. He might dissect, anatomise, and give names; but, not to speak of a final cause, causes in their secondary and tertiary grades were utterly unknown to him. I had gazed upon the fortifications and impediments that seemed to keep human beings from entering the citadel of nature, and rashly and ignorantly I had repined.

But here were books, and here were men who had penetrated deeper and knew more. I took their word for all that they averred, and I became their disciple. It may appear strange that such should arise in the eighteenth century; but while I followed the routine of education in the schools of Geneva, I was, to a great degree, self-taught with regard to my favourite studies. My father was not scientific, and I was left to struggle with a child's blindness, added to a student's thirst for knowledge. [. . .] And thus for a time I was occupied by exploded systems, mingling, like an unadept, a thousand contradictory theories and floundering desperately in a very slough of multifarious knowledge, guided by an ardent imagination and childish reasoning, till an accident again changed the current of my ideas.

[*When I was about fifteen years old . . .*

(pp. 24–25) *The catastrophe of this tree excited my extreme astonishment . . .*] Before this I was not unacquainted with the more obvious laws of electricity. On this occasion a man of great research in natural philosophy was with us, and excited by this catastrophe, he entered on the explanation of a theory which he had formed on the subject of electricity and galvanism, which was at once new and astonishing to me. All that he said threw greatly into the shade Cornelius Agrippa, Albertus Magnus, and Paracelsus, the lords of my imagination; but by some fatality the overthrow of these men disinclined me to pursue my accustomed studies. It seemed to me as if nothing would or could ever be known. All that had so long engaged my attention suddenly grew despicable. By one of those caprices of the mind which we are perhaps most subject to in early youth, I at once gave up my former occupations; set down natural history and all its progeny as a deformed and abortive creation; and entertained the greatest disdain for a would-be science, which could never even step within the threshold of real knowledge. In this mood of mind I betook myself to the mathematics, and the branches of study appertaining to that science, as being built upon secure foundations, and so worthy of my consideration.[2]

Thus strangely are our souls constructed, and by such slight ligaments are we bound to prosperity or ruin. When I look back, it seems to me as if this almost miraculous change of inclination and will was the immediate suggestion of the guardian angel of my life—the last effort made by the spirit of preservation to avert the storm that was even then hanging in the stars, and ready to envelop me. Her victory was announced by an unusual tranquillity and gladness of soul, which followed the relinquishing of my ancient and latterly tormenting studies. It was thus that I was to be taught to associate evil with their prosecution, happiness with their disregard.

It was a strong effort of the spirit of good, but it was ineffectual. Destiny was too potent, and her immutable laws had decreed my utter and terrible destruction. [end of 1831 Chapter II]

After his mother's death, Victor leaves for the University

Clerval's straits; the breakup of the friendship circle (Ch. III)

I.II (p. 27) *Clerval . . . spent the last evening with us.*] He had endeavoured to persuade his father to permit him to accompany me, and to become my fellow student; but in vain. His father was a narrow-minded trader and saw idleness and ruin in the aspirations and ambition of his son. Henry deeply felt the misfortune of being debarred from a liberal education. He said little; but when he spoke I read in his kindling eye and in his animated glance a restrained but firm resolve, not to be chained to the miserable details of commerce.

We sat late. We could not tear ourselves away from each other, nor persuade ourselves to say the word "Farewell!" It was said; and we retired under the pretence of seeking repose, each fancying that the other was deceived: but when at morning's dawn I descended to the carriage which was to convey me away, they were all there—my father again to bless me, Clerval to press my hand once more, my Elizabeth to renew her entreaties that I would write often, and to bestow the last feminine attentions on her playmate and friend.

[*I threw myself into the chaise . . .*

---

[2]Mathematics was revered as platonically ideal science: uncontingent, objective, universal.

Victor meets Professors Krempe and Waldman

A heightened language of fate and destiny in Victor's seduction by modern science (Ch. III)

I.II (p. 28) *I . . . paid a visit to some of the principal professors.*] Chance—or rather the evil influence, the Angel of Destruction, which asserted omnipotent sway over me from the moment I turned my reluctant steps from my father's door—led me first to Mr. Krempe, professor of natural philosophy. He was an uncouth man, but deeply imbued in the secrets of his science. [*and asked me several questions*

I.II (p. 30) *I departed highly pleased with* [Professor Waldman] *and his lecture.*] Such were the professor's words—rather let me say such the words of the fate, enounced to destroy me. As he went on, I felt as if my soul were grappling with a palpable enemy; one by one the various keys were touched which formed the mechanism of my being: chord after chord was sounded, and soon my mind was filled with one thought, one conception, one purpose. So much has been done, exclaimed the soul of Frankenstein,[1]—more, far more, will I achieve: treading in the steps already marked, I will pioneer a new way, explore unknown powers, and unfold to the world the deepest mysteries of creation.

I closed not my eyes that night. My internal being was in a state of insurrection and turmoil; I felt that order would thence arise, but I had no power to produce it. By degrees, after the morning's dawn, sleep came. I awoke, and my yesternight's thoughts were as a dream. There only remained a resolution to return to my ancient studies and to devote myself to a science for which I believed myself to possess a natural talent. On the same day I paid M. Waldman a visit. [*His manners in private . . .*

Victor's obsessive studies deplete his health (Ch. IV)

I.III (p. 36) *the firmness of my nerves*] the fall of a leaf startled me, and I shunned my fellow-creatures as if I had been guilty of a crime. Sometimes I grew alarmed at the wreck I perceived that I had become; the energy of my purpose alone sustained me: my labours would soon end, and I believed that exercise and amusement would then drive away incipient disease. [*and I promised . . .*

[1]The first naming of "Frankenstein" inside the 1831 narrative.

Elizabeth's report of Ernest Frankenstein's vocation (Ch. VI)

I.V (p. 43) *now that he enjoys good health*] He is now sixteen, and full of activity and spirit. He is desirous to be a true Swiss, and to enter into foreign service,[2] but we cannot part with him, at least until his elder brother returns to us. My uncle is not pleased with the idea of a military career in a distant country, but Ernest never had your powers of application. He looks upon study as an odious fetter;—his time is spent in the open air, climbing the hills or rowing on the lake. I fear that he will become an idler, unless we yield the point, and permit him to enter on the profession which he has selected.

Clerval's lament for William (Ch. VII) replacing the reference to Cato and Stoic maxims

I.VI (p. 50) *During our walk, Clerval endeavoured to raise my spirits*] . . . to say a few words of consolation; he could only express his heartfelt sympathy. "Poor William!" said he, "dear lovely child, he now sleeps with his angel mother! Who that had seen him bright and joyous in his young beauty, but must weep over his untimely loss! To die so miserably; to feel the murderer's grasp! How much more a murderer that could destroy radiant innocence! Poor little fellow! one only consolation have we; [*he now sleeps with his angel mother.*

Victor's anguish over the execution of Justine (Ch. VII)

I.VI (p. 56) replacing the rest of the paragraph after *enough to convict her;*] My tale was not one to announce publicly; its astounding horror would be looked upon as madness by the vulgar. Did any one indeed exist, except I, the creator, who would believe, unless his senses convinced him, in the existence of the living monument of presumption and rash ignorance which I had let loose upon the world? [*We were soon joined by Elizabeth.*

end of Ch. VIII and Vol. I (p. 64) *As we returned . . .*] And on the morrow Justine died. Elizabeth's heart-rending eloquence failed to move the judges from their settled conviction in the criminality of the saintly sufferer. My passionate and indignant appeals were lost upon

---

[2]Because Switzerland had a policy of neutrality in foreign conflicts, its citizens were available for paid foreign service.

them. And when I received their cold answers, and heard the harsh, unfeeling reasoning of these men, my purposed avowal died away on my lips. Thus I might proclaim myself a madman, but not revoke the sentence passed upon my wretched victim. She perished on the scaffold as a murderess!

From the tortures of my own heart, I turned to contemplate the deep and voiceless grief of my Elizabeth. This also was my doing! And my father's woe, and the desolation of that late so smiling home—all was the work of my thrice-accursed hands! Ye weep, unhappy ones; but these are not your last tears! Again shall you raise the funeral wail, and the sound of your lamentations shall again and again be heard! Frankenstein, your son, your kinsman, your early, much-loved friend; he who would spend each vital drop of blood for your sakes—who has no thought nor sense of joy, except as it is mirrored also in your dear countenances—who would fill the air with blessings, and spend his life in serving you—he bids you weep—to shed countless tears; happy beyond his hopes, if thus inexorable fate be satisfied, and if the destruction pause before the peace of the grave have succeeded to your sad torments!

Thus spoke my prophetic soul, as, torn by remorse, horror, and despair, I beheld those I loved spend vain sorrow upon the graves of William and Justine, the first hapless victims to my unhallowed arts.

Victor's continuing agony and desire for oblivion (Ch. IX)

II.I (p. 67) new text after *Elizabeth: "what can disturb our tranquillity?"*]

And could not such words from her whom I fondly prized before every other gift of fortune, suffice to chase away the fiend that lurked in my heart? Even as she spoke I drew near to her, as if in terror; lest at that very moment the destroyer had been near to rob me of her.

Thus not the tenderness of friendship, nor the beauty of earth, nor of heaven, could redeem my soul from woe: the very accents of love were ineffectual. I was encompassed by a cloud which no beneficial influence could penetrate. The wounded deer dragging its fainting limbs to some untrodden brake, there to gaze upon the arrow which had pierced it, and to die—was but a type of me.[1]

---

[1]Echoing William Cowper: "I was a stricken deer that left the herd / Long since; with many an arrow deep infixt / My panting side was charged when I withdrew / To seek a tranquil death in distant shades" (*The Task* 3.108–11). For Victor to say that all sufferers are but a "type" of him is to claim status as prototype.

Sometimes I could cope with the sullen despair that overwhelmed me: but sometimes the whirlwind passions of my soul drove me to seek, by bodily exercise and by change of place, some relief from my intolerable sensations. It was during an access of this kind that I suddenly left my home, and bending my steps towards the near Alpine valleys, sought in the magnificence, the eternity of such scenes, to forget myself and my ephemeral, because human, sorrows. [. . .] The weight upon my spirit was sensibly lightened as I plunged yet deeper in the ravine of Arve. The immense mountains and precipices that overhung me on every side—the sound of the river raging among the rocks, and the dashing of the waterfalls around, spoke of a power mighty as Omnipotence—and I ceased to fear, or to bend before any being less almighty . . .

end of the chapter (p. 69) instead of *ran below my window*] pursued its noisy way beneath. The same lulling sounds acted as a lullaby to my too keen sensations: when I placed my head upon my pillow, sleep crept over me; I felt it as it came, and blessed the giver of oblivion.

Ch. X/II.II (p. 70) end of paragraph 1 and beginning of paragraph 2] my slumbers, as it were, waited on and ministered to by the assemblance of grand shapes which I had contemplated during the day. They congregated round me; the unstained snowy mountain-top, the glittering pinnacle, the pine woods, and ragged bare ravine; the eagle, soaring amidst the clouds—they all gathered round me, and bade me be at peace.

Where had they fled when the next morning I awoke? All of soul-inspiriting fled with sleep, and dark melancholy clouded every thought. [*The rain depressed me*

The Creature's story of finding, adoring, and framing Justine (Ch. XVI)

II.VIII (p. 110) *she shall not escape:*] "And then I bent over her and whispered, 'Awake, fairest, thy lover is near—he who would give his life but to obtain one look of affection from thine eyes: my beloved, awake!'

The sleeper stirred; a thrill of terror ran through me. Should she indeed awake, and see me, and curse me, and denounce the murderer? Thus would she assuredly act if her darkened eyes opened and she beheld me. The thought was madness; it stirred the fiend within me—not I, but she, shall suffer; the murder I have committed because I am forever robbed of all that she could give me, she shall atone. The crime had its source in her: be hers the punishment!" [*thanks to the lessons of Felix . . .*

Victor's plans for a second creature (Ch. XVIII)

III.I (p. 118) *I was delighted with the idea of spending a year or two in change of scene and variety of occupation*] I had an insurmountable aversion to the idea of engaging myself in my loathsome task in my father's house, while in habits of familiar intercourse with those I loved. I knew that a thousand fearful accidents might occur, the slightest of which would disclose a tale to thrill all connected with me with horror. I was aware also that I should often lose all self-command, all capacity of hiding the harrowing sensations that would possess me during the progress of my unearthly occupation. I must absent myself from all I loved while thus employed. Once commenced, it would quickly be achieved, and I might be restored to my family in peace and happiness. My promise fulfilled, the monster would depart forever. Or (so my fond fancy imaged) some accident might meanwhile occur to destroy him [*and put an end to my slavery for ever.*

Clerval's imperial ambitions (Ch. XIX)

III.II (p. 123) *The difference of manners which he observed was to him an inexhaustible source of instruction and amusement*] He was also pursuing an object he had long had in view. His design was to visit India, in the belief that he had in his knowledge of its various languages, and in the views he had taken of its society, the means of materially assisting the progress of European colonization and trade. In Britain only could he further the execution of his plan. [*He was for ever busy.*

Victor's apprehensions for his family (Ch. XXI)

III.IV (p. 144) *his longing for oblivion* (replacing the two short paragraphs, *I remember . . . so much misery*)] Yet one duty remained to me, the recollection of which finally triumphed over my selfish despair. It was necessary that I should return without delay to Geneva, there to watch over the lives of those I so fondly loved; and to lie in wait for the murderer, that if any chance led me to the place of his concealment, or if he dared again to blast me by his presence, I might, with unfailing aim, put an end to the existence of the monstrous Image which I had endued with the mockery of a soul still more monstrous. My father still desired to delay our departure, fearful that I could not sustain the fatigues of a journey: for I was a shattered wreck,—the shadow of a human being. My strength was gone. I was a mere skeleton; and fever night and day preyed upon my wasted frame.

The longing for forgetfulness returns

III.IV (p. 145) adding to the end of the chapter] the dashing waves were around: the cloudy sky above; the fiend was not here: a sense of security, a feeling that a truce was established between the present hour and the irresistible, disastrous future, imparted to me a kind of calm forgetfulness, of which the human mind is by its structure peculiarly susceptible.

Victor's secret (Ch. XXII)

III.V (p. 145) new sentences for paragraph 2, on Alphonse's concern] he did not know the origin of my sufferings, and sought erroneous methods to remedy the incurable ill. He wished me to seek amusement in society. I abhorred the face of man. Oh, not abhorred! they were my brethren, my fellow beings, and I felt attracted even to the most repulsive among them, as to creatures of an angelic nature and celestial mechanism. But I felt that I had no right to share their intercourse. I had unchained an enemy among them, whose joy it was to shed their blood, and to revel in their groans. How they would, each and all, abhor me, and hunt me from the world did they know my unhallowed acts and the crimes which had their source in me! [*As for my father*

III.V (p. 146) *I had a feeling that I should be supposed mad, and this for ever chained my tongue*] But, besides, I could not bring myself to disclose a secret which would fill my hearer with consternation, and make fear and unnatural horror the inmates of his breast. I checked, therefore, my impatient thirst for sympathy and was silent [*when I would have given the whole world to have confided the fatal secret.*

there to watch over the lives of those I so fondly loved; and to lie in wait for the murderer, that if any chance led me to the place of his concealment, or if he dared again to blast me by his presence, I might with unfailing aim, put an end to the existence of the monstrous image which I had endued with the mockery of a soul still more monstrous. My father still desired to delay our departure, fearful that I could not sustain the fatigues of a journey: for I was a shattered wreck,—the shadow of a human being. My strength was gone. I was a mere skeleton; and fever night and day preyed upon my wasted frame.

The longing for forgetfulness returns

III.IV (p. 143) adding to the end of the chapter] the dashing waves were around, the cloudy sky above; the bond was not here; a sense of security, a feeling that a truce was established between the present hour and the irresistible, disastrous future, imparted to me a kind of calm forgetfulness, of which the human mind is by its structure peculiarly susceptible.

Victor's secret (Ch. XXIII)

III.V (p. 143) new sentences for paragraph 2, on Alphonse's conceal] he did not know the origin of my sufferings, and sought erroneous methods to remedy the incurable ill. He wished me to seek amusement in society. I abhorred the face of man. Oh, not abhorred! they were my brethren, my fellow beings, and I felt attracted even to the most repulsive among them, as to creatures of an angelic nature and celestial mechanism. But I felt that I had no right to share their intercourse. I had unchained an enemy among them, whose joy it was to shed their blood, and to revel in their groans. How they would each and all, abhor me, and hunt me from the world, did they know my unhallowed acts, and the crimes which had their source in me! [As for my father

III.V (p. 146) had a feeling that I should be supposed mad, and this for ever chained my tongue. But, besides, I could not bring myself to disclose a secret which would fill my hearer with consternation, and make fear and unnatural horror the inmates of his breast. I checked, therefore, my impatient thirst for sympathy, and was silent when I would have given the whole world to have confided the fatal secret.

CONTEXTS

Monsters, Visionaries, and Mary Shelley

Aesthetic Adventures

Much of the descriptive aura of *Frankenstein*—its settings, its psychological terrains, and the contours of its characters—draws on the categories of eighteenth-century aesthetics: "the sublime," "the beautiful," and "the picturesque." Developed against established "mimetic" ideas (the notion that art, visual and verbal, should imitate the external world), these categories emphasized a beholder's cognitive, affective, and psychological response: What can be grasped in understanding? what defeats it? what feelings are aroused? what senses of self are excited or threatened?

Edmund Burke's influential treatise, *A Philosophical Inquiry into the Origin of Our Ideas of the Sublime and the Beautiful* (1757), set forth two contrasting categories. The "sublime," to denote spectacles—vast landscapes; terrifying figures, such as Milton's "Death"; horrific events, such as war and earthquakes; sensations of infinity—that overpower, impress, and terrify the mind with a sense of its insignificance and perishable existence. The sublime threatened the integrity and potency of the self; the "beautiful" reassured, with its emphasis on order, harmony, and an appeal to the affections. In Burke's descriptions, these were gendered aesthetics: the beholder is always assumed to be male, and in the aesthetics of the "beautiful," enjoying his sensation of mastery over an object of attention gendered "she."

This gendering was one provocation to Mary Wollstonecraft's critique of Burke's aesthetics, and the consequences play across *Frankenstein*. To Burke's categories, William Gilpin added a third, "the picturesque," a beauty pleasing not for the harmonies and symmetries that Burke proposed, but for delightful irregularities, asymmetries, quaint roughness. It was a kind of "junior sublime," containable, manageable, enjoyable. A Gothic cathedral is sublime, an English cottage beautiful, a ruined cottage or shepherd's hut picturesque; the Alps are sublime, a formal garden beautiful, and a landscape of winding paths and streams, of little hills and dales, picturesque.

Edmund Burke (1729–1797)
from *A Philosophical Inquiry into the Origin of Our Ideas of the Sublime and the Beautiful* (1757; 5th edition, 1767)

> *Before* Reflections on the Revolution in France *(1790), his internationally celebrated denunciation of the French Revolution (a sublime event, before the Reign of Terror), Burke was a renowned member of Parliament, famous for his powerful oratory (itself a kind of sublime), and in aesthetic theory, for his treatise on "the Sublime and the Beautiful." In* Frankenstein, Shelley *draws on Burkean notions of the "sublime" to render such landscapes as the Alps and the Arctic, and to convey the horrific creation of the Creature. In the oratorical sublime, the Creature competes with his creator in an effort to arouse compassion for his plight—a dynamic Burke addresses in conclusion of his* Inquiry.

Of the SUBLIME

Whatever is fitted in any sort to excite the ideas of pain, and danger, that is to say, whatever is in any sort terrible, or is conversant about terrible objects, or operates in a manner analogous to terror, is a source of the *sublime;* that is, it is productive of the strongest emotion which the mind is capable of feeling. I say the strongest emotion, because I am satisfied the ideas of pain are much more powerful than those which enter on the part of pleasure. [. . .] When danger or pain press too nearly, they are incapable of giving any delight, and are simply terrible; but at certain distances, and with certain modifications, they may be, and they are delightful, as we every day experience. . . .

Of the passion caused by the SUBLIME

The passion caused by the great and sublime in *nature*, when those causes operate most powerfully, is astonishment; and astonishment is that state of the soul, in which all its motions are suspended, with some degree of horror. In this case the mind is so entirely filled with its object, that it cannot entertain any other, nor by consequence reason on that object which employs it. Hence arises the great power of the sublime, that far from being produced by them, it anticipates our reasonings, and hurries us on by an irresistible force . . .

TERROR

No passion so effectually robs the mind of all its powers of acting and reasoning as fear. For fear being an apprehension of pain or death, it operates in a manner that resembles actual pain. Whatever therefore is terrible, with regard to sight, is sublime too, whether this cause of terror be endued with greatness of dimensions or not . . .

OBSCURITY

To make any thing very terrible, obscurity seems in general to be necessary. When we know the full extent of any danger, when we can accustom our eyes to it, a great deal of the apprehension vanishes. Every one will be sensible of this, who considers how greatly night adds to our dread, in all cases of danger, and how much the notions of ghosts and goblins, of which none can form clear ideas, affect minds, which give credit to popular tales concerning such sorts of beings. Those despotic governments, which are founded on the passions of men, and principally upon the passion of fear, keep their chief as much as may be from the public eye. This policy has been the same in many cases of religion. Almost all the heathen temples were dark. [. . .] No person seems better to have understood the secret of heightening, or of setting terrible things, if I may use the expression, in their strongest light by the force of a judicious obscurity, than Milton. His description of Death in the second book is admirably studied; it is astonishing with what a gloomy pomp, with what a significant and expressive uncertainty of strokes and colouring he has finished the portrait of the king of terrors.

The other shape,
If shape it might be call'd that shape had none

> *Distinguishable, in member, joint, or limb;*
> *Or substance might be call'd that shadow seem'd,*
> *For such seem'd either; black he stood as night;*
> *Fierce as ten furies; terrible as hell;*
> *And shook a deadly dart. What seem'd his head*
> *The likeness of a kingly crown had on.*[1]

In this description all is dark, uncertain, confused, terrible, and sublime to the last degree.

Beautiful objects small

I am told that in most languages, the objects of love are spoken of under diminutive epithets. It is so in all the languages of which I have any knowledge. [. . .] The sublime, which is the cause of [admiration], always dwells on great objects, and terrible; [love] on small ones, and pleasing; we submit to what we admire, but we love what submits to us; in one case we are forced, in the other we are flattered into compliance . . .

How WORDS influence the passions

Now, as words affect, not by any original power, but by representation, it might be supposed, that their influence over the passions should be but light; yet it is quite otherwise; for we find by experience that eloquence and poetry are as capable, nay indeed much more capable of making deep and lively impressions than any other arts, and even than nature itself in very many cases. And this arises chiefly from these three causes. First, that we take an extraordinary part in the passions of others, and that we are easily affected and brought into sympathy by any tokens which are shewn of them; and there are no tokens which can express all the circumstances of most passions so fully as words; so that if a person speaks upon any subject, he can not only convey the subject to you, but likewise the manner in which he is himself affected by it. Certain it is, that the influence of most things on our passions is not so much from the things themselves, as from our passions concerning them; and these again depend very much on the opinions of other men, conveyable for the most part by words only. Secondly; there are many

[1]*Paradise Lost* 2.666–73. Death is Satan's son, begot in his incestuous rape of his daughter, Sin.

things of a very affecting nature, which can seldom occur in the reality, but the words which represent them often do; and thus they have an opportunity of making a deep impression and taking root in the mind, whilst the idea of the reality was transient; and to some perhaps never really occurred in any shape, to whom it is notwithstanding very affecting, as war, death, famine, &c. Besides, many ideas have never been at all presented to the senses of any men but by words, as God, angels, devils, heaven and hell, all of which have however a great influence over the passions. Thirdly; by words we have it in our power to make such combinations as we cannot possibly do otherwise. By this power of combining we are able, by the addition of well-chosen circumstances, to give a new life and force to the simple object. [. . .] Words [. . . are] capable of being the representatives of these natural things, [. . .] able to affect us often as strongly as the things they represent, and sometimes much more strongly.

Mary Wollstonecraft (1759–1797)
from *A Vindication of the Rights of Men*

A Vindication of the Rights of Men (1790), by Mary Shelley's mother, was one of the first responses to Burke's conservative attack on the French Revolution. First published anonymously, it made Wollstonecraft's reputation when a second edition bore her name in 1791. Although her primary target was Burke's politics, she anticipated her Vindication of the Rights of Woman *two years later (1792) in her attention to the gender-text in Burke's aesthetic ideology. Shelley registers this system in* Frankenstein, *though not with her mother's critical edge.*

[. . .] ladies may have read your Enquiry concerning the origin of our ideas of the Sublime and Beautiful, and, convinced by your arguments, may have laboured to be pretty, by counterfeiting weakness.

You may have convinced them that littleness and weakness are the very essence of beauty; and that the Supreme Being, in giving women beauty in the most supereminent degree, seemed to command them, by the powerful voice of Nature, not to cultivate the moral virtues that might chance to excite respect, and interfere with the pleasing sensations they were created to inspire. Thus confining truth, fortitude, and humanity, within the rigid pale of manly morals, they might justly argue, that to be loved, woman's high end and great distinction! They should 'learn to lisp, to totter in their walk, and nick-name God's creatures.'[1] Never, they might repeat after you, was any man, much less a woman, rendered amiable by the force of those exalted qualities, fortitude, justice, wisdom, and truth; and thus forewarned of the sacrifice they must make to those austere, unnatural virtues, they would be authorized to turn all their attention to their persons, systematically neglecting morals to secure beauty [. . .]

But should experience prove that there is a beauty in virtue, a charm in order which necessarily implies exertion, a depraved sensual taste may give way to a more manly one—and melting feelings to rational satisfactions. Both may be equally natural to man; the test is their moral difference, and that point reason alone can decide.

Such a glorious change can only be produced by liberty.[2]

William Gilpin (1724–1804)
from *Three Essays: On Picturesque Beauty, On Picturesque Travel, and On Sketching Landscape*

Schoolmaster and vicar Gilpin was a pioneering theorist of "the picturesque," an aesthetic he defined in his Essay on Prints *(1768) as "that kind of beauty which would look well in a picture." He elaborated his principles over several years and gave a summary description in his popular and influential treatise,* Three Essays: On Picturesque Beauty, On Picturesque Travel, and On Sketching Landscape *(1792). If the Arctic and Alpine terrains of* Frankenstein *are sublime, and Elizabeth and home are a beautiful world (though imperiled and problematic), the picturesque emerges in* Frankenstein *not just where we expect it, in the "tourist" episodes in England and the Rhineland; strangely, it also emerges in Victor's adventures as a science student—activities that Shelley, following Gilpin, represents as gendered, with a dedicated*

[1]From Hamlet's misogynist diatribe against Ophelia, when he suspects her of treachery (*Hamlet* 3.1.145–50); a phrase Burke quoted in his *Inquiry* (in a section titled "Perfection not the cause of BEAUTY") to advise women how to appeal to men.

[2]That is, a republican (proto-democractic), non-monarchal political system, the purpose of the French Revolution.

*and excited male pursuer in chase of and out to conquer a nature
gendered as "she."*

from *On Picturesque Travel*

The first source of amusement[1] to the picturesque traveler is the pursuit of his object—the expectation of new scenes continually opening,
and arising to his view. We suppose the country to have been unexplored. Under this circumstance the mind is kept constantly in an
agreeable suspense. The love of novelty is the foundation of this pleasure. Every distant horizon promises something new; and with this
pleasing expectation we follow nature through all her walks. We pursue her from her hill to dale, and hunt after those various beauties,
with which she everywhere abounds.

The pleasures of the chase are universal. A hare started before
dogs is enough to set a whole country in an uproar. The plow and the
spade are deserted. Care is left behind; and every human faculty is
dilated with joy.

And shall we suppose it a greater pleasure to the sportsman to
pursue a trivial animal, than it is to the man of taste to pursue the
beauties of nature? to follow her through all her recesses? to obtain a
sudden glance, as she flits past him in some airy shape? to trace her
through the mazes of the cover? to wind after her along the vale? or
along the reaches of the river?

After the pursuit we are gratified with the *attainment* of the
object. Our amusement, on this head, arises from the employment
of the mind in examining the beautiful scenes we have found.
Sometimes we examine them under the idea of a *whole:* we admire
the composition, the coloring, and the light, in one *comprehensive
view.* When we are fortunate enough to fall in with scenes of this
kind, we are highly delighted. But as we have less frequent opportunities of being thus gratified, we are more commonly employed
in analyzing the *parts of scenes,* which may be exquisitely beautiful, though unable to produce a whole. We examine what would
amend the composition; how little is wanting to reduce it to the
rules of our art; what a trifling circumstance sometimes forms the
limit between beauty and deformity. Or we compare the objects
before us with other objects of the same kind—or perhaps we

[1]That is, "aesthetic pleasure" (note the root, *muse*).

compare them with the limitations of art. From all these operations of the mind results great amusement.

But it is not from this *scientifical* employment that we derive our chief pleasure. We are most delighted when some grand scene, though perhaps of incorrect composition, rising before the eye, strikes us beyond the power of thought—when the *vox faucibus haeret*,[2] and every mental operation is suspended. In this pause of intellect; this *deliquirium*[3] of the soul, an enthusiastic sensation of pleasure overspreads it, previous to any examination by the rules of art. The general idea of the scene makes an impression, before any appeal is made to the judgment. We rather *feel*, than *survey* it.

Samuel Taylor Coleridge (1772–1834)
from *The Rime of the Ancyent Marinere*, IN SEVEN PARTS

> Coleridge's Rime, *written in 1797, first appeared in 1798 as the lead piece in* Lyrical Ballads, *an experimental collection published anonymously with William Wordsworth. Like* Frankenstein, The Rime *is a "frame" tale: a would-be Wedding-Guest is accosted by an Ancyent Marinere, who relates (by strange compulsion, he later reveals) his adventures at sea: voyaging toward the South Pole, their ship became icebound, almost fatally; an Albatross arrived, and the ice broke up; inexplicably, the Mariner shot the Albatross; horrific events ensued, including the death of everyone else on board in boiling tropical seas; the Mariner returned to his home country. He finds he is compelled to tell his tale over and over. The protagonist of Mary Shelley's frame tale, polar explorer Robert Walton, keeps recalling* The Rime; *Victor Frankenstein recalls it, too, on the morning after he animates and abandons his Creature. The version in* Lyrical Ballads *uses a consciously antiqued diction, in imitation of medieval ballads; this version lacked the satirically "explanatory" marginal gloss that framed the poem when Coleridge published under his own name in* Sibylline Leaves *(1817).*

---

[2]"The voice sticks in the throat"—an echo of Virgil's *Aeneid* (12.868), in which warrior Turnus is overcome by terror.

[3]Dissolution; melting.

ARGUMENT

How a Ship having passed the Line[1] was driven by Storms to the cold
Country towards the South Pole; and how from thence she made her
course to the tropical Latitude of the Great Pacific Ocean; and of the
strange things that befell; and in what manner the Ancyent Marinere
came back to his own Country.

I

It is an ancyent Marinere,
    And he stoppeth one of three:
"By thy long grey beard and thy glittering eye
    Now wherefore stoppest me?

The Bridegroom's doors are open'd wide
    And I am next of kin;
The Guests are met, the Feast is set,—
    May'st hear the merry din."

But still he holds the wedding-guest—
    There was a Ship, quoth he—   10
"Nay, if thou'st got a laughsome tale,
    Marinere! come with me."

He holds him with his skinny hand,
    Quoth he, there was a Ship—
"Now get thee hence, thou grey-beard Loon!
    Or my Staff shall make thee skip.

He holds him with his glittering eye—
    The wedding-guest stood still
And listens like a three year's child;
    The Marinere hath his will.   20

[1]The equator.

The wedding-guest sate on a stone,
    He cannot chuse but hear:
And thus spake on that ancyent man,
    The bright-eyed Marinere.

The Ship was cheer'd, the Harbour clear'd—
    Merrily did we drop
Below the Kirk,° below the Hill,   *church*
    Below the Light-house top.

The Sun came up upon the left,
    Out of the Sea came he: 30
And he shone bright, and on the right
    Went down into the Sea.

Higher and higher every day,
    Till over the mast at noon—
The wedding-guest here beat his breast,
    For he heard the loud bassoon.

The Bride hath pac'd into the Hall,
    Red as a rose is she;
Nodding their heads before her goes
    The merry Minstralsy.   40

The wedding-guest he beat his breast,
    Yet he cannot chuse but hear:
And thus spake on that ancyent Man,
    The bright-eyed Marinere.

Listen, Stranger! Storm and Wind,
    A Wind and Tempest strong!
For days and weeks it play'd us freaks—
    Like Chaff° we drove along.   *husks of grain*

Listen, Stranger! Mist and Snow,
    And it grew wond'rous cauld: 50
And Ice mast-high came floating by
    As green as Emerauld.

And thro' the drifts the snowy clifts
    Did send a dismal sheen;
Ne shapes of men ne beasts we ken—
    The Ice was all between.

The Ice was here, the Ice was there,
    The Ice was all around:
It crack'd and growl'd, and roar'd and howl'd—
    Like noises of a swound.   60

At length did cross an Albatross,
    Thorough the Fog it came;
And an° it were a Christian Soul,   *as if*
    We hail'd it in God's name.

The Marineres gave it biscuit-worms,
    And round and round it flew:
The ice did split with a Thunder-fit;
    The Helmsman steer'd us thro'.

And a good south wind sprung up behind,
    The Albatross did follow;   70
And every day for food or play
    Came to the Marinere's hollo!

In mist or cloud on mast or shroud
    It perch'd for vespers nine,
Whiles all the night thro' fog smoke-white
    Glimmer'd the white moon-shine.

"God save thee, ancyent Marinere!
    From the fiends that plague thee thus—
Why look'st thou so?"—with my cross bow
    I shot the Albatross.   80

from VI
[The Mariner's ship brings him to his "own countrée."]

And in its time the spell was snapt,
    And I could move my een:°   *eyes*

I look'd far forth, but little saw
   Of what might else be seen.   450

Like one, that on a lonely road
   Doth walk in fear and dread,
And having once turn'd round, walks on
   And turns no more his head:
Because he knows, a frightful fiend
   Doth close behind him tread.[2]

But soon there breath'd a wind on me,
   Ne sound ne motion made:
Its path was not upon the sea
   In ripple or in shade.   460

It rais'd my hair, it fann'd my cheek,
   Like a meadow-gale of spring—
It mingled strangely with my fears,
   Yet it felt like a welcoming.

Swiftly, swiftly flew the ship,
   Yet she sail'd softly too:
Sweetly, sweetly blew the breeze—
   On me alone it blew.

O dream of joy! is this indeed
   The light-house top I see?   470
Is this the Hill? Is this the Kirk?
   Is this mine own countrée?

We drifted o'er the Harbour-bar,
   And I with sobs did pray—
"O let me be awake, my God!
   Or let me sleep alway!"

The harbour-bay was clear as glass,
   So smoothly it was strewn!

[2]The passage that plays in Victor Frankenstein's mind (I.IV). Percy Shelley reportedly fainted on hearing these lines recited.

And on the bay the moon light lay,
    And the shadow of the moon.   480

The moonlight bay was white all o'er,
    Till rising from the same,
Full many shapes, that shadows were,
    Like as of torches came.

A little distance from the prow
    Those dark-red shadows were;
But soon I saw that my own flesh
    Was red as in a glare.

I turn'd my head in fear and dread,
    And by the holy rood,°   *cross* 490
The bodies had advanc'd, and now
    Before the mast they stood.

They lifted up their stiff right arms,
    They held them strait and tight;
And each right-arm burnt like a torch,
    A torch that's borne upright.
Their stony eye-balls glitter'd on
    In the red and smoky light.

I pray'd and turn'd my head away
    Forth looking as before.   500
There was no breeze upon the bay,
    No wave against the shore.

The rock shone bright, the Kirk no less
    That stands above the rock:
The moonlight steep'd in silentness
    The steady weathercock.

And the bay was white with silent light,
    Till rising from the same
Full many shapes, that shadows were,
    In crimson colours came.   510

A little distance from the prow
   Those crimson shadows were:
I turn'd my eyes upon the deck—
   O Christ! what saw I there?

Each corse lay flat, lifeless and flat;
   And by the Holy rood
A man all light, a seraph°-man,   *angel*
   On every corse° there stood.   *corpse*

This seraph-band, each wav'd his hand:
   It was a heavenly sight: 520
They stood as signals to the land,
   Each one a lovely light:

This seraph-band, each wav'd his hand,
   No voice did they impart—
No voice; but O! the silence sank,
   Like music on my heart.

Eftsones° I heard the dash of oars,   *again*
   I heard the pilot's cheer:
My head was turn'd perforce away
   And I saw a boat appear.   530

Then vanish'd all the lovely lights;
   The bodies rose anew:
With silent pace, each to his place,
   Came back the ghastly crew.
The wind, that shade nor motion made,
   On me alone it blew.

The pilot, and the pilot's boy
   I heard them coming fast:
Dear Lord in Heaven! it was a joy,
   The dead men could not blast.   540

I saw a third—I heard his voice:
   It is the Hermit° good!   *religious recluse*

He singeth loud his godly hymns
    That he makes in the wood.
He'll shrive[3] my soul, he'll wash away
    The Albatross's blood.

VII

This Hermit good lives in that wood
    Which slopes down to the Sea.
How loudly his sweet voice he rears!
He loves to talk with Marineres   550
    That come from a far Contrée.

He kneels at morn and noon and eve—
    He hath a cushion plump:
It is the moss,° that wholly hides   *(parasitic)*
    The rotted old Oak-stump.

The Skiff-boat ne'rd: I heard them talk,
    "Why, this is strange, I trow!°   *suppose*
Where are those lights so many and fair
    That signal made but now?"

"Strange, by my faith!" the Hermit said—   560
    "And they answer'd not our cheer.
The planks look warp'd, and see those sails
    How thin they are and sere!
I never saw aught like to them
    Unless perchance it were

The skeletons of leaves that lag
    My forest brook along:
When the Ivy-tod is heavy with snow,
    And the Owlet whoops to the wolf below
That eats the she-wolf's young."   570

"Dear Lord! it has a fiendish look—
    (The Pilot made reply)

---

[3]The ritual hearing of confession, rendering of penance and absolution.

"I am a-fear'd."—"Push on, push on!"
  Said the Hermit cheerily.

The Boat came closer to the Ship,
  But I ne spake ne stirr'd!
The Boat came close beneath the Ship,
  And strait a sound was heard!

Under the water it rumbled on,
  Still louder and more dread: 580
It reach'd the Ship, it split the bay;
  The Ship went down like lead.

Stunn'd by that loud and dreadful sound,
  Which sky and ocean smote:
Like one that hath been seven days drown'd
  My body lay afloat:
But, swift as dreams, myself I found
  Within the Pilot's boat.

Upon the whirl, where sank the Ship,
  The boat spun round and round: 590
And all was still, save that the hill
  Was telling of the sound.

I mov'd my lips: the Pilot shriek'd
  And fell down in a fit.
The Holy Hermit rais'd his eyes
  And pray'd where he did sit.

I took the oars: the Pilot's boy,
  Who now doth crazy go,
Laugh'd loud and long, and all the while
  His eyes went to and fro,   600
"Ha! ha!" quoth he—"full plain I see,
  The devil knows how to row."

And now all in mine own Countrée
  I stood on the firm land!

The Hermit stepp'd forth from the boat,
    And scarcely he could stand.

"O shrieve me, shrieve me, holy Man!
    The Hermit cross'd his brow—
"Say quick," quoth he, "I bid thee say
    What manner man art thou?"   610

Forthwith this frame° of mine was wrench'd   *body*
    With a woeful agony,
Which forc'd me to begin my tale
    And then it left me free.

Since then at an uncertain hour
    Now oftimes and now fewer,
That anguish comes and makes me tell
    My ghastly aventure.

I pass, like night, from land to land;
    I have strange power of speech;   620
The moment that his face I see
I know the man that must hear me;
    To him my tale I teach.

What loud uproar bursts from that door!
    The Wedding-guests are there;
But in the Garden-bower the Bride
    And Bride-maids singing are:
And hark the little Vesper°-bell   *evening*
    Which biddeth me to prayer.

O Wedding-guest! this soul hath been   630
    Alone on a wide wide sea
So lonely 'twas, that God himself
    Scarce seemed there to be.

O sweeter than the Marriage-feast,
    'Tis sweeter far to me

To walk together to the Kirk
   With a goodly company.

To walk together to the Kirk
   And all together pray,
While each to his great father bends,   640
Old men, and babes, and loving friends,
   And Youths, and Maidens gay.

Farewel, farewell! but this I tell
   To thee, thou wedding-guest!
He prayeth well who loveth well
   Both man and bird and beast.

He prayeth best who loveth best,
   All things both great and small:
For the dear God, who loveth us,
   He made and loveth all.   650

The Marinere, whose eye is bright,
   Whose beard with age is hoar,
Is gone; and now the wedding-guest
   Turn'd from the bridegroom's door.

He went, like one that hath been stunn'd
   And is of sense forlorn:
A sadder and a wiser man
   He rose the morrow morn.

Mary Wollstonecraft

Shelley's mother published the first major English statement of feminist philosophy, A Vindication of the Rights of Woman, in 1792. In a trenchant argument for women's right to education and respect as rationally capable beings, Wollstonecraft itemized the "wrongs" (sufferings) of woman inflicted throughout history, institutionalized by law, social stricture, and "the prevailing opinion" of inferiority to man (what we would call today an "ideology of gender"). The Wrongs of Woman, a novel fashioned on these arguments, opens with its heroine imprisoned in a madhouse by her husband, who has claimed her property and her daughter. The novel involves several stories of wronged women, one of the longest and most searing told by Maria's life-hardened warder Jemima. Hers is a kind of "monster story," a case of how some human beings, fated by social contempt and a physical difference from man (here, woman), are treated monstrously, and may become monstrous in consequence. Shelley read both Rights of Woman *and the novel. Begun in 1796 and left unfinished at Wollstonecraft's death, it was published in 1798 in William Godwin's* Posthumous Works of the Author of A Vindication of the Rights of Woman. *The square brackets indicate his interpolations.*

from *The Wrongs of Woman; or Maria*: Jemima's story

"My father," said Jemima, "seduced my mother, a pretty girl, with whom he lived fellow-servant; and she no sooner perceived the natural, the dreaded consequence, than the terrible conviction flashed on her—that she was ruined. Honesty, and a regard for her reputation, had been the only principles inculcated by her mother; and they had been so forcibly impressed, that she feared shame, more than the poverty to which it would lead. Her incessant importunities to prevail upon my father to screen her from reproach by marrying her, as he had promised in the fervour of seduction, estranged him from her so completely, that her very person became distasteful to him; and he began to hate, as well as despise me, before I was born.

My mother, grieved to the soul by his neglect, and unkind treatment, actually resolved to famish herself; and injured her health by the attempt; though she had not sufficient resolution to adhere to her project, or renounce it entirely. Death came not at her call; yet sorrow, and the methods she adopted to conceal her condition, still doing the work of a house-maid, had such an effect on her constitution, that she died in the wretched garret, where her virtuous mistress had forced her to take refuge in the very pangs of labour, though my father, after a slight reproof, was allowed to remain in his place—allowed by the mother of six children, who, scarcely permitting a footstep to be heard, during her month's indulgence, felt no sympathy for the poor wretch, denied every comfort required by her situation.

The day my mother died, the ninth after my birth, I was consigned to the care of the cheapest nurse my father could find; who suckled her own child at the same time, and lodged as many more as she could get, in two cellar-like apartments.

Poverty, and the habit of seeing children die off her hands, had so hardened her heart, that the office of a mother did not awaken the tenderness of a woman; nor were the feminine caresses which seem a part of the rearing of a child, ever bestowed on me. The chicken has a wing to shelter under; but I had no bosom to nestle in, no kindred warmth to foster me. Left in dirt, to cry with cold and hunger till I was weary, and sleep without ever being prepared by exercise, or lulled by kindness to rest; could I be expected to become any thing but a weak and rickety babe? Still, in spite of neglect, I continued to exist, to learn to curse existence, [her countenance grew ferocious as she spoke,] and the treatment that rendered me miserable, seemed to sharpen my wits. Confined then in a damp hovel, to rock the cradle of the succeeding tribe, I looked like a little old woman, or a hag shrivelling into nothing. The furrows of reflection and care contracted the youthful cheek, and gave a sort of supernatural wildness to the ever watchful eye. During this period, my father had married another fellow-servant, who loved him less, and knew better how to manage his passion, than my mother. She likewise proving with child, they agreed to keep a shop: my step-mother, if, being an illegitimate offspring, I may venture thus to characterize her, having obtained a sum of a rich relation, for that purpose.

Soon after her lying-in,[1] she prevailed on my father to take me home, to save the expence of maintaining me, and of hiring a girl to assist her in the care of the child. I was young, it was true, but appeared a knowing little thing, and might be made handy. Accordingly I was brought to her house; but not to a home—for a home I never knew. Of this child, a daughter, she was extravagantly fond; and it was a part of my employment, to assist to spoil her, by humouring all her whims, and bearing all her caprices. Feeling her own consequence, before she could speak, she had learned the art of tormenting me, and if I ever dared to resist, I received blows, laid on with no compunctious hand, or was sent to bed dinnerless, as well as supperless.[2] I said that it was a part of my daily labour to attend this child, with the servility of a slave; still it was but a part. I was sent out in all seasons, and from place to place, to carry burdens far above my strength, with-

[1]Final weeks of pregnancy.
[2]Dinner: midday meal; supper: evening meal; consequence: importance; compunction: remorse.

out being allowed to draw near the fire, or ever being cheered by encouragement or kindness. No wonder then, treated like a creature of another species, that I began to envy, and at length to hate, the darling of the house. Yet, I perfectly remember, that it was the caresses, and kind expressions of my step-mother, which first excited my jealous discontent. Once, I cannot forget it, when she was calling in vain her wayward child to kiss her, I ran to her, saying, 'I will kiss you, ma'am!' and how did my heart, which was in my mouth, sink, what was my debasement of soul, when pushed away with—'I do not want you, pert thing!' Another day, when a new gown had excited the highest good humour, and she uttered the appropriate *dear*, addressed unexpectedly to me, I thought I could never do enough to please her; I was all alacrity, and rose proportionably in my own estimation.

As her daughter grew up, she was pampered with cakes and fruit, while I was, literally speaking, fed with the refuse of the table, with her leavings. A liquorish tooth[3] is, I believe, common to children, and I used to steal any thing sweet, that I could catch up with a chance of concealment. When detected, she was not content to chastize me herself at the moment, but, on my father's return in the evening (he was a shopman), the principal discourse was to recount my faults, and attribute them to the wicked disposition which I had brought into the world with me, inherited from my mother. He did not fail to leave the marks of his resentment on my body, and then solaced himself by playing with my sister.—I could have murdered her at those moments. To save myself from these unmerciful corrections, I resorted to falsehood, and the untruths which I sturdily maintained, were brought in judgment against me, to support my tyrant's inhuman charge of my natural propensity to vice. Seeing me treated with contempt, and always being fed and dressed better, my sister conceived a contemptuous opinion of me, that proved an obstacle to all affection; and my father, hearing continually of my faults, began to consider me as a curse entailed on him for his sins: he was therefore easily prevailed on to bind me apprentice to one of my step-mother's friends, who kept a slop-shop in Wapping.[4] I was

[3]Sweet tooth.

[4]A shop selling cheap clothing; Wapping, the river-dock area of London, suggests its chief customers were seamen. Lower-class children, usually boys, were apprenticed both to relieve their families of their maintenance and to learn a craft or trade. Typically beginning at age eight, apprenticeships bound the child for seven years of unpaid labor in exchange for training, shelter, food, and clothing. Apprentices were notoriously vulnerable to abuse, often treated as slaves and sometimes quartered in the barn rather than the home.

represented (as it was said) in my true colours; but she, 'warranted,' snapping her fingers, 'that she should break my spirit or heart.'

My mother replied, with a whine, 'that if any body could make me better, it was such a clever woman as herself; though, for her own part, she had tried in vain; but good-nature was her fault.'

I shudder with horror, when I recollect the treatment I had now to endure. Not only under the lash of my task-mistress, but the drudge of the maid, apprentices and children, I never had a taste of human kindness to soften the rigour of perpetual labour. I had been introduced as an object of abhorrence into the family; as a creature of whom my step-mother, though she had been kind enough to let me live in the house with her own child, could make nothing. I was described as a wretch, whose nose must be kept to the grinding stone—and it was held there with an iron grasp. It seemed indeed the privilege of their superior nature to kick me about, like the dog or cat. If I were attentive, I was called fawning, if refractory, an obstinate mule, and like a mule I received their censure on my loaded back. Often has my mistress, for some instance of forgetfulness, thrown me from one side of the kitchen to the other, knocked my head against the wall, spit in my face, with various refinements on barbarity that I forbear to enumerate, though they were all acted over again by the servant, with additional insults, to which the appellation of *bastard*,[5] was commonly added, with taunts or sneers. But I will not attempt to give you an adequate idea of my situation, lest you, who probably have never been drenched with the dregs of human misery, should think I exaggerate.

I stole now, from absolute necessity,—bread; yet whatever else was taken, which I had it not in my power to take, was ascribed to me. I was the filching cat, the ravenous dog, the dumb brute, who must bear all; for if I endeavoured to exculpate myself, I was silenced, without any enquiries being made, with 'Hold your tongue, you never tell truth.' Even the very air I breathed was tainted with scorn; for I was sent to the neighbouring shops with Glutton, Liar, or Thief, written on my forehead. This was, at first, the most bitter punishment; but sullen pride, or a kind of stupid desperation, made me, at length, almost regardless of the contempt, which had wrung from me so many solitary tears at the only moments when I was allowed to rest.

[5]The legal term for a child born outside of marriage. English common law denied bastards rights of inheritance, even of care, and left them to the care of the poor houses. The social and legal contempt is evident in the metaphorical extension of the term to indicate inferiority and falseness.

Thus was I the mark of cruelty till my sixteenth year; and then I have only to point out a change of misery; for a period[6] I never knew. Allow me first to make one observation. Now I look back, I cannot help attributing the greater part of my misery, to the misfortune of having been thrown into the world without the grand support of life—a mother's affection. I had no one to love me; or to make me respected, to enable me to acquire respect. I was an egg dropped on the sand; a pauper by nature, hunted from family to family, who belonged to nobody—and nobody cared for me. I was despised from my birth, and denied the chance of obtaining a footing for myself in society. Yes; I had not even the chance of being considered as a fellow-creature—yet all the people with whom I lived, brutalized as they were by the low cunning of trade, and the despicable shifts of poverty, were not without bowels,[7] though they never yearned for me. I was, in fact, born a slave, and chained by infamy to slavery during the whole of existence, without having any companions to alleviate it by sympathy, or teach me how to rise above it by their example. But, to resume the thread of my tale—

At sixteen, I suddenly grew tall, and something like comeliness appeared on a Sunday, when I had time to wash my face, and put on clean clothes. My master had once or twice caught hold of me in the passage; but I instinctively avoided his disgusting caresses. One day however, when the family were at a methodist meeting, he contrived to be alone in the house with me, and by blows—yes; blows and menaces, compelled me to submit to his ferocious desire; and, to avoid my mistress's fury, I was obliged in future to comply, and skulk to my loft at his command, in spite of increasing loathing.

The anguish which was now pent up in my bosom, seemed to open a new world to me: I began to extend my thoughts beyond myself, and grieve for human misery, till I discovered, with horror—ah! what horror!—that I was with child. I know not why I felt a mixed sensation of despair and tenderness, excepting that, ever called a bastard, a bastard appeared to me an object of the greatest compassion in creation.

I communicated this dreadful circumstance to my master, who was almost equally alarmed at the intelligence; for he feared his wife, and

[6]Termination.

[7]Bowels: tenderness; pity. Wollstonecraft's view that a life in trade, or worse, poverty, necessarily suppresses virtue in favor of pragmatic but dishonest practices.

public censure at the meeting. After some weeks of deliberation had elapsed, I in continual fear that my altered shape would be noticed, my master gave me a medicine in a phial, which he desired me to take, telling me, without any circumlocution, for what purpose it was designed.[8] I burst into tears, I thought it was killing myself—yet was such a self as I worth preserving? He cursed me for a fool, and left me to my own reflections. I could not resolve to take this infernal potion; but I wrapped it up in an old gown, and hid it in a corner of my box.

Nobody yet suspected me, because they had been accustomed to view me as a creature of another species. But the threatening storm at last broke over my devoted[9] head—never shall I forget it! One Sunday evening when I was left, as usual, to take care of the house, my master came home intoxicated, and I became the prey of his brutal appetite. His extreme intoxication made him forget his customary caution, and my mistress entered and found us in a situation that could not have been more hateful to her than me. Her husband was 'pot-valiant,' he feared her not at the moment, nor had he then much reason, for she instantly turned the whole force of her anger another way. She tore off my cap, scratched, kicked, and buffetted me, till she had exhausted her strength, declaring, as she rested her arm, 'that I had wheedled her husband from her.— But, could any thing better be expected from a wretch, whom she had taken into her house out of pure charity?' What a torrent of abuse rushed out! till, almost breathless, she concluded with saying, 'that I was born a strumpet; it ran in my blood, and nothing good could come to those who harboured me.'

My situation was, of course, discovered, and she declared that I should not stay another night under the same roof with an honest family. I was therefore pushed out of doors, and my trumpery[10] thrown after me, when it had been contemptuously examined in the passage, lest I should have stolen any thing.

Behold me then in the street, utterly destitute![11] Whither could I creep for shelter? To my father's roof I had no claim, when not pursued by shame—now I shrunk back as from death, from my mother's cruel

[8]To induce abortion.

[9]Doomed.

[10]Worthless things.

[11]In *Rights of Woman*, Wollstonecraft argued that a man should be legally required to support any woman he impregnated as well as any children produced.

reproaches, my father's execrations. I could not endure to hear him curse the day I was born, though life had been a curse to me. Of death I thought, but with a confused emotion of terror, as I stood leaning my head on a post, and starting at every footstep, lest it should be my mistress coming to tear my heart out. One of the boys of the shop passing by, heard my tale, and immediately repaired to his master, to give him a description of my situation; and he touched the right key—the scandal it would give rise to, if I were left to repeat my tale to every enquirer. This plea came home to his reason, who had been sobered by his wife's rage, the fury of which fell on him when I was out of her reach, and he sent the boy to me with half-a-guinea,[12] desiring him to conduct me to a house, where beggars, and other wretches, the refuse of society, nightly lodged.

This night was spent in a state of stupefaction, or desperation. I detested mankind, and abhorred myself.

In the morning I ventured out, to throw myself in my master's way, at his usual hour of going abroad. I approached him, he 'damned me for a ——, declared I had disturbed the peace of the family, and that he had sworn to his wife, never to take any more notice of me.' He left me; but, instantly returning, he told me that he should speak to his friend, a parish-officer, to get a nurse for the brat I laid to him; and advised me, if I wished to keep out of the house of correction, not to make free with his name.[13]

I hurried back to my hole, and, rage giving place to despair, sought for the potion that was to procure abortion, and swallowed it, with a wish that it might destroy me, at the same time that it stopped the sensations of new-born life, which I felt with indescribable emotion. My head turned round, my heart grew sick, and in the horrors of approaching dissolution, mental anguish was swallowed up. The effect of the medicine was violent, and I was confined to my bed several days; but, youth and a strong constitution prevailing, I once more crawled out, to ask myself the cruel question, 'Whither I should go?' I had but two shillings left in my pocket, the rest had been expended, by a poor woman who slept in the same room, to pay for my lodging, and purchase the necessaries of which she partook.

With this wretch I went into the neighbouring streets to beg, and my disconsolate appearance drew a few pence from the idle, enabling

[12]Eleven shillings, sixpence.

[13]Parishes were responsible for providing for orphans, bastards, and other destitutes; house of correction: prison.

me still to command a bed; till, recovering from my illness, and taught to put on my rags to the best advantage, I was accosted from different motives, and yielded to the desire of the brutes I met, with the same detestation that I had felt for my still more brutal master. I have since read in novels of the blandishments of seduction, but I had not even the pleasure of being enticed into vice."

"I shall not," interrupted Jemima, "lead your imagination into all the scenes of wretchedness and depravity, which I was condemned to view; or mark the different stages of my debasing misery. Fate dragged me through the very kennels of society: I was still a slave, a bastard, a common property. Become familiar with vice, for I wish to conceal nothing from you, I picked the pockets of the drunkards who abused me; and proved by my conduct, that I deserved the epithets, with which they loaded me at moments when distrust ought to cease.

Detesting my nightly occupation, though valuing, if I may so use the word, my independence, which only consisted in choosing the street in which I should wander, or the roof, when I had money, in which I should hide my head, I was some time before I could prevail on myself to accept of a place in a house of ill fame,[14] to which a girl, with whom I had accidentally conversed in the street, had recommended me. I had been hunted almost in a fever, by the watchmen of the quarter of the town I frequented; one, whom I had unwittingly offended, giving the word to the whole pack. You can scarcely conceive the tyranny exercised by these wretches: considering themselves as the instruments of the very laws they violate, the pretext which steels their conscience, hardens their heart. Not content with receiving from us, outlaws of society (let other women talk of favours) a brutal gratification gratuitously as a privilege of office, they extort a tithe of prostitution, and harrass with threats the poor creatures whose occupation affords not the means to silence the growl of avarice. To escape from this persecution, I once more entered into servitude.

A life of comparative regularity restored my health; and—do not start—my manners were improved, in a situation where vice sought to render itself alluring, and taste was cultivated to fashion the person, if not to refine the mind. Besides, the common civility of speech, contrasted with the gross vulgarity to which I had been accustomed, was something like the polish of civilization. I was not shut out from all intercourse of humanity. Still I was galled by the yoke of service,

[14]Whorehouse.

and my mistress often flying into violent fits of passion, made me dread a sudden dismission, which I understood was always the case. I was therefore prevailed on, though I felt a horror of men, to accept the offer of a gentleman, rather in the decline of years, to keep his house, pleasantly situated in a little village near Hampstead.[15]

He was a man of great talents, and of brilliant wit; but, a worn-out votary of voluptuousness, his desires became fastidious in proportion as they grew weak, and the native tenderness of his heart was undermined by a vitiated imagination. A thoughtless career of libertinism and social enjoyment, had injured his health to such a degree, that, whatever pleasure his conversation afforded me (and my esteem was ensured by proofs of the generous humanity of his disposition), the being his mistress was purchasing it at a very dear rate. With such a keen perception of the delicacies of sentiment, with an imagination invigorated by the exercise of genius, how could he sink into the grossness of sensuality!

But, to pass over a subject which I recollect with pain, I must remark to you, as an answer to your often-repeated question, 'Why my sentiments and language were superior to my station?' that I now began to read, to beguile the tediousness of solitude, and to gratify an inquisitive, active mind. I had often, in my childhood, followed a ballad-singer, to hear the sequel of a dismal story, though sure of being severely punished for delaying to return with whatever I was sent to purchase. I could just spell and put a sentence together, and I listened to the various arguments, though often mingled with obscenity, which occurred at the table where I was allowed to preside: for a literary friend or two frequently came home with my master, to dine and pass the night. Having lost the privileged respect of my sex, my presence, instead of restraining, perhaps gave the reins to their tongues; still I had the advantage of hearing discussions, from which, in the common course of life, women are excluded.

You may easily imagine, that it was only by degrees that I could comprehend some of the subjects they investigated, or acquire from their reasoning what might be termed a moral sense. But my fondness of reading increasing, and my master occasionally shutting himself up in this retreat, for weeks together, to write, I had many opportunities of improvement. At first, considering money" ("I was right!" exclaimed Jemima, altering her tone of voice) "as the only means, after my loss of

[15]Suburb north of London.

reputation, of obtaining respect, or even the toleration of humanity, I had not the least scruple to secrete a part of the sums intrusted to me, and to screen myself from detection by a system of falshood. But, acquiring new principles, I began to have the ambition of returning to the respectable part of society, and was weak enough to suppose it possible. The attention of my unassuming instructor, who, without being ignorant of his own powers, possessed great simplicity of manners, strengthened the illusion. Having sometimes caught up hints for thought, from my untutored remarks, he often led me to discuss the subjects he was treating, and would read to me his productions, previous to their publication, wishing to profit by the criticism of unsophisticated feeling. The aim of his writings was to touch the simple springs of the heart; for he despised the would-be oracles, the self-elected philosophers, who fright away fancy, while sifting each grain of thought to prove that slowness of comprehension is wisdom.

I should have distinguished this as a moment of sunshine, a happy period in my life, had not the repugnance the disgusting libertinism of my protector inspired, daily become more painful.—And, indeed, I soon did recollect it as such with agony, when his sudden death (for he had recourse to the most exhilarating cordials to keep up the convivial tone of his spirits) again threw me into the desert of human society. Had he had any time for reflection, I am certain he would have left the little property in his power to me: but, attacked by the fatal apoplexy in town, his heir, a man of rigid morals, brought his wife with him to take possession of the house and effects, before I was even informed of his death,— 'to prevent,' as she took care indirectly to tell me, 'such a creature as she supposed me to be, from purloining any of them, had I been apprized of the event in time.'

The grief I felt at the sudden shock the information gave me, which at first had nothing selfish in it, was treated with contempt, and I was ordered to pack up my clothes; and a few trinkets and books, given me by the generous deceased, were contested, while they piously hoped, with a reprobating shake of the head, 'that God would have mercy on his sinful soul!' With some difficulty, I obtained my arrears of wages; but asking—such is the spirit-grinding consequence of poverty and infamy—for a character[16] for honesty and economy, which God knows I merited, I was told by this—why must I call her woman?—'that it would go against her conscience to recommend a

---

[16]Letter of reference.

kept mistress.' Tears started in my eyes, burning tears; for there are situations in which a wretch is humbled by the contempt they are conscious they do not deserve.

I returned to the metropolis; but the solitude of a poor lodging was inconceivably dreary, after the society I had enjoyed. To be cut off from human converse, now I had been taught to relish it, was to wander a ghost among the living. Besides, I foresaw, to aggravate the severity of my fate, that my little pittance would soon melt away. I endeavoured to obtain needlework; but, not having been taught early, and my hands being rendered clumsy by hard work, I did not sufficiently excel to be employed by the ready-made linen shops,[17] when so many women, better qualified, were suing for it. The want of a character prevented my getting a place; for, irksome as servitude would have been to me, I should have made another trial, had it been feasible. Not that I disliked employment, but the inequality of condition to which I must have submitted. I had acquired a taste for literature, during the five years I had lived with a literary man, occasionally conversing with men of the first abilities of the age; and now to descend to the lowest vulgarity, was a degree of wretchedness not to be imagined unfelt. I had not, it is true, tasted the charms of affection, but I had been familiar with the graces of humanity.

One of the gentlemen, whom I had frequently dined in company with, while I was treated like a companion, met me in the street, and enquired after my health. I seized the occasion, and began to describe my situation; but he was in haste to join, at dinner, a select party of choice spirits; therefore, without waiting to hear me, he impatiently put a guinea into my hand, saying, 'It was a pity such a sensible woman should be in distress—he wished me well from his soul.'

To another I wrote, stating my case, and requesting advice. He was an advocate for unequivocal sincerity; and had often, in my presence, descanted on the evils which arise in society from the despotism of rank and riches.

In reply, I received a long essay on the energy of the human mind, with continual allusions to his own force of character. He added, 'That the woman who could write such a letter as I had sent him, could never be in want of resources, were she to look into herself, and exert her powers; misery was the consequence of indolence, and, as to my being shut out from society, it was the lot of man to submit to certain privations.'"

---

[17]Shops selling garments such as shirts, aprons, underwear.

"How often have I heard," said Jemima, interrupting her narrative, "in conversation, and read in books, that every person willing to work may find employment? It is the vague assertion, I believe, of insensible indolence, when it relates to men; but, with respect to women, I am sure of its fallacy, unless they will submit to the most menial bodily labour; and even to be employed at hard labour is out of the reach of many, whose reputation misfortune or folly has tainted.

How writers, professing to be friends to freedom, and the improvement of morals, can assert that poverty is no evil, I cannot imagine."[18]

"No more can I," interrupted Maria, "yet they even expatiate on the peculiar happiness of indigence, though in what it can consist, excepting in brutal rest, when a man can barely earn a subsistence, I cannot imagine. The mind is necessarily imprisoned in its own little tenement; and, fully occupied by keeping it in repair, has not time to rove abroad for improvement. The book of knowledge is closely clasped, against those who must fulfil their daily task of severe manual labour or die; and curiosity, rarely excited by thought or information, seldom moves on the stagnate lake of ignorance."

"As far as I have been able to observe," replied Jemima, "prejudices, caught up by chance, are obstinately maintained by the poor, to the exclusion of improvement; they have not time to reason or reflect to any extent, or minds sufficiently exercised to adopt the principles of action, which form perhaps the only basis of contentment in every station."

"And independence," said Darnford,[19] "they are necessarily strangers to, even the independence of despising their persecutors. If the poor are happy, or can be happy, *things are very well as they are.* And I cannot conceive on what principle those writers contend for a change of system, who support this opinion. The authors on the other side of the question are much more consistent, who grant the fact; yet, insisting that it is the lot of the majority to be oppressed in this life, kindly turn them over to another,[20] to rectify the false weights and measures of this, as the only way to justify the dispensations of Providence. I have not," continued Darnford, "an opinion more firmly fixed by observation in my mind, than that, though riches may fail to produce

---

[18]This argument usually cites Scripture—e.g., "Blessed be ye poor: for yours is the kingdom of God" says Jesus in his Sermon on the Mount (Luke 6.20)—or more generally, the inscrutable designs of God.

[19]Henry Darnford, a fellow inmate who eventually becomes Maria's lover.

[20]Heaven.

proportionate happiness, poverty most commonly excludes it, by shutting up all the avenues to improvement."

"And as for the affections," added Maria, with a sigh, "how gross, and even tormenting do they become, unless regulated by an improving mind! The culture of the heart ever, I believe, keeps pace with that of the mind. But pray go on," addressing Jemima, "though your narrative gives rise to the most painful reflections on the present state of society."

"Not to trouble you," continued she, "with a detailed description of all the painful feelings of unavailing exertion, I have only to tell you, that at last I got recommended to wash in a few families, who did me the favour to admit me into their houses, without the most strict enquiry, to wash from one in the morning till eight at night, for eighteen or twenty-pence a day.[21] On the happiness to be enjoyed over a washing-tub I need not comment; yet you will allow me to observe, that this was a wretchedness of situation peculiar to my sex. A man with half my industry, and, I may say, abilities, could have procured a decent livelihood, and discharged some of the duties which knit mankind together; whilst I, who had acquired a taste for the rational, nay, in honest pride let me assert it, the virtuous enjoyments of life, was cast aside as the filth of society. Condemned to labour, like a machine, only to earn bread, and scarcely that, I became melancholy and desperate.

I have now to mention a circumstance which fills me with remorse, and fear it will entirely deprive me of your esteem. A tradesman became attached to me, and visited me frequently,—and I at last obtained such a power over him, that he offered to take me home to his house.—Consider, dear madam, I was famishing: wonder not that I became a wolf!—The only reason for not taking me home immediately, was the having a girl in the house, with child by him—and this girl—I advised him—yes, I did! would I could forget it!—to turn out of doors: and one night he determined to follow my advice. Poor wretch! She fell upon her knees, reminded him that he had promised to marry her, that her parents were honest!—What did it avail?—She was turned out.

She approached her father's door, in the skirts of London,—listened at the shutters,—but could not knock. A watchman had observed her go and return several times—Poor wretch!—[The remorse Jemima spoke of, seemed to be stinging her to the soul, as she proceeded.]

[21]This report of washerwomen's slightly more than penny-an-hour wage is historically accurate.

She left it, and, approaching a tub where horses were watered, she sat down in it, and, with desperate resolution, remained in that attitude—till resolution was no longer necessary!

I happened that morning to be going out to wash, anticipating the moment when I should escape from such hard labour. I passed by, just as some men, going to work, drew out the stiff, cold corpse—Let me not recall the horrid moment!—I recognized her pale visage; I listened to the tale told by the spectators, and my heart did not burst. I thought of my own state, and wondered how I could be such a monster!—I worked hard; and, returning home, I was attacked by a fever. I suffered both in body and mind. I determined not to live with the wretch. But he did not try me; he left the neighbourhood. I once more returned to the wash-tub.

Still this state, miserable as it was, admitted of aggravation. Lifting one day a heavy load, a tub fell against my shin, and gave me great pain. I did not pay much attention to the hurt, till it became a serious wound; being obliged to work as usual, or starve. But, finding myself at length unable to stand for any time, I thought of getting into an hospital. Hospitals, it should seem (for they are comfortless abodes for the sick) were expressly endowed for the reception of the friendless; yet I, who had on that plea a right to assistance, wanted the recommendation of the rich and respectable, and was several weeks languishing for admittance; fees were demanded on entering; and, what was still more unreasonable, security for burying me, that expence not coming into the letter of the charity. A guinea was the stipulated sum—I could as soon have raised a million; and I was afraid to apply to the parish for an order, lest they should have passed me, I knew not whither.[22] The poor woman at whose house I lodged, compassionating my state, got me into the hospital; and the family where I received the hurt, sent me five shillings, three and six-pence of which I gave at my admittance—I know not for what.

My leg grew quickly better; but I was dismissed before my cure was completed, because I could not afford to have my linen washed to appear decently, as the virago of a nurse said, when the gentlemen (the surgeons) came. I cannot give you an adequate idea of the wretchedness of an hospital; every thing is left to the care of people intent on gain. The attendants seem to have lost all feeling of compassion in the

---

[22]Passed back to the last parish where the applicant was legally settled.

bustling discharge of their offices; death is so familiar to them, that they are not anxious to ward it off. Every thing appeared to be conducted for the accommodation of the medical men and their pupils, who came to make experiments on the poor, for the benefit of the rich. One of the physicians, I must not forget to mention, gave me half-a-crown, and ordered me some wine, when I was at the lowest ebb. I thought of making my case known to the lady-like matron; but her forbidding countenance prevented me. She condescended to look on the patients, and make general enquiries, two or three times a week; but the nurses knew the hour when the visit of ceremony would commence, and every thing was as it should be.

After my dismission, I was more at a loss than ever for a subsistence, and, not to weary you with a repetition of the same unavailing attempts, unable to stand at the washing-tub, I began to consider the rich and poor as natural enemies, and became a thief from principle. I could not now cease to reason, but I hated mankind. I despised myself, yet I justified my conduct. I was taken, tried, and condemned to six months' imprisonment in a house of correction. My soul recoils with horror from the remembrance of the insults I had to endure, till, branded with shame, I was turned loose in the street, pennyless. I wandered from street to street, till, exhausted by hunger and fatigue, I sunk down senseless at a door, where I had vainly demanded a morsel of bread. I was sent by the inhabitant to the work-house, to which he had surlily bid me go, saying, he 'paid enough in conscience to the poor,' when, with parched tongue, I implored his charity.[23] If those well-meaning people who exclaim against beggars, were acquainted with the treatment the poor receive in many of these wretched asylums, they would not stifle so easily involuntary sympathy, by saying that they have all parishes to go to, or wonder that the poor dread to enter the gloomy walls. What are the common run of workhouses, but prisons, in which many respectable old people, worn out by immoderate labour, sink into the grave in sorrow, to which they are carried like dogs!"

Alarmed by some indistinct noise, Jemima rose hastily to listen, and Maria, turning to Darnford, said, "I have indeed been shocked beyond expression when I have met a pauper's funeral. A coffin carried on the

[23]Parishioners were assessed a "poor tax" to support dependents. By the late 1790s, on the theory that poverty stemmed from indolence, "poor laws" were being proposed in Parliament to prohibit alms-giving (charity) and to require the poor to enter workhouses, where the wages were appallingly low and families typically broken up.

shoulders of three or four ill-looking wretches, whom the imagination might easily convert into a band of assassins, hastening to conceal the corpse, and quarrelling about the prey on their way. I know it is of little consequence how we are consigned to the earth; but I am led by this brutal insensibility, to what even the animal creation appears forcibly to feel, to advert to the wretched, deserted manner in which they died."

"True," rejoined Darnford, "and, till the rich will give more than a part of their wealth, till they will give time and attention to the wants of the distressed, never let them boast of charity. Let them open their hearts, and not their purses, and employ their minds in the service, if they are really actuated by humanity; or charitable institutions will always be the prey of the lowest order of knaves."

Jemima returning, seemed in haste to finish her tale. "The overseer farmed the poor[24] of different parishes, and out of the bowels of poverty was wrung the money with which he purchased this dwelling, as a private receptacle for madness. He had been a keeper at a house of the same description, and conceived that he could make money much more readily in his old occupation. He is a shrewd—shall I say it?—villain. He observed something resolute in my manner, and offered to take me with him, and instruct me how to treat the disturbed minds he meant to instruct to my care. The offer of forty pounds a year,[25] and to quit a workhouse, was not to be despised, though the condition of shutting my eyes and hardening my heart was annexed to it.

I agreed to accompany him; and four years have I been attendant on many wretches, and"—she lowered her voice,—"the witness of many enormities. In solitude my mind seemed to recover its force, and many of the sentiments which I imbibed in the only tolerable period of my life, returned with their full force. Still what should induce me to be the champion for suffering humanity?—Who ever risked any thing for me?—Who ever acknowledged me to be a fellow-creature?"—

Maria took her hand, and Jemima, more overcome by kindness than she had ever been by cruelty, hastened out of the room to conceal her emotions.

Darnford soon after heard his summons, and, taking leave of him, Maria promised to gratify his curiosity, with respect to herself, the first opportunity.

[24]Hired them out as laborers, with part of their meager wages taken in commission, as allowed by law.

[25]At the end of the 18th c., farm workers on a six-day week could expect £15–20 a year.

Active as love was in the heart of Maria, the story she had just heard made her thoughts take a wider range. The opening buds of hope closed, as if they had put forth too early, and the happiest day of her life was overcast by the most melancholy reflections. Thinking of Jemima's peculiar fate and her own, she was led to consider the oppressed state of women, and to lament that she had given birth to a daughter.

Mary Godwin (Shelley), journal entries (1815)

[probably Wednesday 22 February 1815]
[Percy Bysshe Shelley's hand]
[Maie] is in labour, & after very few additonal pains she is delivered of a female child—5 minutes afterwards Dr Clarke comes. all is well. Maie perfectly well & at ease The child is not quite 7 months. The child not expected to live. S. sits up with Maie. much agitated & exhausted. Hogg[1] sleeps here.

Thursday 23 Mary quite well—The child unexpectedly alive, but still not expected to live. Hogg returns in the evening at ½ 7. S writes to Fanny requesting her to come & see Maie. Fanny comes and remains the whole night, the Godwins being absent from home. Charles comes at 11 with some lines from Mrs Godwin[2] [. . .]

Friday Feb^ry 24 Maie still well. favorable symptoms in the child—we may indulge some hopes. Hogg comes at 2. Fanny departs. Dr Clarke calls. confirms our hopes of the child. S. very unwell—S. finishes the 2nd Vol. of Livy 1657 page—Hogg comes in the evening. S. unwell & exhausted.

[Mary Shelley's hand]
Teusday 28th [February] I come down stairs — talk – nurse the baby & read Corinne[3] [. . .]

Wednesday 1st March nurse baby – read Corinne & work—S. & C. out all morning – in the evening Peacock comes – talk about types

[1]Thomas Jefferson Hogg: a close friend of both Shelleys and Percy's friend from college days, expelled with him for *The Necessity of Atheism.* "S." is (Percy) Shelley; "Maie" is Hogg's and Percy's pet name for Mary.

[2]Fanny is Mary's half-sister (Wollstonecraft's daughter by Gilbert Imlay), living with Godwin (whom she believed to be her father) and his second wife, Charles Clairmont's mother.

[3]De Staël's *Corinne, ou l'Italie* (1807), a sensationally popular novel about a female artist, worshipped as a celebrity and doomed to unhappiness.

— editions & greek letters all the evening — H comes – they go away at ½ 11. Bonaparte invades France.[4]

[Thursday 2 March] A bustle of moving[5]—read Corinne—I an my baby go about 3—S & C do not come till six—Hogg comes in the evening

[Friday 3 March] nurse my baby—talk & read Corinne

[Saturday 4 March] read talk and nurse [. . .]

Sunday 5—S & C go to town—Hogg here all day – read Corinne & nurse my baby—in the evening talk—S finishes the life of Chau[c]er—He goes at 11

Monday 6 find my baby dead————

Send for Hogg[6]—talk—a miserable day—in the evening read fall of the Jesuits.[7] H. sleeps here— [. . .]

Thursday 9[th] Read & talk—still think about my little baby—'tis hard indeed for a mother to loose a child— [. . .]

Monday 13[th] stay at home [. . .] think of my little dead baby—this is foolish I suppose yet whenever I am left alone to my own thoughts & do not read to divert them they always come back to the same point—that I was a mother & am so no longer— [. . .]

Sunday 19th Dream that my little baby came to life again—that it had only been cold & that that we rubbed it by the fire & it lived—I awake & find no baby—I think about the little thing all day—not in good spirits—Shelley is very unwell— [. . .]

Monday 20th Dream again about my baby— [. . .] Shelley reads Livy—he has arrived at vol 3—Page 307—Play at chess & work in the evening— [. . .]

Thursday 23[d] [. . .] walk with Shelley & Hogg [. . .] hear that Bonaparte has entered Paris—as we come home meet my father &

---

[4]C. is Claire Clairmont, daughter of Godwin's second wife, and living with the Shelleys; Peacock, a novelist, poet, and essayist, was a close friend of Percy, though he made Mary impatient. Napoleon Bonaparte escaped exile on the island of Elba on 26 February 1815, arrived in France on 1 March, and with an army set off for Paris.

[5]After a quarrel with the landlady, the Shelleys and Claire moved to cheaper lodgings.

[6]"My dearest Hogg," she wrote, "my baby is dead—will you come to me as soon as you can—I wish to see you—It was perfectly well when I went to bed—I awoke in the night to give it suck it appeared to be sleeping quietly that I would not awake it—it was dead then but we did not find that out till morning—from its appearance it evedently died of convulsions—Will you come—you are so calm a creature & Shelley is afraid of a fever from the milk—for I am no longer a mother now."

[7]Isaac D'Israeli's *Despotism; or, the Fall of the Jesuits* (1811).

C.C. [Charles Clairmont] [. . .] C.C. calls—he tells us that Papa saw ~~Shelley~~ us & that he remarked that S. was so beautiful it was a pity he was so wicked—

Percy Bysshe Shelley
from *Alastor; or, The Spirit of Solitude*

> *Shelley wrote this visionary quest-romance in 1815, and published it with other poems (including* Mutability*) in 1816. Its restless, dream-inspired, death-bound visionary traces a mythic parallel to Victor Frankenstein and Robert Walton. The title was proposed by a friend, who explained that "Alastor" is Greek for "evil genius." The excerpt here is roughly the first quarter; the remainder renders the Poet's quest to reunite with his dream-vision, his path coursing far from human habitation, until death releases him from all frustrations. In the final verse paragraph, the frame narrator laments the loss of this "surpassing Spirit" and voices his sense that those "who remain behind" (himself included) are left only with "pale despair and cold tranquility, / Nature's vast frame, the web of human things, / Birth and the grave, that are not as they were."*

Preface

The poem entitled *Alastor* may be considered as allegorical of one of the most interesting situations of the human mind. It represents a youth of uncorrupted feelings and adventurous genius led forth by an imagination inflamed and purified through familiarity with all that is excellent and majestic, to the contemplation of the universe. He drinks deep of the fountains of knowledge, and is still insatiate. The magnificence and beauty of the external world sinks profoundly into the frame of his conceptions, and affords to their modifications a variety not to be exhausted. So long as it is possible for his desires to point towards objects thus infinite and unmeasured, he is joyous, and tranquil, and self-possessed. But the period arrives when these objects cease to suffice. His mind is at length suddenly awakened and thirsts for intercourse with an intelligence similar to itself. He images to himself the Being whom he loves. Conversant with speculations of the sublimest and most perfect natures, the vision in which he embodies his own imaginations unites all of wonderful, or wise, or beautiful, which the poet, the philosopher, or the lover could depicture. The intellectual faculties, the imagination, the functions of sense, have their respective requisitions on the sympathy of corresponding powers in other human beings. The Poet is represented as uniting these requisitions, and attaching them to a single image. He seeks in vain for a prototype of his conception. Blasted by his disappointment, he descends to an untimely grave.

The picture is not barren of instruction to actual men. The Poet's self-centred seclusion was avenged by the furies of an irresistible passion pursuing him to speedy ruin. But that Power, which strikes the luminaries of the world with sudden darkness and extinction, by awakening them to too exquisite a perception of its influences, dooms to a slow and poisonous decay those meaner spirits that dare to abjure its dominion. Their destiny is more abject and inglorious as their delinquency is more contemptible and pernicious. They who, deluded by no generous error, instigated by no sacred thirst of doubtful knowledge, duped by no illustrious superstition, loving nothing on this earth, and cherishing no hopes beyond, yet keep aloof from sympathies with their kind, rejoicing neither in human joy nor mourning with human grief; these, and such as they, have their apportioned curse. They languish, because none feel with them their common nature. They are morally dead. They are neither friends, nor lovers, nor fathers, nor citizens of the world, nor benefactors of their country. Among those who attempt to exist without human sympathy, the pure and tender-hearted perish through the intensity and passion of their search after its communities, when the vacancy of their spirit suddenly makes itself felt. All else, selfish, blind and torpid, are those unforeseeing multitudes who constitute, together with their own, the lasting misery and loneliness of the world. Those who love not their fellow-beings live unfruitful lives, and prepare for their old age a miserable grave.

> "The good die first,
> And those whose hearts are dry as summer dust
> Burn to the socket!"[1]

December 14, 1815.

[1] From Wordsworth's *The Excursion* (1814): these lines (1.531–33) are spoken by "The Wanderer" to the poet-author, about Margaret, a kind woman now dead from grief and poverty.

Alastor; or, The Spirit of Solitude

Nondum amabam, et amare amabam, quaerebam quid amarem,
amans amare.

—*Confessions of St. Augustine*[2]

Earth, Ocean, Air, belovèd brotherhood!
If our great Mother has imbued my soul
With aught of natural piety[1] to feel
Your love, and recompense the boon° with mine;   *gift*
If dewy morn, and odorous noon, and even,
With sunset and its gorgeous ministers,
And solemn midnight's tingling silentness;
If Autumn's hollow sighs in the sere wood,
And winter robing with pure snow and crowns
Of starry ice the gray grass and bare boughs;   10
If spring's voluptuous pantings when she breathes
Her first sweet kisses, have been dear to me;
If no bright bird, insect, or gentle beast
I consciously have injured, but still loved
And cherished these my kindred; then forgive
This boast, belovèd brethren, and withdraw
No portion of your wonted favour now!

Mother of this unfathomable world!
Favor my solemn song, for I have loved
Thee ever, and thee only; I have watched   20
Thy shadow, and the darkness of thy steps,
And my heart ever gazes on the depth
Of thy deep mysteries. I have made my bed
In charnels and on coffins, where black death
Keeps record of the trophies won from thee,

[2]St. Augustine's *Confessions* (c. 400) recounts his conversion to Christianity after a wild youth in Carthage. The epigraph from Book 3, Ch. 1, describes his sexual lust, a misplacement of desire to be fulfilled only by God: "Not yet did I love, yet I loved to love; I sought what I might love, loving to love."

[1]Echoing Wordsworth's *My Heart Leaps Up*: "I could wish my days to be / Bound each to each by natural piety" ("natural piety" is faith grounded in nature); also involved is Wordsworth's use of these lines in the epigraph for the "Intimations" Ode in 1815. "Mother" in 2 and 18 is Wordsworthian "Nature."

Hoping to still these obstinate questionings
Of thee and thine, by forcing some lone ghost,
Thy messenger, to render up the tale
Of what we are.[2] In lone and silent hours,
When night makes a weird sound of its own stillness,   30
Like an inspired and desperate alchymist
Staking his very life on some dark hope,[3]
Have I mixed awful° talk and asking looks   awe-filled
With my most innocent love, until strange tears
Uniting with those breathless kisses, made
Such magic as compels the charmèd night
To render up thy charge: . . . and, though ne'er yet
Thou hast unveiled thy inmost sanctuary,
Enough from incommunicable dream,
And twilight phantasms, and deep noonday thought,   40
Has shone within me, that serenely now
And moveless, as a long-forgotten lyre
Suspended in the solitary dome
Of some mysterious and deserted fane,°   temple
I wait thy breath, Great Parent, that my strain
May modulate with murmurs of the air,
And motions of the forests and the sea,
And voice of living beings, and woven hymns
Of night and day, and the deep heart of man.[4]

There was a Poet whose untimely tomb   50
No human hands with pious reverence reared,
But the charmed eddies of autumnal winds
Built o'er his mouldering bones a pyramid
Of mouldering leaves in the waste wilderness:—
A lovely youth,—no mourning maiden decked

[2]See "Intimations" Ode, stanza 9, in which the poet recalls his "obstinate questionings / Of sense and outward things" and his "shadowy recollections" of a transcendent realm, to which his soul is kindred. As a boy, Shelley experimented in conjuring spirits.

[3]Alchemy is an occult chemistry concerned with converting base metals to gold; influenced by Hellenistic philosophy, this project was part of a general quest for perfection, and pursued by scientists such as Isaac Newton.

[4]An extended figure of the frame-poet as an aeolian lyre, or wind-harp, its strings sounded by the wind.

With weeping flowers, or votive cypress wreath,[5]
The lone couch of his everlasting sleep:—
Gentle, and brave, and generous,—no lorn° bard   *forlorn*
Breathed o'er his dark fate one melodious sigh:
He lived, he died, he sung, in solitude.   60
Strangers have wept to hear his passionate notes,
And virgins, as unknown he passed, have pined
And wasted for fond love of his wild eyes.
The fire of those soft orbs has ceased to burn,
And Silence, too enamoured of that voice,
Locks its mute music in her rugged cell.

      By solemn vision and bright silver dream,
His infancy was nurtured. Every sight
And sound from the vast earth and ambient air
Sent to his heart its choicest impulses.   70
The fountains of divine philosophy
Fled not his thirsting lips, and all of great
Or good, or lovely, which the sacred past
In truth or fable consecrates, he felt
And knew. When early youth had past, he left
His cold fireside and alienated home
To seek strange truths in undiscovered lands.
Many a wide waste and tangled wilderness
Has lured his fearless steps; and he has bought
With his sweet voice and eyes, from savage men,   80
His rest and food. Nature's most secret steps
He like her shadow has pursued, where'er
The red volcano overcanopies
Its fields of snow and pinnacles of ice
With burning smoke, or where bitumen lakes[6]
On black bare pointed islets ever beat
With sluggish surge, or where the secret caves
Rugged and dark, winding among the springs
Of fire and poison, inaccessible
To avarice or pride, their starry domes   90
Of diamond and of gold expand above

[5]Offered to the gods by devoted mourners on behalf of the dead.
[6]Lakes of molten lava or pitch, evoking the landscape of Hell in *Paradise Lost.*

Numberless and immeasurable halls,
Frequent° with crystal column, and clear shrines   *crowded*
Of pearl, and thrones radiant with chrysolite.°   *gem*
Nor had that scene of ampler majesty
Than gems or gold, the varying roof of heaven
And the green earth lost in his heart its claims
To love and wonder; he would linger long
In lonesome vales, making the wild his home,
Until the doves and squirrels would partake   100
From his innocuous hand his bloodless[7] food,
Lured by the gentle meaning of his looks,
And the wild antelope, that starts whene'er
The dry leaf rustles in the brake, suspend
Her timid steps, to gaze upon a form
More graceful than her own.

                    His wandering step
Obedient to high thoughts, has visited
The awful ruins of the days of old:
Athens, and Tyre, and Balbec, and the waste
Where stood Jerusalem, the fallen towers   110
Of Babylon, the eternal pyramids,
Memphis and Thebes, and whatsoe'er of strange
Sculptured on alabaster obelisk,
Or jasper tomb, or mutilated sphinx,
Dark Aethiopia in her desert hills
Conceals.[8] Among the ruined temples there,
Stupendous columns, and wild images
Of more than man, where marble daemons° watch   *spirits*
The Zodiac's brazen mystery, and dead men
Hang their mute thoughts on the mute walls around,[9]   120
He lingered, poring on memorials

[7]Innocuous: harmless; Shelley was a vegetarian.

[8]A journey through the sites of ancient civilizations: Athenian Greece; the Phoenician cities of Tyre (now in Lebanon) and Balbec; cities named in the Old Testament, and in ancient Egypt (Memphis, the home of the great pyramids, and Thebes); and finally Ethiopia, the fabled source of the Nile.

[9]In the Egyptian temple of Isis at Denderah, images of the gods were arrayed along the signs of the Zodiac.

Of the world's youth, through the long burning day
Gazed on those speechless shapes, nor, when the moon
Filled the mysterious halls with floating shades
Suspended he that task, but ever gazed
And gazed, till meaning on his vacant mind
Flashed like strong inspiration, and he saw
The thrilling secrets of the birth of time.

    Meanwhile an Arab maiden brought his food,
Her daily portion, from her father's tent,   130
And spread her matting for his couch, and stole
From duties and repose to tend his steps:—
Enamoured, yet not daring for deep awe
To speak her love:—and watched his nightly sleep,
Sleepless herself, to gaze upon his lips
Parted in slumber, whence the regular breath
Of innocent dreams arose: then, when red morn
Made paler the pale moon, to her cold home
Wildered, and wan, and panting, she returned.

    The Poet, wandering on, through Arabie   140
And Persia, and the wild Carmanian waste,
And o'er the aërial mountains which pour down
Indus and Oxus from their icy caves,
In joy and exultation held his way;
Till in the vale of Cashmire,[10] far within
Its loneliest dell, where odorous plants entwine
Beneath the hollow rocks a natural bower,
Beside a sparkling rivulet he stretched
His languid limbs. A vision on his sleep
There came, a dream of hopes that never yet   150
Had flushed his cheek. He dreamed a veilèd maid
Sate near him, talking in low solemn tones.
Her voice was like the voice of his own soul
Heard in the calm of thought; its music long,
Like woven sounds of streams and breezes, held

[10]The Poet wanders further eastward through Saudi Arabia, Persia (Iran), the Kerman Desert (southern Iran), the Hindu Kush Mountains, the source of the Oxus and Indus rivers, to the legendary Vale of Cashmire (Kashmir is the region of northwest India and northeast Pakistan).

His inmost sense suspended in its web
Of many-colored woof and shifting hues.
Knowledge and truth and virtue were her theme,
And lofty hopes of divine liberty,
Thoughts the most dear to him, and poesy,   160
Herself a poet. Soon the solemn mood
Of her pure mind kindled through all her frame
A permeating fire: wild numbers° then   *metrical poetry*
She raised, with voice stifled in tremulous sobs
Subdued by its own pathos: her fair hands
Were bare alone, sweeping from some strange harp
Strange symphony, and in their branching veins
The eloquent blood told an ineffable tale.
The beating of her heart was heard to fill
The pauses of her music, and her breath   170
Tumultuously accorded with those fits
Of intermitted song. Sudden she rose,
As if her heart impatiently endured
Its bursting burthen; at the sound he turned,
And saw by the warm light of their own life
Her glowing limbs beneath the sinuous veil
Of woven wind, her outspread arms now bare,
Her dark locks floating in the breath of night,
Her beamy bending eyes, her parted lips
Outstretched, and pale, and quivering eagerly.   180
His strong heart sunk and sickened with excess
Of love. He reared his shuddering limbs, and quelled
His gasping breath, and spread his arms to meet
Her panting bosom: . . . she drew back a while,
Then, yielding to the irresistible joy,
With frantic gesture and short breathless cry
Folded his frame in her dissolving arms.
Now blackness veiled his dizzy eyes, and night
Involved° and swallowed up the vision; sleep,   *enwrapped*
Like a dark flood suspended in its course,   190
Rolled back its impulse on his vacant brain.

    Roused by the shock he started from his trance—
The cold white light of morning, the blue moon

Low in the west, the clear and garish hills,
The distinct valley and the vacant woods,
Spread round him where he stood. Whither have fled[11]
The hues of heaven that canopied his bower
Of yesternight? The sounds that soothed his sleep,
The mystery and the majesty of Earth,
The joy, the exultation? His wan eyes   200
Gaze on the empty scene as vacantly
As ocean's moon looks on the moon in heaven.
The spirit of sweet human love has sent
A vision to the sleep of him who spurned
Her choicest gifts. He eagerly pursues
Beyond the realms of dream that fleeting shade;°   *phantom*
He overleaps the bounds. Alas! alas!
Were limbs, and breath, and being intertwined
Thus treacherously? Lost, lost, for ever lost,
In the wide pathless desart of dim sleep,   210
That beautiful shape! Does the dark gate of death
Conduct to thy mysterious paradise,
O Sleep? Does the bright arch of rainbow clouds,
And pendent mountains seen in the calm lake,
Lead only to a black and watery depth,
While death's blue vault, with loathliest vapours hung,
Where every shade which the foul grave exhales
Hides its dead eye from the detested day,
Conduct, O Sleep, to thy delightful realms?
This doubt with sudden tide flowed on his heart,   220
The insatiate hope which it awakened, stung
His brain even like despair.

                                        While day-light held
The sky, the Poet kept mute conference
With his still soul. At night the passion came,
Like the fierce fiend of a distempered dream,
And shook him from his rest, and led him forth
Into the darkness.—

[11]A sounding of the old "ubi sunt?" (Latin: where are?) trope, a voice of elegiac longing, most recently sounded by Wordsworth in the "Immortality" *Ode:* "Whither is fled the visionary gleam? / Where is it now, the glory and the dream?" (56–57).

Mary Wollstonecraft Shelley, with Percy Bysshe Shelley (1817)

from *History of a Six Weeks' Tour through a part of France, Switzerland, Germany, and Holland: With Letters Descriptive of a Sail Round the Lake of Geneva, and of the Glaciers of Chamouni*[1]

[*Frankenstein* scenery: Geneva and the Alps, late spring 1816]

[Mary Shelley] 17 May 1816

[. . .] arrived at Poligny. This town is built at the foot of Jura, which rises abruptly from a plain of vast extent. The rocks of the mountain overhang the houses. Some difficulty in obtaining horses detained us here until the evening closed in, when we proceeded, by the light of a stormy moon, to Champagnolles, a little village situated in the depth of the mountains. The road was serpentine and exceedingly steep, and was overhung on one side by half distinguished precipices, whilst the other was a gulph, filled by the darkness of the driving clouds. The dashing of the invisible mountain streams announced to us that we had quitted the plains of France, as we slowly ascended, amidst a violent storm of wind and rain, to Champagnolles. [. . .] The next morning we proceeded, still ascending among the ravines and vallies of the mountain. The scenery perpetually grows more wonderful and sublime: pine forests of impenetrable thickness, and untrodden, nay, inaccessible expanse spread on every side. Sometimes the dark woods descending, follow the route into the vallies, the distorted trees struggling with knotted roots between the most barren clefts; sometimes the road winds high into the regions of frost, and then the forests becomes scattered, and the branches of the trees are loaded with snow, and half of the enormous pines themselves buried in the wavy drifts. [. . .] as we ascended the mountains, the same clouds which rained on us in the vallies poured forth large flakes of snow, thick and fast. The sun occasionally shone through these showers, and illuminated the magnificent ravines of the mountains, whose gigantic pines were some laden with snow, some wreathed round by the lines of scattered and lingering vapour; others darting their dark spires into the sunny sky, brilliantly clear and azure.

[1]Published in London by T. Hookham Jr. and C. & J. Ollier. Selections are from pp. 88–100 and 173–83.

As the evening advanced, and we ascended higher, the snow, which we had beheld whitening the overhanging rocks, now encroached upon our road, and it snowed fast as we entered the village of Les Rousses. [. . .] departed from Les Rousses at six in the evening, when the sun had already far descended, and the snow pelting against the windows of our carriage, assisted the coming darkness to deprive us of the view of the lake of Geneva and the far distant Alps.

The prospect around, however, was sufficiently sublime to command our attention—never was scene more awfully desolate. The trees in these regions are incredibly large, and stand in scattered clumps over the white wilderness; the vast expanse of snow was chequered only by these gigantic pines, and the poles that marked our road: no river or rock-encircled lawn relieved the eye, by adding the picturesque to the sublime. [. . .] To what different scene are we now arrived! To the warm sunshine and to the humming of sun-loving insects. From the windows of our hotel we see the lovely lake, blue as the heavens which it reflects, and sparkling with golden beams. The opposite shore is sloping, and covered with vines, which however do not so early in the season add to the beauty of the prospect. Gentlemen's seats are scattered over these banks, behind which rise the various ridges of black mountains, and towering far above, in the midst of its snowy Alps, the majestic Mont Blanc, highest and queen of all. Such is the view reflected by the lake; it is a bright summer scene without any of that sacred solitude and deep seclusion that delighted us at Lucerne.

[. . .] every evening at about six o'clock we sail on the lake, which is delightful, whether we glide over a glassy surface or are speeded along by a strong wind. The [. . .] tossing of our boat raises my spirits and inspires me with unusual hilarity. Twilight here is of short duration, but we at present enjoy the benefits of an increasing moon, and seldom return until ten o'clock, when, as we approach the shore, we are saluted by the delightful scent of flowers and new mown grass, and the chirp of the grasshoppers, and the song of evening birds.

[Mary Shelley] 1 June 1816

[. . .] We now inhabit a little cottage on the opposite shore of the lake, and have exchanged the view of Mont Blanc and her snowy *aiguilles* for the dark frowning Jura, behind whose range we every evening see the sun sink, and darkness approaches our valley from behind the Alps, which is observed in England to attend on the clouds of an autumnal sky when day-light is almost gone. The lake is at our feet, and a little harbour contains our boat, in which we still enjoy our evening excursions on the water. Unfortunately we do not now enjoy those brilliant skies that hailed us on our first arrival to this country. An almost perpetual rain confines us principally to the house;[2] but when the sun bursts forth it is with a splendour and heat unknown in England. The thunder storms that visit us are grander and more terrific than I have ever seen before. We watch them as they approach from the opposite side of the lake, observing the lightning play among the clouds in various parts of the heavens, and dart in jagged figures upon the piny heights of Jura, dark with the shadow of the overhanging cloud, while perhaps the sun is shining cheerily upon us. One night we *enjoyed* a finer storm than I had ever before beheld. The lake was lit up—the pines on Jura made visible, and all the scene illuminated for an instant, when a pitchy blackness succeeded, and the thunder came in frightful bursts over our heads amid the darkness.

Percy Bysshe Shelley

MONT BLANC
Lines Written in the Vale of Chamouni

At nearly 16,000 ft. in the French Alps, Mont Blanc is the highest peak in Europe, a must-see on everyone's Grand Tour as the epitome of "the sublime"—a vast scene at once exciting and defeating adequate perception and representation; its summit had been attained only a few times by 1816. In History of a Six Weeks' Tour, Percy said his poem "was composed under the immediate impression of the deep and powerful feelings excited by the objects which it attempts to describe." Mont Blanc is the site of the Creature's first encounter and extended interview with Victor Frankenstein.

I

The everlasting universe of things
Flows through the mind, and rolls its rapid waves,
Now dark—now the glittering—now reflecting gloom—

[2]This weather is also described in the 1831 "Introduction" to *Frankenstein*.

Now lending splendour, where from secret springs
The source of human thought its tribute brings
Of waters,—with a sound but half its own,
Such as a feeble brook will oft assume
In the wild woods, among the mountains lone,
Where waterfalls around it leap for ever,
Where woods and winds contend, and a vast river   10
Over its rocks ceaselessly bursts and raves.

II

Thus thou, Ravine of Arve[1]—dark, deep Ravine—
Thou many-coloured, many-voiced vale,
Over whose pines and crags and caverns sail
Fast cloud shadows and sunbeams: awful[2] scene,
Where Power in likeness of the Arve comes down
From the ice gulphs that gird his secret throne,
Bursting through these dark mountains like the flame
Of lightning thro' the tempest;—thou dost lie,
Thy giant brood of pines around thee clinging,   20
Children of elder° time, in whose devotion   *earlier*
The chainless winds still come and ever came
To drink their odours, and their mighty swinging
To hear—an old and solemn harmony;
Thine earthly rainbows stretched across the sweep
Of the ethereal waterfall, whose veil
Robes some unsculptured image; the strange sleep
Which when the voices of the desart fail
Wraps all in its own deep eternity;—
Thy caverns echoing to the Arve's commotion,   30
A loud, lone sound no other sound can tame;
Thou art pervaded with that ceaseless motion
Thou art the path of that unresting sound—
Dizzy Ravine! and when I gaze on thee
I seem as in a trance sublime and strange
To muse on my own separate phantasy,[3]

[1] The river descending from the glacier on Mont Blanc.
[2] Awesome.
[3] Fantasy or delusion.

My own, my human mind, which passively
Now renders and receives fast influencings,
Holding an unremitting interchange
With the clear universe of things around;   40
One legion of wild thoughts, whose wandering wings
Now float above thy darkness, and now rest
Where that or thou[4] art no unbidden guest,
In the still cave of the witch Poesy,
Seeking among the shadows that pass by,
Ghosts of all things that are, some shade of thee,
Some phantom, some faint image; till the breast
From which they fled recalls them, thou art there![5]

III

Some say that gleams of a remoter world
Visit the soul in sleep,—that death is slumber,   50
And that its shapes the busy thoughts outnumber
Of those who wake and live.—I look on high;
Has some unknown omnipotence unfurled
The veil of life and death?[6] or do I lie
In dream, and does the mightier world of sleep
Spread far around and inaccessibly
Its circles? For the very spirit fails,
Driven like a homeless cloud from steep to steep
That vanishes among the viewless gales!
Far, far above, piercing the infinite sky,   60
Mont Blanc appears,—still, snowy, and serene—
Its subject mountains their unearthly forms
Pile around it, ice and rock; broad vales between
Of frozen floods, unfathomable deeps,
Blue as the overhanging heaven, that spread
And wind among the accumulated steeps;

[4]Where thy darkness or the dizzy ravine . . .

[5]Evoking Plato's allegory in *Republic* 7, which compares the mind to a cave in which
our sense of reality consists of the shadows cast by firelight on its walls, ignorant of the
light of "Reality" outside. Shelley's difficult syntax blurs the distinction of inner and
outer, human mind and Ravine.

[6]The screen of phenomena separating physical from spiritual reality (lifted in sleep, in
daydreams and visions).

A desart peopled by the storms alone,
Save° when the eagle brings some hunter's bone,   *except*
And the wolf tracts her there—how hideously
Its shapes are heaped around! rude, bare, and high,   70
Ghastly, and scarred, and riven.—Is this the scene
Where the old Earthquake-dæmon[7] taught her young
Ruin? Were these their toys? or did a sea
Of fire, envelope once this silent snow?
None can reply—all seems eternal now.
The wilderness has a mysterious tongue
Which teaches awful doubt,[8] or faith so mild,
So solemn, so serene, that man may be
But for such faith, with nature reconciled;
Thou hast a voice, great Mountain, to repeal   80
Large codes of fraud and woe; not understood
By all, but which the wise and great and good
Interpret, or make felt, or deeply feel.

IV

The fields, the lakes, the forests, and the streams,
Ocean, and all the living things that dwell
Within the daedal earth,[9] lightning, and rain,
Earthquake, and fiery flood, and hurricane,
The torpor of the year when feeble dreams
Visit the hidden buds, or dreamless sleep
Holds every future leaf and flower;—the bound   90
With which from that detested trance they leap;
The works and ways of man, their death and birth,
And that of him, and all that his may be;
All things that move and breathe with toil and sound
Are born and die; revolve, subside, and swell.
Power dwells apart in its tranquillity
Remote, serene, and inaccessible:
And *this,* the naked countenance of earth,
On which I gaze, even these primaeval mountains

[7]In Greek mythology, a spirit, usually a personification of natural forces.
[8]Awe-filled questioning.
[9]Daedalus, architect of the labyrinth in Crete, was imprisoned there, and escaped on wings crafted with feathers and wax.

Teach the adverting mind. The glaciers creep   100
Like snakes that watch their prey, from their far fountains,
Slow rolling on; there, many a precipice,
Frost and the Sun in scorn of mortal power
Have piled: dome, pyramid, and pinnacle,
A city of death, distinct with many a tower
And wall impregnable of beaming ice.
Yet not a city, but a flood of ruin
Is there, that from the boundary of the sky
Rolls its perpetual stream; vast pines are strewing
Its destined path, or in the mangled soil   110
Branchless and shattered stand; the rocks, drawn down
From yon remotest waste, have overthrown
The limits of the dead and living world,
Never to be reclaimed. The dwelling-place
Of insects, beasts, and birds, becomes its spoil;
Their food and their retreat for ever gone,
So much of life and joy is lost. The race
Of man, flies far in dread; his work and dwelling
Vanish, like smoke before the tempest's stream,
And their place is not known.[10] Below, vast caves   120
Shine in the rushing torrent's restless gleam,
Which from those secret chasms in tumult welling
Meet in the vale, and one majestic River,
The breath and blood of distant lands, for ever
Rolls its loud waters to the ocean waves,
Breathes its swift vapours to the circling air.

V

Mont Blanc yet gleams on high:—the power is there,
The still and solemn power, of many sights,
And many sounds, and much of life and death.

---

[10]Echoing Psalm 103: "As for man, his days are as grass . . . For the wind passeth over it, and it is gone; and the place thereof shall know it no more" (15–16).

In the calm darkness of the moonless nights,   130
In the lone glare of day, the snows descend
Upon that Mountain; none beholds them there,
Nor when the flakes burn in the sinking sun,
Or the star-beams dart through them:—Winds contend
Silently there, and heap the snow with breath
Rapid and strong, but silently! Its home
The voiceless lightning in these solitudes
Keeps innocently, and like vapour broods
Over the snow. The secret strength of things
Which governs thought, and to the infinite dome   140
Of heaven is as a law, inhabits thee!
And what were thou, and earth, and stars, and sea,
If to the human mind's imaginings
Silence and solitude were vacancy?

23 July 1816

George Gordon, Lord Byron (1788–1824)
from *Manfred, A Dramatic Poem* (1817)

> *Manfred is yet another progeny of the Geneva circle in summer 1816.
> From the ghost-story compact of June, Byron had succeeded only with a
> brief fragment, but in August he was newly inspired by the visit of M. G.
> Lewis, author of* The Monk, *a sensational gothic novel published in
> 1796 (the decade in which* Frankenstein *is set) and* Castle Spectre, *a
> melodrama that was a stage sensation in 1797. Lewis translated most of
> Goethe's (German)* Faust *out loud to Byron, who was "much struck
> with it," especially amidst Geneva's sublime Alpine scenery. The result
> was* Manfred, *its title character, like Victor Frankenstein and like Dr.
> Faustus, an unorthodox scientist, tortured by a secret sin. Written over
> the next half year,* Manfred *appeared several months before* Franken-
> stein, *in June 1817, with Byron's celebrity ensuring a much larger print
> run of 6,000. The excerpts below show Manfred as Frankenstein's twin
> in torment: brilliant, transgressive, isolated, doomed. The Creature, too,
> has a purchase, in the lament that knowledge is sorrow. The common
> godfather is Milton's Satan.*

"There are more things in heaven and earth, Horatio,
Than are dreamt of in your philosophy."[1]

*The Scene of the Drama is amongst the Higher Alps—partly in the
Castle of Manfred, and partly in the Mountains.*

from *Act I, scene i.* Manfred alone.—
Scene, a Gothic Gallery.— Time, Midnight.

MANFRED The lamp must be replenish'd, but even then
    It will not burn so long as I must watch:
    My slumbers—if I slumber—are not sleep,
    But a continuance of enduring thought,
    Which then I can resist not: in my heart
    There is a vigil, and these eyes but close
    To look within; and yet I live, and bear
    The aspect and the form of breathing men.
    But grief should be the instructor of the wise;
    Sorrow is knowledge: they who know the most   10
    Must mourn the deepest o'er the fatal truth,
    The Tree of Knowledge is not that of Life.[2]
    Philosophy and science, and the springs
    Of wonder, and the wisdom of the world,
    I have essayed, and in my mind there is
    A power to make these subject to itself—
    But they avail not: I have done men good,
    And I have met with good even among men—
    But this avail'd not: I have had my foes,
    And none have baffled, many fallen before me—   20
    But this avail'd not:—Good, or evil, life,
    Powers, passions, all I see in other beings,
    Have been to me as rain unto the sands,
    Since that all-nameless hour. I have no dread,
    And feel the curse to have no natural fear,
    Nor fluttering throb, that beats with hopes or wishes,
    Or lurking love of something on the earth.—

[1]So Hamlet rebukes a skeptical college friend, after he's seen his father's ghost (*Hamlet* 1.5.66–67).
[2]What Adam and Eve learn (Genesis 2–3), and what Victor's Creature learns from his reading (see the end of II.V, p. 90).

from Act II, scene ii:
A lower Valley in the Alps.—a Cataract[3]

WITCH   What could be the quest
  Which is not in the power of the most powerful,
  The rulers of the invisible?
MANFRED   A boon;
  But why should I repeat it? 'twere in vain.
WITCH   I know not that; let thy lips utter it.
MANFRED   Well, though it torture me, 'tis but the same;
  My pang shall find a voice. From my youth upwards   50
  My spirit walk'd not with the souls of men,
  Nor look'd upon the earth with human eyes;
  The thirst of their ambition was not mine,
  The aim of their existence was not mine;
  My joys, my griefs, my passions, and my powers,
  Made me a stranger; though I wore the form,
  I had no sympathy with breathing flesh,
  Nor midst the creatures of clay that girded me
  Was there but one who—but of her anon.
  I said with men, and with the thoughts of men,   60
  I held but slight communion; but instead,
  My joy was in the Wilderness, to breathe
  The difficult air of the iced mountain's top,
  Where the birds dare not build, nor insect's wing
  Flit o'er the herbless granite; or to plunge
  Into the torrent, and to roll along
  On the swift whirl of the new-breaking wave
  Of river-stream, or ocean, in their flow.
  In these my early strength exulted; or
  To follow through the night the moving moon,   70
  The stars and their development; or catch
  The dazzling lightnings till my eyes grew dim;
  Or to look, list'ning, on the scattered leaves,
  While Autumn winds were at their evening song.
  These were my pastimes, and to be alone;
  For if the beings, of whom I was one,—

[3]Manfred has summoned the Witch of the Alps, hoping for refuge in natural beauty from the memory that torments him: the destruction of a beloved woman, who seems an intellectual version of Frankenstein's beloved Elizabeth.

Hating to be so,—cross'd me in my path,
I felt myself degraded back to them,
And was all clay again. And then I dived,
In my lone wanderings, to the caves of death,   80
Searching its cause in its effect; and drew
From wither'd bones, and skulls, and heap'd up dust,
Conclusions most forbidden. Then I pass'd
The nights of years in sciences untaught,
Save in the old-time; and with time and toil,
And terrible ordeal, and such penance
As in itself hath power upon the air,
And spirits that do compass air and earth,
Space, and the peopled infinite, I made
Mine eyes familiar with Eternity,   90
Such as, before me, did the Magi, and
He who from out their fountain-dwellings raised
Eros and Anteros, at Gadara,[4]
As I do thee;—and with my knowledge grew
The thirst of knowledge, and the power and joy
Of this most bright intelligence, until—
WITCH   Proceed.
MANFRED   Oh! I but thus prolonged my words,
    Boasting these idle attributes, because
    As I approach the core of my heart's grief—
    But to my task. I have not named to thee   100
    Father or mother, mistress, friend, or being,
    With whom I wore the chain of human ties;
    If I had such, they seem'd not such to me—
    Yet there was one—
WITCH   Spare not thyself—proceed.
MANFRED She was like me in lineaments—her eyes,
    Her hair, her features, all, to the very tone
    Even of her voice, they said were like to mine;
    But soften'd all, and temper'd into beauty:
    She had the same lone thoughts and wanderings,
    The quest of hidden knowledge, and a mind   110
    To comprehend the universe: nor these

[4]Eros, god of love, and Anteros, god of unrequited love, were legendarily raised from
springs in Syria by the 4th-c. Neo-Platonist philosopher Jamblicus.

Alone, but with them gentler powers than mine,
Pity, and smiles, and tears—which I had not;
And tenderness—but that I had for her;
Humility—and that I never had.
Her faults were mine—her virtues were her own—
I loved her, and destroy'd her!

WITCH   With thy hand?

MANFRED Not with my hand, but heart—which broke her heart—
It gazed on mine, and withered. I have shed
Blood, but not hers—and yet her blood was shed—   120
I saw—and could not stanch it.

WITCH   And for this—
A being of the race thou dost despise,
The order which thine own would rise above,
Mingling with us and ours, thou dost forego
The gifts of our great knowledge, and shrink'st back
To recreant mortality—Away!

MANFRED Daughter of Air! I tell thee, since that hour—
But words are breath—look on me in my sleep,
Or watch my watchings—Come and sit by me!
My solitude is solitude no more,   130
But peopled with the Furies;[5]—I have gnash'd
My teeth in darkness till returning morn,
Then cursed myself till sunset;—

George Gordon, Lord Byron

from *Childe Harold's Pilgrimage, Canto the Third* (1816)

[Thunderstorm in Switzerland][1]

XCII

Thy sky is changed!—and such a change! Oh night,   860
And storm, and darkness, ye are wondrous strong,

[5]The classical Greek goddesses of vengeance.

[1]"The thunder-storms to which these lines refer occurred on the thirteenth of June, 1816, at midnight. I have seen among the Acroceraunian mountains of Chimari several more terrible, but none more beautiful" [Byron's note]

Yet lovely in your strength, as is the light
Of a dark eye in woman! Far along,
From peak to peak, the rattling crags among
Leaps the live thunder! Not from one lone cloud,
But every mountain now hath found a tongue,
And Jura answers, through her misty shroud,
Back to the joyous Alps, who call to her aloud![2]

XCIII

And this is in the night:—Most glorious night!
Thou wert not sent for slumber! let me be   870
A sharer in thy fierce and far delight,—
A portion of the tempest and of thee!
How the lit lake shines, a phosphoric sea,
And the big rain comes dancing to the earth!
And now again 'tis black,—and now, the glee
Of the loud hills shakes with its mountain-mirth,
As if they did rejoice o'er a young earthquake's birth.

XCIV

Now, where the swift Rhone cleaves his way between
Heights which appear as lovers who have parted
In hate, whose mining depths so intervene,   880
That they can meet no more, though broken-hearted!
Though in their souls, which thus each other thwarted,
Love was the very root of the fond rage
Which blighted their life's bloom, and then departed:
Itself expired, but leaving them an age
Of years all winters,—war within themselves to wage.

XCV

Now, where the quick Rhone thus hath cleft his way,
The mightiest of the storms hath ta'en his stand:
For here, not one, but many, make their play,

[2]The Jura mountains, to the north and west of Geneva, form the boundary between Switzerland and France; the Alps run to the east and south.

And fling their thunder-bolts from hand to hand,   890
Flashing and cast around: of all the band,
The brightest through these parted hills hath fork'd
His lightnings, as if he did understand,
That in such gaps as desolation work'd,
There the hot shaft should blast whatever therein lurk'd.

XCVI

Sky, mountains, river, winds, lake, lightnings! ye!
With night, and clouds, and thunder, and a soul
To make these felt and feeling, well may be
Things that have made me watchful; the far roll
Of your departing voices, is the knoll   900
Of what in me is sleepless,—if I rest.
But where of ye, oh tempests! is the goal?
Are ye like those within the human breast?
Or do ye find, at length, like eagles, some high nest?

XCVII

Could I embody and unbosom now
That which is most within me,—could I wreak
My thoughts upon expression, and thus throw
Soul, heart, mind, passions, feelings, strong or weak,
All that I would have sought, and all I seek,
Bear, know, feel, and yet breathe—into *one* word,   910
And that one word were Lightning, I would speak;
But as it is, I live and die unheard,
With a most voiceless thought, sheathing it as a sword.

Leigh Hunt (1784–1859)
from *Blue-Stocking Revels, or The Feast of the Violets* (c. after 1831)

Radical journalist, poet, and essayist Leigh Hunt was a close friend of the Shelleys. In a poem to honor women writers and refute the slur of "blue-stocking," Hunt welcomes Shelley to the feast:

And Shelley, four-fam'd,—for her parents, her lord,[1]
And the poor lone impossible monster abhorr'd.
(So sleek and so smiling she came, people stared,
To think such fair clay should so darkly have dared;
But Apollo[2] the very name lov'd so, he turn'd
To a glory all round her, which shook as it burn'd . . .)[3]

Benjamin Spock, M.D.
from *Baby and Child Care* (1945; revised 1957)[1]

Baby and Child Care *was second only to the Bible on U.S. book-shelves in the mid-twentieth century.*

Enjoy Your Baby

Don't be afraid of your baby. You'd think from what some people say about babies demanding attention that they come into the world determined to get their parents under their thumb by hook or by crook. This isn't true. Your baby is born to be a reasonable, friendly human being. . . .

Love and enjoy your children for what they are, for what they look like, for what they do, and forget about the qualities that they don't have. I don't give you this advice just for sentimental reasons. There's a very important practical point here. The children who are appreciated for what they are, even if they are homely, or clumsy, or slow, will grow up with confidence in themselves—happy. They will have a spirit that will make the best of all the capacities that they have, and of all the opportunities that come their way. They will make light of any handicaps. But the children who have never been

---

[1]Percy Bysshe Shelley.

[2]The classical god of poetry (a "glory" is a halo).

[3]*The Poetical Works of Leigh Hunt* (London: Ward, Lock & Co, 1884), pp. 115–16.

[1]Reprinted with permission of Pocket Books, a division of Simon & Schuster, from *Baby and Child Care* by Benjamin Spock, M.D. Copyright © 1945, 1946, © 1957, 1968, 1976 by Benjamin Spock, M.D.

quite accepted by their parents, who have always felt that they were not quite right, will grow up lacking confidence. They'll never be able to make full use of what brains, what skills, what physical attractiveness they have. If they start life with a handicap, physical or mental, it will be multiplied tenfold by the time they are grown up.

A baby at birth is usually disappointing-looking to a parent who hasn't seen one before. Her skin is coated with a soft white wax, which, if left on, will be absorbed slowly and will lessen the chance of rashes during the hospital stay. Her skin underneath is apt to be very red. Her face tends to be puffy and lumpy, and there may be black-and-blue marks from forceps. The head is misshapen from "molding" during labor—low in the forehead, elongated at the back, and quite lopsided. Occasionally there may be, in addition, a hematoma, a localized hemorrhage under the scalp that sticks out as a distinct bump and takes weeks to go away. A couple of days after birth there may be a touch of jaundice, which is visible for about a week. (Jaundice that comes the first day or is very noticeable or lasts more than a week should be reported to the doctor.) At the base of the spine, there is often a bluish-gray spot, the "Mongolian spot," which fades gradually.

The baby's body is covered all over with fuzzy hair, which is usually shed in about a week. For a couple of weeks afterward there is apt to be a dry scaling of the skin, which is also shed. Some babies have black hair on the scalp at first, which may come far down on the forehead. The first hair, whatever its color or consistency, comes out, and the new hair that grows in, sooner or later, may be quite different in all respects.

. . .

Some causes of dissatisfaction. The reasons why parents sometimes get off on the wrong foot with one child are quite varied and are usually hidden under the surface. Two possible factors: . . . the parents may not have felt ready for this pregnancy or there may have been unusual family tensions during it. The baby himself may have got the parents off to the wrong start by being completely different from what they had been secretly expecting—a boy when they were looking for a girl, or a very homely baby when they were anticipating a beauty, or a frail infant compared to their other husky children. The infant may cry for several months with colic and seem to spurn her parents' efforts to comfort her. The father may be disappointed when his son turns out to be no athlete, no scrapper; the mother because he's no student. It doesn't matter that the parents are intelligent people who well know that they can't order the kind of baby they want most. Being human, they have irrational expectations and can't help feeling let down.

As children become a little older they may remind us, consciously or unconsciously, of a brother, sister, father, or mother who made life hard for us at times. A mother's daughter may have traits like her younger sister, who used to be always in her hair—and yet she may have no conscious realization that this is the cause of a lot of her irritation.

A father may be excessively bothered by some particular characteristic in his young son—timidity, for instance—and never connect it with the fact that as a child he himself had a terrible time in overcoming timidity. You'd think that a person who has suffered a lot in trying to overcome what he considers a fault would be more sympathetic with it in his child. Usually it doesn't work that way.

The Story-Telling Compact

Frankenstein was conceived at Byron's residence, Villa Diodati on Lake Geneva, on a rainy night in June 1816, as part of a group project involving Percy Shelley, Claire Clairmont, Byron, and Byron's personal physician, John Polidori. No one has disagreed with Thomas Moore that "the most memorable result . . . of their story-telling compact, was Mrs. Shelley's wild and powerful romance of Frankenstein,—one of those original conceptions that take hold of the public mind at once, and for ever" (1832, *Works of Lord Byron*, 3: 282). Percy and Claire foundered, Byron managed a short, vampiric Byronic tale, and Polidori later "vamped up" a full fable, *The Vampyre*, which inspired Bram Stoker at the other end of the century to *Dracula* (1897), a distant progeny of that evening.

Shelley's account of the compact in her retrospective Introduction of 1831 is complemented by Moore's:

> When the weather did not allow of their excursions after dinner,—an occurrence not unfrequent during this very wet summer,—the inmates of the cottage [Mary, Percy, and Claire] passed their evenings at Diodati, and, when the rain rendered it inconvenient for them to return home, remained there to sleep. "We often," says one, who was not the least ornamental of the party, "sat up in conversation till the morning light. There was never any lack of subjects, and, grave or gay, we were always interested."
>
> During a week of rain at this time, having amused themselves with reading German ghost-stories, they agreed, at last to write something in imitation of them. "You and I," said Lord Byron to Mrs. Shelley, "will publish ours together." He then began his tale

of the Vampire; and, having the whole arranged in his head, repeated to them a sketch of the story one evening,—but, from the narrative being in prose, made but little progress in filling up his outline. [. . .] From his remembrance of this sketch, Polidori afterwards vamped up his strange novel of the Vampire, which under the supposition of its being Lord Byron's, was received with such enthusiasm in France. (*ibid* 3: 281–82)

George Gordon, Lord Byron (1788–1824)

Although Byron conceived his "German ghost-story" as a twin for Frankenstein, *and projected a co-publication, his efforts halted after several days at a fragmentary sketch. He thought this still could please* Blackwood's Edinburgh Magazine *or another periodical; he sent it to his publisher John Murray on 15 May 1819 with this design, assuring him that the report of "the agreement to write the ghost-books is true":*

> Mary Godwin (now Mrs. Shelley) wrote Frankenstein, *which you have reviewed, thinking it Shelley's. Methinks it is a wonderful book for a girl of nineteen,—not nineteen, indeed, at that time. I enclose you the beginning of mine, . . . I never went on with it, as you will perceive by the date. (1832, Works, 4: 149)*

Eager to fill out a slender volume of recent poetry by Bryon, Murray decided to use the resource himself, and so took the "prose" and "post-scribed it" to Mazeppa. *Byron grumbled, unhappy about the genre-pollution of poetry and prose (letter, 20 March 1820). It is a measure of Byron's celebrity that when the* Mazeppa *volume appeared (the end of July 1819), eighteen months after* Frankenstein, *its print run was 8,000 (compared to* Frankenstein's *500).*

A Fragment is also a personal register of a life painfully fragmented in 1816. Byron told Murray that he began it in "an old account-book of Miss Milbanke's, which I kept because it contains the word 'Household,' written by her twice on the inside blank page of the covers, being the only two Scraps I have in the world in her writing, except her name to the deed of Separation" (1832, Works, 4: 149). Lady Byron, née Milbanke, left Byron in January 1816, and they were legally separated in April, never to meet again.

A FRAGMENT

`===================`

June 17, 1816.

In the year 17—, having for some time determined on a journey through countries not hitherto much frequented by travellers, I set out, accompanied by a friend, whom I shall designate by the name of Augustus Darvell. He was a few years my elder, and a man of considerable fortune and ancient family—advantages which an extensive capacity prevented him alike from undervaluing or overrating. Some peculiar circumstances in his private history had rendered him to me an object of attention, of interest, and even of regard, which neither the reserve of his manners, nor occasional indications of an inquietude at times nearly approaching to alienation of mind, could extinguish.

I was yet young in life, which I had begun early; but my intimacy with him was of a recent date: we had been educated at the same schools and university; but his progress through these had preceded mine, and he had been deeply initiated into what is called the world, while I was yet in my noviciate. While thus engaged, I heard much both of his past and present life; and, although in these accounts there were many and irreconcilable contradictions, I could still gather from the whole that he was a being of no common order, and one who, whatever pains he might take to avoid remark, would still be remarkable.[1] I had cultivated his acquaintance subsequently, and endeavoured to obtain his friendship, but this last appeared to be unattainable; whatever affections he might have possessed seemed now, some to have been extinguished, and others to be concentred: that his feelings were acute, I had sufficient opportunities of observing; for, although he could control, he could not altogether disguise them: still he had a power of giving to one passion the appearance of another, in such a manner that it was difficult to define the nature of what was working within him; and the expressions of his features would vary so rapidly, though slightly, that it was useless to trace them to their sources. It was evident that he was a prey to some cureless disquiet; but whether it arose from ambition, love, remorse, grief,

---

[1]The patent language and character configuration of the Byronic hero, elaborated through the rest of this paragraph. There are homoerotic shades that would be legible to Byron's Cambridge circle, and even a homosexual sign system in the "advertised secret," an intimate connection to the East, and a wasting disease.

from one or all of these, or merely from a morbid temperament akin to disease, I could not discover: there were circumstances alleged, which might have justified the application to each of these causes; but, as I have before said, these were so contradictory and contradicted, that none could be fixed upon with accuracy. Where there is mystery, it is generally supposed that there must also be evil: I know not how this may be, but in him there certainly was the one, though I could not ascertain the extent of the other—and felt loth, as far as regarded himself, to believe in its existence. My advances were received with sufficient coldness; but I was young, and not easily discouraged, and at length succeeded in obtaining, to a certain degree, that common-place intercourse and moderate confidence of common and every-day concerns, created and cemented by similarity of pursuit and frequency of meeting, which is called intimacy, or friendship, according to the ideas of him who uses those words to express them.

Darvell had already travelled extensively; and to him I had applied for information with regard to the conduct of my intended journey. It was my secret wish that he might be prevailed on to accompany me: it was also a probable hope, founded upon the shadowy restlessness which I had observed in him, and to which the animation which he appeared to feel on such subjects, and his apparent indifference to all by which he was more immediately surrounded, gave fresh strength. This wish I first hinted, and then expressed: his answer, though I had partly expected it, gave me all the pleasure of surprise—he consented; and, after the requisite arrangements, we commenced our voyages. After journeying through various countries of the south of Europe, our attention was turned towards the East, according to our original destination; and it was in my progress through these regions that the incident occurred upon which will turn what I may have to relate.

The constitution of Darvell, which must from his appearance have been in early life more than usually robust, had been for some time gradually giving away, without the intervention of any apparent disease: he had neither cough nor hectic,[2] yet he became daily more enfeebled: his habits were temperate, and he neither declined nor complained of fatigue, yet he was evidently wasting away: he became more and more silent and sleepless, and at length so seriously altered, that my alarm grew proportionate to what I conceived to be his danger.

---

[2]Symptomatic fever.

We had determined, on our arrival at Smyrna, on an excursion to the ruins of Ephesus and Sardis,[3] from which I endeavoured to dissuade him in his present state of indisposition—but in vain: there appeared to be an oppression on his mind, and a solemnity in his manner, which ill corresponded with his eagerness to proceed on what I regarded as a mere party of pleasure, little suited to a valetudinarian; but I opposed him no longer—and in a few days we set off together, accompanied only by a serrugee and a single janizary.[4]

We had passed halfway towards the remains of Ephesus, leaving behind us the more fertile environs of Smyrna, and were entering upon that wild and tenantless tract through the marshes and defiles which lead to the few huts yet lingering over the broken columns of Diana—the roofless walls of expelled Christianity, and the still more recent but complete desolation of abandoned mosques—when the sudden and rapid illness of my companion obliged us to halt at a Turkish cemetery, the turbaned tombstones of which were the sole indication that human life had ever been a sojourner in this wilderness. The only caravansera[5] we had seen was left some hours behind us, not a vestige of a town or even cottage was within sight or hope, and this "city of the dead"[6] appeared to be the sole refuge of my unfortunate friend, who seemed on the verge of becoming the last of its inhabitants.

In this situation, I looked round for a place where he might most conveniently repose:—contrary to the usual aspect of Mahometan burial-grounds, the cypresses were in this few in number, and these thinly scattered over its extent: the tombstones were mostly fallen, and worn with age:—upon one of the most considerable of these, and beneath one of the most spreading trees, Darvell supported himself, in a half-reclining posture, with great difficulty. He asked for water. I had some doubts of our being able to find

---

[3]Cities (and their religious cultures) successively vanquished and ruined: Smyrna was an ancient Greek city in Turkey; Ephesus was an important Greek city in Asia Minor, famed for the Temple of Diana, goddess of the hunt and chastity; Sardis was the capital of ancient Lydia, near Smyrna.

[4]A horse-driver and a soldier escorting travelers.

[5]Inn.

[6]A self-quotation: "Freedom hallows with her tread / The silent cities of the dead," from the last stanza of *On the Star of "The Legion of Honour,"* first published anonymously in *The Examiner*, 7 April 1816, then in *Poems*, 1816 (late May/early June).

any, and prepared to go in search of it with hesitating despondency—but he desired me to remain; and turning to Suleiman, our janizary, who stood by us smoking with great tranquillity, he said, "Suleiman, verbana su," (i.e. bring some water,) and went on describing the spot where it was to be found with great minuteness, at a small well for camels, a few hundred yards to the right: the janizary obeyed. I said to Darvell, "How did you know this?"—He replied, "From our situation; you must perceive that this place was once inhabited, and could not have been so without springs: I have also been here before."

"You have been here before!—How came you never to mention this to me? and what could you be doing in a place where no one would remain a moment longer than they could help it?'"

To this question I received no answer. In the mean time Suleiman returned with the water, leaving the serrugee and the horses at the fountain. The quenching of his thirst had the appearance of reviving him for a moment; and I conceived hopes of his being able to proceed, or at least to return, and I urged the attempt. He was silent—and appeared to be collecting his spirits for an effort to speak. He began.

"This is the end of my journey, and of my life—I came here to die: but I have a request to make, a command—for such my last words must be—You will observe it?"

"Most certainly; but I have better hopes."

"I have no hopes, nor wishes, but this—conceal my death from every human being."

"I hope there will be no occasion; that you will recover, and ———"

"Peace!—it must be so: promise this."

"I do."

"Swear it, by all that"——— He here dictated an oath of great solemnity.

"There is no occasion for this—I will observe your request; and to doubt me is ———"

"It cannot be helped,—you must swear."

I took the oath: it appeared to relieve him. He removed a seal ring from his finger, on which were some Arabic characters, and presented it to me. He proceeded—

"On the ninth day of the month, at noon precisely (what month you please, but this must be the day), you must fling this ring into the salt springs which run into the Bay of Eleusis: the day after, at the same hour, you must repair to the ruins of the temple of Ceres, and wait one hour."[7]

"Why?"

"You will see."

"The ninth day of the month, you say?"

"The ninth."

As I observed that the present was the ninth day of the month, his countenance changed, and he paused. As he sate, evidently becoming more feeble, a stork, with a snake in her beak, perched upon a tombstone near us;[8] and, without devouring her prey, appeared to be stedfastly regarding us. I know not what impelled me to drive it away, but the attempt was useless; she made a few circles in the air, and returned exactly to the same spot. Darvell pointed to it, and smiled: he spoke—I know not whether to himself or to me—but the words were only, "'Tis well!"

"What is well? what do you mean?"

"No matter: you must bury me here this evening, and exactly where that bird is now perched. You know the rest of my injunctions."

He then proceeded to give me several directions as to the manner in which his death might be best concealed. After these were finished, he exclaimed, "You perceive that bird?"

"Certainly."

"And the serpent writhing in her beak?"

"Doubtless: there is nothing uncommon in it; it is her natural prey. But it is odd that she does not devour it."

He smiled in a ghastly manner, and said, faintly, "It is not yet time!" As he spoke, the stork flew away. My eyes followed it for a moment, it could hardly be longer than ten might be counted. I felt Darvell's weight, as it were, increase upon my shoulder, and, turning to look upon his face, perceived that he was dead!

I was shocked with the sudden certainty which could not be mistaken—his countenance in a few minutes became nearly black. I should have attributed so rapid a change to poison, had I not been aware that he had no opportunity of receiving it unperceived. The day

[7]These locations are involved in the mysterious rites of ancient religion, with the suggestion that Darvell may return from the dead—the hint from which Polidori developed his tale.

[8]According to Pliny (1st-c. Roman historian), storks were so venerated for preying on snakes that it was illegal to kill them; a stork is an old augur of death.

was declining, the body was rapidly altering, and nothing remained but to fulfil his request. With the aid of Suleiman's ataghan[9] and my own sabre, we scooped a shallow grave upon the spot which Darvell had indicated: the earth easily gave way, having already received some Mahometan tenant. We dug as deeply as the time permitted us, and throwing the dry earth upon all that remained of the singular being so lately departed, we cut a few sods of greener turf from the less withered soil around us, and laid them upon his sepulchre.

Between astonishment and grief, I was tearless.

* * * * *

John William Polidori (1795–1821)

In April 1816, set to leave England, Lord Byron engaged as his personal physician and traveling companion a handsome, temperamental twenty-one-year-old prodigy, John Polidori, the youngest-ever recipient of a medical degree from University of Edinburgh. His father, Gaetano Polidori, an Italian émigré in London, had been secretary to the poet Alfieri (a favorite of Byron), and was the Italian translator of the first "gothic novel," Horace Walpole's The Castle of Otranto *(1765). Gaetano's daughter would become the mother of Dante Gabriel Rossetti and Christina Rossetti. Publisher Murray, with his eye on the market, promised Polidori £500 for a memoir of Byron's life abroad. Jealous of the poetic talents of Shelley and Byron, and possessive about Byron, exasperating in his mood swings ("not a bad fellow, but young and hotheaded, and more likely to incur diseases than cure them," said Byron in retrospect), by the end of the summer Polidori exhausted his employer's patience and was let go. In October, he got into a quarrel with the wrong person, an Austrian officer whose tall hat was blocking his view at the La Scala Opera. French novelist Stendhal, Byron, and Byron's Italian friends managed to get him released from jail, and the next day he was banished from Milan. Polidori returned to London to live with his father, flirted with a young Harriet Martineau, took a stab at a career in the law, published a few works of literature, racked up severe gambling debts, and killed himself with a dose of prussic acid in August 1821.*

When Shelley has Frankenstein regard his creature "nearly in the light of my own vampire, my own spirit let loose from the grave, and

[9]Turkish sword with a curved double-edged blade.

force to destroy all that was dear to me" (I.VI), she pays homage to another production of that rainy evening's inspirations, Polidori's "vamped up" version of Byron's sketchy "tale of the Vampire" (as Moore puns the gestation). Part revision, part elaboration, part sequel, Polidori's tale was published, without his knowledge, the year after Frankenstein, *in* New Monthly Magazine *(1 April 1819), as "The Vampyre: A Tale by Lord Byron." It then took up anonymous residence, the same year, in a slender book, issued in London by the firm of Sherwood, Neely, and Jones, arrayed with a scholarly "Introduction" on vampirism and two gossipy (fictitious) "letters" about Byron's life in Geneva and on the Island of Mitylene. Polidori tried to clarify the authorship with the editor of* New Monthly, *explaining (according to Murray, who remonstrated with the editor) "that the whole plan was [Byron's], and that it was merely written out by him." He also put a letter in the next (May) issue, stating that there had been a mistake "in attributing that tale, in its present form, to Lord Byron. The fact is, that though the ground-work is certainly Lord Byron's, its development is mine."*

The ground-work was more than narrative: Polidori's vampyre feeds off of Byron as yet another version—patently excessive—of the already excessive Byronic hero (aristocratic, devastatingly seductive, restlessly wandering, villainous), even coded with coterie information. It was no wonder The Vampyre *was still thought to be Byron's progeny, prompting Byron to complain to the editor of Galignani's* Messenger *for colluding in the error. "I have besides," he added wryly, "a personal dislike to 'Vampires' and the little acquaintance I have with them would by no means induce me to divulge their secrets" (letter, 27 April 1819). As* The Vampire, *or* The Bride of the Isles, *Polidori's tale was staged successfully in London, at the English Opera House, in 1820—just three years before another hit on that stage,* Frankenstein.

THE VAMPYRE; A Tale.

It happened that in the midst of the dissipations[1] attendant upon London winter, there appeared at the various parties of the leaders of the ton[2] a nobleman, more remarkable for his singularities, than his rank. He gazed upon the mirth around him, as if he could not participate therein. Apparently, the light laughter of the fair only attracted his attention, that he might by a look quell it and throw fear into those breasts where thoughtlessness reigned. Those who felt this sensation of

[1]Partying and carousing, night after night.
[2]Fashionable "toney" society.

awe, could not explain whence it arose: some attributed it to the dead grey eye, which, fixing upon the object's face, did not seem to penetrate, and at one glance to pierce through to the inward workings of the heart; but fell upon the cheek with a leaden ray that weighed upon the skin it could not pass. His peculiarities caused him to be invited to every house; all wished to see him, and those who had been accustomed to violent excitement, and now felt the weight of *ennui*,³ were pleased at having something in their presence capable of engaging their attention. In spite of the deadly hue of his face, which never gained a wanner tint, either from the blush of modesty, or from the strong emotion of passion, though its form and outline were beautiful, many of the female hunters after notoriety attempted to win his attentions, and gain, at least, some marks of what they might term affection: Lady Mercer, who had been the mockery of every monster shewn in drawing-rooms since her marriage, threw herself in his way, and did all but put on the dress of a mountebank, to attract his notice⁴—though in vain:—when she stood before him, though his eyes were apparently fixed upon her's, still it seemed as if they were unperceived;—even her unappalled impudence was baffled, and she left the field. But though the common adultress could not influence even the guidance of his eyes, it was not that the female sex was indifferent to him: yet such was the apparent caution with which he spoke to the virtuous wife and innocent daughter, that few knew he ever addressed himself to females. He had, however, the reputation of a winning tongue; and whether it was that it even overcame the dread of his singular character, or that they were moved by his apparent hatred of vice, he was as often among those females who form the boast of their sex from their domestic virtues, as among those who sully it by their vices.

About the same time, there came to London a young gentleman of the name of Aubrey: he was an orphan left with an only sister in the possession of great wealth, by parents who died while he was yet in childhood. Left also to himself by guardians, who thought it their duty merely to take care of his fortune, while they relinquished the more important charge of his mind to the care of mercenary subalterns, he cultivated more his imagination than his judgment. He had, hence, that high romantic feeling of honour and candour, which daily ruins so

³Boredom, world-weariness, with sophisticated French affectation.
⁴Lady Mercer is modeled on the antics of Byron's tempestuous lover of 1811–12, Lady Caroline Lamb. A mountebank is a quack pharmacist, more generally, a pretender.

many milliners' apprentices.[5] He believed all to sympathise with virtue, and thought that vice was thrown in by Providence merely for the picturesque effect of the scene, as we see in romances:[6] he thought that the misery of a cottage merely consisted in the vesting of clothes, which were as warm, but which were better adapted to the painter's eye by their irregular folds and various coloured patches. He thought, in fine,[7] that the dreams of poets were the realities of life. He was handsome, frank, and rich: for these reasons, upon his entering into the gay circles, many mothers surrounded him, striving which should describe with least truth their languishing or romping favourites: the daughters at the same time, by their brightening countenances when he approached, and by their sparkling eyes, when he opened his lips, soon led him into false notions of his talents and his merit. Attached as he was to the romance of his solitary hours,[8] he was startled at finding, that, except in the tallow and wax candles that flickered, not from the presence of a ghost, but from want of snuffing, there was no foundation in real life for any of that congeries of pleasing pictures and descriptions contained in those volumes, from which he had formed his study. Finding, however, some compensation in his gratified vanity, he was about to relinquish his dreams, when the extraordinary being we have above described, crossed him in his career.

He watched him; and the very impossibility of forming an idea of the character of a man entirely absorbed in himself, who gave few other signs of his observation of external objects, than the tacit assent to their existence, implied by the avoidance of their contact: allowing his imagination to picture every thing that flattered its propensity to extravagant ideas, he soon formed this object into the hero of a romance, and determined to observe the offspring of his fancy, rather than the person before him. He became acquainted with him, paid him attentions, and so far advanced upon his notice, that his presence was always recognised. He gradually learnt that Lord Ruthven's affairs were embarrassed,[9] and soon found, from the notes of preparation

[5]Milliners are seamstresses; the "milliner-girl" apprentice was a popular type of an easily seduced young woman.

[6]"Romance" is the popular literary genre of exotic adventure and sometimes love.

[7]In sum.

[8]Byron's first publication was *Hours of Idleness*.

[9]Embarrassed: in serious debt (Byron left England thus, stiffing a number of creditors). Clarence Ruthven, Lord Glenarvon, is the villainous hero of Caroline Lamb's Byron-coded novel *Glenarvon* (1816).

in —— Street, that he was about to travel. Desirous of gaining some information respecting this singular character, who, till now, had only whetted his curiosity, he hinted to his guardians, that it was time for him to perform the tour,[10] which for many generations has been thought necessary to enable the young to take some rapid steps in the career of vice towards putting themselves upon an equality with the aged, and not allowing them to appear as if fallen from the skies, whenever scandalous intrigues are mentioned as the subjects of pleasantry or of praise, according to the degree of skill shewn in carrying them on. They consented: and Aubrey immediately mentioning his intentions to Lord Ruthven, was surprised to receive from him a proposal to join him. Flattered by such a mark of esteem from him, who, apparently, had nothing in common with other men, he gladly accepted it, and in a few days they had passed the circling waters.

Hitherto, Aubrey had had no opportunity of studying Lord Ruthven's character, and now he found, that, though many more of his actions were exposed to his view, the results offered different conclusions from the apparent motives to his conduct. His companion was profuse in his liberality;—the idle, the vagabond, and the beggar, received from his hand more than enough to relieve their immediate wants. But Aubrey could not avoid remarking, that it was not upon the virtuous, reduced to indigence by the misfortunes attendant even upon virtue, that he bestowed his alms;—these were sent from the door with hardly suppressed sneers; but when the profligate came to ask something, not to relieve his wants, but to allow him to wallow in his lust, to sink him still deeper in his iniquity, he was sent away with rich charity. This was, however, attributed by him to the greater importunity of the vicious, which generally prevails over the retiring bashfulness of the virtuous indigent. There was one circumstance about the charity of his Lordship, which was still more impressed upon his mind: all those upon whom it was bestowed, inevitably found that there was a curse upon it, for they were all either led to the scaffold, or sunk to the lowest and the most abject misery. At Brussels and other towns through which they passed, Aubrey was surprized at the apparent eagerness with which his companion sought for the centres of all fashionable vice; there he entered into all

[10]A post-collegiate "grand tour," usually of Europe and the eastern Mediterranean countries, was considered the last phase of a young man's education, often a holiday of adventures, sexual and otherwise, before "settling down."

the spirit of the faro[11] table: he betted, and always gambled with success, except where the known sharper was his antagonist, and then he lost even more than he gained; but it was always with the same unchanging face, with which he generally watched the society around: it was not, however, so when he encountered the rash youthful novice, or the luckless father of a numerous family; then his very wish seemed fortune's law—this apparent abstractedness of mind was laid aside, and his eyes sparkled with more fire than that of the cat whilst dallying with the half-dead mouse. In every town, he left the formerly affluent youth, torn from the circle he adorned, cursing, in the solitude of a dungeon, the fate that had drawn him within the reach of this fiend; whilst many a father sat frantic, amidst the speaking looks of mute hungry children, without a single farthing of his late immense wealth, wherewith to buy even sufficient to satisfy their present craving. Yet he took no money from the gambling table; but immediately lost, to the ruiner of many, the last gilder he had just snatched from the convulsive grasp of the innocent: this might but be the result of a certain degree of knowledge, which was not, however, capable of combating the cunning of the more experienced. Aubrey often wished to represent this to his friend, and beg him to resign that charity and pleasure which proved the ruin of all, and did not tend to his own profit;—but he delayed it—for each day he hoped his friend would give him some opportunity of speaking frankly and openly to him; however, this never occurred. Lord Ruthven in his carriage, and amidst the various wild and rich scenes of nature, was always the same: his eye spoke less than his lip; and though Aubrey was near the object of his curiosity, he obtained no greater gratification from it than the constant excitement of vainly wishing to break that mystery, which to his exalted imagination began to assume the appearance of something supernatural.

They soon arrived at Rome, and Aubrey for a time lost sight of his companion; he left him in daily attendance upon the morning circle of an Italian countess, whilst he went in search of the memorials of another almost deserted city. Whilst he was thus engaged, letters arrived from England, which he opened with eager impatience; the first was from his sister, breathing nothing but affection; the others were from his guardians, the latter astonished him; if it had before

---

[11]Named for the picture of a pharaoh on a French card-deck, Faro was a popular card game, especially with aristocrats.

entered into his imagination that there was an evil power resident in his companion, these seemed to give him almost sufficient reason for the belief. His guardians insisted upon his immediately leaving his friend, and urged, that his character was dreadfully vicious, for that the possession of irresistible powers of seduction, rendered his licentious habits more dangerous to society. It had been discovered, that his contempt for the adultress had not originated in hatred of her character; but that he had required, to enhance his gratification, that his victim, the partner of his guilt, should be hurled from the pinnacle of unsullied virtue, down to the lowest abyss of infamy and degradation: in fine, that all those females whom he had sought, apparently on account of their virtue, had, since his departure, thrown even the mask aside, and had not scrupled to expose the whole deformity of their vices to the public gaze.

Aubrey determined upon leaving one, whose character had not shown a single bright point on which to rest the eye. He resolved to invent some plausible pretext for abandoning him altogether, purposing, in the mean while, to watch him more closely, and to let no slight circumstances pass by unnoticed. He entered into the same circle, and soon perceived, that his Lordship was endeavouring to work upon the inexperience of the daughter of the lady whose house he chiefly frequented. In Italy, it is seldom that an unmarried female is met with in society;[12] he was therefore obliged to carry on his plans in secret; but Aubrey's eye followed him in all his windings, and soon discovered that an assignation had been appointed, which would most likely end in the ruin of an innocent, though thoughtless girl. Losing no time, he entered the apartment of Lord Ruthven, and abruptly asked him his intentions with respect to the lady, informing him at the same time that he was aware of his being about to meet her that very night. Lord Ruthven answered, that his intentions were such as he supposed all would have upon such an occasion; and upon being pressed whether he intended to marry her, merely laughed. Aubrey retired; and, immediately writing a note, to say, that from that moment he must decline accompanying his Lordship in the remainder of their proposed tour, he ordered his servant to seek other apartments, and calling upon the mother of the lady informed her of all he knew, not only with regard to her daughter, but also concerning the character of his Lordship. The

---

[12]The custom was to sequester a young woman at home, until her father arranged her marriage.

assignation was prevented. Lord Ruthven next day merely sent his servant to notify his complete assent to a separation; but did not hint any suspicion of his plans having been foiled by Aubrey's interposition.

Having left Rome, Aubrey directed his steps towards Greece, and crossing the Peninsula, soon found himself at Athens. He then fixed residence in the house of a Greek; and soon occupied himself in tracing the faded records of ancient glory upon monuments that apparently, ashamed of chronicling the deeds of freemen only before slaves, had hidden themselves beneath the sheltering soil or many coloured lichen.[13] Under the same roof as himself, existed a being, so beautiful and delicate, that she might have formed the model for a painter, wishing to portray on canvass the promised hope of the faithful in Mahomet's paradise, save that her eyes spoke too much mind for any one to think she could belong to those who had no souls.[14] As she danced upon the plain, or tripped along the mountain's side, one would have thought the gazelle a poor type of her beauties;[15] for who would have exchanged her eye, apparently the eye of animated[16] nature, for that sleepy luxurious look of the animal suited but to the taste of an epicure. The light step of Ianthe[17] often accompanied Aubrey in his search after antiquities, and often would the unconscious girl, engaged in the pursuit of a Kashmere butterfly, show the whole beauty of her form, floating as it were upon the wind, to the eager gaze of him, who forgot the letters he had just decyphered upon an almost effaced tablet, in the contemplation of her sylph-like figure. Often would her tresses falling, as she flitted around, exhibit in the sun's ray such delicately brilliant and swiftly fading hues, as might well excuse the forgetfulness of the antiquary, who let escape from his mind the very object he had before thought of vital importance to the proper interpretation of a passage in

[13]Modern Britons, from Byron to Felicia Hemans, liked to contrast modern Greeks, oppressed by the Ottoman Empire, to the glorious (though slave-holding) ancient Greeks.

[14]The virtuous martyrs of Islam are promised a paradise of sexual pleasures. In Byron's day, it was popularly thought that Islam denied souls to females, treating them as only creatures of, and for, sense—an "animal suited but to the taste of an epicure."

[15]Evoking the gazelle-like Leila of Byron's eastern tale, *The Giaour* (ll. 473–75), who confounds the Muslim teaching that in women "form was nought but breathing clay" (482), "but dust, / A soulless toy for tyrant's lust" (489–90).

[16]Literally, "with a soul."

[17]Verses "To Ianthe" precede *Childe Harold's Pilgrimage* (1812). "Ianthe" is the pseudonym for Lady Charlotte Harley, the pre-teen daughter of Lady Oxford, one of Byron's former lovers.

Pausanias.[18] But why attempt to describe charms which all feel, but none can appreciate?—It was innocence, youth, and beauty, unaffected by crowded drawing-rooms and stifling balls. Whilst he drew those remains of which he wished to preserve a memorial for his future hours, she would stand by, and watch the magic effects of his pencil, in tracing the scenes of her native place; she would then describe to him the circling dance upon the open plain, would paint to him in all the glowing colours of youthful memory, the marriage pomp she remembered viewing in her infancy; and then, turning to subjects that had evidently made a greater impression upon her mind, would tell him all the supernatural tales of her nurse. Her earnestness and apparent belief of what she narrated, excited the interest even of Aubrey; and often as she told him the tale of the living vampyre, who had passed years amidst his friends, and dearest ties, forced every year, by feeding upon the life of a lovely female to prolong his existence for the ensuing months, his blood would run cold, whilst he attempted to laugh her out of such idle and horrible fantasies; but Ianthe cited to him the names of old men, who had at last detected one living among themselves, after several of their near relatives and children had been found marked with the stamp of the fiend's appetite; and when she found him so incredulous, she begged of him to believe her, for it had been remarked, that those who had dared to question their existence, always had some proof given, which obliged them, with grief and heartbreaking, to confess it was true. She detailed to him the traditional appearance of these monsters, and his horror was increased by hearing a pretty accurate description of Lord Ruthven; he, however, still persisted in persuading her, that there could be no truth in her fears, though at the same time he wondered at the many coincidences which had all tended to excite a belief in the supernatural power of Lord Ruthven.

Aubrey began to attach himself more and more to Ianthe; her innocence, so contrasted with all the affected virtues of the women among whom he had sought for his vision of romance, won his heart; and while he ridiculed the idea of a young man of English habits, marrying an uneducated Greek girl, still he found himself more and more attached to the almost fairy form[19] before him. He would tear himself

---

[18] 2d-c. writer of *Descriptions of Greece*, a compendium of social, cultural, historical, and topographical information.

[19] Byron's favorite romance term for women, e.g., Zuleika in *The Bride of Abydos* (1.285–86); the Maid of Saragoza in *Childe Harold's Pilgrimage* (1.54–55).

at times from her, and, forming a plan for some antiquarian research, he would depart, determined not to return until his object was attained; but he always found it impossible to fix his attention upon the ruins around him, whilst in his mind he retained an image that seemed alone the rightful possessor of his thoughts. Ianthe was unconscious of his love, and was ever the same frank infantile being he had first known. She always seemed to part from him with reluctance; but it was because she had no longer any one with whom she could visit her favourite haunts, whilst her guardian was occupied in sketching or uncovering some fragment which had yet escaped the destructive hand of time. She had appealed to her parents on the subject of Vampyres, and they both, with several present, affirmed their existence, pale with horror at the very name. Soon after, Aubrey determined to proceed upon one of his excursions, which was to detain him for a few hours; when they heard the name of the place, they all at once begged of him not to return at night, as he must necessarily pass through a wood, where no Greek would ever remain, after the day had closed, upon any consideration. They described it as the resort of the vampyres in their nocturnal orgies, and denounced the most heavy evils as impending upon him who dared to cross their path. Aubrey made light of their representations, and tried to laugh them out of the idea; but when he saw them shudder at his daring thus to mock a superior, infernal power, the very name of which apparently made their blood freeze, he was silent.

Next morning Aubrey set off upon his excursion unattended; he was surprised to observe the melancholy face of his host, and was concerned to find that his words, mocking the belief of those horrible fiends, had inspired them with such terror. When he was about to depart, Ianthe came to the side of his horse, and earnestly begged of him to return, ere night allowed the power of these beings to be put in action;—he promised. He was, however, so occupied in his research, that he did not perceive that day-light would soon end, and that in the horizon there was one of those specks which, in the warmer climates, so rapidly gather into a tremendous mass, and pour all their rage upon the devoted[20] country.—He at last, however, mounted his horse, determined to make up by speed for his delay: but it was too late. Twilight, in these southern climates, is almost unknown; immediately the sun sets, night begins: and ere he had advanced far, the power of

[20]Doomed.

the storm was above—its echoing thunders had scarcely an interval of rest;—its thick heavy rain forced its way through the canopying foliage, whilst the blue forked lightning seemed to fall and radiate at his very feet. Suddenly his horse took fright, and he was carried with dreadful rapidity through the entangled forest. The animal at last, through fatigue, stopped, and he found, by the glare of lightning, that he was in the neighbourhood of a hovel that hardly lifted itself up from the masses of dead leaves and brushwood which surrounded it. Dismounting, he approached, hoping to find some one to guide him to the town, or at least trusting to obtain shelter from the pelting of the storm. As he approached, the thunders, for a moment silent, allowed him to hear the dreadful shrieks of a woman mingling with the stifled, exultant mockery of a laugh, continued in one almost unbroken sound;—he was startled: but, roused by the thunder which again rolled over his head, he, with a sudden effort, forced open the door of the hut. He found himself in utter darkness: the sound, however, guided him. He was apparently unperceived; for, though he called, still the sounds continued, and no notice was taken of him. He found himself in contact with some one, whom he immediately seized; when a voice cried, "Again baffled!" to which a loud laugh succeeded; and he felt himself grappled by one whose strength seemed superhuman: determined to sell his life as dearly as he could, he struggled; but it was in vain: he was lifted from his feet and hurled with enormous force against the ground:—his enemy threw himself upon him, and kneeling upon his breast, had placed his hands upon his throat—when the glare of many torches penetrating through the hole that gave light in the day, disturbed him;—he instantly rose, and, leaving his prey, rushed through the door, and in a moment the crashing of the branches, as he broke through the wood, was no longer heard. The storm was now still; and Aubrey, incapable of moving, was soon heard by those without. They entered; the light of their torches fell upon mud walls, and the thatch loaded on every individual straw with heavy flakes of soot. At the desire of Aubrey they searched for her who had attracted him by her cries; he was again left in darkness; but what was his horror, when the light of the torches once more burst upon him, to perceive the airy form of his fair conductress brought in a lifeless corse.[21] He shut his eyes, hoping that it was but a

[21]Corpse.

vision arising from his disturbed imagination; but he again saw the same form, when he unclosed them, stretched by his side. There was no colour upon her cheek, not even upon her lip; yet there was a stillness about her face that seemed almost as attaching as the life that once dwelt there:—upon her neck and breast was blood, and upon her throat were the marks of teeth having opened the vein:—to this the men pointed, crying, simultaneously struck with horror, "A Vampyre! a Vampyre!" A litter was quickly formed, and Aubrey was laid by the side of her who had lately been to him the object of so many bright and fairy visions, now fallen with the flower of life that had died within her. He knew not what his thoughts were—his mind was benumbed and seemed to shun reflection, and take refuge in vacancy—he held almost unconsciously in his hand a naked dagger of a particular construction, which had been found in the hut. They were soon met by different parties who had been engaged in the search of her whom a mother had missed. Their lamentable cries, as they approached the city, forewarned the parents of some dreadful catastrophe.—To describe their grief would be impossible; but when they ascertained the cause of their child's death, they looked at Aubrey and pointed to the corse. They were inconsolable; both died broken-hearted.

Aubrey being put to bed was seized with a most violent fever, and was often delirious; in these intervals he would call upon Lord Ruthven and upon Ianthe—by some unaccountable combination he seemed to beg of his former companion to spare the being he loved. At other times he would imprecate maledictions upon his head, and curse him as her destroyer. Lord Ruthven chanced at this time to arrive at Athens, and, from whatever motive, upon hearing of the state of Aubrey, immediately placed himself in the same house, and became his constant attendant. When the latter recovered from his delirium, he was horrified and startled at the sight of him whose image he had now combined with that of a Vampyre; but Lord Ruthven, by his kind words, implying almost repentance for the fault that had caused their separation, and still more by the attention, anxiety, and care which he showed, soon reconciled him to his presence. His lordship seemed quite changed; he no longer appeared that apathetic being who had so astonished Aubrey; but as soon as his convalescence began to be rapid, he again gradually retired into the same state of mind, and Aubrey perceived no difference from the former man, except that at times he was surprised to meet his gaze fixed intently upon him, with a smile of malicious exultation playing upon his lips: he knew not why, but this smile haunted him. During the last stage of the invalid's recovery, Lord Ruthven was apparently engaged in watching the tideless waves raised by the cooling breeze, or in marking the progress of those orbs, circling, like our world, the moveless sun;—indeed, he appeared to wish to avoid the eyes of all.

Aubrey's mind, by this shock, was much weakened, and that elasticity of spirit which had once so distinguished him now seemed to have fled for ever. He was now as much a lover of solitude and silence as Lord Ruthven; but much as he wished for solitude, his mind could not find it in the neighbourhood of Athens; if he sought it amidst the ruins he had formerly frequented, Ianthe's form stood by his side;—if he sought it in the woods, her light step would appear wandering amidst the underwood, in quest of the modest violet; then suddenly turning round, would show, to his wild imagination, her pale face and wounded throat, with a meek smile upon her lips. He determined to fly scenes, every feature of which created such bitter associations in his mind. He proposed to Lord Ruthven, to whom he held himself bound by the tender care he had taken of him during his illness, that they should visit those parts of Greece neither had yet seen. They travelled in every direction, and sought every spot to which a recollection could be attached: but though they thus hastened from place to place, yet they seemed not to heed what they gazed upon. They heard much of robbers, but they gradually began to slight these reports, which they imagined were only the invention of individuals, whose interest it was to excite the generosity of those whom they defended from pretended dangers. In consequence of thus neglecting the advice of the inhabitants, on one occasion they travelled with only a few guards, more to serve as guides than as a defence. Upon entering, however, a narrow defile, at the bottom of which was the bed of a torrent, with large masses of rock brought down from the neighbouring precipices, they had reason to repent their negligence; for scarcely were the whole of the party engaged in the narrow pass, when they were startled by the whistling of bullets close to their heads, and by the echoed report of several guns. In an instant their guards had left them, and, placing themselves behind rocks, had begun to fire in the direction whence the report came. Lord Ruthven and Aubrey, imitating their example, retired for a moment behind the sheltering turn of the defile:

but ashamed of being thus detained by a foe, who with insulting shouts bade them advance, and being exposed to unresisting slaughter, if any of the robbers should climb above and take them in the rear, they determined at once to rush forward in search of the enemy. Hardly had they lost the shelter of rock, when Lord Ruthven received a shot in the shoulder, which brought him to the ground. Aubrey hastened to his assistance; and, no longer heeding the contest or his own peril, was soon surprised by seeing the robbers' faces around him—his guards having, upon Lord Ruthven's being wounded, immediately thrown up their arms and surrendered.

By promises of great reward, Aubrey soon induced them to convey his wounded friend to a neighbouring cabin; and having agreed upon a ransom, he was no more disturbed by their presence—they being content merely to guard the entrance till their comrade should return with the promised sum, for which he had an order. Lord Ruthven's strength rapidly decreased; in two days mortification ensued, and death seemed advancing with hasty steps. His conduct and appearance had not changed; he seemed as unconscious of pain as he had been of the objects about him: but towards the close of the last evening, his mind became apparently uneasy, and his eye often fixed upon Aubrey, who was induced to offer his assistance with more than usual earnestness—"Assist me! you may save me—you may do more than that—I mean not my life, I heed the death of my existence as little as that of the passing day; but you may save my honour, your friend's honour."—"How? tell me how? I would do any thing," replied Aubrey.—"I need but little, my life ebbs apace—I cannot explain the whole—but if you would conceal all you know of me, my honour were free from stain in the world's mouth—and if my death were unknown for some time in England—I—I—but life."—"It shall not be known."—"Swear!" cried the dying man, raising himself with exultant violence, "Swear by all your soul reveres, by all your nature fears, swear that for a year and a day you will not impart your knowledge of my crimes or death to any living being in any way, whatever may happen, or whatever you may see."—His eyes seemed bursting from their sockets: "I swear!" said Aubrey; he sunk laughing upon his pillow, and breathed no more.

Aubrey retired to rest, but did not sleep; the many circumstances attending his acquaintance with this man rose upon his mind, and he knew not why; when he remembered his oath a cold shivering came over him, as if from the presentiment of something horrible awaiting him. Rising early in the morning, he was about to enter the hovel in which he had left the corpse, when a robber met him, and informed him that it was no longer there, having been conveyed by himself and comrades, upon his retiring, to the pinnacle of a neighbouring mount, according to a promise they had given his lordship, that it should be exposed to the first cold ray of the moon that rose after his death. Aubrey astonished, and taking several of the men, determined to go and bury it upon the spot where it lay. But, when he had mounted to the summit he found no trace of either the corpse or the clothes, though the robbers swore they pointed out the identical rock on which they had laid the body. For a time his mind was bewildered in conjectures, but he at last returned, convinced that they had buried the corpse for the sake of the clothes.

Weary of a country in which he had met with such terrible misfortunes, and in which all apparently conspired to heighten that superstitious melancholy that had seized upon his mind, he resolved to leave it, and soon arrived at Smyrna.[22] While waiting for a vessel to convey him to Otranto,[23] or to Naples, he occupied himself in arranging those effects he had with him belonging to Lord Ruthven. Amongst other things there was a case containing several weapons of offence, more or less adapted to ensure the death of the victim. There were several daggers and ataghans. Whilst turning them over, and examining their curious forms, what was his surprise at finding a sheath apparently ornamented in the same style as the dagger discovered in the fatal hut—he shuddered—hastening to gain further proof, he found the weapon, and his horror may be imagined when he discovered that it fitted, though peculiarly shaped, the sheath he held in his hand. His eyes seemed to need no further certainty—they seemed gazing to be bound to the dagger, yet still he wished to disbelieve; but the particular form, the same varying tints upon the haft and sheath were alike in splendour on both, and left no room for doubt; there were also drops of blood on each.

He left Smyrna, and on his way home, at Rome, his first inquiries were concerning the lady he had attempted to snatch from Lord Ruthven's seductive arts. Her parents were in distress, their fortune

[22]The location of Byron's tale.

[23]A port in south Italy, and a nod by Polidori to his father, the translator of Walpole's *The Castle of Otranto*.

ruined, and she had not been heard of since the departure of his lordship. Aubrey's mind became almost broken under so many repeated horrors; he was afraid that this lady had fallen a victim to the destroyer of Ianthe. He became morose and silent; and his only occupation consisted in urging the speed of the postilions,[24] as if he were going to save the life of some one he held dear. He arrived at Calais; a breeze, which seemed obedient to his will, soon wafted him to the English shores; and he hastened to the mansion of his fathers, and there, for a moment, appeared to lose, in the embraces and caresses of his sister, all memory of the past. If she before, by her infantine caresses, had gained his affection, now that the woman began to appear, she was still more attaching as a companion.

Miss Aubrey had not that winning grace which gains the gaze and applause of the drawing-room assemblies.[25] There was none of that light brilliancy which only exists in the heated atmosphere of a crowded apartment. Her blue eye was never lit up by the levity of the mind beneath. There was a melancholy charm about it which did not seem to arise from misfortune, but from some feeling within, that appeared to indicate a soul conscious of a brighter realm. Her step was not that light footing, which strays where'er a butterfly or a colour may attract—it was sedate and pensive. When alone, her face was never brightened by the smile of joy; but when her brother breathed to her his affection, and would in her presence forget those griefs she knew destroyed his rest, who would have exchanged her smile for that of the voluptuary? It seemed as if those eyes,—that face were then playing in the light of their own native sphere. She was yet only eighteen, and had not been presented to the world, it having been thought by her guardians more fit that her presentation should be delayed until her brother's return from the continent, when he might be her protector. It was now, therefore, resolved that the next drawing-room, which was fast approaching, should be the epoch of her entry into the "busy scene." Aubrey would rather have remained in the mansion of his fathers, and feed upon the melancholy which overpowered him. He could not feel interest about the frivolities of fashionable strangers, when his mind had been so torn by the events he had witnessed; but he determined to sacrifice his own comfort to

[24]Horse-drivers.
[25]Formal receptions where wealthy young ladies were presented at court to royalty.

the protection of his sister. They soon arrived in town, and prepared for the next day, which had been announced as a drawing-room.

The crowd was excessive—a drawing-room had not been held for long time, and all who were anxious to bask in the smile of royalty, hastened thither. Aubrey was there with his sister. While he was standing in a corner by himself, heedless of all around him, engaged in the remembrance that the first time he had seen Lord Ruthven was in that very place—he felt himself suddenly seized by the arm, and a voice he recognized too well, sounded in his ear—"Remember your oath." He had hardly courage to turn, fearful of seeing a spectre that would blast him, when he perceived, at a little distance, the same figure which had attracted his notice on this spot upon his first entry into society. He gazed till his limbs almost refusing to bear their weight, he was obliged to take the arm of a friend, and forcing a passage through the crowd, he threw himself into his carriage, and was driven home. He paced the room with hurried steps, and fixed his hands upon his head, as if he were afraid his thoughts were bursting from his brain. Lord Ruthven again before him—circumstances started up in dreadful array—the dagger—his oath.—He roused himself, he could not believe it possible—the dead rise again!—He thought his imagination had conjured up the image his mind was resting upon. It was impossible that it could be real—he determined, therefore, to go again into society; for though he attempted to ask concerning Lord Ruthven, the name hung upon his lips, and he could not succeed in gaining information. He went a few nights after with his sister to the assembly of a near relation. Leaving her under the protection of a matron, he retired into a recess, and there gave himself up to his own devouring thoughts. Perceiving, at last, that many were leaving, he roused himself, and entering another room, found his sister surrounded by several, apparently in earnest conversation; he attempted to pass and get near her, when one, whom he requested to move, turned round, and revealed to him those features he most abhorred. He sprang forward, seized his sister's arm, and, with hurried step, forced her towards the street: at the door he found himself impeded by the crowd of servants who were waiting for their lords; and while he was engaged in passing them, he again heard that voice whisper close to him—"Remember your oath!"—He did not dare to turn, but, hurrying his sister, soon reached home.

Aubrey became almost distracted. If before his mind had been absorbed by one subject, how much more completely was it engrossed now that the certainty of the monster's living again pressed upon his thoughts. His sister's attentions were now unheeded, and it was in vain that she intreated him to explain to her what had caused his abrupt conduct. He only uttered a few words, and those terrified her. The more he thought, the more he was bewildered. His oath startled him;—was he then to allow this monster to roam, bearing ruin upon his breath, amidst all he held dear, and not avert its progress? His very sister might have been touched by him. But even if he were to break his oath, and disclose his suspicions, who would believe him? He thought of employing his own hand to free the world from such a wretch; but death, he remembered, had been already mocked. For days he remained in state; shut up in his room, he saw no one, and eat only when his sister came, who, with eyes streaming with tears, besought him, for her sake, to support nature. At last, no longer capable of bearing stillness and solitude, he left his house, roamed from street to street, anxious to fly that image which haunted him. His dress became neglected, and he wandered, as often exposed to the noon-day sun as to the mid-night damps. He was no longer to be recognized; at first he returned with evening to the house; but at last he laid him down to rest wherever fatigue overtook him. His sister, anxious for his safety, employed people to follow him; but they were soon distanced by him who fled from a pursuer swifter than any—from thought. His conduct, however, suddenly changed. Struck with the idea that he left by his absence the whole of his friends, with a fiend amongst them, of whose presence they were unconscious, he determined to enter again into society, and watch him closely, anxious to forewarn, in spite of his oath, all whom Lord Ruthven approached with intimacy. But when he entered into a room, his haggard and suspicious looks were so striking, his inward shuddering so visible, that his sister was at last obliged to beg of him to abstain from seeking, for her sake, a society which affected him so strongly. When, however, remonstrance proved unavailing, the guardians thought proper to interpose, and, fearing that his mind was becoming alienated, they thought it high time to resume again that trust which had been before imposed upon them by Aubrey's parents.

Desirous of saving him from the injuries and sufferings he had daily encountered in his wanderings, and of preventing him from exposing to the general eye those marks of what they considered folly, they engaged a physician to reside in the house, and take constant care of him. He hardly appeared to notice it, so completely was his mind absorbed by one terrible subject. His incoherence became at last so great, that he was confined to his chamber. There he would often lie for days, incapable of being roused. He had become emaciated, his eyes had attained a glassy lustre;—the only sign of affection and recollection remaining displayed itself upon the entry of his sister; then he would sometimes start, and, seizing her hands, with looks that severely afflicted her, he would desire her not to touch him. "Oh, do not touch him—if your love for me is aught, do not go near him!" When, however, she inquired to whom he referred, his only answer was, "True! true! " and again he sank into a state, whence not even she could rouse him. This lasted many months: gradually, however, as the year was passing, his incoherences became less frequent, and his mind threw off a portion of its gloom, whilst his guardians observed, that several times in the day he would count upon his fingers a definite number, and then smile.

The time had nearly elapsed, when, upon the last day of the year, one of his guardians entering his room, began to converse with his physician upon the melancholy circumstance of Aubrey's being in so awful a situation, when his sister was going next day to be married. Instantly Aubrey's attention was attracted; he asked anxiously to whom. Glad of this mark of returning intellect, of which they feared he had been deprived, they mentioned the name of the Earl of Marsden. Thinking this was a young Earl whom he had met with in society, Aubrey seemed pleased, and astonished them still more by his expressing his intention to be present at the nuptials, and desiring to see his sister. They answered not, but in a few minutes his sister was with him. He was apparently again capable of being affected by the influence of her lovely smile; for he pressed her to his breast, and kissed her cheek, wet with tears, flowing at the thought of her brother's being once more alive to the feelings of affection. He began to speak with all his wonted warmth, and to congratulate her upon her marriage with a person so distinguished for rank and every accomplishment; when he suddenly perceived a locket upon her breast; opening it, what was his surprise at beholding the features of the monster who had so long influenced his life. He seized the portrait in a paroxysm of rage, and trampled it under foot. Upon her asking him why he thus destroyed the resemblance of her future husband, he looked as if he did not understand her—then seizing her hands, and gazing on her with a frantic expression of countenance, he bade her swear that she would never wed this monster, for he—But he could not advance—it seemed as if that voice again bade him remember his oath—he turned suddenly round, thinking Lord Ruthven was near him but saw no one. In the meantime the guardians and physician, who had heard the whole, and thought this was but a return of his disorder, entered, and forcing him from Miss Aubrey, desired her to leave him. He fell upon his knees to them, he implored, he begged of them to delay but for one day. They, attributing this to the insanity they imagined had taken possession of his mind, endeavoured to pacify him, and retired.

Lord Ruthven had called the morning after the drawing-room, and had been refused with every one else. When he heard of Aubrey's ill health, he readily understood himself to be the cause of it; but when he learned that he was deemed insane, his exultation and pleasure could hardly be concealed from those among whom he had gained this information. He hastened to the house of his former companion, and, by constant attendance, and the pretence of great affection for the brother and interest in his fate, he gradually won the ear of Miss Aubrey. Who could resist his power? His tongue had dangers and toils to recount—could speak of himself as of an individual having no sympathy with any being on the crowded earth, save with her to whom he addressed himself;—could tell how, since he knew her, his existence had begun to seem worthy of preservation, if it were merely that he might listen to her soothing accents;—in fine, he knew so well how to use the serpent's art, or such was the will of fate, that he gained her affections. The title of the elder branch falling at length to him,[26] he obtained an important embassy, which served as an excuse for hastening the marriage, (in spite of her brother's deranged state,) which was to take place the very day before his departure for the continent.

Aubrey, when he was left by the physician and his guardians, attempted to bribe the servants, but in vain. He asked for pen and paper; it was given him; he wrote a letter to his sister, conjuring her, as she valued her own happiness, her own honour, and the honour of those now in the grave, who once held her in their arms as their hope and the hope of their house,[27] to delay but for a few hours that mar-

---

[26]That is, Earl of Marsden, the title held by an elder male relative, now deceased.

[27]Family dynasty; "honour" means, for an unmarried woman, not only virginity but also an untainted reputation.

riage, on which he denounced the most heavy curses. The servants promised they would deliver it; but giving it to the physician, he thought it better not to harass any more the mind of Miss Aubrey by, what he considered, the ravings of a maniac. Night passed on without rest to the busy inmates of the house; and Aubrey heard, with a horror that may more easily be conceived than described, the notes of busy preparation. Morning came, and the sound of carriages broke upon his ear. Aubrey grew almost frantic. The curiosity of the servants at last overcame their vigilance; they gradually stole away, leaving him in the custody of an helpless old woman. He seized the opportunity, with one bound was out of the room, and in a moment found himself in the apartment where all were nearly assembled. Lord Ruthven was the first to perceive him: he immediately approached, and, taking his arm by force, hurried him from the room, speechless with rage. When on the staircase, Lord Ruthven whispered in his ear—"Remember your oath, and know, if not my bride to day, your sister is dishonoured. Women are frail!" So saying, he pushed him towards his attendants, who, roused by the old woman, had come in search of him. Aubrey could no longer support himself; his rage not finding vent, had broken a blood-vessel, and he was conveyed to bed. This was not mentioned to his sister, who was not present when he entered, as the physician was afraid of agitating her. The marriage was solemnized, and the bride and bridegroom left London.

Aubrey's weakness increased; the effusion of blood produced symptoms of the near approach of death.[28] He desired his sister's guardians might be called, and when the midnight hour had struck, he related composedly what the reader has perused—he died immediately after.

The guardians hastened to protect Miss Aubrey; but when they arrived, it was too late. Lord Ruthven had disappeared, and Aubrey's sister had glutted the thirst of a VAMPYRE!

[28]The loss of blood and draining of life are also associated with the victims of vampirism.

God, Adam, and Satan

"Romantic Satanism" names the refusal of Romantic-era writers to view Milton's Satan as only an architect of evil. In *The Marriage of Heaven and Hell,* Blake, for one, argued that Milton is really of the devil's party and the arch-outlaw Satan is the true hero of *Paradise Lost,* the magnificent antagonist of a vengeful oppressor called "God." Blake did not mean that Milton was a closet sinner; he was suggesting Milton's political and imaginative sympathy with this opponent of a tyrant's arbitrary, absolute, and non-negotiable power. In the age of the American and French Revolutions, Blake and others were keenly aware that for all the high argument of *Paradise Lost* about the sin of rebellion against authority, Milton had also written in vigorous defense of Cromwell's regicidal revolt, and that with the Restoration, he was imprisoned and nearly executed for being of the rebels' party. Celebrating the archly rebellious, caustically critical, boldly transgressive Satan, the political readings of *Paradise Lost* by Blake and his contemporaries contested Milton's arguments justifying the ways of God to man.

In *Vindication of the Rights of Woman,* Mary Wollstonecraft identified with Satan's anti-monarchial arguments, but she went further than her male contemporaries in questioning the ways of God to woman. Her sharpest focus was on the praise of Eve's "virtues" of meek submission and ignorant innocence, and the argument for male superiority by virtue of a sex-determined power of "reason." She compares the lot of a woman educated just enough not to bore her husband to Satan's exile in Hell, a place of "no light, but rather darkness visible" (1.63): "would it not be a refinement on cruelty only to open her mind to make the darkness and misery of her fate *visible?*"

301

(her italics). In 1793 William Godwin's *Political Justice* followed Blake and Wollstonecraft in admiring the political heroism of Satan's opposition to inequality of rank and power and his disdain of despotism, as well as his fortitude in his torments—an analysis that also animates Byron's *Prometheus*.

Yet other readings of Satan are sensitive to Milton's moral argument. To William Hazlitt, he was both magnificently heroic and magnificently ambitious. Writing the Preface to *Prometheus Unbound*, even Percy Shelley found the rebellious classical god Prometheus superior to Satan in lacking the sins of pride, envy, ambition, and revenge—thus sparing readers the "pernicious casuistry" of excusing these faults. Even so, Shelley's *Defence of Poetry* admires the "magnificence and energy" of Milton's Satan and summons his voice for the poet's visionary power of creation.

The King James Bible
Genesis, Chapters 2 and 3

Chapter 2

THUS the heavens and the earth were finished, and all the host of them.

2   And on the seventh day God ended his work which he had made; and he rested on the seventh day from all his work which he had made.

3   And God blessed the seventh day, and sanctified it: because that in it he had rested from all his work which God created and made.

4   These *are* the generations of the heavens and of the earth when they were created, in the day that the LORD God made the earth and the heavens,

5   And every plant of the field before it was in the earth, and every

herb of the field before it grew: for the LORD God had not caused it to rain upon the earth, and *there was* not a man to till the ground.

6   But there went up a mist from the earth, and watered the whole face of the ground.

7   And the LORD God formed man *of* the dust of the ground, and breathed into his nostrils the breath of life; and man became a living soul.

8   And the LORD God planted a garden eastward in Eden; and there he put the man whom he had formed.

9   And out of the ground made the LORD God to grow every tree that is pleasant to the sight, and good for food; the tree of life also in the midst

of the garden, and the tree of knowledge of good and evil.

[. . .]

15 And the LORD God took the man, and put him into the garden of Eden to dress it and to keep it.

16 And the LORD God commanded the man, saying, Of every tree of the garden thou mayest freely eat:

17 But of the tree of the knowledge of good and evil, thou shalt not eat of it: for in the day that thou eatest thereof thou shalt surely die.

18 And the LORD God said, *It is* not good that the man should be alone; I will make him an help meet for him.

19 And out of the ground the LORD God formed every beast of the field, and every fowl of the air; and brought *them* unto Adam to see what he would call them: and whatsoever Adam called every living creature, that *was* the name thereof.

20 And Adam gave names to all cattle, and to the fowl of the air, and to every beast of the field; but for Adam there was not found an help meet for him.

21 And the LORD God caused a deep sleep to fall upon Adam, and he slept: and he took one of his ribs, and closed up the flesh instead thereof;

22 And the rib, which the LORD God had taken from man, made he a woman, and brought her unto the man.

23 And Adam said, This is now bone of my bones, and flesh of my flesh: she shall be called Woman, because she was taken out of Man.

24 Therefore shall a man leave his father and his mother, and shall cleave unto his wife: and they shall be one flesh.

25 And they were both naked, the man and his wife, and were not ashamed.

Chapter 3

NOW the serpent was more subtil than any beast of the field which the LORD God had made. And he said unto the woman, Yea, hath God said, Ye shall not eat of every tree of the garden?

2 And the woman said unto the serpent, We may eat of the fruit of the trees of the garden:

3 But of the fruit of the tree which is in the midst of the garden, God hath said, Ye shall not eat of it, neither shall ye touch it, lest ye die.

4 And the serpent said unto the woman, Ye shall not surely die:

5 For God doth know that in the day ye eat thereof, then your eyes shall be opened, and ye shall be as gods, knowing good and evil.

6 And when the woman saw that the tree *was* good for food, and that it *was* pleasant to the eyes, and a tree to be desired to make *one* wise, she took of the fruit thereof, and did eat, and gave also unto her husband with her; and he did eat.

7 And the eyes of them both were opened, and they knew that they *were* naked; and they sewed fig leaves together, and made themselves aprons.

8 And they heard the voice of the LORD God walking in the garden in the cool of the day: and Adam and his wife hid themselves from the presence of the LORD God amongst the trees of the garden.

9 And the LORD God called unto Adam, and said unto him, Where *art* thou?

10 And he said, I heard thy voice in the garden, and I was afraid, because I *was* naked; and I hid myself.

11 And he said, Who told thee that thou *wast* naked? Hast thou eaten of the tree, whereof I commanded thee that thou shouldest not eat?

12 And the man said, The woman whom thou gavest *to be* with me, she gave me of the tree, and I did eat.

13 And the LORD God said unto the woman, What *is* this *that* thou hast done? And the woman said, The serpent beguiled me, and I did eat.

14 And the LORD God said unto the serpent, Because thou hast done this, thou *art* cursed above all cattle, and above every beast of the field; upon thy belly shalt thou go, and dust shalt thou eat all the days of thy life:

15 And I will put enmity between thee and the woman, and between thy seed and her seed; it shall bruise thy head, and thou shalt bruise his heel.

16 Unto the woman he said, I will greatly multiply thy sorrow and thy conception, in sorrow thou shalt bring forth children; and thy desire *shall be* to thy husband, and he shall rule over thee.

17 And unto Adam he said, Because thou has hearkened unto the voice of thy wife, and hast eaten of the tree, of which I commanded thee, saying, Thou shalt not eat of it: cursed *is* the ground for thy sake; in sorrow shalt thou eat *of* it all the days of thy life;

18 Thorns also and thistles shall it bring forth to thee; and thou shalt eat the herb of the field;

19 In the sweat of thy face shalt thou eat bread, till thou return unto the ground; for out of it wast thou taken: for dust thou *art,* and unto dust shalt thou return.

20 And Adam called his wife's name Eve; because she was the mother of all living.

21 Unto Adam also and to his wife did the LORD God make coats of skins, and clothed them.

22 And the LORD God said, Behold, the man is become as one of us, to know good and evil: and now, lest he put forth his hand, and take also of the tree of life, and eat, and live for ever:

23 Therefore the LORD God sent him forth from the garden of Eden, to till the ground from whence he was taken.

24 So he drove out the man; and he placed at the east of the garden of Eden Cherubim, and a flaming sword which turned every way, to keep the way of the tree of life.

John Milton (1608–1674)

When the Civil Wars culminated in the execution of Charles I in 1649, John Milton defended the rebels and served as Latin secretary to the parliamentary government. With the Restoration of the

Monarchy, he was imprisoned, and it was only through the interven-
tion of friends that he was spared execution, let off instead with a
heavy fine and forfeiture of most of his property. Blind, financially
ruined, politically defeated, he began Paradise Lost, *intent to "assert*
Eternal Providence, / And justify the ways of God to men," as its
grand opening paragraph concludes. Published in ten books in 1667,
then twelve in 1674 (the text used here), this epic was the most
important poem in English literature for Shelley's generation, both
for its poetry and its story. Milton unfolds Genesis 1–3 into elabora-
tions of an earlier War in Heaven in which Archangel Lucifer (later
called Satan) led a third of the angels in revolt against God, a deadly
sin of pride. Vanquished and cast into eternal Hell, Satan decides not
to renew futile warfare but to plot insidious revenge; his plan is to
turn God's latest creation, man and woman, against their Creator by
subverting Eve into disobedience.

from *Paradise Lost*

[Satan in Hell: Book I]

his Pride

Had cast him out from Heav'n, with all his Host
Of Rebel Angels, by whose aid aspiring
To set himself in Glory above his Peers,
He trusted to have equall'd the most High   40
If he oppos'd; and with ambitious aim
Against the Throne and Monarchy of God
Rais'd impious[1] War in Heav'n and Battle proud
With vain attempt. Him the Almighty Power
Hurl'd headlong flaming from th' Ethereal Sky
With hideous ruin and combustion down
To bottomless perdition, there to dwell
In Adamantine Chains and penal Fire,
Who durst defy th' Omnipotent to Arms.
Nine times the Space that measures Day and Night   50
To mortal men, hee with his horrid crew
Lay vanquisht, rolling in the fiery Gulf
Confounded though immortal; But his doom
Reserv'd him to more wrath; for now the thought

[1]Irreverent, rebellious, with an implied allusion to the Latin phrase for civil war, *bellum impium.*

Both of lost happiness and lasting pain
Torments him; round he throws his baleful[2] eyes
That witness'd huge affliction and dismay
Mixt with obdurate pride and steadfast hate:
At once as far as Angels' ken° he views   *field of vision*
The dismal Situation waste and wild,   60
A Dungeon horrible, on all sides round
As one great Furnace flam'd, yet from those flames
No light, but rather darkness visible
Serv'd only to discover sights of woe,
Regions of sorrow, doleful shades, where peace
And rest can never dwell, hope never comes
That comes to all; but torture without end
Still urges,° and a fiery Deluge, fed   *intensifies*
With ever-burning Sulphur unconsum'd:
Such place Eternal Justice had prepar'd   70
For those rebellious, here thir Prison ordained
In utter darkness, and thir portion set
As far remov'd from God and light of Heav'n
As from the Center thrice to th' utmost Pole.[3]
O how unlike the place from whence they fell!

[*Satan speaks to his closest allies: Book I*]

"Is this the Region, this the Soil, the Clime,"
Said then the lost Arch-Angel, "this the seat°   *situation*
That we must change for Heav'n, this mournful gloom
For that celestial light? Be it so, since he
Who now is Sovran can dispose and bid
What shall be right: fardest° from him is best   *farthest*
Whom reason hath equall'd, force hath made supreme
Above his equals. Farewell happy Fields
Where Joy for ever dwells: Hail horrors, hail   250
Infernal world, and thou profoundest Hell
Receive thy new Possessor: One who brings

[2]Sinister, sorrowful.

[3]In geocentric cosmology, the distance from the center of Earth to the outermost celestial sphere.

A mind not to be chang'd by Place or Time.
The mind is its own place, and in itself
Can make a Heav'n of Hell, a Hell of Heav'n.
What matter where, if I be still the same,
And what I should be, all but° less than hee   *barely*
Whom Thunder hath made greater? Here at least
We shall be free; th' Almighty hath not built
Here for° his envy, will not drive us hence: *to provoke*   260
Here we may reign secure, and in my choice
To reign is worth ambition though in Hell:
Better to reign in Hell, than serve in Heav'n."

[*Satan, in Hell, just before he addresses his defeated army: Book I*]
                              he above the rest
In shape and gesture proudly eminent   590
Stood like a Tow'r; his form had not yet lost
All her[4] Original brightness, nor appear'd
Less than Arch-Angel ruin'd, and th' excess
Of Glory obscur'd: As when the Sun new risen
Looks through the horizontal misty air
Shorn of his Beams: or from behind the Moon
In dim Eclipse disastrous twilight sheds
On half the Nations, and with fear of change
Perplexes Monarchs.[5] Dark'n'd so, yet shone
Above them all th' Arch-Angel: but his face   600
Deep scars of Thunder had intrencht.

[*Satan alone at the border of Paradise: Book IV*]
                          horror and doubt distract°   *agitate*
His troubled thoughts, and from the bottom stir
The Hell within him, for within him Hell   20
He brings, and round about him, nor from Hell
One step no more than from himself can fly
By change of time or place: Now conscience wakes despair
That slumber'd, wakes the bitter memory

[4]*Forma* is a feminine noun in Latin.
[5]Eclipses were often read as portents of impending disaster. Charles II's censor reportedly objected to these lines as a veiled threat to the Monarch.

Of what he was, what is, and what must be
Worse; of worse deed worse sufferings must ensue.
. . .

"Me miserable! which way shall I fly
Infinite wrath, and infinite despair?
Which way I fly is Hell; myself am Hell.[6]

. . .

So farewell Hope, and with Hope farewell Fear,
Farewell Remorse: all Good to me is lost;
Evil be thou my Good."   110

[Satan sees Adam and Eve: Book IV]

"O Hell! what do mine eyes with grief behold,
Into our room of bliss thus high advanc't
Creatures of other mould, earth-born perhaps,   360
Not Spirits, yet to heav'nly Spirits bright
Little inferior; whom my thoughts pursue
With wonder, and could love, so lively shines
In them Divine resemblance, and such grace
The hand that form'd them on thir shape hath pour'd.
Ah, gentle pair, yee little think how nigh
Your change approaches, when all these delights
Will vanish and deliver ye to woe,
More woe, the more your taste is now of joy."

[Eve recounts her first moments of life to Adam: Book IV]

That day I oft remember, when from sleep
I first awak't, and found myself repos'd   450
Under a shade on flow'rs, much wond'ring where
And what I was, whence thither brought, and how.
Not distant far from thence a murmuring sound
Of waters issu'd from a Cave and spread
Into a liquid Plain, then stood unmov'd
Pure as th' expanse of Heav'n; I thither went

---

[6]When the hero of Christopher Marlowe's *Doctor Faustus* (1616) asks skeptically,
"Tell me, where is this place that men call hell?" the demon Mephostophilis answers,
"Where we are tortured and remain for ever. / Hell hath no limits, nor is circum-
scribed / In one self place. But where we are is hell, / And where hell is there must we
ever be" (Act 1, scene 5).

With unexperienc't thought, and laid me down
On the green bank, to look into the clear
Smooth Lake, that to me seem'd another Sky.
As I bent down to look, just opposite,   460
A Shape within the wat'ry gleam appear'd
Bending to look on me, I started back,
It started back, but pleas'd I soon return'd,
Pleas'd it return'd as soon with answering looks
Of sympathy and love; there I had fixt
Mine eyes till now, and pin'd with vain desire,[7]
Had not a voice[8] thus warn'd me, What thou seest,
What there thou seest fair Creature is thyself,
With thee it came and goes; but follow me,
And I will bring thee where no shadow stays°   *awaits*   470
Thy coming, and thy soft imbraces, hee
Whose image thou art, him thou shalt enjoy
Inseparably thine, to him shalt bear
Multitudes like thyself, and thence be call'd
Mother of human Race . . . what could I do,
But follow straight, invisibly thus led?
Till I espi'd thee, fair indeed and tall,
Under a Platan,° yet methought less fair,   *tropical tree*
Less winning soft, less amiably mild,
Than that smooth wat'ry image.   480

[Adam recounts his birth to Archangel Raphael: Book VIII]

For Man to tell how human Life began   250
Is hard; for who himself beginning knew?
Desire with thee still longer to converse
Induc'd me. As new wak't from soundest sleep
Soft on the flow'ry herb I found me laid
In Balmy° Sweat, which with his Beams the Sun   *fragrant*
Soon dri'd, and on the reeking° moisture fed.   *steaming*
Straight toward Heav'n my wond'ring Eyes I turn'd,

---

[7]Milton's scene alludes to the tale in Ovid's *Metamorphoses* of the beautiful youth Narcissus who, in punishment for his scorn, was made to fall in love with his reflection in a pool, and pine for it in vain. Milton may also be evoking Eve's particular paradise, lost when she is brought to Adam as his inferior.
[8]God's.

And gaz'd a while the ample Sky, till rais'd
By quick instinctive motion up I sprung,
As thitherward endeavoring, and upright   260
Stood on my feet; about me round I saw
Hill, Dale, and shady Woods, and sunny Plains,
And liquid Lapse[9] of murmuring Streams; by these,
Creatures that liv'd, and mov'd, and walk'd, or flew,
Birds on the branches warbling; all things smil'd,
With fragrance and with joy my heart o'erflow'd.
Myself I then perus'd, and Limb by Limb
Survey'd, and sometimes went, and sometimes ran
With supple joints, as lively vigor led:
But who I was, or where, or from what cause,   270
Knew not; to speak I tri'd, and forthwith spake,
My Tongue obey'd and readily could name
Whate'er I saw. Thou Sun, said I, fair Light,
And thou enlight'n'd Earth, so fresh and gay,
Ye Hills and Dales, ye Rivers, Woods, and Plains
And ye that live and move, fair Creatures, tell,
Tell, if ye saw, how came I thus, how here?
Not of myself; by some great Maker then,
In goodness and in power preëminent;
Tell me, how may I know him, how adore,   280
From whom I have that thus I move and live,
And feel that I am happier than I know.
While thus I call'd, and stray'd I knew not whither,
From where I first drew Air, and first beheld
This happy Light, when answer none return'd,
On a green shady Bank profuse of Flow'rs
Pensive I sat me down; there gentle sleep
First found me, and with soft oppression seiz'd
My drowsed sense, untroubl'd, though I thought
I then was passing to my former state   290
Insensible, and forthwith to dissolve:
When suddenly stood at my Head a dream,
Whose inward apparition gently mov'd
My fancy to believe I yet had being,
And liv'd: One came, methought, of shape Divine,

[9]Fall, flowing.

And said, thy Mansion wants thee,[10] *Adam,* rise,
First Man, of Men innumerable ordain'd
First Father, call'd by thee I come thy Guide
To the Garden of bliss, thy seat[11] prepar'd.
So saying, by the hand he took me.   300

[Adam recounts the creation of Eve: Book VIII]

Under his forming hands a Creature grew,   470
Manlike, but different sex, so lovely fair,
That what seem'd fair in all the World, seem'd now
Mean, or in her summ'd up, in her contain'd
And in her looks, which from that time infus'd
Sweetness into my heart, unfelt before,
And into all things from her Air inspir'd
The spirit of love and amorous delight.
Shee disappear'd, and left me dark, I wak'd
To find her, or for ever to deplore°   *lament*
Her loss, and other pleasures all abjure: 480
When out of hope, behold her, not far off,
Such as I saw her in my dream, adorn'd
With what all Earth or Heaven could bestow
To make her amiable: On she came
Led by her Heav'nly Maker, though unseen,
And guided by his voice, nor uninform'd
Of nuptial Sanctity and marriage Rites:
Grace was in all her steps, Heav'n in her Eye,
In every gesture dignity and love.

[Satan, in Eden, finds Eve alone: Book IX]

Much hee the Place admir'd, the Person° more.   *Eve*
As one who long in populous City pent,
Where Houses thick and Sewers annoy° the Air,   *pollute*
Forth issuing on a Summer's Morn to breathe
Among the pleasant Villages and Farms
Adjoin'd, from each thing met conceives delight,
The smell of Grain, or tedded Grass, or Kine,°   *cattle* 450

[10]Home lacks thee.
[11]Residence, throne.

Or Dairy, each rural sight, each rural sound;
If chance with Nymphlike step fair Virgin pass,
What pleasing seem'd, for her now pleases more,
She most, and in her look sums all Delight.
Such Pleasure took the Serpent to behold
This Flow'ry Plat,° the sweet recess° of *Eve*   *plot/retreat*
Thus early, thus alone; her Heav'nly form
Angelic, but more soft, and Feminine,
Her graceful Innocence, her every Air°   *manner, aura*
Of gesture or least action overaw'd   460
His Malice, and with rapine° sweet bereav'd   *ravishment*
His fierceness of the fierce intent it brought:
That space the Evil one abstracted° stood   *withdrawn*
From his own evil, and for the time remain'd
Stupidly good,° of enmity disarm'd,   *stunned*
Of guile, of hate, of envy, of revenge;
But the hot Hell that always in him burns,
Though in mid Heav'n, soon ended his delight,
And tortures him now more, the more he sees
Of pleasure not for him ordain'd: then soon   470
Fierce hate he recollects, and all his thoughts
Of mischief, gratulating,[12] thus excites.
    "Thoughts, whither have ye led me, with what sweet
Compulsion thus transported to forget
What hither brought us, hate, not love, nor hope
Of Paradise for Hell, hope here to taste
Of pleasure, but all pleasure to destroy,
Save what is in destroying, other joy
To me is lost."

[*Adam's soliloquy after the Fall: Book X*]

O voice once heard
Delightfully, *Increase and multiply*,[13]   730
Now death to hear! for what can I increase
Or multiply, but curses on my head?
Who of all Ages to succeed, but feeling
The evil on him brought by me, will curse

---

[12]Exulting in, welcoming.
[13]God's blessing on Adam and Eve (Genesis 1.28).

My Head; Ill fare our Ancestor impure,
For this we may thank *Adam;* but his thanks
Shall be the execration;° so besides   *curse*
Mine own° that bide upon me, all from mee   *curses*
Shall with a fierce reflux on mee redound,
On mee as on thir natural centre light°   *alight*   740
Heavy, though in thir place. O fleeting joys
Of Paradise, dear bought with lasting woes!
Did I request thee, Maker, from my Clay
To mould me Man, did I solicit thee
From darkness to promote me,[14] or here place
In this delicious Garden? as my Will
Concurr'd not to my being, it were but right
And equal° to reduce me to my dust,   *just, fair*
Desirous to resign, and render back
All I receiv'd, unable to perform   750
Thy terms too hard, by which I was to hold
The good I sought not. To the loss of that,
Sufficient penalty, why hast thou added
The sense of endless woes? inexplicable
Thy Justice seems; yet to say truth, too late
I thus contest; then should have been refus'd
Those terms whatever, when they were propos'd:
Thou didst accept them; wilt thou enjoy the good,
Then cavil° the conditions? and though God   *contest*
Made thee without thy leave, what if thy Son   760
Prove disobedient, and reprov'd, retort,
Wherefore didst thou beget me? I sought it not:
Wouldst thou admit for his contempt of thee
That proud excuse? yet him not thy election,°   *choice*
But Natural necessity begot.
God made thee of choice his own, and of his own
To serve him, thy reward was of his grace,
Thy punishment then justly is at his Will.
Be it so, for I submit, his doom° is fair.   *judgment*
And dust I am and shall to dust return.   770
O welcome hour whenever!

[14]Lines 743 to here give Shelley her epigraph for *Frankenstein,* as well as a reference to the admonishment of Isaiah: "Woe unto him that striveth with his Maker" (45.9).

[*Exile from Eden: Book XII*][15]

from the other Hill
To thir fixt Station, all in bright array
The Cherubim[16] descended; on the ground
Gliding meteorous, as Ev'ning Mist
Ris'n from a River o'er the marish° glides,   marsh
And gathers ground fast at the Laborer's heel   630
Homeward returning. High in Front advanc't,
The brandisht Sword of God before them blaz'd
Fierce as a Comet; which with torrid heat,
And vapor as the *Libyan* Air adust,
Began to parch that temperate Clime; whereat
In either hand the hast'ning Angel caught
Our ling'ring Parents, and to th' Eastern Gate
Led them direct, and down the Cliff as fast
To the subjected° Plain; then disappear'd.   lying below
They looking back, all th' Eastern side beheld   640
Of Paradise, so late° thir happy seat,°   recently/home
Wav'd over by that flaming Brand,° the Gate   sword
With dreadful Faces throng'd and fiery Arms:
Some natural tears they dropp'd, but wip'd them soon;
The World was all before them, where to choose
Thir place of rest, and Providence thir guide:
They hand in hand with wand'ring steps and slow,
Through *Eden* took thir solitary way.

William Godwin (1756–1836)
from *An Enquiry Concerning Political Justice* (1793)

Can great intellectual power exist, without a strong sense of justice?

It has no doubt resulted from a train of speculation similar to this, that poetical readers have commonly remarked Milton's devil to be a

---

[15]The end of the poem.

[16]Second highest angels; also, biblical figures with wings, human head, and animal body, who were guardians of a sacred place.

being of considerable virtue. It must be admitted that his energies centered too much in personal regards. But why did he rebel against his maker? It was, as he himself informs us, because he saw no sufficient reason, for that extreme inequality of rank and power, which the creator assumed. It was because prescription and precedent form no adequate ground for implicit faith. After his fall, why did he still cherish the spirit of opposition? From a persuasion that he was hardly[1] and injuriously treated. He was not discouraged by the apparent inequality of the contest: because a sense of reason and justice was stronger in his mind, than a sense of brute force; because he had much of the feelings of an Epictetus or a Cato,[2] and little of those of a slave. He bore his torments with fortitude, because he disdained to be subdued by despotic power. He sought revenge, because he could not think with tameness of the unexpostulating authority that assumed to dispose of him. How beneficial and illustrious might the temper from which these qualities flowed, have been found, with a small diversity of situation!

George Gordon, Lord Byron

Prometheus

> Titan! to whose immortal eyes
>   The sufferings of mortality,
>   Seen in their sad reality,
> Were not as things that gods despise;
> What was thy pity's recompense?
> A silent suffering, and intense;
> The rock, the vulture, and the chain,
> All that the proud can feel of pain,
> The agony they do not show,

[1]Harshly.
[2]Cato the Younger (95–46 B.C.E.), a Roman statesman famed for principle and integrity, was praised for his noble suicide when Caesar vanquished his faction in a struggle for power; Shelley refers to him in I.VI. Epictetus (c. 50–c. 138) was a Stoic philosopher who advocated the brotherhood of man and indifference to material goods.

The suffocating sense of woe,   10
  Which speaks but in its loneliness,
    And then is jealous lest the sky
  Should have a listener, nor will sigh
    Until its voice is echoless.

Titan! to thee the strife was given
  Between the suffering and the will,
    Which torture where they cannot kill;
  And the inexorable Heaven,
  And the deaf tyranny of Fate,
  The ruling principle of Hate,   20
  Which for its pleasure doth create
  The things it may annihilate,
  Refused thee even the boon to die:
    The wretched gift eternity
  Was thine—and thou hast borne it well.
All that the Thunderer[1] wrung from thee
Was but the menace which flung back
On him the torments of thy rack;[2]
The fate thou didst so well foresee,[3]
But would not to appease him tell;   30
And in thy Silence was his Sentence,
And in his Soul a vain repentance,
And evil dread so ill dissembled
That in his hand the lightnings trembled.

Thy Godlike crime was to be kind,
  To render with thy precepts less
    The sum of human wretchedness,
  And strengthen Man with his own mind;
  But baffled as thou wert from high,

---

[1]Jupiter, the king of the gods who torments Prometheus, is also the god of thunder; this is also Satan's name for God (see *Paradise Lost* 1.258).

[2]An instrument of bone-breaking torture; Prometheus was chained by Jupiter to a mountain, where each day an eagle gnawed on his heart, and each night it grew back for renewed feeding; maintaining heroic defiance, Prometheus was eventually liberated by Hercules.

[3]Prometheus, whose name means "foreseeing," prophesied the downfall both of his fellow Titans and of their conqueror, Jupiter. Jupiter offered to end his torture if he would tell him the secret of averting his downfall—a crisis that shapes Percy Shelley's *Prometheus Unbound* (written 1818–19).

Still in thy patient energy,   40
In the endurance, and repulse
   Of thine impenetrable Spirit,
Which Earth and Heaven could not convulse,
   A mighty lesson we inherit:
Thou art a symbol and a sign
   To Mortals of their fate and force;
Like thee, Man is in part divine,
   A troubled stream from a pure source;
And Man in portions can foresee
   His own funereal destiny;   50
His wretchedness, and his resistance,
   And his sad unallied existence:
To which his Spirit may oppose
   Itself—and equal to all woes,
   And a firm will, and a deep sense,
   Which even in torture can descry
   Its own concenter'd recompense,
   Triumphant where it dares defy,
   And making Death a Victory.

Diodati, July, 1816   pub. 1816

William Hazlitt

From Lectures on the English Poets *(1818) by William Hazlitt, a
politically liberal author, essayist, philosopher, painter, and journalist.*

Remarks on *Paradise Lost*
"On Shakespeare and Milton"

I am ready to give up the dialogues in Heaven where, as Pope justly
observes, "God the Father turns a school divine."[1] [. . .] The interest of
the poem arises from the daring ambition and fierce passions of Satan,

---

[1]The discussion in *Paradise Lost* III between the "Almighty Father" and his "only
begotten Son" about Adam and Eve's revolt, and quoting Pope's *First Epistle of the
Second Book of Horace* (1737), 102; a *school divine* is a scholastic theologian.

and from the account of the paradisaical happiness, and the loss of it by our first parents. Three-fourths of the work are taken up with these characters, and nearly all that relates to them is unmixed sublimity and beauty. The two first books alone are like two massy pillars of solid gold.

Satan is the most heroic subject that ever was chosen for a poem; and the execution is as perfect as the design is lofty. He was the first of created beings who, for endeavouring to be equal with the highest, and to divide the empire of heaven with the Almighty, was hurled down to hell. His aim was no less than the throne of the universe; his means, myriads of angelic armies bright, the third part of the heavens, whom he lured after him with his countenance, and who durst defy the Omnipotent in arms.[2] His ambition was the greatest, and his punishment was the greatest; but not so his despair: for his fortitude was as great as his sufferings. His strength of mind was matchless as his strength of body; the vastness of his designs did not surpass the firm, inflexible determination with which he submitted to his irreversible doom and final loss of all good. His power of action and of suffering was equal. He was the greatest power that was ever overthrown, with the strongest will left to resist or to endure. He was baffled, not confounded. [. . .] The sense of his punishment seems lost in the magnitude of it; the fierceness of tormenting flames is qualified and made innoxious by the greater fierceness of his pride; the loss of infinite happiness to himself is compensated in thought by the power of inflicting infinite misery on others. Yet Satan is not the principle of malignity, or of the abstract love of evil, but of the abstract love of power, of pride, of self-will personified, to which last principle all other good and evil, and even his own, are subordinate. From this principle he never once flinches. His love of power and contempt for suffering are never once relaxed from the highest pitch of intensity. His thoughts burn like a hell within him; but the power of thought holds dominion in his mind over every other consideration. The consciousness of a determined purpose, of "that intellectual being, those thoughts that wander through eternity," though accompanied with endless pain, he prefers to nonentity, to "being swallowed up and lost in the wide womb of uncreated night."[3] He expresses the sum and substance of all ambition in one line: "Fallen cherub, to be weak is miserable, doing or suffering!"

---

[2]Paraphrasing *Paradise Lost* 1.49; Hazlitt uses Satan's voice to shape his praise.

[3]Belial, a rebel who is intellectual, worries that to persist against God is to risk total annihilation; and "who would lose, / Though full of pain, this intellectual being, / Those thoughts that wander through Eternity, / To perish rather, swallow'd up and lost / In the wide womb of uncreated night, / Devoid of sense and motion?" (*Paradise Lost* 2.146–51).

[1.157–58]. After such a conflict as his and such a defeat, to retreat in order, to rally, to make terms, to exist at all, is something; but he does more than this: he founds a new empire in hell, and from it conquers this new world, whither he bends his undaunted flight, forcing his way through nether and surrounding fires. [. . .] Prometheus chained to his rock was not a more terrific example of suffering and of crime. [. . .] The deformity of Satan is only in the depravity of his will; he has no bodily deformity to excite our loathing or disgust. The horns and tail are not there, poor emblems of the unbending, unconquered spirit, of the writhing agonies within. Milton was too magnanimous and open an antagonist to support his argument by the by-tricks of a hump and cloven foot. [. . .] He relied on the justice of his cause, and did not scruple to give the devil his due.

Percy Bysshe Shelley

This epic-prophetic verse drama (written 1818–19; published 1820) concerns Prometheus's struggle with tyrant Jupiter.

from *Prometheus Unbound*

Preface

The only imaginary being resembling in any degree Prometheus, is Satan; and Prometheus is, in my judgement, a more poetical character than Satan, because, in addition to courage, and majesty, and firm and patient opposition to omnipotent force, he is susceptible of being described as exempt from the taints of ambition, envy, revenge, and a desire for personal aggrandisement, which, in the Hero of *Paradise Lost*, interfere with the interest. The character of Satan engenders in the mind a pernicious casuistry[1] which leads us to weigh his faults and his wrongs, and to excuse the former because the latter exceed all measure. In the minds of those who consider that magnificent fiction with a religious feeling it engenders something worse. But Prometheus is, as it were, the type of the highest perfection of moral and intellectual nature, impelled by the purest and the truest motives to the best and noblest ends.

[1]Moral reasoning; "interest" means "sympathy for."

ACT I

Scene—A Ravine of Icy Rocks in the Indian Caucasus.
    PROMETHEUS *is discovered bound to the Precipice.* PANTHEA
    and IONE *are seated at his feet. Time, night. During the Scene,
    morning slowly breaks.*

PROMETHEUS. Monarch of Gods and Dæmons, and all Spirits
But One, who throng those bright and rolling worlds
Which Thou and I alone of living things
Behold with sleepless eyes! regard this Earth
Made multitudinous with thy slaves, whom thou
Requitest for knee-worship, prayer, and praise,
And toil, and hecatombs of broken hearts,
With fear and self-contempt and barren hope;
Whilst me, who am thy foe, eyeless in hate,
Hast thou made reign and triumph, to thy scorn,   10
O'er mine own misery and thy vain revenge.
Three thousand years of sleep-unsheltered hours,
And moments aye divided by keen pangs
Till they seemed years, torture and solitude,
Scorn and despair,—these are mine empire:—
More glorious far than that which thou surveyest
From thine unenvied throne, O Mighty God!
Almighty, had I deigned to share the shame
Of thine ill tyranny, and hung not here
Nailed to this wall of eagle-baffling mountain,   20
Black, wintry, dead, unmeasured; without herb,
Insect, or beast, or shape or sound of life.
Ah me! alas, pain, pain ever, for ever!

No change, no pause, no hope! Yet I endure.
I ask the Earth, have not the mountains felt?
I ask yon Heaven, the all-beholding Sun,
Has it not seen? The Sea, in storm or calm,
Heaven's ever-changing Shadow, spread below,
Have its deaf waves not heard my agony?
Ah me! alas, pain, pain ever, for ever!   30

The crawling glaciers pierce me with the spears
Of their moon-freezing crystals, the bright chains

Eat with their burning cold into my bones.
Heaven's wingèd hound, polluting from thy lips
His beak in poison not his own, tears up
My heart; and shapeless sights come wandering by,
The ghastly people of the realm of dream,
Mocking me: and the Earthquake-fiends are charged
To wrench the rivets from my quivering wounds
When the rocks split and close again behind: 40
While from their loud abysses howling throng
The genii of the storm, urging the rage
Of whirlwind, and afflict me with keen hail.

**Percy Bysshe Shelley
from *A Defence of Poetry* (1821, pub. 1840)**

[*On moral sympathy*]

The great secret of morals is love, or a going out of our own nature,
and an identification of ourselves with the beautiful which exists in
thought, action, or person, not our own. A man, to be greatly good,
must imagine intensely and comprehensively; he must put himself in
the place of another and of many others; the pains and pleasures of
his species must become his own. The great instrument of moral good
is the imagination; and poetry administers to the effect by acting upon
the cause.

[*On Milton's Satan*]

Milton's poem contains within itself a philosophical refutation of that
system, of which, by a strange and natural antithesis, it has been a
chief popular support.[1] Nothing can exceed the energy and magnificence of the character of Satan as expressed in Paradise Lost. It is a
mistake to suppose that he could ever have been intended for the popular personification of evil. Implacable hate, patient cunning, and a

---

[1]That is, the "great Argument" to "justify the ways of God to men" and Satan's
punishment for the "Pride," "Envy and Revenge" by which he cast himself "th' Arch-
Enemy" both of God and man (1.24–83).

sleepless refinement of device to inflict the extremest anguish on an enemy, these things are evil; and, although venial[2] in a slave, are not to be forgiven in a tyrant; although redeemed by much that ennobles his defeat in one subdued, are marked by all that dishonors his conquest in the victor. Milton's Devil as a moral being is as far superior to his God, as one who perseveres in some purpose which he has conceived to be excellent, in spite of adversity and torture, is to one who in the cold security of undoubted triumph inflicts the most horrible revenge upon his enemy, not from any mistaken notion of inducing him to repent of a perseverance in enmity, but with the alleged design of exasperating him to deserve new torments. Milton has so far violated the popular creed (if this shall be judged to be a violation) as to have alleged no superiority of moral virtue to his God over his Devil. And this bold neglect of a direct moral purpose is the most decisive proof of the supremacy of Milton's genius.

---

[2] Forgivable.

Frankenstein,
A Romantic Drama
in Three Acts

Richard Brinsley Peake (1792–1847)

Late in August 1823, on the eve of her twenty-sixth birthday, Mary Shelley saw a compressed, reorganized, sensationalized staging of her novel (including some of its very language): *Presumption; or the Fate of Frankenstein,* replete with musical enhancements, comic interludes, and some canny condensations of plot and character. Having opened on 28 July at the English Opera House, it survived some oppositional picketing and leafleting about its impiety, to run for thirty-seven shows, with repeat stagings well into mid-century. 1823 also saw the work published as a sixteen-page performance text by Dicks' Standard Plays (No. 431): *Frankenstein, A Romantic Drama* (London: John Dicks). This included directions for COSTUME, with those for creature and creator seeming only different fashions, rather than signifiers of a non-human demon and a human hero:

THE MONSTER'S APPEARANCE AND DRESS.—Dark black flowing hair—*à la Octavian*—his face, hands, arms, and legs all bare, being one colour, the same as his body, which is a light blue or French gray cotton dress, fitting quite close, as if it were his flesh, with a satin colour scarf round his middle, passing over one shoulder.

FRANKENSTEIN.—Black velvet vest and trunk breeches—gray tunic, open, the sleeves open in front, slashed with black—black silk pantaloons and black velvet shoes—black velvet hat.

A poster for Thomas Potter Cooke as the Creature, in *Frankenstein*, by Richard Brins-ley Peake, staged at the Lyceum Theatre (English Opera House), summer 1823. "From one magazine we get a vivid description of him: his green and yellow visage, his watery and lack-lustre eye, his long-matted, straggling black locks, the blue livid hue of his arms and legs, his shriveled complexion, his straight black lips, his horrible ghastly grin. One daily critic compared him to a wax representation of a victim of the plague in a florentine museum" (Nitchie 224). Shelley attended this performance. (The Harvard Theatre Collection, The Houghton Library)

In the play, Frankenstein's alarmed servant describes the "Monster" as "a hob-goblin, seven-and-twenty feet high!" but the play-poster shows him (though huge) rather human-looking, and on stage the chief sign of un-human difference was skin pigmented blue-grey, a quasi-racializing. From some points of view, even, the two comic gypsy characters might seem more monstrous in fashion and complexion, "Tanskin" actually named for his skin color:

> TANSKIN.—A tight goatskin jacket, leaving the throat and arms bare—a coarse canvas shirt seen through it, with ragged sleeves, extending nearly down to the elbow, and hanging loose there—goatskin breeches, extending half way down the thighs, with ragged under-dress or trousers of canvas, reaching within an inch of the knees—legs bare, sandaled with leather thongs, the hair

The frontispiece to H. M. Milner's *Frankenstein, or the Man and the Monster!* (1826). As Elizabeth Nitchie remarks, though disapprovingly, this image "does not represent him as very terrifying." Milner's play, *Frankenstein; or, The Demon of Switzerland*, also staged in the summer of 1823, at London's Royal Coburg Theatre, starred Richard John O. Smith, who wore a "close vest and leggings of pale yellowish brown heightened with blue, Greek shirt of dark brown, and broad black leather belt" (Tropp). (The Harvard Theatre Collection, The Houghton Library)

confined in a long Italian net—the dress confined at the waist by a belt, in which a knife is stuck—slouched hat.

HAMMERPAN.—Same as Tanskin with the addition of a leather apron—wallet [i.e., pouch]—bald wig—and one eye blind.

After seeing the play, Shelley wrote enthusiastically, and with no little pride, to a friend, and with special attention to the way the creature was signified in the cast of characters:

lo & behold! I found myself famous!—Frankenstein had a prodigious success as a drama & was about to be repeated for the 23rd night at the English opera house. The play bill amused me extremely, for in the list of dramatis personæ came, ——— by Mr T. Cooke: this nameless mode of naming the unameable is rather good. On Friday Aug. 29th Jane My father William[1] & I went to the theatre to see it. Wallack looked very well as F—he is at the beginning full of hope & expectation—at the end of the Ist Act. the stage represents a room with a staircase leading to the F workshop—he goes to it and you see his light at a small window, through which a frightened servant peeps, who runs off in terror when F. exclaims "It lives!"—Presently F himself rushes in horror & trepidation from the room and while still expressing his agony & terror ——— throws down the door of the labratory, leaps the staircase & presents his unearthly & monstrous person on the stage. The story is not well managed—but Cooke played ———'s part extremely well—his seeking as it were for support—his trying to grasp at the sounds he heard—all indeed he does was well imagined & executed. I was much amused, & it appeared to excite a breathless eagerness in the audience. (September 1823; *Letters* 1: 378)

Shelley was impressed as well as amused: when she revised her novel, a memory of Peake's elaborate title prompted her to add these sentences to Victor's strained calm at Justine's trial (p. 56, the paragraph beginning "This speech calmed me . . ."): "My tale was not one to announce publicly; its astounding horror would be looked upon as madness by the vulgar. Did any one indeed exist, except I, the creator, who would believe, unless his senses convinced him, in the existence of the living monument of presumption and rash ignorance which I had let loose upon the world?" (1831; Ch. VII). In my transcription of Peake's half-comic

[1]Jane Williams and William Godwin.

half-gothic playlet from Dicks' publication, I silently correct obvious printer's errata, omit technical stage directions, and supply, in square brackets or occasional footnotes, some variants from the text used in Jeffrey Cox's *Seven Gothic Dramas, 1789–1825* (Ohio University Press, 1992). For some details of stage history, I am indebted to Cox and to Charles Robinson's Chronology in *The Frankenstein Notebooks*.

FRANKENSTEIN.

A ROMANTIC DRAMA, IN THREE ACTS.

BY RICHARD BRINSLEY PEAKE

Number 431.   COMPLETE.   One Penny.

DICKS' STANDARD PLAYS.

FRANKENSTEIN.

BY R. B. PEAKE.

ORIGINAL COMPLETE EDITION.—PRICE ONE PENNY.

** THIS PLAY CAN BE PERFORMED WITHOUT RISK OF INFRINGING ANY RIGHTS.

LONDON: JOHN DICKS, 313, STRAND.

DRAMATIS PERSONAE

First Performed at the Lyceum Theatre, 1823

FRANKENSTEIN

CLERVAL (his friend, in love with
   Elizabeth)

WILLIAM (brother of Frankenstein)

FRITZ (servant of Frankenstein)

DE LACEY (a banished gentleman—
   blind)

FELIX DE LACEY (his son)

TANSKIN (a gipsy)

HAMMERPAN (a tinker)

A GUIDE (an old man)

ELIZABETH (sister of
   Frankenstein)

AGATHA (daughter of De Lacey)

SAFIE (an Arabian girl,
   betrothed to Felix)

MADAME NINON (wife of Fritz)

————————2

Gipsies, Peasants, Choristers, and Dancers (Male and Female)

SCENE—Geneva and its vicinity

ACT I
SCENE I

A Gothic Chamber in the house of Frankenstein. FRITZ *discovered in a Gothic arm-chair, nodding asleep. During the symphony of the song, he starts, rubs his eyes, and comes forward.*

> AIR—FRITZ
> *Oh, dear me! what's the matter?*
> *How I shake at each clatter.*
> > *My marrow*
> > *They harrow.*
> *Oh, dear me! what's the matter?*
> *If mouse squeaks, or cat sneezes,*
> *Cricket chirps, or cock wheezes,*
> > *Then I fret*
> > *In cold sweat.*
> *Ev'ry noise my nerves teazes;*

2As Shelley's letter about the play indicates, the Creature is signified by a blank line.

> *Bless my heart—heaven preserve us!*
> *I declare I'm so nervous.*
> > *Ev'ry Knock*
> > *Is a shock.*
> *I declare I'm so nervous!*
> *I'm so nervous.*

FRITZ. Oh, Fritz, Fritz, Fritz! What is it come to! you are frightened out of your wits. Why did you ever leave your native village! why couldn't you be happy in your native village with an innocent cow for your companion (bless its sweet breath!) instead of coming here to the city of Geneva to be hired as a servant! (*starts*) What's that?—nothing. And then how complimentary! Master only hired me because he thought I looked so stupid! Stupid! ha, ha, ha! but am I stupid though? To be sure Mr. Frankenstein is a kind man, and I should respect him, but that I thinks as how he holds converse with somebody below with a long tail, horns and hoofs, who shall be nameless. (*starts again*) What's that! Oh, a gnat on my nose! Oh, anything frightens me now—I'm so very nervous! I spill all my bread and milk when I feed myself at breakfast! Lauk! Lauk![3] In the country, if a dog brayed, or a donkey barked ever so loud, it had no effect upon me. (*two distinct loud knocks—*FRITZ *jumps*) Oh, mercy! I jump like a maggot out of cheese! How my heart beats!

CLERVAL. (*without*) Fritz, Fritz! Open the door, Fritz!

FRITZ. [It's a human being however—] Yes. It's only Mr. Clerval, master's friend, who is going to marry Miss Elizabeth, master's sister. (*opens the door. Enter* CLERVAL) How d'ye do, sir!

CLERVAL. Good morrow, Fritz! Is Mr. Frankenstein to be seen?

FRITZ. I fear not, Sir, he has as usual been fumi— fumi— fumi—

CLERVAL. Fumigating.

FRITZ. Yes, sir—fumigating; thank'ee sir—fumigating all night at his chemistry. I have not dared to disturb him.

CLERVAL. Mr. Frankenstein pursues his studies with too much ardour.

FRITZ. And what can be the use of it, Mr. Clerval? Work, work, work—always at it. Now, putting a case to you. Now, when I was in the country, with my late cow (she's no more now, poor thing!)

---

[3]Slang, akin to "Lordy!"

if I had sat to and milked her for a fortnight together, day and night, without stopping, do you think I should be any the better for it? I ask you as a gentleman and a scholar.

CLERVAL. Ha, ha, ha! Certainly not!

FRITZ. Nor my cow neither, poor creter. (*wipes his eyes*) Excuse my crying—she's defunct, and I always whimper a little when I think on her; and my wife lives away from me, but I don't care so much for that. Oh! Mr. Clerval, between ourselves—hush! didn't you hear a noise!—between ourselves, I want to unbosom my confidence.

CLERVAL. Well!

FRITZ. Between ourselves—there's nobody at the door, is there?—(*crosses to door*)—No! well, between ourselves, Mr. Clerval, I have been so very nervous since I came to this place,

CLERVAL. Pshaw!

FRITZ. Nay, don't "Pshaw!" till you've heard me out. [My poor Master—I know you are his friend, but he has dealings with the Gentleman in black!]

CLERVAL. Yes, I know—the Notary who comes to consult him on my marriage contract—

FRITZ. Notary—no—somebody deeper than that—] Oh, Mr. Clerval! I'll tell you. One night Mr. Frankenstein did indulge himself by going to bed. He was worn with fatigue and study. I had occasion to go into his chamber. He was asleep, but frightfully troubled; he groaned and groaned, his teeth setting mine on edge. "It is accomplished!" said he. *Accomplished!* I know that had nothing to do with me, but I listened. He started up in his sleep, though his eyes were opened and dead as oysters, he cried, "It is animated—it rises—walks!" Now, my shrewd guess, sir, is that, like Doctor Faustus, my master is raising the Devil.[4]

CLERVAL. Fritz, you are simple;[5] drive such impressions from your mind, you must not misconstrue your master's words in a dream. Do you never dream?

FRITZ. (*mournfully*) I dream about my cow sometimes.

CLERVAL. Your master is a studious chemist—nay, as I sometimes suspect, an alchemist.

[4] 16th-c. German scholar Johann Faust was rumored to have supernatural powers from a bargain with the devil. Christopher Marlowe's late 16th-c. treatment of the subject, *Tragical History of Dr. Faustus*, was refreshed in the 19th c. by Goethe's *Faust*.
[5] A simpleton.

FRITZ. Eh! Ah, I think he is. What is an alchemist Mr. Clerval?

CLERVAL. Does he not sometimes speak of the art of making gold?

FRITZ. Lord, sir! do you take Mr. Frankenstein for a coiner?[6]

CLERVAL. Did you never hear him make mention of the grand elixir, which can prolong life to immortality?

FRITZ. Never in all my life!

CLERVAL. Well, go—find out if it is possible I can see him. I will not detain him. *(crosses to door)*

FRITZ. Yes, sir. Oh, that laboratory! I've got two loose teeth, and I am afraid I shall lose them, for whenever I go towards that infernal place my head shakes like a dice-box. *(goes to door)* Oh, mercy! what's that? Two shining eyes—how they glisten! Dear, dear, why I declare it's only the cat on the stairs. Puss, puss, pussy! How you frighten'd me, you young *dog*, when you know I am so very nervous!   *Exit* FRITZ

CLERVAL. Frankenstein, friend of my youth, how extraordinary and secret are thy pursuits! how art thou altered by study! Strange, what a hold has philosophy[7] taken of thy mind—but thou wert always enthusiastic and of boundless ambition. But Elizabeth—the fair Elizabeth, his sister—what a difference in disposition! Everyone adores her. Happy Clerval, to be now the possessor of Elizabeth, who, unconscious of her beauty, stole thy heart away!

SONG—CLERVAL

Ere witching love my heart possest,
  And bade my sighs the nymph pursue,
Calm as the infant's smiling rest,
  No anxious hope nor fear it knew.

But doom'd—ah! doom'd at last to mourn,
  What tumults in that heart arose!
An ocean trembling, wild, and torn
  By tempests from its deep repose.

Yet let me not the virgin blame,
  As tho' she wish'd my heart despair,

---

[6]Alchemy was the occult pseudo-science of transmuting base metals to gold; a coiner is a counterfeiter. Finding the elixir of immortality was another project of occult science.

[7]An Enlightenment term for science.

> *How could the maid suspect a flame,*
> *Who never knew that she was fair.*

—But Frankenstein approaches.

Enter FRANKENSTEIN, *thoughtfully,*
shown in by FRITZ, *who exits*

CLERVAL. My dear friend!

FRANKENSTEIN. Clerval!

CLERVAL. Frankenstein, how ill you appear—So pale! You look as if your night-watchings had been long and uninterrupted.

FRANKENSTEIN. I have lately been so deeply engaged in one occupation that I have not allowed myself sufficient rest. But how left you my sister, Elizabeth?

CLERVAL. Well, and very happy, only a little uneasy that she sees you so seldom.

FRANKENSTEIN. Aye; I am engaged heart and soul in the pursuit of a discovery—a grand, unheard-of wonder! None but those who have experienced can conceive the enticement of science; he who looks into the book of nature, finds an inexhaustible source of novelty, of wonder, and delight. What hidden treasures are contained in her mighty volume—what strange, undreamed-of mysteries!

CLERVAL. But some little respite—your health should he considered.

FRANKENSTEIN. *(abstracted)* After so much time spent in painful labour, to arrive at once at the summit of my desires, would be indeed a glorious consummation of my toils.

CLERVAL. How wild and mysterious his abstractions—he heeds me not! *(aside)*

FRANKENSTEIN. *(apart)* This discovery will be so vast, so overwhelming, that all the steps by which I have been progressively led will be obliterated, and I shall behold only the astonishing result.

CLERVAL. Frankenstein!

FRANKENSTEIN. Ha! *(to* CLERVAL*)* I see by your eagerness that you expect to be informed of the secret with which I am acquainted. That cannot be.[8]

CLERVAL. I do not wish to pry into your secrets, Frankenstein. I am no natural philosopher; my imagination is too vivid for the details of

[8]What Frankenstein says to Walton, *Frankenstein* I.III.

science. If I contemplate, let it be the charms of your fair sister, Elizabeth. My message hither now—I wish to fix the day for our nuptials. But we must be certain, on so important and happy an event, that we shall enjoy the society of our Frankenstein.

FRANKENSTEIN. Pardon me, Clerval! My first thoughts should recur to those dear friends whom I most love, and who are so deserving of my love—name the day?

CLERVAL. On the morn after to-morrow, may I lead the charming Elizabeth to the altar?

FRANKENSTEIN. E'en as you will—e'en as you will! *(aside)* The morn after to-morrow—ere that—my wonderful task will be completed. It will be animated! It will live—will think!

(crosses in deep reflection—afterwards turns up the stage)

CLERVAL. *(apart)* Again in reverie! this becomes alarming—surely his head is affected. I am bound in duty to counteract this madness, and discover the secret of his deep reflections. (FRANKENSTEIN *sits down—musing*) Farewell, Frankenstein! He heeds me not—'tis in vain to claim his notice—but I will seek the cause, and, if possible, effect his cure. No time must be lost. Fritz must assist me, and this way he went.

Exit CLERVAL

FRANKENSTEIN. Every moment lost, fevers me. What time have I devoted? *(rises)* Had I not been heated by an almost supernatural enthusiasm, my application to this study would have been irksome, disgusting, and almost intolerable. To examine the causes of life—I have had recourse to death—I have seen how the fine form of man has been wasted and degraded—have beheld the corruption of death succeed to the blooming cheek of life! I have seen how the worm inherits the wonders of the eye and brain—I paused—analysing all the minutiae of causation as exemplified in the change of life from death—until from the midst of this darkness the sudden light broke in upon me! A light, so brilliant and dazzling, some miracle must have produced the flash! The vital principle! The cause of life!—Like Prometheus of old, have I daringly attempted the formation—the animation of a Being! To my task—away with reflection—to my task—to my task!

Exit FRANKENSTEIN. *Enter* CLERVAL *and* FRITZ

[FRITZ. Now he's going to blow up his fire again!

CLERVAL. And thus you say for whole days and nights together, without repose, and almost without food he has immured himself in his study.]

FRITZ. Yes—there he is—amongst otamies and phials and crucibles, and retorts,[9] and charcoal, and fire, and the Devil—for I'm sure he's at the bottom of it, and that makes me so nervous.

CLERVAL. Fritz, you love your master, and are, I know, a discreet servant—but his friends and relations are all unhappy on his account. His health is rapidly sinking under the fatigue of his present labours—will you not assist to call him back to life and to his family?

FRITZ. La! I'd call out all day long, if that would do any good.

CLERVAL. I know his mind has been devoted to abstruse and occult sciences—that his brain has been bewildered with the wild fancies of Cornelius Agrippa, Paracelsus, and Albertus Magnus, and—

FRITZ. Oh! Mr. Clerval! how can you mention such crazy tooth-breaking names? There sounds something wicked in them.

CLERVAL. Wicked? Psha, man! they are the renowned names of the earliest experimental philosophers. The sages who promised to the hopes of the laborious alchymist the transmutation of metals and the elixir of life.

FRITZ. O! Ah! indeed! Lack a daisy me!

CLERVAL. *(aside)* I suspect this fellow is more knave than fool—he wants a bribe. Now, sirrah I answer me with candour. What is it you like best in the world?

FRITZ. Milk!

CLERVAL. Simpleton! I mean what station of life would you covet?

FRITZ. Station?

CLERVAL. Yes. Would you like to be master of a cottage?

FRITZ. What, and keep a cow?—the very thing. Why, Mr. Clerval, you're a conjuror, and know my thoughts by art.[10]

CLERVAL. Fritz, I want to discover—but you must be prudent. *(takes out purse and gives a florin to* FRITZ*)* Here's an earnest of my future intentions touching the cow and cottage.

---

[9]Fritz means "atomies," an archaism for skeletons; retorts are laboratory vessels in which to heat substances.

[10]Dicks' has "by heart," but the variant "by art" makes better (punning) sense.

FRITZ. Bodikins! a florin![11] *(examining money)*

CLERVAL. Friend Fritz, you must some time, when Mr. Frankenstein is absent from home, admit me into his study.

FRITZ. Oh, dear, I can't!—don't take your florin back again sir—*(puts up money)*—for he always locks the door. To be sure, there's a little window a-top of the staircase, where I can see when he puffs up his fire.

CLERVAL. Well, they say the end justifies the means; and in this case I admit the maxim. You can peep through that window, and inform me minutely of what you see.

FRITZ. But what is to become of my nerves?

CLERVAL. Remember your cottage—

FRITZ. And the cow!

CLERVAL. Put me in possession of the secret, and both shall be secured to you. Some one approaches.

FRITZ. Mr. Clerval, I'm your man. I'm nervous, and the devil sticks in my gizzard; but the cow will drive it out again. *(Starts.)* What's that? Oh, nothing—oh, dear, I'm so nervous.

Exeunt FRITZ *and* CLERVAL

SCENE II

*Part of the Villa Residence of Elizabeth, at Belrive—Garden Terrace— Entrance into the House—*WILLIAM *discovered sleeping on a garden bench—During symphony enter* ELIZABETH *from house.*

SONG.—ELIZABETH.

The summer sun shining on tree and on tower,
And gilding the landscape with radiance divine,
May give joy to the heart o'er which pleasure has power,
But eve's pensive beauties are dearer to mine.

Through trees gently sighing, the cool breeze of even
Seems sympathy's voice to the ear of despair;
And the dew-drops (like tears shed by angels of heaven),
Revive the frail hopes in the bosom of care.

(during this scene the stage becomes progressively dark)

[11]Two-shilling coin (one-tenth of a pound); "Bodikins!" ("little body!") is a mild oath.

MADAME NINON. *(within)* William! little William!

ELIZABETH. Where can our little favourite have secreted himself?

Enter MADAME NINON, *from the house*

NINON. Heaven bless Mont Blanc and all the neighbouring hills! Why, where is the boy? How angry shall I be with him for staying out so late.

ELIZABETH. Why, Ninon, assuage your friendly wrath—yonder is William.

NINON. *(goes to child)* Fast asleep, I declare, the pretty boy—how like his poor mother, who is gone. La, La, I daresay my Fritz was just such another, only his hair was red. Pretty William—he was the pin basket.[12] Bless the thirteen cantons[13] I nursed him. William—*(kisses him)*—a pair of gloves, sir![14] *(*WILLIAM *waking)* Fie, you little urchin, sleeping so early this beautiful evening.

WILLIAM *rises; all come forward*

WILLIAM. Indeed, dear Ninon, I know not how I fell asleep; but I rose with the sun, and thinking I would lie down with it, I closed my eyes, and——

NINON. Slumbered like a young dormouse?

ELIZABETH. But, William, you have not neglected your books?

WILLIAM. Oh, no; for then I should not be such a scholar as my elder brother, Victor Frankenstein. *(runs to end of terrace)*

ELIZABETH. Alas, poor Frankenstein! he studies indeed too deeply; but love—blighted love, drove him to solitude and abstruse research.

NINON. Ah, madame, may love make you happy! Mr. Clerval was here this morning, and looked as handsome——

ELIZABETH. Peace, Ninon! And yet, why should I check your cheerfulness? Ninon, I have given orders to my milliner to make you a handsome new cap. When your husband, Fritz, comes from Geneva, he may call and bring it.

NINON. Thank you, dear madam; but see——

Re-enter WILLIAM *from terrace, and runs, crossing behind*

[12]Youngest child.

[13]Swiss states.

[14]Cox explains that to give a judge a pair of gloves was to suggest that he not take his seat of office (ancient custom required judges to "take off their gloves").

WILLIAM. Oh, sister—oh, Madame Ninon! two travellers are coming up the hill—such a beautiful lady—but her guide, I think, has fallen from his horse. See—here's the lady, helping the poor man.

Melo-Music. Enter SAFIE, *supporting the Guide, from terrace*

ELIZABETH. Madame, allow me to offer you assistance.

SAFIE. Thanks—thanks, fair lady; it is not for myself I require rest or help, for I am young. But this aged man, my faithful follower, is completely worn with fatigue.

ELIZABETH. Ninon, see him conveyed into the house. Give him your support, and assist to welcome our guests.

NINON. *(crossing to Guide)* Lean on me, old sir—aye, as heavy as you like; bless you my arm is strong. Come, gently—gently—there— there———

NINON *leads the Guide into house,* WILLIAM *following them. By this time the wing lights are turned off*

SAFIE. I can only weep my thanks, of late I have been unused to kindness.

ELIZABETH. Your garb and manner denote you a stranger here—yet you are acquainted with our language, and you appear to have travelled a great distance.

SAFIE. From Leghorn,[15] a wearisome journey. How far am I distant from the Valley of the Lake?

ELIZABETH. But a few leagues.

SAFIE. Then to-night I probably could reach it? *(animated)*

ELIZABETH. I would not advise the attempt till the morning—the sun is down now; you are distant from any inn; your horses are fatigued; permit me to offer in my house refreshment and repose.

SAFIE. No, no; no repose until my purpose is accomplished. Yet my poor follower needs rest; generous stranger, I gratefully accept your hospitality.

ELIZABETH. And be assured such comfort as Eliza Frankenstein can offer shall be freely yours.

SAFIE. You—you mention the name of Frankenstein!

ELIZABETH. I bear that appellation.

SAFIE. How fortunate! happy chance that brought me to your hospitable door. Know you the family of De Lacey?

---

[15]A city on the northwest Italian coast; in July 1822 Percy Shelley drowned at sea on a return voyage from Leghorn to the Shelleys' seaside residence.

ELIZABETH. I knew it well, but years have elapsed since I have heard of them.

SAFIE. I seek their retreat. Exiled from France, they now exist in the Valley of the Lake.

ELIZABETH. So near, and I not acquainted with their residence! Does the gentle Agatha De Lacey yet live?

SAFIE. To-morrow's morn I trust will find me locked in her embrace.

ELIZABETH. What rapturous news for my dear brother, Frankenstein. Let us in and converse further on this subject, which is of deep interest to me. Night approaches.—hark!—the sweet nightingale is pouring forth its evening melody.

SAFIE. On such a night was I torn from Agatha's brother. Felix, Felix! sad was the moment when you last enfolded poor Safie in your affectionate embrace.

SONG.—SAFIE.

*Each mountain was tinged with the sun's latest beam
Sinking red in the fathomless deep;
The pale watch lights of heaven shed their rays o'er the stream;
And nature seem'd lulled into sleep.
All was silent and hush'd over lake, lawn, and fell,
Save the whisper that breathed I the lover's farewell;
When at Fate's stern command two fond hearts doom'd to sever,
And poor Felix and Safie were parted for ever!*

(exeunt into house)

SCENE III

The sleeping Apartment of Frankenstein. Dark. The Bed is within a recess between the wings, enclosed by dark green curtains. A Sword (to break) hanging. A Large French Window; between the wings a staircase leading to a Gallery across the stage, on which is the Door of the Laboratory above. A small high Lattice in centre of scene, next to the Laboratory Door. A Gothic Table on stage, screwed. A Gothic Chair in centre, and Footstool. Music expressive of the rising of a storm. Enter FRANKENSTEIN, with a Lighted Lamp, which he places on the table. Distant thunder heard.

FRANKENSTEIN. This evening—this lowering evening, will, in all probability, complete my task. Years have I laboured, and at length
discovered that to which so many men of genius have in vain
directed their inquiries. After days and nights of incredible labour
and fatigue, I have become master of the secret of bestowing animation upon lifeless matter. With so astonishing a power in my
hands, long, long did I hesitate how to employ it. The object of
my experiments lies there *(pointing up to the laboratory)*—A
huge automaton in human form.[16] Should I succeed in animating
it, Life and Death would appear to me as ideal bounds, which I
shall break through and pour a torrent of light into our dark
world. I have lost all soul or sensation but for this one pursuit. I
have clothed the inanimate mass, lest the chilly air should quench
the spark of life newly infused. *(thunder and heavy rain heard)*
'Tis a dreary night, the rain patters dismally against the panes; 'tis
a night for such a task. I'll in and attempt the wondrous effort.[17]

> *Music*—FRANKENSTEIN *takes up lamp, cautiously looks around
> him, ascends the stairs, crosses the gallery above, and exits
> into door of laboratory. Enter* FRITZ, *with a candle.*

FRITZ. Master isn't here—dare I peep. Only think of the reward Mr.
Clerval promised me, a cow and a cottage, milk and a mansion.
Master is certainly not come up yet. My candle burns all manner of
colours, and spits like a roasted apple. *(runs against the chair and
drops his light, which goes out)* There, now, I'm in the dark. Oh my
nerves. *(A blue flame appears at the small lattice window above, as
from the laboratory)* What's that? O lauk; there he is, kicking up the
devil's own flame! Oh my cow! I'll venture up—oh my cottage! I'll
climb to the window—it will be only one peep to make my fortune.

> *Music*—FRITZ *takes up footstool, he ascends the stairs, when
> on the gallery landing place, he stands on the footstool tiptoe
> to look through the small high lattice window of the labora-
> tory, a sudden combustion is heard within. The blue flame
> changes to one of a reddish hue.*

[16]This mechanization, a revision of Shelley's imagination of the Creature, inaugurated a
durable tradition of stage and cinematic representations.

[17]Cox] to infuse the spark of life.

FRANKENSTEIN. *(within)* It lives! it lives!

FRITZ. *(speaks through music)* Oh, dear! oh, dear! oh, dear! (FRITZ, *greatly alarmed, jumps down hastily, totters tremblingly down the stairs in vast hurry; when in front of stage, having fallen flat in fright, with difficulty speaks)* There's a hob—a hob-goblin, seven-and-twenty feet high! Oh my nerves; I feel as if I had just come out of strong fits, and nobody to throw water in my face—if my legs won't lap up under me, I'll just make my escape. Oh, my poor nerves!   *Exit* FRITZ, *crawling off*

> *Music—*FRANKENSTEIN *rushes from the laboratory, without lamp, fastens the door in apparent dread, and hastens down the stairs, watching the entrance of the laboratory.*

FRANKENSTEIN. It lives! I saw the dull yellow eye of the creature open, it breathed hard, and a convulsive motion agitated its limbs. What a wretch have I formed, I had selected his features as beautiful—! Ah, horror! his cadaverous skin scarcely covers the work of muscles and arteries beneath, his hair lustrous, black, and flowing,—his teeth of pearly whiteness—but these luxuriances only form more horrible contrasts with the deformities of the monster. *(He listens at the foot of the staircase)* What have I accomplished? the beauty of my dream has vanished! and breathless horror and disgust fill my heart. For this I have deprived myself of rest and health, have worked my brain to madness; and when I looked to reap my great reward, a flash breaks in upon my darkened soul, and tells me my attempt was impious, and that its fruition will be fatal to my peace for ever. *(He listens again)* All is still! The dreadful spectre of a human form—no mortal could withstand the horror of that countenance—miserable and impious being that I am! Elizabeth! brother! Agatha!—fairest Agatha! never more dare I look upon your virtuous faces. Lost! lost! lost!

> *Music.—*FRANKENSTEIN *sinks on a chair; sudden combustion heard, and smoke issues, the door of the laboratory breaks to pieces with a loud crash—red fire within. The* MONSTER *discovered at door entrance in smoke, which evaporates—the red flame continues visible. The* MONSTER *advances forward, breaks through the balustrade or railing of gallery immediately facing the door of laboratory, jumps on the table beneath, and from thence leaps upon the stage, stands in attitude before*

FRANKENSTEIN, *who had started up in terror; they gaze for a moment at each other.*

FRANKENSTEIN. The horrid corpse to which I have given life!

Music—The MONSTER *looks at* FRANKENSTEIN *most intently, approaches him with gestures of conciliation.* FRANKENSTEIN *retreats, the* MONSTER *pursuing him.*

FRANKENSTEIN. Fiend! do not dare approach me—avaunt, or dread the fierce vengeance of my arm.

Music. FRANKENSTEIN *takes the sword from off nail, points with it at* MONSTER, *who snatches the sword, snaps it in two and throws it on stage. The* MONSTER *then seizes* FRANKENSTEIN— *loud thunder heard—throws him violently on the floor, ascends the staircase, opens the large window, and disappears through the casement.* FRANKENSTEIN *remains motionless on the ground.—Thunder and lightning until the drop falls*

ACT II
SCENE I

An apartment in the House of Elizabeth, at Belrive.—Table and chairs. The hurried music from the close of the First Act to play in continuance until this scene is discovered, and FRANKENSTEIN *enters, hastily, to centre of stage. Music ceases.*

FRANKENSTEIN. At length in my sister's house!—and safe! I have paced with quick steps, but at every turn feared to meet the wretch—my heart palpitates with the sickness of fear! [He does not pursue me—dreams that have been my food and pleasant rest for so long a space, are now become a hell to me—the change so rapid, the overthrow so complete—] What have I cast on the world? a creature powerful in form, of supernatural and gigantic strength, but with the mind of an infant. Oh, that I could recall my impious labour, or suddenly extinguish the spark which I have so presumptuously bestowed.—Yet that were murder—murder in its worse and most horrid form—for he is mine—my own formation. Ha! who approaches?

Enter ELIZABETH, *they embrace*

ELIZABETH. My dear Victor! my dear brother!

FRANKENSTEIN. Elizabeth! [My love, how sweet is this embrace—]

ELIZABETH. You are come to stay, I hope, until our wedding is over. Clerval will be here presently. Alas! Frankenstein! your cheek is pallid—your eye has lost its wonted lustre. Oh, Victor, what are the secrets that prey upon your mind and form?—The pernicious air of your laboratory will be fatal to you.

FRANKENSTEIN. *(apart)* Fatal indeed!

ELIZABETH. I pray you, for my sake, cease—I understand upon one subject you have laboured incessantly.

FRANKENSTEIN. One subject! *(aside)* Am I discovered?

ELIZABETH. You change colour, my dear brother. I will not mention it—I—there is a wildness in your eyes for which I cannot account.

FRANKENSTEIN. *(starts)* See—see—he is there!

ELIZABETH. Dearest Frankenstein—what is the cause of this?

FRANKENSTEIN. Do not ask me. I—I thought I saw the dreaded spectre glide into the room.

ELIZABETH. Calm your mind, Victor.

FRANKENSTEIN. Pardon me, Elizabeth. I know not what you will think of me.

ELIZABETH. I have intelligence of one dear to you and for whom, prior to your close attention to study, you had the tenderest regard.— Say, Victor, will you not be glad to hear that I have a clue to lead you to your lost love, Agatha de Lacey!

FRANKENSTEIN. Agatha! dearest Agatha! her name recalls my sinking spirits—where—where is she to be found? Oh, would that I ne'er had been robbed of her! 'Twas her loss that drove me to deep and fatal experiments!

ELIZABETH. A traveller! a beautiful Arabian girl, was here but last night; she was seeking Felix de Lacey, the brother of Agatha, to whom she had been betrothed—she gave me the information that the family are but a short distance from hence—the Valley of the Lake.

FRANKENSTEIN. And Agatha there?—Agatha! there is yet life and hope for me—Ah, no. *(aside)* The dreadful monster I have formed!—away with thought! Elizabeth, I will instantly seek her. Agatha's smiles shall move this heavy pressure—to the Valley of the Lake.—Farewell, sister, farewell!

They embrace, and exeunt ELIZABETH, FRANKENSTEIN

[ELIZABETH *remains*

ELIZABETH. Unfortunate Frankenstein!—what can thus agitate him?—he will not hint the mysterious calamity to his affectionate sister—but he flies now to seek her who possessed his first love, and Agatha will sooth his mind to its former peaceful state—Ah love! All potent love!—If care or misfortune prey on my heart, I have only to think of Clerval, and be happy.—

SONG—ELIZABETH

When evening breezes mildly blow,
　　And all day's tumults cease;
Where streams in gentle murmurs flow;
　　And all around breathes peace—
What shall my pensive mind employ,
　　From ev'rything free?
I'll turn to life's best dearest joy,
　　And think of love and Thee!

When pleasure's smile no longer gleams,
　　And sorrow weighs my breast
When hope withdraws its placid beams
　　I sink with care opprest—
Ah whither shall my heart then turn,
　　To what sweet refuge flee?
With passion's fire then shall burn
　　And throb with love and thee.

(Exit)]

SCENE II

A wood in the neighbourhood of Geneva. A Bush—A Gypsy's fire flaming near, over which hangs a cauldron. A group of Gypsies discovered surrounding the fire in various positions. All laugh as the scene discovers them. When TANSKIN, HAMMERPAN, *with others (male and female) advance to sing the following*

CHORUS

Urge the slow rising smoke,
Give the faggot a poke,
For unroofed rovers are we;
Whilst our rags flutt'ring fly,

We the brown skin espy,
Our vellum of pedigree.
Behold each tawny face
Of our hard-faring race,
Whilst the cold blast ne'er can feel;
See our glossy hair wave,
Hear us, loud, as we crave
But dumb only when we steal!

TANSKIN. I tell you it was even so, friend Hammerpan—a giant creature with something of a human shape; but ugly and terrible to behold as you would paint the Devil.

HAMMERPAN. And does this monster any mischief, or is he a pacific monster?

TANSKIN. I never heard of any being harmed by him.

HAMMERPAN. Then why are you so frightened, Master Tanskin? For my part, should he come across my path, let who will fly, I'll stand my ground like an anvil!

TANSKIN. And get well beat for once for your pains. *(flute heard)* What sounds are those?

HAMMERPAN. *(returning to the fire)* Why, 'tis Felix, the son of old De Lacey. The young fellow is much famed for his excellence upon the flute, as the father for his piety, charities, and twanging on the harp, which, together with the beauty of his daughter, seems to have turned the heads and won the hearts of all the surrounding country. But come, my merry wanderers, our meal is smoking. I'faith, I'm in a rare relishing humour for it, so, prithee, dame, ladle us our porridge. Fegs, it scents rarely! *(sniffs)* Leeks, mutton porridge, with a whole dead sheep in it. *The gipsies crowd round the fire with their bowls*

TANSKIN. *(pointing off)* See there! that's he! that's the tall bully. He looks like the steeple of Ingoldstadt taking a walk. See yonder, comrades!

HAMMERPAN. See what?

TANSKIN. *(trembling)* As I'm a living rogue, 'tis he!

HAMMERPAN. One of the Devil's grenadiers, mayhap! Pooh, pooh! old Tanskin, we all know you are a living rogue, but you won't frighten us with your ten feet. Come, give me a drink, I say. *(One of the gipsies gives him a wooden bowl)* Gentlemen Gipsies, here's all your good—ha! ha! ha!——

Music.—The Monster[18] appears on an eminence of the bush, or a projecting rock

Help! murder! wouns! 'tis the Devil himself! away with the porridge!

Music. HAMMERPAN *and all the Gipsies shriek and run off. The* MONSTER *descends, pourtrays by action his sensitiveness of light and air, perceives the gipsies' fire, which excites his admiration—thrusts his hand into the flame, withdraws it hastily in pain. Takes out a lighted piece of stick, compares it with another faggot which has not been ignited. Takes the food expressive of surprise and pleasure. [A flute is heard, without. The Demon, breathless with delight, eagerly listens. It ceases—he expresses disappointment.] Footsteps heard and the monster retreats behind the rock. Enter* AGATHA, *followed by* FELIX, *his flute slung at his back*

AGATHA. Yes, my dear Felix, our father is anxious for your return. He bade me seek you, and conducted by the mellifluous sounds of your flute, the task was not one of great difficulty. Oh, Felix! how delightful is the reflection that both you and my father possess the skill of banishing for a few moments the horrors of our present misery. In the midst of poverty, how consoling it is to possess such a brother as you are. Dear, thoughtful Felix, the first little white flower that peeped out from beneath the snowy ground you brought, because you thought it would give pleasure to your poor Agatha.

FELIX. We are the children of misfortune—poverty's chilling grasp nearly annihilates us. Our poor blind father, now the inmate of yon cottage—he who has been blessed with prosperity to be thus reduced—the noble-minded old De Lacey. Wretched man that I am, to have been the cause of ruin to both father and sister.

AGATHA. Nay, Felix, we suffered in a virtuous cause! Poor Safie, thy beloved—

FELIX. Is, I fear, lost to me for ever. The treacherous Mahometan, her father, whose escape I aided from a dungeon in Paris (where he was confined as a State prisoner), that false father has doubtless arrived at Constantinople, and is triumphing at the fate of his wretched dupes.

---

[18]Cox] Demon [a tendentious substitution throughout].

AGATHA. Nay, Felix—

FELIX. Alas, Agatha! for aiding that escape, my family—my beloved family—are suffering exile and total confiscation of fortune.

AGATHA. But Safie still loves you?

FELIX. That thought is the more maddening! Safie! fairest Safie!—and she was my promised reward for liberating her faithless father—dragged away with him and forced to comply with his obdurate wishes. Oh, she is lost—lost to me for ever! The early passion of each of us has been blighted, our rigorous imprisonment and sudden banishment have driven all trace of thee from thy admirer, young Frankenstein.

AGATHA. Dear Felix, press not more wretched recollections on my mind. I consider Frankenstein lost to me for ever. In abject poverty, dare I hope that the brilliant and animated student could e'er think of the unfortunate Agatha. *(weeps)* Let me dry these unworthy tears and exert a woman's firmest fortitude. My soul is henceforth devoted exclusively to the service of my poor dark father. Felix, you shall behold me no longer unhappy.

> DUETT—FELIX and AGATHA
> *Of all the knots which Nature ties,*
> *The secret, sacred sympathies,*
> *That, as with viewless chains of gold,*
> *The heart a happy prisoner hold,*
> *None is more chaste—more bright—more pure,*
> *Stronger, stern trials to endure;*
> *None is more pure of earthly leaven,*
> *More like the love of highest heaven,*
> *Than that which binds, in bonds how blest*
> *A daughter to a father's breast.*
>
> *(exeunt* AGATHA *and* FELIX)

Music.—The MONSTER *cautiously ventures out—his mantle having been caught by the bush, he disrobes himself, leaving the mantle attached to the rock; he watches* FELIX *and* AGATHA *with wonder and rapture, appears irresolute whether he dares to follow them; he hears the flute of* FELIX, *stands amazed and pleased, looks around him, snatches at the empty air, and with clenched hands puts them to each ear—appears vexed at his disappointment in not possessing the sound; rushes forward afterwards, again listens, and, delighted with the sound, steals off catching at it with his hands.*

SCENE III

Exterior of the Cottage of Old DE LACEY. *A hovel, with a low door, near which are two or three large logs of wood and a hatchet; a small basket with violets on a stool to the right of the cottage door, and a stool to the left of the cottage, whereon* DE LACEY *is discovered seated, leaning on his cane, a common harp at his side.—Music.*

DE LACEY. Another day is added to the banished life of De Lacey! *(rises and comes forward)* But how will it be passed—like the preceding days—in wretched poverty, hopeless grief, and miserable darkness! *(calls)* Agatha! Felix! Alas! I am alone! Hark! 'tis the flute of Felix!—my children come. They must not suppose me cheerless—my harp is here—'tis a fair deceit on them—my harp which has so oft been damped with the tears from my sightless eyes—the sound of it is the only indication I can give that I am contented with my lot!

> *Music—*DE LACEY *returns to his seat and plays the harp. The* MONSTER *enters, attracted by the harp, suddenly perceives* DE LACEY, *and approaches towards him—expresses surprise by action that* DE LACEY *does not avoid him—discovers his loss of sight, which the* MONSTER *appears to understand by placing his hand over his own eyes, and feeling his way. At the conclusion of the music on the harp—occasioned, as it were, by the* MONSTER *having placed his hand on the instrument—a short pause, and during which the* MONSTER, *having lost the sound, appears to be looking for it, when the harp music is again resumed. In the midst of the music (without ceasing) a voice is heard.*

FELIX. *(within)* This way, Agatha.

> *The* MONSTER, *alarmed, observes the little door of the hovel, which he pushes open, signifies that he wishes for shelter, and retreats into this hovel or wood-house by the ending of the harp music by* DE LACEY, *when*

Enter FELIX *and* AGATHA.

FELIX. *(apart to* AGATHA*)* Observe his countenance, beaming with benevolence and love—behold those silver hairs—and, Agatha, I—I have reduced him to this pitiable state of poverty!

AGATHA. Cease, Felix, this self reproach! *(goes to her father)* We have returned, dear father. Have you wanted us? AGATHA *leads her father forward*

DE LACEY. No, no, Agatha! You anticipate all my wants, and perform every little office of affection with gentleness.

AGATHA. Is it not my duty, and am I not rewarded by your kind smiles?

DE LACEY. Amiable girl, let thy poor father kiss thee. *(they embrace)* Felix, my son, where are you? *(*FELIX *comes forward, and takes his hand)* Now I am cheerful—I am happy!—indeed I am, my children! Let me encourage you to cast off your gloom. What—a tear, Agatha!

AGATHA. Nay, dear sir!

DE LACEY. 'Tis on my hand. *(pressing her hand to his lips, which he had held in his while speaking to* FELIX*)*

[*The* DEMON *appears watching them with attention and interest*]

FELIX. *(assuming gaiety)* Now must I to labour again. Our fuel is nearly exhausted. My time has been lately so occupied I have omitted my task in the forest.

Music.— FELIX *takes up a hatchet and chops a log of wood.*

SAFIE. *(at a distance)* Felix!

AGATHA. What voice was that?

FELIX. It cannot be—no—it was but fancy!

Music resumed.— FELIX *chops the log in continuance—at a similar break in the tune the same voice heard again, nearer*

SAFIE. *(without)* Felix! *(no music)*

FELIX. That magic sound! Alas! no—there is no such happiness in store for me!

SAFIE. *(without, louder)* Felix! Felix!

Music.— FELIX *drops the hatchet, rushes forward.—At the same instant* SAFIE *enters, and falls into the arms of* FELIX

FELIX. 'Tis she!—Safie! Beloved of my soul!—Ah! revive!

DE LACEY. Safie, the traitor's daughter? Impossible!

AGATHA. 'Tis, indeed, our sweet Safie!

FELIX. We never will part more! Father! father! would that you could behold her! It is my dear, lost Safie.

*Music—*SAFIE *revives, and crosses to old* DE LACEY, *kneels, and kisses his hand, during which the* MONSTER *appears at the little hovel, watching them, and then retires within again.*

DE LACEY. Bless you, my child! where is your father—where the treacherous friend who devoted us to ignominy?

SAFIE. I have fled from him; he would have sacrificed his daughter, loathing the idea that I should be united to one of Christian faith. [Sickening at the prospect of again returning to Asia and being immured in a harem—ill suited to the temper of my soul now accustomed to a nobler emulation]—I—I have sought the love and protection of my Felix!

FELIX. Faithful girl! Your constancy shall be crowned by eternal love and gratitude.

AGATHA. But Safie, you are fatigued. Come, dear girl, and on my lowly couch, seek repose.

*Music—*SAFIE *affectionately kisses and presses* DE LACEY's *hand, embraces* FELIX, *crosses back to* AGATHA, *and is led into the cottage by* AGATHA *and* FELIX

FELIX. *(who returns with a gun from the cottage-door)* Father, I am wild with joy!—no longer the sad, pining Felix. The sun of prosperity again gleams on us—Safie has returned! I am rich!—happy! But hold! I must procure refreshment for our guest. Our larder is not too much encumbered with provision. I'll to the village—I'll cross the forest—I'll hunt, shoot—and all in ecstasy! Farewell, father! I'll soon be back. Farewell!

Exit FELIX. *Music.—*

[*The* DEMON *ventures out, and looks with kind expression on* DE LACEY.

DE LACEY. Good Felix! Now, by the return of Safie will his hopes be rewarded—yet must he remain in perpetual poverty and unceasing labour. But this instant, did he complain that our store of fuel was consumed—unless he possessed superhuman strength his day's employment must be double—where are my favorite violets?

Music.—DE LACEY *feels for the Basket which contained them—the* DEMON *appears to comprehend his wish, and rushes off*

DE LACEY. My flower basket not yet replenished.—My dear children amply repay my former anxious care—they have toiled for my support throughout our misfortunes—

Music—The DEMON *re-enters cautiously and tremblingly with a handful of flowers, which he gently places in the basket*

DE LACEY. Thanks dear Agatha!—ever watchful of your poor father's comfort—]

DE LACEY *again seats himself on his cottage stool. Re-enter* MONSTER, *examines log of wood, takes up hatchet, intimating he understands the use of it, and rushes off with the hatchet. Music ceases.*

DE LACEY. Agatha!   *Enter* AGATHA *from cottage*
AGATHA. Did you call, father?
DE LACEY. Sleeps your sweet guest?
AGATHA. Fatigue will soon lull her to repose. I should not have left her had I not thought I heard you call me. [Ah, father, some one has punished my negligence by replenishing your basket of violets.
DE LACEY. Did you not fill, Agatha?
AGATHA. No, dear sir.—Ah, Felix has forestalled me.]

Exit AGATHA *into cottage again;* DE LACEY *rises and takes up the basket of flowers from the stool*

DE LACEY. [No person has been here since the departure of Felix.] *(smelling the violets)* How delightful is the perfume!—more exquisite because I am debarred the pleasure of beholding these sweet emblems of spring! The touch and scent elevate my spirits! How ungrateful am I to complain! In the contemplation of thee, oh, Nature, the past will be blotted from my memory!—the present is tranquil, and the future gilded by bright rays of hope and anticipated joy!

*Music—*DE LACEY *replaces the basket of flowers, and returns to his seat, leaning pensively on his cane.—The* MONSTER *enters with a pile of green faggots with foliage on his shoulders and throws them loosely on the stage.—Smiles with gratulation at* *that which he has accomplished.—Approaches* DE LACEY, *falls flat at his feet, then kneels to him, and is about to press his hand.—*DE LACEY *feels around him with his cane and hand, without the knowledge of anyone being near him, and seated all the time—then calls*

Agatha! Agatha! (*Music—The* MONSTER *instantly retreats into hovel, and* AGATHA *enters from cottage door*)—Agatha, child, I pray you lead me in. (*rises from his seat and comes forward*)
AGATHA. Yes, father. Good Heavens! why, Felix could not have returned from the forest so quickly? What a quantity of wood!
DE LACEY. How?
AGATHA. Here is fuel to last us for a long time. [Surely some kind spirit watches over us—or] how could we have been so bountifully supplied? Come, father, to the cottage—come!

*Music—*AGATHA *leads* DE LACEY *into cottage, afterwards comes forward*

—Frankenstein! vain is the endeavour to drive you from my recollection. Each bird that sings, each note of music that I hear, reminds me of the sweet moments of my former love!

SONG.—AGATHA
(flute accompaniment, behind the scenes)

In vain I view the landscapes round,
  Or climb the highest hill;
In vain, in vain, I listen to the sound
  Of ev'ry murmuring rill.
For vain is all I hear or see,
  When Victor dear is far from me.   *(thrice)*
But hark, hark, hark,
  My love, my love is near,
His well-known dulcet notes I hear. (thrice)

Oh, yes, my love is near,
  I hear him in the grove;
Soon will he be here,
  And breathe soft vows of love.
Oh, fly not yet, ye blissful hours,
  Oh, fly not yet away;

> *While love its soft enchanting pours,*
> *Prolong, prolong your stay!* (thrice)
> *Oh, yes, my love is near,*
> *I hear him in the grove,*
> *Soon will he be here,*
> *And breathe soft vows of love!*

Exit AGATHA *into cottage*

SCENE IV

A Wild Forest. Enter FELIX, *with his gun.*

FELIX. Not a shot yet—and, egad, joy has made my hand so unsteady, that were a fine pheasant to get up, I could not bring it down again. Thy return, sweet Safie, has restored me to existence. When I thought I had lost thee for ever, I was occupied by gloomy thoughts, and neither heeded the descent of the evening star nor the golden sunrise reflected on the lake; but now my love fills my imagination, and all is enjoyment!

SONG—FELIX

> *Thy youthful charms, bright maid, inspire*
> *And grace my fav'rite theme,*
> *Whose person kindles soft desire,*
> *Whose mind secures esteem.*
> *Oh, hear me then my flame avow,*
> *And fill my breast with joy—*
> *A flame which taught by time to grow,*
> *No time can e'er destroy.*
> *My tender suit with smiles approve,*
> *And share the sweets of mutual love.*
>
> *When autumn yields her ripen'd corn,*
> *Or winter, darkening, lowers,*
> *With tenderest care I'll soothe thy morn,*
> *And cheer thy evening hours.*
> *Again, when smiling spring returns,*
> *We'll breathe the vernal air;*
> *And still when summer sultry burns,*
> *To woodland walks repair—*

> *There seek retirement's sheltered grove,*
> *And share the sweets of mutual love.*

FELIX *retires up stage. Enter* FRANKENSTEIN

FRANKENSTEIN. In vain do I seek a respite from these dreadful thoughts—where'er I turn my eyes, I expect to behold the supernatural Being!—to see him spring from each woody recess—but on, on to Agatha, and repose.

FELIX. A traveller! and surely I know his air and manner. *(comes forward)*

FRANKENSTEIN. Good stranger, can you direct me to the habitation of old De Lacey?

FELIX. Better than most persons, I trust.

FRANKENSTEIN. How! Felix De Lacey!

FELIX. The same! the same! Frankenstein! Your hand, my friend—'tis long since we have met!

FRANKENSTEIN. Your strange and sudden disappearance from Paris—

FELIX. Makes as strange a story, with which I shall not now detain you. Come to our humble cottage. Egad! I'm overjoyed to see you!

FRANKENSTEIN. And Agatha?

FELIX. Has still a warm corner of her heart for you. Come, we have only to cross the wood.

[—I'm in high spirits, my friend—I've this day recover'd my mistress—but that will make another strange story.—This is indeed a lucky day—Safie is restored—and I ramble out to kill a Pheasant, and pop upon a philosopher who is likely to become a brother-in-law—]

HAMMERPAN. *(without)* Any good Christians in the neighbourhood?

FELIX. What have we here?

Enter HAMMERPAN, *with a long pole,*
tinker's utensils, fire kettle, &c.

HAMMERPAN. Real Christians! human beings! Oh, good gentlemen, have you seen it?

FELIX. It!—what?

HAMMERPAN. Ah! that's it! As I live, an hour ago, I saw it in the forest!

FELIX. What do you mean by *it?*

HAMMERPAN. My hair stood on end like mustard and cress, and so will yours when you see it!

FELIX. Get you gone! you are tipsy!

HAMMERPAN. I wish I was. As I take it, you are Master Felix, of the Valley of the Lake; we've done business together before now.

FELIX. I know you not!

HAMMERPAN. I mended your kettle t'other day. You did me a good turn—one good turn deserves another—I'll put you on your guard—the very devil is abroad.

FRANKENSTEIN. *(aside)* How!

FELIX. *(laughs)* Ha! ha! ha! You romancing tinker! [—and pray how was his worship dressed?]

HAMMERPAN. [Dress'd—why it was stark undressed all but a cloak.] You may laugh, but the other gentleman don't laugh. You may perceive he believes it. *(to* FRANKENSTEIN*)* I saw it—I saw with this one eye.

FELIX. One eye!

HAMMERPAN. Yes, I'm blind of the other—a little boy threw a pebble at it, so I've been *stone* blind ever since, gentlemen. He was ten foot six long, *(holds his pole high up)* with a head of black lanky locks down to his very elbows.

FRANKENSTEIN. 'Tis the demon! *(apart to himself)*

HAMMERPAN. I lifted up my hammer to strike it but I was so tremulous that I knock'd my own head instead.

FRANKENSTEIN. What did this strange object? *(to* HAMMERPAN*)*

HAMMERPAN. It didn't speak to me, nor I to it. I saw it at first in the forest picking acorns and berries—and then, after it had dispersed our tribe, like a ferret among the rats—it took a drink of our broth, and burnt its fingers in our fire.

FRANKENSTEIN. And what became of this creature?

HAMMERPAN. I wasn't curious enough to inquire. My wife was in fits at the sight of the devil—so I was obliged to keep my one eye upon her.

FELIX. Your one eye has been pretty well employed. Come, come, gipsy, we'll cross the wood, and see if this man mountain is to be met.

HAMMERPAN. The good genius of wandering tinkers forbid!

FELIX. *(to* FRANKENSTEIN*)* And now, my friend, we'll on to the cottage.

FRANKENSTEIN. So, so! *(apart)* I will follow ye!

Exeunt HAMMERPAN *and* FELIX

So! the peasants have already been terrified by the ungainly form! Ambitious experimentalist! The consciousness of the crime I have committed eternally haunts me! I have indeed drawn a horrible curse on my head! He may be malignant, and delight in murder and wretchedness! a whole country may execrate me as its pest! Every thought that bears towards my baneful project causes my lips to quiver and heart to palpitate. I must now to the cottage of Felix. Agatha, fairest Agatha, instead of smiles, your lover will meet you with dark and hopeless despondency!

Exit FRANKENSTEIN

SCENE V

Evening.—Interior of the cottage of DE LACEY.—*The thatched roof in sight. A woodfire.—Through an open rustic porch are visible a rivulet, and small wooden bridge—a wooden couch—Music.*—DE LACEY *discovered seated thereon, with* AGATHA *next to him in attendance. The* MONSTER *appears through the portico, watching them, and regards* AGATHA *with rapture.*— AGATHA *kisses her father's hand, takes a small pail or hand bucket, and trips through the portico on to the bridge to procure water. The* MONSTER *having retreated on* AGATHA*'s approach, pursues her on the bridge.* AGATHA, *turning suddenly perceives the* MONSTER, *screams loudly, and swoons, falling into the rivulet. The* MONSTER *leaps from the bridge and rescues her.*

DE LACEY. *(speaks during the melo-music)* Gracious Heaven! *(starting from the couch)*—that cry of horror! Agatha!—Despair!—My sweet child where art thou? Agatha! Agatha!

The MONSTER *appears at the portico entrance, with* AGATHA *insensible in his arms.—The* MONSTER *comes forward, gently places* AGATHA *in her father's arms, tenderly guiding the hand of old* DE LACEY *to support his daughter.—*

[DE LACEY. My child—cold, cold, and insensible!—this mystery— cruel fate—Dead?—no, no, no, her heart still beats.—Kind Heaven has saved me that pang!—Felix, Felix, where art thou? My dear daughter, for your poor father's sake revive![19]]

AGATHA *recovers, and perceiving the* MONSTER, *with a shriek, faints—The* MONSTER *hovering over them, with fondness.—*

[19]This voice and scene evoke, with a happier outcome (for the De Laceys, anyway), Lear's anguish over his daughter's corpse at the end of *King Lear*.

FELIX, *with his gun (loaded) suddenly enters through the open portico, and speaks whilst entering.*

FELIX. Agatha! Victor Frankenstein is here! What horrid monster is this!—Agatha, my father in danger!

Music—The MONSTER *retreats,* FELIX *following him—discharges his gun and wounds the* MONSTER *in the shoulder—who writhes under the agony of the wound from which the blood flows—would rush on* FELIX, *who keeps the gun presented—he is deterred by fear of a repetition of the wound.* FELIX *remaining on the defensive.—*SAFIE, *alarmed at the firing of the gun by* FELIX, *rushes on to* AGATHA *and* DE LACEY.—*Enter* FRANKEN-STEIN *through the portico. The* MONSTER *rushes up to* FRANKEN-STEIN, *and casts himself at his feet, imploring protection.*

FRANKENSTEIN. Misery! the Fiend! Hence, avoid me! do not approach me—thy horrid contact would spread a pestilence throughout my veins!—hence—no, no! You shall not quit this spot—but thus—thus I destroy the wretch I have created!

Music— FRANKENSTEIN *endeavours to stab him with his dagger, which the* MONSTER *strikes from his hand—and expresses that his kindly feelings towards the human race, have been met by abhorrence and violence; that they are all now converted into hate and vengeance.—In desperation, the* MON-STER *pulls a flaming brand from the fire, and in agony of feeling, dashes through the portico, setting fire to the whole of the portico, and the entire back of the cottage—the thatched roof and rafters.*

FELIX. Ha! Frankenstein! 'tis no time to parley[20]—the cottage is on fire! the fierce gigantic figure of terrific aspect waves aloft his torch, as if in triumph of the deed.

The large doors in the centre are suddenly closed from without, as if to prevent escape. A coarse yelling laugh is heard.

FRANKENSTEIN. Ha! 'tis that hideous voice! Quick, quick, let us fly! his hellish malice pursues me, and but with his death or mine, will this persecution cease. Could I but place you beyond his power.

---

[20]Issue angry speech; state terms to a military enemy.

FELIX *and* FRANKENSTEIN *(as soon as the* MONSTER *disappears, having climbed outside of the portico) force open the doors, when flaming faggots[21] are thrown down at the portico entrance, and falling trees on fire block up the entrance.* FELIX *and* FRANKENSTEIN *place the couch longways over the fallen trees, and fiery pile of faggots at the portico entrance, and* FELIX *forces his way through the flames with old* DE LACEY, *and then* SAFIE—*and, lastly,* FRANKENSTEIN *rushes out, bearing* AGATHA *in his arms over the couch, in the midst of which parts of the building fall. The* MONSTER *brandishing the burning brand on the bridge, laughs exultingly, on which the drop falls. Continue the "Presto music" until end of the Act II.[22]*

ACT III
SCENE I

The Garden of Elizabeth, at Belrive.—Morning. (Same as Act I, Scene II.)

Enter CLERVAL *from terrace entrance.*

CLERVAL. What a delightful morning! It is an auspicious commencement of the day which is to make me happy in the possession of my love! Elizabeth yet sleeps, peaceful be her slumbers! Soft, she approaches.

Enter ELIZABETH *from the house.*

Elizabeth, my love, why that look of anxiety?

ELIZABETH. Oh, Clerval! We have had strange occurrences since you quitted me yesterday, our house is full of guests, my brother has brought here the family of De Lacey of whom you have heard me so often speak——

CLERVAL. The family of De Lacey, the relatives of Agatha.

ELIZABETH. By some extraordinary mystery, which is yet unexplained to me, the cottage in which Frankenstein discovered his mistress

---

[21]Bundles of wood.

[22]Cox] *Music* includes a chorus, joined by "groups of gypsies": "Tell us—tell us—what form was there? / (With anxious fear enquiring) / Saw you its Eye—the hideous glare / Terrific dread inspiring! / The fiend of Sin / With ghastly grin! / Behold the Cottage firing! / Beware! Beware! / The hideous glare, / The fiend of Sin / With ghastly grin— / Behold the cottage firing."

and her family was destroyed by fire; they arrived late last night and all appear overcome with fatigue and terror; some dreadful calamity hangs about my dear brother.

CLERVAL. How astonishing is his conduct. Alas! my sweet Elizabeth, in the midst of all this misery I am selfish—I trust these singular occurrences will not postpone our marriage. Consider, our friends are invited, the church is prepared.

ELIZABETH. A few hours may explain all. See now *(looks towards house)* Frankenstein approaches—observe his agitated countenance and restless step; he has not slept since his return—he has armed himself with pistols and appears continually watching.

CLERVAL. We will retire and avoid him for the present. This way, love.

> *Exeunt* ELIZABETH *and* CLERVAL.
> *Enter* FRANKENSTEIN *from house*

FRANKENSTEIN. Oh! how to avoid the powerful vengeance of the monster formed by my cursed ambition. I gave him energy and strength, to crush my own guilty head! My hours pass in dread, and soon the bolt may fall which will deprive me of existence! [The diabolical act I have committed in raising a being, recurs each moment and conscience stricken—I shudder to think — Agatha! Agatha! gladly would I sacrifice my own life to preserve yours—] Yet *he* preserved the life of Agatha—he had some feeling of affection—how were those feelings requited!—by detestation, scorn, and wounds!—his look of everlasting malice! He will watch with the wiliness of a serpent, that he may sting with its venom! There is no hope but in his destruction. *(takes out pistol)* I dare not cease to guard and protect my friends *(going to the door)* Agatha has arisen. *(conceals pistol) Enter* AGATHA, *a locket round her neck, from the house.*

AGATHA. Frankenstein, I behold you unhappy—flying to solitude—and I cannot help supposing that you might regret the renewal of our intercourse.[23]

[FRANKENSTEIN. Agatha! Can you forgive my cold neglect? At the sight of you, my long smothered passion bursts out anew—but I thought you lost—receive me once again with smiles and bring me back to life and hope.

[23]Affectionate relationship.

AGATHA. These transports ill accord with the heavy gloom which pervades you—]

Dear Frankenstein, I still love you, and confess that in my airy dreams of futurity you have been my constant friend and companion.

FRANKENSTEIN. Agatha, you shall be mine! I will then divulge to you the secret which disturbs—nay, distracts me. (*Music, the Harmonica—Distant bells*) Those cheerful chimes announce the wedding day of Elizabeth and Clerval! My care-worn looks will but damp their merriment.

Music—Exeunt FRANKENSTEIN *and* AGATHA; *enter* FELIX *and* SAFIE *from house*

FELIX. Listen, Safie, to those merry village bells; they ring a rare contrast to our last night's misery. Soon, my Eastern rose, will they chime for us; and then away with care. This kiss—(*embracing her*)

SAFIE. Fie, Felix! In open daylight. You will deepen the blush of your Eastern rose.

DUET.—SAFIE and FELIX

Come with me, dear, to my mountain home,
And Hymen[24] shall hallow the peaceful dome.
Leave all the world for love and for me,
And I will be all the world to thee.
Our life shall be all holiday—
Shall be all holiday.
Come o'er the dew-bespangled vale,
Where the violet blue and primrose pale
Peep from the verdant shade.
Come o'er the dew-bespangled vale,
Where the violet blue and primrose pale,
Where the violet blue and primrose pale
Peep from the verdant shade.
Come o'er the dew, &c., &c.

[24]Greek god of marriage.

> *We'll fly to the shady grove,*
> *And sign and whisper, love*
> *Till day begins to fade,*
> *Till day begins, &c., &c.*
> *We'll roam, and I will woo thee, love,*
> *Where birds sing sweetly through the grove—*
> *Where birds sing sweetly thro' the grove*
> *Till day begins to fade.*
>
> *We'll roam, and I will woo thee, love,*
> *Where birds sing sweetly thro' the grove—*
> *While birds sing, &c., &c., &c.*

Music, with the Bells.—Enter MADAME NINON, *leading a group of Dancing Villagers, from the terrace entrance, and* ELIZA-BETH, *with* CLERVAL, *re-enter*

NINON. Now, Madame Elizabeth—now, Mr. Clerval—we are all ready, and the priest is in waiting.

*Music resumed—*ELIZABETH *and* CLERVAL, *as also* SAFIE *and* FELIX, *join the procession, and all the villagers dance off to music along the terrace, except* MADAME NINON

NINON. There they go to be coupled, pretty dears! (*calls*) Fritz! Fritz! Where is my stupid husband? I've stretched my neck out of joint looking for him. I expect him from the market at Geneva with a cargo of eatables and my new-fashioned beehive cap—all for our wedding festival of Mr. Frankenstein, who has brought his bride and family here in consequence, as I am told, of their cottage being accidentally destroyed by fire last night. Oh! here the fellow comes, with a basket on his back, creeping like a snail.

Enter FRITZ, *from the terrace entrance, with hamper at his back containing various articles, a lady's cap, and a live duck*

FRITZ. Here I am, spousy. I've brought your list of articles. (NINON *assists him in putting down his basket.*) There's the trout, and the sugar-loaf, and the melons, and the nutmegs.

NINON. But dear Fritz, where's my new beehive you were to bring from the milliner's at Geneva?

FRITZ. Somewhere, I know. *(looking and examining the contents of the hamper, cautiously opening the top)* The three live ducks are lying a top of the maccaroni, squeezed up under the large Gruyere cheese.

NINON. I hope to goodness my cap is not squeezed up!

FRITZ. It's quite safe, I tell you. I put it at the very bottom of the basket.

NINON. It will be in a nice state for my head, then!

FRITZ. Lord, here's a rummaging fuss for the cap. I was so nervous about it—you cautioned me so, you know. *(still kneeling and searching the hamper)* Oh, dear, where is it now? Oh, la, to be sure, spousy—here it is at last; la, I knew it was safe. *(he pulls the cap out, with a live duck in it)*

NINON. *(takes her cap from him)* Oh, Fritz, it's spoiled! That duck has been laying in it.

FRITZ. Not an egg, I hope, Ninon!

NINON. Alas! see how it is rumpled. *(She takes from the cap two or three of the duck's small feathers, which fall on the stage)*

FRITZ. *(aside)* Ha!—he! he! Cap and feathers![25]

NINON. You careless, good-for-nothing fellow! take the basket in, you sinner! *(having first replaced her cap in the hamper)*

FRITZ. Oh! *(to the Duck)* You look very jolly, my fine fellow, considering you are going to be killed for dinner. Wait till the peas are ready! I never seen such a piece of *quackery* as that cap in all my life! *(draws the basket after him into the house, and comes forward during the duet)*

NINON. My finery destroyed by that varlet! But even *that* shall not disconcert me. My sweet mistress is united to-day to the man of her heart, and in spite of my loss I will be merry, and dance till I can dance no longer.

DUET—NINON and FRITZ
(Welsh air)

NINON.   *Oh! I'll hail the wedding day,*
           And be the gayest of the gay,
           Till age has tripp'd my steps away.
FRITZ. *(Re-entering from house.)*   *Away!*
NINON.   *Your manners were not taught in France.*

---

[25]A feather in one's cap was a piece of finery.

FRITZ.   *La, wife! you never learnt to dance—*
              A horse at fifty—(Aside)—cannot prance—
                                              Ah, nay!

NINON.   *While pipes and tabors playing sweetly,*
              With all my soul I'll foot it featly,

FRITZ.   *Yes, I guess you'll hobble neatly.*
                                              Wife!

NINON.   *Don't wife me, you saucy fellow!*
              Sure you're tipsy——

FRITZ.   *Only mellow.*
              We'll all be so, for that is fun and life!

TOGETHER. *Don't wife me, you saucy fellow.*
              I won't wife you, I'm only mellow.

NINON.   *I ne'er was tipsy.*

FRITZ.   *You ne'er were tipsy, only mellow.*
                                              Wife!

FRITZ *dances her up to the house,* NINON *turns, boxes his ear,
and they exeunt into house*

Music—The MONSTER *appears from terrace entrance, watching about, and retreats as* FRITZ *re-enters from house*

FRITZ. Oh! *(rubbing his cheek)* What's the use of a fine cap to her?
she's so short, unless she stood on a chair, in a crowd—no one
would see her, or her new-fashioned bee-hive either.

During the above speech, WILLIAM *comes from the house,
behind* FRITZ *on tiptoe, and gives* FRITZ *a smart smack on the
back, who being fearfully alarmed, cries out lustily*

Oh, dear! who's that? There now, that's the way just to make me
nervous again. What do you want, Master William?

WILLIAM. I can't get a soul to speak to me in the house—some are
busy—some are going to be married—will you play with me,
Fritz?

FRITZ. I like a game of play—it's so relaxing. When work was over I
used to play with my cow's calf.

WILLIAM. Do play with me, Fritz.

[FRITZ. Lord, my dear, that's very fatiguing.—What a way you've
thrown it—right among the cauliflowers. (*Music—Goes off.* DEMON
suddenly appears at the railing—watches the CHILD—FRITZ *returns)*

Here it is, Master Willy! There's your ball, William Frankenstein.

WILLIAM. Now again.

FRITZ. La—no—you give me more trouble than your brother used in his laboratory—when he—(WILLIAM *throws the ball behind the balustrade)* I won't fetch it—you may find it yourself—

> DEMON *points to* WILLIAM—*intimating that the boy must be dear to* FRANKENSTEIN

WILLIAM. If you are too idle to go—I'm not—

FRITZ. I shan't look—(WILLIAM *goes to the balustrade.—The* DEMON *suddenly seizes him.)*

WILLIAM. Help! help! help!

FRITZ. Ah—that won't do—that won't do, young master—I'm not to be had—

WILLIAM. Help! help!]

Music.—Dances backwards towards the balustrade of terrace, when the MONSTER, *during the foregoing speeches had been watching the child, then disappearing by falling flat on his face between the balustrades of the terrace, waits the opportunity as* WILLIAM *is tripping backwards, and suddenly seizes the child, throws him across his shoulder (à la Rolla[26]), and rushes off, terrace entrance, to hurried music.* FRITZ, *turning round sees them, utters a cry of horror, and speaks through the music*

FRITZ. Help, help, murder! Wife; the devil! Oh, my nerves!

> *Exit* FRITZ, *frightened, into house*

SCENE II

A Country View. Rustic Church in the distance. A large Yew Tree, spread plentifully with boughs. Music.[27]—A Foreground with pathway behind it. The procession, as before, returning from the marriage

---

[26]Cox notes the reference to a character in Sheridan's adaptation of German playwright Kotzebue's *Pizarro*.

[27]Cox] This scene opens with a "Congratulatory Sestetto" sung by Agatha, Safie, Elizabeth, Felix, Clerval, and a bass: *"Since all to beauty's rip'ning bloom / Their cheerful homage pay, / Be not displeas'd that we presume / To hail thy bridal day. / But if, by Time's all conquering hand, / Thy bloom must wear away, / The roses of thy mind shall stand / And never more decay."*

ceremony. The corps de ballet, Villagers, preceding, dancing, followed by FELIX, SAFIE, CLERVAL, *and* ELIZABETH.

NINON. *(heard without)* Oh, mistress! Oh!

FRITZ. I couldn't help it—murder! *Enter* NINON *and* FRITZ

NINON. But where did you leave him?

FRITZ. He left me—Oh dear—*(cries)* Murder! My nerves!

NINON. Oh, wicked Fritz![28]

ELIZABETH. What is the matter, good Ninon?

FRITZ. She says her husband's wicked.

NINON. *(to* ELIZABETH*)* William, your brother William is the matter; the boy is lost. No one can find him. I sent him to that Fritz, that he might be out of the way.

FRITZ. Yes; and now he's out of everybody's way.

ELIZABETH. This is most extraordinary—a frolic of the little rogue.

FRITZ. No, no, it isn't; I saw—my nerves! Oh, dear! I saw—a great something snatch him up. *(cries)* I—oh!—oh—dear! Murder!

CLERVAL. There's Frankenstein.

Enter FRANKENSTEIN, *with a pistol*

ELIZABETH. My dear Victor, know you aught of William? The child has been missed in a most unaccountable manner.

FRANKENSTEIN. My brother missing!

NINON. Fritz was with him.

FRITZ. Oh, master! a great creature—oh! oh! oh!

FRANKENSTEIN. Oh, horror!—the demon!

CLERVAL. Hasten, my friends, one and all—all search. Our pastime is marr'd till the boy is found.

> *Music—All exeunt in consternation at different entrances, excepting* FRANKENSTEIN, *who appears lost in desponding reveri.—He turns; the boughs of the yew tree are pulled apart, and the* MONSTER *is discovered behind it, with* WILLIAM *in his grasp—* FRANKENSTEIN *draws a pistol, and points it—the* MONSTER *holds forth the child, when* FRANKENSTEIN *lowers his pistol, and kneels—The* MONSTER *again shoulders the child, and rushes off within the path—* FRANKENSTEIN *rises, and pursues them in despair*

[28]Cox] Oh wretched fate!

SCENE III

An Apartment in the Villa at Belrive.—A wide folding window open-
ing to the Garden, closed. A table with red baize covering. AGATHA
and NINON *enter.*

NINON. The most unaccountable disappearance of my dear little boy,
at such a moment—on such a day—when we should have been so
merry!

AGATHA. It is indeed strange and fearful; let us hope that William will
soon be discovered, and brought home. *(aside)* The wild phantom
that fired our cottage, surely, is not concerned.[29]

NINON. I can do nothing but think of William—that is your room,
ma'am—*(points)*—you will find it well furnished—with such sweet
blue eyes—everything is comfortable—unhappy little boy! There's
a fine grate in the room—with two little dimples on each cheek!
There's a cabinet in the corner—curly locks! Forgive me, ma'am; I
fostered the pretty child, and I cannot get him out of my head.

AGATHA. Pray leave me, Ninon, and give me the earliest intelligence
of Mr. Frankenstein's return.

NINON. All the festivities of the wedding-day destroyed, till the dear
unlucky urchin is found. *(sobbing)* The sweet little, naughty,
rosy-cheek'd rogue! how I will whip him when he comes home.

> *Exit* NINON. *During the above the* MONSTER *is*
> *seen at the window watching, and disappears*

AGATHA. Frankenstein! what a singular fatality is attached to you—
with wealth and friends, doomed to be miserable!—This mystery!—I feel a heavy foreboding of mischance! a presentiment of
evil pervades my mind. I may regret the day that I have given my
affection to Frankenstein—I may rue the hour that I left our
homely hut.

> *Exit* AGATHA *to Room. Afterwards, enter*
> FRANKENSTEIN, *reflecting—two pistols in his belt*

FRANKENSTEIN. One sudden and desolating change has taken place—
the fangs of remorse tear my bosom and will not forgo their
hold!—pursue the wretch! One might as well attempt to overtake

[29]Involved.

the winds, or confine a mountain torrent. My poor brother—I—I am thy murderer—the author of unalterable evils There is scope for fear, so long as anything I love remains. *(goes to door)* Agatha! she reclines sleeping on yon sofa.

> *The* MONSTER *during the above soliloquy reappears on the balcony of the window—and while* FRANKENSTEIN *is looking in at the door, the* MONSTER *creeps in at the window, crouching beneath the table, unseen*

Sleep on, sweet innocence! I dare not leave you; I will stay and guard your slumber, or the remorseless fiend will snatch your breath away. *(Music—* FRANKENSTEIN *takes out a pistol and primes it—lays it on the table)* The wretch ev'n now may be haunting the room—let me search around.

> *Music—*FRANKENSTEIN *fearfully examines each avenue—The* MONSTER, *unperceived by him, follows his footsteps, making an ineffectual attempt occasionally to gain his loaded pistol.* FRANKENSTEIN *leads on, looking in at door, passes behind table, when the* MONSTER *falls flat before table, still unseen by* FRANKENSTEIN, *who then places the loaded pistol on table, and turns to close the folding large window. While* FRANKENSTEIN *has his back turned, the* MONSTER *snatches up the pistol, hugs it, and escapes into door.* FRANKENSTEIN *having closed the window comes forward*

Oh, Agatha! would that I had banished myself for ever from my native country, and wandered a friendless outcast over the earth, rather than I had again met you—perhaps to bring you in the grasp of my fiendish adversary—perhaps to—— *(pistol shot heard, and a piercing scream)*—My blood curdles! that shriek! *(goes to door)* Ah! What do I behold! My last, last hope!

> *Music—He rushes off into door*

> [*In the large glass—*AGATHA *appears on her knees with a veil over her head.—The* DEMON *with his hand on her throat—she falls—the* DEMON *disappears after tearing a locket from* AGATHA'*s neck. The figure of* FRANKENSTEIN *appears in the glass, kneeling over the body of* AGATHA. *The* DEMON *crosses by the window in a boat with great swiftness—exulting*]

SCENE IV

An Ante-chamber in Belrive. Enter ELIZABETH, *hastily, meeting* NINON.—*Music ceases.*

ELIZABETH. Whence is this fresh alarm?

NINON. I know not madam. Oh, wretched day for poor Ninon! Mr. Frankenstein is stark mad; he ran but out this instant, jumped into his boat, and rowed off rapidly.   *Enter* FRITZ, *alarmed*

FRITZ. Oh, oh, oh!—I've seen it—seen it again! The great creature, it got out of one of our windows and scudded off in a boat, and there's Mr. Frankenstein got another boat, and is going after the great creature like lightning.

ELIZABETH. Where—where are our friends?

FRITZ. Oh, I don't know; there's Mr. Frankenstein gone after the great creature, Mr. Clerval and Mr. Felix have gone after Mr. Frankenstein, and I'm going after them all.

SAFIE. (*without*) Help! ah, help!

   Enter SAFIE, *crosses to* ELIZABETH, *and throws herself into her arms*
      Ah, Madam! Agatha, my sister—the gentle Agatha—I fear, is no more!

OMNES.[30] Agatha!

ELIZABETH. Gracious Heaven! what horrible destiny hangs over us?

SAFIE. Stretched on the ground she lies! [a livid mark on her neck!] Ah! Elizabeth, the spark of life may yet not be extinct.

ELIZABETH. Hasten—hasten to the apartment.

Hurried music. Exeunt hastily ELIZABETH, SAFIE, *and* MADAME NINON

SCENE V

Wild Border of the Lake. At the extremity of the stage, a lofty overhanging mountain of snow. Music.—All the GIPSIES *discovered in various groups.*

   A pistol shot is heard. The GIPSIES *start up alarmed. A second pistol is fired nearer. The* MONSTER *rushes on with the locket worn by* AGATHA, *during the piece. The* GIPSIES *scream out and fly in all directions.* HAMMERPAN *is the verge of escaping, when the* MONSTER *seizes him and* HAMMERPAN *falls down on being dragged back. The* MONSTER *points off stage, to intimate that* FRANKENSTEIN

[30](Latin): All.

is approaching, throws down the locket, commands the gipsy, HAMMERPAN, to show it to FRANKENSTEIN—*the* MONSTER *threatens him, and rushing up the mountain, climbs, and disappears*

Enter FRANKENSTEIN, *with two loaded pistols and a musket unloaded. At the same time* HAMMERPAN *rises and gets near stage wing*

FRANKENSTEIN. In vain do I pursue the wretch, in vain have I fired on him. (*throws his gun from him*) He eludes the bullet. Say, fellow, have you seen aught pass here?

HAMMERPAN. The giant creature, who aroused us in the forest, rushed upon me but this instant, and pointing to the path by which you came, intimated that I should give you this. (*presents locket to* FRANKENSTEIN)

FRANKENSTEIN. 'Tis Agatha's—the murdered Agatha! Malicious fiend! it will joy you to know that my lacerated heart bleeds afresh. Revenge shall henceforth be the devouring and only passion of my soul. I have but one resource—I devote myself either in my life or death to the destruction of the Demon. Agatha! William! you shall be avenged.

HAMMERPAN. See yonder (*points*) the monster climbs the snow.

FRANKENSTEIN. Then this rencontre[31] shall terminate his detested life or mine.

> *Music*—FRANKENSTEIN *draws his pistol—rushes off at back of stage—The gipsies return at various entrance—At the same time, enter* FELIX *and* CLERVAL *with pistols, and* SAFIE, ELIZABETH, *and* NINON *following—The* MONSTER *appears at the base of the mountain,* FRANKENSTEIN *pursuing*

CLERVAL. Behold our friend and his mysterious enemy.

FELIX. See—Frankenstein overtakes him—let us follow and assist him. (*is going up stage with* CLERVAL)

HAMMERPAN. Hold, master! if the gun is fired, it will bring down a mountain of snow. Many an avalanche has fallen there.

> *Music*—FRANKENSTEIN *discharges his pistol.—The* MONSTER *and* FRANKENSTEIN *meet at the very extremity of the* FRANKENSTEIN *fires his second pistol—the avalanche falls and annihilates the* MONSTER *and* FRANKENSTEIN—*A heavy fall of snow succeeds—Loud thunder heard, all the characters form a picture as the curtain falls*

END

---

[31]A "re-encounter" of enemies, a battle.

Reviews and Reactions

"I expected this reception," is the first utterance of Frankenstein's abject Creature. What no one expected was a reception across decades, across centuries. *Frankenstein* has not only refused to go out of print but has also spawned a ceaseless cultural life of sequels, films, plays, parodies, and commercial kitsch, as well as a nearly automatic lexicon for new developments in science, technology, and culture.

Reflecting the reception dynamics inside the novel—its nested frames of tale-reading, tale-telling, tale-listening, and reaction—the initial reception took *Frankenstein* itself as a decidedly monstrous creation. Victor virtually writes the book on horrific communication when he confesses to his new bride, "I have one secret, Elizabeth, a dreadful one; when revealed to you, it will chill your frame with horror, and then, far from being surprised at my misery, you will only wonder that I survive what I have endured." After that embodied secret pops between the election and these nuptial hopes, to murder the intimate confidant, he spills his tale to the local magistrate, who reacts (so Frankenstein reports) the way readers of *Frankenstein* might:

> It is indeed a tale so strange, that I should fear you would not credit it, were there not something in truth which, however wonderful, forces conviction. The story is too connected to be mistaken for a dream. (III.VI; p. 157)

On the same page as the first reviewers, "the magistrate appeared at first perfectly incredulous." Frankenstein tracks the sequel: "as I continued he became more attentive and interested; I saw him sometimes shudder with horror, at others a lively surprise, unmingled with disbelief" and overall, "with that half kind of belief that is given to a tale of spirits and supernatural events" (p. 157). When Frankenstein's last lifetime auditor (recorder, and designated textual executor), Robert Walton, conveys the tale to his sister, he reiterates, with press-agent perfection, the rhetoric, genre, and effect: "You have read this strange and terrific story, Margaret; and do you not feel your blood congealed with horror?" (letter of 26 August 17—, p. 165).

"Do you not . . . ," as if any other feeling were unimaginable! The magistrate's qualified attention—a "half kind" of belief that tilts into incapacity for disbelief—exceeds even Samuel Taylor Coleridge's theory of literary power. It is no coincidence that one of Coleridge's own ventures into the supernatural, *The Rime of the Ancient Mariner*, is cited more than once in *Frankenstein*, or that its conceptual twin, *Christabel*, published in May 1816, was recited with similar horrific effect to the summer company at Byron's villa. Describing the impulse behind both these tales the next year, Coleridge explains his creative fascination with "incidents and agents . . . in part at least, supernatural"—not for the exotic recreation, but as an experiment in

> the dramatic truth of such emotions, as would naturally accompany such situations, supposing them real . . . so as to transfer from our inward nature a human interest and semblance of truth sufficient to procure for these shadows of imagination that willing suspension of disbelief for the moment, which constitutes poetic faith.[1]

Within the novel, the Creature is just such a shadow-imagination embodied into a truth that refuses disbelief. *Frankenstein* solicits the public imagination to poetic faith.

But not without a price. This new species of novel was said to be an unnatural, even impious conception. At the very least, its tale was so "improbable" as to defy the preferred value of the novel in providing moral instruction from a plausible representation of life in the world. Some stated the case directly: the novel was a monster, a "tissue of horrible and disgusting absurdity . . . embodied in the strong and striking language of the insane," warned Murray's *Quarterly*. "Strong and striking" might be praise, but here it's a caution. Even if

---

[1]*Biographia Literaria* (1817), Ch. 14 (*The Longman Anthology of British Literature*, vol. 2a [2006], p. 634). *The Rime of the Ancyent Marinere* led off the 1798 *Lyrical Ballads*. *Christabel* was designed for this project, but Wordsworth rejected it; although known in manuscript and from recitation, it was not until 1816 (with Byron's support) that it was published by John Murray.

Scot's *Edinburgh* could note some "power and beauty," it deemed much else as mangled as Victor Frankenstein's misbegotten creation: "the execution is imperfect, and bearing the marks of an unpractised hand," a confabulation of "hazardous innovations" shockingly, revoltingly, in violation of "the established order of nature as it appears, both in the world of matter and of the mind." *British Critic* expanded the indictment to the author's "diseased and wandering imagination, which has stepped out of all legitimate bounds, to frame these disjointed combinations and unnatural adventures." The deviant author was a Frankenstein and the novel a monster.

This monstrosity reverberated with the extraordinary times. Having judged *Frankenstein* "the most outrageous improbability," Scot's *Edinburgh* admitted a contradiction: "There never was a wilder story imagined, yet, like most of the fictions of this age, it has an air of reality attached to it, by being connected with the favourite projects and passions of the times. The real events of the world have, in our day, too, been of so wondrous and gigantic a kind. . . ." By these lights, *Frankenstein* was swelling a progress on a historical stage already, and amply, filled with things wondrous and gigantic. Scot's *Edinburgh* had intuited what would become the routine invocation of Shelley's fable, as recently as yesterday, to describe any incredible development in science boding peril to our present safety and our human future.

The last pages of *Frankenstein*, sub-headed "Walton, *in continuation*" (p. 165), could not be more aptly tuned to this reception. "Walton disappears 'in continuation' never to return in proper (or signatory) persona," notes critic Garrett Stewart; what happens instead is that "his transcriptive role" gets "absorbed by the reading audience's own reactions." In this absorption (at once transfer and rapture), Shelley generates a reader and a culture of reading. What *Frankenstein* "takes from the discourses of its culture," adds Stewart, must be "correlated with what the narrative sends back into cultural circulation through the very form of its own discourse."[2] *Frankenstein* has prospered in this reflex. To put this another way, Shelley created not just a novel but a myth, in two contrary senses of myth: a foundational fable of cultural knowledge; an imaginary fiction. From this double generativity, *Frankenstein* issues a double-progeny: it is a cautionary tale about scientific egotism and failed social ethics;

---

[2]"In the Absence of Audience: Of Reading and Dread in Mary Shelley," pp. 117–18.

but it is also a complex imagination of conflicts and contradictions. *Frankenstein* continues to fascinate us with the transgressions that literature can entertain, and which, as Coleridge proposed the year after it was published, it is the power of literary imagination *to* entertain.

[John Wilson Croker], *Quarterly Review* 18 (January 1818): 379–85

The Quarterly, *published by John Murray and edited by William Gifford, was one of the most powerful, influential reviews, with a Tory-establishment orientation and the patronage of Church and Court. Among regular contributors were Walter Scott, Robert Southey, and the famously caustic John Wilson Croker. Murray, also Byron's publisher, had been approached by Percy Shelley about publishing* Frankenstein. *When he declined, Mary wrote to Percy, "Of course Gifford did not allow this courtly bookseller to purchase F" (29 May 1817; Letters 1.36). The January 1818* Quarterly *also included an attack (by John Taylor Coleridge) on Leigh Hunt (pp. 324–35), with some thinly veiled jibes at Percy Shelley's pamphlet on atheism. Croker undertook the review of* Frankenstein *(unsigned, a practice meant to convey a corporate opinion) after Scott accepted the same assignment for* Blackwood's. *Percy Shelley was braced for disaster, fearing the novel would suffer the fate of its Creature. Amidst reports of praise elsewhere, he told a friend, "I hear that poor Mary's book is attacked most violently in the* Quarterly review*" (25 July 1818). After the review appeared, he reported to another friend: "*Frankenstein *seems to have been well received; for although the unfriendly criticism of the* Quarterly *is an evil for it, yet it proves that it is read in some considerable degree, and it would be difficult for them, with any appearance of fairness, to deny it merit altogether." By August, Percy Shelley heard from this same friend that at the Egham races he had been asked by a great number of his acquaintances "a multitude of questions concerning* Frankenstein *and its author. It seems to be universally known and read." While Croker used the novel as an occasion for satire, making it seem a kind of farce, he grasped one serious ethical issue in calling the Creature "Frankenstein's hopeful son" as it acquires an education at the De Lacey household.*

Frankenstein, a Swiss student at the university of Ingolstadt, is led by a peculiar enthusiasm to study the structure of the human frame, and to attempt to follow to its recondite sources "the stream of animated being." In examining the causes of *life*, he informs us, antithetically, that he had first recourse to *death*.—He became acquainted with anatomy; but that was not all; he traced through vaults and charnel-houses the decay and corruption of the human body, and whilst engaged in this agreeable pursuit, examining and analyzing the minutiae of mortality, and the phenomena of the change from life to death and from death to life, a sudden light broke in upon him—

[quotes from Volume I, Chapter III]

Having made this wonderful discovery, he hastened to put it in practice; by plundering graves and stealing, not bodies, but parts of bodies, from the church-yard: by dabbling (as he delicately expresses it) with the unhallowed damps of the grave, and torturing the living animal to animate lifeless clay, our modern Prometheus formed a filthy image to which the last step of his art was to communicate being:—for the convenience of the process of his animal manufacture, he had chosen to form his figure about eight feet high, and he endeavoured to make it as handsome as he could—he succeeded in the first object and failed in the second; he made and animated his giant; but by some little mistake in the artist's calculation, the intended beauty turned out the ugliest monster that ever deformed the day. The creator, terrified at his own work, flies into one wood, and the work, terrified at itself, flies into another. Here the monster, by the easy process of listening at the window of a cottage, acquires a complete education: he learns to think, to talk, to read prose and verse; he becomes acquainted with geography, history, and natural philosophy, in short, "a most delicate monster."[1] This credible course of study, and its very natural success, are brought about by a combination of circumstances almost as natural. In the aforesaid cottage, a young *Frenchman* employed his time in teaching an *Arabian* girl all these fine things, utterly unconscious that while he was

"whispering soft lessons in his fair one's ear,"

he was also tutoring Frankenstein's hopeful son. The monster, however, by due diligence, becomes highly accomplished: he reads Plutarch's Lives, Paradise Lost, Volney's Ruin of Empires, and the Sorrows of Werter. Such were the works which constituted the Greco-Anglico-Germanico-Gallico-Arabic library of a Swabian hut,

---

[1]The creature Caliban in Shakespeare's *The Tempest* (2.2).

which, if not numerous, was at least miscellaneous, and reminds us, in this particular, of Lingo's famous combination of historic characters—"Mahamet, Heliogabalus, Wat Tyler, and Jack the Painter."[2] He learns also to decypher some writings which he carried off from the laboratory in which he was manufactured; by these papers he becomes acquainted with the name and residence of Frankenstein and his family, and as his education has given him so good a taste as to detest himself, he has also the good sense to detest his creator for imposing upon him such a horrible burden as conscious existence, and he therefore commences a series of bloody persecutions against the unhappy Frankenstein—he murders his infant brother, his young bride, his bosom friend; even the very nursery maids of the family are not safe from his vengeance, for he contrives that they shall be hanged for robbery and murder which he himself commits.

The monster, however, has some method in his madness:[3] he meets his Prometheus in the valley of Chamouny, and, in a long conversation, tells him the whole story of his adventures and his crimes, and declares that he will "spill more blood and become worse," unless Frankenstein will *make* (we should perhaps say *build*) a wife for him: the Sorrows of Werter had, it seems, given him a strange longing to find a Charlotte, of a suitable size, and it is plain that none of Eve's daughters, not even the enormous Charlotte of the Variétés herself, would have suited this stupendous fantoccino.[4] A compliance with this natural desire his kind-hearted parent most reasonably promises; but, on further consideration, he becomes alarmed at the thoughts of reviving the race of Anak,[5] and he therefore resolves to break his engagement, and to defeat the

---

[2]Swabia is a region of southwest Germany. Lingo is a character in Samuel Foote's play *The Agreeable Surprize*, the role constituting the London debut in 1803 of popular stage comedian Charles Mathews. Mahamet is Muhammad, the prophet of Islam; Heliogabalus was a notoriously eccentric decadent Roman emperor of the 3rd c. Wat Tyler led the Peasants Revolt of the late 14th c. and was the subject of a drama by Robert Southey (before he became Poet Laureate). Jack the Painter was John Aitken, alias James Hill, alias James Hinde, alias James Actzen, a thief, renegade, and traitor to England in the American War, who was hanged at Portsmouth on 10 March 1777.

[3]Of Hamlet's eccentric behavior, his father's advisor Polonius correctly surmises, "though this be madness, yet there is method in't" (*Hamlet* 2.2.207–8).

[4]In the parody of Werter, at the Variétés in Paris, the Charlotte is ludicrously corpulent. [Croker's note; referring to a staged version of *The Sorrows of Young Werter*, a popular novel by Goethe, which the Creature reads.]

[5]The race of Anak (the Anakim) are giants or their descendants, mentioned in various books of the Old Testament.

procreative propensities of his ungracious child—hence great wrath and new horrors—parental unkindness and filial ingratitude. The monster hastens to execute his promised course of atrocity, and the monster-maker hurries after to stab or shoot him, and so put an end to his proceedings. This chase leads Frankenstein through Germany and France, to England, Scotland, and Ireland, in which latter country, he is taken up by a constable called Daniel Nugent, and carried before Squire Kirwan a magistrate, and very nearly hanged for a murder committed by the monster. We were greatly edified with the laudable minuteness which induces the author to give us the names of these officers of justice; it would, however, have been but fair to have given us also those of the impartial judge and enlightened jury who acquitted him, for acquitted, as our readers will be glad to hear, honourably, acquitted, he was at the assizes of Donegal.—Escaped from this peril, he renews the chase, and the monster, finding himself hard pressed, resolves to fly to the most inaccessible point of the earth; and, as our Review had not yet enlightened mankind upon the real state of the North Pole, he directs his course thither as a sure place of solitude and security; but Frankenstein, who probably has read Mr. Daines Barrington and Colonel Beaufoy on the subject,[6] was not discouraged, and follows him with redoubled vigour, the monster flying on a sledge drawn by dogs, according to the Colonel's proposition, and Prometheus following in another—the former, however, had either more skill or better luck than the latter, whose dogs died, and who must have been drowned on the breaking up of the ice, had he not been fortunately picked up in the nick of time by Mr. Walton, the master of an English whaler, employed on a voyage of discovery towards the North Pole. On board this ship poor Frankenstein,

[6]With an address to the Royal Society in 1773 advancing the open polar sea theory (to which Robert Walton subscribes), Daines Barrington, a judge and member of the Royal Society with an amateur passion for geology, antiquities, and polar geography, got the Admiralty interested in polar exploration (which had been privately funded). Colonel Beaufoy reprinted Barrington's papers on polar matters in 1818. Sir John Barrow, Second Secretary to the Admiralty and frequent contributor to the *Quarterly*, wrote several articles on polar exploration, one in this same issue. Croker, First Secretary to the Admiralty, did not participate in this enthusiasm, wryly suggesting that if the Creature had been apprised of the open sea theory, he would not have depended on escape across ice. J. T. Coleridge's article on Hunt included a snide reference to a polar expedition of 1818, wishing that Leigh Hunt's verses could be among "the stores of the Dorothea and Isabella, if, in spite of our hopes and predictions, they should chance to be frozen up in the polar basin" (334); the *Dorothea* was the flagship, captained by David Buchan.

after telling his story to Mr. Walton, who has been so kind to write it down for our use, dies of cold, fatigue, and horror; and soon after, the monster, who had borrowed (we presume from the flourishing colony of East Greenland) a kind of raft, comes alongside the ship, and notwithstanding his huge bulk, jumps in at Mr. Walton's cabin window, and is surprized by that gentleman pronouncing a funeral oration over the departed Frankenstein; after which, declaring that he will go back to the Pole, and there burn himself on a funeral pyre (of ice, we conjecture) of his own collecting, he jumps again out the window into his raft, and is out of sight in a moment.

Our readers will guess from this summary, what a tissue of horrible and disgusting absurdity this work presents.—It is piously dedicated to Mr. Godwin, and is written in the spirit of his school. The dreams of insanity are embodied in the strong and striking language of the insane, and the author, notwithstanding the rationality of his preface, often leaves us in doubt whether he is not as mad as his hero. Mr. Godwin is the patriarch of a literary family, whose chief skill is in delineating the wanderings of the intellect, and which strangely delights in the most affecting and humiliating of human miseries. His disciples are a kind of *out-pensioners of Bedlam*, and, like "Mad Bess" or "Mad Tom," are occasionally visited with paroxysms of genius and fits of expression, which makes sober-minded people wonder and shudder.

We shall give our readers a very favourable specimen of the vigour of fancy and language with which this work is written, by extracting from it the three passages which struck us the most on our perusal of it. The first is the account of the animation of the image. [quotes I.IV, from its opening to ". . . so miserably given life."]

The next is a description of the meeting in the valley of Chamouny. [quotes II.II, from "It was nearly noon when I arrived at the top of the ascent" to "furious detestation and contempt."]

The last with which we shall agitate the nerves of our readers is Captain Walton's description of the monster he found in his cabin. [quotes the last letter, from "Great God! what a scene has just taken place!" (changing the oath to "O!") to "The monster continued to utter wild and incoherent self-reproaches."]

It cannot be denied that this is nonsense—but it is nonsense decked out with circumstances and clothed in language highly terrific: it is, indeed,

—————————"a tale
Told by an ideot, full of sound and fury,
Signifying nothing—"[7]

but still there is something tremendous in the unmeaning hollowness of its sound, and the vague obscurity of its images.

But when we have thus admitted that Frankenstein has passages which appal the mind and make the flesh creep, we have given it all the praise (if praise it can be called) which we dare to bestow. Our taste and our judgement alike revolt at this kind of writing, and the greater the ability with which it may be executed the worse it is—it inculcates no lesson of conduct, manners, or morality; it cannot mend, and will not even amuse its readers, unless their taste have been deplorably vitiated—it fatigues the feelings without interesting the understanding; it gratuitously harasses the heart, and wantonly adds to the store, already too great, of painful sensations. The author has powers, both of conception and language, which employed in a happier direction might, perhaps, (we speak dubiously,) give him a name among these whose writings amuse or amend their fellow-creatures; but we take the liberty of assuring him, and hope that he may be in a temper to listen to us, that the style which he has adopted in the present publication merely tends to defeat his own purpose, if he really had any other object in view than that of leaving the wearied reader, after a struggle between laughter and loathing, in doubt whether the head or the heart of the author be the most diseased.

[Walter Scott], *Blackwood's Edinburgh Magazine* 12 (March 1818): 613–20

A frequent reviewer for the Quarterly *and* Blackwoods, *Scott was best known as a novelist.* Waverly *(1814),* Old Mortality *(1816),* Rob Roy *(1817),* The Heart of Midlothian *(1818), and* Ivanhoe *(1819), were published unsigned, although his identity was an open secret. These works were a major force in raising the status of the novel (regarded as a low-culture genre) and set the pattern for historical fiction in the*

[7]*Macbeth* 5.5.26–28; Macbeth's sense of life.

nineteenth century. Scott had given an admiring review in the Quarterly
to Jane Austen's Emma *(1815). Hoping for his notice, the Shelleys sent
him* Frankenstein *on publication, Percy indicating that he was acting on
behalf of a friend. Scott was not alone in taking him to be the author.*

Blackwood's *was founded in 1817 as a Tory-conservative rival to the
Whig-liberal monthly, the* Edinburgh Review. *Popularly called Maga, it
became infamous for attacks, inaugurated in 1817 and signed "Z.," on
"The Cockney School" of poets and essayists (suburban Londoners Leigh
Hunt, John Keats, William Hazlitt) and later, by force of political and moral
censure, Byron and Shelley. Scott's own enthusiasms were less predictable,
and his influence was considerable: announced in the February issue, this
review of* Frankenstein, *unsigned, headed the March 1818 issue, and was
almost immediately quoted by the publishers in their advertisement in the*
Morning Chronicle. *Mary Shelley wrote Scott to thank him warmly for the
"favourable notice," but added, "I am most anxious to prevent your continuing in the mistake" of believing Percy Shelley to be the author. Her stated
motive was to spare any fault to the poet for this "juvenile effort . . . to
which—from its being written at an early age, I abstained from putting my
name—and from respect to those persons from whom I bear it" (14 June
1818), but she may have hoped for due credit in Scott's favor.*

REMARKS ON FRANKENSTEIN, OR THE MODERN PROMETHEUS; A NOVEL.

Did I request thee, Maker, from my clay,
To mould me man? Did I solicit thee
From darkness to promote me?——

Paradise Lost.

This is a novel, or more properly a romantic fiction, of a nature so
peculiar, that we ought to describe the species before attempting any
account of the individual production.

The first general division of works of fiction, into such as bound
the events they narrate by the actual laws of nature, and such as, passing these limits, are managed by marvellous and supernatural
machinery, is sufficiently obvious and decided. But the class of marvellous romances admits of several subdivisions. In the earlier productions of imagination, the poet, or tale-teller does not, in his own
opinion, transgress the laws of credibility, when he introduces into his
narration the witches, goblins, and magicians, in the existence of
which he himself, as well as his hearers, is a firm believer. This good
faith, however, passes away, and works turning upon the marvellous

are written and read merely on account of the exercise which they afford to the imagination [. . .] In this species of composition, the marvellous is itself the principal and most important object both to the author and reader. To describe its effect upon the mind of the human personages engaged in its wonders, and dragged along by its machinery, is comparatively an inferior object. [. . .]

A more philosophical and refined use of the supernatural in works of fiction, is proper to that class in which the laws of nature are represented as altered, not for the purpose of pampering the imagination with wonders, but in order to shew the probable effect which the supposed miracles would produce on those who witnessed them. In this case, the pleasure ordinarily derived from the marvellous incidents is secondary to that which we extract from observing how mortals like ourselves would be affected. [. . .] Even in the description of his marvels, however, the author who manages the style of composition with address, gives them an indirect importance with the reader, when he is able to describe with nature, and with truth, the effects which they are calculated to produce upon his dramatis personæ.[1] [. . .]

In the class of fictitious narrations to which we allude, the author opens a sort of account-current with the reader; drawing upon him, in the first place, for credit to that degree of the marvellous which he proposes to employ; and becoming virtually bound, in consequence of this indulgence, that his personages shall conduct themselves, in the extraordinary circumstances in which they are placed, according to the rules of probability, and the nature of the human heart. In this view, the *probable* is far from being laid out of sight even amid the wildest freaks of imagination; on the contrary, we grant the extraordinary postulates which the author demands as the foundation of his narrative, only on condition of his deducing the consequences with logical precision. [. . . A] good illustration [. . .] is the well known Saint Leon of William Godwin.[2] In this latter work, assuming the possibility of the transmutation of metals, and of the *elixir vitae,* the author has deduced, in the course of his narrative, the probable consequences of the possession of such secrets upon the fortunes and mind of him who might enjoy them. Frankenstein is a novel upon the same plan with Saint Leon; it is said to be written by Mr Percy Bysshe Shelley, who, if

[1]Recall Coleridge's comments in Ch. 14 of *Biographia Literaria* (p. 370).
[2]*St. Leon, a Tale of the Sixteenth Century* (1799).

we are rightly informed, is son-in-law to Mr Godwin; and it is inscribed to that ingenious author. [Scott gives a summary, with ample quotations of the Preface and the novel. He pauses over a potential blasphemy in describing Frankenstein's "creation (if we dare to call it so), or formation of a living and sentient being," then proceeds to a long quotation from I.IV.] The result of this extraordinary discovery it would be unjust to give in any words save those of the author. We shall give it at length, as an excellent specimen of modern chemistry, as well as of the style and manner of the work. [quotes I.IV from "It was on a dreary night of November" to the verse from Coleridge; then resumes the plot summary. Of the death of Justine, he comments:] It does not appear that Frankenstein attempted to avert her fate, by communicating his horrible secret; but, indeed, who would have given him credit, or in what manner could he have supported his tale? [Summary resumes, including the following comment about the episode of the Creature's education at the De Lacey household.]

The most material part of his education was acquired in a ruinous pig-stye—a Lyceum which this strange student occupied, he assures us, for a good many months undiscovered, and in constant observance of the motions of an amiable family, from imitating whom he learns the use of language, and other accomplishments, much more successfully than Caliban, though the latter had a conjuror to his tutor.[3] This detail is not only highly improbable, but it is injudicious, as its unnecessary minuteness tends rather too much to familiarize us with the being whom it regards, and who loses, by this *lengthy* oration, some part of the mysterious sublimity annexed to his first appearance. The result is, this monster, who was at first, according to his own account, but a harmless monster, becomes ferocious and malignant, in consequence of finding all his approaches to human society repelled with injurious violence and offensive marks of disgust. [Plot summary resumes; Scott's last long quotation is of the end of the novel starting from the Creature's "Fear not that I shall be the instrument. . . ."]

Whether this singular being executed his purpose or not must necessarily remain an uncertainty, unless the voyage of discovery to the north pole should throw any light on the subject.

So concludes this extraordinary tale, in which the author seems to us to disclose uncommon powers of poetic imagination. The feeling with which we perused the unexpected and fearful, yet, allowing

[3]In *The Tempest,* magician Prospero, an exiled Duke of Italy, has taken command of Caliban's island and of Caliban, whom he teaches how to speak.

the possibility of the event, very natural conclusion of Frankenstein's experiment, shook a little even our firm nerves; although such and so numerous have been the expedients for exciting terror employed by the romantic writers of the age, that the reader may adopt Macbeth's words with a slight alteration:

> "We have supp'd full with horrors
> Direness, familiar to our 'callous' thoughts,
> Cannot once startle us."[4]

It is no slight merit in our eyes, that the tale, though wild in incident, is written in plain and forcible English, without exhibiting that mixture of hyperbolical Germanisms with which tales of wonder are usually told, as if it were necessary that the language should be as extravagant as the fiction. The ideas of the author are always clearly as well as forcibly expressed; and his descriptions of landscape have in them the choice requisites of truth, freshness, precision, and beauty. The self-education of the monster, considering the slender opportunities of acquiring knowledge that he possessed, we have already noticed as improbable and overstrained. That he should have not only learned to speak, but to read, and, for aught we know, to write—that he should have become acquainted with Werter, with Plutarch's Lives, and with Paradise Lost, by listening through a hole in a wall, seems as unlikely as that he should have acquired, in the same way, the problems of Euclid, or the art of book-keeping by single and double entry. The author has however two apologies—the first, the necessity that his monster should acquire those endowments, and the other, that his neighbours were engaged in teaching the language of the country to a young foreigner. [. . .] We should also be disposed, in support of the principles with which we set out, to question whether the monster, how tall, agile, and strong however, could have perpetrated so much mischief undiscovered, or passed through so many countries without being secured, either on account of his crimes, or for the benefit of some such speculator as Mr. Polito,[5] who would have been happy to have added to his museum so curious a specimen of natural history.

---

[4]"I have supp'd full with horrors, / Direness, familiar to my slaughterous thoughts, / Cannot once start me" (*Macbeth* 5.5.13–15).

[5]Proprietor (recently deceased) of what he boasted was the largest traveling menagerie in Europe.

But as we have consented to admit the leading incident of the work, perhaps some of our readers may be of opinion, that to stickle upon lesser improbabilities, is to incur the censure bestowed by the Scottish proverb on those who start at straws after swallowing *windlings*.[6]

The following lines, which occur in the second volume, mark, we think, that the author possesses the same facility in expressing himself in verse as in prose. [Quotes the verse from P.B. Shelley's "Mutability," p. 71 above.] Upon the whole, the work impresses us with a high idea of the author's original genius and happy power of expression. We shall be delighted to hear that he has aspired to the *paullo majorica;*[7] and, in the meantime, congratulate our readers upon a novel which excites new reflections and untried sources of emotion. If Gray's[8] definition of Paradise, to lie on a couch, namely, and read new novels, come any thing near truth, no small praise is due to him, who, like the author of Frankenstein, has enlarged the sphere of that fascinating enjoyment.

(Scots) *Edinburgh Magazine and Literary Miscellany*, new series II (March 1818): 249–53

Evolving from Scots Magazine, *this periodical was newly formed in 1817 with the participation of many from London literary circles, including William Hazlitt and Shelley's father, William Godwin. This reviewer (anonymous) treats Godwin's influence on the novel as a problem rather than an advantage, and is shocked to see the word "Creator" applied to "a mere human being." At once moved by the Creature's plight and dismayed by its genesis, the reviewer uses terms for it and the novel that seem exchangeable: "extraordinary"; "disjointed and irregular"; "the execution is imperfect, . . . bearing the marks of an unpractised hand."*

Here is one of the productions of the modern school in its highest style of caricature and exaggeration. It is formed on the Godwinian manner, and has all the faults, but many likewise of the beauties of

[6]Whole bundles.
[7]Latin: "more important matters." Virgil's *Eclogue IV* has the line, which may be translated: "Of matters somewhat more important let us sing."
[8]18th-c. poet Thomas Gray.

that model. In dark and gloomy views of nature and of man, bordering too closely on impiety,—in the most outrageous improbability,—in sacrificing every thing to effect,—it even goes beyond its great prototype; but in return, it possesses a similar power of fascination, something of the same mastery in harsh and savage delineations of passion, relieved in like manner by the gentler features of domestic and simple feelings. There never was a wilder story imagined, yet, like most of the fictions of this age, it has an air of reality attached to it, by being connected with the favourite projects and passions of the times. The real events of the world have, in our day, too, been of so wondrous and gigantic a kind,—the shiftings of the scenes in our stupendous drama have been so rapid and various,[1] that Shakespeare himself, in his wildest flights, has been completely distanced by the eccentricities of actual existence. Even he would scarcely have dared to have raised, in one act, a private adventurer to the greatest of European thrones,[2]—to have conducted him, in the next, victorious over the necks of emperors and kings, and then, in a third, to have shewn him an exile, in a remote speck of an island, some thousands of miles from the scene of his triumphs; and the chariot which bore him along covered with glory, quietly exhibited to a gaping mechanical rabble under the roof of one of the beautiful buildings on the North Bridge of Edinburgh. [. . .] Our appetite, we say, for every sort of wonder and vehement interest, has in this way become so desperately inflamed, that especially as the world around us has again settled into its old dull state of happiness and legitimacy, we can be satisfied with nothing in fiction that is not highly coloured and exaggerated; we even like a story the better that it is disjointed and irregular, and our greatest inventors, accordingly, have been obliged to accommodate themselves to the taste of the age, more, we believe, than their own judgment can, at all times, have approved of. The very extravagance of the present production will now, therefore, be, perhaps, in its favour, since the events which have actually passed before our eyes have made the atmosphere of miracles that in which we most readily breathe.

---

[1]That *Frankenstein* is set in the 1790s amplifies the reviewer's echo of famous sentences from Edmund Burke's *Reflections on the Revolution in France* (1790): "Everything seems out of nature in this strange chaos [. . .] this monstrous tragicomic scene."

[2]World conqueror Napoleon Bonaparte, by now exiled to the Island of St. Helena in the Atlantic.

[Plot summary (249–52). The reviewer admires the tour of Chamounix: "This part of the book is very beautifully written; the description of the mountain scenery, and of its effect on Frankenstein's mind, is finely given." The reviewer is also moved by the Creature's narrative: "a very amiable personage he makes himself to be. The story is well fancied and told"; he is described as originally "really a good-natured monster," indeed, "a worthy monster" and is pitied in Felix's attack: "the poor monster is abused and maltreated."]

Such is a sketch of this singular performance, in which there is much power and beauty, both of thought and expression, though, in many parts, the execution is imperfect, and bearing the marks of an unpractised hand. It is one of those works, however, which, when we have read, we do not well see why it should have been written;—for a *jeu d'esprit*[3] it is somewhat too long, grave, and laborious,—and some of our highest and most reverential feelings receive a shock from the conception on which it turns, so as to produce a painful and bewildered state of mind while we peruse it. We are accustomed, happily, to look upon the creation of a living and intelligent being as a work that is fitted only to inspire a religious emotion, and there is an impropriety, to say no worse, in placing it in any other light. It might, indeed, be the author's view to shew that the powers of man have been wisely limited, and that misery would follow their extension,— but still the expression "Creator," applied to a mere human being, gives us the same sort of shock with the phrase, "the Man Almighty," and others of the same kind, in Mr Southey's "Curse of Kehama."[4] All these monstrous conceptions are the consequences of the wild and irregular theories of the age; though we do not at all mean to infer that the authors who give into such freedoms have done so with any bad intentions. This incongruity, however, with our established and most sacred notions, is the chief fault in such fictions, regarding them merely in a critical point of view. Shakespeare's Caliban (though his simplicity and suitableness to the place where he is found are very delightful) is, perhaps, a more *hateful* being than our good friend in this book. But Caliban comes into existence in the received way which common superstition had pointed out; we should not have

---

[3]French: *play of the mind,* a clever exercise.

[4]Kehama, the villain of Robert Southey's epic poem, which Shelley read 1814–15, is routinely described in terms that would strike Christians as blasphemy: "Almighty," "Omnipotent," "King of Men," "the Man-God."

endured him if Prospero had created him. Getting over this original absurdity, the character of our monster is in good keeping;—there is a grandeur, too, in the scenery in which he makes his appearances,—the ice-mountains of the Pole, or the glaciers of the Alps;—his natural tendency to kind feelings, and the manner in which they were blighted,—and all the domestic picture of the cottage, are very interesting[5] and beautiful. We hope yet to have more productions, both from this author and his[6] great model, Mr Godwin; but they would make a great improvement in their writings, if they would rather study the established order of nature as it appears, both in the world of matter and of mind, than continue to revolt our feelings by hazardous innovations in either of these departments.

Belle Assemblée 2d series 17 (March 1818): 139–42

As the French name may suggest, this was a magazine for ladies of fashion. It also included social news, and reviews of drama and literature. The unsigned review of Frankenstein *led its March section on "Literary Intelligence."*

This is a very *bold* fiction; and, did not the author, in a short preface, make a kind of apology, we should almost pronounce it to be *impious.* We hope, however, the writer had the moral in view which we are desirous of drawing from it, that the *presumptive*[1] works of man must be frightful, vile, and horrible; ending only in discomfort and misery to himself.

But will all our readers understand this? Should not an author, who has a moral end in view, point out rather that application which may be more generally understood? We recommend, however, to our fair readers, who may peruse a work which, from its originality, excellence of language, and peculiar interest, is likely to be very popular, to draw from it that meaning which we have cited above.

[5]In Shelley's day, this adjective carried the sense of "engaging the moral sympathies and affections."
[6]The author is assumed to be male.

[1]This word may have caught Peake's notice. He published his play under the title *Presumption; or the Fate of Frankenstein.*

The story of *Frankenstein* is told in a letter from a Captain Walton to his sister, Mrs. Saville, residing in England. Walton is almost as much of an enthusiast as the wretched Frankenstein, whom, as the Captain is in search of finding the north west passage, and penetrating as far as possible to the extremities of the pole, he meets, engaged in the pursuit of the demon-being of his own creation; Walton rescues Frankenstein from the imminent danger of losing his life in this pursuit, amongst the floating flakes of ice; and after this Prometheus recovers, in part, his bodily strength, and relates his history to Walton. Frankenstein is a Genevese; (these people are not naturally romantic) but Frankenstein's mind has been early warped by a perusal of those authors who deal in the marvellous. [Plot summary follows.]

This work, which we repeat, has, as well as originality, extreme interest to recommend it, and an easy, yet energetic style, is inscribed to Mr. Godwin; who, however he once embraced novel systems, is, we are credibly informed, happily converted to what he once styled *ancient prejudices.*

We are sorry our limits will not allow us to a more copious review of *Frankenstein.* The few following extracts will serve to shew the excellence of its style and language.

> [Then follows a set of excerpts, with these uppercase headlines:
> ENTHUSIASM OF FRANKENSTEIN IN HIS WORK OF FORMING MAN;
> DESCRIPTION OF FRANKENSTEIN'S MAN WHEN FIRST ENDOWED WITH LIFE;
> HIS REPENTANCE AT HAVING FORMED HIM;
> ARGUMENTS HELD OUT BY THE MONSTER;
> FRANKENSTEIN'S AGONY ON THE DEATH OF ELIZABETH;
> THE MONSTER'S REFLECTIONS OVER THE DEAD BODY OF FRANKENSTEIN.]

The British Critic new series 9 (April 1818): 432–38

Famous for hostile reviews of Godwin, Leigh Hunt, and Percy Shelley, this Tory, High-Church monthly was founded to oppose the dissenting, reformist slant of other monthly reviews.

This is another anomalous story of the same race and family as Mandeville;[1] and, if we are not misinformed, it is intimately connected with that

---

[1] Godwin's novel *Mandeville: A Tale of the Seventeenth Century* was published in 1817.

strange performance, by more ties than one. In the present instance, it is
true, we are presented with the mysteries of equivocal generation,
instead of the metaphysics of a bedlamite; but he who runs as he reads,
might pronounce both novels to be *similis farinæ*.[2] We are in doubt to
what class we shall refer writings of this extravagant character; that they
bear marks of considerable power, it is impossible to deny; but this
power is so abused and perverted, that we should almost prefer imbecil-
ity; however much, of late years, we have been wearied and ennuied by
the languid whispers of gentle sentimentality, they at least had the comfortable property of provoking no uneasy slumber; but we must protest
against the waking dreams of horror excited by the unnatural stimulants
of this later school; and we feel ourselves as much harassed, after rising
from the perusal of these three spirit-wearing volumes, as if we had been
over-dosed with laudanum, or hag-ridden by the night-mare.

No one can love a real good ghost story more heartily than we do;
and we will toil through many a tedious duodecimo[3] to get half a
dozen pages of rational terror, provided always, that we keep company
with spectres and skeletons, no longer than they maintain the just dignity of their spiritual character. Now and then too, we can tolerate a
goule, so it be not at his dinner-time; and altogether, we profess to
entertain a very due respect for the whole anierarchy of the dæmoniacal
establishment. Our prejudices in favour of legitimacy, of course, are
proportionably shocked by the pretensions of any pseudo-diabolism;
and all our best feelings of ghostly loyalty are excited by the usurpa-
tion of an unauthorized hobgoblin, or a non-descript fe-fa-fum.

It will be better, however, to say what little we mean to add on
this point, by and by, when our readers are fairly put in possession of
the subject, and enabled to form their own estimate of our opinions.
In a sort of introduction, which precedes the main story of the novel,
and has nothing else to do with it, we are introduced to a Mr. Walton, the Christopher Sly[4] of the piece, with whose credulity the hero
of the tale is afterwards to amuse himself. This gentleman, it seems,
has had his imagination fired by an anticipation of the last number of
the Quarterly Review, and is gone out to the North Pole, in quest of
lost Greenland, magnetism, and the parliamentary reward. In justice

[2]Same sort.

[3]An economical production (printing 12 pages to one side of a sheet); see p. 1, above.

[4]A drunken, disorderly tinker in the preliminary "frame" to Shakespeare's *The Taming
of the Shrew*, the main tale of which appears as his "dream."

to our author, we must admit that this part is well done, and we doubt whether Mr. Barrow, in plain prose, or Miss Pordon herself, in more ambitious rhyme,[5] can exceed our novelist in the description of frozen desarts and colliding ice-bergs. While employed in this pursuit, and advancing into a very high latitude, one day, . . . [Quotes Walton's letter on the discovery of Frankenstein.] After proper applications, the stranger is recovered, and of course a strong attachment takes place between him and his preserver; and, in due season, after much struggling with melancholy and sullenness, he prevails upon himself to tell his own story. [Summarizes Frankenstein's story, then comments on the Creature's education.] Some of the steps in his intellectual progress, we confess, made us smile. He learns to read by accidentally finding *Paradise Lost,* a volume of *Plutarch's Lives,* the *Sorrows of Werter,* and *Volney's Ruins;* and his code of ethics is formed on this extraordinary stock of poetical theology, pagan[6] biography, adulterous sentimentality, and atheistical jacobinism:[7] yet, in spite of all his enormities, we think the monster, a very pitiable and ill-used monster, and are much inclined to join in his request, and ask Frankenstein to make him a wife [. . . Comments on the end of the novel.] After a short conversation, which Mr. Walton was not very anxious to protract, he takes his leave, with the very laudable resolution of seeking the northern extremity of the globe, where he means to collect his funeral pile, and consume his frame to ashes, that its remains may afford no light to any curious and unhallowed wretch who would create such another. We cannot help wishing, that our ships of discovery had carried out the whole impression of his history, for a similar purpose.

We need scarcely say, that these volumes have neither principle, object, nor moral; the horror which abounds in them is too grotesque and *bizarre* ever to approach near the sublime, and when we did not hurry over the pages in disgust, we sometimes paused to laugh outright; and yet we suspect, that the diseased and wandering imagination, which has stepped out of all legitimate bounds, to frame these disjointed combinations and unnatural adventures, might be disciplined into something

---

[5]At age 16, Eleanor Anne Porden (1795–1825) wrote *The Veils, or The Triumph of Constancy* (1815), lauded by the Institut de France. Her long poem *The Arctic Expeditions* was published in 1818; in 1823, she married Arctic explorer John Franklin; in 1825, she died of tuberculosis.

[6]Christian terminology for pre-Christian (i.e., classical).

[7]The reactionary term for the philosophical and political principles of the French Revolution, which also disestablished the Church.

better. We heartily wish it were so, for there are occasional symptoms of no common powers of mind, struggling through a mass of absurdity, which well nigh overwhelms them; but it is a sort of absurdity that approaches so often the confines of what is wicked and immoral, that we dare hardly trust ourselves to bestow even this qualified praise. The writer of it is, we understand, a female; this is an aggravation of that which is the prevailing fault of the novel; but if our authoress can forget the gentleness of her sex, it is no reason why we should; and we shall therefore dismiss the novel without further comment.

Gentleman's Magazine (April 1818): 334–35

The first journal to use the military term "magazine" for a compendium of news and essays, Gentleman's was founded in the eighteenth century.

This Tale is evidently the production of no ordinary Writer; and, though we are shocked at the idea of the event on which the fiction is founded, many parts of it are strikingly good, and the description of the scenery is excellent.

In the pride of Science, the Hero of the Tale presumes to take upon himself the structure of a human being; in which, though he in some degree is supposed to have succeeded, he forfeits every comfort of life, and finally even life itself. [Quotes the Preface on the circumstances of composition and identifies one of the "friends" mentioned as "a Noble Poet."]

Monthly Review new series 85 (April 1818): 439

A respectable review begun in the eighteenth century for university-educated gentlemen, the Monthly was losing readers by the mid-Regency to the newer quarterlies and reviews aimed at the emerging business and professional classes.

An uncouth story, in the taste of the German novelists, trenching in some degree on delicacy, setting probability at defiance, and leading to no conclusion either moral or philosophical. In some passages, the writer appears to favour the doctrines of materialism: but a serious examination is scarcely necessary for so excentric a vagary of the imagination as this tale presents.

The Literary Panorama and National Register, new series 8 (1 June 1818): 411–14

This novel is a feeble imitation of one that was very popular in its day,—the St. Leon of Mr. Godwin. It exhibits many characteristics of the school whence it proceeds; and occasionally puts forth indications of talent; but we have been very much disappointed in the perusal of it, from our expectations having been raised too high beforehand by injudicious praises; and it exhibits a strong tendency towards *materialism*.[1]

The main idea on which the story of Frankenstein rests, undoubtedly affords scope for the display of imagination and fancy, as well as knowledge of the human heart; and the anonymous author has not wholly neglected the opportunities which it presented to him: but the work seems to have been written in great haste, and on a very crude and ill-digested plan; and the detail is, in consequence, frequently filled with the most gross and obvious inconsistencies.

[Summary follows, and concludes:] Frankenstein dies on board the vessel of Walton; and the fiend may, for any thing we know to be the contrary, be wandering about upon the ice in the neighbourhood of the North Pole to this day; and may, in that case, be among the wonderful discoveries to be made by the expedition which is destined there.

We have mentioned that there are gross inconsistencies in the minor details of the story. They are such, for example, as the following: the moment Frankenstein has endowed with life the previously inanimate form of the being which he has made, he is so horror-struck with the hideousness of the form and features, when they are put in motion, that he remains fixed to the spot, while the gigantic monster runs from the horizontal posture in which he lay, and *walks away*;

---

[1]The doctrine that gives matter primary position over immaterialities such as mind, soul, and spirit; in its most radical version, the assertion that reality is only material. Cf. *Monthly Review*, above.

and Frankenstein never hears any more of him for nearly two years. The author supposes that his hero has the power of communicating *life* to dead matter: but what has the vital principle to do with *habits,* and actions which are dependent on the moral will? If Frankenstein could have endowed his creature with the vital principle of a hundred or a thousand human beings, it would no more have been able to walk without having previously acquired the habit of doing so, than it would be to talk, or to reason, or to judge. He does not pretend that he could endow it with *faculties* as well as life: and yet when it is about *a year old* we find it reading *Werter,* and *Plutarch* and *Volney!* The whole detail of the development of the creature's mind and faculties is full of these monstrous inconsistencies. After the creature leaves Frankenstein, on the night of *its birth,* it wanders for some time in the woods, and then takes up its residence in a kind of shed adjoining to a cottage, where it remains for many months without the knowledge of the inhabitants; and learns to talk and read thro' a chink in the wall! "*Quod mihi ostendit,*" &c.[2]

We have heard that this work is written by Mr. Shelley; but should be disposed to attribute it to even a less experienced writer than he is. In fact we have some idea that it is the production of a daughter of a celebrated living novelist.

Blackwood's Edinburgh Magazine XIII (March 1823): 283–93

> *This is the opening of a review of Shelley's next novel* Valperga *(published February 1823).*

We opened the packet, which we knew to contain this book, with great expectations. Frankenstein, at the time of its appearance, we certainly did not suspect to be the work of a female hand; the name of Shelley was whispered, and we did not hesitate to attribute the book to Mr Shelley. Soon, however, we were set right. We learned that Frankenstein was written by Mrs Shelley; and then we most undoubtedly said to ourselves, "For a man it was excellent, but for a woman it

---

[2]Latin: "In which it would have to be shown to me."

is wonderful." What we chiefly admired, in that wild production, was vigour of imagination and strength of language; these were unquestionable attributes, and they redeemed the defects of an absurd groundwork and an incoherent fable; and, moreover, they tempted us, and every body else, to forgive the many long passages of feeble conception and feeble execution, with which the vigorous scenes were interwoven.

London Morning Post
Reviews of *Presumption; or, the Fate of Frankenstein*

Tuesday, July 29, 1823
THEATRE
English Opera

A new three act piece, described as "a romance of a peculiar interest," was last night produced at this theatre, entitled, Presumption, or the Fate of Frankenstein.

The fable represents Frankenstein, a man of great science, to have succeeded in uniting the remains of dead persons, so as to form one being, which he endows with life. He has, however, little reason to exult in the triumph of his art; for the creature thus formed, hideous in aspect, and possessed of prodigious strength, spreads terror, and carries ruin wherever he goes. Though wearing the human form, he is incapable of associating with mankind, to whom he eventually becomes hostile, and having killed the mistress and brother of Frankenstein, he finally vanquishes his mortal creator, and perishes himself beneath a falling avalanch.

Such is the outline of the business of a drama more extraordinary in its plan, than remarkable for strength in its execution. There is something in the piecemeal resurrection effected by Frankenstein, which, instead of creating that awful interest intended to arise from it, gives birth to a feeling of horror. We have not that taste for the monstrous which can enable us to enjoy it in the midst of the most startling absurdities. To Lord BYRON, the late Mr. SHELLEY, and philosophers of that stamp, it might appear a very fine thing to attack the Christian faith from a masked battery, and burlesque the resurrection of the dead, by representing the fragments of departed mortals as starting into existence at the command of a man; but we would prefer the comparatively noble assaults of VOLNEY, VOLTAIRE, and PAINE. In the first scene in which ————— (so the creature of Frankenstein is indicated in the bills) makes his appearance, the effect is terrific. There are other parts in which a very powerful impression is produced on the spectators, but to have made the most of the idea a greater interest ought early in the drama to have been excited for Frankenstein and the destined victims of the non-descript, and he himself would have been an object of greater attention if speech had been vouchsafed. The efforts to relieve the serious action of the Piece by mirth and music were generally successful, and the labours of Mr. WATSON the composer we often loudly applauded.

The acting was very grand. WALLACK as Frankenstein, displayed great feeling and animation; T. P. COOKE as ————— (or the made up man), was tremendously appalling. The other performers did as much as could be expected in the parts allotted to them, and the piece though it met with some opposition at the close had a large majority in its favour, and was announced for repetition.

Wednesday, July 30, 1823
ENGLISH OPERA HOUSE

At this Theatre last night, Presumption, or the Fate of Frankenstein, was again performed. Whatever may be thought of Frankenstein as a novel, or of the principles of those who could indite such a novel, there can be but one opinion of it as a drama. The representation of this piece upon the stage is of astonishing, of enchaining, interest. In the novel the rigid moralist may feel himself constantly offended, by the modes of reasoning, principles of action, &c.—But in the Drama this is all carefully kept in the back ground. Nothing but what can please, astonish, and delight, is there suffered to appear; Frankenstein despairingly bewails his attempt as impious, and suffers for it; partial justice is rendered; and many more incidents in the novel might have been pourtrayed, of harrowing interest! though without infringing good taste. As it stands, however, as a drama, it is most effective; and T. P. COOKE well pourtrays what indeed it is a proof of his extraordinary genius so well to pourtray—an unhappy being without the pale of nature—a monster—a nondescript—a horror to himself and others;—yet the leaning, the bias, the nature, if one may so say, of the creature is good; he is in the beginning of his creation gentle, and disposed to be affectionate and kind, but his appearance terrifies even those to whom he has rendered the most essential service; the alarm he excites creates hostility; he is miserably assailed by man; and revenge and the malignity are thus excited in his breast. Instead of being longer kind or gentle he becomes ferocious, sets fire to the cottage where his services had been so ungratefully requited (and this scene is admirably managed), and perceiving that Frankenstein, the author of his existence, shuns and abhors him as much as others, he becomes enraged against him, and seeks his destruction and that of all dear to him, in which he too fatally succeeds. Too much cannot be said in praise of T. P. COOKE, his development of first impressions, and naturally perceptions, is given with a fidelity to nature truly admirable. Take for instance the pourtraiture of his first sensations on hearing music, than which nothing can be finer. The acting of WALLACK, the unhappy Frankenstein, is painfully interesting; he looks, he seems to feel the very character he assumes, so abstracted, so wretched, so care-worn. Upon the whole, though from diversity of taste this Piece may meet with some opposition, it cannot fail to stand its ground in ultimate conjunction with other pieces. The applause predominated in a more marked degree last night.

The pleasant Afterpiece of Where shall I Dine? followed, and kept the house in a continued laughter.

George Canning, Remarks in Parliament (16 March 1824)

George Canning (1770–1827) served as Foreign Secretary from 1822 to 1827. His reference to Frankenstein *in the debate on the "Amelioration of the Condition of the Slave Population of the West Indies" (16 March 1824) testifies to the novel's entrance into general cultural lore, a status relayed back when John Murray published the speech in a separate pamphlet the same year. The text here is from Hansard's Parliamentary Debates, 2d series 10 (1824), column 1103. Just after the debate, Shelley was happy to report to E. J. Trelawny, "Parliament is met here and Canning is making a figure. . . . They are introducing some amelioration in the state of the slaves in some parts of the West Indies—during the debate on the subject Canning paid a compliment to* Frankenstein *in a manner sufficiently pleasing to me" (Letters, ed. Bennett, 1: 416–17). Of this latest fame, Shelley told several friends how "pleasing" it was to her ("gratissimi a me" she said to Byron's mistress, Teresa Guiccioli).*

To attempt to shorten the road between desire and attainment is nine times out of ten to go astray, and to miss the wished-for object altogether. I am fully persuaded that freedom, when acquired under the regulations prescribed by government, will be a more delightful as well as a more safe and stable possession than if it were bestowed by a sudden acclamation.

In dealing with the negro, Sir, we must remember that we are dealing with a being possessing the form and strength of a man, but the intellect only of a child. To turn him loose in the manhood of his physical strength, in the maturity of his physical passions, but in the infancy of his uninstructed reason, would be to raise up a creature resembling the splendid fiction of a recent romance; the hero of which constructs a human form, with all the corporeal capabilities of man, and with the thews and sinews of a giant; but being unable to impart to the work of his hands a perception of right and wrong, he finds too late that he has only created a more than mortal power of doing mischief, and himself recoils from the monster which he has made.

Such would be the effect of a sudden emancipation, before the negro was prepared for the enjoyment of well-regulated liberty. I, therefore, Sir, would proceed gradually, because I would proceed safely. . . .

Knight's Quarterly Magazine 3 (August 1824): 195–99

This short-lived journal (1823–24) was published by Charles Knight and staffed by a group of young Eton-educated men. In a 50-page feature article, "The Anniversary," the staff, writing under pseudonyms, turns to a variety of subjects, including Percy Shelley's character and poetry, and three endeavors by Mary Shelley: her edition of Shelley's Posthumous Poems (1824), her recent novel Valperga (1823), and Frankenstein, which had been reissued in 1823 under her own name.

I do not think I ever was so much disappointed in any book as in Valperga; I had the very highest expectations of the maturing of the genius which could produce such a work as Frankenstein. [. . .] This induced me to read Frankenstein again—for I thought I must have been strangely mistaken in my original judgment. So far, however, from this, a second reading has confirmed it. I think Frankenstein possesses extreme power, and displays *capabilities* such as I did hope would have produced far different things from Castruccio [the hero of Valperga].

It is, I think, the best instance of natural passions applied to supernatural events that I ever met with. Grant that it is possible for one man to create another, and the rest is perfectly natural and in course. I do not allude to the incidents, for they are thrown together with a haste and carelessness so apparent as to be almost confessed; but the sentiments—both of thought and passion—are given with a truth which is equal to their extraordinary vigour. I am surprised to see by the preface that Dr. Darwin, and some of the physiological writers of Germany supposed the creation of a human being "as not of impossible occurrence." I can understand that it might be possible to put together a human frame—though with the very greatest difficulty—both from the intricacy and minuteness of the conformation, the most trifling error in which would be fatal, and from the difficulty of preventing putrescence during the process, without drying up the form like a mummy, which would incapacitate it from all purposes of *life*. But, granting that a frame could be so constructed, I cannot conceive how Dr. Darwin, who, however over-rated by his friends, was certainly a man of considerable powers of mind, I cannot conceive, I say, how he could contemplate the possibility of infusing the principle of life, when of such principle we are wholly ignorant. Many attempts have been made to say where life dwells—to prove that such or such a part is infallibly vital; but whoever could say what life itself was? This is one of the most strange of those mysteries which are hidden from human reason. The simplest operations of nature are, in their cause and process, equally inscrutable;—the whole progress and vegetation from the seed rotting in the earth, to the shoot, the sapling, the tree, the blossom, the fruit—is as utterly inscrutable by man as are the causes of his own production and existence.

The most unskillful thing in the book is the extreme ugliness of the being whom Frankenstein creates. It is not natural, that to save himself additional trouble from the minuteness of the parts, he should create a giant. He must have known the vast danger of forming one of such bodily power, whose mind it would take a considerable time to mould into humanity. Besides, though it is highly natural that the features which had been chosen individually as perfect, and which appeared so even when conjoined in the lifeless figure, should, on their being vivified, have an incongruous and unearthly aspect; yet, it is not at all probable, that one with Frankenstein's science should have formed a creature of such "appalling hideousness." It is utterly inconceivable also, that he should have let the monster (as he is somewhat unfairly called) escape;—one of the thoughts which must, one would imagine, have been uppermost in his mind during his labours, would have been the instructing his creature intellectually as he had formed him physically.

In the account which the creature gives of his instruction by means of watching the polished cottagers, the hastiness of the composition is the most apparent. Indeed, nothing would require such extreme trouble and carefulness as a correct representation of the mind of one who had (from whatever circumstances) reached maturity without any acquired knowledge. Those things which, from having been known to us before the period to which our remembrances reach, appear to be part of our innate consciousness, would be perfect novelty to such a being. Not only speech would be non-existent but even sight would be imperfect in him. In short, it would require much thought and some physical knowledge, joined (as I before said) to the greatest care, to render such a description at once full and accurate. In Frankenstein what there is of it is sufficiently interesting in itself, but it suggests so frequently how much more it might be wrought out, that it brings strongly into view its own imperfectness.

For my own part, I confess that *my* interest in the book is entirely on the side of the monster. His eloquence and persuasion, of which Frankenstein complains, are so because they are truth. The justice is indisputably on his side, and his sufferings are, to me, touching to the last degree. Are there are any sufferings, indeed, so severe as those which arise from the sensation of dereliction, or, (as in this case) of isolation? Even the slightest tinge of those feelings, arising as they often do from trivial circumstances, as from passing a solitary evening in a lone and distant situation—even these, are bitter to a severe degree. What it must be, then,—what *is* it to feel oneself *alone in the world!* Fellow-feeling is the deepest of all the needs which Nature has implanted within us. The impulses which lead us to the physical preservation of our life are scarcely stronger than those which impel us to communion with our fellows. Alas! then to have no fellows!—to be, with feelings of kindliness and beneficence, the object of scorn and hate to every one whose eyes lighted on us!—to be repaid with blows and wounds for the very benefits we confer!—The poor monster always, for these reasons, touched me to the heart. Frankenstein ought to have reflected on the means of giving happiness to the being of his creation, before he *did* create him. Instead of that, he heaps on him all sorts of abuse and contumely for his *ugliness,* which was directly *his* work, and for his crimes to which his neglect gave rise.

But whence arises the extreme inferiority of Valperga? I can account for it only by supposing that Shelley wrote the first, though it was attributed to his wife,—and that she really wrote the last. Still I should not, from internal evidence, suppose Frankenstein to be the work of Shelley. It has much of his poetry and vigour—but it is wholly free from those philosophical opinions from which scarcely any of his works *are* free, and for which there are many fair openings in Frankenstein. It is equally to be observed that there are no religious reflections—and that there are many circumstances in which a mind at all religiously inclined would not have failed to have expressed some sentiments of that nature. It may be, that Mrs. Shelley wrote Frankenstein—but, knowing that its fault was extravagance, determined to be careful and correct in her next work; and, thence, as so many do from the same cause, became cold and common-place. At all events, the difference of the two books is very remarkable.

London Literary Gazette, 19 November 1831 (740)

This review of the 1831 Frankenstein *is notable not only for the alacrity of its appearance but also for its enthusiasm about this unusual work from a "female," if not conventionally "feminine," pen.*

Vigorous, terrible, and with its interest sustained to the last, *Frankenstein* is certainly one of the most original works that ever proceeded from a female pen. The merits our feminine writers possess, are tact, feeling, the thoughtfulness born of feeling, a keen perception of the ridiculous, or touching appeal to sympathy. Not one of all these is the characteristic of the work before us; it appeals to fear, not love; and, contrary to the general *matériel* in the writings of women, has less of the heart in it than the mind. The character of the enthusiastic young student, with whom knowledge is a passion, is powerfully drawn; and we know, in all our imaginative literature, few scenes more appalling than where Frankenstein is pursuing his monstrous and vindictive enemy over the frozen deserts of the ocean. We remember being greatly struck with this work on its first appearance; and our second reading has revived all our early impressions: the romantic excitement of its pages well repays their perusal. We should recommend them on the same principle that physicians prescribe alternatives. A clever frontispiece represents the moment when Frankenstein rushes away in horror from the frightful shape to which his science has at length communicated life.

Percy Bysshe Shelley
The Athenæum 263 (10 November 1832): 730

In The Athenæum, *a progressive London weekly, Shelley's cousin, Thomas Medwin, unconstrained by Sir Timothy Shelley's prohibition on his widowed daughter-in-law from publishing anything on his son, produced a series of "Shelley Papers," which included this heretofore unpublished review of* Frankenstein, *of fresh interest in the wake of the 1831 publication. Percy Shelley insists on using the term "Being" for the Creature (instead of the more usual one in the reviews, "monster"), and indicts social failure: "Treat a person ill, and he will become wicked." Anticipating that such a novel might receive some harsh initial reviews, Shelley planned to submit his review anonymously for publication in 1818, but (perhaps because the reception was better than he anticipated) he never did. Some variants in his manuscript from the text Medwin prepared for* The Athenæum *are noted.*

"ON FRANKENSTEIN"
By the Late Percy Bysshe Shelley

The novel of "Frankenstein, or the Modern Prometheus," is undoubtedly, as a mere story, one of the most original and complete productions of the day. We debate with ourselves in wonder, as we read it, what could have been the series of thoughts—what could have been the peculiar experiences that awakened them—which conduced, in the author's mind, to the astonishing combinations of motives and incidents, and the startling catastrophe, which compose this tale. There are, perhaps, some points of subordinate importance, which prove that it is the author's first attempt. But in this judgment, which requires a very nice discrimination, we may be mistaken; for it is conducted throughout with a firm and steady hand. The interest gradually accumulates and advances towards the conclusion with the accelerated rapidity of a rock rolled down a mountain. We are led breathless with suspense and sympathy, and the heaping up of incident on incident, and the working of passion out of passion. We cry "hold, hold! enough!"[1]—but there is yet something to come; and, like the victim whose history it relates, we think we can bear no more, and yet more is to be borne. Pelion is heaped on Ossa, and Ossa on Olympus.[2] We climb Alp after Alp, until the horizon is seen blank, vacant, and limitless; and the head turns giddy, and the ground seems to fail under our feet.

This novel rests its claim on being a source of powerful and profound emotion. The elementary feelings of the human mind are exposed to view; and those who are accustomed to reason deeply on their origin and tendency will, perhaps, be the only persons who can sympathize, to the full extent, in the interest of the actions which are their result. But, founded on nature as they are, there is perhaps no reader, who can endure any thing beside a new love story, who will not feel a responsive string touched in his inmost soul. The sentiments are so affectionate and so innocent—the characters of the subordinate agents in this strange drama are clothed in the light of such a mild and gentle mind—the pictures of domestic manners are of the most simple and attaching character: the father's[3] is irresistible and deep. Nor are the crimes and malevolence of the single Being, though indeed withering and tremendous, the offspring of any unaccountable propensity to evil, but flow irresistibly from certain causes fully adequate to their production. They are the children, as it were, of Necessity and Human Nature. In this the direct moral of the book consists; and it is perhaps the most important, and of the most universal application, of any moral that can be enforced by example. Treat a person ill, and he will become wicked. Requite affection with scorn;—let one being be selected, for whatever cause, as the refuse of his kind— divide him, a social being, from society, and you impose upon him the irresistible obligations—malevolence and selfishness. It is thus that, too often in society, those who are best qualified to be its benefactors and its

[1]Shakespeare, *Macbeth* 5.8.34.

[2]Various mountains in Greek mythology; Virgil, *Georgics* 1.281–82.

[3]Shelley's manuscript reads "pathos" rather than "father's" (*The Prose Works of Percy Bysshe Shelley*, ed. E. B. Murray [Oxford, 1993], Vol. 1, p. 283).

ornaments, are branded by some accident with scorn, and changed, by neglect and solitude of heart, into a scourge and a curse.

The Being in "Frankenstein" is, no doubt, a tremendous creature. It was impossible that he should not have received among men that treatment which led to the consequences of his being a social nature. He was an abortion and an anomaly; and though his mind was such as its first impressions framed it, affectionate and full of moral sensibility, yet the circumstances of his existence are so monstrous and uncommon, that, when the consequences of them became developed in action, his original goodness was gradually turned into[4] inextinguishable misanthropy and revenge. The scene between the Being and the blind De Lacey in the cottage, is one of the most profound and extraordinary instances of pathos that we ever recollect. It is impossible to read this dialogue,—and indeed many others of a somewhat similar character,—without feeling the heart suspend its pulsations with wonder, and the "tears stream down the cheeks."[5] The encounter and argument between Frankenstein and the Being on the sea of ice, almost approaches, in effect, to the expostulation of Caleb Williams with Falkland. It reminds us, indeed, somewhat of the style and character of that admirable writer, to whom the author has dedicated his work, and whose productions he seems to have studied.[6]

There is only one instance, however, in which we detect the least approach to imitation; and that is the conduct of the incident of Frankenstein's landing in Ireland.[7] The general character of the tale, indeed, resembles nothing that ever preceded it. After the death of Elizabeth, the story, like a stream which grows at once more rapid and profound as it proceeds, assumes an irresistible solemnity, and the magnificent energy and swiftness of a tempest.

The churchyard scene, in which Frankenstein visits the tombs of his family, his quitting Geneva, and his journey through Tartary to the shores of the Frozen Ocean, resemble at once the terrible reanimation of a corpse and the supernatural career of a spirit. The scene in the cabin of Walton's ship—the more than mortal enthusiasm and grandeur of the Being's speech over the dead body of his victim—is an exhibition of intellectual and imaginative power, which we think the reader will acknowledge has seldom been surpassed.

[4]Manuscript: into the fuel of an . . .

[5]Manuscript has no quotation marks.

[6]Another representation of a male author, this by someone who knew better.

[7]Manuscript: landing and trial in Ireland.

Frankentalk: Frankenstein in the Popular Press of Today

The child in William Blake's *Songs of Innocence* (1789) who asks, "Little Lamb who made thee?" might be alarmed by the answer today. In an op-ed piece for the *New York Times* (27 February 1997), William Safire confessed to the "head-breaking thoughts about good and evil, God and humanity" provoked by "the creation of Dolly, the lamb formed by cellular biologists in Scotland and fused into life by electric shock, as was the Monster in Mary Shelley's *Frankenstein*." Dolly the cloned ewe had just taken her first breath, a scientific sibling to the "frankencat" that debuted at the New York Cat Show in 1995—featuring furry stubs instead of legs. It wasn't the little lamb or kitty-pillow that seemed monstrous, but the science and scientists that created them: Who had the rights of creation and miscreation? What about untoward consequences and misapplications?

"Frankenstein" speaks dreams and nightmares about our future in a technological world, where a matrix can be a mother. "The *Frankenstein* Myth Becomes a Reality: We Have the Awful Knowledge to Make Exact Copies of Human Beings" blared an article in the *New York Times Sunday Magazine*, 1973. Shelley's myth spawned twin referents: the physically terrifying creature of filmdom, and the terrifyingly ambitious, ethically challenged creator. The cultural logic that likes to call the Creature "Frankenstein" is less a misrecognition than an intuition of the intimate bond between creator and creature, agent and result. From the 1820s into the twenty-first century, "Frankenstein" has been invoked to name, warn about, and mock a wealth of new designs, doubtful notions, and alarming developments.

402

from the *Oxford English Dictionary*: Frankenstein

The name of the title-character of Mrs. Shelley's romance *Franken-stein* (1818), who constructed a human monster and endowed it with life. Commonly misused allusively as a typical name for a monster who is a terror to his originator and ends by destroying him. Also attribute: *Frankensteinian*.

1838] GLADSTONE: "They [mules] really seem like Frankensteins of the animal creation" (Murray's *Handbook of Sicily*
[1864], p. xlvi)

1889] S. WEBB in G. B. Shaw, *Fabian Essays*: "The landlord and
the capitalist are both finding that the steam-engine is a
Frankenstein which they had better not have raised" (p. 38)

1907] *Saturday Review*: "Is Great Britain creating for herself
something of a Frankenstein monster on the Nile?" (6 April,
p. 414)

1958] ISAAC ASIMOV, *Naked Sun*: "Do you know robots
started with a Frankenstein complex against them? They were
suspect. Men distrusted and feared robots" (xiv.172)

1971] *Daily Telegraph*: "There are now growing indications that
the Nationalists in South Africa have created a political
Frankenstein which is pointing the way to a non-White political revival" (3 May).

Just Plain English

If languages are living things, as the philologists like to say, then English is a sort of Frankenstein creature, originally built of spare parts—
a little French, a little Anglo-Saxon, some Norse and Danish.

—Charles McGrath, *New York Times*, 26 December 2004

Science

The Bomb

On 6 August 1945, the news that an atomic bomb had been dropped
on Hiroshima reached the United States. "For all we know," said H.
V. Kaltenborn on his popular network-radio broadcast that night,
"we have created a Frankenstein."

"What Scientists Can Do to Fight the Frankenstein Myth"

At the annual meeting of the American Association for the Advancement of Science two weeks ago, President Bill Clinton echoed a refrain from his State of the Union address in which he tempered his enthusiasm for scientific progress with a call to "see that science serves humanity, and not the other way around." This disquieting sentiment—that science, like Dr. Frankenstein's monster, is poised to wreak havoc on its creator—has a currency today that should alarm us as scientists. More than alarm us, it should spur us to action.

— Mildred S. Dresselhaus, *The Scientist,* 2 March 1998

"A Frankenstein Monster Ended Up Being a Lamb"

Cloning, before it happened, was another one of those science fiction bugaboos, a prospect whose horror quotient ranked just below that of reanimated corpses or a walking, talking Frankenstein monster. It was not supposed to be possible: the laws of nature, scientists said, precluded it.

— Ed Regis, reviewing Gina Kolata's
The Road to Dolly, and the Path Ahead, New York Times, 1997

"Take Action: Stop Frankenstein Science!"

The US Food and Drug Administration [has drafted its] report on xenotransplantation (animal-to-human transplantation), which is intended to provide guidance on the production, testing, and evaluation of products used in xenotransplantation.

— PETA [People for the Ethical Treatment
of Animals] newsletter, 5 April 2001

"Frankenstein Is Alive and Well!"

To these mad scientists, it's just "embryo research." In 1818, Mary W. Shelly [*sic*] authored a famous horror novel which detailed the exploits of a young medical student whose name was Victor Frankenstein. In the story, young Frankenstein created a "monster" from the parts of dead human bodies. It was only fiction. More horrible now is the fact that modern "Frankensteins," subsidized by our tax dollars, and with the approval of some congressmen, are using parts from human beings, who, in most cases, have been murdered. Oh, they don't call it murder. To these mad scientists, it's just "embryo research."

— Wayne Jackson, *Christian Courier,* 1 March 1999

Letter to the Editor of the New York Times

The early debates over heart transplantation did not evoke images of Frankenstein, and objections to it were not about its ostensibly unnatural character. Rather, . . . critical problems were addressed by ethicists and others.

—David J. Rothman, 17 March 1998

"Frankenstein fears after head transplant"

Professor Robert White, from Cleveland[,] Ohio, transplanted a whole monkey's head onto another monkey's body, and the animal survived for some time after the operation. The professor . . . believes the operation is the next step in the transplant world. And he raised the possibility that it could be used to treat people paralysed and unable to use their limbs, and whose bodies, rather than their brains, were diseased. . . .

The arguments against head and brain transplants were outlined by Dr. Stephen Rose, director of brain and behavioural research at the Open University. "This is medical technology run completely mad and out of all proportion to what's needed."

The issue of who someone who had received a head transplant would "be" is extremely complicated, said Professor Rose.

—BBC News, 6 April 2001

Playing God

[George W. Bush] should announce his support of embryonic stem cell research and the careful oversight called for by scientists and doctors who are disinclined to play God. At the same time, he should convene a White House conference on bioethics; that would focus world attention on both the opportunities in genetic exploration and America's awareness of the real dangers of the slippery slope to Frankenscience.

—William Safire, *New York Times*, 5 July 2001

"Dr. Frankenstein on the Hill"

House Republicans called in a latter-day Dr. Frankenstein this week in an absurd attempt to stampede the Senate into passing a ban on all human cloning, even that intended for the most beneficial purposes. The witness was Dr. Panayiotis Zavos, one of the small band of scientists who have been titillating and terrifying anyone who will listen by proclaiming that they will soon produce the world's first cloned human baby. The very thought, House Republicans hope, may push Congress to impose a ban on all human cloning lest the dreaded deed happen here instead of abroad.

—Editorial, *New York Times*, 18 May 2002

"Hurray for Frankenstein!"

British parliamentarians welcome the biotech future

The "Frankenstein Report" is what outraged critics are calling a new report, Human Reproductive Technologies and the Law, that signals welcome sanity on the cloning front in Western world politics. The report was issued on March 24 by the cross-party Science and Technology Committee of the British House of Commons. What's got the critics' knickers in a twist?

First, the U.K. Members of Parliament dare to suggest that a wide range of current and potential interventions in human reproduction can, in fact, be done ethically. For example, the MPs find "no adequate justification for prohibiting the use of sex selection for family balancing." Family balancing means using pre-implantation genetic diagnosis (PGD) to select and implant embryos of a specific sex to ensure the desired proportion of girls and boys among your children.

The report also says it's OK to create cloned human embryos for research aimed at producing immune-compatible transplant tissues and cells. British regulatory authorities have already approved human cloning research proposals. The Brits even go as far as suggesting that cloning for human reproduction might be ethically acceptable.

For example, what would be wrong with this scenario? An embryo with a defective gene is created by normal *in vitro* fertilization. Stem cells are taken from the embryo and the faulty gene is replaced with a healthy one. A nucleus from the corrected embryonic stem cells is then installed in an enucleated egg, which matures into an embryo that is then implanted into his mother's womb. An instant healthy child, thanks to cloning technology.

The MPs' report notes, sensibly, "If there is to be a total prohibition of any form of reproductive cloning, it is important that it is supported by principled arguments why such a technique should be banned even if it were shown to be safe, effective, and reliable." . . . .

The report does take note of the concerns of biotech critics, including the eugenics fears expressed by anti-biotech activist groups like Human Genetics Alert: "With the ability to select the characteristics of and even genetically engineer children according to consumers' desires comes the concern that human beings are becoming just another designed object/commodity within the industrial market system." The MPs tartly reply, "If ensuring that your child is less likely to face a debilitating disease in the course of their [*sic*] life can be termed eugenics, we have no problem with its use."

Finally, and most importantly, the U.K. report [argues that] the . . . highly speculative fears that sex selection will lead to sexism, or genetic engineering will socially marginalize the disabled, or clones will suffer psychological maladjustments, should not trump the known and sought-after benefits of biotechnological progress. . . .
—Ronald Bailey, *Reason Online*, 30 March 2004

"Church alarm over picking sex of babies"
As details emerged of the extent of the disagreements among the MPs on the Commons science and technology select committee over the report—said by one to be like creating "Frankenstein" babies—the Church of England and Roman Catholics claimed the work was deeply flawed.
—Stephen Bates, *The Guardian*, 25 March 2005

Letter to the Editor of New York Times Magazine
Which is the real monster? chimeric stem-cell science or the political use made of it by opponents to all embryonic-stem-cell research? Evoking the sound of "the scuffling of strange new feet in laboratory basements" [Jamie Shreeve's article, 10 April 2005] invites us to see the researchers as monster-creating Dr. Frankensteins. Images like this risk inflaming the public to unthinkingly torch the whole hopeful enterprise.
—Stephen E. Levick, M.D.

"Frankenstein" Neanderthal
Anthropologists have built a "Frankenstein" Neanderthal skeleton, the first and only full-body reconstruction of the species. . . . Gary Sawyer, an anthropologist at the American Natural History Museum in New York, and his colleague Blaine Maley of Washington University pieced together the skeleton using bones mostly from an individual known as La Ferrassie 1. La Ferrassie 1 was missing its rib cage, pelvis and a few other parts, so Sawyer and Maley had to scrounge

around to fill in the gaps. . . . Still, as the scientists pieced together the bones, something didn't look quite right. A rotund, bell-shaped torso, produced by a flared lower ribcage, and a pelvic region that looked slightly wide and feminine, began to form in front of their eyes.

"The biggest surprise by all means is that they have a rib cage radically different than a modern human's rib cage," said Sawyer. "As we stood back, we noticed one interesting thing was that these are kind of a short, squat people. These guys had no waist at all— they were compact, dwarfy-like beings." Other bits and replacement pieces, mostly the ends of bones, were collected from half a dozen other Neanderthals. The remaining gaps were filled in with reconstructed human bones. The finished product is "like Frankenstein," Sawyer said.

—Bjorn Carey, *MSNBC News*, 10 March 2005

A non-surgical procedure

"It's not a Frankenstein thing," Bill Redfern joked, as a medical attendant at Shady Grove Adventist Hospital in Rockville cuffed him flat to a medical table by his calves and thighs. Green rubber hoses poked from the blue cuffs wrapping the legs of the 73-year-old Maryland accountant. Several wires linked his chest to a large gray box near the head of the table. A switch was flicked, and the machine began a pulsing sound, an unfamiliar whoosh-CLICK! whoosh-CLICK! At each pulse, three sets of cuffs strapped to Redfern's legs rapidly inflated and deflated, one after another, so powerfully that his body jerked upward. . . . [T]he bizarre-looking procedure, which is administered over a period of seven weeks, also has a unique selling point to patients with coronary artery disease: it's nonsurgical. That means less risk, lower cost, less pain, less time in the hospital. And it seems to work.

—Ranit Mishori, *Washington Post*, 31 May 2005

In stitches

Getting stitches once meant a week spent looking like Frankenstein. No more. Today, doctors are increasingly turning to two alternatives: glue and staples. Both make treatment less traumatic and require less follow-up.

—Karen Springen, *Newsweek*, 6 June 2005

Frankenfood

"Seeds of Discontent"

Biotech companies are facing a growing furor in Europe over genetically altered food. Last fall, protesters in Ireland dug up fields of gene-spliced sugar beets. In Iowa, members of the environmental group Greenpeace spray-painted rows of genetically engineered soybeans. British activists shivered naked on the rooftops of London to protest what they called a genetic coverup, and others carried life-size, inflatable Frankenstein monsters through the streets to protest genetically modified foods.

—Julia Flynn and John Carey, with
William Echikson, *Business Week*, 2 February 1998

Frankentaters

It was a study conducted on genetically altered potatoes by a scientist in Scotland in August 1998 that set off what has now become a voluble and forceful movement by protesters against planting what they call "Frankenstein food" in Britain.

—Warren Hodge, *New York Times*, 7 June 2000

McFrankenfood

The judge ran down the ingredients of several McDonald's products, including Chicken McNuggets, which in addition to well-known additives common to processed foods, contain some less-familiar substances like TBHQ and an "anti-foaming agent." "Chicken McNuggets, rather than being merely chicken fried in a pan, are a McFrankenstein creation of various elements not utilized by the home cook."

—*New York Times*, 26 January 2003

"Of Frankenstein Fish and the Call of the Wild: A Trout's Tale"

BOZEMAN, Mont. . . . the hatchery-bred fish have killed off many of the wild trout, an outcome nobody wanted. These fish compete with the wild ones for food, and even though they are more vulnerable to disease, they usually outnumber the wild fish by such a high ratio that they threaten the native species. The so-called Frankenstein fish also interbreed, narrowing the genetic diversity because [when] they propagate, they do so with a less varied genetic map.

—Timothy Egan, *New York Times*, 2 June 1998

"GM Industry Puts Human Gene into Rice"

Scientists have begun putting genes from human beings into food crops in a dramatic extension of genetic modification [GM]. The move, which is causing disgust and revulsion among critics, is bound to strengthen accusations that GM technology is creating "Frankenstein foods" and drive the controversy surrounding it to new heights.

Even before this development, many people, including Prince Charles, have opposed the technology on the grounds that it is playing God by creating unnatural combinations of living things. . . . [S]cientists caution that if the gene were to escape to wild relatives of the rice it could create particularly vicious superweeds that were resistant to a wide range of herbicides. [One professor states,] "I do not have any ethical issue with using human genes to engineer plants," dismissing talk of "Frankenstein foods" as "rubbish." He believes that European opposition to GM crops and food is fuelled by agricultural protectionism. . . . Pete Riley, director of the anti-GM pressure group Five Year Freeze, said: "I am not surprised by this. The industry is capable of anything and this development certainly smacks of Frankenstein."

—Geoffrey Lean, *Independent Digital*, 24 April 2005

"Wine: Sorting Berries"

The newest Big Idea. . . . micro-oxygenation to make red wines accessible at an early age; and the use of reverse osmosis (RO) to remove water from wine so as to concentrate its flavour and enhance its mouthfeel and palate weight. Unfortunately, in the second case, alcohol levels also rise, as does volatile acidity, which makes some wines take on balsamic vinegar-like character. So no wonder there's a Luddite rebellion developing in winemaking circles which blames RO for producing "Frankenstein wines," which, once poured, soon "die in the glass."

—*Financial Mail* (South Africa), 14 March 2003

"In Vino Veritas: Frankenstein Wines?"

As more vintners use high tech to standardize their products, a few small purists emphasize old methods and distinctive flavors.

—Alice Feiring, *Fortune Small Business*, February 2004

Frankenburger

Andy Puzder figures he'll be forever famous—or infamous—for creating fast food's first edible Frankenstein: the Monster Thickburger. That's the 1420-calorie burger sold at Hardee's and Carl's Jr. since late last year.
—Bruce Horovitz, *USA Today*, 13 May 2005

Frankenfruit

The Orange Blossom Festival is a chance to taste UC Riverside varieties so exotic they may be unnamed. For nearly a century, UC Riverside has been creating Frankenstein-like citrus in its groves and laboratories—all in an effort to build the tastiest, hardiest fruits.
—Susannah Rosenblatt, *Los Angeles Times*, 20 May 2005

Automotive
"Frankenstude" redefines the hot rod

Frankenstein's Dragster. . . . Frankenstude—a reconstructed Studebaker, to say the least—pays the ultimate tribute to the American symbol of speed, power and uncompromising individuality. . . . Although it became an object of disgust shortly after its debut [1951], the bullet-nosed Studebaker still holds an iconoclastic position in American culture. "When Jim Henson put the Muppets in a car to go to Hollywood in the Muppet Movie, he chose a bullet-nosed Studebaker. . . . [H]e didn't just randomly pick this car," says Steve Andersen, the owner of Frankenstude.
—Kendra Ramic, *A&E*, 25 July 1997

"Frankenstein Hybrid Honda Power: VTEC Head Meets LS Block"

In the world of boxing, the bout between Mike Tyson and Evander Holyfield brought two well-trained fighters with opposing styles into the ring. . . . If we could apply our hybrid "Tyson-Holyfield" theory to our motor, we would have the best of both worlds—brute torque force and extended high-rev stamina. It exists and it's called the Frankenstein engine. . . .

The Transformation

We happened to stop by Pann Auto Performance in San Diego and visited Carl Batac, the company's resident auto surgeon who was about to perform this miracle surgery. . . . Horsepower, torque and rpm are the keys to molding our Frankenstein motor. We extracted our torque from the LS, pulled out the rpm from the VTEC and horsepower came from the combination of the two. People say, "You can talk the talk, but can you walk the walk." So with the Dynojet as our referee the proof is now on paper. Frankenstein lives.

   —undated online story in *IT Tech*, sometime after 1997

And Now . . . the Frankenstein of All Cars; The Mitsuoka Motor Company in Tokyo Has Built 8,000 Mutant Motor
   —*The Independent* (London), 1 November 2003

"The birth of a Frankenstein car"

The Logan, built from parts of various Renault cars, is about to embark on the bumpy road to emerging markets. . . .

   —Christopher Condon, *Financial Times*, 20 July 2004

Government Programs and Budgets
Frankenocracy

[T]he U.S. Department of Energy is . . . out of control like a bureaucratic Frankenstein's monster. Almost everything the huge federal agency has touched since it went into business on Oct. 1, 1977, has been left in shambles.

   —Senior Editor Kennth R. Sheets,
   U.S. News & World Report, 15 October 1979

"The Fiscal Frankenstein"

Some really scary, grinning ghouls and goblins were around this Halloween. You ain't seen nothing yet. The Thing they have been conjuring up on Capitol Hill out of hot air, tumbleweed and the dried bones of Southern senators is Jaws III with knobs on, a fiscal Frankenstein with three fathers that, once animated, will devour its own creators. . . . It is a crude, clanking monster with the eye of a Cyclops and the moral sense of a skunk. . . . It cannot touch the billions in tax loopholes for the wealthy and large corporations, which will increase by 192 billion dollars between 1984 and 1989, outpacing inflation. Its mean eye can see only the programs for the really poor, the farmers, schoolchildren, sick veterans, black-lung coal miners and the like. These groups will have to bear a share of automatic spending cuts equal to twice their share of the overall budget. It has no eye for the big weapons contracts, but its gaze will burn into national defense by damaging military readiness. It will handicap the war against terrorism and slow research into AIDS and cancer. . . . The grotesque nature of the beast is merely a reflection of the grotesque failure of the President and Congress to control spending or raise the money to pay for it. . . . The world's most prosperous democracy needs a Frankenstein to frighten it to its senses.

—Harold Evans, Editorial Director,
U.S. News & World Report, 11 November 1985

U.S. House of Representatives debates a Simplified USA Tax Act

Mr. ENGLISH of Pennsylvania: Mr. Speaker, the American tax system is a Frankenstein's monster that terrorizes individual taxpayers while casting a cold shadow over the productive sectors of the U.S. economy.
—*Hansard's Congressional Record*, 2 October 1998

Thatcher's Frankenstein's monster

Margaret Thatcher's legacy—political, social and cultural—is vast. But underpinning it all is an appalling economic legacy which the country has never recovered from . . . part of a vile experiment conducted on the British economy, involving privatisation, deregulation, trade union legislation and tight monetary policy. It was Margaret Thatcher's Frankenstein's Monster.

—opinion piece, BBC News, 29 April 1999

Back to the '80s: Big budget deficits are back.

NEW YORK. Skinny ties, feathered hair and legwarmers may not be coming back—hopefully—but at least one hallmark of the 1980s is here again: big budget deficits that could endanger the government's fiscal future, even if they help the economy in the short run. . . .

Will Frankenstein's monster wreck the budget?. . . [A]fter much grandstanding in Congress, the resulting stimulus package will probably include elements of both parties' plans. So a multibillion-dollar Frankenstein's monster of tax cuts and spending plans could stumble out of Congress this summer.

—Mark Gongloff, *CNN/Money*, 6 February 2003

Frankenbudget

The Senate yesterday delayed action until late January on a $328 billion bill to fund most non-military government operations, after the Democratic leader decried the measure as a "Frankenstein's monster."
—Helen Dewar, *Washington Post*, 10 December 2003

Frankenblueprint

With his proposal for a White Clouds Wilderness Idaho Rep. Mike Simpson has created a blueprint for a new Frankenstein that could threaten all of the nation's wilderness areas.
—*Idaho Mountain Express*, 16 July 2004

Frankenlegislation

HARRISBURG—Warning that the state Legislature and the Department of Labor and Industry have inadvertently created a "Frankenstein monster," a group of Western Pennsylvania lawmakers yesterday argued in vain for the repeal of the state's uniform construction code.
—Bill Toland, *Pittsburgh Post-Gazette*, 17 June 2004

Deregulation should loosen up the electricity market for private customers. However, a shortcircuiting history between management and unions in the energy monolith makes it more a slumbering Frankenstein awaiting a bolt from the heavens than an active agent of deregulation.
—*Financial Times*, 10 February 2005

Political Campaigns

Franken-primary

WASHINGTON, DC. . . . Both parties see victory in the south as essential to victory in the presidential election. They are beguiled, in particular, by the super-primary in at least 14 states in or bordering upon the south in the second week of March 1988. Yet, like Dr Frankenstein, southern Democrats, the creators of this primary, may have fashioned a creature that will end up turning on its master. The regional vote is set, but disagreement continues over whether it will have its desired effect. Will southerners anoint the kind of candidate envisioned by the regional primary's proponents, or will the plan produce something quite different?
—*The Economist*, 21 February 1987

"Mad Dr. Dean jolts Kerry campaign to life"

Ever since last Monday's audition for "An American Werewolf In Des Moines," the Vermonster has been in sleep mode. . . . [H]e talked in a voice so evenly modulated that Diane Sawyer kept dropping in tape of the Howlin' Howard roar every five minutes like Baron von Frankenstein frantically clamping the electrodes to the monster and getting no response.

—Mark Steyn, *Chicago Sun-Times*, 25 January 2004

Globalization and World Affairs

Frankenations

Nations that once relied on the West for aid and trade now are challenging their benefactors where it hurts most—in the pocketbook. . . . South Korea, Taiwan, Hong Kong and Singapore [have] become Frankenstein monsters, considered dangerous by the nations that helped them industrialize. The capital and expertise poured by the West into these and other backward or relatively poor countries help produce a flood of cheap exports—textiles, shoes, electronic equipment, even ships and steel. These goods, the output of somewhat low-paid but highly organized and sophisticated labor forces, undersell Western producers in their own markets, create unemployment and arouse powerful opposition from unions, industrialists and politicians.

—*U.S. News & World Report*, 16 October 1978

FrankenChina

In 1969, as Richard Nixon shared with Charles de Gaulle his idea of an opening to China, the French President told him: "Better to deal with the Chinese now, when they need you, than later, when you're forced to because of their strength." . . . Then he added this chilling caveat: "in the long haul, looking way down the line—this is the deep background—15 years from now, we may have created a Frankenstein."

—William Safire, *New York Times*, 9 July 1998

Meeting on a hopeful note . . .
"it is far from looking like a Frankenstein"

GENEVA—Heading into the World Trade Organization meeting scheduled for Wednesday in Cancun, Mexico, trade ministers from

146 nations have been dogged by a string of missed deadlines and a lack of progress on major issues. . . . Still, there are hopeful signs. . . . "We have been adding a lot of flesh to the bones of the skeleton," said Uruguayan ambassador Carlos Perez del Castillo, chairperson of the WTO's general council. "Although the end product may not look like Miss Universe, I can assure you that it is far from looking like a Frankenstein that will turn against us."

—Naomi Koppel, Montreal *Gazette*, 8 September 2003

Canadian Parliament, on allying in the war against Iraq

Hon. Hedy Fry (Vancouver Centre, Liberal): I may be wrong in my perception, but yesterday's heroes are today's monsters. Are we creating sort of a Frankenstein syndrome here? Iraq, we know, was very active against Iran. Where did Iraq get the weapons of chemical and biological warfare to do that? The Taliban was created in order to get rid of the great Communist scourge when Russia was within Afghanistan and today the Taliban are monsters. Does he see a pattern here? Does he feel that manipulative interests in other countries' "democratic institutions" or non-democratic institutions can lead to a sort of Frankenstein syndrome?

—10 February 2002

"We Finally Got Our Frankenstein . . . and He Was in a Spider Hole!"

Thank God Saddam is finally back in American hands! . . . We were so cozy with dear old Saddam that we decided to feed him satellite images so he could locate where the Iranian troops were. . . . and sure enough, as soon as we sent him the spy photos, he gassed those troops. And we kept quiet. Because he was our friend, and the Iranians were the "enemy." A year after he first gassed the Iranians, we reestablished full diplomatic relations with him! . . . We had a virtual love fest with this Frankenstein whom we (in part) created.

And, just like the mythical Frankenstein, Saddam eventually spun out of control. He would no longer do what he was told by his master. Saddam had to be caught. And now that he has been brought back from the wilderness, perhaps he will have something to say about his creators.

—Michael Moore, *MichaelMoore.com*, 14 December 2003

"America's Frankenstein Monsters"

George W Bush is trying to create yet another monster in the Middle East like his father's predecessor, Ronald Reagan, . . . who supported and sustained the resistance movement in Afghanistan against Soviet intervention. Al-Qaeda and other resistance groups then fighting against the Soviets in Afghanistan earned great ovation and respect from the US policy-makers, and Ronald Reagan called them "the moral equivalent of the founding fathers." The US blinded by its hatred for the Soviets fully armed an insurgency which also had Saudi Money and Arab manpower as its constituents and finally was able to push back the Soviets. . . . Refusing to learn lessons from the past the US is doing the same in the Gulf. It is now supporting and sustaining "Mujaheedin-i-Khalq" . . . Not long ago they were branded as terrorist organization in the US, whereas presently they have a safe haven in Iraq. . . . British author and feminist, Mary Wollstonecraft Shelley, must be very proud in her grave that playing "Fritz" of her story most US Secretaries of State have no pangs of conscience in choosing their tools to realize their objectives in the Gulf.

—Syed Javed Hussain, *Pakistan Observer*, 29 April 2005

"Bolton is Bush's Frankenstein monster"

Too little attention has been paid to the most important aspect of the Senate Foreign Relations Committee hearings on the nomination of Undersecretary of State John Bolton to be the ambassador to the United Nations. . . . [I]n spite of his incompetence and his egregious misuse of information to push his unsubstantiated claims . . . winning at any cost has morphed into the overriding Bush administration objective as party polarization has turned Washington D.C., politics into a no man's land where the nation's needs are the main casualty. Nowhere are these two points made more clearly than in the case of Bolton, who turns out to be President Bush's Frankenstein's monster, a figurative stitching together of the administration's worst traits.

—Walter Williams, *Seattle Post-Intelligencer*, 11 May 2005

Meanwhile in Europe . . .
"The Franco-German monster"

Rather like Frankenstein's monster, the Franco-German relationship has a habit of appearing dead for long periods, only to spring to life and start crashing around once more.

—*The Economist*, 25 October 2003

"Chirac has subdued Bolkestein's monster—but he's not safe yet"

President Chirac had won his battle against the monster that has been terrorising his country. The creature's name is Bolkestein's directive. In the manner that Frankenstein's monster terrorised the locals, Bolkestein's directive has come to crystallise everything that France fears in the European Union—and its new constitution in particular.

Blame Bolkestein, or at least the draft EU directive that bears his name, if France votes "non" in the referendum on the constitution on May 29, as polls suggest that it might. [Ed.: It did.] Frits Bolkestein, a Dutch member of the last Commission, merely sought to implement a 45-year-old commitment to open European frontiers for the service industries that now account for 70% of its economy. . . . For France, this new Frankenstein's monster lurched out of the northern mists this winter to symbolise the free-market misery that Britain and its allies in Central Europe are trying to foist on the Continent in the guise of a constitution.

Left-wing opponents have succeeded in demonising the directive as the harbinger of the hell of "social dumping" . . . this means invasion by cut-price Polish plumbers, Estonian electricians and Slovenian surgeons, who will push French professionals out of business. . . .

- *Frankenstein's monster*: Stitched together in Ingolstadt, Germany, in 1818 in "days and nights of incredible fatigue" (in the words of Mary Shelley, his author).

    Bolkestein's directive: Stitched together in Brussels, Belgium, in 2004 in "days and nights of incredible fatigue" (in the words of a Commission official)
- *Frankenstein's monster*: Made from human parts retrieved from German graveyards.

    Bolkestein's directive: Made from ideas retrieved from British economic doctrines
- *Dr Frankenstein*: Swiss scientist whose project ran out of control, turning evil.

    Mr Bolkestein: Dutch liberal whose evil project ran out of control
- *Frankenstein's monster*: "A hideous phantasm" (Mary Shelley).

    Bolkestein's directive: "The ugly liberal nightmare" (Henri Emmanuelli, senior French socialist)
- *Frankenstein's monster*: Put to death after struggle on Arctic mountain.

Bolkestein's directive: Put to death after struggle at Brussels summit.
—Charles Bremner, *Europe*, 24 March 2005

"No debate on 'Frankenstein' directive"

The proposed legislation was known as the Bolkestein Directive, after Fritz Bolkestein, the former EU internal market commissioner responsible for the original draft. But Dublin MEP Proinsias de Rossa dubbed it the "Frankenstein directive" because, as drafted, it would have undermined most existing collective agreements, national labour laws, environmental codes and public services.
—Bernard Harbor, *Irish Times*, 27 May 2005

Scandals, Sports, and Pop Culture

Frankenpress

Where to draw the line? The voice on the other end of the phone told the *Newsweek* reporter she had a hot tip. Alexander Haig, a Republican candidate for president, had been spotted parking his car in a zone reserved for the handicapped. Haig the Heartless? Wheelchairgate? It was a sign of how conditioned the press has become to playing character cop that the reporter actually briefly considered calling around to check the story out. With the revelations last week about the Rev. Pat Robertson's personal life, the hulking "character issue" was turning into the Frankenstein monster of American presidential politics. And just as in the movie, the monster eventually turns on its creator—in this case, the press.
—Jonathan Alter, *Newsweek*, 19 October 1987

Frankengate

It is sometimes argued that the Iran-contra scandal was even worse than Watergate: because Reagan's men aimed to circumvent laws passed by Congress, it was a direct affront to the Constitution they had sworn to uphold. And in setting up what amounted to a private CIA to carry out that and other schemes, they were creating a Frankenstein's monster.
—Larry Martz and Robert Parry, *Newsweek*, 17 July 1989

"If you create Frankenstein, you can't be real surprised if he eats the village. It's not his fault. You created him." —Steve Stone, former Cubs broadcaster commenting on the Cubs' preferential treatment of Sammy Sosa

—*Houston Chronicle*, 17 December 2004

Call the mortician for the Cincinnati Deads, uh, Reds. Even Dr. Frankenstein would declare no hope of reviving their season.

—Todd Jones, *Columbus Dispatch*, May 23, 2005

For those individuals looking to cheat and steal an edge on their rivals, gene doping has become the ultimate aim, and the prospect of genetically modified athletes competing like so many Frankenstein monsters was again raised in the United States Congress on Wednesday.

—Duncan Mackay, *The Guardian*, 29 April 2005

Frankenball

Kerry Wood created his own personal Frankenstein's monster on May 6, 1998, when he befuddled the Houston Astros with pitches that defied gravity and had more angles than a carnival pitchman. Ever since the young Texas whiz kid struck out 20 and became a national celebrity in the blink of an eye, he has struck out time and again in trying to win Cubs fans' hearts.

—Mike Kiley, *Chicago Sun-Times*, 8 April 2005

"A modern Dr. Frankenstein rushes ahead into the unknown"

SHIPHAM, England—Steve Grand, maverick artificial-life expert and designer of the breathtakingly innovative computer game Creatures, is not one to shrink from brazen pronouncements. "I am an aspiring latter-day Baron Frankenstein," is how Mr. Grand describes himself in his recent book, *Creation: Life and How to Make It*.

—Sarah Lyall, *New York Times*, 2 February 2002

Frankentecture

"There is a downside to all traditions, especially evident when they are most successful," writes Charles Jencks. . . . Today Jencks distinguishes between post-modernism proper . . . and "pomo"—"mass-produced, cliched and too big." The Disney Corporation's patronage . . . was, says Jencks, the kiss of death for post-modernism. One is reminded of John Ruskin, lamenting the influence of *The Stones of Venice*: "There is scarcely a public house near the Crystal Palace but sells its gin and bitters under pseudo-Venetian capitals." Maybe Jencks, like Ruskin, shivers when he sees the "Frankenstein monsters" he unwittingly created?

—*Building Design*, September 6, 2002

Frankenchic

Fashion designers are generally sensitive people with a good sense of humor. But when it comes to making new collections, they are a lot like Dr. Frankenstein. They create a monster, and then they have a few regrets.

—Cathy Horyn, *New York Times*, 4 January 2005

FrankenJolson

Mark Nadler [is] a frenzied, piano-banging, jabbering encyclopedia of show business lore who suggests a Frankenstein-like resurrection of Al Jolson, wired from head to toe with the voltage turned on high.

—Steve Holden, *New York Times*, 10 February 2005

FrankenSpears

These days, with a few notable exceptions, you have to search pretty thoroughly to find the last skeletal vestiges of the blues poking through the accumulated layers of puppy-fat and clutter of piercings on pop's plump, satiated body. At times, it seems as if the form has more to do with the unnatural experiments of some fiendish cultural Frankenstein in a dust-free, sterile Swedish laboratory. What else could explain Britney Spears?

—Andy Gill, London *Independent*, 24 June 2005

Welcome to the House of Frankenstein Wax Museum

Doctor Frankenstein, according to Mary Shelley, created a monster from the dead. Here in the House of Frankenstein Wax Museum there are many "monsters." The creatures roaming the halls of this house are not living . . . yet they are not dead. For as you shall see for yourself, they move and talk and sometimes they even SCREAM! Be warned the House of Frankenstein is not just another Wax Museum. No indeed. When you walk the steps of the haunted stairs you are on your own. Don't turn back, there is no turning back, you must finish this journey of terror.

OPEN APRIL 15 THROUGH HALLOWEEN 2005

Big Business

"Frankensteins, Einsteins and Philistines"

Consumer Finance specialist Beneficial Bank has conducted a survey to determine the population's attitudes to finance and financial planning, the results offering retailers some useful pointers on targeting customers with appropriate credit packages. Three distinct character types were identified: Frankensteins, Einsteins and Philistines. The first (38% of those surveyed) are said to get in a monster muddle with their money and have little idea how much they owe, or how their bank or building society finances stand.

—*Carpet & Floorcoverings Review*, May 1998

A Smarter Frankenstein: The Merging of E-Learning and Knowledge Management

Take an e-learning course. Chunk it into discrete learning bites. Surround it with technology that assesses a learner's needs and delivers the appropriate learning nuggets. Add collaborative tools that allow learners to share information. What do you get? Something that looks a whole lot like knowledge management.

Traditionally seen as separate disciplines whose practitioners might engage in a friendly watercooler chat now and again, training and knowledge management are converging into a new, technology-fueled creature. The beast combines formal training as represented by e-learning and the free-floating knowledge swirling through organizations that KM practices seek to snare and share. But, like Frankenstein's monster, the technologies that fuse the two practices are outpacing management's ability to anticipate their combined impact.

—Tom Barron, *Learning Circuits*, August 2000

"Attention Moguls: It's Time To Play Frankenstein"

NEW YORK—Want to really scare Rupert Murdoch this Halloween? Then dress up as Steve Case, the man who stitched together that Frankenstein's monster known as AOL Time Warner. AOL is the behemoth that gives Murdoch nightmares: a rival media conglomerate with its own cable distribution arm.

—Mark Lewis, *Forbes.com*, 31 October 2001

Frankenron

America's "most innovative company" (per *Fortune*), Enron was created by preacher's son Ken Lay (or as George W. Bush called him, "Kenny Boy") and administered by the Harvard-educated macho man Jeffrey Skilling, whose Gordon Gekkoid business philosophy advocated unlimited greed. Enron contributed mightily to Bush campaign coffers, but once its $30 billion debt emerged from a maze of creative accountancy, the corporation went from being the New Economy poster child to its Frankenstein monster.

—J. Hoberman, on *Enron: The Smartest Guys in the Room*, in *Tracking Shots*, 19 April 2005

"Frankenstein's monster must be destroyed, says ex-Equitable boss"

A former boss of Equitable Life yesterday described the £3.7 billion lawsuit brought by the insurer against him and others as a "Frankenstein's monster that should be strangled" before it did any more damage.

—Rupert Jones, *The Guardian*, 19 April 2005

"Airline industry Frankenstein could creak to life"

Airline mergers, like airline bankruptcies, have a slim record of success, yet these two solutions are becoming the chief restructuring tools of the US airline industry. In the proposed merger between US Airways and America West, both methods are coming to the fore. For some observers, that suggests double trouble. As one former senior airline executive puts it, "it is like combining two one-legged men. They are not going to be a track star, even if they are ambulatory."

—Caroline Daniel, *FinancialTimes.com*, 15 May 2005

Frankenspace

The International Space Station is a mess. It is the Frankenstein monster of too many decades and too many economic ups and downs and too many administrations with varying priorities. Construction is years behind schedule and tens of billions of dollars overbudget.

—*Columbus Dispatch*, 3 June 2005

Frankentrak

AMTRAK, Budget-cutters and fiscal conservatives . . . say that what Congress cobbled together in 1971 from the fading passenger operations of the major freight railroads was not a phoenix but a Frankenstein.
—Matthew L. Wald, *New York Times*, 12 June 2005

"Frankenpine"

The Adirondack Park Agency, a powerful group charged with protecting New York's six-million-acre state park, decided last week that a cellphone tower could be constructed near Lake George. The tower, a 104-foot fake pine tree . . . the new Frankenpine of Lake George.
—*New York Times*, editorial, 11 July 2005

"Who Said It?"

"I'm older than dirt, I've got more scars than Frankenstein, but I've learned a few things along the way."

BARBARA BUSH
JOHN McCAIN
SANDRA DAY O'CONNOR
ROBERT REDFORD

Answer: Sen. John McCain, R-Ariz., asked on the *Today* show if his health would be a factor in 2008 if he runs for president.
—*San Antonio Express-News*, 3 February 2006

Further Reading and Viewing

Mary Wollstonecraft Godwin Shelley: Biography, Letters, Journals

The Journals of Mary Shelley, 1814–1844. Ed. Paula R. Feldman and Diana Scott-Kilvert. 1987; Johns Hopkins University Press, 1995.

The Letters of Mary Wollstonecraft Shelley. Ed. Betty T. Bennett. 3 vols. Johns Hopkins University Press, 1980–88.

Garrett, Martin. *Mary Shelley.* Oxford University Press, 2000.

Mellor, Anne K. *Mary Shelley: Her Life, Her Fiction, Her Monsters.* Methuen, 1988.

Nitchie, Elizabeth. *Mary Shelley, Author of "Frankenstein."* Rutgers University Press, 1953.

Schor, Esther, ed. *The Cambridge Companion to Mary Shelley.* Cambridge University Press, 2003. Includes five essays on *Frankenstein.*

Seymour, Miranda. *Mary Shelley.* Pantheon, 2001.

Smith, Johanna. *Mary Shelley.* Twayne, 1996.

St. Clair, William. *The Godwins and the Shelleys: The Biography of a Family.* Faber, 1989.

Sunstein, Emily. *Mary Wollstonecraft Shelley: Romance and Reality.* Little, 1989.

Walling, William. *Mary Shelley.* Twayne, 1972.

Other Texts of *Frankenstein*

Rieger, James, ed. *Frankenstein (the 1818 text).* University of Chicago Press, 1974. An introduction biased against Mary Shelley's talents and authorship, but interesting documentation of the revisions of the mid-1820s.

Robinson, Charles. *The Frankenstein Notebooks: A Facsimile Edition of Mary Shelley's Manuscript Novel, 1816–17 (with Alterations in the Hand of Percy Bysshe Shelley) as it Survives in Draft and Fair Copy Deposited by Lord Abinger in the Bodleian Library, Oxford.* Garland, 1996. 2 vols. An extraordinary resource, indispensable for all arguments about authorship and revision.

Smith, Johanna M., ed. *Frankenstein.* 1831; Bedford Press, 2000.

Web Sites

(Digital texts enable word searches; links to other information, images, bibliographies.)

Mary Shelley: http://www.rc.umd.edu/reference/mschronology/mws.html
The 1818 text: http://www.boutell.com/frankenstein/
The 1831 text: http://www.sangfroid.com/frank/index.html
Reviews of *Presumption; or, The Fate of Frankenstein* (1823):
                http://www.rc.umd.edu/reference/mschronology/
                reviews/mprev.html
Film versions: http://us.imdb.com/
                full credits, and some reviews

Critical Issues

Baldick, Chris. *In* Frankenstein's *Shadow: Myth, Monstrosity, and Nineteenth-Century Writing.* Clarendon Press, 1987.

Behrendt, Stephen C., ed. *Approaches to Teaching Shelley's* Frankenstein. Modern Language Association, 1990. Readable as "approaches to reading." Nineteen essays on a range of topics; bibliography; filmography.

———. "Language and Style in *Frankenstein.*" Behrendt (ed.), 78–84.

———. "Mary Shelley, *Frankenstein,* and the Woman Writer's Fate." In *Romanticism and Women Writers: Voices and Counter-Voices.* Ed. Paula R. Feldman and Theresa M. Kelley. University Press of New England, 1995, 69–87.

Bennett, Betty T. "*Frankenstein* and the Uses of Biography." Behrendt (ed.), 78–84.

Bloom, Harold. "*Frankenstein* Or, The New Prometheus." Afterword, Signet edn. of *Frankenstein,* 1965; rpt. *The Ringers in the Towers: Studies in Romantic Tradition.* University of Chicago Press, 1971, 118–29.

Botting, Fred. *Making Monstrous: "Frankenstein," Criticism, Theory.* Manchester, 1991.

Brooks, Peter. "'Godlike Science / Unhallowed Arts': Language, Nature, and Monstrosity." Levine and Knoepflmacher, 205–20.

———. "What Is a Monster? (According to *Frankenstein.*)" *Body Works: Objects of Desire in Modern Narrative.* Harvard University Press, 1993, 199–220.

Brown, Marshall. "*Frankenstein*: A Child's Tale." *Novel* 36.2 (2003): 146–73.

Bugg, John. "'Master of Their Language': Education and Exile in Mary Shelley's *Frankenstein.*" *HLQ* 68.4 (2005): 655–66.

Butler, Marilyn. "The First *Frankenstein* and Radical Science." *TLS* 9 (April 1993): 12–14.

Cantor, Paul. "The Nightmare of Romantic Idealism." *Creature and Creator: Myth-Making and English Romanticism.* Cambridge University Press, 1984, 103–32.

——— and Michael Valdez Moses. "Teaching *Frankenstein* from the Creature's Perspective." Behrendt (ed.), 127–32.

Carson, James P. "Bringing the Author Forward: *Frankenstein* through Mary Shelley's Letters." *Criticism* 30 (1988): 431–53.

Clubbe, John. "The Tempest-Toss'd Summer of 1816: Mary Shelley's *Frankenstein*." *Byron Journal* 19 (1991): 26–42.

Conger, Sydny. "Aporia and Radical Empathy: *Frankenstein* (Re)trains the Reader." Behrendt (ed.), 60–66.

Cragwall, Jasper. "The Shelleys' Enthusiasm." *HLQ* 68.4 (2005): 631–54.

Duyfhuizen, Bernard. "Periphrastic naming in Mary Shelley's *Frankenstein*." *Studies in the Novel* (1995): 477–92.

Ellis, Kate. "Monsters in the Garden: Mary Shelley and the Bourgeois Family." In Levine and Knoepflmacher, 1979, 123–42.

Favret, Mary A. "The Letters of *Frankenstein*." *Genre* 20 (1987): 3–24. Cf. *Romantic Correspondence: Women, Politics, and the Fiction of Letters*. Cambridge University Press, 1993, 176–96.

Feldman, Paula R. "Probing the Psychological Mystery of *Frankenstein*." Behrendt (ed.), 67–77.

Ferguson, Frances. "The Gothicism of the Gothic Novel." *Solitude and the Sublime*. Routledge, 1992, 97–113.

Gigante, Denise. "Facing the Ugly: The Case of *Frankenstein*." *ELH* 67 (2000): 565–87.

Gilbert, Sandra, and Susan Gubar. "Horror's Twin: Mary Shelley's Monstrous Eve." *The Madwoman in the Attic: The Woman Writer and the Nineteenth-Century Literary Imagination*. Yale University Press, 1979, 213–47.

Griffin, Andrew. "Fire and Ice in *Frankenstein*." Levine and Knoepflmacher, 1979, 49–73.

Hobbs, Colleen. "Reading the Symptoms: An Exploration of Repression and Hysteria in Mary Shelley's *Frankenstein*." *Studies in the Novel* 25.2 (1993): 152–69.

Homans, Margaret. "Bearing Demons: *Frankenstein's* Circumvention of the Maternal." *Bearing the Word: Language and Female Experience in Nineteenth-Century Women's Writing*. University of Chicago Press, 1986, 100–19.

Jacobus, Mary. "Is There a Woman in This Text?" *New Literary History* 14 (1982): 117–41; rpt. *Reading Woman: Essays in Feminist Criticism*. Columbia University Press, 1986, 83–109.

Johnson, Barbara. "My Monster / My Self." *Diacritics* 12.2 (1982): 2–10; rpt. *A World of Difference*. Johns Hopkins University Press, 1989.

Kincaid, James, R. "'Words Cannot Express': *Frankenstein's* Tripping on the Tongue." *Novel* 24.1 (Fall 1990): 26–47. See also *Annoying the Victorians*. Routledge, 1995, 181–205.

Knoepflmacher, U. C. "Thoughts on the Aggression of Daughters." Levine and Knoepflmacher, 1979, 88–119.

Komisaruk, Adam. "'So Guided by a Silken Cord': *Frankenstein's* Family Values." *Studies in Romanticism* 38 (1999): 365–85.

Levine, George. "The Ambiguous Heritage of *Frankenstein*." Levine and Knoepflmacher, 1979, 3–30.

——. "*Frankenstein* and the Tradition of Realism." *Novel* 7 (1973): 14–30; cf. *The Realistic Imagination: English Fiction from* Frankenstein *to* Lady Chatterly's Lover. University of Chicago Press, 1981.

—— and U. C. Knoepflmacher, eds. *The Endurance of* Frankenstein: *Essays on Mary Shelley's Novel*. University of California Press, 1979.

London, Bette. "Mary Shelley, *Frankenstein*, and the Spectacle of Masculinity." *PMLA* 108 (1993): 253–67.

Marshall, David. *The Surprising Effects of Sympathy*. University of Chicago Press, 1988.

Mellor, Anne K. "Choosing a Text of *Frankenstein* to Teach." Behrendt (ed.), 31–37.

———. "*Frankenstein* and the Sublime." Behrendt (ed.), 99–104.

———. "Possessing Nature: The Female in *Frankenstein*." *Romanticism & Feminism*. Ed. Anne K. Mellor. Indiana University Press, 1988, 220–32.

Michie, Elsie B. "Production Replaces Creation: Market Forces and *Frankenstein* as Critique of Romanticism." *Nineteenth-Century Contexts* 12.1 (Spring 1988): 27–33. Cf. Behrendt (ed.), 93–96.

Moers, Ellen. "Female Gothic." *Literary Women*. Doubleday, 1976; rpt. in Levine and Knoepflmacher, 1979, 77–87.

Newlyn, Lucy. *"Paradise Lost" and the Romantic Reader*. Oxford University Press, 1993.

Newman, Beth. "Narratives of Seduction and the Seductions of Narrative: The Frame Structure of *Frankenstein*." *ELH* 53.1 (1986): 141–63.

Oates, Joyce Carol. "*Frankenstein*'s Fallen Angel." *Critical Inquiry* 10.3 (March 1984): 543–54.

O'Rourke, James. "The 1831 Introduction and Revisions to *Frankenstein*: Mary Shelley Dictates Her Legacy." *Studies in Romanticism* 38 (1999): 365–85.

Poovey, Mary. "My Hideous Progeny: Mary Shelley and the Feminization of Romanticism." *PMLA* 95 (1980): 332–47; rpt. *The Proper Lady and the Woman Writer: Ideology as Style in the Works of Mary Wollstonecraft, Mary Shelley, and Jane Austen*. University of Chicago Press, 1984, 114–42.

Rauch, Alan. "The Monstrous Body of Knowledge in Mary Shelley's *Frankenstein*." *Studies in Romanticism* 34 (1995): 227–54.

Richard, Jessica. "'A Paradise of My Own Creation': *Frankenstein* and the Improbable Romance of the North Pole." *Nineteenth-Century Contexts* 25.4 (2003): 295–314.

Richardson, Alan. "From *Emile* to *Frankenstein*: The Education of Monsters." *European Romantic Review* 1.2 (Winter 1991): 147–62.

Rovee, Christopher. "Monsters, Marbles, and Miniatures," in *Imagining the Gallery: The Social Body of British Romanticism*. Stanford University Press, 2006.

Rubenstein, Marc. "'My Accursed Origin': The Search for the Mother in *Frankenstein*." *Studies in Romanticism* 15 (1976): 165–94.

Scott, Peter Dale. "Vital Artifice: Mary, Percy, and the Psychopolitical Integrity of *Frankenstein*." Levine and Knoepflmacher, 1979, 172–202.

Shaw, Debra B. *Women, Science, and Fiction: The Frankenstein Inheritance*. Palgrave, 2000.

Sherwin, Paul. "Creation as Catastrophe." *PMLA* 96 (1981): 883–903.

Small, Christopher. *Ariel Like a Harpy: Shelley, Mary and Frankenstein*. Gollancz, 1972; rpt. as *Mary Shelley's Frankenstein: Tracing the Myth*. University of Pittsburgh Press, 1973.

Spivak, Gayatri Chakravorty. "Three Women's Texts and a Critique of Imperialism." *Critical Inquiry* 12 (1985–86): 243–61.

Sterrenberg, Lee. "Mary Shelley's Monster: Politics and Psyche in *Frankenstein*." Levine and Knoepflmacher, 1979, 143–71.

Stevick, Philip. "*Frankenstein* as Comedy." Levine and Knoepflmacher, 1979, 221–39.

Stewart, Garrett. "In the Absence of Audience: Of Reading and Dread in Mary Shelley." *Dear Reader: The Conscripted Audience in Nineteenth-Century British Fiction*. Johns Hopkins University Press, 1996, 113–32.

Tropp, Martin. *Mary Shelley's Monster: The Story of* Frankenstein. Houghton Mifflin, 1976.

Veeder, William. *Mary Shelley and* Frankenstein: *The Fate of Androgyny*. University of Chicago Press, 1986.

Walling, William. "*Frankenstein* in the Context of English Romanticism." Behrendt (ed.), 105–11.

Wolfson, Susan. "Feminist Inquiry and *Frankenstein*." Behrendt (ed.), 50–59.

———. "Reconstructing *Frankenstein*." *Review* 20 (1998): 1–15.

Zonana, Joyce. " 'They will prove the truth of my tale': Safie's Letters as the Feminist Core of Mary Shelley's *Frankenstein*." *Journal of Narrative Technique* 21.1 (Spring 1991): 170–84.

On the Stage and Film Versions

Branagh, Kenneth. *Mary Shelley's* Frankenstein: *A Classic Tale of Terror Reborn on Film*. Newmarket Press, 1994.

Dixon, Wheeler. "The Films of *Frankenstein*." Behrendt (ed.), 166–79.

Forry, Steven Earl. *Hideous Progenies: Dramatizations of Frankenstein from Mary Shelley to the Present*. University of Pennsylvania Press, 1990.

Heffernan, James A. W. "Looking for the Monster: *Frankenstein* and Film." *Critical Inquiry* 24 (August 1997): 133–58.

La Valley, Albert J. "The Stage and Film Children of *Frankenstein*: A Survey." Levine and Knoepflmacher, 1979, 243–59.

Film and TV Versions

1910   *Frankenstein.* "A Liberal Adaptation from Mrs. Shelley's Famous Story for Edison Productions." 11 minutes. Silent. Mad scientist, lab-science, the animation, Frankenstein's (VF) wedding, final confrontation. Directed by J. Searle Dawley.

1915   *Life without a Soul.* Silent.

1920   *The Monster of Frankenstein.* Italian. Silent.

1931   *Frankenstein.* Fixing the image of the Creature as bolted and inarticulate, though pathetic. Directed by James Whale. Boris Karloff (C), Colin Clive (F: called "Henry"). Based on the stage play by Peggy Webling.

1935   *The Bride of Frankenstein.* Directed by James Whale. Boris Karloff (C), Colin Clive (VF—"Henry"), Elsa Lanchester (Mary Shelley, the Bride). Begins with the summer of 1816. *Bride of* refers to genesis, not possession.

1939   *Son of Frankenstein.* Basil Rathbone (son of), Boris Karloff (C), Bela Lugosi assisting.

1942   *The Ghost of Frankenstein.* Cedrick Hardwicke (another son of), Lon Chaney Jr. (C), Ralph Bellamy, Evelyn Ankers, Lionel Atwill (another son), Bela Lugosi (still assisting).

1943   *Frankenstein Meets the Wolf Man.* Patric Knowles (F), Lon Chaney Jr. (W), Bela Lugosi (now promoted: C), and the incomparable Maria Ouspenskaya.

1944   *House of Frankenstein.* A Creature Feature. The gang's all here.

1945   *House of Dracula.* More Creatures.

1948   *Abbott and Costello Meet Frankenstein.* Aka *The Brain of Frankenstein.* Bud Abbott, Lou Costello, Lon Chaney Jr. (C), Bela Lugosi (Dracula). The gang's all here. Directed by Charles T. Barton.

1957   *The Curse of Frankenstein.* Christopher Lee (C), Peter Cushing (F). The first of Britain's Hammer series. Dir. Terence Fisher.
        I Was a Teenage Frankenstein. After the Michael Landon hit, *I Was a Teenage Werewolf.*

1958   *Frankenstein's Daughter.*
        The Revenge of Frankenstein. Hammer. Peter Cushing (F), Michael Gwynn (C).
        Frankenstein 1970. Near-futurism. Boris Karloff.

1960   *How to Make a Monster.* Don't try this at home.

1964   *Frankenstein Meets the Space Monster.*
        The Evil of Frankenstein. Hammer. Peter Cushing (F).

1966   *Frankenstein Created Woman.* Hammer. Peter Cushing (F).
        Jesse James Meets Frankenstein's Daughter.
        Frankenstein Conquers the World (Japanese), Nick Adams is C.
        Munster, Go Home! Fred Gwynne as the Creaturely Munster. Spawned the TV series *The Munsters.*

1967   *Mad Monster Party.* A puppet version.

1969   *Frankenstein Must Be Destroyed.* Hammer. Peter Cushing (F).

1970   *Dr. Frankenstein on Campus.* You always knew it.
        Dracula vs. Frankenstein. It had to happen.
        Horror of Frankenstein. Satire.

1971   *Lady Frankenstein* (Italian: *La Figlia* [daughter] *di Frankenstein*). Joseph Cotten (F).

1973   *Frankenstein.* TV. Robert Foxworth (F), Bo Svenson (C).
        Frankenstein and the Monster from Hell. Peter Cushing returns, for the last time (F).
        Andy Warhol's Frankenstein. Not. Directed by Paul Morrissey. 3-D.
        Blackenstein. First there was *Blacula* (1972), then . . .
        Spirit of the Beehive. Spanish. A child is haunted by Whale's *Frankenstein.*
        Frankenstein: The True Story. Not. TV. Leonard Whiting (F), Michael Sarrazin (C), Jane Seymour as she-Creature. Scripted by Christopher Isherwood.
        Young Frankenstein. Sublime satire. Directed by Mel Brooks. Gene Wilder (F), Peter Boyle (C), Madeline Kahn, Cloris Leachman, Marty Feldman (Igor).

1975   *Death Race 2000.* Satiric near-futurism; David Carradine as a race-car driver named Frankenstein.

Rocky Horror Picture Show. Dir. Jim Sharman. Tim Curry as the outrageous transvestite from Transylvania, Dr. Frank-N-Furter. Preceded by *The Rocky Horror Show* on the London stage, also spiced with Curry. "Why don't ya come up to the lab and see what's on the slab . . . ?"

1976   *Terror of Frankenstein.*

1980   *Dr. Franken.* Robert Vaughn (F), Robert Perault (C).

1986   *The Bride.* Sting (F), Jennifer Beals.
      Gothic. Directed by Ken Russell. Summer of 1816. Natasha Richardson, Gabriel Byrne, Julian Sands. Surreal.

1987   *The Monster Squad.*
      Making Mr. Right. Comedy. Frankie Stone, tired of the singles scene, gets involved in educating an android (John Malkovich), and they fall for each other. Dir. Susan Seidelman.

1988   *Haunted Summer.* . . . of 1816. Eric Stolz as Percy Bysshe Shelley. Dir. Ivan Passer.

1990   *Frankenhooker.* Do the math.
      Frankenstein Unbound. Aka Roger Corman's *Frankenstein Unbound.* Based on Brian Aldiss's novel. Raul Julia (F), John Hurt, Bridget Fonda.

1991   *Waxworks II: Lost in Time.*
      Frankenstein: The College Years (TV). Written by Bryant Christ and John Trevor Woolf; directed by Tom Shadyac. Favorite student Mark inherits the key to his professor's secret lab, where he and a friend discover and revive the body of "Frankenstein." They find they have produced a popular football star. Right place, right time.

1993   *Frankenstein.* TV. Randy Quaid (C).

1994   *Mary Shelley's Frankenstein.* Not. Directed by Kenneth Branagh (also F), Robert De Niro (C). Spectacular on the sublimities, and De Niro is poignant.

1995   *Mr. Stitch.* Rutger Hauer as F.

1997   *The Creeps.* Mad scientist steals the original manuscript of *Frankenstein.*

1998   *Gods and Monsters.* The demons in the mind of a dying James Whale—the director of *Frankenstein* and *The Bride of Frankenstein*—closeted homosexual, in the homophobic Hollywood of the 1950s, still traumatized by the horror of trench warfare in WWI. Ian McKellan is brilliant. Dir. Bill Condon.
      Billy Frankenstein. Directed by Fred Olen Ray. When the Frank family inherits an old castle, Billy learns he's a distant relative of Dr. Frankenstein. They visit and discover they're not alone. . . .

1999   *Alvin and the Chipmunks Meet Frankenstein.* Working at an amusement park in their "second full-length animated feature!" the furry critters encounter the real Dr. Frankenstein at the new attraction, "Frankenstein's Castle." Straight to video.
      Rock 'n' Roll Frankenstein. Directed by Brian O'Hara. Story by Brian O'Hara and Vito Cannella. Music agent Bernie Stein, his scientist nephew Frankie, and stoner roadie Iggy create a superstar from the remains of dead rockers. But Iggy screws up by stealing the private parts of Liberace instead of Jim Morrison's. Their monster is on the way to stardom when his Liberace side awakens, with tragic results. What's not to love?